The Last Innocent Hour

THE LAST INNOCENT HOUR

A NOVEL

Margot Abbott

ARROW

Arrow Books Limited
20 Vauxhall Bridge Road, London SW1V 2SA

An imprint of the Random Century Group

London Melbourne Sydney Auckland Johannesburg
and agencies throughout the world

First published in Great Britain by Century in 1991
Rowan edition 1992

1 3 5 7 9 10 8 6 4 2

Printed and bound in Great Britain by
Cox & Wyman Ltd, Reading

ISBN 0 09 999270 1

To the friends, old and new, in California, New York and places in between, who encouraged, listened, read, criticized, inputted, badgered, joked, and otherwise got me through this incredible marathon.

BOOK ONE

BERLIN, 1946

CHAPTER 1

With a start, Lieutenant Sally Jackson awoke, as the vibrating transport plane fought its way across the Atlantic through the April storm. Disoriented, she had to think for a moment to remember where she was. Then she pushed up the window shade and quickly pulled it down again when she saw the gray, roiling clouds, the heavy rain beating against the little porthole.

The clouds, the rain, the darkness, especially the darkness, had been part of her nightmare. She remembered the dream-rain, filling her mouth and eyes, and she rubbed her hands across her face. She had been having the dream for a year, ever since Frank Singleton had talked her into returning to Berlin with the special military intelligence unit, D-6. She could blame it all on her boss with his fatherly advice and honest fondness of her. And his manila envelope of obscene photographs. The photographs that had fueled her nightmare were photographs the Nazis themselves had made of their brutal advance through the Soviet Union, with the "special action groups" of the SS following the Wehrmacht.

The airplane took another dip, the interior fixtures rattled and creaked with the strain and the cabin lights flickered. Sally hadn't eaten for—what was it?—days, hours, at least, but her stomach rolled and dipped with the aircraft and she felt that if she had to inhale one more mouthful of stale, tobacco-scented air, she would throw up.

She tried tucking one foot underneath her, but all she managed was to jar her sleeping seatmate, a restless Army Air Force major whose elbow jabbed into her ribs. Sally shoved him back, hating the idea that his might be the hand she would grab if the plane went down. Wiggling around, she found a position that she could convince her body was comfortable, and closed her eyes.

The images of her dream were there, waiting for her, the walls of dirt rising up to the gunmetal sky, her white flesh glowing against the rich Ukrainian soil; the man in the black-and-silver uniform leaning over her. She opened her eyes. Better to be about to die in a rickety C-54 than already dead in a Russian ditch.

Her seatmate breathed, snuffled. He sounded as though he had a cold. She glanced at him. He wasn't a bad-looking man, her age, thirtyish, maybe younger, and as rumpled as she was. AAF officers, the fly-boys, tended to be younger than those in the other branches. She wondered if he had nightmares. She could decipher enough from his battle ribbons and insignia to know that he had been in the Pacific. He was a major and his outfit was . . . oh, forget it.

Uniforms and military men.

As far as she could see, everyone on the plane was in the military, including herself, and the array of uniforms, ranks, battle ribbons, patches and other insignia was vast. They seemed to be all Americans and primarily army men in their brown-on-brown uniforms. She compared them to German uniforms, which were beautifully tailored, carefully designed costumes for the master race. Brutality called for ugliness of dress, not all that black-and-silver flash. She approved of the practicality of American uniforms. No flash there.

A naval officer in his winter blues came down the aisle toward her, steadying himself on the backs of the seats. His tunic was open, his tie loosened, a tired, middle-aged man. He smiled at her when he saw her watching him and quietly walked past. Naval uniforms were nice, those heavy wool coats and the whites. Sally remembered her brother in his dress whites. How handsome and old-fashioned he had looked in them, as though he were on his way with Commodore Perry to Japan to woo Madame Butterfly.

Sally squirmed in the narrow seat, trying to find a comfortable spot. Give up, there wasn't one. She closed her eyes, her thoughts still of Eddie.

Her brother, a naval officer, an Annapolis graduate, a father and husband, had been bayoneted by a Japanese soldier after the surrender of Corregidor in May of 1942. Sally had learned of his death months later when one of his pals, who had escaped into a rice field during the confusion caused by too many prisoners and too few guards, had telephoned her from San Diego.

By that time, she had already seen pictures of the Americans as they surrendered after the terrible siege. Classified photographs, stolen from the Japanese, and not for public consumption because of their demoralizing content. She could understand why. She had gone back to look at the pictures, searching among the thin, haggard men for her brother, wondering if she would recognize him if she found him.

Still, they weren't the worst photographs Sally's job at the State Department had required her to look at and study in the past five years. Frank Singleton had shown her the worst as a kind of emotional blackmail that day in April 1945 when he had asked her to join D-6.

The unit, part of army intelligence, was to return to Berlin within a year of the armistice to gather information about the SS. Sally's German, her knowledge of Berlin, and her experience there would all be useful, but it was her newly honed interpretative skills that were most needed. She was, Frank told her, very good at looking at pictures.

"You'll have to join the army, Sally," he had told her. "But they'll make you an officer."

She had refused. Yes, her German was fine. But she didn't want to join the army, not as an officer or anything else. She didn't want to leave Washington. She was all right at the State Department, safe in her little cubicle, with her daily routine and her nice, dull life. She remembered nothing of Berlin and she knew nothing about the SS, never had. But most especially she did not want to return to Berlin.

Frank should know why. He'd been her father's friend and knew everything there was to know about her, she said, almost sarcastically. But his big, ugly Charles Laughton face remained expressionless, and Sally immediately felt guilty for her nastiness.

Frank didn't answer. Instead he handed her the manila envelope and walked away, to stare out the window, his back to her.

Opening the envelope, Sally drew out about a dozen black-and-white photographs, all eight-by-tens. She couldn't really tell what the first one was and she picked it up and turned it so that she was looking at it lengthwise. She quickly put it back down on the pile.

She stared at the painting on the wall behind Singleton's desk: flowers, lavender and green, in a glass vase. Strange choice for a man's office, but perhaps Elizabeth had picked it out . . .

"Sally," Singleton said gently, startling her. She looked up at his kind, heavily lined face. "I'm sorry for the shock tactics, but I didn't know how else to show you."

"No." She touched the stack of pictures. "Are they all like this? Those are . . ." She stopped short. In the almost five years she had worked for Frank Singleton, she had seen terrible pictures from the war, photographs of soldiers and civilians burned and hanged and blown to bits, but nothing, not even the pictures of charred tank crews in North Africa, shocked her as much as this photograph had.

"Bodies," Frank said, just as Sally managed to speak again.

"Dead," he said, at the same time. She looked at the next picture. "Who are these people? Where is this place?"

"That photograph was taken at a camp outside Weimar. The living are citizens of that city, who claim not to have known what was going on. The dead, well, the dead are mostly Jews. Left unburied when the German army fled."

Frank and Sally both studied the photographs as she went through the pile. When she had finished, she looked up at him, feeling she had aged a hundred years since she opened the envelope.

"Well, these certainly are effective. I kind of wish you hadn't shown them to me, I will admit." She tried to smile. "A person could go her whole life without needing to see these. Did this really happen?"

"Yes, Sally, it did," said Frank.

"I've heard the rumors."

"If you are the person of conscience I know you are, I simply don't see how you can refuse to do whatever can be done to bring the men who did this to justice."

Sally didn't want to listen to Frank. The photographs made her slightly nauseous. "Think of the smell," she said, looking at the first photograph again. Frank was silent and finally she asked him, "Who did this?"

"The SS ran the camps, Sally. The SS. And General Heydrich seems to have designed the system. We're not entirely clear about the details of his involvement yet."

"I see," she said, nodding, as though she did. "Did we know this was going on? Did anybody?"

"Yes."

"What did we do?"

"We're winning the war."

Sally didn't reply, nodding again as though she understood.

Just then the telephone rang and Frank picked it up. Sally sat for a moment, trying not to listen, then took the stack of horrible pictures and shuffled through them again, dividing and sorting them, applying some of the methods she had devised to study photographs. She thought it would help her regain her detachment. It didn't.

The dead continued to stare up at her, out of cavernous eye sockets, their shaved heads making their bony faces bizarre and robbing them of their individuality. Their bodies were frail bones with stretched-over worn skin, and Sally had to fight not to push the photographs away.

Who had known about this?

A stack of bodies with a foot sticking out here, a hand there, a stack four feet high, leaned against the wall of a barracks.

"Oh, God," said Sally softly.

She hadn't been listening to Frank's telephone conversation and she didn't immediately notice when he hung up the phone. His silence finally made Sally look up. His head was turned toward the window and tears were running down his baggy face.

"Frank, what was it? Is it Elizabeth?" Sally asked, getting quickly to her feet.

"No," he smiled sadly. "Thank God, it's not Elizabeth." He faced Sally. "It's FDR, Sally. He died this afternoon, down in Georgia."

Sally, unable to think of anything to say, stood for a time, still clutching the photographs, then very carefully she replaced them in the envelope. "I'll go to Berlin, Frank," she said, as gently as she could. "Whenever you want me to."

She felt absolutely inadequate, against both his grief and the magnitude of the crime represented by the photographs. And never had her guilt over her past so consumed her.

"What? Oh, yes, thank you, my dear, thank you. I'm sorry. I loved that old son of a . . ." And Frank had covered his face.

"I'll go," said Sally, backing away from his desk. "I'll . . . we can talk about it later." She reached the door and opened it to escape into the corridor. But all the way back to her office, people were stopping to talk and cry and comfort one another. Sally hurried past them, her head down.

Roosevelt was the President who had sent her father to Berlin, she remembered, thinking about how long he had been in office. She was sorry, especially that he hadn't lived to see the end of the war, which would surely happen any day now, but she didn't feel any sorrow for him personally and the grief of the people around her irritated her.

Later, during dinner at Mrs. Wallace's boardinghouse that evening, her friend Denise Brothers said in her broad Texas accent that she thought people were so upset because they were frightened. FDR had led them through so much, perhaps they thought they wouldn't be able to carry on without him. *That* Sally could understand and she nodded at Denise.

"You really are a wise woman," she told her.

"Oh, silly," Denise said, her fair freckled skin flushing. "I only went through eleventh grade." But Sally could see that she was pleased at the compliment.

Watching the newsreels of FDR's funeral train and the people crying in the streets, Denise had cried, along with most of the other people in the movie theater. Only Sally had stared stony-eyed at the screen and later, while they were drinking Cokes at the neighborhood drugstore, Denise had asked her why.

"Don't you feel sorry?"

"Sure I do," Sally said, stirring the crushed ice with her straw. "But I just don't cry easily, I guess. I don't feel as much."

"You cover everything up, Sal."

"No. I just don't feel things like other people do."

Denise didn't say any more, sipping her soda, her cherry-red lips like a flower around her straw, her big brown eyes on Sally. When she finished her Coke, she reached for Sally's wrist.

"You cover it all up, like these old scars." And without waiting for an answer, Denise stood up, smoothing her yellow-and-white summer dress over her hips. She was a tiny thing, born and bred on the windy plains of the Texas panhandle, and the first friend Sally had had in years.

Sally followed Denise out of the drugstore and the two women walked all the way home to Mrs. Wallace's without saying a word to each other. Sally started thinking again, as she had every day since she had seen them, of the photographs Frank had shown her. Those were worth crying over, howling over.

For the great old, tired President finally going to his well-deserved rest, in a place he had known and loved, death was almost a blessing and he was not to be pitied.

To die naked and abused under those gray eastern skies; to die cowed and confused, starving and dirty; to die and be so afraid, unimaginably afraid—those were deaths that were worth crying about.

But crying was such an insufficient response to such overwhelming evil, and so Sally's eyes had stayed dry. It would have helped if she could have talked to Denise about the photographs, but they were classified and she remained silent. Instead, she had started having the nightmare.

The DC-3 dipped and the cabin lights flickered. Sally hugged her overcoat around her. She could feel a rawness scratching at the back of her throat, and she wondered if she should dig out the flask of brandy from her carry-on bag under the seat. After all these death-filled years, she knew that she had not been surprised at Frank Singleton's photographs. Shocked. Angered. Frightened. But not surprised.

It was as though, on that July afternoon over ten years ago, when she had sat opposite Christian in her newly decorated sitting room in the house in Lichterfeld and had listened to his terrible, bloody story of the weekend, she had seen a vision of the awful future. No, she had not been surprised.

Bending over, she scrambled around under her seat for the flask. She wanted the warm comfort of the alcohol against the cold of the cabin and the memories this trip was reviving. Her fingers brushed something in the bag and she paused.

Gathering the bag and her shoes into her arms, she climbed over the major into the aisle. She apologized for disturbing him, but he just waved at her, too sick to care.

Sally slipped on her shoes and stood in line for the WC. Finally, she locked the flimsy door behind her, relieved that the place had a door at all. It was noisy, cold, and even more jarring in the little cabinet than in the cabin, but it was private.

She put her bag on the floor, sat down on the closed seat of the toilet, and pulled out two photographs, one a regular snapshot, one a five-by-seven. She sat for a long moment, the pictures loose in her hands, before she finally looked at them.

She really had no idea why she had brought the pictures with her. Yesterday, before she left Mrs. Wallace's boardinghouse, she had, at the last moment, dug her photograph album out of a box and found these two pictures, the larger one folded behind the other.

Now here they were and she couldn't throw them away, so she tucked them back into her bag, making sure they were stuck way down at the bottom.

The storm followed the plane across the Atlantic, through the stopover in Great Britain and all the way to France. There, Sally and a large group of assorted American armed forces personnel waited for sixteen hours in a Quonset hut on the airfield outside Paris for the rain and fog to lift. She had managed to wash her face and brush her teeth, but after nearly three days of flying and sitting in airports, she felt filthy. But she was too numb with fatigue and too sick, with the cold her seatmate had given her, to care.

The Quonset hut, large enough for a regiment, was empty and drafty and poorly lit. Sally dared not go in search of aspirin or hot tea for fear of missing her Berlin flight, and so she sat glumly on a hard bench with her coat wrapped around her, sinking fast into self-pity. Her little flask of brandy was long empty. When she used to travel as a child, safe in her parents' care, her mother had always had the proper medication handy: aspirin, tea, or whatever else was needed to provide comfort, if not instant cure. If she could not travel with her mother, she should have, at least, packed as she did. Sally searched her pocket for a handkerchief and blew her nose noisily, then lay down on the bench to try and sleep, her camel's hair over-coat her blanket, her big leather bag her pillow.

A door slammed somewhere and she awoke. Her cold was worse, her throat hurt, she ached all over, and she now had a nasty, hacking cough. With the thought of looking for some water, she struggled to sit up. It wasn't worth it and she sank down again with a little self-pitying moan. Cursing the infectious major, she retreated into sleep.

"Ma'am," said a midwestern voice. Sally did not move. "Lieutenant?" insisted the voice.

"What?" she answered grumpily, swallowing against a cough.

She sensed someone bending over her and opened her eyes, blinking against the ceiling lights. His face was in shadow, the lights a halo around his head.

"Need some help?" he asked.

"Leave me alone," she muttered, closing her eyes.

"That's a bad cold."

"Brilliant," she said ungraciously, and dozed off, or thought she did, until she felt a cool hand on her forehead. It felt good, and she let it stay.

"Fever, too." It was the same voice. She opened her eyes. She lay on her side and the man sat down next to her head, bending over her, his hand on her forehead. She tried to sit up.

"Don't. It's okay," he said, gently pushing her back down. She closed her eyes. "Ache?"

"All over," she said, breathing through her mouth. "I'm so thirsty." She rubbed her stuffed nose.

"Hang on," he said, patting her shoulder before he got up. Sally swallowed against the dryness in her throat. She was very cold. She dozed again.

"Lieutenant," said the voice. "Can you sit up and drink something?"

She struggled to do as she was asked, inclined to trust the calm, friendly voice.

"C'mon, you'll feel better." He sat beside her as she pulled herself up. "Found you this." He tucked a worn gray blanket around her, putting his arm across her shoulders to do so.

"What time is it?" she asked, leaning into his arm.

"O-three-hundred," he answered, removing his arm to lean forward and pull a tall silver thermos out of his bag. He untwisted the cap and offered it to Sally.

"What is it?" she asked.

"It's tea and brandy. Perfect for what ails you. Now drink it, and here, take these. They're aspirin. Put your hand out." Sally complied and he put two tablets into her palm.

"I can't taste it," she complained, then, as she felt the warm liquid coat her throat, said, "Oh, thank you." She swallowed the pills, then held the cup in both her gloved hands and sipped from it.

"Finish it."

She looked at him. He was watching her so seriously that she had to smile, in spite of her sore throat. He had dark-blond hair and a mustache under an almost too-large nose. His eyebrows were strong half-circles above his eyes, which were very big. He was not particularly handsome, but Sally immediately liked his face, his serious expression. He looked to be about her age. He was a captain.

He smiled back at her and she liked even more what the smile did to him, the crinkles around his eyes, the way his mouth curved up.

"Any temp?" the captain asked, reaching to feel her forehead. She flinched. It was instinctive and the rudeness of it made her blush. "Hey, I'm not going to hurt you," he said with a laugh. She smiled sheepishly and allowed him to cover her forehead with his big hand. "Not as bad as I thought."

"I notice you're a doctor," she said, looking at the medical symbols on his lapel.

"Yep. Hope you don't think I pour brandy down just anybody's throat? Although it is a good way to meet girls."

"I'm not a girl," she said seriously.

"No?"

"I'm a lieutenant."

He laughed gently at her little joke. "So you are. And about the prettiest one I've seen in a while."

"Well," said Sally, standing up, "you must not get out much."

The captain stood and took the blanket from her. He was very tall, with broad shoulders, loose-limbed in his wrinkled uniform.

"By the way" the captain held out his right hand. "Tim Hastings, Wichita."

She shook hands with him. "Sally Jackson, San Francisco."

"Nice to meet you, Sally Jackson. Ah, this must be your flight." He had to raise his voice to be heard over the scratchy PA system. Hastings had the most beautiful green eyes she had ever seen, the laugh lines around them adding to their character, and quite against her will, she wondered if he was married. She decided instantly that he was; men like him always were. But the warm eyes were obviously interested in her. Must be medical interest, she concluded and turned away from them, busying herself with gathering her things together.

"Yes. I'm going to Berlin."

"Me too."

"Really?" she said, sniffling. She dug into her bag for another handkerchief. He was going to Berlin too.

Sally had taken care of herself for years now and was both proud and jealous of her independence, seldom asking for or accepting help. But she was sick, she told herself, as Tim Hastings took charge of her luggage, of checking them both in, and of finding their seats. She was sick, so it was all right to allow him to help. She did feel bad, and by the time she fastened her seat belt, she was exhausted. She fell asleep before the plane gained its cruising altitude.

When she awoke, she found herself nestled against the captain's shoulder. He was reading a thick book and as she let herself rest against him, she read a page. It was *Anna Karenina*. She sat up.

"Hi," he said.

"I seem to have used you as a pillow."

"That's okay, Lieutenant." He closed the book, but kept his finger in his place.

"Think I'll go clean up," she said, and he stood up so she could get out.

"Not much room for you, is there?" she said, watching him unfold himself into the aisle.

"Just think of it as cozy," he replied.

"You really from San Francisco?" he asked her when she got back.

"Originally. I was in Washington—for the duration. Are you really from Kansas?"

"A farm boy like my dad and his dad before him."

"I've never met anyone from there. Sounds exotic."

"Yeah, sure it is, the heartland of America."

"Cornfields."

"Wheat. Lots and lots of wheat. Real, real flat." His voice was just as flat, and she smiled at the sound. "But I'd rather talk about the City by the Bay," he continued. "One of my favorite places. Went to med school there."

"At U.C.?"

He nodded. "Yep. I was in Hawaii for the duration, treating poor saps with shellshock, uh, battle fatigue, as we call it now. A real euphemism if there ever was one."

"My brother was in Hawaii before . . . before . . ." she trailed off. "What kind of a doctor are you?" she asked abruptly. He made a wry face.

"Now I've torn it. You'll never use me as a pillow again."

"Why?" she asked, laughing at him, at his deadpan manner, that broad, lazy voice.

"I liked being your pillow."

"No, I mean, why . . . what kind of doctor are you?"

"I'm a shrink," he drawled, grimacing.

"A psychiatrist? That's okay. I'm broad-minded; I don't care."

"You're very progressive. Most people throw drinks in my face. Of course, it allows to me to gauge the depths of their neuroses, but it does hurt my feelings."

"You don't look like one, that's why," Sally said shyly.

"You think that's it?" She nodded. "You know you could be right. Farm boys aren't the shrink type, are they? Maybe I ought to cultivate a German accent."

"Viennese, you mean."

"Of course."

"And a beard."

"Especially a beard," he said, rubbing his chin. "I could start right now. Vronsky had a beard."

"Vronsky?"

"*Anna Karenina*." He indicated the book in his lap.

"Oh, yes. I read that. The ending made me mad. I threw the book across the floor. Imagine her killing herself like that."

"Don't tell me."

"What?"

"I'm a romantic, so don't tell me the ending."

"It ends like everything ends," she muttered and turned to look out the porthole. It was still raining. "I wonder if we'll outrun the rain?"

When Tim Hastings climbed out of his seat to go clean up, Sally considered her past experience with other members of his profession. She had lied. She did care what kind of a doctor he was. Most of the psychiatrists she had met had been unpleasant men.

She remembered the brusque young man at Los Angeles General who had failed to hide his disgust and disapproval of her. She remembered police and a woman yelling. There had been sirens and people roughly handling her. After the wild ambulance ride she had been thrust into the chaos of a Los Angeles New Year's Eve emergency room. Happy 1936.

She remembered the glaring lights that had burned her eyes as she tried to turn her head to escape them. She had been very weak, slipping in and out of consciousness. When she came to, she was in a small cubicle, her bandaged, aching arms on top of the sheet, which was tucked around her so tightly that it impeded her breathing. She had been very frightened and began to weep.

That was how the young doctor found her when he snapped the curtains open. He had smiled a frozen smile at her and picked up each bandaged wrist, carefully inspected the wrappings. Then he had taken her pulse by placing two fingers under her jaw. Finally, picking up his clipboard, he told her she would be all right. But not once had he looked at her face.

Ignoring him, she had turned her head to stare at the curtained wall. It was heavy cotton and fairly clean.

"Got someone at home?" he asked. "Someone to take care of you?"

She shook her head. Obviously, if she had had someone at home, someone to take care of her, she wouldn't be here. Alone, that's what she was. And she started to cry again.

"Miss, we can't let you go unless someone comes for you. It's the law. You'll be sent to County." He waited for her to stop crying. She didn't. "Okay, if that's the way you want it." Abruptly, he left the cubicle and her weeping.

In the end, unable to stop crying, she had managed to give them Eddie's telephone number in San Diego. She couldn't bear the idea of either him or her father seeing her in this state, but she knew that of the two, Eddie was the better choice as a rescuer.

He had arrived the next morning, trim and so normal-looking in his naval blues. Without asking her any difficult questions, he had gotten her discharged from the hospital, had her prescriptions filled, and had even gone to her nasty little apartment in Santa Monica to settle things there. Then he had bundled her into a car and had driven her all the way home to their father's house in Palo Alto.

Lowell Jackson had opened the door of the Spanish-style house, but he stepped back when Sally made a move to embrace him. In his face, in his eyes, she saw and understood the fear and pain her actions had caused him. Again.

"I'm sorry, Daddy," she had said, standing helplessly on the red tile steps, her bandaged wrists feeling heavy.

Her father had reached out to pat her shoulder, but he just could not touch her and backed away as she entered the house. Both of them had retreated into formal politeness and the pretense that all was well.

That was when she started seeing a psychiatrist. She had seen a certain logic in the situation, but had stopped going as soon as she could. The doctor was kind, but he seemed to feel she wasn't trying hard enough, that, with some willpower, she ought to be able to overcome her little problems. Perhaps he was right, but she got tired of disappointing him as well as everyone else, so she quit.

Neither her father nor Eddie ever got up the nerve to ask her about the incident until years later, when Eddie and Barbara were visiting on leave before they went to their new posting in Manila. That was right before the invasion of Poland in September of '39.

Eddie was the one who finally broached the subject. Sally had always supposed her father and brother were too frightened by her moods, and besides, her family didn't ask questions about such deep, emotional, troublesome subjects.

Hell, neither one of them had ever talked to her about what happened to her in Berlin. It had been hard enough for her father to come to the hospital.

Eddie and Sally had been doing the dishes after a fine huge meal. Barbara had gone upstairs to check on Stevie and had not come back down.

"Listen, Sal," Eddie said, waiting for her to hand him a plate. He was drying. "Do you mind if I ask you a question? You don't have to answer, but I figure we might not see each other for a long time and . . . well, I have some idea of what was going on, but I'd just like to know."

She held the dinner plate under the running water. She knew what he was going to ask. "Okay," she said in a small voice, watching the water run off the white-and-blue rim.

He reached over, turned off the water, gently took the plate out of her hands, and placed it on the drainer. It was very quiet in the kitchen. There was a low whir from the fridge.

"Did you . . . did you really try and kill yourself?"

The phrasing of the question had struck her as funny, and she laughed harshly. "Oh, Eddie, it certainly wasn't an accident. You just don't pick up an old razor blade and slit your wrists open for fun."

Above the sink, her reflection in the dark window laughed back at her. She knew she had hurt him.

"Who found you?" he asked in an even voice, staring down at the spotless sink.

She swallowed, trying to dispel the great weight in her chest. Carefully wringing out the dishrag, she paused, then hung it over the porcelain divider between the two parts of the sink. She coughed slightly and wished for a cigarette. Finally, she answered her brother. "A man."

"A man?" he had echoed. "Who?"

"What does it matter?" she said, and realized they had been whispering. She glanced at her brother and saw his face. "A stranger. Matt. Walt. Some name like that."

He turned and looked at her, his forehead wrinkled in confusion. "A stranger? How could. . . ?" He stopped, as understanding flooded his face, and as the full implication of that strange man in his sister's room dawned on him, he blushed.

Sally smiled sadly at him. "You shouldn't have asked if you didn't want to know. I was in his room, Eddie. Some guy. There were a lot of guys in those days. You shouldn't have asked."

"No, Sal, no," he said, reaching for her hands. "I had to know. It's haunted me. Why would you do such a thing? All of it. That hospital. How sick you were. How you might have succeeded . . ." His voice faltered. "You could have done it and maybe I'd have never known."

"Oh, sure, Eddie," she said, extricating her hands from his. "A stiff in a lousy L.A. hotel was not going to go unnoticed for very long." She had been purposely cruel because his tears had frightened her. "Besides, there was so much blood."

"Sally . . ."

"I'm sorry," she said. She looked again at her reflection in the dark window.

"Why?" he whispered after a pause.

"Why, what?" she answered, facing the sink again. "Why the man? There were a lot of them. Bet you didn't know that. I wanted . . . I don't know what. But it never worked. And, truthfully, I never expected it to."

"But why the razor blade? Why try and kill yourself?"

She bent her head and studied the green-and-yellow linoleum on the floor.

"Was it because of Berlin?" he asked, still whispering. "Was that it?"

She turned her head and slowly raised it to meet his eyes. They were light blue, lighter than her own, clearer than hers, and his lashes were long and thick, oddly feminine in his wide, square face. Looking at her brother, Sally realized how much she cared about him, yet how little she knew him. Still, he was the only person in the entire world who loved her in spite of everything. She knew that about him.

"Yes." She took a deep breath and looked again at the linoleum.

16

"Berlin," she repeated so softly that the word was only a brush of sound in the quiet kitchen.

Without a word, Eddie opened his arms and they stood there, holding one another, for a long time. It was the last time she had seen him, but she knew, that if she was sane at all now, he had helped her become so with his embrace.

CHAPTER 2

B erlin was a city of rubble.

Sharp, perilously suspended stone walls stood without obvious support. Vast fields of broken gray stone stretched as far as Sally could see. All the parks, the greenery, were gone. The setting sun cast the plane's shadow onto the silent and frightening ruins. The shadow plane, slipping effortlessly across the shells of buildings, the blocked streets, the burned cars and tanks still visible here and there, was the only moving thing in this huge dead city. Surely people, even feisty, stubborn Berliners, could not be alive down there.

The devastation produced in Sally a dull emptiness and the violence of the destruction frightened her profoundly. She stared out of the small porthole, angry at the tears that started to her eyes.

She reminded herself of the pictures Frank Singleton had shown her. The people down there had let those things happen. And that frightened her as well.

On the ground, things weren't much better, although the military bustle at Tempelhof Airport was reassuring. As were the American uniforms and voices, busy, purposeful, and energetic. Sally had never been particularly chauvinistic, and she experienced mixed feelings as she watched the activity: gratefulness at the no-nonsense attitude and dislike of a certain callousness in the midst of the colossal ruins.

Waiting for her bags, she saw Tim Hastings's tall figure disappear through a door to the outside. He glanced around at the last moment and, spotting her, waved. Sally raised her hand and he was gone. He would be here too, in Berlin. The thought was oddly comforting.

She found a ride to her billet, and as the driver drove cautiously through the narrow passageways cleared in the rubble, she began to feel a sense of dislocation. She could not tell where she was, the streets had either changed so much, or had entirely disappeared.

"Are we going toward Neukölln?" she asked the driver.

"No, ma'am, Dahlem."

Sally sat back. Her head ached and she dug her handkerchief out of her bag and blew her nose. She closed her eyes.

18

It was nearly dark when the driver let her out in front of the building she would be living in. As she got out of the car, she could smell the terrible air, even through her stuffy nose. She grimaced.

"You'll get used to it, Lieutenant," the driver said, seeing her expression. He carried her bags up the steps of the building and into the entry hall, then came back.

Sally stood on the top step and studied the block of rubble across the street, the flattened buildings and twisted concrete. She had heard that, during heavy bombings, the heat had made sidewalks warp. She hadn't believed it. But she was sure that she would be seeing a lot of things she would never have believed.

"This city used to have the best air," she said to the driver. "Berliner air," she added in German.

"It's the dead," he said. "Lots of them still buried in the rubble, in the canals. It's not so bad now, but when the wind comes from the right direction . . . phew."

There was nothing to say in response, so she turned to look at her new home. The block of nineteenth-century apartment buildings—all still standing—had been built for middle-class families and now quartered single American women. The women were Red Cross and UNRRA workers, military nurses and doctors, and administrators who were trying to organize the various programs the military government of occupation had brought along with it.

The entry hall was surprisingly crowded with furniture, all of it worn and old. The place looked like a junk store, a rummage sale of good, solid, middle-class nineteenth-century Berlin furniture, but, for all the clutter, everything was clean and the stuffy air smelled of furniture polish.

A thin, middle-aged woman came striding across the faded, patched carpet, her hand outstretched. "Hello, you must be Lieutenant Jackson," she said. "I'm Dr. Mavis Chambers. I'm with the Red Cross. In refugee relief."

"Do I qualify? I sure feel like one," said Sally, with an attempt at humor.

Dr. Chambers laughed, causing her glasses, round ones with thin frames, which were slightly too large for her narrow face, to fall down her long nose.

"I bet you do," she said, shoving her glasses back up. "I bet you do. I am also the official greeter of our little home away from home here. So, you've come to work with D-6?"

"Yes," said Sally, glad someone knew about her. Then she coughed. She still felt rotten and searched in her pocket for a hand-kerchief.

"That sounds bad."

"It is," Sally said, blowing her nose. It hurt.

"Well. I've been working with the boys, and your new boss, Colonel Eiger, asked me to keep my eye out for you. He's a good egg. Come along, I'll show you to your room. I imagine you'd like to get to bed."

She gestured toward Sally's bags. "Can you carry one? I'll get the other." They started off up the marble stairs, lugging Sally's suitcases. "It's the air on those planes. You'd better get right in bed. I think tomorrow you're going to have to hit the floor running."

Sally's room, her home for the next year or so, was on the second floor, down a short hall. Mavis waved at a closed door. "The WC. There's one on each floor. Bath, too, but separate, down that way."

The doctor opened a door and flipped on a light switch. Sally dropped her bag by the door and sat on the nearest bed.

"I really do feel terrible," Sally said, pulling off her cap and gloves. "I guess I should go to bed." She smiled weakly at Mavis. "I feel as though I haven't slept in a week."

"Traveling does that to me, too. I'll find you some tea while you get undressed. Do you have aspirin? Do you need some help with your bags?"

"No," Sally said, standing to take off her coat. "I've got overnight stuff, and aspirin, in this bag."

"Well, for goodness' sake, hang your uniform up. Your boss is regular army, and a stickler for the niceties of army life."

Then she was gone, closing the door behind her, before Sally could tell her she had met Colonel Eiger. Nevertheless, Sally followed Mavis's suggestion and hung up her rumpled uniform in the huge wardrobe that took up almost all of one wall. Next to it was a small sink, with a mirror over it, and she washed her face and brushed her teeth. Though the water ran hot and cold, it tasted of chemicals. She took two aspirin, swearing as the flaky tablets scratched her raw throat. After pulling her pajamas out of the bag and putting them on, Sally climbed into her single bed. There were two beds in the room and they faced a good-sized window. Tomorrow she'd see what was out there.

Sally had met Colonel Eiger after she joined the WACs, toward the end of her four-week basic training at Fort Des Moines. She still had to do her officer's training, but hadn't received her assignment, and she had gone to her CO's office expecting to be given her orders.

Instead the CO had introduced her to the colonel and had quickly retreated.

Standing square against the window of her CO's office, his arms crossed, the colonel did not look pleased to see Private Jackson.

"Sit down, Private," Colonel Eiger growled. Sally quickly complied, sitting in a chair facing him. "I'll get to the point," he said. "I read your file back in D.C. and I don't want you on my team. I don't want a woman, and if I did, I wouldn't want one with your background. I don't trust you. How could I?"

Sally sat stiffly under his attack, glad for once of the protocol of military behavior into which she could retreat and remain silent and motionless.

The colonel continued. "But the brass and your boss at State convinced me that I should come to talk to you and see for myself exactly what kind of a person you are. I was coming west anyway, so I agreed."

Eiger left his spot by the window and walked to the desk, where he could look down into Sally's face. He leaned on the corner and folded his arms again. "So tell me, Private."

"Sir?" Sally looked up at him. The colonel was of medium height and build, although he had a broad chest. His uniform, with its impressive array of battle ribbons on his left breast, was perfectly tailored. His thinning red hair was cut so short, the color barely showed. He had pronounced cheekbones, a long, sharp nose, and deep-set pale eyes with golden eyelashes. His intense gaze frightened Sally.

"Talk, Private. Who are you? Why should I let you on my team?" Sally detected a slight Southern accent.

"What do you want to know, sir," asked Sally, "if you've already read my file?"

"How old are you?"

"Surely that's in my file, sir." Sally couldn't see why she should answer. The man had already made his conclusions about her.

"No sass, Private. Answer the question."

"Thirty-two," said Sally, keeping her voice steady and expressionless.

"Ever been married?" Sally, surprised by the question, hesitated. "Well?" insisted Eiger.

"Yes, I was married. For a short time, a long time ago. To a German," she added defiantly, knowing that was what he was interested in.

"Why?"

"Why what, sir?"

"Why'd you marry a Kraut, Private?"

"I didn't, sir. I married a German and I married him because I loved him." She raised her chin, then added: "Sir."

The colonel grunted and walked around the desk to sit in the chair. He leaned back, one arm extended to the desk where his fingers lightly tapped the wood.

"You are close to being way out of line."

"Yes, sir. I'm sorry, sir."

"It's all in your file," he said. "I just wanted to hear your version."

Sally looked at his hand, the powerful fingers tapping one after another.

"A messy, unsuitable marriage that ruined your father's career and you . . . a stint in several hospitals for various reasons, including the incident in Los Angeles. Was that your only attempt? I asked that, but no one could tell me."

"That was a long time ago," said Sally.

"And what have you accomplished since?" Sally was silent, staring at the light swirls on the wood of the desk. "What, Jackson? Tell me."

"My work." Damn. She raised her head and looked at him. "I've done what I could. And what happened in Berlin was . . . it happened then and is no longer relevant." She bit off the words, hearing her father's well-bred, highly educated tones in her voice.

"All right, about your work—it's why I'm talking to you. I read some of your reports. I agree with Singleton that you're becoming a top-notch analyst of visual material. And I read your report on Heydrich. It was and will be very useful to us in our work in Berlin."

After General Heydrich's assassination by Czech commandos in the spring of 1942, Frank Singleton had asked Sally to write a analysis of the Reich Protector's career in the Third Reich. Sally had done her research and the writing in two weeks, and when she was finished, had walked the completed report over to Frank herself. She dropped off all the research materials in the various offices on the way, and had thrown her notes away, as well. She wanted to rid her office of every shred of paper referring to Reinhard Tristian Heydrich.

"Look, Private," continued Colonel Eiger. "I don't mean to bully you, but I can't afford to take along someone, no matter how talented, who's nuts. You can see that." He looked down at his hands, which were out flat on the desk. "There's something else; it's about your . . . your loyalties, shall we say."

"Colonel Eiger," said Sally angrily, "I deeply resent that remark.

If you are so . . . I didn't ask to do this," she said, standing up. "You think I look forward to this job, looking at pictures of godawful things, being in the army? Going to Berlin, for God's sake. Do me a favor, throw me out."

"Whoa, simmer down, Private," Eiger said calmly. "Besides, once in, you'll find it difficult to get out of the army." And, for the first time during their meeting, he smiled.

"Tell me, then, why did you agree to do this? C'mon, sit back down and tell me."

Sally deliberated for a moment, then sat. What the man had said about her was true, but there was more.

"I don't see why I have to be forever justifying myself," she said, trying to control her anger.

"You can't see why you could be a liability for D-6?" asked Eiger.

"I would more likely be an asset," she snapped back.

"All right," he said, holding up one hand, palm out, "then tell me why."

"You've already dismissed me," Sally said, sitting up straighter, looking him in the eye. "You came here as a gesture. You've already decided. Why the hell should I tell you anything? Sir."

Eiger looked at Sally for a long moment, then said, "Okay, I'll try to put aside my preconceived notions about you. If you'll be honest with me. You convince me that I don't have to worry about these two points, and I'll agree to have you on my team."

"With an eye on me," said Sally.

"No. If you're part of the team, you're part of the team. No probation. No conditions. We have to trust each other." Sally nodded, and he continued, "Now, tell me why you agreed to go back to Berlin."

Sally took a deep breath. She wanted to tell him—the truth—as far as she could.

"I owe it. My brother died at Bataan and the ship my sister-in-law and niece and nephew were on was torpedoed in the Pacific. The kids were babies." She wondered if she should tell him about Frank's photographs. "Is that enough? There is probably more, but those reasons are all either in the past or indirect ones."

"Sorry."

"What for?"

"Your family. The kids. That stinks."

"Yeah." Barbara, Stevie, and Ellie, the niece she had never seen, had been evacuated from Manila in 1942, as the Japanese were moving in. Sally didn't think they ever knew what happened to Eddie;

nor that he knew what happened to them. Her father had died quietly and quickly of a heart attack before Pearl Harbor, so he never knew either. Only Sally knew how her family had been decimated.

Colonel Eiger was watching her intently. Picking up a pencil from the desk, he started rolling it back and forth between his thumb and forefinger. "What about the ah—incident in L.A.?"

As Sally searched for the words, she clutched one wrist with the other hand. "I did what I did. Because it seemed to be the only way out at a time I was in despair. I don't know much now, but I do know one thing for certain. I don't want to die. If I die, the bastards win. But I'm alive. That's a victory for me, Colonel, and it was hard-won."

She leaned forward. "The main reason I'm here is that my boss showed me some photographs. I don't understand them. Why we let them happen. I want—I *need* to do something."

"Photographs?" He eyed her. "Of the camps?"

Sally nodded.

"My outfit liberated a small POW camp in southern Germany. I think I understand what you mean." Eiger nodded, the fingers twirling the pencil paused for a moment. "Yeah, well. Now, what about your loyalties? What if—" he started to say, but Sally interrupted him.

"Oh, Colonel, please. You aren't looking at the facts realistically if you can think there's the slightest question of that."

"What about you and . . ."

Sally stood abruptly and walked to the window. "God, it's stupid to think that just because . . . that I can't differentiate between right and wrong. Well, maybe the edges got blurred, but that's what happens when you try to cover up, try *not* to see. I was young, which I realize is not an excuse, but, well, I won't go into all of that."

He was silent. She glanced at him. There was no condemnation in his expression, but he rolled his lips together tightly. Looking at his tanned face above the khaki shirt, the tight knot of his tie, his military haircut, Sally wondered if she would ever be free of these hard military men.

"I'll tell you something funny, Colonel. After all my experiences there and here, I find . . . I find I hate . . ." she trailed off.

"What? What do you hate?" asked Eiger in a quiet voice.

Sally stared out the brown slats of the blinds at the brown-and-green of the base. There were big whitewashed stones lining the paths and the sun beat off them in a blinding glare. "Uniforms, Colonel. Uniforms." She turned away from the window, holding her arms wide, exhibiting herself, smiling at the irony. "And look at me now."

"It's funny how things turn out, Jackson," the colonel said, throwing the pencil on the desk. "Smoke?" he said, pulling out a pack of Luckies.

"Thanks," she said, taking one.

"I was going to be a farmer. I'm from west Texas and my dad had a nice little farm. Raised barley, corn, had some cows, chickens, the whole bit. Then the drought came. The bank foreclosed and there went the farm. Really busted me up, because of all my father's sons—there were four of us—I was the one that really loved farming. My mom died having another kid and as the hard times got harder, the family drifted apart. My dad died of a heart attack too."

"So how did you wind up in the army?" Sally asked.

"I was on my way to California, a typical dust-bowl Okie from Texas, and I stopped in a little pissant town on the border of New Mexico. My old Ford, my dad's old Ford, had had it. I saw a recruiting poster and went and talked to the man and decided to do it. I didn't mean to stay, but with one thing and another, here I am. Even got some college. Found a wife, an old army brat, so she understands the life." Colonel Eiger smiled at Sally, the smile softening his stark features. "So, Jackson, you never know, maybe the army'll be good to you, too."

"Maybe, sir." She stood as the colonel slapped both hands on the desk and pushed himself up.

"C'mon, let's go get some lunch. I want to hear about General Reinhard Heydrich. I'll tell you about D-6." He grabbed his hat off the coat rack behind the desk, then turned to Sally. "Thanks for being frank with me. We won't have to discuss it anymore and it doesn't go any further than here."

He regarded her seriously for a moment. "I admire you, Private."

"Sir?" replied Sally.

"To be going back, after being wounded, so to speak. So, you run up against any problems, you let me know. Deal?"

"Yes, sir."

"That's an order."

"I understand, sir."

"Good." He started for the door, then turned. "Now, about your commission. It helps with pay, although I understand you don't have those particular problems. Can't do better than a first lieutenant for you. Some of the team received their bars in battle, so I don't want to insult them. As you can imagine, the living conditions aren't great. There are American women working in Berlin—nurses, doctors, and the like. The city is still dangerous, so we've got you bunking in a dorm. It won't be the Adlon. Hope you can manage."

"Yes, sir. Sounds fine."

"Good," said the colonel briskly. Putting on his hat, he led Sally out into the noonday sun.

Exhaustion was Sally's first impression of the defeated Berliners, just pure exhaustion, which wasn't surprising, considering that they had gone through weeks of night-and-day bombing, and through the horrors of the Soviet invasion less than a year ago. Now, they struggled in their ruined city, in their ruined country, just to get enough food to survive. They were Berliners, and Sally frowned, remembering the energy and self-confidence of the pre-war city.

"They brought it on themselves," Dr. Chambers said, seeing Sally's expression. "Save your pity for those who really deserve it. You'll see soon enough."

They were on their way to the office, sharing the backseat of a sedan, driven with great style and panache by a young private from the motor pool.

"I knew Berlin before," Sally said. She noticed a young man with an old, tired face dully watching the jeep as it passed. He wore a Wehrmacht coat, the insignia removed. "All this destruction—was it really necessary?"

"They killed so many children," Mavis Chambers said instead of answering, her low voice tight with her emotional control. "And not only that, they kidnapped them and tried to breed them. As though human beings were chickens. Just look what they did to their own kids, look at them—starving, half-animal orphans." She pushed her glasses up on her nose. "But perhaps the worst thing was the indoctrination of an entire generation. Separating them from their families, turning them against their parents, subverting their morals, and teaching them to hate before sending them out to die, brutalizing them. It's evil, evil. And we will all reap the consequences."

They finished the ride in silence. Soon they pulled up in front of the former minor ministry building that housed their offices. As Mavis had said, it was quite close to their living quarters, and Sally realized, with a not unpleasant jolt, that it was also close to the suburb where she and her father had lived.

Mavis led Sally into the building. It was large and liberally covered with marble. They climbed up the wide staircase, which looked more appropriate for the foyer of an opera house than for a government agency. Most of the splendor was hidden behind crowded benches and file cabinets. Mavis indicated the double doors on either side.

"You're through there and I'm over there," she said, waving her hand at one set of doors and then the other. "When I'm here," she added. In the center of the foyer, at a large desk, sat a burly American sergeant.

"Come meet Sergeant Taveggia," Mavis said and introduced Sally to the man. He stood and saluted Sally and she returned the salute, still feeling a bit silly doing so. Would she ever get used to it?

"This is as far as I can go. Security," said Mavis. "I'll see you back at our quarters this evening. The sergeant will take care of you."

Sally thanked the doctor and turned to the sergeant, who handed her a key.

"The colonel said I was just to send you back. You keep going down the hall there until you come to room 208 and that'll be your office. This key will open it."

Going through the set of double doors the sergeant had indicated, Sally found herself in a short gloomy hallway. She walked down it and turned the corner, continuing down the corridor, past closed, silent doors. Where were the people? she wondered. Later she learned that because of air-raid damage, most of the offices in this wing were unusable, the doors sealed.

After the small, dark room at the pension, Sally was pleasantly surprised at her office. She didn't expect anything like this clean, sunny room. Opposite the door, a stretch of windows ran down the length of the wall above a waist-high sill. She walked over to the windows and looked down at the street.

The desk, which was at the end of the rectangular room, sat at right angles to the windows. She studied the intercom with its row of buttons, sitting under a crook-neck lamp.

Suddenly cheered by the pretty room, she sat in the desk chair and opened a few drawers. The place was a palace compared to the cubbyhole in Washington where she had worked through the war. She sniffed and pulled out her handkerchief. Now, if only her cold would go away.

Suddenly the intercom came alive with a nasty little buzz. Sally pushed the lever above the small red light and said, "Hello."

"Lieutenant Jackson?" asked a male voice on the other end.

"Speaking," replied Sally.

"I'm Colonel Eiger's aide, Master Sergeant Chester Dolan."

"Nice to meet you, Sergeant."

"Does the lieutenant see the file on her desk?"

"Yes, Sergeant, but I haven't opened it. I just got here."

"That is understood. But, if you would bring the file directly to a meeting in the conference room, it would be appreciated."

"Now?"

"That would be fine, ma'am. Down the hall, third door on your right," he said, and rang off.

Sally opened the file, glanced at the photographs inside, and closed the cover. She stood and smoothed down her tunic, fleetingly considered lipstick or a comb, but decided she had better hurry. She picked up the file and headed toward the conference room.

CHAPTER 3

M aster Sergeant Dolan, a thin man with a neat, narrow mustache, stood and saluted when Sally entered his office, then offered his hand.

"Lieutenant Jackson?" He spoke with a soft Southern drawl.

"Yes, Sergeant," she said, shaking hands.

"You'd better go right in," he said, as he walked to a closed door and opened it. He announced her and stood aside.

Sally entered, but stopped just a step or two past the doorway. Another long rectangular room with windows at one end and a huge table down the center. Five uniformed men sat around the table. They all turned to watch her enter, making her terribly self-conscious

"Come in, Lieutenant." Colonel Eiger, leaning back in a comfortable desk chair, one hand fiddling with a pencil on the table, nodded at her.

"Hello, Lieutenant, welcome to Berlin. Everyone—Lieutenant Sally Jackson. Actually, if I remember correctly, Sarah Wentworth Jackson. Isn't that correct, Lieutenant?"

"Yes, sir."

"What's the Wentworth for? Old family name?"

"Yes, sir."

"Well, good, good. Sit down, Lieutenant. We'll get you some coffee. Dolan, grab the lieutenant a mug, will you?"

Sally sat in the closest chair and set the folder on the table. A mug of coffee appeared in front of her. Across from her sat a handsome young lieutenant with combat ribbons on his chest. His hair was dark brown, curly, and longer than was usual in the military. She smiled at him.

"Doug Finkelstein," he said, standing and reaching across the table to shake her hand. Then he touched the shoulder of the man sitting next to him, a captain smoking a pipe. "This is Nelson Armbrewster," Finkelstein said, his accent revealing his New York background. "He's from Yale, so watch out for him."

Armbrewster took his pipe from his mouth. He wore round, thin-rimmed glasses, and had a horsy, but not unattractive face.

29

"Glad to have you with us, Lieutenant Jackson. I for one find all-male companionship a trial."

"I'm Max Tobin," the man sitting next to Sally introduced himself. He was older than the others, of average build, and had smooth brown hair and very thick glasses. He was also a captain. "I read your Heydrich report. Good work."

Smiling her thanks, Sally looked down past him at the last man. Sitting with his fanny low on his chair, his long legs stretched out in front of him, was her doctor from the plane, Tim Hastings.

When her eyes met his, he grinned. "How's your cold?" he asked.

"Fine. I didn't realize—"

"Well, we didn't talk about jobs."

"You two old buddies from somewhere?" the colonel asked.

"We met on the plane," Hastings explained. "She had a lousy cold. About gone now?" Sally nodded. "Good."

"Good God," Armbrewster muttered.

"To business, folks," Colonel Eiger said. "Lieutenant, what do you think of the photographs in that folder?"

"They're appalling," Sally said, opening the file. "Where were they taken?"

"That's rather what we hoped you could tell us," Armbrewster said.

Sally looked around the table; the eyes on her were friendly, but intent. She understood what was going on; it was a test. She had told Colonel Eiger in Iowa that she had seen pictures like these. Quickly she leafed through the four photographs. Two of them were from the camps, two were not. She took the first two and laid them on the table.

"These," she said, "are from a concentration camp, probably British photos, taken when they liberated Dachau."

"Bingo," Doug said.

"A quick decision, Lieutenant," Hastings drawled from down the table. Sally leaned forward so she could see around Max Tobin.

"I've been analyzing all sorts of photographs for nearly five years, Captain," she said in a businesslike voice.

"This sort of material would never have crossed your desk," Nelson Armbrewster protested.

"Not so," Sally said. She looked at him for a moment, then said, "I recognized them. My boss in D.C. showed me similar photos. He did it to encourage me to volunteer for this job."

"An effective ploy, I imagine," Armbrewster said dryly.

"I'm here, aren't I?" she replied, copying his tone of voice.

"You are, Lieutenant," Colonel Eiger said. "Now tell us about the other two. Why aren't they from Dachau as well?"

"Do you mind if I smoke?" she asked.

"Go right ahead," the colonel said.

Sally reached for her bag, then realized she hadn't brought it and looked around. The colonel, interpreting her glance, tossed his pack of Luckys down the table. She thanked him and lit one. When she was ready, figuring that she had stalled long enough, she picked up the two pictures.

"Well, let's see," she mused, already sure of what she would say. "Primarily, the sky . . ."

"There was no sky showing in the others," Armbrewster said.

"No, Captain, you're correct, but what I was going to say was . . . that the light is different. These two were taken at a different time of year, and probably, place. Also the ground is different, allowing, of course, for the disturbance to it."

She was silent for a moment, looking at the pictures of the long, ugly gashes in the earth filled with dead people. The dream . . . she pushed the memory away. "And there is the difference in situation." She looked across the table at Doug and Nelson. "Sometimes you get so involved analyzing shadows and light sources and all that you forget to look at the content."

"And what about it?" Captain Tobin asked in his soft voice.

Sally shook her head, then leaned back in her chair and took a deep drag on her cigarette. "Did Germans—are these German? Taken in Poland or Russia, early in the war?"

"Yes, Lieutenant, they are," Tobin said.

"Excellent," Armbrewster said. "Now tell us how you knew."

Sally pointed to a faint shadow in the foreground of one of the pictures. "There. I'd guess that was the photographer. A member of the SS group that did the killing, no doubt. The bodies are naked, but not as thin, or as . . . old as the camp victims."

"Old?" Doug asked.

"They haven't been dead for as long, I would guess," she said, hoping he wouldn't want her to go into detail. He was the soldier, for God's sake. He was the one who should recognize a corpse that had been lying around for some time. The young captain was silent, so Sally continued.

"I'm making an intuitive guess about the place—the sky and quality of light, the sense of emptiness, of space makes me think of the east. And finally, in this one"—she picked up the second picture—"you can see the silhouette of a soldier—SS enlisted man, I'd

31

say, from the shape of his cap. Was this an Einsatzgruppen commando unit?"

"Very good, Lieutenant," the colonel said, "and to answer your question, yes, they are from a roll of film recovered from the body of an SS noncom. These are the only two photographs that could be recovered."

Because of his ready confirmation of her identification, Sally's suspicion that this was a setup was confirmed. The men around the table relaxed, pulled out cigarettes, got up for more coffee. Max Tobin took a handkerchief out of his pocket and started to clean his spectacles.

"Glad to have you with us, Lieutenant," he said quietly, almost shyly.

Feeling very pleased, Sally smiled at him. Beyond Max, Tim Hastings, still slouched in his chair, winked at her. She ducked her head and turned away abruptly to stuff the photographs back in the envelope.

Over the next few weeks, Sally came to know her colleagues and to understand more fully the task D-6 had been set. Although their work was not directly connected to the military tribunal currently in session at Nuremberg, they had been asked to contribute some input to that trial and to the smaller trials being held throughout the American sector. With that, they began to wade through the mountains of documents the Third Reich had left behind.

The focus of D-6's work was the SS. Hitler's palace guard, the administrators of the concentration camps, the nucleus of the new race. From a small group of bodyguards in makeshift uniforms, the SS had grown into a monolithic organization with influence in virtually every sphere of the life of the nation and the occupied lands. Little was known about its organization, and that was part of the information D-6 was collecting.

Sally was particularly useful in identifying the ranks and outfits of SS men in photographs, and in the attempt to identify the men themselves. That information was passed on to another group in military intelligence, who in turn started the hunt—or not. There was no problem finding evidence; the problem was in sifting through it.

All of this work had to be done in a country that had had all of its services destroyed, its citizens traumatized. Making the situation even more difficult was the increasingly tense relationship between the Western Allies and Soviet Russia. Already, in the spring of 1946, the line between former enemy and former friend was quickly blurring. But much of that Sally wouldn't come to understand until she had lived in the midst of it for a time.

On that first morning, as they were filing out, Colonel Eiger asked her to have lunch with him and led her into his office.

"I apologize about the setup," he confessed. "I wanted the guys to be impressed with you, Lieutenant." He bit into one of the ham-and-Swiss sandwiches that had materialized—thanks to Sergeant Dolan. "I knew they were resisting the idea of a woman working with us. I figured you could give them a little demonstration and show them what you could do. Thanks for not disappointing me. I am impressed that you identified the two Ukrainian pictures as well. Good work."

"Thank you, sir," said Sally, "but that was not very difficult. Try proving that two people in two different pictures taken twenty years apart are the same person, especially when you can only see one face from the side—if the picture is blown up five or six times."

"I see what you mean," said Eiger. "Well, it served our purpose. Now, how are your quarters? Things are still pretty rough here, although you should have seen it six months ago."

"I can imagine—or, rather, I can't imagine."

"How's that?"

"Well, flying into Tempelhof—I'd read about the bombing, but seeing the results, even a year afterward . . ."

"And we've all been clearing up like crazy. Especially the Russians, they're much better housekeepers than we are. Do you know those bastards have actually dismantled factories and set them up in the USSR?" He let out an abrupt laugh, then began to tell Sally about his attempts—unsuccessful—to bring his wife to Berlin when he found he would be stationed here for over a year. "Although," he added, "I'm not sure I'd want her to see this place."

Their sandwiches and coffee finished, he picked up a pencil and began to fiddle with it. "Tell me about your years here before the war," he said, catching Sally unawares.

"What do you want to know?" she said, resentful of his tactics. She had just begun to like him.

"Did you like it? How aware were you of what the Nazis were up to? You were here four years, weren't you?"

"Three, just barely," she said. "Can I bum another cigarette? I promise to buy you a pack."

"Sure. You'll have to remind me to tell you about our PX." He held out his pack for her. "I'm still waiting," he said, when they both settled back in their chairs. She watched him manipulate the pencil.

"I was here almost three years, and yes, for most of the time, I

33

liked it. I loved the city. Did you know I was born here? My father was working on his doctorate then. We came back to Germany for summers when I was a child. That's when I learned to speak the language. I have a real Berliner accent."

"That ought to come in handy," he said.

"Being a Berliner, Colonel, is sort of like being a New Yorker. You know, being tough and resourceful, with a sense of humor. Not believing anything anyone tells you. And very proud of the city."

"Yet they voted for Hitler."

"No, they didn't. The Nazis never took Berlin. The Communists were much the stronger party. Red Berlin, the Nazis called it. The Nazis were always nervous about their support in the city. Hitler was supposed to hate the place."

"Those were Berliners under Hitler's window, carrying torches."

"True. Something happened to them. Maybe their history—they've always been subjugated by some king or dictator. That's partly why the capital of the republic was in Weimar. I don't know what happened, Colonel."

"Don't expect you to. But, back then, what did you think of the government?"

"Well," she said, thinking carefully through the conflicting feelings the conversation had aroused in her, "I was one of those foreigners who, at first, thought everything was just great. You've got to understand that it all seemed so . . . so terrifically healthy. This was early, in '33 and '34."

"What happened to change your mind?"

"I wish I could say it was some sort of political awakening, but it wasn't. The trouble I got into . . . it was . . ." She stopped, not knowing what to say. "I was a naive kid, really. Not that I'm so wise now. Just not a kid anymore."

"Yeah, I sure know what you mean. But you never admired them for, you know, making the trains run on time?"

"No, I was just, or I tried to be, neutral. I had lived in Italy as a child and we traveled a great deal. I suppose I had the notion that the host country's politics were none of my business. That was how I was raised. Also, I just wasn't interested in politics. My father never talked to me about his job, either, so I didn't have that advantage. Looking back, though, I can clearly see how much he disliked, hated, really, what was going on."

"I see," said Colonel Eiger thoughtfully, still playing with the pencil.

"Sir?" Sally said tentatively. "What do the rest of the fellows know about me?" She laughed nervously. "Lord, I really sound like I have a past, don't I?"

"Let's look at it this way, Lieutenant. The men know you lived here and who your dad was. Your past is part of why you're here now."

"You sound as though you have a specific plan for me."

"No. It's just what I said. Your experience here, especially your . . ."—he paused, searching for the right word—". . . your friendship with Heydrich makes you a valuable eyewitness for us."

"Heydrich's dead. I mean, if you're expecting me to identify someone." Sally thought of the photograph she had seen of his Mercedes, the door hanging open, a small team of Gestapo agents investigating the broad street around it. The commandos had thrown a grenade under the big car, which had disabled it, but Heydrich, as grievously wounded as he was, had jumped out and run after his attackers waving his side arm. She could imagine him doing that, his will had been so strong, his discipline so fierce.

"No, of course not we don't expect you to identify anyone," the colonel was saying. "But you were here. At the very least you know what the lay of the land was."

"Hardly," Sally laughed bitterly. "I saw what was in front of my nose and then I did my best to ignore it."

"Well, Lieutenant, that may be. But you'll be there if we need you, and meanwhile you are the best picture person we've got."

"I'm the only one."

He grinned at her and she had to grin back at him. "Right," he said, tossing the pencil onto his desk and standing up. She stood as well. "I'd say you see a little farther now," he continued. She looked at him, questioning. He held his hand up in front of his face. "Than in front of your nose, Lieutenant."

"Yes, sir. Well, you can't say I don't learn." He laughed out loud at that and came around the desk.

"I believe Finkelstein had an interview with a guy we think was a guard at a work camp. You should sit in, okay? Learn something interesting about the Krupps and the business they ran. God, what a time we live in, Lieutenant. What a time."

She stopped on her way to the door. "Colonel?"

"Yes?"

"Do they know I knew the general? Do they know about my marriage?"

"They know about the general. Not about the other. I figured that was private."

"Yes, Colonel. Thank you."

* * *

One beautiful morning a week later, Mavis, as promised, took Sally to visit a DP camp outside of Berlin. The camp was being closed down shortly because of the growing tension between the Allies, and there weren't as many people sitting in front of the barracks or standing in line at the kitchens.

"You should have seen it a month ago," the doctor said, as they got out of the jeep. She had driven them, handling the recalcitrant machine with ease. She pulled her large bag out of the back, waving off Sally's offer of help. "I'm so used to lugging this thing around, I'd feel lost without it. Listen, I'll be in here for a while." She indicated the whitewashed building in front of them. "I've got some paperwork to do. It'll take me about half an hour. Then I've got my rounds. Stay close and you can come with me on those. All right?"

The camp was laid out in a grid, much like an army base, and, as Mavis had explained, that was exactly what it had been. Sally walked around the grounds, stopped, facing the gate to smoke a cigarette. Some of the DPs eyed her, one or two drifted closer, but none approached. Still, their keen interest in her smoking made her throw the cigarette down half-smoked and walk away without stamping the fire out. She heard the scuffle behind her, but didn't turn to watch. It was too disturbing.

The hospital where Mavis took Sally was emptying day by day, as patients either got well and were sent to other camps, or didn't get well and were sent to other hospitals. Some were still dying of malnutrition.

"The effects of that will last for years," Mavis said, peering into the eyes and ears of a teenage girl who, because of her thinness, looked twelve. "These kids, even if they live, will suffer from tooth decay, respiratory ailments, backaches." The doctor stood up, smiling at the girl, who obviously did not understand English. "We learned that after the last war, from the blockade of Germany." As she went from patient to patient, carefully, efficiently examining them, Mavis told Sally about her Quaker parents, who had sailed to Germany with powdered milk for the starving children of the defeated and humiliated country in 1918.

"They were heroes," Sally said.

"I know. I have a lot to live up to. But I'm afraid I've got none of their nobility of character. I get too mad," she said, pulling off her examining gloves.

"Still," said Sally, looking about the neat ward, with its scrubbed wood floor and white bedsteads, "it must be worth it to know you've saved even just one person, let alone a whole ward."

"These? Save these? Oh, my dear, these children are all dying. I don't expect to save any of them. Not a one."

Sally was sitting on the front steps of the hospital when Mavis came out.

"Ready to go?" the doctor asked.

Sally stood up and followed Mavis to the jeep. "Mavis, all those kids! How can you manage? I'd be in despair."

"And I'm not?"

"You don't seem to be."

"Well, perhaps not. I guess I still have hope."

"For what?"

"Maybe I'll save one of them." Mavis put her arm through Sally's. "They're as comfortable as we can make them, clean and fed and gently treated. And you know what? I've even seen one or two of them smile."

"That's the saddest thing I've ever heard. I couldn't do it," Sally said.

"Well, you have the worst of it." Mavis climbed into the jeep and Sally walked around to the other side.

"Me?"

"Yes. Looking at those gruesome photographs." Sally had told Mavis about the colonel's setup. "I'd rather treat real people. You never get anything back; none of those people ever, ever smile at you."

"No, no, they don't. But I don't think I could take care of those kids like you do, not without breaking down."

"Well, they are sending me on R and R, so maybe they think I am. Come, on, climb in. Let's go."

Sally sighed with relief as they passed under the chicken wire and wood arch of the camp gate, glad she didn't have to go back.

CHAPTER 4

There." Sally pointed excitedly at the apartment house Lisa Mayr
had lived in. "There it is. Number twenty-three, you can even
can even see the number."

"Almost looks normal," Doug Finkelstein said. He had unexpectedly agreed to accompany Sally when she decided she should try
and find Christian's family. She explained that they were old friends
of her family, which was the truth, just not the entire truth.

As Doug stopped the car in front of the building, a man in a
well-worn Wehrmacht overcoat came out of the front door and
down the steps. Sally quickly got out of the car and walked up to
him.

"Good afternoon," she said in German. The man looked at her,
his expression guarded, but noncommittal.

"Good afternoon, miss," he answered.

"Do you live in this building?"

"Why?" he answered, immediately suspicious, his gaze going
past Sally to the car and Doug.

"I wonder if you could help me find someone?"

"No, no, no one. I know no one here," he said, moving off.

"But, please . . ." Sally tried, but she was talking to his back as
he hurried down the scattered sidewalk and away.

"That was real successful," she remarked as Doug came up to
her.

"Yeah," he said, "you really won his heart."

"Bad approach." Going up to the door, she gave it a push and
entered the building. The hallway was dark, dingy, and dank with
water and smoke stains. Heavy gouges marred the wood paneling
and the marble floor was cracked. It was very quiet.

There was a door on either side of the entry. The concierge had
lived on the right. Sally knocked on the door; no one answered. She
knocked again. Nothing.

"Nobody home," Doug said softly. Something about the place
discouraged loud conversation.

"Damn," Sally said, "but I'm not really surprised."

"Your friend could have moved away before the war started."

"Yeah," she agreed. She would have to try every tenant in the building. Surely someone would know something. She walked across the hall to the other door.

But before she could knock, two kids, a boy and a girl, raced in from outside, nearly knocking Doug over with their energy. They stopped and looked at Doug and Sally, but did not respond to Sally's smile.

"Hi," she said nervously, taking a step toward them. They backed away. Sally stopped her advance. The boy was about eleven and the girl about eight. The girl, after a good long look at Sally, finally spoke.

"Lady GI?" she said in English.

"Yes," said Sally.

"Gum?" the boy asked. Sally patted her coat and searched her bag.

"Sorry," she said, holding out her empty hands. They both looked at Doug, who was close to the front door. He shook his head. The kids shrugged and started up the stairs.

"Wait!" Sally called. In German, she added quickly, "Maybe we can trade something."

The kids stopped, peering at her over the railing. "What?" the boy said, putting his hands on his hips.

"Information," Sally said. "I can pay you for it."

"About what?" The boy was impatient.

"We don't know anybody," the girl said.

"A friend of mine," Sally said, opening her purse. She found two quarters and held them out on her hand. "As a sign of good faith," she said. "Two now and two after—if you can help me."

The children looked at each other, obviously considering. Quickly grabbing the quarters, the girl hid them in her clothing.

"A friend from before the war," said Sally. "An older lady lived here. She was a friend of mine. I came here to visit." She looked around at the ruined entry hall. "It was very nice."

"We weren't here then," the boy said.

"But maybe my friend or someone from her family has come by," Sally said into their young, closed faces. "I just want to know how she is."

"The name, miss. What was the name?" asked the boy.

"Mayr was the family name. My friend's name was Lisa." The children studied each other for a moment, then shook their heads. "Frau Doktor Mayr?"

"Not here now," the boy said, although Sally was sure she had detected a flicker of recognition at the name.

"Were they Jews?" the girl asked.

"No," Sally answered evenly.

"Good, because if they were, they wouldn't come back," the little girl said.

"Yes, I realize that."

"I'm going to wait in the car," Doug told her and went out the door. Sally felt rather than heard a sound behind her. She turned back to the children in time to see the boy's eyes shift to his right. He and the girl moved up the stairs. Looking toward the door on her left, Sally saw it closing. She stared at it for a moment, unsure of what she had seen, then she looked up at the children. They stood, almost lost in the shadows, watching her. She and the two kids stared at each other for a long moment, all three of them waiting to see what she would do.

"You'll remember the name?" she called, hating the way her voice echoed in the dank hall.

"Yes." The boy's voice was nearly inaudible.

"Do we get the money now?" the girl piped.

"Okay," Sally agreed, smiling. They were just kids, after all, and had been through more than kids should. She couldn't be angry with them for watching out for themselves. It was probably one reason they were still alive. She tossed two more quarters through the damp air to them. Snap. Snap. The boy caught them and handed them to the girl, who stowed them away with the first two.

"If you hear that name—Lisa Mayr—will you call me?" Sally asked them, and pulling a notebook from her purse, tore out a page. "Here's where I live." She recited the address as she wrote it, then did the same with her phone number. "Just in case you hear something." She held the paper out toward the boy. "I'll pay."

The children whispered together, then the boy said, "What will you pay?"

"Anything you like," Sally said, "that I can get. Food, money, clothes. Chocolate?"

"Chocolate?" The girl was obviously unfamiliar with the word.

"I know what that is," the boy said.

"If you call me with news of my friend," Sally said.

The boy nodded, then he and the girl disappeared up into the dark of the broad staircase. For a few minutes, Sally stood in the entry hall and listened, but she could hear nothing. She stared at the door that had opened and closed so mysteriously, wondering if she had the guts to knock on it. She took a step toward it, then, unaccountably, felt deeply frightened. At that moment, Doug came through the front door, startling her so that she yelped.

"Sorry," he said, laughing at her, "what happened?"

"Oh, nothing," she said, pulling at the strap of her shoulder bag, at the belt of her coat, calming herself. "I was just spooking myself. C'mon, let's get out of here."

In the car, he asked her if the kids had been of any help and she told him about her deal.

"You'll never hear from them," Doug said, starting the car.

"Maybe," Sally murmured, thinking about that closed door. Who had been behind it? Recalling the response of the man in the Wehrmacht coat, she decided that if anyone had been there, he—or she—had probably been too wary of her. Maybe, next time she went hunting, she shouldn't wear her uniform.

"I hate seeing kids like that," she said sadly. A line of women in shabby coats and kerchiefs were clearing a site of bricks across the street.

"Yeah," said Doug, "but at least they're alive." He glanced at her. "The place must have looked real different to you." Sally was silent, then shook her head.

"It was a long time ago."

Annaliese, in a pale-yellow dress the same color as her hair, white lace ruffles at her neck and down the front, leaned over the balustrade and cried, "Congratulations!"

Colored confetti fluttered down, catching the light from the wall sconces, twinkling in the sound of laughter, landing on the upturned faces of Sally and her new husband, as they climbed the stairs to the party.

It had been a long time ago.

Sally had always been a loner, so it was a new experience to be part of a team. She liked it and she also liked the men she worked with. Still, she spent most of her time alone and she began to go for walks, going farther and farther as the damp spring turned into a dry summer. The Mayr apartment was the first of the sites she visited from her past. Next, she found the house, or what was left of it, where she had lived with her father. Another day she stood staring at the hole in the ground where the apartment building Sydney and Brian Stokes had lived in had once been. But she was more distressed than she would have imagined to see the Adlon Hotel, her first home in Berlin, a ruin.

It was a fine June evening as she stood across the street and studied the broken facade of the grand old hotel, remembering all those happy times with David Wohl after her fencing lessons. Now, weeds grew over the ruins.

41

She turned away and walked quickly down the Friedrichstrasse into the American sector, wishing she could find some company. And she realized that she missed Denise, her friend back at Mrs. Wallace's boardinghouse. She was about to go back to her room, when she remembered that Doug Finkelstein had mentioned a restaurant set up by an American of German descent that was supposed to be decent. She paused to take her bearings. It wouldn't be a long walk, and the evening was still pleasant, the light still good.

Having found the restaurant easily, Sally stood in the doorway for a moment. It was busy, Occupation officers only. Heading toward the tiny bar through the door to her right, she ran her fingers through her hair, hoping she didn't look too disheveled. The men glanced up at her, but turned away. There were other uniformed women present, so she felt comfortable enough to take a seat at one of the round tables. A waiter came over at once, to take her order.

"A martini?" she asked hopefully, pleased when he nodded. Sally looked around the little room and a memory stirred. She had been here before, also with David Wohl. Turning in her seat, she recognized the distinctive window moldings, strange feathered designs, covered in white paint. The bar had been a place frequented by the newspaper crowd. Sally sat back in her chair and felt, for the first time since she returned, that she had found someplace familiar. She took her cigarettes from her bag and lit one.

"So this is what you do with your weekends." Tim Hastings stood in front of her, a cigarette dangling from his lips, a beer stein in one hand.

"Hi," she said, pleased to see him. "Have a seat."

"Thanks." Tim sat down. "You here alone?"

"I was out walking."

"Walking?"

"Yeah. Don't they walk in Wichita?"

"Not if they can help it. Where've you been walking to?"

"A sentimental journey. I've been seeing how many places I remember are still standing."

"And?"

"This is about it." Sally looked up at the waiter as he placed her martini on the table. "Thank you," she said in German. She told Tim how David Wohl and the others used to fall silent when one of the waiters came near.

"And now we talk about anything in front of them."

"Do we?"

"I hope not," Tim said, swallowing some beer. "So, you were here before the war?"

"I was," she answered, looking at his intelligent face for a sign of censure. "My dad was the ambassador here in the early thirties. Didn't you know that?"

"The ambassador? Nope, I didn't. Where'd you think I'd hear that? That's fascinating."

"The colonel said you all knew."

"Probably before I arrived. Is it classified?"

Sally shrugged. "I don't think it matters. It was one reason they hired me."

"So, tell me about it. Who'd you meet? How long were you here for?"

"Three years. From '33 to '36. Hitler. William Shirer. Maestro Joaquim von Hohenberg."

Tim whistled. "I'm impressed, even with the last guy, who I've never heard of."

"He was one of the last of the great fencing instructors of the Italian school, which was taught to the officers of the Austro-Hungarian Empire." She raised her glass to him and drank.

"Fencing? You fenced?"

"I did. I was pretty good."

"Why'd you stop?"

"You play any sports, Captain? Basketball, maybe? Lacrosse?"

He laughed at that and shook his head. "Naw. Baseball. Left field. The king of the pop-ups. Foul-Ball Hastings, they called me. Really. You laugh, but it's the gospel. You know how all ball players used to have nicknames. That was mine. But I liked the left field. All because of Mary Anna Caswell."

"And what did she have to do with it?" For some reason Sally felt obscurely jealous of Mary Anna Caswell.

"She used to sit in the grass beyond the fence, and when things were slow, which seemed to be most of the time, I'd wander over and we'd, you know, talk. Sometimes, she'd bring me a hot dog."

"Baseball and hot dogs and a pretty girl. I assume she was pretty."

"As a picture. Snub nose and blond curls." He shook his head and took a long drink of beer. "What a gal. Now you, you're amazing. How'd you get into fencing? That's interesting. It's such a weird thing for a girl to do."

"In school," she said shortly and fell silent. Then, embarrassed at her brusqueness: "I had forgotten about this place. I liked it." Sally looked around at the tables and the handsome little bar, the newly glazed windows. "I was afraid there would be so many ghosts."

43

"Are there?"

"A few." She sipped her martini.

"Do you have any friends left?" Tim asked.

Sally laughed. "None. Not a one in the world."

"I meant here," he said, laughing with her.

"I don't think so—most were foreigners and they're gone, of course. And as for the few Germans, I haven't been able to find anyone. Not that there were that many to find . . . I mean, that I'd want to find."

"Maybe they've left too," he said.

"Yeah," said Sally, looking away from his green eyes. She took a sip of her martini. "Wow, this is good." And she took another sip. Tim laughed. "What?" she said.

"Oh, nothing, I just like to see you enjoying yourself."

And Sally, realizing that she was, grinned at him.

"So, tell me, Doctor, sir, what's a pop-up?" she said; then twisted in her seat, looking for the waiter. "And what does a person have to do to get another drink?"

CHAPTER 5

The knocking brought Sally out of a deep sleep, and she found herself halfway around her bed before she was entirely awake. She stood near the foot of her bed, confused, her heart beating wildly. It was late on a Saturday afternoon and she had lain down for a short nap. She looked at her watch, staring at it until her sleepy eyes focused: it was nearly six.

"Sally? Are you there?" the voice outside called.

"What is it?" she replied, opening the door.

"Oh, I'm sorry," said the woman, whose name Sally couldn't remember. She was a nurse and lived across the hall. "You were asleep."

"It's okay." Sally pulled her shirt down over her bare legs. "I slept too long."

"You've got a visitor."

"Who?"

"A woman, a German," Margie said. That was her name, Margie Allen. She'd raised her eyebrows when she said the visitor was German.

"Oh," said Sally, "well, I better comb my hair."

"And put on a skirt," Margie said, walking away.

Dressed in a short-sleeved blouse and slacks, her hair brushed, Sally walked down the stairs to the small reception area on the first floor. The door to the parlor was slightly open, and pushing it open, she entered.

Across from her in the long, sparsely furnished room stood Annaliese Mayr, Christian's younger sister. Astounded, Sally gasped as Annaliese took a step toward her, then stopped.

"Hello, Sally," Annaliese said, "do you remember me?" She spoke German, reminding Sally that Annaliese had never learned any English.

"Of course I do." Sally couldn't stop staring. "I don't believe it."

Annaliese shrugged. "It's only me."

"You look—" Sally broke off when she saw Annaliese's questioning look. "Great. This is such a surprise. I've been looking for

45

you." She smiled at Annaliese, unsure of how to proceed. "Please, why don't you sit down?"

"I got your message two days ago." Annaliese said, following Sally to the sofa.

"From the children?"

"The children?"

"The kids at your old building—number twenty-three?"

"Oh, Sally," laughed Annaliese, "we haven't lived there in years."

"Then how did they find you? Who found you?"

"You know how it is," said Annaliese vaguely. She touched Sally's arm. "You look well. I like your hair."

Sally's hand floated to her hair at the back of her neck. "I just got it cut. Too short, I think. But, how are you? And what about your mother? I've been so worried about all of you."

"Have you, Sally? How sweet of you. May I smoke?" Annaliese opened her handbag, a well-worn, but good-quality, brown leather envelope.

"Oh, certainly." Sally took her cigarettes out of her trouser pocket. "Have one of these if you like. I'll go see if I can find us some coffee." She started toward the door, then stopped. "Or would you rather have something else?"

"Coffee would be fine."

When Sally returned, Annaliese stood at the window at the far end of the room, her slim figure silhouetted against the fading evening light. She turned as Sally entered carrying a tray with two mugs of coffee, a pot of powdered milk, and a saucer of sugar cubes. Annaliese was dressed in a dark-red suit with a round collar on which she had pinned a small bunch of white-and-black fake flowers. She wore a black straw hat that looked fresh and stylish.

She bore a striking resemblance to her brother. Sally had never seen it before, but it must have always been there. Annaliese's hair and eyes, the line of her jaw, even her nose, everything was a softer, feminine version of Christian's features. Sally couldn't stop looking at her.

"Don't you love summer evenings like this?" Annaliese said, walking purposefully down the room toward Sally. All of a sudden, Sally knew Christian's sister had come to get something. Or—and her heart beat quicker when she thought of it—to tell her something.

"They remind me of childhood summers," said Sally. "Look, why don't we go upstairs? My room's not much better, but it is a little more comfortable."

Annaliese smiled and picked up Sally's cigarettes. "I'll bring these, shall I?"

In Sally's room, they made themselves comfortable, one on each of the twin beds, their coffee mugs on the small nightstand between them.

"How long have you been here?" Annaliese asked.

"Since late April," Sally replied. "Do you want milk in that?" She indicated the mug of coffee.

"Is it real?" asked her visitor. Sally shook her head.

"Then this is fine," said Annaliese, taking a sip. "And how long will you be here?"

"I don't know. As long as it takes."

"As what takes?"

Sally looked at the coffee in her mug, then said abruptly, "My job." She didn't want to talk about it with Annaliese. "What about you? Are you working?"

"No," said Annaliese, "I am in a—a situation that requires me to be at home. I do not mind. It works out to be easier and cheaper all the way around. What is your job?"

"Research," said Sally, then she grinned. "You know I am in the army?"

"No! This I can't imagine. Must I salute you?" Annaliese giggled, sounding more the girl Sally remembered.

"Please," Sally said. They smiled at each other, relaxing at the little joke.

Annaliese made herself more comfortable against the headboard, kicking off her shoes and folding her legs to one side, looking neat and self-contained. "Did you ever marry again?"

"No, did you marry?"

"Yes." Annaliese took a long drag on her cigarette, then, picking up the ashtray from the nightstand, snubbed the Camel out. "He's dead."

"Oh, I'm sorry . . ."

"It's over now," said Annaliese, interrupting. "He died a long time ago. In Africa. I can barely remember back that far."

Sally was silent, unsure of what to say. Annaliese's expression was grave, her pale-blue eyes remote. "You have to go forward and not look back, in such times as these." Swinging around, she put her bare feet flat on the floor, stood up and smoothed her straight skirt.

She walked around the room looking at Sally's things. Her blond hair was carefully waved, so that it formed a halo around her thin face. Her makeup was tastefully applied, and she wore small gold earrings. She was a very attractive woman.

"Where do you live now?" Sally asked.

"In the Russian sector. Off Neue Königstrasse, beyond Alexanderplatz." Annaliese stopped in front of the small, unused fireplace in the corner where Sally had arranged her books on the mantel. "Did you always read so much?" Then, before Sally could answer: "I have a child."

Annaliese walked back to the bed and sat down facing Sally. "Her name is Klara and she is four years old." Her face relaxed as she spoke of her little girl. "She's a wonderful child. Oh, I know all mothers think that of their children. But Klara and I have gotten to know each other well because of the hardships we have faced together, so I can say this about her."

"You're very lucky," Sally said.

"Yes, but it has been, at times, very difficult."

"I can imagine."

"Can you?" Annaliese studied Sally with her chill blue eyes. "Where were you during the war?"

"I didn't mean . . ."

"Where were you? I'm interested," Annaliese said, reaching for another cigarette, then stopping. "May I?"

"Of course," said Sally. "I spent the war in Washington, at a desk."

"Ah," said Annaliese ironically. "And you can imagine how it has been for us."

"Annaliese, I didn't mean to insult you or condescend."

"What do you want?" said Annaliese harshly.

"Nothing."

Annaliese looked at Sally through the smoke from her cigarette. She drew on it deeply, more intensely. "Nothing? Don't be silly. Everyone wants something. Well, if I have it, I will give it to you, but for a price. You understand."

"I don't want anything from you. Honestly, I don't," said Sally, dismayed.

"We weren't such good friends, Sally. I wonder that you would think of me at all."

"I know, but . . ."

"When I heard you were in Berlin, I tried to remember us together, but the only thing that came to mind was that party Mother gave you, remember?"

"Yes, of course I do."

"That was all. We weren't friends. Not then. Not later. But of course, it's not me you want, is it?" Annaliese smiled a mirthless smile at Sally, and Sally, unable to help herself, looked away. "You don't care about me or my mother."

"Of course I do," Sally protested.

"You want to know about my brother, don't you?" Still Annaliese smiled. "Maybe you came all the way back here just to find him. I think you did, but the question is why?" Her voice dropped to a whisper. "Perhaps you came back for revenge. No? You couldn't still love him, not after all these years and all the things he's done."

"What do you mean by that?" Sally suddenly felt cold, afraid, as though a ghost had entered the room.

"You know." Annaliese's eyes caught and held Sally's. "What he did to you. I know all about it."

"How?" whispered Sally.

"He told me. I remember the morning after you'd been attacked. I found him crying on the stairs at my mother's, leaning against the wall, like a child. It was terrible, what happened to you, but I thought you both were fools, stupid fools. Not to see. Not to understand how impossible it was for you.

"He was such a romantic—so many young men were then. And he needed a girl who was practical. You just weren't the right sort for him. You weren't what he needed then. You knew that, didn't you? You both knew that. But you fools, you thought you could ignore everything."

Annaliese reached across the space between the beds and took Sally's hands. "I did not know you well but I loved my brother then and I wished you both well. I am very sorry for the terrible thing that happened to you, and I wish you had never met each other."

"We were young," said Sally, wanting to free her hands, but not wanting Annaliese to know how uncomfortable she was.

"Yes, but you destroyed him. If he hadn't been with you, he wouldn't have . . ." Her voice trailed off. She let go of Sally's hands and leaned back. "Here I am, talking about what can't be changed. And I said we had to look forward. You can see how useless it is to look back."

"Yes."

"Do you have anything else to drink?" Annaliese stood up, looking around the room. "Oh, what is this?" she said, spying the bottle of brandy on the floor under the little sink. "Good. I'll pour us both a drink." She looked around for glasses.

"I only have the one glass," Sally said, getting up quickly. "Here, I can wash out my coffee mug."

"I'll do it." Annaliese reached for the mug. She rinsed it, then poured the brandy, handing the mug back to Sally. "I'm sorry to be so hard," she said, not sounding sorry at all. "I've gotten very nasty."

Sally took a sip of brandy. It wasn't very good, but she welcomed the sharpness. "Why are you here?"

"You were looking for us. I wanted to know why."

"Your mother was kind to me. I'll never forget that, and because . . . because I wanted to see if I could do anything."

"Because of my brother."

"Yes. And no. Because of your mother, too. Maybe more."

Annaliese walked to the window and pushed it open. "Mama's dead," she said, not turning around. "An air raid. She was buried in a shelter, left there. My sister Marta died in London, also in a raid, but one of ours. That was all in '42, a long time ago. But Ursula is still alive in Copenhagen. I have many Danish nieces and nephews." She reached for a cigarette. "What about your family? I mostly remember your brother. What was his name?"

"Eddie," Sally said dumbly. At the news of Lisa's death, she had stood up, the mug of brandy still in her hand. She looked down at it. Lisa dead too.

"Yes, Eddie, that's it. I remember him at the lake those summers. Didn't he go into the navy?"

"Yes." Sally drained the mug.

"He died," said Annaliese flatly. Sally looked up at her. "I can recognize your expression. I've seen it so often. You get used to it."

"No, I don't think so. Not really. Not ever." Sally sank down on the bed. Lisa dead. She hadn't realized how much she had counted on Lisa Mayr's being alive and safe somewhere. "I'd hoped that your mother had gone back to Denmark to stay."

"She came back. She was a Berliner." They were silent for a moment, then Annaliese said in a gentle voice, "I'm sorry about your brother. I never thought of Americans dying."

"We died."

"Yes. You've grown hard too," said Annaliese.

"Yes."

"You were a sweet girl, Sally." She smiled a true smile that thawed the ice in her eyes. "You always were. Nice. Honest. So was your brother."

"So was yours," said Sally, although her voice caught on the words.

Annaliese smiled a funny half-smile. "Was he? He might have been once. Yes, I think he was, back then. But he wound up a real bastard."

Sally looked at the ugly utility light on the nightstand. "Annaliese," she started, but had to stop and swallow, her voice felt so raspy. "Annaliese, is he still alive?"

Annaliese shrugged. "I don't know. The last time I saw him was before the Russians came. I begged him to get me and Klara out of the city. He could have, too. He was on his way south on some official matter—he said—and he could have taken us. He didn't even come to the apartment where I lived. I had to run into him on the Mühldamm. I asked him right there, but he left us to the Russians. I didn't care so much for me, you understand. My generation is finished. But I'll never forgive him for Klara's sake. She is all the hope I had left, she is all that is left that is good. And my brother left her to die. I hate him for it. So, no—I don't know if he lived and I hope he didn't. He probably changed out of his pretty uniform and ran away somewhere. All those supermen, so called, did that. Big, strong men. They ran out on their women and children, leaving us to . . ."

Picking up her glass, Annaliese drank the last of the brandy. "You must meet my Klara. I want you to, because I want you to help her. That's the real reason I came to see you."

"I'll be glad to," said Sally. "I'll do anything I can for her. Just tell me."

Annaliese laughed sadly. "I just thought . . ."

"What?"

"You were almost her aunt."

Sally slid to the foot of the bed and leaned forward, looking up at Annaliese. "I thought that too. Let me be, please? For your mother's sake. I'd be happy to do whatever I can for Klara. For you, too."

"What do you want? Why be so altruistic?"

"I loved your mother, Annaliese. Your family was the best part of my childhood. I've lost them all, too. As well as my own. There's nobody left, Annaliese. And Christian, I loved him. I can't say I didn't, that it was all wrong. There's no one left now."

"You and me."

"And your daughter."

Annaliese reached to touch Sally's face. "I see," she said gently, a bright gleam in her eyes. Annaliese looked at Sally for a long while, her expression inscrutable, then, suddenly, she glanced out the window. It was dark. "I had better go. Here, I'll give you my address and a phone number. The Russian officer, a colonel, downstairs from me has a telephone and allows me a message on emergencies. Perhaps next Saturday you will come to meet my Klara."

"I will be happy to," Sally said, handing her the small notepad from her table. Annaliese wrote quickly and handed the pad back to Sally. "There, now you know where we are."

"Yes," said Sally. "And what can I bring? Powered milk? Clothes?"

Annaliese thought for a moment. "A coat," she said. "We eat sufficiently, but I have no coat for her."

"Good," Sally said. "I'll do what I can. Now, do you have a way home?"

"Yes," Annaliese said, opening her bag and checking her lipstick. "I have a ride."

Sally walked Annaliese downstairs. After they said good-bye, she stood in the door of the building and watched Annaliese walk across the street and get into a black sedan. Sally couldn't really see the driver, but he wore a military cap and she wondered about the Russian colonel Annaliese said lived downstairs from her. She knew there were German women living on the largess of the occupying armies, and she knew that if she were in the same position, with a four-year-old daughter, she might do the same thing. Her own life and the choices she had to make suddenly seemed so simple compared with those Annaliese faced.

Upstairs again, Sally crossed the room in the dark, and leaning on the windowsill, she studied the shell of the building across the street. It was a bright night, and the shadows cast on the ruin by the moon were sharp-lined and black.

Somehow, she felt less alone. She suspected that Annaliese had information about Christian, for which she would just have to wait patiently. Meanwhile, she knew Annaliese would exploit their connection for her daughter. But, she, Sally, would use it too. Perhaps she could help Christian's niece. After hearing how he abandoned her, Sally realized just how much he must have changed. The man she had loved would never have left his sister and niece in the path of an invading army.

What had happened to him? And the same old questions followed that one: Where had he been when she was lying nearly dead in that Berlin hospital? Why hadn't he ever contacted her?

Sally thought of Annaliese's description of him the morning after, sitting on the steps of the apartment crying. She could see him, had seen him, crying in his uniform, had seen the incongruity of the military trappings and his tears.

Sally turned abruptly from the window. "I'm so . . . so *sick* of this," she said angrily to the dark room. She balled her hands into fists and pushed them against her forehead, the heels of her hands against her eyes, making sparks and dark colors appear, until her head hurt.

Later that night, Sally lay awake in the moonlit room, listening to the silence stretching out around her. Christian was in her thoughts, as he had been since she first flew over the ruins of the city.

As she turned on her side, her eyes fell on her bag sitting on the foot of the other bed. The photographs were still there, at the bottom, where she had put them three months ago.

She sat up and scrambled across her bed to grab the bag. In the dark, she opened it and pulled out the photographs. She didn't look at the pictures in her hand for a long time. She thought of nothing. Just sat in the dark holding the pictures, until, finally, she turned on the little lamp above her nightstand.

The photograph on top was a group shot, taken on the flag-stone terrace of the green house on the lake. There were several adults and many children of various ages in the picture. She turned it over: "Lake Sebastian, 1923."

In front, sitting cross-legged on the ground, was Sally, aged ten. She was a sturdy-looking little girl, with long, messy braids and no shoes. She wore a dress with a flowered pattern, and she looked at the camera with her head slightly ducked, her expression grave.

Her family was behind her: her beautiful mother, seated grace-fully on a wicker chair, her full skirt fanned out; her father, standing straight and tall, in a light summer suit, his arms crossed; Eddie, tanned and stocky, sitting on a step above Sally. His grin was enormous.

Sally smiled at him. How familiar they all looked, how dear, and yet, so distant. She barely remembered her father as young as he was here; she couldn't remember her mother's voice, nor her brother's.

The Mayr family took up the major portion of the photograph. There were eight of them: Herr Doktor Mayr and Lisa, the parents; Marta, Ursula, Annaliese, and Elizabeth, the daughters; and Kurt and Christian, the sons. There had been another son as well: Thomas, who had died at Passchendaele in the First World War.

With a start, thinking of Thomas, the hero, Sally realized that nearly all of the people in the photograph were dead. She closed her eyes and leaned her head back, enumerating the list. Elizabeth of illness later that same year. Herr Doktor and Kurt . . . the first by his own hand in 1933, the second in a street fight in 1927. Lisa and

Marta in air raids. Eddie bayoneted by a Japanese soldier. Her father of a heart attack before Pearl Harbor, and her mother four years after the picture was taken, in the accident in New York. Just me and Ursula and Annaliese. And him.

Sally lowered her head to look down at the fair young man with the grave expression, his elbow on his bare knee, his chin in his hand. Christian.

What of Christian? Was he still alive?

She slid the family photograph behind the other she held in her hand. It was one of those pictures taken in nightclubs by young women in short skirts, and indeed, in the lower-right-hand corner was the name of a club, in German, embossed in gold art-deco lettering: The Blue Parrot.

A crowded tabletop took up the bottom part of the photo. Glasses, full ashtrays, and empty plates surrounded a small lamp with parrots painted on the shade. Seated at the table was a younger, plumper, prettier Sally, dressed in a sparkling, low-cut evening gown, which showed off her round arms and shoulders and cleavage. Her hair was dressed close to her head, but some curls had escaped and framed her face above her ears.

She was leaning close to Christian. They had pushed their chairs together for the picture, Christian with his arm along the back of Sally's chair, his fingers lighting against her bare shoulder. They were happy and drunk, their cheeks shiny, their smiles wide. The Sally in the picture gazed up at Christian adoringly, her large eyes, heavily made up, bright. Her head was tilted back in order to look into his face, and there was a voluptuous abandonment in the posture. Her bare arm lay on the table and a wedding ring was clearly visible on her finger.

Christian gazed out of the photograph, his expression guarded but friendly. His fair hair was parted on the right and combed straight back from his high, square forehead. He had straight eyebrows and a long, straight nose; his mouth was wide and thin-lipped, especially when he was not smiling. His features were stern and regular and his handsomeness could be forbidding. But when he smiled, as he was doing in the photograph, his face lit up, all the straight lines curving, the hard planes softening. He was, at any rate, smiling or not, a very handsome young man.

He was also an SS-Hauptsturmführer, a captain, and was wearing, in the photograph, the flashy silver-and-black dress uniform that was, even then, a symbol of cruelty and hatred.

Sally studied him, as though she could tell from his face, photographed over eleven years ago, if he lived. But she knew, whether he lived or not, that the memory of him would continue to weigh on her.

She shouldn't have come to Berlin. Not without knowing whether he was dead or not. In 1935, he was already a captain, a protégé of Heydrich, and, according to Annaliese, he had still been alive in 1945, and involved with important errands. He had, it seemed, prospered in the SS, even after the death of his mentor, Reinhard Heydrich. No doubt he had remained in the SD, the state security service, and no matter where he was, he was sure to have been implicated in some aspect of the evil the SS had perpetrated all over Europe.

He had left his sister and niece in Berlin in the path of the revengeful Russians. Perhaps he had been killed or captured during the invasion. Holding one photograph in each hand, Sally searched Christian's two faces, the boy's and the young man's, and she hoped, fervently hoped, he had died.

You are beautiful and I will love you forever, she had said to him that day by the lake. Neither of them ever forgot her valiant, youthful promise, but now—the love destroyed, his beauty mocked by the ugly significance of his uniform, she hoped he was dead.

CHAPTER 6

Sally pushed her chair away from her desk. It was the middle of a dark, muggy summer day and she had been working hard since early that morning writing the Tiechmann report. At last she was finished, and she was sure it was complete and would accomplish its purpose—the conviction of a Waffen-SS officer accused of murdering 189 American prisoners of war. An eight-by-ten black-and-white photograph, a blowup of a snapshot, lay on Sally's desk, propped against her dictionary. She looked at it for, she hoped, the last time, and put it in the green file that contained her report. She knew her evidence would be instrumental in convicting Klaus Tiechmann, and although she felt strongly that he should be punished, she couldn't help but feel ambivalent about his possible execution. At any rate, that would not be her decision.

Tiechmann had been identified by an American serviceman in a POW camp. The enlisted man was the only survivor of the group the major had machine-gunned after they surrendered in the Ardennes Forest. After the armistice, Tiechmann changed his SS uniform for that of a Wehrmacht officer, hoping to pass as regular army. Unfortunately for him, the American survivor, who had pulled guard duty at the POW camp, spotted him one night at chow.

The SS man was taken from the POW camp and interned at the prison near Munich where he was awaiting trial. He was still denying his SS background, and, because he was one of the few SS men who had not had his blood type tattooed on his upper arms, he was close to being convincing. Except for the American soldier, there was virtually no proof available to the Americans that the man was SS, let alone the commander of the particular unit that had massacred the American prisoners.

Until a photograph, found in a burned-out tank two years earlier, miraculously made its way onto Sally's desk. Working with the army photo-lab technicians, Sally had been able to identify the German definitely as the man who the American enlisted man said he was.

Someone knocked on her door and when she called for him to enter, Sergeant Taveggia shouldered his way into the room. He carried a battered cardboard carton that had once held powdered milk. "A Gift of the United States" was stamped on the side.

"Where do you want these, Lieutenant?" he asked.

"What is it?" Sally asked, standing and moving the lamp from the corner of her desk. "Put it here."

"I don't know. Dr. Chambers asked me to deliver it to you," Taveggia said, depositing the box. "She said she found them or something." He put his fists on his hips, obviously not disposed to leave until he got a look at what was in the box, so Sally took her Swiss Army knife out of her leather bag and slit open the top. She pulled the flaps apart and looked in.

"It's full of photographs," she said, reaching in and taking out a handful. The pictures were of all sizes, small 2-by-1-inch proofs, snapshots, and portraits; black-and-white, colored, and tinted photos among them. Sally started shuffling through the handful she held, quickly glancing at them. She frowned.

"What are they?" the sergeant asked, picking up a few pictures and holding them gingerly.

"I'm not sure. Here, look at these," she said, handing a few photos across the desk to him. He put the ones he held back in the box and fanned out the batch from Sally in his big hands.

"They're all families, aren't they?" he said.

"Yeah. Look, someone with her dog."

"And here's a house. With a car in front." They both held pictures out for each other. "Looks like the one I've got of my '38 Chevy. My wife took it the day I brought the car home. Look, I carry it in my wallet." And pulling his wallet from his back pocket, he slipped the snapshot out of its slot and held it out. He was right. It was the same kind of picture.

"These are all like that. Pictures people carry in their wallets, aren't they?"

"Yep, looks that way to me, ma'am," said the sergeant. "Where do you suppose they came from?"

"I hate to think," Sally said, reaching for her phone. While she waited for her call to Mavis to go through, Sergeant Taveggia left.

Mavis came on the line, and when she heard Sally's voice, asked, "You get my package?"

"Yes, it's here on my desk."

"Impressive, isn't it?"

"Where are they from, Mavis?" Sally picked up one of the photographs. It was of an older woman and a child, grandmother and grandchild, perhaps. Solemnly, the two stared out at Sally.

"They're from a place called Auschwitz. Ever hear of it?"

"The camp in Poland, isn't it? The big one," replied Sally.

"That's it. A Russian friend of mine was part of the gang that liberated it and he found the photos. He took some with him. Why, he couldn't say, but then, when he had them, he didn't know what to do with them, so I told him about your work with photographs, and there they are."

Sally dropped the photograph back into the box. Suddenly, the photographs frightened her; there were so many of them and they were so silent, so mute.

"I'm not sure what I could do with them, Mavis," she said.

"Well, I know you have a lot to do, but I thought you might take a look at them. Maybe later. You know the whole problem of DP identification is immense. Certainly photographs could be a source of information to help people track down relatives or, in this case, find out what happened to them."

"What happened to these people; who are they?"

"Oh, I thought you realized—they died. They're probably primarily Jews who went to the gas chambers," Mavis said calmly. "The Germans sorted and stored all their possessions."

The next day, Sally ran into Mavis in the entry hall, where the doctor was on her way out. Tomorrow, she told Sally, she'd finally be leaving for the States for her often-postponed R and R.

"Mavis, were you just going to sneak away like this, without saying good-bye?"

"Too busy," replied the doctor, then patted Sally's cheek. "I'll be thinking of you, my dear."

Sally said good-bye and was all the way back into the building before she remembered the pictures. She turned and ran out the door, down the steps.

"Mavis!" she called, stopping the older woman as she was climbing into the car. "Those pictures you dumped on me . . ."

"I remember, Sally," said the doctor.

"Well, they sat there for a while and then Sergeant Dolan and I counted them. There were over two thousand of them. Two thousand, Mavis!"

"And you want to know the thing that really was horrible?"

"What?" said Sally, not really wanting to know any such thing.

"My Russian friend, the one who handed them on to me? He said the pile he got them from was the size of a large room."

Sally stared at her in silence, her mind conjuring up a room filled to the ceiling with photographs. "Where did they all come from?"

"From the camp, I told you that." Mavis sounded irritated.

"I know that, but . . ."

"The people that the Germans sent to the camp had them."

"Obviously, but what I don't understand is: *Why* were the pictures collected? Why weren't they destroyed? It doesn't make sense, Mavis. Why did the Germans keep them?"

"Millions of people, millions, Sally, went up the chimneys at that camp, and you want sense. Oh, my dear . . ." Her voice petered out. Then she looked back up at Sally. "I've got to go now. Goodbye." Mavis got into the backseat of the olive-green sedan, leaving Sally standing on the sidewalk. Sally watched the car pull away, then turned and walked slowly into the building and up the stairs.

In her office, Sally found messages from the colonel, Tim Hastings, and Annaliese. She picked up the phone and asked to be connected to the number Annaliese had left for her. Annaliese and her daughter may have been through horrors, but they were alive. One little girl. Sally thought of the children represented by the photographs she had handled—one little girl left.

Annaliese answered on the first ring, as though she had been waiting for the call. She and Sally arranged to meet near the Brandenburg Gate on Saturday and then drive into the Tiergarten and see if they could find a spot for a picnic, Sally supplying the food and the car.

Next, Sally called Tim, who wasn't in, and finally, she called her boss, who was. He wanted to know what the content of the box was. The box of pictures was beginning to figure quite prominently in her life. Sally explained its history to Colonel Eiger.

He was more interested in the doctor's Russian source. "Who do you suppose her Russian pal was?"

"Don't know, sir," said Sally, wondering the same thing. "Mavis did say 'he' when speaking of him."

"That's interesting," said the colonel, musing. "Well, she gets around. We're going to be the worse for her absence. The people she knew."

Then, getting down to business, Colonel Eiger told Sally that he was sending her to Munich the next week for the Tiechmann trial. It was to be her first public appearance as a member of D-6 and only the second in which a member of the team had been instrumental in the evidence presented. The colonel again asked Sally to be sure about her material and her judgment. Reiterating what she had told him before, she said she was sure there could be no question that the man in the photograph found in the tank was Tiechmann. And because the picture was of a group of Waffen-SS men whose insignia was identified as being that of the unit accused of the massacre, Sally believed his connection with them could not be denied.

She finished her report to the colonel, adding that Captain Tobin had also come up with the paper proof that the panzer unit had been present in the Ardennes Forest. They had even found a company clerk's list of names of the men. Heading that list was SS-Obersturmführer Klaus Tiechmann, Iron Cross First Class.

"Sounds good, Sally," the colonel said, and she knew he meant it because he had used her first name.

"Thank you, sir," she said. Hearing a knock on her door, she turned around to find Tim Hastings, hands in pockets, leaning against the doorjamb. She smiled at him. The colonel, after telling her a few more details about her trip, hung up abruptly, and Sally replaced her receiver.

"Nice seeing you, Jackson," said Tim.

"It has been a while," Sally replied. "Just tried calling you, but you weren't there."

"Nope," he said, not volunteering any information. "You miss me?"

"Barely noticed you were gone," she said. He grinned at her, letting her know he saw through her wisecrack. "So, where have you been?" She stood, tidying up the papers on her desk, placing the Tiechmann file in the center. "Scuttlebutt says Nuremberg."

"Yep," said Tim, walking and taking a chair. "Got back this morning."

Sally perched on one corner of her desk, folding her arms across her chest. "What was it like?"

Tim put one leg up, propping the ankle on his other knee. He studied his light-brown sock for a moment before answering. Then he looked up at Sally and she saw that his eyes had become dark, almost gray, reflecting his mood. She also noticed that they were not focusing on her, but on his memories of the trials. She imagined herself leaning forward and kissing him. That would regain his attention quickly enough. But she didn't, of course, although the image stayed in her mind.

"I'll tell you what it's like," he was saying. "It's a mess like you've never seen."

"A mess?"

"The amount of material those guys are trying to go through—it's staggering. I figure that what they ought to do is just throw all of it at the defendants. Don't bother hanging any of the bastards, just bury 'em in the paper they created."

"Do you think any of them will get off?"

"Fritsch, maybe. He's just small potatoes." Then Tim laughed. "Von Papen probably. In honor of his survival." He stood up, uncoiling his long body from the chair. He was very close to her, although he still seemed not to be aware of her.

"Did you see them? Speer and Göring and the lot?"

"As big as life," he said and turned to look at her. There. Now she had his attention. She shifted her body slightly away from him. "Listen, you doing anything for dinner?" he asked.

"Eating it, probably."

"Sassy, aren't you?" He touched her cheek. "One of the things I like about you, Jackson," he said, his eyes warm on her.

"What? My being rude?" Her heart was pounding, which irritated her. Why was she acting like a sixteen-year-old? She walked behind her desk.

"Yeah, so what about dinner? I'll buy."

"Oh, dinner. I don't think I'd better. I'm going to Munich Monday. My first appearance, you know. The colonel wants my finished report tonight."

"Sure, okay," he said, retreating to the door. He pulled it open, then stopped. "Sal, you know, I was thinking about you—"

"Tim, please, don't."

"You don't know what I was going to say."

"No, but it doesn't matter. Don't say anything. Tim, please. Not now."

"You gonna tell me when you're ready?" He smiled as he asked the question, but she could hear the irritation in his voice underneath the geniality.

"Probably never. Not because of you," she added quickly. "You're great. It's just that . . . Well, we're friends, aren't we?"

"Right. Got it." And with that he was gone.

Damn. She'd made him mad. Sally slumped into her chair and absently kicked her shoes off. She was a clumsy fool. She liked him and he was obviously interested in her and she had just refused to go to dinner with him. Why?

She just wasn't interested in starting anything. That was it. She was here to work, and besides . . . She opened one of the files on her desk. The report was virtually finished; it just needed a little polishing, and she could do that tomorrow before the picnic. After all, Tim had only asked her to dinner.

I'm so afraid, she thought and paused, her hand still on the report, her eyes gazing unseeing at the two chairs at the end of the room as she argued with herself. It wasn't the dinner, of course; it wasn't even the possibility of bed, which, frankly, she would welcome. It was the possibility of feelings, of feeling for another person, for Tim.

She didn't want to feel. Not yet.

The Saturday with Annaliese and Klara was a treat. As Annaliese had said, her daughter was delightful.

"She has your mother's nose," Sally said, then leaned down to the little girl. "Did you know that? That you have the same nose as your grandmother?"

Klara, who was shy with Sally, merely shook her head, her blue eyes wide in her little face. She would not speak to Sally, but studied her intently.

Sally drove Annaliese and Klara into the ruined Tiergarten, happy to see signs of regrowth, although it would take years for the trees to regain their former beauty. She found a small patch of grass underneath a statue of some forgotten Hohenzollern prince who was missing his head and right elbow. The July day was bright and clear and warm as the two women spread out the blue-flowered cloth Annaliese had brought and set out Sally's lunch, which included two huge oranges.

Klara happily ate the sandwiches and potato salad from the cafeteria in the basement of Sally's office building. When she had finished, Sally handed her an orange. The little girl took it slowly, obviously unfamiliar with it, causing Sally to remember a similar occasion with Christian. She leaned over and broke the peel. And, like her uncle, on the lawn in front of the lake so many years ago, Klara smelled the orange's pungent fragrance and smiled up at Sally.

Annaliese, too, enjoyed the treat, exclaiming how long it had been since she had tasted one. Sally sat watching Annaliese wiping the last of the orange juice from Klara's thin little face and she felt unaccountably happy—and sad. She might have been Klara's aunt. She might have lived all of her life here in this city. If the Nazis hadn't taken over; if they hadn't started the war; if, if, if.

She said none of that to Annaliese, who talked to Sally of her time in Vienna before the war, describing in loving detail the parties and balls she had attended and the dresses she had worn.

As the three of them were walking back to the car, Klara rewarded Sally for the picnic by taking her hand for a moment. The little girl, blinking in the sun, looked up at Sally, smiled shyly, then darted around to her mother.

"She's a great kid," Sally said in English.

"What did she say?" Klara asked her mother.

"I said you were a wonderful child," Sally repeated in German.

Klara looked around her mother's skirt at Sally. Sally nodded and Klara rewarded her again with a smile.

"Oh, I almost forgot," Sally said when they reached the car. "About the coat. I asked someone who has gone back to the States to send me one, so you ought to have it by the fall. Is that all right?"

"Of course it is," Annaliese said, her hand curving across the back of her daughter's head. "Did you hear that, sweetheart?" She bent her head. "Aunt Sally is having a coat sent to you all the way from America."

Sally watched them, the mother, elegant in gray sweater and slacks, her blond hair shining in the sunshine, and the little girl in her hand-knit jacket and navy skirt, her hair fluffy and unsubstantial as golden smoke; and her heart ached with her own proud isolation. Then the two blond heads lifted and smiled at her, including her in their delight in the news of a new coat, and she laughed.

"That's right," she said, opening the car door, ushering her passengers into the vehicle. "And you know what it's going to look like?"

Klara, seated between the two women on the front seat, shook her head, and the three of them conjured up the perfect winter coat.

Standing next to the car on Pariser Platz, Sally said good-bye to Annaliese and Klara. She and Annaliese shook hands, and when Sally turned to leave, she thought she saw, out of the corner of her eye, a familiar figure. She turned quickly to look, but the man had gone. She stared after him, frowning.

"What is it, Sally?" said Annaliese.

Sally looked at her. Annaliese was watching her intently. "Nothing," she said, "nothing." She didn't like the feeling that crept over her, a feeling that she could not trust the German woman. Then she shook her head. She was being paranoid. She laughed. "I'm sorry," she said. "I think I just saw a ghost."

Annaliese smiled. "It happens often these days," she said.

That was when the feeling that someone was watching her began, someone with very blond hair, someone tall, someone, in fact, very much like Christian. Sally began to see him, or men who looked like him, everywhere. Even in Munich, in court, the next week, she looked up into the gallery of the small, crowded courtroom and saw, or thought she saw, someone. She became, alternately, angry with herself and frightened, and then angry again. But she spoke to no one about her fears, her imaginings. How could she? What could she say? She would have to tell everything, and she couldn't do that. The men knew she had been in Berlin. They did not know about Christian; no one but Colonel Eiger did.

"I'm going crazy," she said out loud into her empty dim room. "I'm really going crazy."

She lay rigid on her narrow bed, still dressed except for her shoes. Reading on her bed after dinner she had fallen asleep, and had had a disturbing dream, full of menacing images that faded as she awoke. She reached for her cigarettes on the little nightstand and knocked a glass off with her fumbling. She heard it break on the hardwood floor and quickly sat up, jerking her legs around to the floor on the other side of her bed. Her heart was pounding. It was the dream. She leaned back and tried to turn on the wall sconce above the nightstand, but nothing happened. No comforting light came on.

Sally padded over to the door in her stocking feet. Pulling it open, she saw that the hall was dark as well. Then from around the corner, where the stairs were, came a bobbing light, followed by a person carrying a flashlight. It was Margie Allen, the nurse who worked for the Red Cross.

"Lights are out all over the neighborhood," she said when she came up to Sally, handing her two candles. "They ought to be on soon."

In her room, Sally found a saucer on her table and some matches and lit the candle, sticking it into the saucer with its own wax. She watched the fat, stubby candle burn steadily. Well, she couldn't clear up the glass in the gloom. She would just have to wait until the lights went on, or morning arrived.

It was stuffy in the darkness. She was still in her uniform, so she undressed down to her slip. Crawling across her bed, she found her cigarettes and lit one, then went to the window.

She pushed open the heavy shutters and, leaning on the sill like an Italian housewife, looked out. The night was very still, the air heavy and warm, threatening a storm. The gutted building across the way, with its almost delicate walls, no longer looked forbidding;

she had seen it so often. The other buildings on the block retained all or most of their walls and the resulting stone corridor magnified sound so that when the occasional car passed slowly along the street, it could be heard long before it came into sight and long after it turned. One came along as Sally watched.

She finished the cigarette and flicked it into the darkness, watching the tiny light fall. Then, from below in the street, Sally heard a sound that she immediately recognized as a shoe scraping on cement.

Someone was in the street.

She backed away from the window, frightened, trying to see between the shutter hinges and the wall. She could see the figure of a man down at the corner, under the useless, bent street lamp. Was it her imagination, or did he seem to be looking in her direction?

Just then, the lights came on in the building, startling her and causing her to bump her elbow. She swore and rubbed the injured spot. When she looked back at the corner, now illuminated by light from the windows at that end of the building, the dark figure was gone. But in the moment as the lights came on, before she hit her elbow, she had seen his hair. It had shone in the light—yellow.

She retreated, leaving the window and its mystery, went to the sink and splashed cool water on her face and arms, then she remembered the broken glass.

Getting her little wastebasket, she crouched over the glass and picked up the larger pieces. Then, slowly, she stopped, her hand carefully holding a shard. She looked at it. There was a memory, that was what had frightened her when she broke the glass—a memory.

A hand, her hand, carelessly knocking a glass off a bedside table. She could remember that. The memory-glass fell, as if through water, and shattered on the floor, a hardwood floor as well, like the one in her room. That floor, the one in her memory, was—where? She remembered that the glass shattered because it was crystal.

Oh, yes, she remembered that, and she also remembered his hair, smooth across his forehead—usually he combed it straight back—but then, it had fallen forward. He lay stretched out, fully dressed in his wicked black-and-silver uniform, a glass of something on his chest, his head against the back of the big armchair, not the bed.

Sally closed her eyes, the piece of broken glass falling unnoticed onto the floor. No. Not the bedroom, but her father's study in the house in Lichterfeld. The study with the tall cabinet of highly polished wood that reflected Christian's shiny hair. Not the bed upstairs, but the cabinet. That night . . .

Sally stayed crouched over the pieces of glass and waited for the feelings to ebb. She covered her face, although she did not cry, and felt fear, anger, hurt, and, strangest of all, regret course through her. And finally a feeling that not only surprised her, but made her ashamed: desire.

Quickly, she cleared away the mess, changed into her nightgown and red, plaid robe, and sat at her table to write a letter to her friend, Denise Brothers, now back in Texas with her ex-marine husband.

If the man in the street had been Christian, what then? Did she want to see him? She rolled her pen between her fingers as Colonel Eiger did, thinking about the answer to that question. Back in Washington, in his hot office, Frank Singleton had asked her whether or not she wanted to confront her ghosts, or rather, ghost. Frank thought it would help her, and maybe it would.

Sally stood up, tossing the pen on the table. She got her big leather bag and sat with it between her legs on her bed. She took out the nightclub picture.

Many people, including her co-workers, would condemn her for the relationship that picture represented. There were people, including dear friends, who had condemned her for it back then. David Wohl, especially, had been angered by what he saw as her unreasoning obsession with Christian.

Christian. He had been her first love and her first lover and her husband. Sally laughed at herself. He had been her only lover, ever. Those men in Los Angeles—that hadn't been love, nothing like it. She knew what love was; what it could be.

But she and Christian had been so . . . so dramatic about their love. They had tried to ignore the context of it. She had tried to ignore his uniform. But even as she thought that, Sally knew she was lying to herself. The danger his uniform represented attracted her, although she had been attracted to the man underneath long before he put it on.

That was what was so seductive about the memories of him. Her sensual memories of him were crystal-clear and popped up to haunt her at odd moments. Even now, she could remember the feel of his cheek under her hand, the creases at the side of his mouth when he smiled. Sally laid the photograph on the bed in front of her and wrapped her arms around herself. It hurt to remember him. It hurt to remember how much they wanted each other, the things they did, and how it all went so very, very wrong. Sure, she could blame everything on Heydrich, but truly she knew she and Christian were guilty as well. Yes, they had been young and in love, but they also

66

had been blind, stubbornly so. Youth and love and blindness were no excuse for consorting with evil.

But Sally felt she had been punished enough for loving Christian. Surely the pain, the scars on her wrists, her solitariness, her inability to love would exonerate her. Why couldn't she believe that?

And Christian, what about him? She didn't ever know if he was still alive, not even his sister knew. And if he was, what then? Sally looked at him in the photograph, remembering him instead in his khaki shorts and well-worn white blouse that last summer at the lake. How had that laughing boy, with the beautiful golden-brown skin, turned into the SS man in the picture? And, assuming he was still alive, what was he now?

The lake.

She remembered: Eddie, about thirteen, coming after her in the little rowboat, leaning over the side and yelling at her to climb out before she caught pneumonia and died and he got blamed for it.

You are beautiful and I will love you forever, she had said to Christian that day, before the boys came tumbling out of their hiding places, laughing and ridiculing her fervent expression of love. He had sat there impassively and she had run straight into the freezing lake, thinking only of escaping him.

Christian. Golden hair and tanned skin. He was beautiful, even as a kid. Unlike me, she thought, dumpy and plain with all that messy, curly brown hair. Mama despaired of my looks. How proud she would have been to have a child as beautiful as Christian had been.

Leave it. Thoughts of him hurt, he hurt her. Unlike Eddie, who never did. Who apologized and meant it. Who smuggled her up the back stairs so that no one ever found out. She had caught a horrible cold, but her mother never knew how. Eddie kept his promises, always. He saved her neck a dozen times. He had been dead four years and she still couldn't believe he wasn't somewhere off in the world on one of his ships and they would see each other again.

"Edward Lowell Jackson," she said into the empty room, as she hugged her loneliness to her. She thought about sitting up or getting ready for bed, but still she just lay there. After a while, she stopped thinking and she slept. Her dreams, when they came, were not about her dead, beloved brother but were full of shiny water and a golden-haired boy and menace. Somehow, everything always seemed to come back to him.

CHAPTER 7

On a muggy August afternoon, Sally returned to the old Mayr apartment to give the children the second payment. Even though Annaliese claimed they hadn't given her a message, Sally still felt the kids had put them together.

She borrowed a car, but went alone this time. Apprehensively, she pushed open the door of the building. Inside, the foyer was as dark and quiet as before. She took a few steps into the middle of it.

"Hello," she called out quietly. "Children?" she said, in German. "I have the quarters for you."

A door opened above her, but no one came down; there were no footsteps.

"Please, lady," a man's voice said behind her. Sally started and turned. "What are you doing?"

She saw an older man, jowly, dark hair turning gray. He had large pouches under his eyes and thin eyelashes.

"I was looking for two children," she stammered.

He inspected her. "You go away from here," he said finally, raising his head. "You come in here to take our German children."

"No, you don't understand."

"Go, you go. You take everything from us. You go from here." His voice was intense, although he did not raise it, as if he did not want to disturb the other inhabitants of the building. Whoever they were.

"They—the children—helped me find some friends who used to live here," Sally tried to explain.

"You are ridiculous. All of you. Women in uniforms. Go, go."

She went. He watched from the door as she walked down the steps and got into her jeep. Nuts to him. She started the car, knowing her defiance only covered her relief at being out of the building. Especially with the information Annaliese had given her.

The day before, Annaliese had telephoned Sally with a cryptic message regarding "someone we used to know," which resulted in Sally's traveling that very evening to Annaliese's apartment in the Russian sector. Tim Hastings had at the last moment appeared in Sally's office, and when she told him of her plans, had refused to allow her to make the trip alone at night.

The first surprise was Annaliese's flat, which was well-furnished, well-heated, and well-stocked with food and drink. The second surprise was a large Russian colonel, which explained the first surprise. Annaliese seemed to expect Sally's censure, but Sally found she was inclined to thank the Russian for his protection of Klara and her mother rather than condemn Annaliese for accepting it.

During the evening, after a generous supper, Annaliese drew Sally into her bedroom, to "freshen up," she told the men. Instead, in a nervous whisper, Annaliese said that she had heard her brother was alive.

Annaliese lowered her eyes for a long time, as if to control herself. Then she looked up at Sally, and said in a whisper, "It's just a rumor, you understand." Annaliese drew deeply on her cigarette.

"He's alive," Sally repeated flatly. "Who told you?"

"No one in particular. Someone passed on something that he heard someone else say. It's all very vague."

"I see." The SS, it was rumored, had an organization that helped members escape. Perhaps Annaliese had heard from them. Sally slowly turned her head to study Annaliese, and her expression was so unpleasant that Annaliese took a step away. Sally grabbed her arm. "Where is he?" she whispered.

"Sally!" Annaliese said, pulling free. "You hurt me."

"I'm sorry."

"I can't tell you any more. I do not know any more."

"Have *you* seen him?"

"I haven't, and really, I know nothing else about him except that he is alive. I told you how I feel about him. I hate all of them. I wonder that you were interested, except perhaps to catch him, to punish him. But"—she shrugged casually—"that's all I know."

Searching Annaliese's face, Sally saw that it was a lie. She was not surprised. She only wondered what Annaliese hoped to gain. If she didn't care about her brother, why should she lie; and if she was shielding him, why tell Sally anything at all? The comment about punishing Christian must have been an attempt at information; perhaps Annaliese was . . . Then Sally remembered Klara.

"Okay," she said, holding up her hands, "no more questions."

"Good," said Annaliese. "Sally, I like you. I did not before. We could be honest about this, I think. You were never my friend. And at first, I thought you meant—well, I could not imagine why you wanted to see me. But I see that you are a good person. You Americans . . ." She gave a little laugh. "I also see how much you care for my daughter. For this, I will tell that even if I did know more about my brother, I could not tell you." She looked into Sally's face, her

69

expression earnest, her blue eyes clear and candid. "Do you understand why?"

Sally nodded slowly. "I'm still the enemy," she said, and Annaliese smiled sadly and kissed Sally's cheek.

Out of nowhere, a restaurant had opened up in the basement of the building on the corner down from Sally's office. The Americans who filled the buildings in the neighborhood gratefully adopted it, naming it the Dive. It was simple and basic: a bar, round tables covered with blue-and-white-checked cloths, a painted brick wall with a sentimental view of the Bay of Naples. The fare was also simple and basic; just beer and wine and whatever food was on hand, although the menu improved with the American patronage.

That evening, Sally and Tim went to the Dive after work. He had stopped by her office, where she had been sitting for an hour smoking, after her encounter with the old man.

"You look green."

"I had a funny turn with a local this afternoon. An ex-golden pheasant, I should think."

"A what?" He came into the office and stood in front of her desk.

"A party man. They called them that because of the brown uniforms. They'd put a lot of tinsel and gold braid on them."

Tim laughed. "That's great. You never think of Germans as having a sense of humor."

"Doesn't go with death camps, does it? Do you suppose they laughed, anyone laughed there? I wonder if anyone has laughed in the last six years." Max Tobin had brought films of the camps back from Nuremberg, and that morning they had all watched the silent black-and-white pictures of unbelievable horror. The film had preyed on her mind, as she was sure it had on her colleagues'.

"Let's go get that beer," Tim had said, not letting her talk about the movies.

"I was there, Tim, and I did nothing. Ever."

"What could you have done, one twenty-year-old American girl?" he'd asked. When she turned her face away from him, he'd grabbed her, her bag, her tunic, and literally pulled her out of her office into the hall.

"C'mon," he said angrily, "you don't want to wallow in your misery." Sally stopped walking, pulling against his hand.

"Wallow? Wallow?" she exclaimed, her voice rising on the second word.

"Yes, wallow. Good God, you've spent years poring over photographs of this stuff. How can you bear to look at them? Doesn't it give you the creeps?"

"No. No, it does not."

"Dammit, Sally," Tim said. "Stop it, just stop it. Don't take it all so personally."

"I do," she said, "when someone murders several million of my species, I take it very personally. I don't know how else to take it. And yes, I feel damn guilty for my part in it, regardless of how logical it is to feel that way. Logic has nothing to do with it." Hearing her voice lose control, she shut her mouth.

Tim was silent for a moment, then reached out and fixed the collar of her tunic, turning it right side out, patting it down, his hand lingering on her shoulder. "I know," he said, "I feel pretty much the same way. Those movies gave me bad dreams too." He smiled. "Let's go have a beer. After all, since I'm rescuing you, you can pay. Okay? Okay?" he repeated, pulling her into him, hugging her.

"Okay," she answered, feeling the pull of him, his humor and easygoing attitude, his attractiveness. She let herself rest for a moment, her face turned into his chest so that she couldn't see any of the ugly world around them, then, with a deep breath, she stepped away from him.

"It helps, doesn't it?" he said softly, his hands on her shoulders. "We can help each other, can't we?"

And she nodded, unable to look at him for fear he would see how much she cared.

Outside, the sun had finally put in an appearance, just in time to set. Sally watched their shadows walk before them. "I guess it's my guilt," she said.

"Yeah," he replied, touching her arm, "we all feel it."

"No," she said, "not a generalized guilt, but a specific . . . Oh, Tim," she said, and they stopped at the top of the steps that led down to the bar in the basement. He looked down at her, his face full of concern. Sally glanced at him, then at the ground, letting go of his arm.

"I'm being awfully dramatic, aren't I?" she said and he just smiled. "It's my past, the one here. There was a man. I knew him all my life. I loved him." There—she had said it, she had told someone.

She looked down the street toward their office building. The block was, at that moment, deserted and silent, the last rosy glow of sunset warming the battered gray bricks. Sally could hear Tim's breathing, it was so quiet.

"He, this man, was SS." She held her hand up quickly, to stop him from commenting, although he did not seem inclined to do so. "He was one of Heydrich's protégés. And I loved him. I married him." That said, she took a deep breath and expelled it.

Two young women came around the corner, chattering noisily, and a U.S. Army staff car drove past, pennants snapping.

"Feel better?" asked Tim.

"Yeah, I guess so."

"Good," he said, taking her arm. "Let's go get that beer."

She didn't let him lead her down the steps to the restaurant, but stood on the top stair, her eyes almost level with his.

"No condemnations?" she asked.

"Nope," he answered, then grinned his corn-fed grin at her. "I've heard worse." And he continued down the steps. This time she followed, feeling infinitely cheered, not knowing quite why.

"I don't know, Sally," Hastings said as they settled themselves at a small, rickety table. "It sounds to me as though you are taking on way too much guilt."

"But I was there. I knew some of the men responsible. I even liked them." Embarrassed, she turned her head away from him. "Some of them, anyway. And I did know." She looked at his kind face. "I heard about the beatings in the cellars of the Prinz-Albrecht Strasse and I knew about the anti-Jewish laws and I saw the SA push people off the curbs. Including Americans who were too slow to salute when that damned flag went by. But I was safe. Daddy's position protected me, I thought. I thought it was *their* problem, a German problem, and they had to fix it themselves. I was just an impartial observer . . . for a while."

Tim moved his chair closer to hers. The bar, filled with uniformed Americans, was becoming crowded and noisy. "Sally," Tim said, putting his hand on her arm, "you are not responsible. Okay . . . all of us, as a civilization, are responsible. But we are all also hurt by it. But you personally did not dream up, build, or use the damned gas chambers. Besides, it's the height of egotism to take the blame for the deaths of six million people. Why not take responsibility for the full fifty million who died in the war altogether?"

She smiled. "You're right. But I can't help it."

"Yeah. I guess I know the feeling. We think we go through life solitary, not hurting anyone. Then we discover that we've had an effect on someone, even hurt them. I've experienced that a lot in my career. Patients I should have helped, or who I thought I had helped, but didn't."

Sally took a long drink, then, putting her stein back on the table, said softly, "There were three people. A young woman my age named Marlene, her little girl, and her mother. They—"

She was interrupted by Nelson Armbrewster's well-bred voice. "Well, look who's here, and so very serious." He stood behind Sally and clapped his hands onto her shoulders. He leaned forward, his weight heavy on her, his word slightly slurred. "Telling secrets? Making plans for a rendezvous?"

"Beat it, Armbrewster," Tim said evenly, his hand firmly on Sally's arm.

"It's that way, is it? We have wondered who would—"

"Nelson," said Tim warningly. "Don't say something you'll be sorry for."

"Right. You're right, old man. I apologize, Lieutenant, for impugning your honor. I had forgotten we are all officers and gentlemen here." Saying this, he pulled himself upright and saluted Sally.

"Thank you, Nelson," she said.

"The question is—were *they*? Gentlemen? Officers, yes. But gentlemen? I think not." He looked from Tim to Sally and back to Tim. "Know what I mean, old man?"

"I think so, Nelson. I think so." The films again.

"Knew you would. Thanks." And he patted Tim on the shoulder and walked carefully away.

Sally and Tim watched him.

"Funny how differently everyone takes it, isn't it?" Tim said. "The different things we do to live with the knowledge."

"What about you?" Sally leaned her head on her hand, looking sideways at Tim. "How do you keep on going?"

He took a long time to answer, rubbing his thumb against the condensation on his nearly empty beer stein. Finally he looked up, "I think I'll have another beer." And he ambled over to the bar.

"That's your response?" said Sally, when he returned carrying another beer for her as well as one for himself.

"Isn't it a good one?"

"I suppose, but—"

"No. No." He stopped her from speaking. "The human heart and brain can only accommodate so much evil and unhappiness. I have had my fill for the day. It may be callous of me, but I'm not going to help those poor people by being maudlin tonight. Nor are you. So we will drink and talk about good things—life and jazz and sex and when the hell we are going to get a decent meal in this town. Okay?" He spoke intensely, one hand grasping Sally's arm. His words brought tears to her eyes—why, she could not say—but he noticed. Gently, he touched her cheek. She smiled at him.

"Good," he said, picking up his beer. "Now, let's talk about jazz. Do you like it or not?"

"I don't know . . ." she started to say.

"Nope, can't be lukewarm about it. Yea or nay."

"Yea, I guess so. I liked Glenn Miller. I thought he had a very romantic sound."

"No, no, no," he said, waving his hand at her. "Not those guys. You gotta listen to Basie or Ellington to know what it's about."

"What?"

"You know, life. Music. Sex. Life. Sex. Or do you know?"

"I know." Sally drank her beer, feeling herself blush under his scrutiny.

"I am a shrink, you know, so you can tell me everything." He leaned his head on his hand, his eyes bright. "Everything. Don't leave a thing out."

"No," she said, smiling in spite of herself.

"Not a thing. I wanna know it all. Every filthy detail. Everything. And don't you worry, I won't condemn or judge or even think about what you tell me. I'll barely listen to you. Honest. Except if there's anything about tattoos. I can't stand stuff about tattoos. Other than that, c'mon, spill the beans, Sal ol' gal."

By this time, she was giggling, and all she could do was shake her head.

"Ah, resistance. I know what that was. You're shy. You're blushing. You don't wanna tell me. Don't worry. I'll figure it out from your silence. Your giggling. Shall we talk about why you're giggling? It could be significant. After all, you are past your adolescence."

"Do you use this technique on all your patients?" Sally asked through her laughter.

"Yep. It's good to hear you laugh." And without warning, he leaned forward and kissed her, his mustache offering a pleasant contrast to the softness of his lips. They parted and looked at each other. "You're not afraid of me, are you?"

"A little," she whispered.

"I'm just a Kansas farm boy."

"With a Ph.D. and a passion for jazz."

"And baseball," he said. "Don't forget baseball. Did you know I have an apartment?"

"So I heard. Do you have a kitchen?"

"And a living room, a bath . . ."

"Hot water?"

"Yep. Well, most of the time. What's today? Well, it doesn't matter, it's past seventeen hundred hours." They both laughed.

"What else do you have?" She leaned forward. He looked at her and his mouth curved very slightly.

"I've got a bedroom, too," he said. "At least, I did the last time I looked under the mess."

Sally looked away from him. "I think they want us out of here," she said, reaching for her big leather bag.

Tim looked around at the empty bar. "Right," he said, standing up. "You're good at that."

"What?" she asked.

"Changing the subject. Must be your upbringing. Living in embassies and all."

"Must be."

Tim stumbled a little over the steps up, as they headed toward the door, and Sally took his arm.

"Watch it, Doctor," she said, emphasizing the title, teasing him.

"Am I being insulted?" he said, his hand on the door. He raised one eyebrow snootily.

Sally laughed. "Probably. But you deserve it."

"Oh, why? For seeing through your conversational techniques? You think I don't know when I'm being rejected?"

Sally, standing against the wall of the narrow hallway, hitched her bag up on her shoulder. "You haven't been rejected yet," she muttered.

"What?" He leaned toward her. She shook her head, smiling. "C'mon, Sally." He grabbed the strap of her bag and gave it a shake. "Talk."

"No. Never mind," she said. Now she was getting embarrassed.

"Wh-at?" he asked again, breaking the word into two syllables, like a kid would. He was close to her in the small space and she could smell the beer on his breath. His green eyes laughed at her and then, suddenly, they didn't, and he kissed her again, his hands cupping her face. She put her arms around him and kissed him back. When it was over, they stood together for a moment, arms around each other. She could feel his heart thudding away in his chest. He was so warm, so solid, and it had been so long since she had kissed anyone that she thought maybe the one kiss was enough right now. She closed her eyes and took a deep breath, breathing him in. His arms tightened around her.

"I said, I haven't rejected you yet," she whispered into his chest.

"Oh." He nodded. Paused. "Well. Will another kiss maybe sway the vote in my favor?" He touched her shoulder, the back of her neck.

"It's too much," she said, her skin tingling under his touch as she backed out of his arms. "Does that make sense?"

"Sure." Another pause. "What the hell, to show you how chivalrous a kid from Kansas can be, I'll drive you home. But I warn you, I've got a lot of patience I didn't have ten years ago. So watch yourself, Lieutenant," he teased, lightly tapping her nose. "Understand?"

"Yes, sir," she answered, suddenly unaccountably happy.

Her happiness frightened her. Her attraction to Tim and his interest in her frightened her. She trusted neither emotion, and although she didn't avoid Tim in the next few days, she didn't seek out his company.

Still, when he smiled at her, catching her eye as she hurried into her seat at the weekly unit conference, her stomach flip-flopped and she lowered her head to her notes, certain the other men had noticed and that her face was bright red.

"You going to come with us, Sally?" Finkelstein asked, startling her. "We're going to the Officer's Club Friday night."

"All of you?"

"Sure. You too. It'll be fun."

"Sounds good," she said, as the colonel took his seat and the meeting started. It did sound good; she'd be able to spend time with Tim without being alone with him.

And, of course, nothing went as she had planned.

(HAPTER 8

So," Tim Hastings said in his usual laconic voice, "*did* you sleep with Heydrich?"

Furious, Sally socked him as hard as she could on his shoulder. He yelled and scrambled to keep the car steady, hold her off, and rub his arm at the same time. "Shit. Don't. You'll kill us."

"Good," she yelled, "then you'll leave me alone." Suddenly, she was thrown against her side of the front seat, as Tim swerved to avoid another car. He pulled to one side of the street and turned off the motor.

"All right," he said, "go ahead, beat me up." He spoke calmly and it infuriated her. "I've come this far, I don't want to die in a traffic accident."

"Did you hear what you said to me?" she said, trying to match his control.

"What? Everything I've said to you, ever since I've know you, has made you angry. What was it this time, what?"

"That crack about—"

"Oh, that. Christ, Sally, that was a joke. A bad joke." He turned to her. "I'm sorry. I was out of line."

He was driving her home after a long evening drinking martinis at the Officer's Club with their colleagues from the unit. Sally had been several drinks ahead when Hastings finally showed up, and during that time, Armbrewster had quizzed her about Heydrich. The worst part was not that she had gotten teary and the guys had quickly sent her off with Hastings when he arrived, but that she could not quite remember what she had said about her relationship with Heydrich.

She rubbed her eyes. She remembered that feeling from the bad days in Los Angeles, the headache, the sense that her skin was layered in sand.

"I shouldn't drink," she said. "Who asked me that? About Heydrich?"

"Armbrewster."

"Of course." Tim was silent and she wondered if he was, at last, disgusted with her. Really, she couldn't blame him.

Outside the Officer's Club, she had accused him of treating her like a patient and he had lost his temper and said she had better stop acting like one and she had called him a shrink and had stomped off. She hadn't gotten far; there was nowhere for her to go except home and no other way to get there at that moment except in Tim's car, and so she had turned and walked back to his car.

She had tapped on the window of the car, and as she slid into the seat beside him, had asked him why he had never told her he played the clarinet.

"You're finding out everything about me," she said, "and I know so little about you."

"I'm pretty boring. Just a hick from the Midwest. Not like you."

"Right," she had said sarcastically. That was when her hangover had settled in and his question, "So, did you sleep with Heydrich?" had hit her like a fist.

"I'm sorry I socked you," she said then. He grunted. "If you only knew how frightening that man was, you wouldn't make jokes like that." Tim still didn't reply, letting her go on. "I'm sorry to be such a pain in the neck. Tim, I . . . I don't want you to think badly of me."

"Sally, listen. I think we're friends. And I think you trust me a little. What's more, I think you need to trust me. Everybody needs to trust someone, don't they?" He said the last as though he didn't quite believe it himself.

"Even you, Timothy Hastings. Who does the shrink talk to?"

He was silent for a very long time. "You're right. I'll tell you my trouble. It's very simple. My wife left me and took my boys. She did it without really telling me why. I figured it out—well, some of it. You never figure all of it out. She had big ideas about life, what she wanted from it. A big house, position. She was ambitious; I wasn't. There was a lot of silence between us. Anyway, she found someone else she wanted to marry. So my sons have a new father, and from what I hear, he's not a bad guy. Owns a bunch of service stations, several commercial buildings, is too old to be drafted. Me, I'm thirty-six years old and I've worked like hell to get where I am. Some people, my ex-wife among them, would say that where I am doesn't look so hot next to several gas stations and a lot of real estate, but it's okay for me. I like my work. It's hard and I'm good at it.

"Took me a long time to get over her and what she did. So I haven't been interested in getting to know another woman since Nancy dumped me. I've slept with a couple, but I didn't want to know about them. You . . ." He laughed, shaking his head. "Believe me, I don't understand it. But you interest me. I like you. And, to tell the truth, I'm just as glad we haven't been in the sack."

"Great," Sally said softly, teasing him.

"I told you, Sally." Tim was serious. "I'm patient. I can wait." And he gave her a long look that she couldn't hold; she had to look down.

"So what about this guy you were married to?" Tim asked. "You still upset because he was SS?"

"That's not reason enough?"

"Maybe. You tell me."

Sally shoved her hands deep into the pockets of her jacket. "Well, we've gone this far, haven't we?" She took a deep breath.

"He was a German, in the SS. I married him in 1934, and we were together for . . . just months. I got . . . well. Anyway, it all went wrong. It was horrible. I came back to the States. We were divorced in '36. I went crazy, I guess. And I . . . I went to bed with men afterward until I . . ."

It was chilly in the car and she started to shake. She pulled her hands out of her pockets and wrapped her arms around herself. "It's cold, isn't it," she said, trying to talk and keep her teeth from chattering at the same time. "God, I'm so scared," she blurted out past her clenched teeth.

"Of what?" Tim asked gently. "Of me? Of what?"

Sally tried to laugh, feeling the shaking deep inside her body. "Everything," she said, her teeth clenched so tightly her jaw hurt. "The worst things I haven't told you."

"You don't have to."

"No, I want to. You're right, I need to. But I'm afraid you'll be disgusted or frightened of me. You won't like me," she said in a small voice.

"I will, I promise," Tim said patiently. "And believe me, Sally, you couldn't tell me anything that would shock me. I used to think I'd heard it all, listening to those marines back from the Pacific. But Jesus, after a month here, listening to refugees, how much can one shrink take?"

She laughed at his little joke, hearing the truth behind it. "God, I'm cold."

He slid across the seat and put his arms around her, just holding her. "Go on, Sal, talk to me. Tell me about you. I want to know, and not just because I'm a doctor."

Sally broke from him. "It was when I was in Los Angeles . . ."

"Sleeping around."

"Yes. Trying not to be empty. Not to feel dead."

"I know the feeling." He was so close to her, not moving, his presence warming her so that she could take a deep breath.

"On New Year's Eve—uhmm, several months after I . . . got back from Germany—I met this guy and went with him to his hotel. And sometime, while we were there, before or after the sex—I don't remember—I guess I decided that since I felt dead, I might as well be dead. So I went into the bathroom and took the razor blade out of his safety razor and slit my wrists."

"Oh, God, Sal." Tim breathed the words out, his hand on the back of her neck.

"It was hard to do, and I'd never have managed as well if I hadn't been drunk. On the other hand, I probably would have succeeded. My left was easy, but the blood scared me, and I bobbled doing the right wrist. There was a lot of blood, though, and I probably would have bled to death if the guy hadn't found me. It was so bloody. It confused me, the blood did. He called the ambulance and all.

"Funny, I can't remember his name and he saved my life. So I went back to my father's house—he let me come—and I tried to be a good girl."

"And you've been trying all this time?" His hand moved to stroke the back of her head, gently calming her.

"Yeah. Stupid. I was a good girl all my life, before . . . everything."

"Aren't you tired of being a good girl?" Tim asked, in a tender, teasing tone that didn't obscure the fact that he was serious about his question.

"I'm getting there," she said.

He leaned over and gave her a sweet, brief kiss, then held his cheek against hers. It was an oddly comforting gesture, and Sally relaxed, leaning her head against his shoulder.

"Your story frightens me," he said, his voice muffled. "I've had patients try that. Some succeeded. Guys who were sent to the hospital at Pearl, marines from the islands and sailors and airmen who had spent ten days in the water, fighting off sharks." He moved so that he could see her face. "You'd think they'd be happy to be alive, but some of them weren't. I didn't understand, I still don't, why death should be so attractive. And I'll tell you, it scares me. There was one kid . . . Listen, Sally, we all carry demons with us."

"When you get that close to death," she said, "I think you never trust life again. It's valuable, more valuable than ever to you. But you never trust it. Does that make sense? I look at the scars and I know how easy it would be to suddenly *be* no more."

"Do you ever think of doing it again?" he asked.

She looked at her wrists for a long time before she answered, as though she could see the thick scars through the cloth of her shirt and jacket.

"No. At first, I didn't care if I was alive or not, but now I think there's been enough death."

"Glad to hear it."

"Besides," she said softly, moving away from him to her side of the seat.

"What besides?" He started the car.

"There might be more to live for. Now. Maybe." She turned her head and looked out the window at the shapes of darkened buildings. Tim was silent. She sneaked a look at him. His eyes flicked from the road ahead, toward her, and back to the road. But he smiled, the corners of his mouth turning up fleetingly, and she knew he understood what she was trying to say.

CHAPTER 9

O n Sunday morning, Sally awakened early and lay on her side, watching the sunlight that had worked its way in through her double-shuttered windows. She could see the short row of books on the little mantel in the corner. In one, a battered copy of *Gone with the Wind,* were the photographs of Christian that she had brought from the States. Somehow, this morning, thinking about them didn't bother her. Nothing did, not even Annaliese's sketchy news of her brother's survival.

Turning onto her back, she stretched. Yesterday, Saturday, she had spent the day puttering around, doing chores, writing letters, and then, last night, Tim had called. They had chatted for a few minutes about nothing in particular. He had just called to say hello and to tell her that he would be busy all day Sunday at the American hospital, where he continued his work with GIs.

Trying not to think about how much she had looked forward to seeing him, Sally quickly got out of bed, pulled on her robe, and went to the window to open the shutters. That's what happens when you care for someone, she thought. She spent all her time missing him. Damn.

She leaned out to secure the outer shutters, latching them to the hook on the wall. It was a chilly day, bright and sunny. It felt like fall at last. Sally closed the window and looked over at the travel clock on her nightstand. It wasn't even eight o'clock yet. She sighed. It would be a long day, and she sat on the foot of her bed thinking about how she could spend the time.

What she really wanted was to see Tim. She fell back on the bed. The thought frightened her, but she also knew it was true.

She wanted to find out about how his heart had been broken and she wanted to ask him about the marines who didn't want to live and she wanted to hear about his children. And—let's be honest, she told herself—she wanted to kiss him again. Her fear made her laugh at herself, at her predictability. She would telephone him; maybe he hadn't left for the hospital yet. Maybe they could meet that evening. Try to see if they could have a normal time together. And wouldn't he be surprised to hear from her?

She showered and dressed, putting on navy wool slacks and a red-and-navy sweater over a white shirt. The thought occurred to her that Tim had never seen her out of uniform; nor she, him. She remembered his back and shoulders under his shirt, moving away from her down the hall. And she smiled.

Then she went into the hall to telephone, but swerved instead into the dining room for coffee. She lingered, eating a hard roll, before she ventured back to the phone. Two times she picked up the receiver and replaced it again. She gave herself a mental slap, put the receiver to her ear and dialed. It rang. And rang. And rang.

He wasn't there. She had waited too long. Sally looked at the receiver as though she could see down the line to Tim's apartment. How dare he, after all the nerve it had taken her. Shaking her head, amused and frustrated, she decided to walk over to the office.

In her office, she shed her coat and bag, then walked to the corner and looked down the hall toward Tim's office, knowing he wouldn't be there. He wasn't, but there was light spilling from the open door of Colonel Eiger's office. Curious, she walked down the hall and looked in.

"Hello?" she called.

"Who's that?" the colonel called from the conference room.

"Sally," she replied, and walked in.

"Say, Sally, do you know anybody at *Life* magazine?"

"*Life*? As a matter of fact, I do. An old pal," she said, slowly. "At least I think he's still there. Why?"

The colonel was standing, his back to her, at the table on which lay a black-and-white picture. Several more were in his hand, and as he turned, he thrust them at her.

"Look at these. What do you think of them? Are they good enough for *Life*?" he asked. Sally cringed: the pictures were still damp from the developer and the colonel's fingerprints were all over them. Carefully she took them from the colonel and laid them out separately on the table.

Later, thinking about that moment, she recalled how innocently she had begun to move the photographs about, relating them to each other, making conclusions in her mind about them.

Those photographs were the reason she had come to Berlin, although she wouldn't realize it for several days.

The photographs were of a German action, and unlike most of the material she had seen, the focus was on the perpetrators, not the victims. SS officers, noncoms, and soldiers were portrayed, their rank and unit markings clear, sharp, most of their faces identifiable. Sally turned her head toward Colonel Eiger, who stood next to her, his arms crossed.

"Where. . . ?" she started to ask, trying to control her excitement.

"Czech refugee. Evidently she was in a camp in the east. A girl named Mala something. She's in very bad shape, malnourished, bad lungs, and an infected wound on her leg. Medics can't figure out how she's managed to stay alive.

"She hitched her way here on a DP train and collapsed at the station. Couple of MPs brought her to the hospital. She wouldn't go with them without making sure they were Americans. Wouldn't take their word for it. Had to see their ID cards before she'd allow herself to pass out.

"So, when the docs undressed her, they found three rolls of film in a pouch around her waist. She tried to explain the stuff, but she doesn't speak English, of course, and it took a while to rustle up someone who could speak Czech. They found a patient who talked to her, got her name and where she was from, that she'd shot the film, and some rigmarole about *Life* magazine."

The colonel held up his hand to ward off Sally's question. "Wait until you hear. So, we finally got an interpreter and Finkelstein talked to her this morning and her story's a beaut. After the Germans leveled her town, she hid the film, then took off for Prague."

"Where'd she hide it?"

"Wouldn't say. Evidently somewhere no one ever looked because the film was still there after the war. Meanwhile, she was caught in a roundup and wound up at Auschwitz."

"She went from Poland back to Czechoslovakia to get this film?" Sally asked, incredulous.

"Guess so, because here she is with it. Finkelstein says she told him that after the camp was liberated in '45, when she could walk, she went back to Czechoslovakia. To get the film and bring it to us. And you wanna know why she wanted Americans to get the film?"

"Does it have something to do with *Life* magazine?" Sally said, touching an edge of a photograph.

"She wants *Life* to publish them."

"Why?"

"Pictures, Sally. All those great *Life* pictures. You know, war pictures, the baby in the ruins of Peking, that Spanish Civil War stuff they published."

"Where'd she see a *Life*?"

"She told Finkelstein that during her hike back to Czechoslovakia, she spent a couple of cold nights in someone's ruined house, up in the attic, along with a pile of old *Life* magazines. Not only did they give her something to sit on but a reason for going on. Or something like that. Anyway, those are from the first roll." He pointed at the pictures on the table.

Sally's eyes followed his gesture to the photographs. One showed two soldiers and a noncom standing over a line of bodies. In the background, a lone bare tree loomed stark against the horizon. In another, a group of women and children as herded down a street by men carrying rifles. There were bayonets on some of the guns. They were beautiful photographs, well-composed, the light throwing the buildings and people into sharp relief. They had to be good enough for *Life*.

"Look," she said, picking up two of the pictures carefully by their edges, "these look as though they are consecutive. Did Doug get the name of the town?"

"Some small place—Layzaky?" Colonel Eiger grimaced. "They're sending over a report with the particulars and the correct spelling."

"There are two more rolls?"

"Yes," said the colonel, "Sergeant Dolan's bringing them up as soon as they're ready. Ah, this may be him," he said in response to footsteps in the outer office, and left the conference room.

"What year was this?" said Sally. "And how in God's name did she manage to evade capture? Do you realize what these guys would have done to her if they had caught her? I wonder where she got the camera—hey!" She called to the colonel, then went to the door between the two offices. "Can I go talk to her? I'd like to meet her. Is she well enough for visitors?"

"You can't," said Colonel Eiger.

"Here you are, sir," said Sergeant Dolan, handing over a big manila envelope.

"Thanks, Sergeant," replied the colonel.

"Why, Colonel?" asked Sally.

"She's being operated on. I think they have to take her leg off. Here," he said, handing her the envelope.

"What happened?" she asked softly.

"The wound. Gangrene. It was too far along."

"Is she going to be all right?"

"Don't know, Sally. Don't know."

Sally nodded and turned back to the table. She gathered all of the photographs into a stack and sat in front of it. She would look at each one individually before she began trying to make a story out of them. She was excited. Rarely had she ever had more than two or three photographs of the same event, and certainly she had never had so many pieces of destructive evidence in her hands.

"So, you think you know somebody to send them to?"

"Yes. One of their war correspondents, David Wohl."

"Hey, I know him. Met him in Italy. New Yorker. Funny guy. Real nuts. Never saw a guy drink so much. You know him? Small world, isn't it."

"Sure is, Colonel," she said, happy to hear about David, even at such a remove. She got up to go get her loupe from her office.

"Sally," the colonel said. "What are you doing here on a Sunday, anyway?"

"Oh," she said, "nothing. Just bored. Wandering around."

"Good, good," he said, not really listening to her.

Sally stood back and studied the wall of photographs she had just finished creating on the corkboard in the conference room. It was late Tuesday afternoon, and she had been working since Sunday morning on Mala's film, trying to re-create the sequence, and she thought, looking at them critically, that she had.

It began with a shot of the village's main street, its only street, in the late-afternoon light, peaceful and nearly deserted. There was a tiny church and one or two other buildings. Lezaky, which was the name of the village, was small, more a hamlet, really. It had had less than ninety inhabitants, all miners, but now it had none. The town did not exist anymore. It would never glow in the sunset again.

In the last pictures, near the window, was the end of Lezaky. Taken from some distance away in early-morning light, the few buildings were disappearing in flame and smoke. Again Sally marveled at the bravery of the Czech girl who had relentlessly recorded the death of her village—and of her family.

Mala had been only sixteen when she took the pictures. She had, the patient who had talked to her reported, learned to take pictures from her elder brother, who had a studio in Prague. Max Tobin was trying to track him down or his business.

On the evening the Germans came to Lezaky, Mala had, evidently, been wandering around with her camera, looking for likely subjects.

Lezaky had been an old village, and it had never grown, like its neighbor, Lidice, fifty miles to the west. There the people were also miners, but in Lezaky the young people tended to leave the town for Prague and wider horizons.

Mala had the instincts of all great photographers, and when she saw disaster driving up the road from Prague that June of 1942, she had turned her camera to face it. She also realized her danger well enough to hide while she took her pictures, many of which seemed to have been shot from above the action.

Sally lit a cigarette and leaned against the long table, studying the photographs. Heydrich again. Lezaky had been destroyed as part of the brutal retribution wrought by the Gestapo after Heydrich's assassination.

Someone whistled long and low behind her. Sally turned; it was Nelson Armbrewster. She nodded at the expression on his face.

"Something else, aren't they?" she said.

"Indeed," he answered. He moved closer to the wall, his hands behind his back, and began looking in earnest. "Jesus," he exclaimed, "if we can only identify a quarter of these bastards . . ."

But Sally was only half-listening to him. Something in one of the photographs near the window had caught her eye. She walked to it, studied it, then turned and grabbed her loupe from the table. She placed it on the photograph and looked. More light, she needed more light.

"Sally?" said Nelson, but she ignored him, unpinning the particular picture from the wall and bringing it to the window.

"Need a blowup," she muttered, feeling dread growing in her, icy cold, and returned to the wall, bending to look at the photographs that surrounded the empty space. She peered closely at them, forcing her mind to stay blank, ignoring the coldness in her stomach.

"Recognize someone?" Nelson asked facetiously.

Sally raised her head and looked at him, hating him. He must have read it in her face, for he was silent. Sally picked up her grease pencil and made a set of brackets on the photograph, indicating the area she wanted enlarged, then she walked out of the room, leaving behind a perplexed and curious Nelson Armbrewster.

Sometime later, the enlargement in her hand, Sally stood in the cement corridor outside the darkroom in the basement. She held the photograph up in the glaring, uncovered light bulb. She could not be absolutely sure and it was driving her crazy. But more than anything, she wanted very, very much not to be able to recognize him. Her arms dropped to her side and she stood, feeling helpless, sick to her stomach, in the middle of the bleak hall. The darkroom door opened.

"You all right, Lieutenant?" asked the young soldier who had developed all of Mala's pictures and had just made the enlargement for her. "Did I get what you wanted?"

"Yes, Henry," she said, "they're fine." She looked at him and tried to smile. "So am I," she said. "Thanks."

Upstairs in her office, she placed the enlargement and the original next to each other on her desk and lit a cigarette. She sat heavily in her chair, then, as though pulled by a magnet, her eyes were drawn across the room to the box of Auschwitz pictures she had shoved into the corner. All those photographs that she had looked at, those of the victims and others of the perpetrators, all of them recording countless acts of stupidity and evil . . . And with all those thousands of pictures, it now came down to one single picture and whether she could see Christian in this picture of a man committing a murder.

She could identify the man's rank: Obersturmbannführer, lieutenant colonel. The face was thin, the mouth tight and Prussian-grim, and resembled other Germans, Wehrmacht and SS. The Czech girl had caught him as he was wiping his forehead with the back of a gloved hand shading his upper face, his cap pushed back. It could be Christian but Sally couldn't be absolutely sure.

But she was sure she must tell her suspicions to her commanding officer. She snubbed out her cigarette, then reached for the phone and asked to be connected to the colonel. After speaking to him, she reached for her bag and headed back to her quarters. It was time to bring her own photographs out of hiding.

Chester Dolan was typing as she entered his office. He looked up at her and smiled. He cocked his head.

"You feeling all right?" he asked softly.

Sally nodded, then shook her head. "I think the roof's about to fall in on me, Chester."

"Anything I can do?"

"Pick up the pieces?"

"Can do, Lieutenant," he said. Then he reached out and, after the briefest hesitation, patted her arm.

"He's expecting me," Sally said. She went into the conference room to take a couple of pictures from the wall. Then she knocked on the door to the colonel's office and went in. Timothy Hastings sat in the battered armchair in front of Colonel Eiger's desk, one ankle on the other knee.

"Oh," Sally said, surprised to see him. "I thought—"

"That's okay, Sally," Colonel Eiger interrupted her, "Hastings was on his way out."

Tim came up out of the chair easily. "Just dropped by. See

88

you." He walked past Sally to the door. She held a hand out.

"Wait," she said quietly, "maybe . . ." She looked at Eiger. "I wouldn't mind if he stayed, if that's all right? He knows about some of this."

"Fine with me," the colonel said. "Do you want to stay, Hastings?"

"Sure," said Tim without hesitation, and went back to his chair.

Sally sat on the hard chair at the other corner of the colonel's desk, the photographs on her lap. She could hear Sergeant Dolan typing in the outer office; it was a comforting, normal sound. She looked at her colonel. He was silhouetted by the late-afternoon light behind him as it shone in through the half-closed wooden blinds. The fall weather was beautiful, although Sally hadn't noticed until now.

"This might take a while," she said and he nodded. "First," Sally started, taking the 8-by-10 original of Mala's picture and handing it to Eiger, "you should see this." He looked at it, grunted and handed it on to Tim. "That man is a Lieutenant Colonel, an Obersturmbannführer and the commander of this action group. I say that because there is no one of higher rank in any of the photographs. Because they are SS, their insignia is easy to see, even in their gray field uniforms—the silver on black on their collar tabs stands out."

Tim, holding the photograph by the edges, looked from it to Sally and back again. "This was one of the Czech girl's?"

Sally nodded. "Although Lidice was the most famous of all the towns destroyed by the SS, there were many others. Well, you know that. This little place—barely a village—was supposed to have harbored a radio used by the commandos who killed Heydrich. So while one group of SS and Gestapo was destroying Lidice, another, smaller team went over to take care of Lezaky in the same way. They shot all males over twelve, took the women and children to camps, and blew up the buildings.

"The difference here was Mala and her camera. You've been in to see her work?" Both men nodded. "I know you've read Doug's interview with her and Max's reports . . ." Sally trailed off, looking down at the file on her lap. She took the enlargement out and handed it to Eiger. "I think I can identify the commander, this man." Tim looked at her, she could feel his eyes and his sharp interest on her, but she kept hers on the photograph in the colonel's hand.

"I had Henry do the blowup to make sure. I thought I might be able to identify him positively. But there's still a question in my mind. If only he'd taken his cap off."

"She waited, didn't she," said the colonel, staring at the pic-

"She tried to catch him so he could be identified." He laid the photograph down. "So who is he?"

"I *think* he is Christian Robert Mayr," Sally said.

"Your husband," said Colonel Eiger.

"Yeah," said Sally, and stood up abruptly, spilling the photographs onto the floor. "Oh, damn!" She bent to pick them up. "That was stupid. Look, one went under the desk. Can you reach it? God, that was stupid."

"I've got it," Tim said, kneeling in front of her.

"I'm sorry to be so clumsy." She grabbed for the one of her and Christian in the nightclub, not wanting Tim to see it yet.

"That's all right," said Colonel Eiger. He was standing behind his desk.

Sally and Tim stood up together and he handed her the photographs.

"Thanks." She wouldn't look at him.

He sat back in his chair. Sally laid out the sequence on the colonel's desk, adding the enlargement to them. She put the pictures down deliberately, carefully, and then stood back, allowing Colonel Eiger to see them easily.

"Is it your husband?" he asked gently, looking up at her.

"Yes, Colonel, I think it is."

"Sally," said Tim, almost in a whisper.

"It's okay," she said, trying to smile, to let him know she was calm. "It doesn't surprise me either. Not really." She looked down at the pictures and touched the edge of one with her fingertips. "I wish it did. But Chris——, he was a protégé of Heydrich's. Had worked for him for years. He was already a Hauptsturmführer the last time I saw him, a Captain at twenty-one. It makes sense he would have been sent out to do this, to have this rank."

The colonel and Hastings looked at the sequence of three pictures she laid out. Simply, they showed a child being shot out of a tree by an SS officer. In the first, the officer pointed his handgun, his Luger, at the child, visible only as a white blot in the branches of the tree. In the second, the officer wiped his forehead, ignoring the crumpled body of the child several feet away. The child, a boy, was in dark shorts, his thin legs splayed, his arms folded under his body. The last picture of the sequence showed another SS soldier dragging the body away. It was the second photograph that Sally had had enlarged.

"So, you can identify this bastard," said the colonel, tapping the middle picture with his knuckle. "Do we know where he was? Is he alive? Did he survive?"

"I might," said Sally, "that is, I know how we might find out. You know the German woman I visit occasionally? Tim's been with me. She's his sister and she told me he was still alive, although she claims not to have seen him since '45, just before the end of the war."

"When did she tell you this?" Eiger asked.

"The night we were there," Sally answered, indicating Tim.

"But Sally, that was a month ago," Tim said softly.

"I didn't know whether to trust her or not. And we didn't have these pictures then," she said, answering his unasked question. "This is so . . ." She stopped for a moment, then spoke briskly. "I have these to help identify him more positively." She held out the two personal pictures and sat down, carefully smoothing her uniform skirt over her knees.

Eiger looked at the new pictures, looking from them to Sally and back. He handed them on to Tim. Out of the corner of her eye, Sally watched Tim take the prints. She didn't want to see his reaction to the nightclub photograph, to the naked longing on her twenty-one-year-old face.

"Tell us about him," said the colonel.

Sally cleared her throat and looked down at her lap. "He was born in 1913, in Berlin," she began, speaking softly. "Like me," she added. "He's a month older than I am. His father was a professor, who died the year Hitler came to power. His mother . . ." Sally stopped, remembering Lisa Mayr. "I'm sorry, Colonel," she said softly. "Lisa Mayr was very dear to me. She was killed in an air raid. Her daughter told me. I . . . it is difficult to betray her."

"Not him?" asked the colonel.

"Yes, him, even him," she answered.

"But look at what he's done," said Eiger.

"It could be him. I'm not sure."

"He was, is, SS, Sally," said Tim.

Her hands in fists in her lap, Sally spoke in a whisper. "I know. I've tried to see him killing that child, but I can't, and I'm afraid . . . I'm afraid. I don't want to see him there." And she lowered her head, letting the coldness spread around her heart, killing all feeling, turning her soul to ice.

When she raised her head, she was calm again. "As I said, he was one of Heydrich's protégés. He was ambitious. And he believed in much of the Nazi line. He was idealistic, you see, back then. So it is possible that he would, eventually, have come to this, shooting children out of trees." Her voice was hard and impersonal and she was pleased she could speak so professionally.

"His sister claims he's alive?" said Eiger.

"Yes. I might have even seen him. At any rate, I think Annaliese knows much more."

"Why didn't you tell me any of this?" Eiger asked.

"I don't know. There didn't seem to be anything to tell. It could have been my imagination. There wasn't anything specific."

"You didn't need to identify him now."

"Oh, yes. Yes, I did. I do."

"Why, Sally?" asked Tim.

"Mala's pictures. Those Auschwitz pictures Mavis left me. All the damn pictures! I've been looking at pictures for years now. It's become an avalanche of photographs, all of hell.

"How could I reconcile the man I knew, the boy I knew, with those Einsatzgruppen pictures you had me identify my first day? I just don't understand it.

"But I can't be silent any longer. I feel guilty. I feel so . . . But I just couldn't do this alone any longer."

"You're not alone," murmured Tim and moved toward her. She raised her hand from her lap, stopping him. She could not bear his tenderness at that moment.

"Is this your family?" Eiger asked, looking at the photograph taken on the lake.

"Mine and his."

"Yes, I recognize you. Is this him?"

Sally craned her neck to look to where Eiger was pointing. "No, that's his older brother Kurt. He was an early National Socialist and was killed in the street fighting in '27. That's Christian."

"A good-looking boy," said the colonel.

"Yes. He was."

"Looks like an SS recruiting poster." The colonel had picked up the nightclub photograph. "I can see the attraction."

"Why was my loving him not enough?" Sally said quietly. "Isn't that egotistical of me? But I used to wonder . . . He promised my father he would bring me to the States. I don't know if he meant it, if he was lying. What he was thinking?

"I had a powerful rival—what woman has ever been able to win against boots and flags and all that hoopla? When have any of you ever chosen us over those other things—brotherhood, duty, and honor? Honor.

"Not that we don't fall for it ourselves. Hell, death is a fascinating thing and a good-looking guy in a uniform—and he was a very handsome man—could be irresistible. But Christian . . . he was also . . . kind and funny and honest. Sweet. He was. He was sweet.

Generous, too, toward me. Well, all of this is about how he was toward me, how I saw him. How I loved him, even while he wore that uniform."

She looked at the enlargement of Mala's brutal photograph, at the tight mouth and thin face.

"What happened to him?" she whispered.

BOOK TWO
BERLIN, 1933 – 1934

SNAPSHOTS

I spend my working days looking at photographs of strangers. It is an uncommon job and one I never would have anticipated. Not that I anticipated any other sort of job in its place. When I was young, I never thought about the future. I think it frightened me. Now I just let it come, knowing there isn't a lot I can do about it.

The photographs fascinate me, all of them. I can study them for hours, these captured moments of other people's lives. I concentrate on the faces, trying to see through that moment when the shutter clicked and all those human thoughts and emotions were frozen forever.

I don't like photographs without people in them. Fortunately, there are other departments to study those. I stay with the faces. They are what are important, what I want to see clearly. Which is one reason the Czech girl's, Mala's, photograph of the Obersturmbannführer is so upsetting: I can't see the man's face. Even if he turns out to be Christian, I would rather be able to see his face. Then, maybe, I could understand why he was in that place, doing those things. Whoever he was.

Is.

Does this make any sense at all?

I have looked at pictures of terrible things, things my mind can still barely encompass. I had such a sheltered life, in spite of the separations, in spite of the sophistication of my parents. Until my mother died, that is. But even after that, when I was put into a boarding school, the sheltering continued.

Of course, everything changed when I went to Berlin with Daddy in 1933.

I am reminded of an old Chinese curse I read somewhere: May you live in interesting times. I think of it and laugh. What a curse it is. Interesting times, indeed.

There is death all around us these days. And although I keep myself apart, I feel guilty. I suppose I feel I must atone for my stupidity as a girl. I wish I didn't, but I do. I still feel such a fool for having let Heydrich befriend me, for having been so naive, for believing Christian. I look at my hand and hate it because I shook Hitler's hand with it.

So, studying the pictures, however horrible they are, is my attempt at penance. And understanding. Neither comes easily, of course. Oh, to be honest, I don't have an inkling of either. I mean, I *knew* Reinhard Heydrich.

He was a man who kept things secret. He loved secrets. He also loved power. Did he love National Socialism? I couldn't tell you. He was one of the administrators of the Final Solution, so he believed in something. But, beyond his own personal, secret power, I couldn't tell you what that was. I can't explain him, arranging, organizing all that death, while loving Mozart. It makes no sense.

I can't understand why they did the things they did. I could give you reasons, but they don't suffice. Reason is not at work in this situation.

If you meet someone who thinks he can explain what happened to us in the last dozen years, hand him one of those pictures the British took at Dachau and ask him to explain it. He can't. Nobody could.

I keep looking at the pictures, as terrible as they are. Searching, I guess. A terrible mystery, an *awful* mystery, took place here on planet Earth and I, like a visitor from Mars, search the artifacts for evidence. I also think, and I've never admitted this to anyone, that I have been looking for him.

It has been at the back of my mind that I might, someday, stumble across a photograph of him grinning at some poor, elderly Jewish man being shaved by SS men half his age. I once had an opportunity to study a photograph of an Einsatzgruppen unit, one of the special squadrons sent to conquered Russia expressly to murder as many Jews as possible. They were a tough-looking group of men, a dozen of them, all murderers. I searched the faces, praying he wouldn't be among them.

I have learned to read photographs, although I also have learned that they can be deceiving. A picture of a German soldier, in stove-shuttle helmet and greatcoat, reaching up to take a tiny child from someone's arms. It seems to be one of those shots of the compassionate soldier. You've seen them, the battle-weary man cradling the lost child. Then, one day, I came across the complete photograph of which mine was a detail.

The arms are those of a woman and she is handing down the child—obviously, from her expression, against her will. She is handing her child into the arms of the enemy. She is on a train, packed into a train, on her way to a camp.

I don't know why the soldier is taking the baby until I look more closely. Ah. The child is dead. Once I realize that, I can see it in the baby's limpness. And what I took for compassion is merely efficiency, taking out the bodies before the train leaves. Still, there is a terrible tenderness in the soldier's hands, reaching up to take the dead child. Things are seldom black and white, not even in black-and-white photographs.

I brought my photos of the two families, of the nightclub, to Berlin with me probably for the same reason people carried their snapshots onto the cattle cars—as talismans, and for company. We keep albums to mark the passing of the years, our personal signposts, but it's the pictures we carry in our wallets or set up in empty hotel rooms that show whom or what we really care about.

I don't often look at my own pictures, having spent so much time trying to put the memories behind me. Because that's what photographs are, of course, memories made concrete. Then there are the memories for which we have no photographs. These memory-snaps flash into our minds when we least expect them. We carry them with us everywhere. Even, I imagine, into a gas chamber.

Taking out the family photograph I brought with me to Berlin, I study it, searching the faces, as I do the photographs of strangers, trying to see beyond the gray images. I stop, realizing that I am looking for a shadow. I imagine I can see the future in our faces, the death that is so close to us. I close my eyes, trying to remember, trying to be back there, back on the porch of the Mayrs' house on the shore of Lake Sebastian. I should be dispassionate about this, if I really want to learn from this photograph, but I can't.

I could never be dispassionate about the Mayrs. Any of them. They all touched me, from my envy of the sisters' pretty white dresses and the comfort of Lisa's generous, almost impersonal mothering to all I felt about Christian.

Everyone I have ever truly cared for, except perhaps for Graziella, the nursemaid who cared for me in Rome, is in this picture. Eddie. My parents.

I like the way my parents look in this photograph. I wish, though, that I could see my father's eyes. I wish, oh, how I wish, that I could talk to him.

He had, Eddie told me once, spied for the United States during the Great War. I didn't know if I believed it, but now I search my father's regular features, trying to see if his was the face of a spy. I shake my head. There's no way of knowing, except that he was a secret man. At least, to his children.

My mother's inheritance provided my parents with their comfortable, independent way of life, and I never heard my father discuss whether living off his wife that way bothered him. But that summer,

I learned later, he was thinking seriously of taking up an appointment offered to him by the State Department. They wanted to send him to Vienna. He went, alone, to find a house, leaving the rest of us in Gramercy Park, and my mother and I followed later. Eddie was left behind in prep school.

My parents were a handsome couple, and although they do not touch each other in the photograph, they seem connected to each other. They fit together in their light, sophisticated clothing, their relaxed postures. I am pleased at this observation because I have come to the conclusion that my parents cared more about each other than they did about Eddie and me. Not a bad thing, this fascination they had for each other, but I do think Eddie and I sometimes felt like guests in our family. Well-treated guests, but guests all the same.

In front of everyone, on the lower step, sitting next to me, is Christian, his elbows on his skinny knees. He is my age, almost exactly, only a month older, and my best friend.

Christian. Narrow face, straight eyebrows, long nose, and a shock of hair falling across his forehead. His face is as familiar to me as my brother's. I try to look at him as a stranger would, trying to see him without feelings, but I can't.

I do see how skinny he was, and I remember that, for most of our childhood, he was shorter than I was. He looks unsmilingly at the camera. He wasn't always so serious. He looks very small, sitting so compactly on the bottom step, separated somehow from the rest of his family.

I try to see past the adult, who stands so much more clearly in my memory, to this boy. I try to forget the picture from Czechoslovakia that may or may not be him. It is hard; the later memory gets in the way.

We were such good friends, our interests and abilities meshing, balancing. We loved to read and study the sky at night. He knew all the constellations, and I, the myths about them. He was crazy for cowboys and I had a mother who had actually grown up on a ranch in Texas. I was nuts about the movies and he had to admit that Douglas Fairbanks could fence well. I would push him into adventures and he would follow without shame and then find the way to extricate us from trouble. We shared apples, books, jokes, and each other's languages and a passion for ancient Egypt. We fought and made up and stood up for each other against our elder brothers.

I never doubted that we would be friends forever. But I never thought we would grow older or that the world would change so.

The summer afternoon's light is gentle on us and the old photograph gives our skin a luminescence, a softness that threatens to break my heart as I look at us. We were all so young, so stupidly, blessedly secure in our world. I put the photograph down and lay my hand on it. It is precious. I feel its slickness under my hand.

We lost it, didn't we? All that golden summer innocence. But then, nothing lasts. I've learned that lesson. Nothing lasts, except, sometimes, by some strange fluke, things. Like photographs. And I remember the room of photographs, the box in my office, the wall of them in the conference room.

No, I never could have imagined these flimsy black-and-white images could come to dominate my life so.

Sometimes, I feel that they are all I have left and are the only connections I have to life, to people. I laugh. Photographs are all I have left of him and are what I will use to condemn him.

Evidence.

Perhaps one of the strangest pieces of evidence is my passport, which, in the space where it asks for my place of birth, reads: "Berlin, Germany." None of my family was born in the same place as any of the others.

My mother's childhood was spent on a huge ranch in Texas. Her father, an Anglo, had met and married her mother during a visit to Argentina. He brought his black-haired, tawny-skinned wife back to his family, and was immediately rejected by them. So Mama was brought up with no family, except her parents.

My mother went away to Smith College in the East, and while she was there, an aunt, her father's sister, whom she'd never met, died, leaving Mama a sizable fortune, which included a good chunk of Texas real estate. Mama never returned to Texas. Perhaps that was what her aunt had intended.

My father's family was respectably poor. He was born in San Francisco, his father a refugee from a wealthy patrician family in the East and his mother the daughter of a banker. Daddy was an only child and fled, as soon as he could, from the gentile poverty of his parents. He was very well educated, first at Stanford and then at the university in Berlin.

He and Mama met in Paris, where he was researching the French Revolution. She always said it was her influence that pointed him toward Charlotte Corday, Marat's murderer. Father wrote a biography of Corday that was not only a critical and professional success, but a popular one as well. He probably hated that.

Eddie was born in England, while they were visiting, and about a year before I was born they moved to Germany, to Berlin, where

101

Daddy finished his research for his thesis. I had a nursemaid, to leave Mother time for her artistic pursuits. I don't think my mother liked children very much. Not that she was mean or thoughtless; I just don't think she knew what to do with us. My father had even less to do with us.

We moved to Rome the year after I was born. When I was three, Mama took Eddie back to the States for school and remained there for the rest of the First World War.

I never thought much about my mother's leaving me alone with my father all that time, until I started seeing a psychiatrist. He was very interested in those years, and I finally faced the emptiness in me that seemed to stem from those lonely years without her.

Logically my father and I should have grown close to one another in the two years we lived alone together in the chilly marble villa in the Roman suburb, but we didn't. What would a man like my father, fluent in several languages, an acknowledged authority on eighteenth-century European history, especially that of the Hohenzollerns, and an aficionado of early-Renaissance painting, with a particular affinity for Cimabue, what would a man like that have to do with a child of three or four?

The answer is: nothing. He left me in Graziella's care.

Anyway, when my father and I returned to America after the war, we all lived together in New York City, except for the two-year stint in Vienna. But when Mama was killed crossing Third Avenue on a rainy afternoon, my father, unable and unwilling to take care of Eddie or me, sent both of us off to boarding schools.

My parents had first visited Lake Sebastian when they lived in Berlin at the time I was born and began returning to it after the war. I spent every summer there between the ages of six and fourteen.

Perhaps the main reason for my feelings about the Mayrs was because of Lisa Mayr's warm acceptance of me. With so many children of her own, she just seemed to include me, effortlessly, in her affections. And I adored her in return.

I did love my own mother, although I always felt I was a disappointment to her. I was not a pretty little girl, with my messy hair and my big feet. And Mama was accomplished at so many things. She painted and played the piano and sang in a wonderful, rich alto voice. She read poetry out loud at parties and was a good cook and decorator.

I did none of these things, although I always liked to look at pictures and never complained about hours spent tramping through museums and churches. It wasn't until I started playing the piano that she took an interest in me. And it wasn't until I started to show

102

some talent for it that we began to get to know each other.

And then she was gone, hit by a skidding taxi. I remember that, only the day before, she had given me *Pride and Prejudice* to read after I'd told her that I'd read *Jane Eyre* and *Wuthering Heights*. I missed her dreadfully. And because I had lost her once already, when she had left my father and me in Rome, it took me years to get over the notion that one day, if I was good enough, she would come back.

In the miserable months after her death, while my father locked himself away, leaving Eddie and me alone with our grief, the only connection I had with anyone was letters from Germany, from Lisa and from Christian. He wrote me twice, short letters, not very informative, but enough to let me know he was thinking of me. Lisa wrote often, and it was her letters that allowed me to grieve. I would sit at the upstairs hall window, facing east, facing Germany, and cry to be with her, not realizing I was crying for my own mother.

Christian was my best friend, away from the lake as well. We would write sporadically during the year, but at the start of each summer, one of us would race around the lake to the other's house to pick up right where we had left off the last September.

At first, we were friends because we were so close in age, born the same year, just months apart, and later because we were so similar, both loners, both serious readers, both inclined to daydream. His sisters, Marta, Elizabeth, and Ursula, were too old to be friends with me, and Annaliese was too young.

There were two milestones in our early friendship. The first happened when we were both ten and the next four years later, during the last summer we both spent at the lake.

The summer we were ten, Christian started spending more and more time with the boys, including Eddie and Kurt. There was a gang of them and they went off together, secretly, privately, leaving me out. I began following them, just as secretly, and discovered that they had found a pond deep in the forest behind the Mayrs' house. Every day, they went there and had, as I saw with my envious, lonely eyes, great fun—swimming, horsing around, and even smoking cigarettes.

So, to get back at them, I stole their clothing. I did it three times over the next several weeks—sneaking up on them, in spite of their guards, and spiriting away their things. I always left the clothes somewhere for them to find, but they did have to run, naked, through the forest to do so.

Naturally, they could not allow this to continue and they planned a terrible revenge. They sent Christian to lure me to it.

He arrived one hot afternoon, while I was sitting in the window seat in the dining room, reading, and invited me for a walk. I went, of course. I hadn't seen him in a while and I was reading a wonderful book about Howard Carter's spectacular find in Egypt that I wanted to tell him about.

"I'll take you to a secret place," he said. I babbled on about Tutankhamen as we walked, single-file, along the lake. Finally he turned into the woods, up a rise and over, to the edge of a small meadow covered with wildflowers. There was a convenient fallen log for us to sit on.

Saying nothing, Christian put his arm around my shoulders, which really surprised me. It stopped me in mid-sentence. We sat in uncomfortable silence. Or, at least, I was uncomfortable. I didn't know what was expected of me or what would happen next. I turned my head slightly to look at him. I had never been so close to him and drank in the sight of his golden eyelashes and the almost transparent down on his smooth, tan skin.

"You are so beautiful," I blurted out in German, "and I love you forever." I was thinking of the handsome young Egyptian king and the small dried bouquet of flowers Carter had found on his sarcophagus.

I heard laughter. Horrified, I saw Eddie, Kurt, Christian's older brother, and their other pals come tumbling out of their hiding places behind the trees and scrubs, laughing and repeating my declaration in the most scathing manner.

I swung my arm at Christian, smacking him hard against his shoulder, and sending him sprawling off the log onto the grass. Then I ran. I didn't think about where I was going, my only thought was to escape.

I ran down the path straight for the lake. And found myself cornered. I turned to face the boys as they came up.

"What?" I yelled at them. "What do you want?"

"Your dress," Kurt cried.

"Yeah, yeah," they all yelled. "You're always stealing our clothes. Let's see how you like it. You give it to us or we'll come and get it."

I rolled my lips together, considering. They were right. I had to acknowledge their victory. I had stolen their clothes and they had the right to punish me by taking my dress. So I reached behind my back to unbutton my dress. It was hard. My fingers felt huge and clumsy and the buttons would not slide through the buttonholes, but finally I finished, letting my arms drop to my sides. I kept my head down as I pushed the dress down to where I could step out of it. I was left in my plain step-ins, which buttoned at my shoulders. I was adequately covered, but acutely embarrassed to be in my underwear. I raised my head and looked at Christian. He stood behind the boys, his hands in his pockets, his weight on one foot, his head cocked. He stuck his chin out defiantly when I called his name.

"Here," I said, holding out my dress imperiously. Someone snickered, but the boys fell silent as Christian walked forward to take the dress.

"I hate you," I hissed in German, and whipped the dress at him. Then I turned and ran into the lake, walking, then swimming, heading straight for the freezing center.

I ignored the cold and the shouts behind me and just swam as fast as I could away from them all.

At one point, I turned and looked back. In the distance, the boys were in a flurry of activity, some running toward the Mayr house, others leaping about in excitement. They looked funny and I was pleased that I had caused so much action.

Floating on my back, I looked up at the sky and stuck my arms up into the air, into the sunshine. Already, I was so cold that the sun barely warmed my arms. Lake Sebastian was in the Bavarian Alps, and although it warmed up enough for swimming near the shore, the deeper water farther out never did.

Eddie and Kurt came after me in the Mayrs' little rowboat. I yelled at them when they reached over the side for me, fighting so violently that they backed away from me.

"C'mon, Sal," Eddie said. "Please. It's freezing. Don't go any farther."

I kept swimming, although my arms and legs were becoming heavier and heavier with the cold. I stopped when I heard Eddie apologize.

"Not you," I said, my teeth chattering.

"What, then?" said Kurt.

"I want *him* to," I said.

"My dumb brother."

"Yes. If you promise to get him to apologize, I'll come back," I promised. "And I won't tell anyone what you did to me."

"You started it," protested Kurt.

"We promise," said Eddie, who had realized that our parents would not consider five boys' forcing me out of my dress to be the same as my stealing their clothing. The boys were the ones who would be in terrible trouble.

I allowed Kurt and Eddie to haul me into the boat. I sat on the bottom, my arms wrapped around myself, feeling the goose bumps, and shaking with cold. Eddie wrapped his shirt around my shoulders, but the thin cotton did little to warm me.

At the little dock in front of our house, the other boys stood waiting. After Kurt had delivered my demands to his brother, Christian approached me, still carrying my dress. He held it out to me wordlessly, and just as silently I took it from him. I was shaking too hard to get into it, my hair plastered across my chest and shoulders, my tortoiseshell clip lost in the lake. I put the dress over my shoulders, on top of Eddie's shirt, and glared at Christian.

He stood in front of me, his eyes downcast, his hair falling forward into his face. "I'm sorry," he mumbled. "Please forgive me."

"No," I said loudly. Kurt, Eddie, and Christian all protested, but I merely turned and walked away on my frozen, numb legs, my anger propelling me.

Christian came to visit me while I was convalescing from the bad cold I got in the lake. But I refused to see him. Only my tears convinced my mother of my determination not to let him near me, and she finally sent him away.

I wouldn't talk to him for the rest of the summer. That might have been the end of our friendship, but fortunately, Christian sent me a card during the year, at Easter time. It was a pretty card, covered with lilacs, old-fashioned looking. He didn't say much in it, but by that time I missed him, and enough time had passed. So I decided to forgive him and sent him a treasured postcard of the Statue of Liberty.

FOURTEENTH SUMMER

After my mother died, everything changed. Daddy, who had accepted a position at Stanford, arranged for me to enter Mary Rose, a small boarding school near Palo Alto, which had a fine music program. Eddie was still at Phillips Exeter in the East, and so the Jackson family was tucked, safely, and separately, away. Perhaps it was better than staying on in the house in Gramercy Park, where my mother's presence haunted every corner, but we all retreated, any chance of reaching out to each other gone.

Daddy said we wouldn't return to Germany that summer. It was too expensive and too far and, I imagine, although he never said, too painful a prospect for him. But, for me, to be deprived of my mother and the Mayrs in one year was too much to be borne. For the first time in my life, I let him know how much I wanted something, and in the end, he gave in.

Eddie was going to spend the summer with his roommate in Maine, but he saw Daddy and me off from New York in June of 1927. Daddy spent most of the trip staring out of windows or trying to read. He and I were alone together again and had just as difficult a time talking to each other as before.

It would be the pattern of our relationship all our lives, except for a brief time in Berlin. I think, with the wisdom of adult hindsight, that he blamed me for my mother's death. I do know I always felt I was not the person he wanted with him. He must have loved my mother very much.

That summer, I didn't think about my father. I never received any comfort from him—and never considered offering him any. All I wanted was to be with Lisa Mayr, in her friendly kitchen or at the dinner table with her large noisy family.

Nothing turned out as I expected. Germany seemed finally to be pulling itself out of the inflation and unemployment that had plagued it since the end of the Great War, but families such as the Mayrs continued to suffer economically. Not that I paid any attention to any of that. Money was another thing I was blind about. I wanted to get home, that was how I thought of Lake Sebastian, and the closer we got to it, the more impatient I became.

We stopped for a week in Stuttgart to visit an old friend of Daddy's. I was barely polite to our host and hostess, but I think they believed my brusque behavior was because of Mama's death. Perhaps it was.

Finally, we set out on our last lap of the journey, by train, to Lake Sebastian.

We were met by Hermann Grune who, with his wife Grete, had taken care of us and the house since my parents' first visit to the lake. They both muttered, as they always did, about the changes Germany was going through. Hermann blamed the Communists, and Grete the lack of morals; and both agreed that things had been much better during the Kaiser's day.

We had a light supper and even my father seemed happier. I kissed him good night and he patted my shoulder, an almost indulgent show of affection from him. In my room, after changing into my nightgown, I went to the window to look across the lake toward the Mayrs' house. My heart sank. There were no lights, nothing. Grete came in to check on me and I asked her about the ominous darkness.

"Ah, no, Sally, there's no one there, and I'm not at all sure any of them will be there this summer. Herta"—that was the Mayrs' housekeeper—"had a letter saying not to open the house."

I was stunned. I could no more imagine a summer here without them than I could imagine going to bed hungry. And after all the fuss I had raised to get here. The next morning I ran around the lake on the familiar path, just as I had imagined doing, only to discover that Grete was right. The house was locked up tight, the furniture still under covers. I sat on the front steps almost an hour, trying to come to terms with this horrible new development. Obviously, there was nothing for me to do but wait, which I did with absolutely no grace at all.

I thought music might help. Our house had an old upright in the front parlor and one of the summer rituals was the visit from Herr Leidecker, a short, stout man, to tune the piano. My mother had always planned to move a better instrument into the house, but summer after summer she—and I—played on the stiff old keys, worn smooth as silk.

Anyway, that summer, the summer after my mother's death, I hadn't touched the old piano, and hadn't even realized Herr Leidecker had never come, until one afternoon, wandering around the house, I sat down and tried some chords. Some pianists absolutely will not play on a piano that is not tuned regularly. I was not so fussy, maybe because I never took my playing very seriously, but even I could not stand the sour noise I was making. It depressed me even more and I closed the cover, running my hands along the smooth, shiny surface. The two elaborate candle holders at each end of the box were empty now. My mother had kept white candles in them, and sometimes, at night, she would turn off all the lights in the room and play by the light of the flames.

I remember Daddy sitting by the open window, the one that faced the forest, Eddie sprawled on the sofa, and me sitting quietly in a chair behind Mama, ready to turn the pages for her. The smell of the candles and her perfume mixed with the clean pine scent of the forest outside. She would play anything then: Schumann or Brahms; Victor Herbert or Cole Porter; and, sometimes, the best of all—the sweet, sensual music of Argentina that her mother had taught her.

It wasn't to be borne. Losing her and the Mayrs, being alone here all summer, with only my distracted father, who was too lost in his own misery to notice mine. I put my head down on the piano and cried.

Finally, one evening at dinner, Grete told us that Hermann had seen Frau Doktor Mayr arrive that afternoon with one of her children on a stretcher. I looked up at her, my fork poised halfway to my mouth.

"Who was on the stretcher?"

"Your friend," she answered. "The handsome one."

I jumped up, ready to race to Christian's side, but my father's calm voice stopped me.

"Sit down, Sally," he said gently. "No one would welcome you at this hour."

"What's happened?" I said. "And where's everyone else?"

"Tomorrow we'll find out soon enough. You'll have to live through one more night," said Daddy, spooning up his soup. "It sounds as though our friends have had as trying a year as we have."

"She didn't write you about coming, did she, Daddy?" I asked him. "Didn't she usually write you and ask about your summer plans? But this year she didn't?"

"You're right, my dear. She didn't. I hadn't noticed," he added, falling silent, his spoon motionless in his soup. I turned away. I couldn't help him. I just couldn't.

The next morning the news about the Mayrs was all over town and Grete passed it on to me as soon as she came back from marketing. The Mayr household had been overwhelmed with tragedy over the past few months. First, Kurt, just sixteen, had been killed in a riot in Berlin, fighting for a small, radical political party called the National Socialists. Then, one after another, all of the members of the family still living at home had been stricken with flu. The same kind of flu that had swept through the world after the war, coming back to touch those it had missed.

"And Christian, Grete? What do they say about Christian?"

"He is with Frau Doktor here," said Grete, handing me some tomatoes to lay out on the sill. "He was very, very ill. In fact, Frau Doktor Mayr told Herta that he had nearly died. They were not going to come this year, because of the sickness and also money problems, but she decided that the lake would make her son well again."

Hearing that, it was all I could do not to run right around to them. Christian was sick, he had almost died. What if he had died and I had never seen him again? My heart reeled at the idea of losing him. Not him, too.

And Lisa. How she must be suffering, having lost Kurt and now fighting to keep Christian alive. The news of their financial problems, as usual, made no impression on me.

Unsure of whether I would be a help or a bother, I finally decided a note was the way to let Lisa Mayr know I was here and I wanted to help. I sent it via Grete, who passed it on to the Mayrs' housekeeper. Then all I could do was wait some more.

Finally, a note came for me from Lisa Mayr asking me to come by that afternoon around teatime. Would I? Would I! I don't think she could have kept me away much longer.

Lisa Mayr had changed more in the one year since I had seen her than in all the other years together. She had cut her braids off, and her hair was threaded with gray. She wore wire-rimmed glasses and she moved slowly, like an old woman. It shocked me, making real all I had heard about the troubles the Mayrs had gone through.

I hugged her, and we stood for several minutes, our arms around each other. When she pulled back from me, I saw that she had tears in her eyes.

"You have grown so, Sally," she said, her hands holding my shoulders. "No more the hoyden, huh?"

"I'm so sorry about everything," I said, wanting her to know, wanting to share whatever I could.

She put her hand on my cheek. "I know, lovie," she said, "I know. And you and your father, how are you?"

I shrugged, not wanting to talk about us.

"The loss of your beautiful mother must be unbearable, yes? Oh, my poor little dear, what a tragedy. What a dreadful year. What a dreadful year." And she hugged me again, rocking me in her arms, and I felt better than I had in months.

"You were sick too," I said, worried about her. She looked tired, run down.

"I was, but already, after only three days here, I feel so much better. And now, seeing you, that is a good, strong tonic."

"And Christian?" I said, afraid to ask after him, yet needing to.

"Christian, God willing, will be fine. He improves daily, although the trip was harder on him than I imagined it would be. I will take you up to see him, but first, I must warn you: he is very weak and you must be careful not to tire him. This time, you can only stay a moment."

I looked up the stairs, frightened at what I would find. Lisa put a hand on my shoulder. "Come, my dear, we'll go up."

Lisa stopped outside Christian's bedroom door, pushed it open, and called softly, "Darling, look who's come to visit you." She turned back to me and stepped aside. "Go on, dear."

Slowly, I walked past her into the dimly lighted room. All I could see was the still figure on the narrow bed under the curtained windows. I stood at the foot. It was a boy's bed, painted green with yellow trim. Long ago, Christian, Kurt, and I had all carved our initials on the headboard, and there they still were, worn into the wood above Christian's head. I let myself look at him. He was so thin and he lay so still that I feared he had died. I turned to his mother.

"He looks better, doesn't he," she said, with eyes only for her son.

"Yes, Lisa," I said, willing life into Christian's motionlessness. I'll do anything, I thought, praying to his closed face. If you die, your mother will die, and I—God only knows what would happen to me. I became aware of my own body, my strength and youth, the miracle of my breath and blood. I'll make him well, I promised.

By the next afternoon, Christian was able to stay awake long enough for me to greet him. Again, I stood in the doorway of his room. His breathing was noisier than it had been the day before, and that worried me. Not knowing if he was awake, I tiptoed into the room and stood at the side of his bed, unsure of what I should do. There was a sour smell and the window next to the bed had been opened a crack, but no breeze came in to stir the curtains.

Christian turned his head and, seeing me, smiled. Quickly, I knelt beside the bed.

"Hello, Sally," he said in English, his voice thin.

"How are you? Are you all right?" I whispered, afraid to startle him. Could speaking loudly tire him?

"Better," he said. "It's nice to see you." His face looked much older, the strain of his illness and the unhappy events of his family's year showing up in the dark circles under his eyes and his thinness.

"And you too. Oh, Christian, I was afraid you wouldn't come, then when you did and I heard about Kurt and you, I thought you . . ." I stopped, afraid of overpowering him with my babble, my tears welling up.

He pulled his arm out from under the covers and laid his hand on mine. I lowered my cheek against his long fingers. They felt very warm.

When I looked up, he was asleep again. I stood, my knees aching from kneeling on the hardwood floor. His mother had said sleep was good for him. Feeling protective, I gently replaced his arm under the covers. This was my chance, and I leaned over to kiss him. I think I had a certain *Saturday Evening Post* cover of a battlefield nurse and a wounded, dying soldier in mind.

For a moment, I hesitated, then, daringly, I kissed him on his mouth. I had never done so and I was intrigued by the softness of his lips. I considered doing it again, but in that instant, as I hovered over him, he opened his bright-blue eyes and looked straight into mine. His eyes were clear and warm as summer air.

I turned beet-red, but he—he smiled. A very small smile that barely touched the corners of his mouth. There was something in that smile that I did not understand, and in a panic I fled the room.

Less than two weeks later, Christian was helped down the stairs to sit on the porch. He lay on a wicker chaise longue, covered with a light blanket. I stood waiting, my hands behind my back, holding a surprise. When his mother and Herta left, he raised his head and smiled at me.

"God," he said, "I want a cigarette."

"Christian!" I was shocked. "I didn't know you smoked."

"All the fellows do," he said in an offhand manner. "What do you have there?"

"I have a surprise for you."

"What? Another kiss?"

"No," I said, gently swatting his shoulder.

"Owww," he protested. "Remember, I'm not well. You have to be kind to me."

"I have been. Waiting hand and foot on you." And, laughing, I held my hand out, offering him the orange.

His eyes widened as he reached for it. "Where did you get it? I haven't seen one in—in years." He held it to his nose. "Hmmm. Smells great. Thank you, Sally."

"Do you want me to peel it?" I asked. He nodded and I took the orange from him and sat on a chair close to him. The pungent smell filled the porch when I broke into the fruit. I handed him a section at a time to eat until he waved me off.

"I can't," he said, "I'm too full."

I looked at how much of the fruit was left, remembering when he could have devoured two of them in a flash, and again I was sharply reminded how sick he had been.

"I'll take it to Herta for you," I said, getting up in a hurry, not wanting him to see my tears. It frightened me so much to think how close he had been to death.

He began to mend quickly after that day, his youth and the calm, nurturing atmosphere surrounding him doing their good work. I came every day, happy to spend time with Lisa, too.

It was a very hot summer and I wanted to swim. The water was cold, but if I stayed away from the deep water, it was bearable. Lisa was reluctant to allow Christian in, but he and I convinced her, and as the days stayed hot and dry, she agreed. We would take a late-morning swim along the shore below the Mayrs' house, then come out and lie on the warm grass in the sun. We would talk then, lying next to each other.

I remember how quiet the lake was that summer in the heat, the evergreens so incongruous, the shining water turning gold. I even remember our bathing costumes, his one of those old-fashioned navy suits with a top, and mine a heavy knit red one with a belt clasped with two small seashells. It was scratchy in the heat and took forever to dry. I hated that suit, but I wouldn't have missed one of our swims for anything.

Christian grew healthier almost in front of my eyes, taking on that lovely, toasty color he did when he tanned.

I told him my feelings about Mama's death and he talked about Kurt. When he talked about his brother, he told me, for the first time, about the National Socialists and their charismatic, energetic leader, Adolf Hitler. Kurt had taken Christian to a student meeting at the university in Berlin, and both boys had been impressed by Hitler's speech.

"Even if I do go to university—" he began one morning, lying on his stomach, his hands folded under his head.

113

"If?" I interrupted him. College had always been one of the things we talked about doing.

"I'm not sure. Why should I? There is no guarantee that there will be a job for me when I come out. And everything is changing anyway. The old ways are dying. Nobody cares about an old-fashioned education. Perhaps the Communists will finally have their way and take over. Perhaps the Kaiser will return, but one thing is certain: things will not remain as they are. And what am I to do? Beg in the streets? March? Join a Freikorps? I don't want to be a stormtrooper. I told Kurt that."

"You could emigrate," I suggested. "To Canada. The States. Your English is almost decent enough," I added, unable to resist the dig.

"Better than your German," he said automatically. "I've thought of it, but I'm a German, for better or worse. I don't want to go somewhere else. Well, maybe for a visit . . . I'd love to see Texas, be on the prairie.

"But I am smart, I think. Ambitious. I could do something, something great for Germany if only they will let me. I should be able to do something other than speak mediocre English."

"It's better than mediocre."

"Well, thanks."

"Maybe the army," I said, trying to be helpful, and was astonished by the vehemence of his answer.

"Never," he cried. "That pack of useless aristocratic Prussian lackeys."

"You're a Prussian, aren't you? Well, weren't you born in Berlin? That makes you a Prussian."

"Makes you one too," he snapped back. "Oh, you know what I mean." He stood and walked to the lake and sat on a stone step, his legs in the water.

I propped up my head on my hand to watch him. "What would you do, if you could do anything?"

He thought for a long time and when he answered, he didn't turn to face me. "I've got one idea, but you must promise not to tell anyone. Ever?"

"Of course," I said, crawling over the grass to sit next to him.

"Okay." I had taught him the phrase years ago and he used it even when speaking in German. "I don't want to be a professor, like our dads. But I would like to travel. I also don't want to be in the military. But I think I'd like to live in all kinds of places, like you have. So maybe I could be a diplomat. Well, what do you think? Is that stupid?"

"No, it's not." I was feeling proud of him. "You can serve your country and travel too."

"Oh, it's useless. And I can't even join the army. Your stupid treaty has made that impossible."

"You'll think of something. But I think you shouldn't give up on college. Maybe you'll find what you want to do there," I added hopefully.

He just snorted and without another word ran into the water and swam away.

Late in August, we swam out to a little platform together, and lying next to me in the sun, he talked again about the Nazis, telling me how three years ago they had tried to take over the government in Bavaria and how Hitler had gone to jail.

"My father says they're all thugs. He disapproves of them and was very upset with Kurt. But at least they tried to *do* something."

"Was Kurt a Nazi?"

"Yes. Although Father didn't know how deeply involved he was until after Kurt was dead. The Nazis gave Kurt and the other fellows who died during the same riot a big funeral with a torchlight procession and my father refused to go. We got into a huge argument."

Christian dropped his head onto his hands and stayed that way for some time, his face hidden from me. "What's going to happen to me?" he muttered.

I started across the lake for a while, then reached down, cupped some water in my hand and flicked it onto his back.

He howled and grabbed at me. "That's cold!"

I rolled away. "You were getting a sunburn," I protested, as he scrambled after me. I sat up, to stand up, but he got me from behind, putting his arms around me, his legs on either side of me, holding me tight against him.

"Come on, Christian. Let me go."

"Maybe," he said and rubbed his chin against my shoulder.

"Stop it." I tried wiggling to free myself, enjoying the contact between us, but extremely nervous about it.

"Okay," he said. "I'll let you go—if you give me another kiss."

"No," I squealed, wiggling in his arms. "Never!"

"Come on, you'll like it."

"I will not."

"Okay." And he began to tickle me. I hate being tickled to this day, and I fought like crazy to get away from him. Finally, worn out by flailing around and laughter, we both took a rest.

"I thought you were supposed to be sick."

"I'm not anymore." And he let go of me. "Why don't you move?" he asked when I didn't.

"Maybe I don't want to," I answered, amazed at my own courage. Talk was as far as I could go and I could only wait for him to take the next step. He did—bending his head down to mine, finally, he kissed me.

The buzzing of the insects in the grass, the quiet lap of the water against the bank, and the bright hot sunshine are all mixed up in my memory of how he felt and smelled, his hot smooth skin, the damp wool of his suit. I think I must have squeezed my eyes tightly closed because I thought I had gone blind, that the kissing and the sun had blasted away my eyesight.

THE DANCE

Carefully, I lifted the tissue-wrapped bundle out of the deep bottom drawer of my steamer trunk and laid it on my bed. Even more carefully, I unpeeled the tissue, layer by layer, until the dress was uncovered. A pale-pink satin slip to go under a drift of even paler petals of chiffon, with one satin-covered button at the back of the neck. It was the most beautiful dress I had ever owned. I reached back into the drawer for the shoes, also pale-pink satin, with small mother-of-pearl buckles. As I laid the shoes next to the dress on the tissue paper, I wondered if I could ever live up to such a beautiful outfit.

It was my first dancing dress to wear to my first dance on the last evening of the summer. Christian and I were going together and I wanted everything to be perfect.

That evening, I stood in front of my bedroom mirror and considered my reflection critically. I was pleased. The color of the dress suited me and the style made me look slimmer and taller than I was. I had gathered my hair into a bow at the nape of my neck, brushing the end into fat curls. It almost frightened me to see how pretty I looked, and I turned quickly to go downstairs.

My father came into the hall as I came down the stairs. He looked at me for a long moment, then said, "What'd you do to your hair?" Immediately, my hand flew to my head. "It looks nice, Sally," he said and smiled at me as his hand reached toward me, brushing my shoulder, trying to touch me, yet unable to do so.

Christian arrived exactly on time. He was in a dinner jacket, his hair combed back from his forehead. He was very polite to my father and, even more strangely, to me. It made me terribly nervous.

We walked slowly, without speaking, down toward the village. The silence between us grew until I couldn't bear it any longer.

"It's a nice evening," I said, trying to break the silence.

He grunted, ambling along, hands in his trouser pockets, his coattails bouncing along behind him. His hair had come unglued from whatever it was he had stuck it down with and was reverting to its usual style, parted slightly to one side, hanging in his face. He didn't look at me once the entire walk.

The main street of Lake Sebastian was strung with Japanese paper lanterns and looked magical. In front of the Boating Club, a dance platform had been set up and a small band was already playing. Refreshment tables were set up in the Boating Club and people were carrying glasses of beer and cider. Christian asked me if I wanted anything and I shook my head. He finally looked at me.

"Come on," he said, "let's go talk for a while. Okay?" I nodded and he led us down to the lake, where the club's small fleet of rowboats was beached. We walked out to the end of the short dock. There was a built-in bench, but I was reluctant to sit on it for fear of snagging my chiffon dress.

"You want a cigarette?" asked Christian, offering me one from a battered pack.

"Sure," I said, reaching for one. I didn't smoke, although some girls at school did, in secret, of course. "I mustn't get caught," I said, shielding the flame of his match with my hand, trying not to touch him.

"Nobody's going to see us here," he said, "and so what if they do?" My cigarette lit, he turned away from me, to face the dark lake. A breeze touched us from the lake and I shivered.

"Cold?" he said. "Want to go back?" He flipped his cigarette into the lake.

"Oh, no," I exclaimed, throwing my cigarette after his, glad to be rid of it.

"Here," he said, taking off his jacket.

"No," I protested, "I'm fine."

"Shut up," he said, and swung the jacket around my shoulders. Then he pushed me gently down onto the bench. "Have a seat. There. Better?"

I nodded, wondering where he had learned to do these things, not looking up at him as he stood with his hands on my shoulders. Things were changing too quickly between us; time was flying by too fast. He let go of me and moved back to the railing. Now I could look at him.

"I've been thinking about your brother," he said.

"Eddie? Why Eddie?" I had told Christian about a letter my father had recently received from my brother, in which he announced that he wanted to attend Annapolis after he graduated next June.

"He already knows what he means to do with his life. I've been trying to decide what I should do and I've been thinking about the navy. But it is so difficult here, with the restrictions. If my grades are good enough and if I can get someone to sponsor me, I might be able to get in." He stood leaning against the railing, one foot crossed over the other, his arms folded. He looked tall and slim and older than his fourteen years.

The Treaty of Versailles had restricted the number of prospective naval officers Germany could train when it ruled on the other aspects of the country's military forces.

"Has Eddie planned to do this for a long time?" he asked.

"I don't know," I answered. "He doesn't write much, and when I saw him in New York he didn't mention it."

"Perhaps I will try anyway."

"But I thought you didn't want a military career."

"The navy's different, and besides," he continued in a bitter voice, "what else am I good for?"

"Oh, for heaven's sake, Christian, you're the most—well, I think you can do anything. You're smart. You know you are. That's what I think."

"Perhaps," he said, falling silent. I turned my head to stare out at the lake, missing it already, missing him.

"It's been fun here this year," he said in an emotionless voice.

"Yes," I answered. He was silent for a long time. I continued to study the water.

"I wonder what will happen next year," he said in the same strange voice.

"We'll be back," I answered. There was more silence. "Christian—"

"I'd like—" he said at the same time. We laughed and he gestured. "Go ahead."

"No," I said. "You first."

"No, I insist," he said, "you're the lady." That stopped me cold. I returned to my study of the lake. "What is it?" he asked. I shook my head. "Come on, Sally, now what?" He flung his arms out from his body, then slapped them along his sides, the white of his dress shirt flashing through the growing darkness. "What did I say?"

I started to cry. I could not believe it myself, nor could I forgive myself. After all these years of being his friend, of making him forget I was a girl, I was crying.

"Sally!" He moved to sit next to me on the bench. He didn't touch me. I pulled my legs up in front of me, under his jacket, and turned so that my back faced him.

"What did I do?" He sounded so worried that I had to say something.

"Nothing, Christian, not really . . . I'm sorry. It's just . . . oh, I don't know. I guess I don't want to be a lady."

"What?" he said, absolutely confused.

"Everything tonight . . . this summer . . . is so different," I stammered. "We've got so old," I wailed, my voice sailing out into the night air on the last word. That was bad enough, but then he made it worse. He laughed.

"You're an insensitive toad, Christian Robert Mayr," I said with all the dignity I could muster.

"I know," he said, sounding smug. "Do you have a handkerchief?"

"You know I don't," I said.

"Well, don't wipe your nose on my jacket; here, take this." He nudged me and I turned far enough to take the handkerchief from him.

"Thank you," I said frostily.

"You are welcome," he said. We had been speaking English, and now he switched to German.

"I'm sorry, honestly I am." He sighed. "Everything is so confused, like you said. My whole life, my family. Do you realize I am the only son my father has left? Do you suppose that is an easy thing to bear?

"I'll tell you, Sally, when I became ill, after Kurt was killed, I knew my father wished I would die."

"Christian, no."

"He wouldn't come to see me. My mother said she kept him away so that he would not become ill, but I could see in her eyes that she was lying. He . . . Thomas . . . was his favorite, the oldest son, the hero. I think Kurt and I both knew that. And when Thomas died . . . my father changed. I was very young, but I could feel it. He changed toward Kurt and me, especially after the war ended. My father said something, once, I remember him standing in the downstairs hall. Then he was silent. But I think he blamed us for living, and now I feel he blames me for being left.

"He disagreed with Kurt, but Kurt was sure and strong and could make my father laugh, even though he'd made him angry. I don't make him laugh or angry or anything. I'm not smart like Marta, or brave like Thomas. Nothing." He fell silent. I sat next to him silently, not knowing what I could say.

I touched his shoulder. "My father is the same. Ever since my mother died, he's hated me. It's the same, Christian."

He nodded. "This has been a good time, with you here, this summer. I hope you believe that. Do you?"

"Yes. Oh, yes."

"So, I thought we might write each other more often. I have

many friends at school, but I can't talk to them as I talk to you."

"Oh," I said, turning to face him, sliding my feet back to the ground, "I know just what you mean. I feel the same. No one understands the way you do."

"Then you will write me?" he said eagerly.

"Of course, I will, you idiot," I said, "and will you write me?"

"I promise," he said. He reached a hand out toward my head and I, thinking he was going to cuff me or grab my neck as he sometimes did, flinched. But his arm came up around me and the hand I had been retreating from gently took hold of my face. We stared for a long moment at each other, then slowly he lowered his face to mine and kissed me.

"Do you want to dance?" he asked me after the kiss ended.

I raised my head and heard the sound of the band, an accordion, a violin, some sort of brass, float over to us from the dance floor. "Oh, yes," I answered, and gave him back his jacket.

There was a crowd on the dance floor, townspeople and summer visitors of all ages and dressed in all manner of finery, from evening dresses to dirndls. Christian led me into the crush, then turned and held up his left hand. I put my right hand into his, put my other hand on his shoulder, feeling the smooth fabric of his dinner jacket. He put his hand carefully around my waist.

He drew me close to him. He was not a good dancer yet, but then, neither was I. It didn't matter. There were so many other couples that all we could really do was move in our own space.

We danced silently for several dances. I remember I felt as if we were alone on a private dance floor, and that the fact that we were not lent a sense of security and excitement. Eventually, he put both of his arms around me and I did the same, laying my cheek against his shoulder, feeling protected and secure. I closed my eyes, trusting him to guide me, shutting out the other dancers, all of my senses concentrated on Christian.

In the middle of a waltz, Christian bent his head and rubbed his cheek against my hair. "Let's leave," he said, his voice sleepy. "It's getting late."

I didn't want to leave, but he was right. We had to get home.

We walked off down the street. We didn't speak. At the fork in the path, Christian led us off toward the lake, instead of toward my gate. I didn't protest, wanting to stay with him. I also felt a languid helplessness, as though the dancing and fancy clothes and my feelings toward him had all conspired to turn my brain to mush. I was very happy.

On the path, he started into the woods, and I recognized the

121

place where we turned off for the meadow. I stopped.

"Come on," he whispered, taking my hand, pulling me toward him. Then he kissed me, his lips brushing along the side of my face to my neck. I shivered and stepped back from him, not letting go of his hand. "Are you afraid of me?"

"No."

He kissed my hand and put his arm around my waist. "Don't you want to kiss me? I want to kiss you. I want you."

Wanting. He was talking about wanting me. I didn't really understand about wanting. He noticed my hesitation and pressed his advantage.

"You're so pretty, Sally. You feel so good. Please, come with me." His hand brushed my breast. I shivered and his hand came back. I backed away.

"It's late," I said apologetically.

He looked at his watch, holding it up to catch the light. "Just half past eleven."

"We have to be home at midnight."

"Yes." He stood in front of me, not moving. "Sally?" I heard his feet shift in the leaves and grass of the forest floor. I shivered. "Are you scared?"

"Yes." I always had to be honest with him. "I'll ruin my dress," I added.

He laughed nastily and dropped his hands from my arms. "You girls." Then he disappeared, leaving me alone in the dark. I heard his footsteps on the ground and a rustle and then nothing.

"Christian, where are you?" I called, but not too loudly. The forest was big and dark and I didn't know who or what else might be in it.

"Come here," he whispered, taking my hand. I jumped, literally starting back from him. He laughed quietly. "It's me. Shhh."

"Where . . ."

"Shhh. Come on." He led me down the path toward the meadow. We stopped at the edge. "There, can you see?" He pointed.

The moon was full and bright and blue light and dark shadows covered the meadow. In the center, beyond the fallen log, two people, a man and a woman, were standing their arms around each other. The man had a shirt and trousers on; the woman was naked, her body gleaming in the moonlight. I backed up, bumping into Christian.

"What are they doing?" I whispered in a panic.

"What do you think, stupid?"

I gasped. "We shouldn't be watching."

"They can't see us," he said. "Don't be afraid."

We stood next to each other, not touching, and watched the couple. Their arms still entwined, they slowly sank to their knees, the man's hands lost in the darkness of the woman's unbound hair. The woman pushed the man's shirt off his shoulders. His bare skin glowed despite the dark.

"Don't you think they'd be uncomfortable?" I whispered, my embarrassment lost for a moment in my curiosity of the logistics.

"Maybe they put something down first."

The couple were on the ground, the man on top of the woman, and although I couldn't see all of them, the man's naked back and the woman's pale legs glowed in the moonlight. We were too far away to see anything more, but I found it a ritual too private to be witnessed, and I had to turn away. Christian came after me down the path. Perhaps he felt the same way, because he followed me without a word.

I stopped at our gate and looked out at the lake. Parts of it glittered in the moonlight, and parts were as black as pitch. "Do you know . . . about that, all of that?" I blurted out.

He had his hands in his trouser pockets. He shrugged without removing them. "Yeah, sure, I do."

"Did you take me there . . . did you know they would be there?"

"No. How would I? I don't even know who they were." He peered at me, trying to see my face in the shadows of the trees. "Are you upset?"

"Yes. But not at you. Not angry. I . . . I don't know. I've never . . ." I was having a very hard time talking about it with him. "I'll never tell anyone," I said.

"Me neither."

"Christian, did you mean, when you said you wanted me, did you mean like *that*?"

"No. Well, yes, I guess so. I don't know." There was a pause. "Have you ever. . . ?"

"A lot of fellows I know have. Or claim that they have."

"With whom?"

"Women. Or their family maids."

"Maids?" I imagined Christian kissing Herta and giggled. "That must be revolting."

"Yeah, I guess so." Another long pause.

"I don't know anything," I said passionately. "Nobody's ever told me anything. Please tell me."

"Me?"

123

"Please. You're my best friend."

"Your mother is supposed to do that."

"I don't have a mother."

"You're a girl. Ask my mother. You should have a woman tell you."

"Why?"

"It's different for girls."

"Why?"

"Oh, God, Sally, I don't know." He turned and walked away a few steps.

"Who told you? Your father?"

"Can you imagine that? No, Kurt told me. We used to talk about it when we were kids. He did it. Then he told me all about it."

"Who did he . . ."

"A woman."

"A prostitute?" I said the word carefully, imagining scarlet lips and a huge purple velvet hat.

"No. A girl. I met her once. I . . . but he got . . . but then he died."

"That's sad. I wonder if she was . . . expecting."

"Sally! I thought you didn't know anything about this."

"Well, I read books." I tried to tuck up a lock of my hair. Then I noticed he was watching me and his expression froze my hand.

"You've done it," I said, "haven't you? I can tell when you're lying."

"Yes, once. I wish I hadn't," he said in a low voice, almost too softly for me to hear him. "I'd rather it had been with you."

"Oh." It was all I could say. I swallowed, feeling slightly giddy. And elated. As well as embarrassed. He seemed to be waiting for an answer. "Thank you," I said. "But I think I'm still too young. And I really think I ought to wait until I'm married."

"You wouldn't, even if you loved someone?"

"Well . . . if we were engaged . . . Or he was going off to war, or something like that. A separation." Then I realized what I had said. Christian and I were going to be separated. He didn't move and I sensed that he was, again, waiting. "Oh, Christian, I wish . . . I just can't. I'm . . . Would you want to love a girl who had given herself to another?" I asked dramatically.

"I guess not. You're right." He sounded convinced. And relieved.

"I hope you're not angry with me."

"Of course not."

"I'd better go in."

"Yes," he said and turned to leave.

"Christian," I called. He stopped and I ran the few steps to him. I couldn't tell him how I felt, my emotions were so roiled up. Instead, I put my arms around his neck and kissed him, feeling his body along mine as I stretched on my toes to reach his mouth. He didn't hesitate, but put his arms around me, holding me tight, his mouth responding to mine. That kiss made me dizzy and when I let go of him, I almost tripped.

"Careful," he said, laughing in a low voice, his arms still around my waist.

"I like you so much, Christian. I would rather . . . with you then anyone. Ever. It's all so confusing."

"Too much change."

"Yeah." I stood for a moment, my hand on his chest. I could feel his heart beating wildly and it amazed me that he felt as crazy as I did. I dropped my hand and walked away from him, turning back when I got through the gate. He was still standing there, looking after me, a shadow except for his white shirtfront and pale head, a stray moonbeam hitting and lighting his golden hair.

I love you, I thought, although I didn't speak the words. You're beautiful and I'll love you forever, I thought in German, and ran up the path to the house.

FENCING

Christian and I wrote to each other, but when I didn't return to Germany the next summer, the letters petered out. It was bound to happen, but the knowledge that I would probably never see Christian again created a secret hollowness in my heart that never went away.

I finished high school with a wonderful year in Switzerland while Daddy was with the State Department in Austria. I liked being back in Europe and using my German. But the best thing that happened to me was fencing.

Fencing attracted me because it was an individual sport and I was hopeless at team sports. I also liked the mystery and romance of it, and I got a secret thrill out of doing something that men did. It made feel adventuresome to take on the sport by which Zorro, Robin Hood, and countless German university students had measured their manhood. I liked the anonymity of it too, the large masks worn to protect the face, that hid it as well, and the tight, padded jacket that obscured my breasts. In my fencing costume, with the mask on, my identity—my sex—was whatever I wanted it to be.

Although there had always been female fencers, they were usually aristocratic women with the resources to pursue the sport privately. It was an unusual sport for a high school, but it was an unusual school. Our German master, an Austrian who had lost the bottom half of his left arm in the war, had been a champion before the war. He was a romantic figure to all of us girls with his dark hair, high forehead, and brooding manner, so that when he offered, God knows why, to start a fencing club, several of us signed up. Our headmistress was not wholly approving, but the school's penchant for modern ideas and physical education was unshakable.

A dozen of us started in Herr Kempner's fencing salle, although by the end of the semester only five remained. All the better. Those of us who stuck with him received a unique introduction to the art of the blade. Herr Kempner did not treat us as the pampered, protected young ladies we were, but instead drilled us as he had been drilled.

He had not fenced since his injury and worked very hard to

126

overcome his disability. Because I tried so hard, he singled me out for attention, and sometimes I would stay after and talk with him about his championship days and the training he received. He was always absolutely correct in his treatment of me, and I felt comfortable with him and his formal manner.

I thought about him in later years, every time I put on my fencing gear, trying to see him in a more realistic light than I had at seventeen. But he remained something of an enigma. I wonder now what became of him—whether he stayed safely in Switzerland, or if he returned to Vienna, to be swept away in the German maelstrom.

After Switzerland, I went to a small women's college near San Francisco. It, too, had a fencing team, and I happily found myself more advanced than most of the other girls. I got even better as my self-confidence grew, and I began to represent my college in local tournaments.

The college was on a beautiful campus and the classes were small, the teachers personal, and I probably received a good education, although I remained a mediocre student.

Still, I made friends and was enjoying myself. I especially loved our trips into San Francisco, where we saw some wonderful operas. I began dating and fancied myself in love with a Stanford student of my father's, but when the boy began hinting about long-term plans, I let the relationship fade away.

I continued my music, halfheartedly planning for a teaching career; however, as much satisfaction and joy as the piano gave me, nothing seemed to be changing for me. My life was the same as it had been: school, vacations, the music, and my silent, distant father and never-present brother. There was something missing in me, I felt a sense of dislocation, as though I didn't belong, although if anyone had asked me where I did belong, I couldn't have answered. At a piano? In a fencing salle? Those were the places where I felt most at home, where I lost my sense of isolation.

Then, in 1933, two days before Daddy and I were to leave for Annapolis for Eddie's graduation, Daddy received a telephone call from President Roosevelt, offering him the ambassadorship in Berlin.

My father was a modest man, who hated fuss, but I know he was proud and surprised to be asked. He couldn't understand why he should be chosen and had to be convinced of his suitability for the job. He talked it over with his colleagues at Stanford and saw the President himself on our trip east.

Eddie thought it was terrific, and I did too, although I was, in my turn, quite taken aback when Daddy asked me to accompany him. He had been told that a bachelor ambassador was at a disadvantage, and he asked if I would come and act as his hostess.

American ambassadors, unlike diplomats from other countries, were expected to rent their own living quarters as well as the embassy building, and to provide the expenses for the usual social demands from their own pocketbooks. Daddy's money—separate from my inheritance from Mama—was quite sufficient for this, especially considering the simple way both of us lived.

Well, of course, I agreed to go. I was tired of college and dormitory living and I was eager to return to Germany. I could pursue my fencing and music there. I was also very flattered that my father had chosen me, that he thought I was grown up enough to go with him.

I didn't let myself think about seeing Christian or his family again until I came upon an old battered copy of a Karl May book about old Shatterhand that Christian had given me.

Standing with the little book in my hand, I thought of the lake and the people there, memories whirling through my mind. Maybe, maybe . . . I grew excited by the possibilities.

It was a busy summer, with Daddy traveling to Washington for his briefings, and Eddie setting out for his first posting in Norfolk. I had returned to California to pack and ready a shipment for Germany. It was the first time I had been given an important task and I wore myself out trying to warrant my father's trust.

Happily, all went well, and I recrossed the United States in August to sail for Europe. I think I slept away the entire ocean crossing, I was so exhausted.

When my ship, the *Bremen,* a fairly new German liner, docked in Hamburg, Daddy was there to meet me. He hugged me fiercely, surprising me with this uncharacteristic display of emotion.

What surprised me even more were all the reporters from German and American papers that met the ship. They liked the fact that I spoke German and that my father and I were polite to them. Daddy introduced me to his protocol officer, and we made our way to the Berlin train. Two reporters followed us closely, although Daddy had told them he wasn't giving any interviews. That was all right, they told us, they wanted to talk to me. One, a woman, wanted to know where I got my coat, which was a navy wool with brass buttons, shoulder tabs, and a high collar. I told her I had bought it in New York after envying my brother for his watch coat. The other reporter was an American man who wanted to know if I was aware of the problems Jews were facing in the Third Reich. The protocol officer held off both reporters, and my father and I got onto the train.

We entered Berlin from the north, and by the time we were met by the American consul general and his wife at the Lehrter Bahnhof, I was in love with the city. I was prepared to love it, of course, but the bustle and energy, contrasted with the age and dignity of the buildings, completely captured my imagination.

We got into one car—my trunks went in another with the protocol officer—and drove to the Adlon Hotel, where Daddy was staying for the time being. I tried responding politely to the questions the consul's wife addressed to me, but I kept my nose to the window of the car. There was greenery over the tops of the buildings to my right, and above the green, I saw the ruined dome of the Reichstag. It had been burned the previous February, as Mrs. Bushmuller, the consul's wife, informed me.

We crossed Unter den Linden with its broad double rows of trees. The avenue was alive with traffic and lights in the summer dusk. At one end of the wide Pariser Platz, I could see the magnificent Brandenburg Gate, the famous symbol of Prussian military might. The traffic was intense but orderly, and it took our driver some time to get us across to Number One Unter den Linden, which was the address of one of the most famous hotels in Europe—the Adlon.

Daddy had been staying in a smaller hotel, he told me, but decided to give me the gift of a few nights at the Adlon. "To get a sense of what Berlin used to be," he said sadly. I was too happy to be there to question what he meant. I thought he was just bemoaning the passing of the mythical pre-war world that older people were always going on about.

I had my own rooms, connected to his by a large sitting room, and after I had said good night, I sat at my window in the dark, watching the Unter den Linden traffic flashing by for hours. I don't really know why Berlin affected me so. I was not untraveled. I had seen New York and Paris. Maybe it was the fact that I had been born there; maybe it was my still-strong connection with our German summers; and certainly it was the knowledge that Christian and his family lived there. But I also liked the city for itself.

I once talked about this attachment one can have for cities with my friend Sydney Stokes. She, for instance, was crazy about Rome, which she visited for the first time in her university days. We decided that only reincarnation could explain this illogical love of a foreign place, this sense of belonging.

The next morning, Daddy and I went out to the house he had rented, because he wanted us to get situated as fast as possible. The embassy itself was on the Wilhelm Platz, close to the Adlon, and in the same neighborhood as the Chancellery and Dr. Goebbles's immense Ministry of Propaganda. Those buildings were still being renovated and expanded to the proper National Socialist proportions.

Daddy didn't want to live in the center of the city, and the living quarters in the embassy building were much too grand for us. He wanted and found a comfortable house on a quiet street in the suburb of Lichterfeld. Since most Berliners lived in apartments, Daddy had had a difficult time finding the house, a two-story building that stood on the corner of a wide street, surrounded by a black wrought-iron fence.

The house was new, built just before the Great War, and it had three bathrooms and a modern kitchen. It was large enough for the modest entertaining Daddy intended us to do, but not so big that the two of us would be lost in it.

The entry hall had black and white tiles and a lovely curving staircase up to the second floor. On the first floor, there was also a study for Daddy along one side, and next to it were two rooms connected by sliding doors that could be made into one long reception room. I put my piano in the far one. On the other side of the house, a sitting room and a dining room ran the length of the house, with a smaller morning room off the dining room. All three rooms opened onto a terrace, beyond which the lawn and gardens sloped down to a stand of trees. The property backed onto a disused military academy, so there were virtually no neighbors to disturb us.

Upstairs, there were four bedrooms. I took one, Daddy took another, and the others were to be for guests. There was also a small sitting room with a tiled stove, an old-fashioned touch in such a modern house. I used that room a great deal, especially in the winter, when the stove made it warm and cozy.

We returned that afternoon to the Adlon for a fancy tea. How I liked hearing German spoken, although the Berliners, with their distinctive accent, the accent Christian had insisted on teaching me, were not the most polished or classic of German speakers. For years, I had only spoken the language in classrooms, and I liked hearing the different permeations of a living language.

Daddy smiled across the table at me. "You like it here already, don't you?"

"Oh, yes," I said. "Don't you?"

He pursed his lips. "I've always felt comfortable here. But now . . ." He stopped as two couples, the men in fancy brown uniforms with bright-red armbands loudly proclaiming their loyalties, walked past our table.

"What would you like to do today? Tomorrow, I must return to work and I believe you've been invited to tea at the British embassy. You can call Mrs. Bushmuller in the morning."

We talked about decorating and when we might move into our house and agreed that we should do so as soon as possible. Daddy then informed me that he was going to leave all the details of our living situation in my hands.

"I assume you can keep a checkbook. I'll give you a budget. And I will trust your taste. You saw the apartments on the Wilhelm Platz. I don't want to live in those."

"You want your house in Palo Alto," I said, daring to tease him a little.

"I guess I do. But you know what kind of impression we want to present."

"Simple. Tasteful and unostentatious," I said.

"Exactly, my dear. Now, may I have another cup of tea? Perhaps you'd like to hear some music this afternoon?"

MOVING IN

The next morning, I interviewed a prospective butler, sent over by Mrs. Bushmuller. An Italian named Vittorio Centanni, he was middle-aged, but seemed old to me, and rather ordinary-looking, with lots of dark, graying hair and well-tended hands. His clothes, though, were impressive, and I learned he had been a butler in England for many years. He was polite and businesslike, and since he had worked for the American ambassador in London for six years, I felt confident about hiring him. I was very lucky to have found him, as I discovered later. He helped enormously in making the house what we wanted it to be, and he was always discreet and formal without being pompous or condescending. He even found a valet for my father, a young German named Friedrich Diederhof, who was called Rick and could also act as chauffeur.

The tea the next afternoon with Lady Harcourt-Greves at the British embassy appeared to be attended by no one under forty-five. I did my duty, smiling, making polite conversation, handling my teacup, saucer, linen serviette, as the British called it, spoon, and pastry with adroitness. The party had a mixture of nationalities, including wives of German dignitaries, as did most of these affairs.

Everyone was politely interested in me, commenting on how young I was to be my father's official hostess. I answered their questions about our living quarters as well as I could, and listened to their useful advice about hiring servants and setting up accounts with grocers, butchers, and the rest. In fact, the ladies gave me so much advice that I began to lose my self-confidence. I had never run a home before, and here my father expected me to run a mansion. I began to wonder if I had been right to hire the butler so quickly.

"Can I refill that for you?" I looked around to find a slender woman of medium height, who seemed to be only slightly older than I. She wore a gray dress and beautiful rosy pearls.

"No, thank you. I'm fine."

"Well, let me take it for you." She reached for my cup and saucer.

"That's okay," I said. "I need something to hang on to."

She smiled. "That's understandable with this lot badgering you."

"Oh, I'm not . . ." I stopped when I saw the humor in her face and I smiled back at her. "They have been—a bit."

"You need a small recess. Come with me." And she led me out of the room. "I'll show you some pictures. British embassies are famous for their art. Did you know that?"

Upstairs, she took me into a sitting room. On the far wall as we entered hung a Turner. The subject was a common one for the painter—the Thames River, painted at night, fog swirling across the water, the demarcation between sky and water and land invisible. It was very beautiful.

"Oh, it's wonderful," I gasped.

"Knew you'd appreciate it," she answered and we grinned at each other.

Then, leading the way, she took me down the hall into one of the bedrooms. I was extremely nervous, but her self-confidence prevailed. I stopped in the doorway, looking at the signs of occupation, brushes and combs on a dressing table, slippers under the bed. Could this be Lady Harcourt-Greves's very bedroom?

"Are you sure we should be in here?" I whispered.

"Absolutely not," she said, "but look." And she pointed to a small picture in a carved frame, heavy with gold leaf. It was a pencil drawing of a little girl in a Tudor cap looking straight out at us, her canny expression belying her age. The picture drew me into the room and across the carpet. I stood in front of it and smiled.

"You recognize it?" she asked.

"Holbein," I said. "Is it Elizabeth?"

"Bravo. Of course, it's not proved, but Lady H-G swears she knows a queen when she sees one. Even a queen at five or whatever age the darling is." She moved closer to the picture. "And she is a darling, isn't she?"

"Imagine living with such wonderful pictures."

We admired the drawing a moment more and went back downstairs, discussing paintings. At the foot of the stairs, she stopped.

"By the way, I'm Sydney Stokes," she said, holding out her hand. "We weren't properly introduced."

"Sally Jackson." We shook hands. Her fingernails were long and scarlet and she wore a large modern ring, swirls of gold among which a clear blue sapphire nested.

"You're the American ambassador's daughter, aren't you?" she said. I nodded. "You've just now come from college in California. You fence. Play the piano. And you are redecorating the house in Lichterfeld. It's very pretty. Let me know if I can help."

I laughed, surprised at the spy network. "Word gets around fast," I said, a little nonplussed.

"It does indeed. The secret service should give tea parties," Sydney replied.

"And you?" I asked diffidently.

"I'm Lady H-G's assistant."

"Do you live here? I mean in the embassy?"

"Good Lord, no. I'm married. To a fabulous man. I must tell you immediately that he's a newspaperman for the Perth *Star*."

"Australian?"

"Hmmm. He is, as well." She took my arm and steered me back toward the tea party. "Everyone here thinks he's dreadfully provincial. A peasant. He is, of course. Which is one reason why I adore him. Dads was livid. Mummy more so. Another reason why I adore him."

Laughing, we walked back into the reception room. The large room had two fireplaces along one wall and French windows along the other. Women were scattered about standing and sitting.

"How long do you think you'll stay?" Sydney asked, after we had gotten our tea.

"Until I can properly leave."

"No," she said, laughing. "I meant, in Berlin."

"Oh, well, I guess as long as my father does," I said. "And you?"

"Oh," she said, her eyes peeping over her teacup, "I'm here for as long as Brian is or until I get preggers. I shall have to scamper home at that point."

"Oh," I said, not quite understanding what she meant. I tried a safe question. "How long have you been married?"

"Just half a year." She smiled. "I met Brian in Italy. He's lovely. Lady H-G, who's a dear friend of my mother's, decided she couldn't do without me, so I've kept my job here. We have a sweet little flat. Mummy took one look and told me how sorry she was for me." We both giggled.

"We'll have you round one of these evenings. You'll have to spend enough time at dos such as this one."

"This is my first." I frowned at my teacup. "And, I'm sorry to say, I don't like tea." I looked around at the elegant, formal room. "Imagine that, the walls didn't fall in on me."

Sydney laughed. "Such blasphemy, Sally. Well, I'm glad to meet you. I seldom enjoy these things at all. We can band together and have some fun." She pushed her hair behind one ear. Her hair was ash blond and she wore it in a smooth pageboy, quite unlike the prevailing fashion, but it suited her high cheekbones and strong jaw. "There are a lot of Americans here, did you know? But if there's anything I can help you with, just let me know."

"Well, there is something you could do for me right now."

"And what is that?"

"Tell me who is this lady advancing on me?"

"Oh, dear, that's Magda Goebbels. She's not too bad, if a mite stiff. At least she dresses well. For a German. Her husband's the Minister of Propaganda. Perhaps you've seen his building? I'll tell you more about him later." She held out her hand to Frau Goebbels.

Sydney was a godsend, filling me in on the gossip, a necessity in the multi-layered society of Nazi Berlin, and helping me keep my sense of humor in spite of dull parties and duller suppers. Not that all of it was boring, but the glamour quickly wore off.

Perhaps, if I had been at all interested in politics, I would have always found something to fascinate me. But looking back, I see I was a vacuous, if charming girl, and I wonder that Sydney Stokes was interested in being my friend. My true self, lonely and hungry for beauty and love, I kept hidden from everyone.

Sydney did invite me to her home for dinner, and I spent a very pleasant evening with her and her lively husband, Brian. He had brown curly hair and a nose too large for his face, with boyish freckles scattered across it, and he spoke with a strong Australian accent, although he claimed that it had been tamed by contact with his British wife.

"That's how she corrupts me," he said soulfully.

He and Sydney seemed an odd match, but it was obvious how much they enjoyed and stimulated each other. They were a delightful couple and entertained me enormously, keeping me laughing and well-fed.

They lived in a two-bedroom flat on the twelfth floor of a brand-new building. The living/dining-room space was large and furnished with modern pieces in blond wood and light fabrics. An absence of clutter and only one large abstract painting on the wall made it as different a space as I could imagine from the traditional furnishings of the British embassy.

Daddy had plunged right into his job, leaving me to handle the housekeeping. Vittorio suggested that we start with the main sitting room and I agreed.

I had hired, with Vittorio's welcome advice, a cook, two maids, as well as Rick. All of the staff except Vittorio were German. The two maids lived in the attic rooms, Vittorio had a room tucked away at the rear of the second floor, where there was a back stairs, and the cook, Frau Brenner, lived in a room near the kitchen. Rick lived over the garage. So the house was full to the rafters, in spite of our small family. Of course there were marines assigned to guard us, although Daddy didn't believe we needed them and felt they would only make the house more obviously important. A small, snug hut was built for them near the front gate, half-hidden behind a section of hedge. They actually lived in a barracks somewhere. I never cared enough to ask.

With all of the extra help, we cleaned the entire house before I called in painters and paperhangers. Sydney and I discussed color and patterns and she took me to the man who had made the British embassy's draperies. She and I spent a wonderful, slightly hysterical time buying furniture, trying to complement what was coming from California—which was not much. We choose modern stuff because it seemed to suit the house better, and I was very pleased with the final effect.

The sitting room had blue-and-white Chinese carpets and navy draperies over white sheers. The walls were pale blue and the moldings white. Three large boxy sofas were arranged in a square in front of the fireplace. We had them covered in a navy-and-white stripe. To relieve all of the blue and white, there were two pale-green occasional chairs at one end of the room and a dark, forest-green armchair in front of the bookshelves at the other end. I put a mirror over the fireplace and kept a space on the opposite wall for one of Daddy's California landscapes, which was coming in the shipment from the States.

The day we finished, Sydney and I stood back happily and surveyed the room. We had to agree: it looked cool and elegant and very modern.

"Just right for an American home," said Sydney.

"C'mon, let's go upstairs and move some furniture around."

Daddy's study was finished about the same time, with dark-green draperies. The furniture and carpet were all still to come from California, so aside from the painting and draperies, there was nothing else for me to do. We kept the dining room simple and traditional. A long table that could, with leaves, seat twenty-four and a handsome sideboard were the only furniture, and I used pale-green wallpaper, printed with paler fronds of water plants. It too was cool and elegant, especially by candlelight.

My job as official hostess began, even before the decorating was finished, at a reception in the old living quarters in the embassy. It was a small event, at the cocktail hour, for various people in the German government whom my father needed to meet socially.

I stood, shaking hands and greeting people with my father, in the embassy entry hall on the second floor, as the first crush of guests arrived. After a time, I went into the sitting room to chat with people and make sure they were provided with drinks. The Adlon had supplied the hors d'oeuvres. It was a cool evening.

I thought everyone was managing well and then I noticed a very tall, very blond man in an ill-fitting suit standing rather forlornly in the far corner, next to the windows. He was staring out at the dusk and he caught my eye because he seemed to be so out of place. Just then my father came up to me and I asked him who the man was, wondering how he had gotten past me at the door.

"Reinhard Heydrich," said my dad, "a major, I believe, in the SS."

"SS?" I said.

"The fellows in the black uniforms. The Chancellor's body-guards." I nodded. I had seen the guards in their handsome black-and-silver outfits. No wonder this poor fellow's clothing looked so forlorn; he was used to wearing a uniform. "He works with Himmler, the SS Reichsführer, who is based in Munich. Heydrich has been here trying to get in to see various people in the Gestapo. The secret police," he added, seeing my look. "I really can't imagine why he's here, except, perhaps, because of Diels, the Gestapo chief, who, I believe, has not yet arrived." My father looked around the room.

"Well, I can at least get the poor man a drink," I said, and went off to do so.

He was not at all approachable, did not even turn around as I came up to him. He stood very still, his hands clasped behind his back, but there was a quality of great suppressed energy about him. I stopped several feet away, not wanting to disturb him.

"Good evening," I said softly. "You're Major Heydrich?" I held out my hand. "I'm Sally Jackson."

He turned his head to look at me, glanced at my outstretched hand as though he had never seen one before. I almost snatched it back. But manners won out, and he uncoiled his hands and held one out. We shook. His hand was very warm, belying his cool appearance.

"Colonel," he said, not smiling. I cocked my head. "Colonel Heydrich."

"Oh." I felt more embarrassed than I should have for the slightness of the mistake. "I am sorry. Is it a recent promotion?"

"Yes," he said.

I was standing with my back to the rest of the room and could not look away for help or rescue. "Congratulations," I said.

He smiled, almost. "Your father is the ambassador," he said, and it took several seconds for me to realize that he was speaking English.

"Yes, he is," I answered in German, then switching to English. "You speak English."

"Obviously. I have been studying it for many years at school."

"Just 'studied,'" I said unthinkingly. His face, already quite expressionless, froze up several degrees more. "Oh, I am sorry," I said quickly. "I didn't mean to insult you. Your English is very good, and I find it such a relief to speak it. It is tiring to always speak someone else's language, isn't it?" I babbled on, not expecting an answer, hoping someone would come and rescue me from this silent, inexpressive, cold man. "I had a friend as a child, a German boy, and he and I always corrected each other. In fact, it was a contest with us, and we never let the other get away with the tiniest mistake."

"Your German seems competent," said the colonel.

"Thank you," I said to the backhanded compliment, "but I think learning another language is awfully difficult, don't you? Especially if you only learn it in the classroom, and never have native speakers to talk to."

"It's a matter of the ear, I think," he said. I was encouraged; he was answering me.

"What do you mean?" I said, wanting him to continue talking.

"Learning another language is the same as learning music," he said. "You must be able to hear the language before you can truly speak it. In music, if you play a note mechanically, without hearing it, it will, no doubt, be flat or sharp." He spoke quickly, with some of that suppressed energy I had noticed in him already. His voice was high and thin and suited his cold demeanor.

"Yes, of course. Unless it is a modern composer's music. Are you a musician, Colonel?" I asked.

"Yes," he said. "I grew up in a musical household. My father is the director of a conservatory."

"How lucky you are," I said. "What instruments do you play?"

"Violin. And piano. But mostly violin."

"Do you play in a group, an orchestra?" I asked.

"Sometimes. At the moment, I play alone." I nodded, my stock of questions empty. He wasn't helping at all, with his almost impolite reticence.

"I admire people who can do several things well, who find the time in their lives to do a job as well as play a sport well or paint.

Here, you are, one assumes, fairly successful in your job." He gave me an interesting look, one I could not interpret, a mixture of irony and amusement and anger. Or contempt? "Well, you're a colonel and busy doing whatever it is you do and you also play the violin. You must admit the two things are unusual in one person. I don't do anything. I mean, I don't have a job, not a real one. All I've ever done is go to school, and not with any great success, and the only thing I've ever managed to do even moderately well is play the piano. . . and become a decent fencer."

For the first time in our lopsided conversation, Heydrich looked at me, really looked at me. It was a penetrating look, with his pale, deep-set blue eyes, that made me actually take a step back, out of its range. As though pleased at my reaction, he smiled slightly.

"How fascinating," he said. "I have seen two girl foil fencers at a fencing hall in Hamburg. They were, I believe, Romanians. Are there many girl fencers in America?"

I shrugged. "About two hundred, nationwide," I said. "All of us are connected with college teams or programs, but it's a sport that is becoming more and more popular with girls. I know at my university, our team grew from five of us to thirteen in three years."

"How old were you when you started?" he asked, his manner much more relaxed, although his attention was still focused on me like a searchlight.

"Seventeen," I said. "The German master at my school in Switzerland had been a famous fencer, and one winter asked in hall if anyone would be interested in learning."

"That is interesting. Your weapon is the foil, I assume."

"Yes, although I've had some training on the épée. Which I liked very much. Colonel," I said, forestalling his next question, "do you fence too?"

"Saber and épée," he said. "Did you compete?"

"In college." And I told him about making it into the regionals. We talked a little about competitive fencing and how difficult the physical and psychological aspects of it were. Then he asked me if I had ever fenced against a man.

I laughed. "Just in fun, in practice bouts, at the regionals," I said. "I liked it, although I seldom won. Once, though, I was paired with a fellow who was very tall—well, about like you—and trying to keep out of his reach I did the best I think I've ever done. I remember how fast I had to think. It was quite an exhilarating experience. Especially, when I finally made the touch."

"Yes," said Heydrich thoughtfully, "I can see how interesting an experience that would be. There are so few times when a woman

139

can be in such a situation." He looked at me speculatively, then asked, "And do you plan to continue?"

"I brought my equipment with me," I said, "but I'm setting up our house and it's kept me so busy . . ." I heard someone come up to my right, and turned to find my father with a tall, dark man in an elegant suit. He had a scar across his cheek, a smaller one on his chin. I glanced at the colonel, but he had turned his intense interest to the newcomer.

"Father," I said, remembering my manners, "have you met Colonel Heydrich? We've been discussing fencing."

The colonel leaned forward from his waist and shook hands with my father. "Excellency," he said, every inch the soldier. His eyes, though, strayed back to the stranger. Evidently he had the social skills, he just chose when to use them.

"I believe you know this gentleman," my father said, indicating the dark man. "Rudolf Diels."

Heydrich and Diels shook hands, both of them behaving impeccably. It wasn't until later that I learned that they knew each other very well and were deadly rivals. Heydrich's boss, Heinrich Himmler, the Reichsführer-SS, was in direct competition for the control of the police of Germany with Diels's boss, Hermann Göring, the head of the State of Prussia. Within three years, Himmler and Heydrich and the SS would oust Diels and take over his Gestapo. The most amazing part of the entire story is that Rudolf Diels would survive not only the SS and the Gestapo, but the war.

Someone came up behind me and asked me how I liked Berlin, and I turned to answer, my duty done with the colonel. It was a relief to be free of him, but as I moved away I had to admit he interested me. I had never met anyone so fiercely determined to ignore the social niceties. Of course, his behavior had changed when my father and Herr Diels appeared. I realized that Heydrich had decided at once that I was a nobody and had only barely put up with me, until I brought up a subject that interested him.

Toward the end of the reception, a guest I was saying goodbye to urged me to visit her hairdresser. The best in the city, she claimed.

"Please, my dear," she said, and held out a gloved hand, "would you button this?" As I began fastening the tiny jet-black buttons, I felt someone watching me, and looking up, over the woman's shoulder, I saw the colonel's eyes boring into me from across the room. The lady with the buttons noticed and turned to see.

"What an extraordinary young man," she said in a delighted whisper. She put a hand on my arm. "My dear, I believe you have made a conquest. How handsome he is. Very Aryan."

I did not believe I had made anything of the kind. I knew what it felt like to have a fellow stare at me from across the room when his intentions were romantic. It had happened to me once or twice. But the colonel's interest was different. He came over to me.

"I will telephone you tomorrow. I am only in Berlin a short time," he said and, seeing my expression, added quickly, "and I know of a fencing hall where you might practice."

"Oh, thank you, Colonel," I said, embarrassed by what I had imagined he was going to suggest. "I would really appreciate it."

"Good evening, Miss Jackson," he said, and taking my hand, bowed and clicked his heels in the best officer-class manner. He had decided I was worth knowing after all.

And that was how I met Reinhard Heydrich.

PARTY DAY AT NUREMBERG

There seemed to be continuous marching going on in the streets, boys, girls, soldiers, and civilians. Almost every time I went anywhere, I had to wait to let a parade, large or small, pass. Martial music filled the air and men broke into song at the slightest provocation. They sang very well, and Sydney Stokes and I made jokes about SS choir practice. It seemed as though the Nazi takeover were nothing more than a continual musical comedy being performed in the streets. I guess that's what I wanted to see.

There were signs on the Jewish stores urging good Germans not to buy, and signs on some restaurants forbidding Jews to enter. They were disturbing, but I listened to the rest of the foreign diplomatic community who dismissed these displays as the excesses of the more radical members of the party. Or, as one blustering, superior Englishman put it, "those people" needed to be taken down a peg, don't you know.

I also heard about the random brutality of the SA troops and rumors of their secret dungeons and prisons. The Americans I talked to, my father's secretary, a young man from the Midwest, the naval attaché, Mr. Bushmuller, and others, simply reaffirmed my attitude. We Americans, the Defenders of the Free World, who had had to come get Europe out of its mess, felt superior to all of these folk in their half-baked uniforms and marching music that wasn't a jot on John Philip Sousa.

Besides, none of it touched me personally. I had no reason to be threatened, and it was none of my business—it wasn't my country. My father, after hearing me make fun of Hermann Göring on the phone to Sydney, had told me to keep my opinions to myself. "However much the Reich Air Minister may deserve your approbation," he added, and I understood that Göring's already well-known excesses were repulsive to my democratic father.

That fall, I experienced the first crack in my complacent acceptance of the new order, when Sydney and Brian Stokes took me with them to the first Party Day at Nuremberg. At first, it struck me as a cross between a Boy Scout jamboree and a Shriner's convention. Not as elaborately stage-managed as later Party Days, this one was more homespun, more an expression of the pride the rank and file felt at their victory. Of course, it was as organized as a German group could want to be.

The three of us stood on a street among the crush as a detachment of SS went by. They had just been christened the Adolf Hitler Brigade and were commanded to protect the Führer always. Sydney and I joked about the handsome men as they marched by, like using that silly, difficult goose step. They all were so serious, like little boys playing soldiers instead of the real thing, their white belts gleaming in the sun, their uniforms spanking new, their determined faces, slightly ridiculous. That they were deadly I missed completely.

Sydney and I spent several hours wandering through the streets of the city, dodging the advances of drunk Brownshirts, following after Brian as he interviewed the ubiquitous man in the street. Late that afternoon, Brian led us to an ancient beer hall, its medieval timbered front completely covered with red, white, and black bunting. Someone had told him that Röhm, or even Hitler, might show up to speak to the storm troopers who favored the place.

Inside, the din was incredible, the air smoky, and it smelled strongly of centuries of spilled beer. The rafters, as high as an American college gymnasium, were black from years of the smoke of open fires, candles, and cigarettes. The crowd, mostly brown-uniformed SA men, was so happy, so full of self-confidence and a sense of belonging that the three of us couldn't help but be swept up in the exuberant atmosphere. Brian steered us toward tables along the wall and wedged us in alongside the group of noisy fellows already there. They good-naturedly made way for us, making tame comments about Sydney and me. An overworked, red-faced, middle-aged barmaid made her way down the line and Brian shouted out our order.

Our tablemates commented to each other on Brian's accent, then one of them, a barrel-chested young man sitting next to me, said something I could not hear.

"Excuse me," I said, putting my hand behind my ear. He smiled and moved closer and spoke again.

"Are you English?" he asked.

I touched my chest and shook my head, to indicate I was not, then I pointed at Sydney, next to me, and nodded. The German pointed at me and shrugged.

"American," I answered, then had to repeat it. He leaned forward to listen and when he finally heard, he sat up straight. He smiled and turned to his companions, who had been watching his progress with interest. They all laughed too when he told them what my nationality was. Or maybe the fact that Sydney and I were foreigners of different varieties was amusing.

The young man leaned back toward me. "And the man?"

I started to answer when, several rows over, a table burst into song, which infected everyone in the place. Soon, my new friend, who boasted a surprisingly good tenor voice, had joined in. He turned toward his friends, all of whom were singing with all their hearts, waving their huge beer mugs, the beer splashing about.

Sydney, Brian, and I watched, mesmerized by the spectacle, by the sensation of being in the center of so much sound. It was, as well, a thrilling experience to be surrounded by so much unbounded masculinity. I could smell the sweat of the young man next to me, and as he swayed to the music, his arm and thigh brushed against me. He was so much bigger than I, and from him, from all the men in the huge room, I felt such a sense of strength, of great violence held in check, that I began to be frightened. Excited.

Disturbed by both feelings, I looked to Brian and Sydney for reassurance, but they were caught up in the moment; Brian, I'm sure, translating it into a story. Besides, they had each other, and Sydney was hanging on to her husband for dear life. I sat by myself in the maelstrom of masculine sound and smell, feeling my own sense of myself invaded by the noise and sweat. I could have screamed, and no one would have heard me, not even my friends just a few feet away across the worn slab of table.

Then, just as suddenly as it had started, the singing stopped. Not at a natural break, but men began to murmur and whisper and point to the front of the room. Here and there, groups began standing, some even stepping up on the benches. Evidently someone important had entered the beer hall. Brian jumped up on the bench to see, and all of the young men at our table stood up.

Then the word came back, jumping from group to group like a forest fire: it was Ernst Röhm, the head of the SA and Hitler's oldest comrade. The excitement level in the room rose several points. My tablemate turned and tugged my arm, forcing me to my feet.

"Look, look," he cried, "the Commander!" The rest of his words were lost in the cheering. The room grew quieter; the visitor was speaking.

"Who is it?" I could hear Sydney ask, as she tugged on Brian's coat.

"Röhm," Brian replied.

The quiet spread, and we could hear Röhm clearly, although we never saw him. He spoke conversationally to his men, calling them his comrades. The crowd cheered like crazy after that and Röhm was unable to continue for several minutes. The men started yelling his name, their cries melding into a chant.

"Röhm! Röhm! Röhm!"

When they finally allowed him to continue, he talked for only a short time more, telling them that this festival of National Socialist brotherhood, which the Führer promised would take place yearly, proved how powerful they had become, what a long, hard, dangerous road they had marched.

"Adolf Hitler will lead Germany to a new revolution," Röhm promised. "But," he cried, "let us not forget one basic truth. Without the Führer, there is no National Socialist party!" Everyone cheered their agreement. "And without you," he continued, "without each and every one of *you*, my brave street fighters, there would be no Adolf Hitler!"

The response to that about took the roof off the building. The cheering went on for a good ten minutes, and then they broke into a song. It was the "Horst Wessel Lied," the marching song that immortalized the pimp supposedly slain in street fighting against the Communists. They stood facing their commander, whom we could not see, their faces stern and suffused with joy, with determination, and with absolute conviction. When they were finished, they raised their arms in the salute Hitler stole from Mussolini, and thundered their heils to the heavens.

I stood sandwiched between the young men and my friends, my arms wrapped protectively around myself. Sydney had her arms around Brian's waist, as he stood on the bench. I saw the concern I was feeling mirrored in both their faces.

The young man turned to me after the heils died down, his face red with excitement.

"American," he said, "what did you think of that?" And, not giving me a chance to answer, he grabbed me and kissed me, a long, sloppy, openmouthed kiss. When he let me go, he watched me expectantly. I could hear his friends laughing. I wiped my mouth with the back of my hand, keeping a smile frozen on my face. Never in my life had I sensed such danger and never had I felt so aware, so alive. I was conscious of the other men around us, waiting, their tension palpable in the smoky heat of the hall. I couldn't see my friends, and I hoped to God Brian wouldn't try being noble.

"And here I thought," I said to them in German, "that you Europeans were such great experts in love." I turned to face the young man. "You kiss like an American," I said, and, making a fist, socked him lightly, but not too lightly, on his big, beefy, brown-shirted arm. Then I picked up my beer stein, raised it to him, and drank.

He hesitated a moment, digesting what I had said and done. I felt as though I were waiting for a wild animal to make up its mind to attack me or not. I drank some more beer. One of his compatriots called out to him: "Maybe you need more practice, Klaus," and the rest of the table laughed.

"He should go visit his uncle in Chicago," cried someone else, to more laughter. Finally, Klaus smiled at me, looking quite human again, showing dimples at the side of his wide mouth. He was actually rather good-looking; hardly older than I was. I smiled back and we all sat down to drink more beer.

It was a hour later before we felt we could leave, and in that time, as he drank more beer, Klaus and I became friends. He was only a big, uneducated, working-class guy, enjoying himself with his buddies. Finally, as I struggled to get out over the bench, he apologized for grabbing me, explaining that it was the heat of the moment. I patted his shoulder, trying to keep him away from me, and followed Sydney and Brian out of the beer hall. I hoped I'd never see my new friend again.

It took forever to get through that large room, fighting our way through hundreds of sweaty, booted men. Finally, as we burst through the front door, the cool evening air cleared my head, restoring my sense of perspective.

When we were alone, on the train back to Berlin, we talked about what it was that had frightened us. Brian said he thought that Hitler would be furious over all the attention Röhm had received, and he was sure something in the party would give. He pointed out that although the Nazis had not yet been a year in power, the cracks were beginning to show between the different factions. Hindenburg was the last bit of paste holding the Nazis together. Once he died—he was high in his eighties—everything would fall apart. That was fine, Brian told us, but when they went down, they would take as many as they could with them.

"Besides," he added, "Göring doesn't want Röhm to gain any more power, Himmler wants the SS to have it all, and Goebbels is taking over more and more of whatever he can get ahold of. The power plays are absolutely Byzantine."

Sydney offered that, obviously, all the energy these young men had was not going to be contained by a three-day camp-out.

"They're used to bashing Commie heads in the street," she said. "If they have to stop doing that, what are they going to do? I mean it," she said, when Brian shrugged.

"No one will be safe."

I never looked at the marching crowds in the same way again.

A TELEPHONE CALL

Decorating the house seemed to take forever, although I enjoyed the work, both the fun of choosing furniture and colors and the responsibility. Daddy and I had moved in as soon as we could and our shipment from the States arrived shortly after that.

As I expected, Daddy's study furniture and books, took up most of the crates, but there were also several containing paintings and some other homey things.

I spent too much money on my own bedroom, buying a handsome walnut bedspread and yards of lace and chintz. Because I hadn't had a room of my own since the house in Gramercy Park, I reveled in every inch of it.

One day, as I was standing on a chair, hanging the curtains, a maid poked her head around the door.

"Telephone for you, miss." She was a big, horsy girl named Edda, whose timid manners belied her size and health.

Downstairs, I went into the small, funny telephone cabinet under the staircase. There was one telephone on Daddy's desk, and I had kept this one for the rest of us. The little booth afforded the user privacy, although it was stuffy and uncomfortable. A dim light came on when the door opened, and it had a built-in chair, complete with carved back and petit-point cushion. The old-fashioned, elaborate telephone, covered with gold squiggles, lay on the small built-in desk.

"When I identified myself, a German man's voice said, "Please hold for Colonel Heydrich," and the line went dead.

Slowly, I sat down on the chair, perching on the hard cushion, my mind an absolute blank, I was so surprised. I stared at the booth's paneling until I heard the line come alive again.

"Miss Jackson?" I recognized the colonel's high-pitched voice. As he had the other night—as he always would—he spoke to me in English. His accent, like that of many Germans who spoke English, was British, and it was not unpleasant to listen to. Without any preliminaries, he launched into the reason for his call.

"Miss Jackson, I must attend a most tedious event Thursday evening—the opening of the First Reich Art and Culture Exposition.

I find these affairs a great waste of time, but I am told I must go. I understand that you know something of art. This is true?"

"Well, I took some courses, but it was my mother . . ."

"Ah, good," he said, interrupting me smoothly. "Perhaps if you accompanied me, you might lessen the boredom for me. I am not an uneducated person, but I know little of the fine arts. What do you say? I shall send a car for you Thursday at six-thirty. This is another irritation; why must they plan these things at such an inconvenient time?"

"I would think any time would be inconvenient for you, Colonel," I said dryly.

He laughed, making me feel absurdly triumphant. "This is very true, Miss Jackson. I am afraid I am not very good in society. My wife tells me this all the time."

Wife? What wife? Where was she and why was he asking me, Sally, to an art exhibit if he was married? He had fallen silent and I said nothing.

"Miss Jackson? Are you there?" he said sharply.

"Yes, Colonel, I'm here."

"Well, then, will you come with me?"

"No, Colonel, I don't think it would be . . ." I searched for the correct word, "appropriate."

"Appropriate," he repeated, "appropriate. What do you . . . ah, it was my mention of my wife, was it not?" He chuckled. Chuckled! I started to speak, but he continued. "My wife, Lina, is in Munich, with our son. I am here, alone. I know few people and no respectable young ladies to whom I may extend an invitation for an extremely respectable evening out. There, you see, I am completely honest with you. I can, of course, go to this function alone or with someone from my office, but I was interested in talking to you. And I will bring with us a chaperon." He stopped, and I heard him say something muffled in German to someone. I waited, twisting the telephone cord.

"So, what do you say?" His voice betrayed his impatience.

"All right, Colonel, I'll go with you." In spite of his unpolished manner, I was flattered by his attention and intrigued by him, he was so different from anyone I'd ever known.

"Thank you, Miss Jackson. Someone will telephone you tomorrow with the arrangements, yes? Good-bye," he said and hung up.

I took the receiver away from my ear and looked at it. "Goodbye," I said to it, somewhat nastily. But I'd been working hard, up to my elbows in curtains, wallpaper paste, selecting pots and pans for the kitchen, and I actually looked forward to an evening out, even an evening looking at Nazi art.

Thursday evening a medium-sized black sedan arrived exactly at six-thirty to take me to the museum. The driver, a polite, reticent young man, wore civilian clothes that did not hide his military bearing. He drove very carefully through the busy traffic.

The exhibition was in a renovated palace near the Dom, Berlin's main cathedral. Outside, red and black banners waved, and a huge white one with red lettering announced the show. The crowd of people entering the building included a few members of the press corps. The car drove past the main entrance, turned down a side street, and pulled up at a smaller entrance. Two men in SS uniforms were standing, waiting. One of them hurried across the sidewalk to open my door.

The other man waited by the building, and when I had climbed out of the car I saw it was the colonel. He looked very different in his uniform, and I almost did not recognize him. He moved toward me.

"Good evening, Miss Jackson," he said, taking off his cap.

"Good evening, Colonel," I replied, holding out my hand. He bent over it, clicking his heels. When he straightened up, he saw my face and looked almost angry.

"You are amused," he said, his eyes going cold and hard.

"Oh, no, I'm sorry," I said, putting my hand lightly on his arm. "I just was surprised at how different you look. I almost didn't recognize you."

He cocked his head at me. "I came straight from work and must return to it, therefore I had no time to change. And," he said, managing a small smile, "you have seen my best suit, which is perhaps the worst suit in Germany."

"I meant no disrespect." I was relieved to discover a germ of humor in him, especially one about himself.

"No, of course you did not. I must become accustomed to your irreverent—is that the word?—irreverent American sense of humor. Now we will go," he said, gesturing toward the door. The other SS man hurried to open it, and Colonel Heydrich and I walked into the museum, the aide following at a discreet distance.

I turned my head to look at the aide. His face was bland and ordinary. "Our chaperon?" I asked Heydrich.

Heydrich inclined his head. "As promised."

We were in a bare entry hall, dim corridors stretching out to the right and left. In front of us, through a pair of swinging doors, came a man in evening dress. He bustled up and greeted us, obsequiously, in German. He was middle-aged, his graying hair combed straight back from his broad forehead.

"Good evening, Colonel Heydrich," he said, holding out his hand. "It is indeed a privilege to welcome you." Heydrich shook hands with the man, but said nothing, only nodding curtly. "You will tell the Reichsführer that I am always at the service of the SS?" the man continued. "And if there is anything you desire"—his eyes swept over me—"a private room for supper, perhaps?"

I felt my face go red and Heydrich fixed his icy blue eyes on the director. "Are you now a whoremonger, Herr Director?" he said, and with his hand grazing my back, led me through the swinging doors, which the aide held open. The man hurried in front of us down a short corridor to a second pair of swinging doors. Heydrich stopped several feet away from the door. Still embarrassed by what the director had said, I did not look at him, but stood smoothing down the front of my black velvet evening coat with my gloved hand.

The coat had small rhinestone buttons in the shape of bows all the way down and a small stand-up collar. The cuffs were as large as those of a seventeenth-century Cavalier's coat, with black braid and three more buttons on each. I loved the coat, and touching it restored some of my courage. Still, I was even less sure of the outing than I had been. Would everyone who saw me with the colonel think what the director had thought? I knew nothing about Heydrich's reputation. I had not told my father that I was going out with him, and I wondered if that would turn out to have been a mistake.

Heydrich was watching me and I smiled sheepishly at him, aware that he knew what I was thinking.

"Do you want to continue?" he said softly, turning his body so that he stood very close to me, concealing me from the aide.

I did not look at his face, my eyes flitting over the front of his uniform, the buttons, the red-and-gold swastika pin on his tie. "It'll be fine."

"Yes," he answered. He raised his hand, turning it palm up. His fingers were very long, like those of a figure from an El Greco painting, the nails short and well-kept. "I apologize for the clumsy oaf. His manners are even worse than mine."

I looked up at him, conscious of his great height. He was smiling and I smiled back. I was beginning to like him.

"Damn the torpedoes, full speed ahead," I said, taking his arm.

"What?" he said, startled. "What is this that you say?"

"An old American war cry, Colonel," I replied, feeling suddenly very gay and carefree.

He repeated Admiral Farragut's quotation, laughing at it, and his high, dry laughter carried through the doors into the main hall of the exhibition.

The pictures in the exhibition were awful. I walked silently next to Heydrich as we worked our way through the galleries at a steady pace. The other viewers, party officials, officers and their wives, strolled along more happily, their fulsome praise gushing over the exhibits.

Many of the paintings were huge canvases, and the sculpture was, all of it, enormous. Nearly everything celebrated the National Socialist view of life, family, and the world. Happy children frolicked in their mother's arms, stalwart fathers looking on; half-naked farm girls coyly bathed; and, in picture after picture, brown-shirted soldiers of all ages fought and sang and looked into the distant National Socialist future with far-seeing blue Aryan eyes. It was utterly depressing.

The colonel and I entered a room empty of all pictures except one displayed at the far end. The walls were hung with red draperies, and there were Nazi banners arranged behind the painting, which was cleverly lit so as to point up its dramatic subject.

"Ah, I recognize this one," said Heydrich, almost in relief.

Red velvet ropes were strung along both sides of the room and in front of the painting, creating a walkway. The other people walked slowly, reverently along, whispering.

All along, our progress had been unheeded, no one coming close or crowding us. It was no different now. I looked behind for the young aide. He was there, unobtrusively bringing up the rear, his hands clasped behind his back. He did nothing, but no one walked between him and Heydrich. I wondered how they knew, how it worked. Surely, if Heydrich was from Munich, these Berliners wouldn't know who he was, and SS uniforms weren't exactly a rarity in the city.

The colonel and I made our way up to the painting, standing alone before it. The aide stood to one side, the line of people stopped behind him. I turned my attention to the picture.

I nearly laughed out loud, managing in the nick of time to stifle myself. Turning the laugh into a cough, I clapped my gloved hand over my mouth so hard that I smeared lipstick on it. Heydrich looked at me, his face impassive except for the merest twitch around his thin mouth.

"Control yourself, Miss Jackson," he said dryly, and turned his attention to the picture. I took a deep breath, my hand on my chest, calming myself. This was not the place to get the giggles. Nor was he a man to insult. But the picture . . .

It was of Hitler, as had been several pictures in the museum, but here, here the Führer, standing against a huge swirling swastika banner, was portrayed as a knight, his armor indeed shining. His forelock hung disarmingly over his forehead, as he clutched the enormous banner and stared, as all good heroes do, into the distance. The huge three-quarter-length portrait was in the typical superrealistic style of the rest of the exhibition. Hitler as Parsifal. I wondered if he had actually posed for the painting.

"He should have shaved the mustache," I said quietly, the laughter bubbling up against my will. "But then, maybe no one would recognize him," I added, controlling myself with great difficulty. I covered my mouth again, turning toward Heydrich, trying to hide my hilarity from the reverent group behind the aide. Heydrich quickly took a firm hold of my arm.

"Come," he said, and led me briskly down the velvet-rope corridor. I kept my head down and dug a handkerchief out of my little handbag, using it to cover my giggles. I hoped everyone would think I was overcome with some deep emotion, not with hilarity.

Without letting go of me, Heydrich gestured to his aide, who moved up to us. "Champagne," he said, and the young man turned and left. I tried to compose myself. But everywhere I looked there were more of those silly pictures reminding me of the pseudo-heroics of the Hitler portrait. People were beginning to stare at us. Fortunately, the aide returned quickly with two glasses of champagne. Heydrich let go of me and took them both, looked around briefly and led me over to a long sofa that crouched under a closed window. He sat me down and stood over me.

Taking a deep breath, patting my face vaguely with my handkerchief, I looked up at the colonel, who loomed over me in his black uniform. He was watching me intently, his face, as usual, quite empty of expression. I tried another deep breath. "Are you going to give me one of those?" I said, gesturing toward the champagne in his hands.

He sat down next to me and handed me a glass. "Are you quite all right now?" he said, turning so that he faced me, his long-booted leg extended in front of me, but he did not touch me. I leaned against the sofa, sinking back against the softness of the cushion. The seat was very wide and my feet barely grazed the floor.

"What an uncomfortable sofa," I said, squirming to sit up straighter. I looked at Heydrich out of the corner of my eye as he raised his glass and took a sip of champagne. He had one of those

Prussian-soldier haircuts, shaved up to the top of his ears, and very short on top. It was not attractive. Because his hair was so light and his skin so fair, he almost looked hairless, like a pink baby mouse. That struck me as being funny, and I was convulsed all over again. Heydrich watched, exasperated.

"I am sorry," I said, "it's inexcusable of me. I don't know what came over me."

"You needn't apologize," he said, taking a sip of champagne.

"No, my behavior is inexcusable, I just couldn't help myself when I saw that mustache . . ." I couldn't go on, overcome with the blasted giggles. "Oh, my," I said when I was finished. I felt exhausted with the tension of holding in my laughter. I drank some champagne. It was very cold and fresh and tasted good.

"It's like giggles in church," I said, sighing.

"Yes," he said. He turned, facing the room. We sat for several minutes in silence.

The champagne glass—a wide one—prompted a memory. "My mother once told me—when I was very young—that champagne should always be drunk out of flutes. You know, the tall glasses. It has something to do with the bubbles."

"That is advice for an aristocrat's child. Or a reprobate's."

"Yes. She wasn't a reprobate. At least, not when I knew her. She might have been in her youth. But she was something of an American aristocrat. If there is such a thing. She died," I added, when he didn't ask, "in an automobile accident."

"I know."

I thought for a moment about that. He knew my mother was dead. The knowledge made me nervous, or, I should say, even more nervous than I already was, because certainly my behavior up to that moment had been giddy with nervousness. I leaned forward and carefully put my champagne glass on the floor, then I took out my compact and checked my makeup. My mascara was smudged under my eyes from the tears of my laughter, and I used my handkerchief to wipe it off. I flicked the puff over my nose, replaced it, and snapped the compact shut. Heydrich was watching me.

"I really made a fool of myself, didn't I?" I said.

"Yes," he said.

"Do you always say what you mean?"

"Usually."

"Well, I've said I was sorry," I said.

"Yes," he repeated, still watching me.

"What are you looking at?" I blurted out.

He laughed softly, then shook his head, but he didn't answer.

154

Instead, he drank the last of his champagne and stood up.

"Come," he said, holding out his hand to me, "I think we have both had enough of this art." The emphasis he gave the last word, almost mocking it, made me look sharply at him. His expression was not unfriendly, and although I could not decipher it, I felt he was not so much angry with me as . . . what?

"Come along, Miss Jackson," he said patiently, still holding out his hand.

"Are you angry with me?" I asked, tilting my head.

He smiled. "No, I am not; now stop flirting with me and come along."

Speechless at last, I reached up, took his hand and let him pull me up.

We exited the way we had come, through the back door, where the aide had the car waiting. The colonel helped me into the back-seat, then leaned in through the open door. He was wearing a very pleasant after-shave, tart and lemony, and the scent filled the small space.

"It has been a most diverting evening, Miss Jackson," he said politely, in fact so politely that I strongly doubted his sincerity. "I will be interested in hearing your opinions of our great and heroic German art."

Taking a leaf out of his book, I merely answered, "Yes." Heydrich closed the car door and, pulling on his cap, raised his arm and saluted as the car pulled away.

I watched him turn quickly and, together with the silent young aide, walk to another car. What an odd evening. What an extremely odd man. I had expected him to be furious with me over my behavior. After all, it was the leader of his country whom I had insulted by my laughter. My father would have chastised me for my nondiplomatic giggles. But Heydrich had remained impassive and even a little amused. I shook my head. Obviously, there was a lot more to him than I had imagined at first. And I had not been flirting with him.

He was so secretive. He hid everything, from the fact of a wife and child in Munich to his thoughts, and even his smiles. And why had he asked me along with him? I pushed back the cuff of my coat and looked at my little watch. The whole thing had taken just under two hours.

I'd gotten all dressed up for that? Some terrible pictures and one glass of champagne? No dinner? Well, he had said that he was returning to work. Which led me to wonder just what exactly was his work. What did a secret policeman do?

A day or so later, I caught my father in his library as he was about to leave for a meeting. It was late afternoon and he had stopped home to change into evening clothes, as he was going on to a reception at the Russian embassy that evening. I was not accompanying him because he anticipated a working evening. He was, as usual, trying to do three things at once, including carrying on a conversation with his secretary at the embassy.

"Damn," he said when he hung up. "Sometimes I wish I had decided to live on the Wilhelm Platz. It would be more convenient for me, I can tell you. What is it, dear?" he said, truly noticing me for the first time, but continuing to fuss with his papers.

"I don't know if I told you that I went to an art exhibition—God, was it ghastly . . ." I stopped at my father's upraised hand.

"Sally, I'm in a hurry, can you get on with it?"

"I'm sorry, Daddy." I came straight to the point. "Do you know anything about Colonel Heydrich?"

He looked up at me, his spectacles reflecting the banker's lamp on his desk. "Heydrich?" he repeated.

"Yes, you know, the man at our cocktail party. You introduced him to Dails."

"Diels," he said, absentmindedly correcting me. "Yes, I remember now. Why do you ask?"

I shrugged. "I was just curious."

"You went out with Heydrich?" he said, proving that he had listened to me.

I nodded. "To an art exhibition." My father looked at me for a moment, almost as though he had never seen me before, then he picked out a paper from the stack on his desk and laid it carefully in his open briefcase.

"I don't know specifically what he does," he said, closing the case. He walked around the desk. I saw his overcoat draped over the leather sofa in front of his desk and picked it up for him. He took it from me and put it on. "But I know enough," he said, buttoning up the coat, "and I don't think it's a good idea for you to go out with him."

"Oh, Daddy, I'm not, not really. It was just the once. And it was just the exhibit. He didn't even give me any dinner. I'm not interested in him romantically. Besides, he's married."

"Now I know I don't want you to see him," he said in the mild tone he used when admonishing me.

"I don't expect to," I said. "I was just curious."

"Your car is here, sir," Vittorio announced, opening the door wide.

"Thank you, Vittorio. I'm coming," my father said, and then he was gone. I remained where I was, perched on the wide back of his leather sofa, staring at the closed door, feeling disappointed.

THE MAESTRO

My second day in Berlin, I wrote a short note to the Mayrs, saying I was in the city, and sent it to the last address I had for them. When I hadn't received a reply by the next week, I got a cab and went around to their apartment. They no longer lived in the building, but the concierge remembered them.

They were all gone, she told me. Herr Doktor Mayr had died, quite recently, in fact, and Frau Mayr had gone abroad, with a daughter, the concierge said.

"And Christian Mayr, the son?" I asked, and opened my purse. I handed her what I hoped was an appropriate amount. She sniffed and tucked the money into the pocket of her black cardigan. She was a short, fat woman, with black hair in complicated curls around her face.

"Yes, yes," she said. "The son. He went away when the doctor died."

"What did Dr. Mayr die of?"

She shook her head. "It was a terrible thing," she said, dropping her voice. "I will not speak of it. A terrible thing." And she turned and went back into her flat.

I was left with more mysteries. How had Herr Doktor Mayr died that the woman would call it "a terrible thing"? What had happened, and where had Christian gone? I turned away, wondering how I could find him or his mother. Musing on the fact that it had been such a long time since I had had any contact with them, perhaps they were better left in the happy past.

As promised, Colonel Heydrich had found me a fencing hall, a salle. The fencing master was a man I had heard of, a former officer who had run the most influential—and fashionable—salle in Vienna at the turn of the century. He was so legendary that I had just assumed he was dead.

On the afternoon of my first visit, I pulled up in front of the building in which the hall was located. I told our chauffeur I'd catch a cab home, since I didn't know how long I would be. I was nervous and very excited about the prospects of working with this man, although I could not imagine that I was a good-enough fencer for him to bother with. After all, he had coached the Emperor of Austria's sons.

I lugged my foil in its canvas case and the bag of other paraphernalia out of the car. Fencing gear was not heavy, just bulky and hard to fit into tight spaces like automobile backseats. I looked up at the building. It was an ugly building, with rows of columns arbitrarily scattered across the facade and other architectural details that seemed to be an unsuccessful attempt to temper the building's stolid, forbidding appearance.

A young man walked by in front of me, and as I hitched my gear up to carry it into the building, he stopped and turned. I ignored him.

"Say, miss!" he called, in an unmistakable New York accent, "don't I know you from someplace?"

I stopped and turned toward him. He stood with his hands in the pockets of his baggy tweed slacks, his equally baggy jacket flapping behind him. He wore a blue-and-brown-patterned sweater under the jacket and a green, red, and yellow muffler wrapped loosely around his neck. A brown disreputable hat was pulled down on top of his unruly dark curly hair. To complete the picture, a toothpick stuck out of his mouth.

I smiled. "I'd remember you," I said, and turned to go inside.

"Wait, hold on." He walked up to me. "I know I've seen you somewhere."

"Well, you figure it out," I said, "I've got an appointment." And I left him on the sidewalk.

The building had a large square inner courtyard, with a glass skylight over it. When I looked up, I could see that six or seven stories opened onto the courtyard. I looked around for a concierge, and not finding one, put my bag down to dig out the paper with the address on it.

"May I help you, Fräulein?" a voice behind me asked.

I turned to find an elderly man in a long black apron peering out at me from the corridor.

I asked him for the fencing hall, and although he shook his head in disbelief, he sent me up to the top floor. I heard him muttering as I carried my gear up the broad, well-worn marble steps. Obviously, he did not approve of my being there, but I was so happy to be returning to the sport that I could dismiss him.

I heard the sound of blades and footfall as I approached a double door on the sixth floor. Panting, I put my bag down for a rest. The climb up had convinced me that I could not waste another day—I had to get back in form. As I stood there catching my breath, the door opened and three young men came out, talking excitedly, and ran into me. For several moments, I was surrounded by them as we all tried to sort ourselves out. Finally, one of them held the door open for me.

"You are a fencer?" he asked. I nodded.

"Good, good. We'll have a bout sometime," said another. They all laughed good-naturedly. One of them had picked up my bag.

"I'm sure you are much too advanced for me," I said, taking my bag. I heard their laughter as they disappeared down the stairs.

The foyer of the fencing salle was a tiny beautiful example of baroque design. The walls were white with delicate powder-blue and gold-leaf embellishments on the plaster cupids and curlicues around the doorjambs and windows. A painting on the high ceiling showed a celestial gathering of assorted gods and goddesses. In one corner was a stove, also painted white and covered with blue and pink flowers. In fact, the entire room was so feminine, so unlike what I expected in a fencing hall, that I stopped dead in my tracks. The place was very quiet and nothing moved but the dust motes dancing in the sunlight streaming in from the two windows along the wall to my right.

I took a few tentative steps into the center of the room. To my left, in a shallow alcove, hung a large painting, larger than life size, of a fencer clad in the classic white jacket and knee breeches and a white powdered wig. He stood in a formal salute, his blade held out and angled down. I walked closer.

"That is Prince August Wilhelm," said a voice behind me. I turned.

Behind me stood a small, wiry old man, clad all in black. He wore a fencing jacket and long pants. His face was heavily lined, almost painfully so, and his hair, although steel-gray, was plentiful and well-cut.

"He was our founder, in 1785," he said, indicating the painting with a small graceful gesture. Then he held out a hand to me. "You must be Fräulein Jackson. Welcome."

"Thank you," I answered, shaking his hand, which was like shaking hands with a coiled spring, all cool steel and suppressed energy and strength.

"I am Joaquim von Hohenberg."

"I am honored, sir. My first fencing master often told us about you, and I am very, very pleased that you have agreed to take me on."

"I am so glad to have another young lady here," he said.

"There are other girls?" I asked, eagerly.

"Oh, yes, at present we have three. One young lady, one of our best, recently left for . . . personal reasons. We hope she will return when she is delivered of them, but who can tell what one's interests may be then, eh?" He laughed delicately. "Now, come let me show you to the changing room. You are prepared to do some exercises today? Yes, I see you are. Good, good."

We went through a door at the end of the hall and entered a long corridor with a rounded ceiling. The maestro, which was what he was called, pointed out the changing room and showers. "You can leave your belongings safely there," he said. "Please join me in the hall when you are ready—through that door there." He pointed toward a door at the end of the corridor.

The changing room, which was empty of people as well as their belongings, was only slightly more utilitarian than the foyer. A dozen full-sized lockers stood along one wall. They too had been painted white to blend more felicitously with the white walls. Three of the lockers had padlocks on them. I opened a free one.

It felt good to put on my uniform. I slid my foil out of its canvas sheath. I hadn't handled it for several months and I tried a few fast parries. That felt good too, if a little rusty.

I braided my hair, which was still long and only barely more manageable than it had been in my girlhood, and wound it into a knot at the base of my neck. I covered it with a net and pinned everything securely in place. Picking up my mask, gloves, and foil, I looked at myself in the full-length mirror. Good. At least, I looked serious, even if my fencing was not going to measure up.

I was quite nervous about the level of my technique and abilities. Maestro, I remembered, had been an important fencing master for over forty years.

The fencing hall was half the size of an American gym but twenty times more beautiful. I pushed open the door and paused to take in the plaster work, the tall windows, and the beautiful parquet floor. The room was a long wide rectangle with a high ceiling. The windows ran along one narrow end, there were mirrors along the other. Two risers stood behind a fancy railing along the near wall. In a corner were several stacks of gilt chairs, presumably for the spectators. The wall opposite was hung with paintings, one of which looked to be another of the prince whose portrait dominated the foyer. The whole effect was of light and space and quiet, an elegant place for an elegant sport.

The maestro, neat and small in his black clothes, stood at the far end of the hall. He raised a hand and beckoned to me. "Let me see your foil," he said, his hand out toward me. As I handed it to him, he grasped the hilt, slashed the air one or two times, then, holding his left hand horizontal to the ground, carefully balanced the foil on it. "It is well-balanced and light," he said. "A good blade. Have you used it long?" He handed it back to me, hilt first.

"It's the only one I've owned," I said. "I bought it my first year in college, when I decided to try to get on the fencing team." Maestro nodded. "I had to replace the blade once, but it has served me well."

"Perhaps while you remain in Europe, you might consider buying another," he said, and I nodded. "Good." He smiled. "You are nervous?" I nodded. "Good. I will, I think, leave you to warm up. I have never met an American fencer before, and I am very interested in seeing what you do. Is this agreeable?" I nodded again. "Good. Well, then, you may begin. I will get out of your way."

Feeling self-conscious, I put my foil and other gear down near the wall and proceeded to stretch. It took a longer time than usual for me to feel ready, partly because I had not done anything for several months and partly because of my nervousness. But I took solace in my routine and its familiarity.

When I had finished, Maestro, who had been sitting on one of the gilt chairs pulled from the stack in the corner, walked onto the floor. I went to put my gloves on. When I turned back to him, foil and helmet in hand, he smiled.

"You do not need your helmet just yet," he said. He had a foil in his hand. "Come, we will begin." And, raising his foil, he saluted me. I followed suit and we began.

Later, after I had followed him through dozens of combinations, he stopped. I was exhausted, although I tried hard not to show it, but he looked as fresh as when we had started. He suggested I take a short break and then we would have a bout or two.

"There is water through that door," he said, gesturing toward a door to the right of the spectators' section. When I had returned, he had his own mask in hand, and I got mine.

He won, of course; I didn't even get close to him. He patted my shoulder. "Not bad, Fräulein," he said. "You will change and we will talk, all right?"

I nodded glumly, sure that he would tell me I wasn't good enough. It seemed to me that I was clumsy, slow, and just short of inept. In the changing room, I sat down and untied my shoes, swearing at myself.

After I had showered and changed and packed up my gear, I went out to the foyer. A stranger was waiting there, a man in a neat pair of gray slacks and navy sweater. He led me through a door nearly invisible in the plaster work on one wall. He also took my foil and bag. The maestro's office, too, was all white and blue, with a lovely Oriental rug on the floor. One wall was filled with the maestro's awards, trophies, and medals. Under a window, on a round table covered with a white cloth, a lunch of tea and little sandwiches had been laid out.

Maestro rose from behind his desk and came toward me. He took my hand, clasping it in both of his.

"You are hungry?" I nodded. "Good, good," he said, smiling. "You worked very hard. Come, let me get you something." Keeping hold of my hand, he led me to a chair. "You have met Horst? No? He is my assistant and we must thank him for this delicious tea. Or would you prefer coffee?"

"Tea is fine," I said, then noticed the coffeepot. "Oh, may I change my mind?"

"Of course, my dear. Lovely young ladies may always change their minds. It is a rule."

"I have heard that Americans prefer coffee, so I asked Horst to be sure to have some on hand." Maestro sat in the chair opposite me and placed a huge damask napkin across his lap. "Now," he said, when I had been supplied with coffee, "we will talk about your fencing." My face must have expressed succinctly my low opinion of my abilities, and Maestro laughed. "No, no, no," he said, leaning forward and tapping my hand. "This pretty face should not look like this. Things are not so desperate. Not at all. But first, we will talk."

We did, for over an hour, first about my abilities and what I needed to work on, and then about the sport. He wanted to know all about competing in the States and about my instructors and fellow fencers, but most of all, he wanted to know why I wanted to continue.

"Do you intend to compete?" he asked.

"Oh, no."

"It is just for the exercise? You do not go dancing enough?" His eyes twinkled as he said this. I laughed.

"Not at all, Maestro."

"Then why, my dear? Why?"

"I like it," I said, shrugging. "I just like fencing. It makes me feel . . ."

"What? What?" He leaned forward, his chin up, peering into my face.

"Strong," I said. "It makes me feel strong."

"Ah, good. Good." And he tapped my knee and leaned back, the interrogation over.

"You are very fast, which, I must confess, surprises me. But you are very sloppy. I think you know this, yes?" His bright eyes flashed at me across the tea table and I sheepishly nodded. "Do not despair! Sloppiness is the fault of your instructors. Perhaps in the United States of America you do not have such traditional fencing masters as me?"

"Nowhere near, Maestro," I agreed, laughing.

He grabbed my hand and gave it a shake. "Good, you laugh easily. This is good. We will work very small. Very fine. In great detail and I will make you very angry with me, but you will improve one hundred percent. You will be strong. Good?"

"Good."

"I will tell you a secret. Fencing, the art of the blade, looks . . . elegant, graceful, but it is swift and brutal, yes? You must be strong here,"—he tapped my forehead—"as well as here." He tapped my chest, above my heart. "Girls, young women, are very strong. They must be for the babies. The blade is an excellent method for them to be swift and brutal without muscles, without looking . . . ugly." He exploded into laughter and patted my arm. "You know I speak the truth, don't you?"

"Yes, Maestro."

We talked briefly then about payment, lower than I imagined, and days and times. I would come three times a week for a month and work with him and then see.

Maestro walked me to the front door and bade me good-bye. Horst had followed with my fencing gear and I offered to take it. "I will carry it downstairs for you," he said. "Next time, we will have a locker for you, so you can leave it all here." After he had handed over my things, he started to leave, then turned back.

"Shall you see Colonel Heydrich soon?" he asked softly.

"What?" I said, surprised. "Oh. I don't think so, although I should phone him to thank him. But I don't have his number in Munich. Oh, dear. Do you think he's in the directory?"

This time it was Horst who was surprised and amused. "Yes, of course he is," he said. "At the Brown House."

"The Brown House?" I said.

"Yes, Fräulein," he said, and giving me a brief salute, started back into the building.

"Horst," I called. He turned. "Do you know Colonel Heydrich?"

He didn't answer and I wondered if he had heard me. Then he spoke. "Of course, Fräulein. Sometimes, he fences here. You will see." And he disappeared into the building.

The day had grown colder as well as darker during my lesson. I looked at my watch. It was almost six. I looked up and down the street for a taxi. Seeing one in the distance, I managed to transfer my bag to my other hand and wave. The taxi drove toward me and stopped. Because my foil started to slip out of its bag—I hadn't fastened it properly—I didn't notice that the taxi already carried a passenger until I was halfway into it.

"Damn," I said.

"I was gonna offer you a ride, but if you're gonna curse at me . . ." It was the young, scruffy-looking man who had shouted at me before I went into the hall.

"I didn't," I said, still hanging in and out of the taxi. "I mean, I was, I didn't mean you. Well, not exactly."

He leaned forward and took my bag. "I'll leave you to handle the weapon," he said. "What the hell is that thing, anyway?" And seeing that I hadn't moved one way or the other, he said, "Are you coming in or getting out? Make up your mind, this is on my tab." But still I hesitated, and he added, "I'm harmless, I'm offering you a free ride, and I'm an American. What more do you want?"

"You're a New Yorker," I said.

"Yeah, well, you can't win 'em all," he said, working the toothpick in his mouth.

"Are you a reporter?" I asked, climbing into the car, settling the foil against my shoulder.

"Yeah," he said, "how'd you guess?"

"The toothpick," I said, gesturing at it. "I saw it in some movie."

He took the toothpick out of his mouth and regarded it. "Too much, huh?" I nodded. "Just to show you how much I trust your judgment, on such short acquaintance, I'm gonna toss it. Drop it from my persona." And he wound down the window and threw the thing away. "Now," he said, "where do you wanna go?"

"San Francisco?" I said hopefully.

"Well, sure you do," he said. "But how about someplace we can go by cab?"

"Home, I guess," I said.

"Really? Do you have to? Why don't you come have dinner with me? Steak. Beer. At this steak house I know. You can meet all the rest of the glamorous newspapermen that hang around there till all hours. How about it? I'll even pay for you." He held up his hand. "Wait, I'd better check." He reached into his jacket front and pulled his worn leather wallet out of his pocket. He counted his money. By this time, the driver had turned around and was unabashedly watching the proceedings.

"Sorry," the young man said. "Unless you pay for the taxi?"

I laughed. "It's a deal," I said.

"Luigi's," he said, with no attempt at a German pronunciation. "And step on it. I'm starving. Would you believe the best dive in town is called Luigi's?" He leaned back as the car started, and pulling out a beat-up pack of cigarettes, offered it to me.

I shook my head. "I don't smoke," I said.

"Mind if I do?" I shook my head again and he lit up. With the cigarette hanging out of his mouth, he put out his hand.

"David Wohl," he said. "And I know who you are. I figured it out, and where I last saw you. You're Sally Jackson, aren't you? The new ambassador's kid." I nodded, enjoying him. "*And* I saw you at that do the night at that museum, so-called, looking at those pictures, so-called. Weren't they the worst?" He took a long drag on his cigarette and blew the smoke out in a good solid stream. "So, why were you with Heydrich?"

I laughed. "How do you know all that? You know, everyone I've met here knows more about me than I do."

"Yeah, well, Berlin's that kind of town."

"Maybe you can tell me about the colonel. Nobody'll talk about him."

"Sweetie, kid," he said, leaning away from me dramatically. "You really are an innocent. That guy's the head of the SS's secret police."

"But he's in Munich," I said, remembering what Horst had said. "Mr. Wohl, what's the Brown House?"

"Phew, what's this Mr. Wohl stuff? David, please." He looked out the front window. "Hey, c'mon, we're here. Now, were you supposed to get this or was I?"

"Me," I said, opening my purse.

"Great," he said and got out of the cab on his side, leaving me to wrestle my fencing stuff out by myself. "What the hell is that thing, anyway?"

"A foil," I said. "I'm a fencer. I was at a class."

"I'm impressed," David said, leading the way into the restaurant. "I didn't know dames did that."

"I doubt if they do," I muttered.

We checked my gear with a surprised hatcheck girl and I made a stop in the ladies' room, and called home to let them know I wouldn't be home for dinner. I was enjoying myself. When I rejoined him, David was talking to a man at the entrance to the bar. He did not introduce me, but abruptly broke off his conversation, put his hand on my back, and almost shoved me into the bar.

"Do I have the plague?" I asked him sweetly.

"Huh?" he said. "Oh, you mean why did I whisk you away. Listen, that guy you don't wanna know. Forget it. A real crumb."

"Then why are you talking to him?"

"Oh, kid, we reporters have to talk to all kinds of people, good guys and bad guys." We sat down at a round table. David looked around for a waiter. "Boy, am I starved."

"Am I a good guy or bad?" I asked facetiously, but he took me seriously. He had been leaning back in his chair, looking left and right, and when I asked my question, he leaned forward, regarding me intently.

"That depends, kiddo."

"On what?" I said, taken aback.

"On what you were doing going out with Colonel Heydrich of the Munich SS."

"I don't see that *that's* any of your business," I said sharply. "You certainly are nervy."

"It's my job. And the daughter of the American ambassador dating an important Nazi is news."

"I'm not dating him," I said, hitting each word through clenched teeth. The waiter appeared next to me with a menu. I grabbed it from him and hid behind it. There was silence for a moment at the table. I lowered my menu-screen. David grinned at me.

"Wanna beer?" I nodded, recognizing the peace offering. "Two beers," he said to the waiter in English. "Know what you want to eat? Steak?" I nodded again. "Steak for both of us," he said, "medium rare, with everything." The waiter nodded and, retrieving the menus, retreated.

"So if you're not dating him, what was going on? C'mon, tell me. Let me get my facts straight."

"You don't mean you're going to write about me?" I asked nervously.

"Naw, don't worry. I just wanna know what my competition is like."

I looked at him for a moment. The thought that he was jealous of Heydrich rather delighted me, and I grinned.

"Oh, God," he said, "now I've done it. I'd recognize that cat-that-ate-the-canary smile anywhere."

"Tell me, David," I said, nodding at the waiter as he placed two large mugs of beer in front of us, "what newspaper do you work for?"

"I'll answer, but I'm not through with the other subject, you understand. I'm just retreating for a while. I'm with the mighty New York *Telegraph*. Ever hear of it?"

"Read it all the time."

"Sure you do, especially since you can't get it over here. Smallest paper in the East. To give you an idea—I'm the European Bureau chief. As a matter of fact, I'm the European Bureau."

"Why are you in Berlin?" I asked. "And not Paris or London?"

"Well, I think Berlin's the place where the news is happening right now. I've only been here about a month, and I'll move on when I need to. So, have you lived all over the world?" he asked, moving his arms aside as the waiter arrived with the food.

For the rest of the meal, we talked about our childhoods and families. David had grown up in Brooklyn, a first-generation son of a hardworking immigrant family. He had gone to public schools and to City College in Manhattan, and his first newspaper job had been, classically, selling papers on street corners when he was nine. He loved the business, every aspect of it, and was poetically describing the printing presses of *The New York Times,* which he had visited once on a school outing, when the waiter arrived with the check.

We had had many beers, more than David could pay for, and I wound up digging some money out of my purse. I didn't mind. He was funny and bright and I liked his big brown eyes.

We collected my fencing gear and the doorman waved us down a cab.

"Do you always lug this stuff around with you?" David asked, as we struggled to get into the taxi. It was a smaller car than the first one we had been in—or seemed that way. Maybe it was the beer that took up the space.

The drive went on forever, and I guess I dozed off. Anyway, the next thing I knew, I was being kissed, and someone's hands were very busy about my person.

"Hey," I yelled, scaring David—and the taxi driver. "David," I said to him in a shocked voice.

"What? What?" he said, untangling himself from me and my foil, which was somehow mixed up in all of this. "What's wrong, what are you yelling about?"

"You took advantage of me," I said. I had expected more of him.

"No, I didn't," he said indignantly.

"Yes, you did. You got me drunk and took advantage."

"You drank the beer. You asked for it, and you were the one who started making eyes—not me."

"I did no such thing," I said in measured tones. I pushed my hair off my face. "Where's my hat?" I squirmed to look behind me.

"Here it is," said David, tossing it in my lap.

"Thank you," I said evenly.

"You're welcome," he replied in like manner. He sat against the opposite corner, as far away from me as he could get. We rode awhile in silence.

"You mad at me?" I asked. I looked at him, but his head was turned toward the outside. "We've been friends for such a long time."

"Long enough," he growled. "Is it because I'm Jewish?" he said in a low tone.

"What?" I said, not sure whether to take him seriously.

"Is that it? You don't kiss Jews, just true-blue Aryan Nazi fascists, am I right?"

"David . . ." I said.

"Course, he's tall and blond and I'm short and dark . . ."

"Shut up," I said, "just shut up. You've got everything wrong." The cab pulled up to the iron gate in front of the house. "Go on in," I told the driver in German.

"Good German accent, too," said David.

"Shut up, and you're not short and dark." When the cab stopped in front of the door, I jumped out and rang the bell. Vittorio opened it immediately. "It's me," I said to him. "Can you pay for this? I'll pay you back."

"Of course, Miss Jackson," he replied.

"And then, please, show Mr. Wohl into the kitchen, where I'll be making some coffee," I said grandly, leaving the men to sort out my fencing equipment.

Vittorio brought David down the hall through the padded swinging door into the kitchen. When they entered, Frau Brenner stuck her head around the door and asked what was going on at this impossible hour of the night. I placated her and sent Vittorio off to his bed. Neither of them wanted to leave David and me alone—especially in the kitchen—but I convinced them everything was dignified and respectable.

David sat at the long marble-topped table while I puttered around making coffee. I explained how I had met the colonel at the reception, and how I had felt sorry for him because he seemed to be so socially inept. David laughed.

"Inept!" he said. "Boy, he's inept all right. Like a killer shark is inept."

I didn't answer and, putting the sugar bowl down in front of him, went to get spoons. When the coffee started to perk, David got up to take care of it. As we sat across from each other with our coffee, I asked him to tell me, please, what he knew about the colonel.

"The SS is still a small organization, compared to the SA. The SA is huge, and those are the guys who fought in the streets, the guys who have been Nazis since the twenties," he said, stirring his coffee. He had put three huge spoonfuls of sugar into it and a great slug of milk. "They want a piece of the pie, since they helped win it. There's even been talk of Röhm ousting Hitler. And I've heard that both the army and Hindenburg hate that idea. Hitler they think they can control, but Röhm's another matter.

"Anyway, the head of the SS, Heinrich Himmler, hired Heydrich two years ago or so to start a security service for the SS. You know they started as Hitler's bodyguards? Now they're the elite, supposedly. Himmler's keeping recruiting pretty select, but to be powerful he has to have a large organization. Anyway, the scuttlebutt says that Himmler is consolidating his power bit by bit. And Heydrich's SD, the secret security service, is helping him do it.

"The SS, well, Himmler and Heydrich, have already gobbled up the police force in Bavaria and most other states—oh, by the way, the Brown House is the Nazi party headquarters in Munich. Anyway, they're involved right now in a fight with Göring over Prussia. If they succeed, Sally, that means your pal, Heydrich, will probably be the head of the security police of the entire country. Including the Gestapo."

"But I thought Diels was the head of the Gestapo," I said, wanting David to know I wasn't entirely uneducated about German politics.

"Fouf," he said, blowing the sound out of his lips, "he's on his way out. Be a wonder if he's still alive in the morning."

I couldn't believe he really meant that and I looked at him skeptically over my coffee cup.

"These boys are tough, and they're only gonna get tougher the more power they get. Always remember that, kid, when it comes down to it, what the National Socialists stand for is not jobs or militarism or stupid, half-baked racial notions, but how much power they can get. And why?" He shrugged. "Who knows. I guess it makes 'em feel good or something." He took a sip of coffee.

"You know who they really remind me of? Dillinger. Capone. This whole country's gonna be like Chicago during Prohibition."

"Want a cookie?" I said and got up before he could answer. What he had told me disturbed and troubled me, although I was glad for the information. Especially about the colonel. Then I laughed, thinking about how I had botched up our date. I got a round tin of English tea biscuits out of the pantry and, prying the top off, set it down before David.

"What are you giggling about?" he said, reaching out and touching my arm. I sat down and told him about my giggle fit at Hitler's portrait. He laughed along with me, although he was surprised that Heydrich hadn't been angry at me.

"Maybe he was being diplomatic, because of who I am," I said.

"Sure, I guess that's it," he said, clearly not agreeing with me. He stuck his wrist out to look at his watch. "Jesus, look how late it is. I'd better take off."

I was sitting on the table at an angle to him, and when he stood up he was very close to me. He hesitated a moment, but he turned away.

"David," I said. He turned back. "Are we friends?" I asked.

"Sure are, kid," he said with a smile. He picked his hat off the table. "Ah, I'm sorry," he said, studying the brim. "About the misunderstanding in the taxi."

"Oh, that's okay," I said. "And, anyway, like I said, you're not so short," I added. I hopped off the table before he could answer. "Ohh," I moaned, "I can feel my fencing muscles coming awake."

"At this hour! You'd better get them to bed, along with the rest of you. I'll call you, all right?"

After I had walked him to the front door, I went back to clean up our tea party, and I wondered what my father would say if he knew I had entertained a man there at such an hour. A Jewish reporter straight from New York, too. And one who had kissed me, and kissed me seriously, in the taxi. Gentlemen didn't do that, especially to a girl they had met only hours before.

I turned the kitchen lights out and walked quietly in my stocking feet through the hall to the stairs. The house was absolutely silent and I stood for a moment at the foot of the staircase listening to the deep silence.

I liked David and when it came down to it, I had liked his kisses too. I just hadn't liked being, well, grabbed when I was, well, drunk, like that. Carrying my shoes, I hurried up the stairs and sneaked past my father's room.

I talked to Sydney about David the next day as we window-shopped on the Kurfürstendamm. She knew him and happily approved, although, as she said, he was a little gauche.

"But," she said, "he's intelligent, if uncultured. Let's go in here," she suggested. We were in front of a small but very elegant lingerie shop. "He's also Jewish." She looked at me sideways, waiting for my reaction.

"I know. He told me."

"Does it matter?"

"I don't think so." I stared at a lime-green satin garter belt. "Looks very uncomfortable, doesn't it?"

"Pretty, though. I'd buy it and keep it to dress up my lingerie drawer."

"I don't think it matters—his being Jewish," I said, returning to the subject. "At least, it shouldn't. I keep wondering what my father would say. You know, an American man living here, studying, I think, came to him at home the other day and asked that Daddy intercede on behalf of a German friend of his, a Jew, who has been in prison for ages and has never been charged with anything."

"How ghastly."

"Daddy can't do anything, of course, because the poor guy in jail is German. But he was feeling very frustrated. I think his American sense of right goes beyond any feelings of prejudice. He said something like, 'It's not right that they keep that fellow locked up without a trial, even if he is a Jew,' something like that."

" 'Even if he is a Jew,' " repeated Sydney. "Well, that's a concession, I suppose. My father won't even go that far. He is extremely anti-Semitic and makes no excuses about it."

"Are you?"

"No. Yes." Sydney sighed. "But I am less so than my parents. I've had Jewish friends, and I don't think they have ever met anyone Jewish socially."

"Well, now we know David." I nodded toward the shop. "Let's go in, shall we?" We pushed open the door. "David's rather like Brian, isn't he?"

"What?" said Sydney, absentmindedly fingering a pale-blue pair of step-ins. "Do you still wear these?" she asked.

"Not since I was twelve. Brian's very intelligent and somewhat uncultured, isn't he?" I said, smiling at her.

"Touché, Fräulein," she said, "Oh, look at this slip. Isn't it lovely." As Sydney told the salesgirl hovering in front of us her size, the door opened and two new customers entered. I saw the other salesgirl look up, and smile, an embarrassed sort of smile. I turned. The two new customers were young men. They were in SS uniforms. The salesgirl went up to them.

"May I help you, gentlemen?" she asked.

I watched surreptitiously from behind a mannequin that wore an ivory camisole and no head. I was very interested in the SS men, after meeting Heydrich and then hearing so much about the pure evil of the organization. They didn't look evil; just arrogant. And well-groomed.

"Heil Hitler," one man replied, raising his arm from the elbow and casually letting it fall. The other man remained somewhat apart, his back to the store. Perhaps he felt uncomfortable in so feminine a shop. I turned back to Sydney and the peach silk slip she was looking at. She wasn't sure she liked the wide bands of lace on the hem and the bodice.

"The color goes with your hair," I said to her. The two SS men moved to the other counter, which, considering the smallness of the shop, was close enough for us to hear them. The one man was being very arrogant, almost rude, to the salesgirl who, it seemed to me, was doing her best to serve them.

"I'll take it," said Sydney to our salesgirl, who took the slip off to wrap it. "Good lord, what are they doing here?" she whispered, for the first time becoming aware of the SS men. We wandered over to the counter near the door, away from them, and studied a display of hosiery. "They're awfully good-looking, aren't they?" she said under her breath to me in English. "I have heard that they must submit a full-length photograph of themselves in a bathing suit when they apply. Can you imagine?

"Who are they?" Sydney asked the salesgirl, who came up with her change and wrapped slip.

"The rude one is a prince," said the salesgirl in a low, excited voice. "The Kaiser's youngest son, I think. He has been here before, buying presents for his girlfriends. The other one I don't know.".

The salesgirl went ahead of us to open the door. As Sydney went through first, I took one last look at the two men. The door swung shut behind me and I was on the sidewalk walking beside my friend before what I had seen, or rather, whom I had seen, had sunk into my brain. Sydney looked at me.

"What is it, Sally?" she asked, putting her hand on my arm. "You look as though you've seen a ghost."

"I think I have," I said. "I think I have."

I turned to walk back to the shop. "I have to find out." We were only half a block away, but by the time we had walked back, the young men were gone. We could see them down the block, their black shoulders and peaked caps bobbing above the crowd.

For the first time in a very long time, I thought of him, of Christian; I was almost certain the second man had been he. Then the thought struck me, that if he was in the SS, surely I could find him. And I knew just the person who could track him down for me.

LUNCH WITH THE GENERAL

"Can you meet me at Horcher's around one?" I asked Sydney. "I want to celebrate. I've finished everything. The house is done and I'm going to treat myself to a big, expensive lunch. You too, if you can come."

"I'd love to," said Sydney. "Lady H-G and the ambassador have left for a holiday, so no one is nipping at my heels. And when are you going to invite me over to see the finished house?"

"We'll talk about it. I guess I should plan some parties, although Daddy did say he didn't want to get too social."

Horcher's was a famous restaurant on the corner of the Friedrichstrasse and Unter den Linden. In warmer weather, there were tables set up outdoors, but now, in the winter, window panels surrounded us. It was a lovely spot, right in the middle of a busy and fashionable street, yet protected and warm.

Sydney arrived just as I was being seated at a table next to the window. She wore a very chic black suit I'd never seen, and we happily discussed it, and the silly, tiny hat she had on, stopping our conversation only long enough to order lunch. She had fish and I ordered veal, and after a short exchange with the waiter, she ordered us a bottle of wine.

I complained that I could never wear hats the way she could, and she suggested that I could if I cut my hair to a more manageable length. Although I was not convinced, I enjoyed being absorbed in such feminine concerns.

We had finished our lunch and ordered coffee and were deep in a discussion of what sort of party I should give, both of us agreeing on an small housewarming to begin with, when Colonel Heydrich, accompanied by a woman, walked past us outside and entered the restaurant. Sydney saw my expression and turned to see what I was looking at. We were far away from the door, and Heydrich did not see me sitting dumbfounded in front of my coffee cup. The headwaiter led him and his companion to a table close to ours.

He studied Sydney with great interest, not noticing me at all. She looked stunning, sitting relaxed in her chair, a cigarette in one hand, the smoke rising lazily over her smooth hair, past the little hat.

The hat, a fold of black velvet, had a tiny sprig of red holly perched on one side, and she wore red lipstick of the same shade.

"Hello, Colonel," I said, grinning at him.

He started, which pleased me. I suspected he was a hard man to catch unawares. "Fräulein Jackson."

His companion was seated, the waiter pushing in her chair, and Heydrich had started to sit.

"Colonel Heydrich, this is Mrs. Stokes," I said, causing the colonel to pop back up again. Sydney turned and smiled at him.

"Yes. Mrs. Stokes. May I present my wife? Lina, Fräulein Sally Jackson," he said to her, "whom I have told you about."

"I'm pleased to meet you, Frau Obersturmbannführer Heydrich," I said. She was not exactly what I had imagined, but she *was* blond and blue-eyed. I had assumed he would be married to a well-educated, ambitious, modern woman, but Lina struck me as being very provincial and unsophisticated, dowdy, in fact.

She wore a blue dress with a lace collar and pin. Her hat was plain navy felt with a short dark-green feather curled around the brim. She wore no makeup and her hair was in a knot at the back of her head. Noticing my scrutiny, she smiled at me. It lit up her face and I smiled back. She had that fresh-faced, clean-scrubbed look that fair-skinned people get in the cold air, which makes their cheeks go bright red and their pale eyes shine.

Our two tables were at the end of the restaurant, and we conversed very briefly—in German; Lina didn't speak any English—before the waiter returned for their order. It seemed that she and Heydrich were searching for a house in Berlin.

"I have never been here," she said, "but I have read about Horcher's, of course, and I knew I had to come. I will admit I almost had to blackmail Reini into bringing me. He hates going out to eat. Poor lamb, he doesn't look at all happy, does he?"

We all dutifully looked at Heydrich, who was sitting up straight in his chair, his elbows on the table, his long fingers laced in front of his face. He gave a little laugh to show he didn't mind being made fun of. Reini? That's what she called him?

"Where have you looked for a house?" asked Sydney, and she and Lina started an involved conversation about neighborhoods, shops, schools, and so on.

"Congratulations on your transfer to Berlin," I said to the colonel, assuming it meant a promotion.

"Thank you," he said. He unlaced his fingers in order to move a fork into proper alignment.

"I meant to write you," I said as he swung his pale eyes around to me, "to thank you for recommending me to Maestro von Hohenberg."

"Ah, so you have gone."

"Yes, just last Thursday. I'm going again, for my first real lesson, tomorrow morning."

"Congratulations to you; he does not take everyone," said Heydrich.

I felt pleased. Perhaps I had, at last, impressed him favorably. "I think he's only interested in me because I am an American—and a girl," I said modestly. Heydrich smiled.

Across the space between our tables, Lina had handed Sydney a snapshot of her son. The colonel retreated behind his fingers.

"Let me see," I said, holding out my hand. Sydney passed me the picture. The boy was a sturdy blond toddler, reaching out his hand, palm forward, to the camera. "He looks just like you," I said to Frau Heydrich.

"That's what my mother says," she said. "Of course, my husband's says he looks like him."

"Well, he's a very handsome boy," I said, handing the picture back, just as the waiters arrived with the couple's lunch.

Sydney and I stopped in the ladies' room before we left. She left first to collect our coats and I repaired my lipstick and gave a quick pat to my hair. Maybe I *would* cut it. This important decision distracted me so that, when I exited the rest room, I nearly ran into the person leaving the telephone cabinet.

It was the colonel and he calmly asked if I was all right.

"I'm fine, Colonel," I said in a low voice. "I'm glad to be able to talk to you in private for a moment. Would you know how I would go about finding someone who I think is in the SS?"

He brought his head up straight again, regarding me with a speculative, glittering eye. He paused for the briefest moment, then said, "You could give me his name and I will find him for you."

We spoke quietly, like conspirators. I didn't mean to keep my question secret from anyone, and certainly not from Sydney, but I did. I think, for some reason, I was embarrassed.

"Thank you," I said, pulling on my red leather gloves. "His name is Christian Robert Mayr."

"The boy you learned to speak German with," said the colonel.

I looked at him, surprised that he would remember, but pleased. I hadn't thought he'd been listening to me so carefully. "What a memory you have," I said. He smiled a tight smile, his thin lips curving upward. He even looked a little smug.

Later, I would discover that his photographic memory was famous, or rather, infamous, among his friends and enemies. And what he did not actively remember, he kept in an ever-growing set of files. It was said that he had files on everyone: even on his boss, Himmler, even on Hitler—the boss of them all. I don't think that he ever met anyone whom he did not mean to use. That day, I think Heydrich filed both Christian and me away in his memory, keeping us until we might serve a purpose.

"Colonel," I said, as I turned back to him. "Now, another favor. Sydney—Mrs. Stokes—says I should cut my hair. What do you think?"

I was, I suppose, teasing him, and making fun of myself, although he didn't know me well enough to know that, and, of course, he didn't know how I had been thinking about cutting my hair all afternoon. Perhaps it was the assumption of a more intimate relationship, perhaps he had never been asked such a question by a girl, but from his reaction, I suspected that I had caught Reinhard Heydrich unawares again. I felt triumphant, as though I had won something by tripping up, just for a moment, this cold, powerful man.

He took a step toward me, his expression confused. "Miss Jackson?" he said tentatively.

"Oh, my goodness, Colonel," I laughed. "I didn't mean to upset you. It's nothing. Please." I touched his arm. "Honestly, it's nothing. I shouldn't have bothered you. I am sorry."

He looked at me for a long moment, then finally spoke. "I see."

"More American irreverence," I said and smiled, then turned and walked away.

"Miss Jackson," he called. I turned back. "Don't cut it too short. Perhaps to here," he said, holding his hand level just above his shoulder, at his chin. He was very serious.

"Thank you, Colonel Heydrich. That is a good idea," I said. "Good-bye."

"Good-bye, Miss Jackson."

On the street, Sydney turned and grabbed my arm. "What was that all about?"

"Oh, I just asked him whether I should cut my hair."

"You did what?" She threw her head back and peals of laughter rang out, causing passers-by to look at her. "Oh, Sally, you are a case," she said when she had recovered. She tucked her arm through mine. "And what did the good colonel suggest?"

"He said maybe shoulder length."

* * *

Maestro stood in the center of the hall, his back toward me as I entered from the dressing rooms. He was speaking to Horst, who saw me and nodded toward me. Maestro turned.

"Good afternoon, Sally," he said affably. "Shall we do our little drills?" I put my helmet on a chair and advanced into the hall. Maestro's little drills were strenuous and demanding, but even after only two weeks, I could feel my strength growing. I did not think that my fencing technique was much better, but I was stronger. When we had finished, Maestro saluted me.

"Now for a small bout, yes?" he said.

"Okay," I said ruefully. I hated these little bouts of his. I had had six classes with him and had fenced him each class and I had yet to get my blade anywhere near him. I was learning a great deal, but felt inadequate. I realized Maestro was, well, a master, and I'd never get near him, but it still rankled.

I picked up my helmet and put it on. Maestro did the same. Not that he needed to; I never came anywhere near his face, but he stuck to the rules. Helmets to be worn, along with jackets and gauntlets, at all times.

We came to attention, saluted each other and began. Because we were alone in the salle and because of the helmet, it was very silent, except for the slap of our feet and the swish and clatter of the blades. I could hear my breathing, which was not as ragged as it had been two weeks ago, and I could see Maestro through a fuzzy scrim. I liked it; as I always had liked the sensation of being hidden.

But I was getting tired of never getting a touch. Maestro, with an elegant parry, touched me lightly on my right shoulder. "Wake up, Sally," he called, as he regained his guard position. I tried a lunge; he successfully parried and attacked, scoring yet another hit, this time in the middle of my chest.

Then a tactic I had learned from Herr Kempner and had never used leapt into my mind, and without thinking, I used it. Maestro's blade was heading for my left flank. My blade, with a short move across my body, stopped his, and—and here was the dramatic part—I used my blade, held straight up, to force his down, as I went down on one knee. Then, much faster than it takes to tell, I came up from the floor and, at the same time, lunged and touched him on his right shoulder.

Maestro reacted quickly, but I still touched him, fair and square. A touch, a touch, I sang to myself. I couldn't see his face, but I guessed he was surprised.

He pulled back into guard position, then stood straight. I did as well. He pulled his helmet off; he was laughing.

"Sally, Sally," he said, coming toward me. I took my helmet off. "How you surprised me. I haven't seen anyone attempt that in years. Where did you learn it, my goodness?"

"Years ago," I said, trying not to sound too pleased with myself. He patted my upper arm.

"Well done, my dear, that was very resourceful. Although you realize it is an uncertain maneuver to use in competition. And, in some cases, you realize your landing on your knee would count against you?"

"I got tired of never getting a touch," I said happily.

"Of course you did; why else do you think I never let up on you? Now, I let you go early. Go have your shower. You have done well."

Absolutely pleased with myself, I walked away from him, pulling the net and pins out of my hair and tossing them into my helmet. I had finally had my hair cut, although I still pinned it back for fencing. I was running my fingers through it, fluffing out the curl, when I saw Heydrich, like a shadow, standing at the entrance to the dressing rooms.

I stopped, smiling at him. I couldn't help it. I felt so triumphant at my accomplishment. He stood with his arms crossed in front of his chest, his cap shadowing his face. He smiled back at me, not much more than a tightening of his cheek muscles, his mouth curving slightly up toward his cheekbones.

"Did you see?" I asked, my pleasure with myself overcoming my surprise at his presence.

"I did," he said, speaking English to me as he always did. "It was well done, and a complete surprise. In a competition, you would have so surprised your competitor, he would be rattled and possibly make mistakes. An excellent tactical move. You are doing well here," he added, stating a fact.

I nodded. "Thank you for recommending it to me. And what are you doing here?" I asked, finally thinking about something other than my touch.

"This is my fencing salle, as well," he said. "You know the SS has fencing clubs?" I didn't, but I nodded. "We work in another hall, a larger one, a gymnasium." He chose the word carefully, and continued, "But I like to come here for individual work."

"You have a lesson now?" I said.

"Yes, and I had better go change." He turned away, then stopped and came back. "I nearly forgot. I had a reason for seeing

180

you." He reached into his jacket and pulled out a buff-colored envelope. "This is for you. From my wife."

He smiled. Another one of those tight smiles. "And from me, as well," he said, handing me the envelope between his index and third finger. "I see you took my advice—your hair. It looks very—"

Just then, Horst came through the door that led to the office. Seeing Heydrich, he immediately stopped and saluted, his arm straight out. Heydrich returned the salute in that less strenuous manner I had seen him use before, a quick bend of the elbow, his palm facing the other man.

"A moment, Obersturmführer," Heydrich said. "Good day, Sally." His mouth almost made a smile and then he walked briskly along the corridor, past Horst, who stood holding the door open. I stared after the two of them as the door closed. Horst—what was his last name?—was an SS officer, a lieutenant? It had never occured to me that Horst might also be in the SS. And the thought led me to wonder if Heydrich had done anything about finding Christian.

Inside the dressing room, I opened the envelope. It was an invitation to a musical evening. Lina Heydrich had written it out by hand, her writing loopy and round. For a moment, the musical part confused me and then I remembered that the colonel played the violin. I wondered if he was any good.

I didn't really know if I wanted to get any closer to him or to his wife, but I couldn't deny that he interested me a great deal and I found his attention very flattering. Flattering and a little frightening.

I'd accept their invitation, out of curiosity if nothing else. At least, I'd get a chance to ask him about Christian.

Outside, David Wohl was waiting with a taxi, as he had the weeks before. We went to Luigi's. It had become our usual practice, and the headwaiter, Luigi's brother Mario, recognized us and gave us the same table under a really bad mural of the Roman Forum. I sat back in the chair while David placed our orders, which were always the same, beer and steaks, and thought how lucky I was to have met two such different, interesting men. David was more comfortable, but, I thought, smiling, perhaps more dangerous. He turned and saw my smile.

"What's that about?" he asked.

I shook my head, embarrassed at being caught with such thoughts in my mind. I would have liked to talk to David about them, about Heydrich too, but I sensed that I couldn't.

I was twenty years old and I had never had a real boyfriend.

Most of the girls I'd known in college were engaged, and many of them had been going steady with boys for at least a year. That didn't mean they were no longer virgins, but in midnight conversations in the kitchen of the sorority house, hints had been dropped about this and that. The consensus seemed to be that the boys wanted it badly and would take whatever they could get, but once they got it, they never look at you again.

When I thought about my future, I imagined I would marry, although I did not view the prospect with any real excitement. But what else would I do? At least I knew that before I took that step I wanted something else. A great love affair, some drama, I wanted to be swept away. I wanted to feel passion, even to be hurt, and then I'd settle down to a nice, quiet life somewhere in the States.

An affair with a married man would, of course, fulfill all those requirements, but even in twenty-year-old naïveté, I realized Heydrich was not a proper prospect. David, on the other hand, was a boy to marry, although I wasn't sure my father would agree. I looked at David across the table and wondered if he would kiss me again and if his kiss would stir me.

"Hey, kiddo," he said, "you look pretty tonight. What gives?"

I laughed at him. "Thanks a lot, fellow," I said and told him about my touch. I did not tell him about Heydrich's invitation.

I had to tell my father, though, at breakfast the next morning. He studied the invitation, read it, then turned it over as though there might be an additional message on the back. His eyes met mine across the breakfast table. He looked tired to me, although he was as neat and well-groomed as ever.

"The Heydriches," he said. He was silent for a moment, thinking, then looked at me. "What do you think, Sally? Do you want to go?"

I shrugged. "I don't know, Daddy. They aren't really the kind of people I'd like to be friends with. I have nothing in common with them. Except for fencing, of course. Maybe Frau Heydrich feels she ought to have me over because of that. I think it would be interesting to go. I certainly don't think it will be fun."

"He is an important man," he said, and handing me back the invitation, picked up his day-old copy of the London *Times*. "And will be more so. Since we are guests in his country, I suppose it wouldn't do to insult him, but I wouldn't become too friendly."

I attacked my grapefruit, flattered again that my father was willing to trust me. I did feel just a bit sorry that he hadn't refused me permission. I really didn't want to spend an evening with Lina Heydrich, and I had no interest in listening to amateur violin music. The violin had never been my favorite instrument. Well, now that you're a grownup, I told myself, you should do things to broaden yourself.

The invitation reminded me of my own music, neglected for so long, and after breakfast I went into the morning room and opened the little grand piano I had rented. I had never played it before, but I was pleased with it and had a good practice session.

A MUSICAL EVENING AT HOME

"Do you like the kitten, Fräulein?" asked Paul. He was three years old, a sturdy, towheaded, solemn boy. He had been brought into the Heydriches' drawing room to meet me before being taken off to bed. The kitten in question, a little ball of black-and-white fluff, filled the child's arms.

"He's very nice," I said, going down to their level. "May I pet him?"

"Her," said Paul. "She's a girl kitten."

"Oh, I didn't know."

"Come, darling," said Lina, "say good night, it's late."

"Good night, Fräulein," the little boy said dutifully.

"Good night, Paul," I replied, "sweet dreams." And off he went with his mother. His father came up to me with a glass in his hand, which he handed to me.

"Thank you, Colonel," I said, looking at it. It was a martini, if the glass and olive were any indication. Heydrich picked up his own drink, a martini as well. He gestured toward the sofa.

"Please, sit down," he said, following his own advice by settling into an easy chair, crossing one leg over the other. He wore shoes, not boots, I noticed. "By the way, Miss Jackson, I am no longer a colonel."

"That must mean you're a general," I said. He almost smiled. "Congratulations." We were silent. I sipped my martini. I had never had one before and it surprised me, although I kept from choking. He arched an eyebrow at me.

"I'm sorry. It's my first martini. I didn't expect it to be so strong."

"Ah. Perhaps you should try another."

When I finished the first one, I accepted another. This time, I found the smoothness of the liquor very pleasant, but took only a small sip.

We heard the front doorbell ring just as Lina entered the room. "That must be the admiral and Erika," she said, turning toward the hall. I sat forward and placed my glass on the table in front of the sofa. I could hear the new arrivals talking to the maid and then to Lina. Heydrich stood.

"Isn't it cold out," a woman was saying as Lina brought the guests into the drawing room. The sofa's back was to the door, so I had to turn to see them. They were an older couple, the man short with a shock of white hair and black eyebrows, the woman small-boned and delicate, with soft brown, graying curls.

"This is Fräulein Sally Jackson," said Lina. "Miss Jackson, Admiral and Frau Canaris." The admiral, whose name I had heard before, came around to the front of the sofa. He was carrying a violin case.

"How do you do, Fräulein," he said, "I have met and admired your father." We shook hands and then I repeated the process with his wife, who immediately asked me about the house we lived in. It seems a cousin of hers had lived in it before the war and she was interested to hear about its latest inhabitants. She took a moment to greet Heydrich, handing him a violin case.

"Here, Reinhard," she said, "put this somewhere safe." She sat next to me, talking about the garden, and the handsome flagstone terrace behind my house. We settled in. Heydrich and the admiral talked by the drinks table. Lina moved back and forth between us.

Dinner was called and we rose to file across the hall into the dining room. By the time we came back, we were all comfortable with each other, warm and well-fed. I was a little nervous about the piece we were going to play. It was a Mozart, not terribly difficult, but I had not received a copy of the score until that morning and had only had time to read through it twice.

"Well, shall we?" said the admiral, and we took our places. There were three music stands set up by the piano, and the others began tuning up. They asked me to hit an A on the piano. Lina, her part of the evening essentially completed, settled into the armchair and pulled her knitting from a basket at her side.

She grinned sheepishly at me as though embarrassed to be caught doing something so domestic. While we were dining, someone had started a fire in the fireplace next to the sofa. The room was very cozy now, with the curtains drawn against the darkness, and Lina's knitting needles going click-clack.

"Are you ready for us?" said the admiral. He wore small wire-rimmed glasses perched on the end of his nose. His jacket—he was not in uniform—was open and his entire appearance was almost elflike, with his strange dark eyebrows. Heydrich, standing in front of a wooden music stand, waited, stiff as usual, buttoned up in his uniform, his violin under his chin.

Erika Canaris had a viola, and she had set her music on the

second wooden stand. The admiral, in the center, counted off, "One, two, three," softly, and I started to play.

"Well, that was fine," said Frau Canaris, when we had finished.

"Well done, my dear," her husband said to me, his violin still under his chin. "You play well."

"Thank you. It was fun." I looked at Heydrich, who was studying his music. "I think this part, the . . . third measure after B, I think it was a little slow."

We all found the spot, and I played the measure lightly through.

"It was me. My fingering—there, I think I've got it," I said.

"Shall we try again?" he said, looking at the three of us. The Canarises raised their bows and I waited for the downbeat.

"You are the metronome here, Sally," said Heydrich, looking around at me over his raised bow arm. "You lead." He smiled slightly. "We will follow."

And we played the pretty little piece again. And again. Before I knew it, it was nearly eleven.

"I must go," said the admiral. "I have to go to the office. I'm expecting a telephone call."

"From England?" Heydrich asked.

Canaris looked at him sharply, all signs of comradeship gone. He actually stiffened, then, relaxing, laughed. "Yes, Reinhard, yes." He rapped the younger man lightly on his arm with his bow. "I won't even begin to ask how you know, but I can see I've got some leaks to plug."

Heydrich smiled and turned to put away his violin. I leaned forward.

"May I call for my car?" I asked Lina.

"Of course," she said, getting up. Heydrich turned and moved quickly to her.

"Stay," he said, putting his hand on her shoulder and gently pushing her back into the chair. "I'll do it. You've worked hard enough." And he quickly left the room.

The Canarises left in a flurry of good-byes and handshakes. Lina and I stood in the entry hall as I buttoned up my coat and put on my gloves.

"I hope you weren't bored," Lina said. "We are very domestic here."

"Oh, no," I said, meaning it, "I enjoyed the whole evening very much. I liked the family atmosphere. And the music was wonderful.

I've never played with other instruments before. I enjoyed it."

She smiled at me, although it didn't quite reach her eyes, and turned to fuss with her hair in the mirror. I wondered what I had done to upset her, if she was indeed upset.

"Good," she said, tucking a stray wisp of hair behind her ears. "I hope you will come back."

Heydrich came into the hall. "The car will be here shortly. Perhaps, Miss Jackson," he said, turning his head toward me, "you would like to attend a fencing competition next Saturday?" Lina, who couldn't speak English, looked curiously at him. He translated for her, and she smiled with that same controlled smile.

"Oh, I don't think I can," I said, not wanting to offend her, thinking she would not like my accepting her husband's offer.

"Oh, yes, Fräulein, it is very exciting," she said, turning to me. She touched my arm. "Really. The SS teams are very good. I know you would enjoy it."

"Will you come too?" I asked.

"Of course," she said, "I never miss one of Reinhard's bouts."

"Will you be competing?" I asked Heydrich.

"In saber—for my Munich team. We will be fencing the Berlin team and one or two others—all SS. It will be my last competition with my old teammates."

"Thank you, General," I said, "I would like to come."

"Good, I will have someone call you." Heydrich turned as we heard a car pull up outside. "Your car is here."

Heydrich walked me out to the car. His house was in a tree-rich cul-de-sac and there were no streetlights. I could see the outline of the car and Rick, our chauffeur, who jumped out when he saw us coming. It was very cold and I shoved my hands into my pockets, pulling my neck into my coat collar.

"You play very well," said the general, reaching for the gate, allowing me to walk in front of him.

"Oh, thank you. I had such a good time. It was fun."

"Fun?"

"Well, I like to play alone, of course, practicing and all, but it's more fun to play with people. Don't you think so?"

"Mozart fun? It is an interesting idea." He stood back as Rick opened the door of the car. I stepped toward it, but stopped and turned.

"General, I wonder if you remember my asking you . . ."

"About Mayr."

"Yes. Were you able to find him?"

He took hold of my elbow and helped me into the car. "Come

along, Miss Jackson, we mustn't send you home with a cold." Rick closed the door and hurried around the car to get in the driver's seat.

I rolled down the window. "You haven't answered my question."

"Good night, Miss Jackson," Heydrich said, bending over to look in the window. "I know. We will discuss it at a more suitable time."

"General . . ."

"Good night, Miss Jackson." His voice was, as usual, level, with an undercurrent of humor. Again, I got the impression that I was amusing the hell out of him.

"Sally," I said briskly, lightly touching his hand, which rested on the window. He held very still, quietly repeated my name, then broke away and rapped on the front window. Rick put the car into gear and I rolled my window back up.

When the car came to the end of the street, I looked back to see him standing outside his garden gate, black except where the light escaped from his house to touch his pale face and hair.

"Did you have a pleasant evening, Fräulein?" asked Rick.

I turned to face forward, slightly embarrassed at being caught staring back at the general.

"Very nice. Thank you."

"I am glad to see you met such a respectable couple."

"You are?" I was startled, both by his familiarity and the comment itself.

"So many foreigners only stay with other foreigners. I know you enjoy the company of the Jewish newspaperman and the British couple, but I am happy for you that you have met such a good German family. You will learn much more about us that way." His eyes met mine in the rearview mirror. "You don't mind my talking this way do you, Fräulein?"

"No," I said, shrugging. "But watch the ice."

"Yes, Fräulein. Of course."

The rest of the ride was in silence.

Little Paul took sick at the last minute, and Lina begged out of the tournament. I went alone, expecting to be able to slip in unobtrusively. I did not want to be there watching Heydrich without his wife, but I was curious and eager to see some good fencing.

The call I received from the general suggested that I arrive around one o'clock. The field of competitors would be narrowed down by that time; Heydrich, no doubt, would have made the cuts.

I took my coat off, placing it on the empty seat next to me—Lina's?—and looked around. It all looked familiar. There were four strips, the measure of ground the fencers had to stay within during their bouts, but only two had pairs in them. Each pair had three men watching them, two judges and a chairman. The table of scorekeepers and additional judges was on my right, and spectators lined the sides of the room, sitting on wooden risers. I saw very few women besides myself, and nearly all of the men in the audience were in uniform. Rectangular black banners, emblazoned with the silver SS lighting flashes, hung at both ends of the gym, with smaller banners, proclaiming the names of the two teams in Gothic script, below them.

Five or six men in white fencing jackets and long white pants were gathered. They talked to each other, fiddled with their equipment, or stood silently watching the empty playing area. There was Heydrich, standing apart, his helmet in the crook of his left arm, his saber hanging blade down from his right hand. He was concentrating on the judges as they talked to one another.

One of the judges walked into the center of the gym with a sheet of paper in his hand. It appeared that the results of the last bout had been contested, and now he was reading us the final outcome of the judges' deliberations. It did not surprise me that General Heydrich was one of the participants of the bout in question.

I had overheard Maestro and Horst discussing the fact that Heydrich was a poor loser. There had been an incident where he had lost and had shockingly thrown his saber on the ground. I watched him as he was named the winner. He did not smile, but the tension left him and he stood more easily.

The next two pairs of fencers were called and they advanced to their respective strips. The judges took their places and the fencing began. One fencer of the pair closest to me was particularly exciting, aggressive and as fast as lightning.

Saber means the target is anything above the waist, the area, in other words, accessible during a cavalry charge. It calls for a heavier blade and, usually, a more aggressive technique than foil fencing does. And if the two opponents are both energetic and powerful, the attacks can be brutal. Twice I had seen men injured during saber bouts in college, even though the blades they used were blunt and had protective tips.

Maestro always stressed the need for finesse, for not forgetting style and technique in the drive for hits. I could just imagine what he would say about these young men. They fought as though it were real, as though they were true enemies dueling to the finish.

I had also heard rumors that dueling, outlawed during the Weimar Republic, had been making a secret comeback. Seeing these aggressive, and excellent, fighters, I believed it. These young men were not there for the elegance of the sport; they were fighters.

The bout lasted about forty-five minutes and the ferocious fellow won, leaving his opponent with a bloody right hand where he had misjudged a parry. He turned and walked to the Berlin end of the hall, as the spectators clapped. With his helmet off, I could see that he was young, probably younger then Heydrich.

Meanwhile another bout was coming to the finish across the gym, and as I turned my attention to it, one fencer lost his footing and went down. I stood up, along with everyone else. The downed man's opponent stood over him, with his blade to the man's throat. Though the blade had a tip on it, and the beaten man's throat was somewhat protected by the bottom of his helmet, all that seemed to be incidental for a long, long moment. There were just the two men, one with the sword at the other's throat. We all stood motionless, as we waited for the winner to move.

Finally, he did, tapping the beaten man's chest lightly and backing away, a proper hit scored, and we all sat down in relief. I glanced down at the Munich team to find Heydrich's eyes on me. I smiled at him, shaking my head to show how impressed I was by what had just happened. He nodded slightly, then looked away.

By the time Heydrich walked out to the strip for his bout with the young fencer from Berlin, the overall scores were nearly even for each team, and the atmosphere in the hall was almost unbearably tense.

The Berliner scored an almost immediate hit on the general. Heydrich was the underdog. His opponent was younger and faster and seemed inspired by his previous wins. But after that first hit the Berliner never scored another one.

Heydrich attacked from the start, never backing off, nor did he let the younger man's speed overwhelm him. Pressing the advantage of his longer reach and longer legs, he soon managed a hit with a simple and elegant glissé, slipping under the other man's parry easily. The Munich team and their partisans in the stands cheered.

The hit seemed to give the general confidence, and throughout the rest of the bout he acquitted himself well, finally winning, much to the crowd's confusion. The bout had been a grueling one, and I looked at my watch to discover it was after five o'clock.

I had to leave, and I gathered up my coat and took advantage of the pause to climb out of the bleachers. Heydrich must have seen me, for he met me by the door. He had a white towel around his neck. His face was red and his hair mussed, but he looked pleased. Almost, I might say, happy.

"General," I said, putting out my hand. "Congratulations. That was a terrific bout."

"Thank you, Sally," he said, shaking my hand, then wiping his face with the towel. "He was good, wasn't he. Tough. I liked that. Made me work." On the last word, he made a fist, grabbing hold of his excitement. "Did you see that last hit? So smooth. Perfect." He laughed and I laughed with him, caught up in his boyish excitement. It was the loosest, the freest I was ever to see him. "Do you have to go?" he said, pushing his hair off his face.

"Yes. I wish I didn't. I have to meet my father. We've got a reception this evening."

"With the Italians. I know. Don't bother. They're useless," he remarked casually, briskly, turning to look toward the arena as another set of bouts began. "What did you think of the other bouts?"

I was about to answer when a cheer went up from the crowd. We both moved forward to try and see what had happened, craning our necks to see over the crowd. He, with his great height, had no problem, but all I could do was stand on tiptoe and catch a glimpse of a white blur of action, as one fighter forced his opponent off the strip. I tried to follow and almost toppled over except, naturally, by instinct, I grabbed Heydrich's shoulder, steadying myself against him.

He let me. He didn't move, either away from me or toward me. I think he barely noticed me until the bout was finally stopped and things calmed down. I stood flat on the ground and he turned to look down at me, a strange expression on his face: surprise, excitement, suspicion, all mixed together.

We were very close to each other, hemmed in by the tall crowd of young men.

"I'm sorry," I said, sure he was angry, insulted. "I couldn't see."

He moved closer to me, a hand on each end of the towel around his neck. I could smell him, soap and clean sweat and the canvas of his fencing jacket. "No matter." He looked down at me for a long moment. "No matter," he repeated, then surprised me by laughing.

"What?" I said, now absolutely confused by this man.

"Nothing. Nothing. Come, I'll walk you out." And he put his arm around me, lightly, to lead me out. "It is fun, isn't it?" he said, reaching in front of me to push the doors open.

"I'll say. But I'd rather be doing it than watching."

He laughed and put a hand on my shoulder as we walked to

the stairs. "Yes, of course, I knew you would feel that way. We should fence someday." He moved his hand, caressing my shoulder and my back, but dropped his hand before I could politely move away.

And truthfully, I don't know if I wanted to move away from him. I was very impressed by the fierceness of his fencing, as I had been impressed by his playing. I also liked him like this, red-faced and with his hair ruffled. And so I made him laugh again by saying: "Of course. It would be an honor to beat you, General." And that was how we parted.

THANKSGIVING IN BERLIN

O n Thanksgiving Day, my father and I hosted a dinner for the American staff of the embassy and for a dozen or so other Americans living or passing through Berlin. We had turkey and cranberry sauce and yams and pumpkin pies, and after a slow start, the younger guests overcame their self-consciousness in the face of my father's staid manner. When the turkey had been picked clean and the older guests were leaving, several of the younger staff suggested we all go find somewhere to dance.

We appointed a tall, thin fellow named James, the naval attaché, as a guide. He took us to two nightclubs, both fairly ordinary, although there was a very good pianist in the second, playing Cole Porter and Rodgers and Hart.

"Come on, James," Kay, one of the girls, said, "this is deadly. Let's go somewhere exciting." She was married to one of the military men with us.

James, all shiny black hair and elegantly tailored evening suit, raised one eyebrow. "Are you all sure?" And when we confirmed our willingness to be led, he took us on an extraordinary tour of what was left of the fabled decadent nightlife of the Berlin of the twenties. The Nazis were doing their best to rid the capital, which was condemned throughout Germany for its evil ways, of these picturesque spots, but in the last months of 1933, the older, evil ways had yet to be entirely replaced by newer ones—if you knew where to look for them.

The last place James took us is the one I remember particularly. I think James saved it, working us up to it. It was on the second floor of a nondescript building. The staircase was dimly lit with a green light and the walls were covered with an embossed velvet paper. Green, too, I think, although it was hard to tell in the light. Everything looked green, even our skin. It was hideous, but we all giggled and made silly jokes as we stumbled up the stairs. By that time, we were pretty giddy from drink and the things we had seen.

"Halt!" said a voice. Before us on the tiny landing stood a large creature, a man, it seemed. It was hard to tell, as he was wearing a nun's habit.

Kay, who was in front of me, burst out laughing, and instantly we were all in hysterics. He seemed quite funny-looking at first glance, although, when I dared to look again, he actually was more sinister-looking than funny, with manicured nails and rouged cheeks.

"He looks like Hermann," whispered one of the men, and he was right. The nun did look like Göring, although of course none of us had ever seen the Reich Air Minister in a nun's habit.

We all started giggling again and James rounded on us, shushing us energetically.

"Shut up, all of you. He won't let us in."

But the nun held the door and we filed past him, controlling our giggles successfully. Once we were in the anteroom, the nun bustled past us to pull a velvet cord.

The eight of us, five men and three girls, looked around as we waited. The place was decorated in the style of the nineteenth century, with dark-paneled walls, velvet wallpaper, and elaborate wall sconces.

"It looks like a whorehouse in Tombstone," said someone in a Western drawl.

"Yeah," agreed another. "Where's Bill Hart when you need him?"

"Gentlemen—and ladies," said a voice and we turned. A woman dressed in a beautiful evening gown had entered the room. She was very beautiful, with deep-red hair and huge diamond earrings. Her dress was exquisite, a complicated spiral of silver-and-black beading with a spiderweb across the back. She spoke German but instantly switched to English when told of our nationality.

"We welcome Americans. We have entertained your countrymen before, but never, I believe, your countrywomen." She bowed her head in the direction of us girls. We had instinctually grouped together when she entered, as though the three of us had to defend ourselves against her superior beauty and style. "Now, what may we offer you?" We all looked at her blankly. I glanced at James. He was trying not to smirk too broadly. "Champagne, perhaps, while you look over our offerings?"

"Champagne," agreed James.

The woman turned and left the room, and we were instantly after James to tell us what was going on.

"It is a whorehouse, isn't it?" Kay's husband asked. His wife moved closer to him and he put his arm around her shoulders.

"My God, man," exclaimed an attaché who resembled Calvin Coolidge, even to the rimless eyeglasses. "We have women with us."

194

"Oh, don't worry about us," Jackie, the third girl, said. "We'll be all right."

Kay and I laughed, agreeing with her, but I am sure we both felt the same deep apprehension.

"Good girls," said James. "Don't worry, we won't let it go too far. But just think of the stories you can tell your grandchildren."

"I'm just worried about the stories we might have to tell Ambassador Jackson," said Calvin Coolidge.

"Simmer down, we'll have some champagne and leave," Kay's husband said.

"Ladies, gentlemen." A girl, no older than thirteen or fourteen, called from the doorway. She wore a simple sleeveless dress with a pale satin bodice and a skirt of tulle. It looked like a nineteenth-century ballet costume; she reminded me of a Degas dancer. Her brown hair was arranged in a single braid that hung down her back. She was very pretty. With a smile she led us into another room and left.

This room also was furnished as a nineteenth-century parlor, and on a large table in the center were four bottles of champagne, kept cool in two silver buckets. James did the honors and we all gratefully drank down our first glass and asked for more.

The young girl returned with a tray of snacks: red and black caviar and toast, salmon, strawberries, bonbons. She set the tray on the table and offered the different plates around.

Then an extraordinary thing happened. A nun, a real woman this time, rushed into the room and headed straight for the girl, who turned to face her, fear and apprehension on her pretty face.

"What did I tell you?" the nun snapped in French. "Didn't I forbid you this room? Didn't I? Have you disobeyed me again? Answer me, you evil child!" And she hit the girl across her face. Hit her so hard, that the girl spun around and landed against a chair.

"My God," exclaimed Calvin, and he and the other men took a step forward.

"Please, gentlemen," the nun said, switching to English. "Please, you do not understand. Do not interfere. This child is not as she seems." She went to the girl and pulled her head up. "She appears to be so good, so pure. A child, untouched and perfect." She caressed the girl's face, her thumbs moving gently across the child's cheeks. "But in reality, she is corrupt and stupid. Oh, don't waste your pity on her, gentlemen, she is quite undeserving of it." She dug her fingers into the girl's face.

"She is not worthy of the smallest mercy. Isn't that so?" She shook the girl's head.

"Yes, Sister," whispered the girl, in a small, frightened voice.

"Madam, please—" said one of the men.

"HELL," cried the nun, stopping him in his tracks. "Hell is where this evil creature is going. It is only fear for my own mortal soul that keeps me from sending her." She had let go of the girl, who immediately jumped away. The sister grabbed the girl's braid and hauled her back, yanking so hard that tears came to the girl's eyes.

I winced and must have made a noise because the nun turned her attention to me.

"Don't pity her. Don't. Look at her," she said, pushing the girl to face me, ripping her bodice, uncovering the pale small breasts. "She looks innocent, but you know looks are deceiving. She has sinned and she must be punished." She threw the girl to the floor and, from her robes, pulled a small white, knotted cord. She brought the cord down across the girl's back and shoulders, raising a welt, a darker pink than the child's skin.

One of my companions gasped. I heard them move, but I couldn't take my eyes off the girl, bent and whimpering on the floor, the vertebrae showing through the thin skin where her shoulders and neck met. Several strands of brown hair lay across the skin and I almost reached out to stroke them away. Perhaps sensing my attention, she turned her face to me.

"Please, Fräulein," she whispered, her eyes bright with tears. I felt my throat constrict sympathetically, felt contradictory emotions, felt I wanted to stop her stupid tears, her stupid helplessness. Then, with a gesture both graceful and pathetic, she held her hand out to me, palm up. And in that perfect gesture, I knew it was all a charade. That she had been deceiving us all.

I laughed. As I had at the art gallery, only here, after a turkey dinner, dancing, drinks, and caviar, I threw my head back and laughed out loud.

"Sally."

"Really, for heaven's sakes."

"What the—"

"Oh, can't you see, all of you," I said, collapsing on a chair. "It's all theater. How absolutely silly." I leaned down toward the girl, who still crouched on the floor. "Oh, I didn't mean to insult you. Do you speak English?" I switched to German. "You are a good actress. Both of you. But what a silly play. I think you've got us all wrong."

The girl got up, arms akimbo, looking quite upset. One of the

196

men handed her a glass of champagne and another gave one to the nun, who had visibly changed character.

The woman in the silver dress glided into the room. She spoke to James, who shrugged, and seemed to be explaining what had happened. They both turned to look at me, and she came over.

"Fräulein Jackson, we have amused you?"

"I am sorry if I spoiled things."

"Don't apologize. We allow our guests nearly every mood and reaction. Even humor."

"Thank you. You're very gracious."

She smiled down at me. "May I bring you some more champagne?"

"Oh, no, thank you, I'm fine." I felt acutely embarrassed at the idea that this elegant woman should wait on me. She was so cool and composed, every shining hair in place, her makeup discreet and tasteful. She turned to speak to the two actresses and I watched the diamond earring sparkle against her skin, fascinated by the light against her cheek. She turned back toward me and arched an eyebrow, questioning. She did not look as though it was four in the morning. I imagined that I did.

"Fräulein," she murmured, "can I help you in any way?"

"Oh. No. Thank you." I took a step away from her. She almost smiled. "Yes. Is there. . . ?" I stopped. "I would like . . ." I gestured toward my face and hair.

She understood immediately. "Of course. Come with me." And she led me from the room.

I turned back to touch Calvin's arm. "Don't you guys leave without me."

We went down a short, dimly lit hall, through a curtain of tinkling crystal beads and stopped in front of a door. I glanced around the hall, which was plainer than the one on the other side of the beads, more utilitarian.

"Fräulein," said my guide, after opening the door to reveal a thoroughly modern bathroom, gleaming with white porcelain and silver chrome. "If I may say something . . ." She paused and I nodded, curious to hear what she had to say. "It has been my experience that people often laugh when they are not amused, but are nervous, uncomfortable, or frightened. Do you suppose this might be the explanation for your behavior?" She stood very close to me. I could smell her dusting powder and see the texture of her skin, dull and pale, like pale-pink velvet. Her mouth was pale too, as though her lipstick had worn off her large lips. I took a step back, turning slightly, my heart pounding unaccountably.

"I've offended you?" she said. She spoke softly, warmly. "I'm sorry."

I didn't know what to say and I smiled halfheartedly and retreated into the bathroom. When I came out, she was gone and I returned to the parlor. We left shortly after that, pausing in the smaller anteroom while James paid the bill, which was exorbitant. The elegant woman handled the practical side as smoothly as the rest of our visit, handing the money to an assistant and engaging James in conversation. At some point, two women came into the room carrying our coats. Two of the men in our party engaged them in conversation. I studied the two girls, wondering if they were actually prostitutes, but decided they weren't.

I wandered to the door to the outside hall, where the man/nun had been, and cracked it open. There was another door on the other side of the small landing, and as I watched, two men came out of it and started down the stairs. They were in civilian clothing, with heavy overcoats and soft-brimmed hats on their heads.

One of the men stumbled and the other one paused to be sure he was all right. While the clumsy man was righting himself, waving the other impatiently away, he turned to face the door and looked right into my face. It was Reinhard Heydrich. And he was very, very drunk. I could see it in his slackened features, the way his heavy eyelids hung over his eyes, the looseness of his posture. I barely recognized him.

We stared at each other for an interminable second, until I jerked out of sight behind the door. I heard the two men continue down the stairs and I hoped fervently that Heydrich had been too drunk to recognize me. But somehow, although I had not known him long, I suspected that he would never get that drunk.

The elegant hostess came up to me with my coat and held it out for me to slip into. I did so, although it made me very uncomfortable to be so close to her. She let her hands linger on my shoulders. I could smell her perfume and, underneath it, her.

"Do you know him?" she asked quietly in German.

I turned my head quickly to meet her eyes. "He comes here often," she said. I nodded as though I understood everything that was going on. I was still more concerned about the fact that Heydrich had seen me here. What would he think of me?

"Ready, Sally?" said James, coming up behind me.

Our party bustled out, more subdued than we had arrived, but generally satisfied with the foray into Berlin's nightlife. As I left, the hostess stopped me again.

"Listen," she said. "You stay away from him. I'll tell you something and you must promise never to breathe a syllable of this to anyone." I nodded again. She came closer and said, her mouth almost touching my ear, her breath warm and lush against my face: "It is hard to find a girl who will go with him. Do you understand? He hurts them. No one wants to go with him, no matter how much money he pays."

"Why let him?" I whispered.

"He is very powerful and very, very dangerous. Do you understand? Now, go on, your friends are waiting."

I looked around; everyone was gone. I could hear them down the stairs and I hurried after them without saying anything to the woman, frightened by her, frightened by being alone with her, by what she had said, by how I had felt.

Three days after the visit to the fancy whorehouse I ran into Lina Heydrich in a hat boutique of the K'damm. I was alone, having a great deal of fun trying to find a hat that would set off my shorter hairstyle.

I had on a navy felt, with a shiny black feather coiled along and over one side, that I liked very much. I turned my head from side to side, judging the effect. And saw Lina across the shop.

She waved energetically at me and I raised my hand. As she started toward me, all I could think of was whether Heydrich "hurt" her. Although I did not know what that actually meant, I could imagine, but I tried not to as I rose to greet her.

"What a cunning little hat," she said. "It suits you, my dear."

"Do you think so?" I turned to look at myself in the mirror. Lina leaned down to do the same.

"Yes, of course. It looks like you, too." She laughed. "I am being so presumptuous, I know, but there it is. It looks like you."

"Well, in that case," I said, taking off the hat and handing it to the hovering salesgirl.

"I just came in here to look, you know. Oh, not that Reinhard isn't generous, but although his job is prestigious and important, he doesn't get paid very much. Last month we had to borrow money from my parents, and you can imagine how embarrassing that was. I hope you don't mind my telling you this?"

"I never suspected," I said, trying to hide how embarrassed I was. "Your house is so comfortable."

"Thank you, my dear. That is encouraging to hear. Now, are you going to look at another hat? Oh, look at that one, isn't it pretty?"

I tried on a few more hats, trying to keep the conversation impersonal. I wished she hadn't told me about their financial situation. I hated knowing it, because it meant that either she was lying to me or he was lying to her. James had told us how expensive that "house" we visited was. And "hurting" girls who didn't want to go with him must cost Heydrich a great deal, too. I hated all of this.

I asked the salesgirl to send the hat as I paid for it. While we waited for my change, I told Lina about the fencing tournament, and although she was obviously proud of her husband, she confessed that she really didn't like watching him fence.

"Did you know he gets up five every morning and practices for an hour? But he does look dashing in his jacket, doesn't he?" Without waiting for a reply, she went on. "Dear Sally, I know most wives would be jealous of a friendship between their husbands and a girl like you. You are so . . . so independent. So free."

"I'm not really. Not at all."

"You are. Especially compared to me. To most German girls. We only think of getting married and having children—"

"American girls are the same," I interjected.

"Yes, but not you. You do all these things, and you are, at the same time, pretty and kind, and I can see you like children. Well, what I am trying to say, dear Sally, is I know it is dangerous, but I am not jealous of you and Reinhard. And do you know why?"

I shook my head, hoping my face wasn't bright red.

"First, because I trust you. You notice, I don't say I trust my husband. He is a man, and men, well . . . I had four brothers, so I know. But you are a good girl, from a good family, and I trust you. But, second—and I hope you will forgive him for telling me this—but he told me about your young friend. The boy in the SS, that you knew as a child, young Mayr."

"Do you know him?" For the first time, I was fully focused on Lina's pale face and she smiled at me, knowing she had my entire attention.

"I have met him. He is very good-looking, but you knew that." Her eyes twinkled.

"He used to be. But thin, and a bit gawky."

"I don't imagine he is any longer," laughed Lina. "No, I don't."

"Did you tell him about me? When will I see him?"

"Well, Reinhard loves secrets, so I do not know for sure. But Christmas would be perfect, wouldn't it? You will come to our Christmas party? Perhaps play something? It is very informal, very homey. All the younger people come. I know you have obligations with the diplomatic community and their fancy affairs, but you'll enjoy our more relaxed party. And I am sure that is when Reinhard will give you your *present*. All two meters of him," she said, giggling at me like a fifteen-year-old over Clark Gable. I couldn't help it, I joined her, excited at the prospect of actually seeing my old friend, now so tall and handsome and grown up.

I saw the general before the holidays started in earnest. He had asked me to play with him and the admiral and Frau Canaris at the Christmas party he and Lina were giving. We met twice to practice the Bach the admiral had picked out, once at the Canarises' house, just around the block from the Heydriches', and once at Lina and Reinhard's.

At the end of the second session, Admiral Canaris was called to the telephone and then had to leave. His wife followed almost immediately. I meant to leave as well, but before he left to show Frau Canaris out, Heydrich handed me some music.

It was a Haydn concerto for piano and violin and I realized, with a thrill of nervousness, that he wanted to play it with me. I set it on the stand and read quickly through it. It was difficult, but beautiful. I would hate to ruin it, especially playing with the general.

He came back into the room. "What do you think?" he said, leaning on the curve of the piano.

"Do you think I can play this? I haven't played such serious, difficult music for some time."

"That is the trouble with you, Sally. You don't push yourself. Sure, it is fun to play jazz for your young friends, but you are wasting your ability, your time, if you don't make yourself tackle more challenging music. Now, don't look like that."

"Like what?"

"Like a schoolgirl being chastised by her Latin teacher."

I laughed. "My Latin teachers were always chastising me." I tapped two fingers against the middle C and D. "You are so much better a player than I am," I said after a silence.

"Of course I am," he answered, pushing away from the piano, picking up his violin. He wore civilian clothes—brown flannel pants, a pale-blue shirt under a navy sweater. He was not a slim man and the sweater showed the bulk of his hips and midriff. "I work at it. I work at everything to be the best. You understand?"

And he launched, without a word, into a Mozart violin concerto, playing it through, flawlessly, beautifully, with perfect technique right to the end. I'd never seen him play that way, pouring so much passion into the music that I feared the violin would break.

He played with so much energy that he had to move, taking steps forward and back, swaying from side to side. I was astounded to hear him and to watch him, to see him lose himself in the music, surrender to Mozart. Except for the moment after the fencing, he had seemed to be a man who—even as drunk as he had appeared the other night—would never lose control of his emotions.

And, for the first time, I let myself imagine him as a lover, in spite of what the madam had said. He was not cold and bloodless as he seemed, but fiery and passionate. Yes, I had seen that in his fencing, but now I saw that he was capable of great beauty and sensitivity. His playing made my heart pound.

With a quick gesture, bowing up and down, one-two, he was finished. He seemed dizzy for a moment, standing next to the piano bench, his hair fallen down into his eyes, his face shiny with sweat.

"You see," he said fiercely. "You see? That is what you must do. Do you see?"

I nodded. "Oh, yes," I said, although I could not imagine myself ever being capable of getting such passionate beauty out of my instrument.

"Now, we will play the Haydn. I am not overly fond of Haydn, but I chose this piece because I thought you . . ." He stopped and turned away. He put his violin on the piano and pulled his handkerchief out of his trouser pocket and patted his face and wiped his hands. Then he folded the handkerchief, put it back. He picked his instrument up.

"Come. We'll try it. Slowly. Like this." And he beat out a moderate, steady beat on the edge of the music stand with his bow.

Helpless before the force of his personality, his energy, and his passion, I played. I didn't play well, and he made me do it again and would have made me start a third time, if Lina hadn't come in and rescued me.

"Look, the poor thing's exhausted," she cried, and she was right. I was, but I was also exhilarated. And excited. I smiled up at both of them.

"I should go home."

Lina sent Heydrich to call a car for me and walked me to the door. It was almost seven in the evening and I could hear the bustle in the kitchen and from upstairs, where the nanny was giving Paul his bath. Lina might not have hats, but she did have the servants her husband's position required. I got into my navy coat and pulled on my gloves.

"I think my hands and arms ache," I said.

"Poor dear. Reinhard," she said, as he came into the entry hall, his navy sweater flecked with snow, his pale skin reddened by the cold outdoors. "You can't drive this poor girl like you do your men. Or yourself. Look, her hands ache." She had her arm around me, playing the role of mother-comforter.

"Let me see," he said, holding out his own hands. "Take your gloves off." I did and laid my hands onto his palms. He felt my hands, lightly squeezing and massaging them.

"Does it hurt?" he asked. "They are tired. You should not play for a day or two and then warm up carefully. It is just like fencing. You cannot expect your muscles to function immediately at top performance if you have not been using them. You know this."

"Reinhard, don't be so hard."

"I am because Sally understands. Don't you?" he said, his serious eyes on me, my hands still in his. I looked up into those cool, distant eyes of his and remembered how he had closed them, feeling the music he was pouring out of his violin, his soul.

"Button your coat, my dear," said Lina.

I looked into her face as she did up my top button. "You are both so kind to me. I feel quite overwhelmed." She smiled at me, making her full cheeks into rosy apples.

"Here's the car." The general walked out with me, holding my arm. It was snowing and the walk was getting icy.

"You should have a coat on," I said.

"I'm all right." Putting his arm around my shoulders, he shepherded me down the walk, through the gate and into the car.

In bed, later, my hands really were achy and I got up to find some liniment. I sat on the closed toilet seat and rubbed it into my fingers and the muscles of my forearms. I couldn't understand how I could have done this. After all, I had been playing the piano for years, but somehow, under the general's instruction, I had pushed myself farther than ever before.

Maybe, if I did well, he would let me see Christian. Maybe he would truly forget about our encounter on Thanksgiving. I smiled ruefully at my bargain. All right, I would believe it. It was a good incentive, although I knew that playing well enough to satisfy Heydrich was incentive enough.

A CHRISTMAS PRESENT

I dressed with great care for the Heydriches' Christmas party in a dark-red velvet dress, quite plain, with a sweetheart neckline and a full skirt cut on the bias. It had long, high-puffed sleeves. My only jewelry was my mother's diamond stud earrings. I wore my hair loose and smiled at myself in the mirror as I sprayed on perfume. Gathering my black velvet evening coat, which I hoped would be warm enough, my small purse, and a lace scarf for my hair, I went downstairs to pick up my music from where I had left it on the piano. I had been practicing the Bach all day and felt well-prepared.

I left my wrap and things in the entry hall, and when I came back down the hall from the music room, I found my father—he was going to dine with the Bushmullers—in front of the mirror, straightening his white tie. He glanced at me.

"That's a pretty dress, Sally," he said.

"Oh, this . . . it's new . . . thank you," I stammered, flustered by his compliment.

"You're going to General Heydrich's?"

"You knew that," I bristled. Vittorio appeared and picked up my coat to help me on with it.

"Yes. I suppose . . ." My father watched me get into the coat. "What is it, Daddy?"

He considered for a moment, then smiled at me. He did not do that often and it took me aback. "The house is very comfortable. You did well."

I nodded, suddenly touched by his unexpected compliment, and almost moved toward him, but he had turned to pick up his coat. I put my scarf over my head and walked to the door, pulling on my gloves.

"And, Sally." I stopped.

"Yes, Daddy."

"Don't be late." He stood in the center of the black-and-white-tiled floor, the staircase curving away behind him. He was, as usual, straight and upright, his expression a blank. But his eyes were on me, and in spite of his closed face, I could feel his concern. I wanted,

I think, at that moment, for him to say something, ask me why I was going, how I was, something. But he didn't, and I smiled at him and went off.

"Your dress is very attractive," said the general, handing me a glass of punch. We stood in the sitting room, which looked lovely, lit with many tall red candles, the fire crackling merrily in the fireplace. The wood floor beyond the rugs shone, reflecting the flickering light. The room smelled of evergreen and the fragrant logs on the fire. Someone was playing the piano and all about us were the sounds of people having a happy time. There were about forty guests scattered through the room, most of them young.

"Thank you, General." The punch was sweet, some fruit juice mixed with a sweet wine. I didn't like it, but I wanted to drink something. "How do you think we played? It went well, didn't it?"

"Yes. We did all right."

"Have you performed before like this? You seem to be used to it."

He was silent for a moment, tasting the punch, his hand curved around the little crystal glass. "When I was a boy. For my parents' friends."

"Oh. I never did. Although I've been playing since I was little. But my mother was so good. I'd sit next to her and turn the pages."

He had nothing to say to this and looked down at the cup of punch in his hand and grimaced. "I hate this kind of sweet stuff. I thought we were serving champagne." He looked above the heads of the people around us. "Ah, I think I see a server. Shall I get you some as well?"

"Please," I said.

"Good," he said and, taking my punch cup, moved off through the crowd, which had grown in the few minutes we had been talking. I glanced around and a man, dark-haired, with wire-rimmed glasses, in uniform, caught my eye. He smiled and came toward me.

"Fräulein," he said, bowing slightly from the waist, reaching for my hand. "My compliments on your playing. It was exhilarating."

"Thank you. It's kind of you to say so." I gave him my hand and he was tipping his head to it, when he glanced over my shoulder and froze almost imperceptibly. He was obviously too well versed in drawing-room manners simply to fling my hand away, but he let go of it quickly.

"Chief," he said, standing straighter. Heydrich stood next to me and handed me a glass of champagne. "I was complimenting

205

Fräulein Jackson on her playing. May I compliment you as well? And thank you for giving me the privilege of being present. It is an honor."

"You may, Sturmbannführer," Heydrich said. "And I am pleased you are so pleased."

The Sturmbannführer bowed slightly to me and left us alone.

"Now, how are you doing with the Haydn? Shall we have a practice next week?" he asked, ignoring what had just happened.

"I'd like to," I replied, doing the same, "but I'm afraid I have too many obligations."

"Parties."

"It is the holiday time. New Year's and all."

"You should refuse to waste your time on these frivolities. Well, then after the first of the year." His eyes went to someone behind me. "Here comes my wife."

I turned to see Lina approaching. She was wearing an unattractive white dress shot with silver. As usual, she wore no makeup and she looked, with her light coloring, washed out. She was beaming at me, though, and I returned her smile. She put her arm around my waist.

"There's someone to see you in the entry," she said softly. I looked at her quizzically. "A young man," she added. "Very handsome and very, very tall."

"Christian?" I said to Heydrich. He smiled. "He's here?"

"Well, he was," said Lina, giving my waist a squeeze, then releasing me. "Now go. It took Reini forever to find him."

"I should . . ." I said, handing the general my glass without thinking. I waved my hands at my face, my dress.

"You look lovely," said Lina. "Doesn't she, dear one?"

"Yes. Now go, so I can go get some more champagne," said Heydrich. I started away from them, then stopped and quickly kissed each of them. I had to put my hands on Heydrich's shoulders to reach his cheek. He did not move or bend his head down to help me.

I quickly made my way through the guests. The door to the entry hall was closed and I hesitated before opening it, then took a deep breath and went through, my heart beating crazily.

The entry hall was several degrees colder than the sitting room. It was lit by a lamp on a small table near the foot of the stairs, although there was light spilling down from the landing above.

He stood across the small hall, looking at a colored portrait of Paul Heydrich and Lina. He wore a suit, not evening clothes, and he carried his overcoat and hat. I would realize what this meant later and understand better why he behaved the way he did. He had been summoned, not invited, to this party, and had been left waiting, like a tradesman, in the front hall.

But, at that first moment, all I realized was that Christian was there, in person, in front of me, and how happy that realization made me. I closed the door behind me, as he turned. We looked at each other for a moment.

"Hello," I said, not moving.

"Hello," he answered. Another moment of silence. He looked uncomfortable, ill at ease, so I moved to him and hugged him. He responded clumsily, his coat and hat in his hands, and I stepped back to look at him, still holding on to his arms.

"It's been forever," I said. "I never thought it would be so long before I saw you again."

"Six years," he said. Then he smiled for the first time. "It is good to see you, Sally." He took a step back from me.

"Can you stay? Do we have time to talk?"

Christian shrugged. "If you like. I have a few moments."

"Here. Give me those." And taking his coat and hat, I draped them over the banister.

"We can go in the dining room. It's freezing in here." I led the way. The tall tree stood at the other end of the room, a strange, dark shape against the bare window until I turned a light on, revealing the glass ornaments, the silver tinsel, and the small red candles in their holders, ready to be lit at the proper moment. The dining table, extended to its full length with several leaves, was laid with a red cloth, with a centerpiece of holly branches and red candles in silver holders. There were swastikas in small white circles on the candles, and here and there, small rosettes of red, black, and white. Serving plates and bowls stood ready for the feast. I could hear the kitchen staff through the swinging door on the far side of the fireplace.

"It's been a long time," he repeated, standing near the door.

"Yes," I agreed. I walked down the table, looking at the decorations.

"And your family?"

"Oh, fine, fine. Do you know about Daddy?" I asked. He shook his head. "He's the ambassador here."

"Yes, I think I heard this." And you didn't call me, I thought, as he continued, "And your brother, Eddie?"

"Eddie went to Annapolis. You knew that, I think. He's a lieutenant now."

"Good." There was an awkward silence.

"What about your family? Your mother. I tried to find her. How are they all?"

He was silent, looking down at the toes of his shoes. "My mother is with Ursula in Denmark. Marta is in England. Annaliese is, I think, today in Vienna." He looked up at me. "My father is dead. He killed himself last January. Shot himself in the mouth."

I stared at him, shocked at the news and at the image his cold, hard words had conjured.

"Why?" I whispered, across the Christmas greenery, the silver, the red candles.

Christian's eyes, icy and distant, remained on me for a long moment, then moved away. He shrugged. "He didn't like the new government," he said, pulling a cigarette case out of his breast pocket, offering it to me. I shook my head. He took a cigarette for himself.

The memory of smoking with him by the lake came into my mind, but looking at his face, I sensed he wouldn't welcome the reminder.

"Christian," I said softly. "Are you all right?"

"Of course," he said, blowing out smoke. "What do you mean?"

"Nothing," I said, and fell silent. I couldn't think of anything to say to him, he seemed such a stranger. This meeting was so different from what I had imagined. I sighed. It wasn't his fault. It had been a long time and we weren't kids any longer. *His father had shot himself in the mouth.* I moved to banish the image. "Come along," I said in English, reaching out for his arm. "I'll bet you'd like a drink."

Much to my surprise he pulled away from me. Firmly, politely, but still, he pulled away. "No, thank you," he said. "I must go. My job . . . I must get up early. I have to go to Munich." He turned toward the door. I stared after him, hurt by his rudeness, at his rejection of my company. And perplexed.

"Christian," I said. He stopped. Why? I wanted to say. Why don't you want to stay with me? Why aren't you glad to see me? What have I done? Instead, I tried a smile. "I didn't even ask you where you live, what you do"—I tried a laugh—"if you're married."

"I live in Berlin. I've just moved here," he said, turning to face me. "I am not married. As for my job—didn't you know? I work for General Heydrich," he said flatly. "In the SD. And now I must go." He turned and left the room. I followed.

"I knew you were in the SS," I said. "I saw you in a shop one day. Or, at least, I thought it was you. You were with a prince or count, also in uniform." Then, a thought: "Your father . . ." My voice petered out as I saw his face.

"Yes," he answered, in perfect imitation of his boss. He picked up his overcoat from the banister and put it on.

"Will you call me?" I said, trying for a flippancy I didn't feel. "I'd hate to have you disappear from my life again."

"I do not think that would be such a good idea." He pulled on his gloves with short, jerky motions, then picked up his hat.

"Why?" I said, trying to keep my voice calm.

He carefully put his hat on, pulling down on the brim in front. It dipped over his right eye. He walked past me to the front door.

"Christian," I said. "We've known each other forever. You're like my brother. You were my friend, the best friend I ever had. I don't deserve to be treated like this."

He stopped and turned toward me. I was trying very hard not to cry.

"I'm sorry, Sally," he said, his voice softer than it had been. "That was all a long time ago. I've changed. You've certainly changed." And he almost grinned at me, his eyes flicking down my body. "But I think you know why I just can't be seen with you."

"I don't understand," I said. "Is it an SS rule? What's wrong with me?"

He almost laughed. "Nothing. Nothing."

"Then what?" I beat my fists into my skirt. "Tell me. Please."

His hand was on the doorknob, and he stood motionless for a long moment. Then he grinned at me, really grinned, so that, for the first time, I saw the boy I had known. "One thing about you is still the same, you always were impatient and demanding. And I *am* sorry, Sal," he said, switching to English again. "I don't mean to hurt your feelings. But Heydrich is my boss. I can't do anything to jeopardize my job. This is not the best job, but it was difficult to find. I do not want to lose it." He switched back to German. "You don't know how it has been here. You can't know." He clamped his mouth shut tight, as though he feared he had let me see too much emotion.

"What on earth do you mean? What's your job got to do with me?"

"Sally," he said, "don't be so naive." And he turned and left the house.

I stared after him, absolutely mystified. Heydrich? Heydrich was his boss and he couldn't see me because of it? What sense did that make? Then comprehension dawned. I almost laughed at the absurdity of it. He thought Heydrich and I . . . how could he? How could he? I could easily set that straight, and I hurried to the door to catch him. If only he had asked me or been clearer or I had been brighter.

I stood on the front porch and peered through the darkness. A small car was just pulling away from the curb and I ran down the brick path to the gate.

"Christian, wait," I called, but the car sped away, its headlights flashing on the snowy trees and fences of the dark suburban street. It was very cold. I looked up at the sky. The stars were clear and crisp, the moon a delicate sliver of silver. It was a beautiful winter night and I started to cry, holding on to the top of the wooden gate.

I didn't hear anyone behind me until he spoke. Heydrich had come to see how the reunion was going.

"What is it?" he said.

I shook my head. How could I tell him what Christian thought about us? He'd laugh at me.

"Come along," he said. "You'd better come in."

But I shook my head again. I didn't want to go back to the party. I wanted to die. Or at least go home.

"Aren't you freezing?" he said patiently. I nodded. "Then come in."

"I don't want to. Please, you go. I'll be along."

He expelled a breath in exasperation. "You really are most irritating." I wasn't facing him so I heard rather than saw him unbutton his coat, take it off, and put it over my shoulders. "You can return it to me when you decide to come inside," he said, and walked away.

I hugged the coat around me, folding my hands into it. It smelled of the tart, lemony after-shave he used. "Thank you," I said.

Then, "General?" I heard his footsteps stop.

"Yes," he said. His voice sounded very far away in the silent cold darkness.

I turned to face him. Away to the left, I could see the warm glow through the curtained windows of the sitting room.

"Christian doesn't want to see me. He wasn't glad to see me at all," I said in a rush and started to cry again, lowering my face into his coat.

After a moment, Heydrich walked forward and put his arms loosely around me, holding me, but keeping us separate. I dropped my head into my hands and it rested against his chest.

"I'm sorry," I said, "I'm sorry." He was silent and I pulled back so I could speak more clearly. "He told me he didn't want to see me because of you. Because you are his boss and it would jeopardize his career and it was so hard to get. And it's all mixed up with his family and his father's death. Did you know Professor Mayr shot himself in the mouth? Oh, God, I thought he'd be as happy to see me as I was to see him." I paused for a moment. "I've loved him all my life and he doesn't want to see me because he thinks there's something going on between you and me."

"Us?" The general's voice was calm.

"Yes, isn't it stupid?" I took a step back from him, out of his arms. "As though that were possible. You're so much older and married and there's never even been a hint of anything romantic between us, has there."

I looked at his face, although I couldn't see his features. His white shirt gleamed in the dark, emphasizing his stillness. I wished very much I could see his face so I could understand what he thought about what I had just said. Was he insulted or amused or angry? By his silence, I did not think he was amused. Had I gotten Christian into trouble?

"You aren't angry at him, are you?" I said, my voice sounding small and young. "I haven't gotten him in trouble, have I?"

"No," he said, as calmly as before, "you haven't gotten him into trouble." He reached out a hand, hesitated, then gently touched my cheek. "Come inside. I'm freezing. I want a drink. We can talk about this . . . misunderstanding. Come." His hand dropped to my shoulder and I let him lead me back up the walk into the house.

The fire was going in the dining room in preparation for the next phase of the party. I glanced at the clock on the mantel. It was eleven forty-five, much later than I had expected. I walked to the fireplace, stretching my hands out toward the heat. I was very cold.

The general went to the swinging door, pushed it open and asked someone for brandy. It was brought to him and he carried a glass to me.

"Here," I said, holding out his jacket to him. "Thank you." He inclined his head and, placing his glass on the mantel, put the jacket on, buttoning it, patting the lapels into place, and checking to make sure his cuffs showed the proper amount of white shirt. I carried out my own repairs, taking from my small handbag a comb, a handkerchief, a tiny compact, and a lipstick. I used them all and felt better afterward.

"So," he said, sipping his brandy, "your reunion with your childhood friend was not as you expected. I suggest that perhaps you romanticized this meeting."

"Perhaps," I said reluctantly. We stood side by side, our backs to the fire, our brandy glasses in our hands.

"Nevertheless, I will agree that this idea of his of our love affair needs to be dealt with." He mocked the words *love affair*.

211

"Although," he continued with a wry smile, "I do not think it such a ridiculous notion as you seem to. I am not that much older than you."

My relief at his little joke must have been quite visible. He turned his face forward and, bringing his brandy glass up, paused before drinking from it. "I ought to feel insulted by your attitude," he said, and took a sip. "But I don't. Now, you will agree that I have never shown you the slightest romantic overture. Always treating you as a friend and even acting as a protector."

I nodded, and he continued. "I have always been aware of your status as the daughter of the diplomat of a powerful nation, and I have also been aware that you have not had the slightest interest in me other than a sort of . . . fascination, fueled, I am sure, by your knowledge of my position as head of the secret service. Still, I think we may continue to be friends."

I ducked my head, studying the bottom of my brandy glass.

"I know young Mayr well," he continued. "I recruited him a year ago, straight from the university. He is good at what he does. And no, he does not beat up Jews. He works in an office. He has a secretary. He is not special, although he is very good-looking. And he is from a good German family. I would, if I were your father, much prefer you to take up with him, than Mr. Wohl.

"Now, before everyone tumbles in here—I shall speak to your young friend, and assure him that my feelings toward you are—what is that wonderful word—avuncular? Yes, avuncular. And that he is dishonoring you by imagining anything more."

"Don't you think that's a little strong?" I said. His tone of voice was disturbing, thin and tight and ironic. "I wouldn't feel dishonored if I were in love with you." I hoped to disarm him, though I didn't appreciate his comment about David Wohl.

"A nice compliment. Thank you. It is appreciated," he said and drank the last of his brandy.

The door to the hall opened and Lina entered, Paul in her arms, followed by the guests. She looked at us but said nothing. Then the waiters entered, laden with trays of food and drink.

"Darling," called Lina, "you forgot to light the tree candles." She caressed her son's hair with her cheek. Heydrich, saying nothing, smiled at the boy and went to take care of the tree. "Things didn't go well?" Lina asked, and I shook my head. "Reinhard will take care of it."

"So he says."

TEA WITH THE CHANCELLOR

The New Year's season brought another round of parties, which at least kept me—and my father—busy and kept me from brooding about the unsuccessful meeting with Christian. I decided that I would enjoy myself. I was the daughter of the Ambassador of the United States to the Third Reich and I would enjoy myself. I danced and flirted with the men and was polite and well-mannered with the women and found myself to be popular. I was invited to all the parties, including a huge, flamboyant New Year's ball given at the Italian embassy, at which I danced with the general. I hadn't expected to see him; he hadn't expected to attend.

"My boss is better at this," he told me, referring to the clerkish Reichsminister-SS, Heinrich Himmler. "Usually I get him to go."

"Don't you like company? Being in society?"

"No." He looked down at me. "Pretty dress," he said, almost to himself.

"Thank you."

"I'd rather stay behind the scenes."

"Not attracting attention."

"That's it," he said and I realized he was absolutely serious.

Sydney asked what had happened with Christian, and I had flippantly told her an abridged version of the disastrous reunion. How could I care so much, I asked her, when I hadn't seen him in years, when he had turned out to be such a prig?

But to myself, I had to admit finally that I had set great store on seeing my childhood friend again and the tall, cold stranger he had turned into had disappointed me mightily.

Toward the end of January I spent another pleasant musical evening at the Heydrich house, playing Strauss. The general was taking Lina and Paul to his parents' home for a short holiday and the party was a small send-off to their vacation.

Heydrich's behavior toward me was as correct as it had always been, and we stayed away from any personal topics. Until, taking advantage of a moment when he was helping me into my coat as I was leaving, he told me that he had talked to Christian.

"When?" I asked, eagerly, turning to face him. "What did he say?"

"Last week. Nothing. I can't order him to see you, Sally."

"No, of course not. Well"—I shrugged, covering my disappointment—"I guess that's it."

"Yes," he said, stepping back from me.

"Thank you, General, for trying."

He nodded and started to turn away, then, noticing he had my music case in his hands, stared down at it. "You never call me by my name. Have you noticed that?"

"Oh." It was all I could think of to say.

"Am I so impersonal?"

"No. Yes. I'm sorry. You are a formal person. At least to me. It goes with being avuncular," I said, cocking my head to see his reaction.

"Yes, of course, I forgot." And he thrust my music at me. "And there is the boy to be gotten over, I suppose?" His voice was thin and sharp, like the dagger he wore with his dress uniform.

"Yes, the boy," I laughed, holding my case in front of me like a shield against his words.

That might have been it, except for the Chancellor of Germany and a visit I made to Munich.

I was introduced to Hitler for the first time during the holiday season, when I was presented to him at a huge reception for the diplomatic corps. The Chancellor had bowed over my hand, said something pleasant, and I had moved on.

Then Daddy and I went to Munich at the end of February, for a holiday. The weather was freezing but clear, and one afternoon, while Daddy was napping in his room, I went out for a walk. I came upon a small crowd of people standing outside a restaurant. I approached the crowd cautiously, not wanting to backtrack around the block, and relaxed when I sensed how happy and excited they were. I learned that they were expecting their Führer on a sentimental visit to a favorite haunt of the old days.

The motorcade arrived; the SS guards jumped out to hold back the crowd; and the Führer and his companions climbed out. Hitler, in a dumpy brown coat and a brown felt hat, smiled and waved at the crowds. He looked very happy and relaxed.

Someone in front of me yelled out Hitler's name. I was on tiptoe, trying to see what was going on, and when Hitler turned around at the sound of the man's voice, he saw me. And recognized me. He made a small gesture, causing an aide to appear at his shoulder, and, glancing back at me, whispered to him.

214

The members of the crowd around me eyed me speculatively, probably wondering who the hell I was. I was wondering if I should quietly back out of the way, although my curiosity held me to the spot. The Chancellor continued into the restaurant and I turned to go when I found the aide, a young SS man, at my side.

"Fräulein Sally Jackson," he said, bowing and clicking his heels. "The Führer presents his compliments and invites you to take tea with him."

"Oh," I said. It surprised me that not only had Hitler recognized me, but he had remembered my first name. "Thank you," I said to the handsome young man, who smiled at me and offered his arm. I took it and he led me through the dispersing crowd into the restaurant.

The Chancellor's party—about a dozen people—were arranging themselves around two large round tables at one end of the second room. The tables were on a sort of platform set off by a balustrade. Waiters, wearing knee pants under their red aprons, were scurrying around to the orders of a man in a green loden coat, who must have been the owner.

My escort brought me to the Chancellor's table, where there seemed to be no seats left. The company was all men, except for a small, pretty blonde who sat at the second table.

"My Führer," said my escort, "Fräulein Sally Jackson."

The Chancellor stood, causing all the other men at his table to follow suit. "How nice of you to join us, Fräulein," he said. "Please, have this seat." He gestured at Hess, who sat next to him, to move. Hess, in turn, motioned a heavyset, balding man out of his chair.

I said something polite and appropriate as the heavy man, who looked very much like a mean peasant, stood behind me and pushed my chair in for me. He went away, for which I was grateful, and got a chair at the other table, but I noticed he kept an eye on us.

The Chancellor introduced me to our tablemates, although I can't remember anyone beside Rudolf Hess, whom I had seen on newsreels, and Heinrich Hoffmann, the photographer.

"I have enjoyed meeting your esteemed father," said my host. "He is a learned and well-spoken man."

"Thank you," I said, "I know he will enjoy hearing that." Daddy would, too. He had once been kept waiting by the Chancellor, and although the slight did not offend him personally, he was extremely angry about the snub to the representative of the United States. But, he told me, it was indicative of the way the Nazis treated the United States, alternatively wooing and insulting us.

A waiter brought pots of tea, coffee, and chocolate. Hitler, who was served first, took hot chocolate, and I had a cup of coffee. Next came trays of cakes, sandwiches, and pastry. I took a plain-looking sandwich.

"Oh, no, my dear young lady," cried the Chancellor. "You must have more than that one." He snapped his fingers and the waiter returned.

"Please, sir," I said, smiling. "I had a very late lunch. You must understand I did not expect to be having this tea."

"I see. But I also know that you modern women are all starving yourselves in order to be fashionable." He laughed. "For myself, I like women who are sturdy, and who like their tea cakes," he said, lowering his voice as though he were imparting a secret. "But I will not insist." And he waved the tray away.

Pulling the white porcelain sugar bowl to him, he spooned two teaspoons of sugar into his chocolate. "I must say, Fräulein," he continued, after a satisfied taste of his concoction, "I am impressed at how well you speak German."

"Thank you, I appreciate such compliments because yours is a difficult language."

"Is it?" he said, pausing for a moment. "This must be why so few foreigners take the trouble to learn it well, although I know many Germans who speak English or French extremely well."

He fell silent, becoming engrossed with ladling whipped cream onto his éclair. The gentleman to my left leaned forward.

"Where are you from in the United States, Fräulein?" he said. He spoke loud enough for Hitler to hear and I understood he was keeping the conversational ball rolling for his Führer.

"California—San Francisco."

"Is this so?" said Hitler, putting down his fork. He turned in his chair to face me and fixed me with his pale eyes. He slapped the table. "I have read every one of Karl May's wonderful stories about the American West. Did you know that?" He didn't wait for an answer, but hurried on. "I read them as a boy and after I had read them, I played them out. Can you imagine? But, what fun it was! I have never forgotten the excitement of those stories—the cowboys, the wagon trains, the Indians. Especially the Indians—ah." He shook his head in nostalgic remembrance. "Old Shatterhand. He was a friend to me."

Someone across the table, which had become silent during his little speech, asked, "Did you wear a feather, my Führer?"

"A feather?" said Hitler, looking up sharply, searching for an insult. "Oh, no. I was a cowboy—always." Relieved, the company laughed. People at the second table were turning in their chairs, craning their necks to see and hear what was going on.

Hitler continued, "I like best, I think, the beautiful descriptions of the canyons and prairies. And of the snow-covered mountains. I have always loved nature, you know, and I thought of myself alone under the vast sky. In the times of struggle, I admit, yes, I will admit, that I sometimes cheered myself thinking of Old Shatterhand, of how he had persevered in spite of the dangers."

The monologue continued in that vein, and I managed to keep smiling and nodding and drinking my coffee while the Chancellor of Germany waxed on and on about the beauties of a West created by a writer who had never seen it.

I studied Hitler as he talked. He was an ordinary-looking, middle-aged man, unremarkable except for the odd little mustache and his pale, piercing eyes. The mustache, of course, had already amused me and his eyes had been staring out at me from posters plastered on every kiosk throughout the city, but I was surprised by the beauty of his hands and the graceful way he used them. They were an anomaly on his middle-aged body.

Thoroughly bored and needing to go the ladies' room, I sneaked a look at my watch and saw I also had to get to the hotel to meet my father. I was wondering how I was going to free myself when an SS man, an officer, entered the room and came toward our party. He leaned over to speak to the aide who had shown me in and who was seated at the other table. When he stood up straight, I got a good look at him. It was Christian.

"But California, Fräulein," Hitler was saying, moving, finally, on to another topic. "California is surely not the true West. After all, Hollywood is in California. Can there be any cultures further apart than the prairies and Hollywood?" He asked this of the whole table, who obligingly laughed at the irony of his comment.

"But one thing I do want to know is this—have you ever seen a real wild Indian?" asked the Chancellor, leaning toward me again.

"No, not really," I admitted, trying to keep an eye on Christian.

"No? What a shame." He paused, noticing the other conversation. "What is it?" he called, obviously irritated. The seated SS officer looked up, then stood and hurried over to Hitler, Christian following at a respectful distance. The officer leaned toward his Führer and they whispered. The rest of the party at the table talked quietly among themselves, trying to look as though they didn't care. The whispered conversation came to an end.

Hitler, turning to face the rest of us, sighed. "I wish Heinrich would not bother me when I'm trying to relax. Am I never again to be allowed these precious moments, just to talk and be with friends?"

He was actually sulking, one arm stretched out on the table, his head dropping, the famous dark lock of hair over his forehead. He stared for a long minute at the tablecloth, then, picking up a crumb, popped it into his mouth. Quickly, he pushed his chair back and stood. Christian and the other officer slammed into a heel-clicking, arm-wrenching salute, which was ignored, because when the Chancellor pushed his chair back, he had bumped my chair, making me jog the elbow of the man next to me and, in turn, causing him to spill almost the entire glass of water he was drinking over himself and me.

I leapt up. He did too. Hitler jumped out of the way. Everyone at the table jumped up. Everyone at the other table jumped up. For all I know, the entire restaurant did. Waiters flew forward with napkins and towels. My damp tablemate whipped out a huge white handkerchief.

"Please, Fräulein, I am desolate," said the Chancellor, raising his hands, as though he feared being soaked himself.

I smiled at him. "It's nothing. Please. It's only water." I looked down at my suit. I was very wet. "I think I'd better get back to my hotel. They can dry and press my suit there."

A storm of apologies, protests, and remedies broke out. The entire situation was becoming farcical and I didn't know whether to laugh or yell at them all to shut up. In spite of the confusion, I noticed that Christian was gone.

The young woman from the other table appeared at my elbow. "Come," she said, "let me take you to the ladies' room." I gratefully retreated with her.

She was my age, with a round face and merry blue eyes. Her only makeup was lipstick and her hair was loosely pulled back into a roll at the nape of her neck. A black felt hat that sported two flat daisies sat over one eye, and she was dressed in a becoming black-and-white-patterned long-sleeved dress with a wide, embroidered collar and black patent leather belt. She looked like a shop girl with little money but lots of style.

When we got into the ladies' room, she turned to me and, holding out her hand, almost shyly, she introduced herself. "I am Eva Braun."

"Sally Jackson," I replied, shaking hands with her, noticing her nails were very well groomed. Mine never were.

"You're American?" She opened her bag and pulled out a pack of cigarettes, holding them out to me.

"Yes," I said, shaking my head to the cigarettes. "And thanks

218

for helping, although I really think I should go to the hotel and get out of this skirt."

"I hope it is not ruined." She handed me a hand towel, and the washroom attendant came over with several more. "It is very smart."

"Thank you. It's wool, it ought to be okay," I said, using the towel to blot up whatever water I could. I was wet through to my skin.

"Okay," she said. "I've heard that expression in American films?"

"Probably."

"It means all right or fine?"

"Yes."

She smiled. "Okay," she repeated. "My first American word." She had her purse with her and opened it, moving to the mirror. The room was narrow and badly lit. Eva fussed with her hair, her cigarette hanging from her red lips. "My hair is a mess. I wish I could bleach it, but he wouldn't like it. Men. What do they know." She giggled. "Do you perm yours?"

"No. This is all my own curl."

"You're lucky. I'm fussing with mine all the time."

"Well, I think mine is too curly."

"Oh, no, it's wavy. And very pretty."

"Thank you. I guess we're never satisfied with what we've got."

"That's what he always says," she said, giggling. "Is your suit going to be okay?" She smiled when she said her new word.

"It is," I said, handing the towel to the attendant and fishing in my bag for a coin to put in her saucer.

Finishing her cigarette, Eva walked to the stall and tossed it in. Then she fished in her bag for a mint.

"He doesn't like me to smoke," she said, snapping her bag shut. "We have been in here long enough to make those men feel better. I hope you realize I only dragged you in here to get you away from them. They were all behaving so helplessly. They're so impractical, aren't they?"

"You rescued me," I said. "Thank you."

She paused, her hand on the doorknob. "Okay?" she said, and laughed.

"Now," she asked as we reentered the restaurant, "do you have a car?" I shook my head, not looking at her, searching for Christian. She must have followed my look. "Looking for the handsome one?"

"Oh, no," I said quickly. "I thought I knew him, but I must have been mistaken."

"Well, you ought to meet him. I wonder if . . . let me see what

I can do. That would be so romantic, if you met at the Führer's tea table."

When we reached the table, she went to the heavyset man and spoke to him. My attention was taken up with trying to extricate myself from the party without offending anyone. The man Eva had spoken to whispered to the Chancellor.

"Good," he said emphatically. Hitler turned to me. "Fräulein Jackson, we have a car to take you to your hotel." Eva, back in her seat at the second table, nodded at me. The arrangements were made and I was escorted out to the sidewalk.

Christian was in the passenger's seat in the front, another uniformed man in the driver's spot. He wore a kepi, the distinctive cap of the SA. Christian was arguing with the Chancellor's aide, who stood by the car.

"I'm under orders from Reichsführer Himmler," Christian said.

"This is a Führer order, Obersturmführer, it supersedes all others," snapped the aide and wheeled around to go back into the restaurant.

"We don't have time to ferry girls around," Christian muttered as I came up to the car.

"Even me?" I said. Christian's expression was a perfect example of shock and surprise. I was very pleased. He made a move to get out of the car. "Don't bother," I said, opening the door myself.

"Surprise, surprise," I said in English, then very politely told the driver the name of my hotel and we started off. Christian was still silent.

"I'm Sally Jackson," I said to the driver. His eyes met mine in the rearview mirror. He grinned. He had a very short haircut and looked bald under his kepi-style hat. But his cheeks were rosy and his eyebrows black crescents above brown eyes.

"Hans Behrends," he said.

"You are not SS?"

"Not bloody likely. SA. Unlike my pansy friend here, who started with the men and went over to those intellectuals and pretty soldier boys in the SS. Eh, Mayr?" From his bantering tone, I could tell this was a subject they had gone on at each other about before.

"Shut up, Hans," said Christian. "We have an important passenger here. A girlfriend of the high and mighty. Let's just deliver her as ordered."

"Is he telling the truth?" Hans asked, his eyes again on mine via the rearview mirror. "Are you really somebody important's girl?"

"No," I snapped.

"Then what were you doing there?" asked Christian.

"Tell me, Hans," I said, folding my arms along the front seat between the two young men. "Do you fellows in the SA condemn people, friends, without listening to their side of it?"

"Of course not, but that's the SS for you," remarked Hans. "It's all that time they spend on their tailoring. Weakens whatever brains they had. Which wasn't much."

"All right," Christian protested. "All right."

I leaned back against the backseat. "I'm not talking to you," I said imperiously. "I'm talking to Hans. Go on, Hans, tell me what you think."

"Not me," he said, laughing. "I don't know what's going on here, but I know enough not to get involved."

"You will agree that making such accusations is quite dishonorable," I said.

"I will," he agreed.

"Dishonorable," said Christian. "It's not at all."

"Oh," I said, leaning forward, "then how would you describe it, Rottenführer Mayr?" I knew he'd understand the English insult.

"You were always a bratty, irrational kid," he said. "And you haven't changed a bit."

"Haven't I?" I said calmly, giving him a superior smile.

He looked at me, then letting his eyes travel down my wet skirt, said slowly, with a sly smile, "Yeah, you're still as sloppy as ever."

"Oh!" I yelled, and hit him on the head and shoulders with my purse. He laughed and yelled for me to stop, holding his hands up and ducking his head. I knocked his cap off.

"Hold on, you two," cried Hans, pulling the car to the side of the street, "you're going to get us killed, which I wouldn't mind, but I'm fond of my old car here." He switched off the ignition and watched Christian scrambling for his cap. "I take it you know each other?"

"Oh, yes, we certainly do," said Christian, shaking his cap, running his sleeve across the shiny bill.

"That is a matter of interpretation," I said.

"No, I recognize your uppercut," said Christian. I feigned another hit and he cringed. "What a violent girl you are. Always were. Have to be careful what you say to her, she'll beat you up," he said to Hans. "You'd never think it, she looks so sweet and feminine." They both turned to look at me. I made a face at them.

"Well," said Hans, "now that we're all such good pals, why don't we go drink some beer. That is, if you'd like to, Fräulein. The Führer order was to deliver you wherever you wanted to go."

Christian remained silent, intent on polishing the bill of his cap.

"All right, but I need to go to the hotel and change." And let my father know, I added to myself.

At the hotel, Christian got out and opened the door for me. We walked up the steps together and into the lobby. It was a small, exclusive, utterly respectable place and people turned to look as we entered. We walked in silence across the lobby toward the elevator.

"You want to come up?" I gestured toward the open door. The boy stood, bored, waiting, in it.

"All right." And Christian followed me into the elevator.

"Sally," he said, touching my arm lightly. He stood behind me as we faced the doors. "I am sorry."

"What you thought was wrong," I said quietly.

"Well, when I saw you at the fencing match . . ."

"You saw me there? Why didn't you say something?"

"You know why. I thought . . ."

"That's no excuse." I noticed the elevator boy watching us and held my next question until we got out of the car on my floor. "Christian, are you afraid of Heydrich?"

Christian came to a stop and, holding his cap in his right hand, studied the silver trim as though he had never seen it before. "Don't be silly. He's my boss. If he were your . . . if you were his girlfriend, I wouldn't dare interfere." He buffed the bill again.

"Stop playing with that hat. Did he order you to come to the party?" I said, taking a step toward him.

"He did. I was very angry about it. I was very busy that week. Doing a special officer's course. I've just been promoted."

"Congratulations. Did he speak to you afterward? He told me he would clear things up. What's your rank?"

"Obersturmführer. A lieutenant in English. And no, he did not speak to me about you. In fact, I haven't seen him in several weeks."

"Then he lied to me. Why would he lie to me? I thought he liked me, that we were friends."

"I was away. Maybe he tried and couldn't find me." He suddenly grinned at me. "I was glad to see you."

"Was?"

"Am," he said, and I grinned back.

"Christian." I reached out to touch his sleeve. "You really don't believe that Heydrich is anything to me, do you? Now that you've talked to me?"

"No."

I breathed a great sigh of relief. "Thank you," I said. We smiled at each other again, and for a moment I was totally unaware of the hall around us.

Hans was a delightful, funny companion. He wasn't at all handsome, but so full of humor about everything, even the SA, even the National Socialists, that I grew very fond of him in the few hours we three spent drinking beer together.

But Christian . . . Christian was quieter, with less to say, and my impression of his seriousness was proved correct. He was a serious person. His sense of humor was there, but buried, and he was slow to laugh, although he was obviously fond of his friend. Underneath his pleasant good mood was a sadness, and, remembering his father's suicide, the scattering of his family, I thought I understood why.

"This is great," I said, starting on my second beer. "Thank you for bringing me." The steins were huge and the boys had each drunk two to my one. This beer hall was smaller than the huge one I had been to in Nuremberg, with low ceilings and multilevels complete with carved railings and screens. A vine, one with pretty shiny leaves, had been trained to snake its way along the ceiling, in and out of the carvings. We sat in an alcove, at a round table with built-in benches, in front of a mullioned window that looked out at the early evening traffic. It seemed as though spring had come early, and the golden light bathed the two young men, one next to me, one opposite, in its friendly glow.

"My pleasure," said Hans. "Believe me, you must be pretty special to get Mayr into a bar. He wouldn't come if I asked him. You know why? Because he's working all the time."

"He's gotten to be so serious. He didn't use to be," I said, mocking Christian, but meaning it.

"He's always been, as long as I've known him, which has been a couple of years now."

"We live in serious times," said Christian, draining his beer stein.

"Are you kidding?" yelled Hans. "These are glorious times. Exciting. On the move. Boy, I'll tell you. We should be happy—Sally, I keep telling him this, but he won't listen—we should be happy and privileged to live now. Look at us, I'm a farmer's kid, no school past eighth grade, no prospects, the old man's farm gone bust . . ."

"And what are you doing now in the SA, Hans? Playing chauffeur," Christian said, interrupting. "I keep trying to get him to join us," he added to me. "The SS is where careers are made. The SA was fine, is fine, for the past, but you're all a bunch of street bullies, good for nothing but bashing people's heads."

223

"Hey, watch it, sidewalk soldier."

"That's all window dressing. And you know I never was in the LAH. The Leibstandarte Adolf Hitler," he said, turning to me. "The Führer's bodyguard."

"Yeah, they wouldn't have you. Probably would get blisters in your pretty boots."

"Oh, give it a rest, Hans."

Hans fell quiet, hearing something in Christian's voice. His eyes flicked to me, and he smiled, a flirtatious, mischievous smile. "So, you live in Berlin?" he asked.

Christian grunted in exasperation and sat back. "I need another beer," he said and raised his hand. The barmaid, a young, plump redhead covered with freckles, appeared almost instantly.

"Yes, Herr Oberst," she said, bending to pick up the old steins, allowing the three of us a fair glimpse of her plump, freckled cleavage.

"Another score, Herr Oberst," teased Hans. "You come with me, Sally. We'll leave our pal here with his newest conquest."

"You'll have to get past me," said Christian good-naturedly, sitting low on his bottom, his legs stretched out under the table.

"You'd risk dirtying your pretty uniform?" cried Hans. "I abdicate. I'll take the barmaid, she's more my type. No offense, Sally." And he stood up, bending over, grabbed my hand, kissed it and nearly jumped out of the booth.

"He's crazy," I said, laughing.

"Yeah," laughed Christian.

"I like him. He's fun."

"He's a good friend. We even lived together for a time. Before I was sent to Bad Tolz—officer's training school," he added when he saw my blank expression.

We fell silent. "Do you want another . . ." He gestured at my beer stein, which was still not empty.

"No. I'm fine. I should . . ." I raised my arm to look at my wristwatch. "My father will wonder . . ."

"Of course. I'll take you back."

In front of the hotel, in the blue dusk, Christian walked me up the steps, under the archways. It had grown colder as the sun set, and felt more like February again.

He said good-bye formally, touching his forefinger to the bill of his cap.

"Wait," I said. "Will you call me?"

He looked at me with that serious, steady look, then smiled, making my heart jump. "Of course I will. I know where you are, don't I?" He reached his hand out to me, as though he would touch my face, moving instead to pat my shoulder. "I have to move the car." I nodded. "Give my regards to your father. I look forward to seeing him again." And he was gone, taking the steps two, three at a time with his long legs. I stood and watched the little car pull away.

When I turned to make my way through the revolving door, I felt I had been ambushed by that last smile. I looked down, surprised at my shaking hands.

FATHER SPEAKS UP

S ally, *Tierce*," cried Maestro, impatiently slapping my blade away.
"We stop!" he said, and pulled his helmet off. I could see he was
angry and it upset me. He had always been patient with my mistakes.

"Please, Fräulein, you go home. I can see your mind is not on
your fencing. You are atrocious today. No timing. No strength. You
are staying out too late dancing, no doubt. You have no dedication.
No one does today," he said, turning and stalking out of the hall.

I stood where I was and watched him leave, not really sorry he
had called my lesson off. I was tired, and partly for the reason he
had said. I was staying out too late, but I was not enjoying myself.
Most of the time. Last night, my father and I had had dinner at the
Adlon with a group of Americans, including a senator from home,
and the men had talked politics the entire time. I had spent the evening trapped by their wives, all of them middle-aged and stiffly cor-
seted, trying to keep my head above the discussions of maids and
casserole receipts and how dirty everything was in Europe.

I swished my blade through the air, once, twice. I lunged,
imagining I was running some grande dame through. I stayed too
long in the lunge and lost the impetus to pull myself out of it. Letting go, I sat down on the floor. It was an extremely clumsy movement, and I laughed at the spectacle I must have made of myself. I
held my blade up to be sure I hadn't bent it, then got up and, my
burst of energy over, listlessly wandered out of the hall to the changing room.

I had to admit the maestro was right. I wasn't concentrating
on the fencing because I was thinking about the afternoon ahead,
which I planned to spend with Christian, skating. It was our first
meeting since Munich and I was excited and a little nervous.

Showered, brushed, and dressed, tiredness gone, I ran down
the stairs into the day. It was sunny and windy, with clouds scuttling
past high above the city. The air smelled and felt cool and fresh.
Spring!

I looked at my watch. I had an hour before I was to meet Christian here in front of the salle. So I went to the nearby coffee bar and
there, sitting in the sunshine in the big window, reading a two-day-

old copy of the *Herald-Tribune*, his hat on the back of his head, was David.

I knocked on the window next to his head, startling him. He laughed and waved at me to come in. Inside, the bar smelled of coffee and chocolate. I ordered and went to David's table.

"Hi, there, stranger," he said, getting up slightly.

I waved him down and sat, pulling off my coat and hat and gloves. "Hello. It has been a long time. Where've you been?"

"Here. Where've you been?"

"I've been spending a lot of time at parties. Went to Munich." I leaned forward and whispered dramatically, "I met the Führer."

"No!"

"Shared a pot of chocolate. Wish I had one now," I said, leaning back, looking around to see how my order was doing. "Today Maestro said I was so bad because I'd been dancing all night. Wish he'd been right. You should have seen the group of our fellow citizens I was with last night. David, they shouldn't let such people out of the country."

"Why don't you ask your dad to let up on you. You're just a kid."

"Yes, but I'm also useless, so I feel I ought to do something to justify my existence."

"And boring parties do?"

"No, but I am working for my board, aren't I? And it's not all boring parties."

"Speaking of which, are you still having your musicales with the cozy chief of the secret police and the cozy head of naval intelligence? Boy, too bad you're not a spy. Say, that's not a bad idea. Has anyone approached you?"

"You're such a jerk. I'm starving. Where's my order?" I turned again to look and see what the counterman was up to, then turned back to David. "And yes, I have been playing music, but mostly with the general."

"Herr Obergruppenführer himself. What an honor."

"Fräulein!" called the counterman, and I got up to get my coffee and bun.

"Are we going to fight? Because if we are," I said, overriding him, "I'm moving. I feel too good today." I took a big bite of the bun, which was gooey with jam, and licked my fingers.

David laughed and reached across the table. "Here, you missed a spot." He wiped my cheek with the little paper napkin.

"Thanks."

"Don't you fence on Saturday mornings?"

"I was, but Maestro threw me out. Said I wasn't concentrating."

"Weren't you?" He had returned to his paper, sitting sideways to the little table. I couldn't read the headlines. The NRA and Roosevelt something something.

"No. Doesn't the States seem far away?" I said to him.

"What? Oh. Yeah. Well, it is."

"All those people out of work. Do you think Roosevelt can really help?"

"God, I hope so." He drank some of his coffee, really looking at me for the first time. "You do look happy. You must be in love or something." He started reading his paper again, and didn't see me blush.

I picked up my coffee cup, my elbows on the table. "Or something," I muttered.

"Oh, yeah? Who's the guy? Anyone I know?"

I didn't answer. I wanted his full attention, although I wasn't sure about the wisdom of telling David my news. I wasn't even sure what the news was. Just that I was happy. I was seeing Christian, who had finally smiled at me with something of the warmth of his old smile, and I was happy.

"You mean it." David finally lowered the paper. "You are in love."

"No, I'm not."

"Who is he?" A horrified expression started to spread across his face. "Not Herr SS-Ober—"

"Oh, David. Honestly. Heydrich's married. And at least thirty."

"And a fascist and the head of the secret police."

"David!"

"What? You don't want me to mention that? Am I being impolite? Undiplomatic?" He smiled when he spoke, but there was anger in his eyes. Had been ever since I rapped on the window. It took a moment for the truth to sink in: he was angry with me.

"No. You're not. You're right. I'm sorry. I didn't mean it that way. I just . . . you're my friend, aren't you? Aren't you?"

"Yeah. Sure. So, who's the guy? Go on, torture me."

"He's that old friend of mine, the one I've known forever. I told you about him. I just met him again, ran into him in Munich. And I'm meeting him in about half an hour to go skating and have tea at the big ice rink in the Tiergarten. That's why I'm happy. Because it'll be fun. Not a chore. Now, why are you mad at me?"

"I'm not," he said, and got up and went to order himself another coffee.

"Yes, you are," I said, when he came back. He took a long time to answer, putting four sugar cubes into his coffee and a big dollop of cream, stirring it, sipping it, carefully laying the spoon down.

"I'm not mad at you, Sally." He smiled. "Honest. Tell me about the guy, what's his name—Christian? See, I remembered. Is he a student? What's he do? How'd you run into him in Munich? With the Führer?"

"Well, yes. Sort of." I told him about the tea party and the accident and the blonde in the bathroom, whom, to my disappointment, David had already heard about, and explained how Christian's car became my limousine. "And so he and I, and his friend, Hans, who is in the SA, but seemed a nice fellow, went and had a beer."

David looked up from his cup at me, suddenly, his brown eyes intently studying my face. "In the SA? And your friend? Delivering messages—and girls—is he a storm trooper too?"

I froze. Opened my mouth. Closed it. Looked out the window, then back at the table, at the bar. "No-o-o," I said.

"Sally. Tell me. Your dear, long-lost friend of your childhood bosom is . . . in the navy! The Wehrmacht. Or maybe he's just an ordinary cop. No? Well, what?"

"Shut up, David. Just shut up," I whispered, almost hissing at him, leaning across the table. "Yes, he's in the SS. There, are you happy?"

"No. No, I'm not happy. Not happy at all." He slouched back, his legs stuck out into the aisle. There weren't many customers in the little café, but a man and woman looked up at us.

"SS. Your friend, your dear pal, the guy you've been mooning about all these years, is in the SS? I don't believe it."

"I haven't been mooning," I said, trying to get a word in. He ignored me.

"I don't believe you can be so damned stupid. So goddamned naive. Don't you know anything? Don't you pay attention? Oh, Jesus, Sally, being cute and pretty is one thing, but it is finally no excuse for being stupid. I thought you were . . . oh, forget it. Just forget it." And he grabbed his coat and stormed out of the café, his yellow-and-red muffler streaming behind him.

I sat, stunned. No, I thought, no! I saw him walking quickly away, and I knew if he got away, he'd be gone from my life and I couldn't let that happen. I jumped up, grabbed my things, and ran after him.

I caught him at the end of the block. He was trudging along, his head bent, the battered old felt hat he'd been wearing all along pulled down over his face.

"David," I said softly. "Slow down, will you."

He stopped, but didn't look at me. I didn't know what to say and we both stood dumbly for several seconds, our hands in our coat pockets, staring in opposite directions down the street at the Saturday shoppers. I touched his sleeve.

"I don't mean . . ." I said.

"I know . . ." he said.

"I'm sorry if I offended you."

He laughed. "Don't be stupid. You haven't offended me. I'm just jealous. And I'm mad at myself because of it."

"I don't understand."

David looked at me for a long time before he answered. "Sally, I'm Jewish."

"It doesn't matter. Not to me."

"Maybe. Maybe. But it does matter to other people. These guys you spend so much time with."

"Christian's not anti-Semitic."

"Sally, he's in the SS. That's like saying a . . . a Jesuit doesn't believe in the Immaculate Conception!"

"But so what if Christian doesn't like you?"

"It's not a question of liking me. I don't care if he—"

"I like you. I'm not—"

"Thank you. But you're the same way. Believe me, this is something I know about." He turned away from me, the cold, bright sun hitting his face. He had tears in his eyes. I looked at him in wonder, overwhelmed at the hurt in his face.

"Oh, David, what have I done?"

"Nothing. Not really. Nothing. You've tried real hard."

"David, I don't believe Jews are less equal or less than human, like the Nazis do. I don't agree with that. It's stupid. Human beings should all have a chance."

He laughed. "You're a good little democrat, Sally. Well-raised by your broad-minded father, but I will note one thing for you. How come you've never asked me to go to one of those fancy dos with you? How come you haven't introduced me to your father? How come you've never invited me back to your house? How come, Sally?"

I stared at him, feeling the truth of what he said go right down to my toes. I felt almost sick. He was right. I raised my head.

"You're right. I didn't mean—"

"Nobody means to, Sally, especially you nice, well-brought-up ones who believe all men are actually equal," he said sadly and walked away.

"You could give me a chance," I said loudly. I heard him stop. "Here's what I'll do. I'll introduce you to my father. He isn't exactly a barrel of monkeys, but you're right. He should meet my friends, meet you. If you'll come to dinner on . . ." I thought quickly through the week. "Come on Tuesday. I'll ask Brian and Sydney too. I haven't introduced them to him either. He should meet all my friends."

I walked toward him. "David, will you do something for me?"

"What?" He took a few steps toward me. "What do you mean?"

"Will you meet Christian?"

"Sally."

"It's important to me. You're right about all the politics. I don't know anyone who is righter than you are. Except maybe my father. You two ought to have a lot in common. But you're also dismissing a friend of mine because of circumstances."

"Circumstances? Presumably he chose to be in the SS."

"Meet him. Just meet him. And," I added in a small voice, "let him meet you."

"You really like this guy?"

"I don't know—yes. I just met him again. I used to be crazy about him. Now, he's older. Serious. I don't know."

"Good-looking, I'll bet." I was glad to hear some of David's sarcastic humor creep back into his voice, but before I could answer, a voice called my name and I turned to find Christian coming up behind us. He wore a charcoal-gray suit over a dark-maroon sweater, his overcoat was a rough black-and-white tweed, and a pale-gray muffler was draped casually around his neck. He looked like a fashion plate.

"Bingo!" said David.

"Christian!" I said, a little too brightly. "Hello. Don't you look elegant. Where'd you come from? Is it time?"

"I'm early. I was walking to the address, and here you are."

"Yes. I ran into David. We were just talking. Christian Mayr, this is my friend . . ." I turned toward David, not sure what to expect.

"David Wohl," he said, putting out his hand.

Christian smiled and took it. "Christian Mayr." They shook and backed a step away from each other, measuring each other, leaving me in the middle.

"You're an American?" said Christian in his careful English.

"Yep. A New Yorker."

"Yes? I would like to go there someday."

"Great city. Berlin's a great city, too," David offered, being generous.

"Yes. You are here long?"

"Almost a year."

"I thought David could come with us. If it's all right." Christian looked disappointed, although he covered his feelings well. I was pleased that he was looking forward to spending the time alone with me, but I wanted to prove to David that Christian was not a bigot. "He's got nothing to do, and I'd love for my friends to get to know each other."

"Of course," said Christian. "We must all do as the lady desires. You will come with us, Mr. Wohl?"

"Call me David, and I wouldn't think of it," David said. "I'm sure you kids want to be alone."

"Come with us, please. It'll be fun," I pleaded, taking his hand. "I'll bet you're a great skater."

"I'm not bad," he said, allowing me to pull him forward. "You sure you won't mind?" he asked Christian.

"I'm pleased to meet an American friend of Sally's," Christian said politely.

"That's settled, then," I said, and stood between them, my hand tucked into the crook of each of their elbows. They both smiled down at me, and I could see they were indulging me. I didn't care. I didn't care if they were wary, circling each other. I didn't care if they really didn't like each other now. I just wanted them to let us have a good time, and then, maybe, they would like each other.

"I got thrown out of fencing," I said, to change the subject. We ended up walking all the way to the ice rink, talking about fencing and then about New York, and Christian and I told David about the lake. Well, I did most of the talking, and by the time we got to where we were going, we were starving, so we went straight into tea and wound up not skating at all.

Christian was very reserved, with that same seriousness I had noticed before. He was polite and interested, although, as the afternoon went on, he began to talk more. But there was always something distant about him, as though he was being very careful about his manners or about what he said. He loosened up most of all when David started talking about boxing. Knowing nothing about that sport, I couldn't contribute, but I felt I had done my best to carry the afternoon.

"I'll be right back," I said, standing up to go to the ladies' room. When I came back, David was gone and Christian was sitting slouched in his chair, one arm along the table, his fingers restlessly moving a salt cellar back and forth.

"What happened?" I said. "Where did David go?"

"He left. Let's go too, Sally. I've paid the bill." And he stood and shepherded me from the restaurant. In the foyer, as we adjusted our coats and mufflers and pulled on gloves, I asked him again.

"What happened? Did David have a meeting or something?"

"No." He slung his muffler around his neck. "I'm afraid I insulted him. I apologized, but he was angry and left."

"Why? What did you say?"

"I'm sorry, Sally. I didn't realize. I should have realized . . . from his name, but I just didn't expect it. I forget about foreigners."

I grabbed his arm. "Christian, what did you say? Something about the Jews, about David being Jewish?"

He looked embarrassed, he wouldn't meet my eyes, but he nodded. "I am sorry, Sally. I think we should go now." And he took my arm.

"Wait. Tell me what happened." I refused to budge.

"I'll show you. Come on." And he led me outside, down the steps leading down to stone pedestals that stood on either side of the walkway. "Look," he said, pointing, and there, half covered with vines, was a discreet sign: "No Jews Allowed."

I'd seen the signs, although they came and went, depending on the party policy. I'd ignored them. They didn't apply to me, and anyway, I was an American.

"Did you tell David he wasn't allowed in here?"

"No, of course, not. I'm not that . . ." He waved his arm, dismissing the idea. A couple got out of a cab just then, the man in military dress. So Christian took my arm and drew me away as they went up the path to the tearoom.

"He asked me about the restrictions, how bad I thought they would get. I told him I thought they were ridiculous, but they were spreading. 'Like here,' I said. 'Here?' he asked. And then I said something stupid like, 'Look around, you don't see any, do you?' I am sorry, Sally. I didn't mean . . ." Christian stopped and turned toward me. "Perhaps you can let him know. He is a good fellow, very funny and smart, and I enjoyed talking to him. Now I think it is getting late, so I should find you a taxi." And taking my arm again, he led me down the sidewalk.

"Christian, are you only upset because of the social situation? Do you care that he is Jewish? Did that offend you?" I spoke quietly, trying to look into his face in the darkening light. I wanted to understand this.

"Your friend is an intelligent, interesting fellow," he said, sounding almost irritated. "I can see why you like him. But there is more to it than his being or not being Jewish. Oh, how can you understand? You're a foreigner."

"Then tell me. Help me understand," I said.

He didn't answer me right away, but deliberated before he spoke. "You know how it was here. We almost had a revolution. The Communists nearly took over the country. I wanted to join the navy, but I was refused entry to Kiel because there was no space and my family knew no influential person. You see, to become an officer, you must already be a member of the elite—or, at least, know a member.

"I went to college, studying history, philosophy, English, anything I wanted because I knew it didn't matter. There would be no job for me when I came out. Except perhaps schoolteacher in some elementary school in some small boring town somewhere.

"Then Heydrich came to a class I was in, an English-literature class. He was looking for someone who could speak and read English well, and that's how I found my job. Or rather, it found me.

"It would be easier for me now to find a job, to join the navy, because the elite has changed. But now, I don't need to. I am a member of it. And I am also working for the betterment of my country as much as if I were in the navy. Perhaps more. So I am satisfied."

"I understand that, but—"

"I do not wish to talk about this anymore. It is late. It is getting very cold and I must go." And without another word, he walked me to the nearest taxi stand and packed me off.

In the taxi home, I decided I didn't like him very much. And he hadn't answered my question about the Jews.

I tried phoning David that evening, after dressing for dinner, but he wasn't anywhere to be found and I went into the piano room and played through the Haydn to cheer myself up.

When I got ahold of David the next day, he made a joke of the whole incident, not letting me apologize.

"So how's Heydrich?" he asked lightly.

"I don't know."

"You seeing him?"

"No plans." We were silent for a few moments, the sound of the wires in our ears. I knew what he was asking. I tried to answer him. "Christian's kind of a prig, isn't he? Didn't used to be."

234

"Well, people change, doll. You're probably different from the person he remembers."

"Oh, don't remind me." I laughed and reminded him of our dinner date.

I called Sydney to tell her all about what had happened and how cold Christian had become. I said I didn't think I wanted to see him again. She agreed that it was for the best. And, of course, she and Brian would love to come meet my father.

We had drinks in the music room and Daddy did his best to be sociable, although I'm afraid he treated us all like undergraduates. All through dinner, we were on our best behavior, Brian and David curbing their usual irreverence. When Daddy left us to go upstairs, we went back to the music room, pulled the sliding doors shut and played dance records. We felt as though we'd been let out of school. We had a good time, though, dancing and drinking a little too much.

After Sydney and Brian left, David and I sneaked into the kitchen to raid the icebox. The big room was dark except for a faint light coming through the long, rectangular window over the sink. I padded on stocking feet across the linoleum to the icebox and pulled it open. Moving things about, I looked for some ice cream.

The dress I was wearing was new. Full length, it had a flower pattern, violets and purples on black, and it was cut on the bias, close to my body, until it flared into a full skirt. The style was more sophisticated than I was used to wearing, with its scooped neck and back and fancy ruffled sleeves.

And as I leaned over to look in the icebox, David came up behind me and ran his hands along my sides. I jumped and jerked away.

"Sally, Sally, it's only me," he said, his hands on my shoulders.

I laughed nervously and turned to face him, the round tub of ice cream in my hand. "I'm sorry," I whispered. "You startled me. Want some ice cream?" I held it up.

"No," he said, and put his hand on top of mine and pushed it and the tub down. I realized he was going to kiss me. And I didn't want him to. Not yet.

"Don't," I whispered, as his head came toward me. He hesitated, his lips no more than an inch from mine, and then he backed away. He turned and walked to the table, his back to me. "I'm sorry," I said, still in the wedge between the icebox and its door.

"No, I'm sorry. I shouldn't have."

"David. Listen, I'm just so confused." I took a few steps toward him.

"I know, Sally. You don't have to explain."

"I want to. I don't understand."

"Sally, put the ice cream away; no, better yet, bring it here. Come on, give it to me." He waved me forward and I obeyed. "Good girl, now go close the icebox before the whole thing melts. You got a spoon around here?" He started opening drawers. "Ah, here we go."

I did as I was told. I leaned my head against the white porcelain corner of the icebox. It felt good. I had really drunk too much. Maybe that was why I was so confused. I sighed and slowly turned to face David. Things were so complicated and I didn't like it. I guess my face looked as woebegone as I felt because he sort of chuckled, then reached his arm out to me.

"Oh, kid, come here," he said. I went to him and he folded me against him. "Now, don't worry about me. I'm a lot tougher than that. I've had myriads of women refuse me, believe me, and with a lot less class than you just did. It's okay. These things work out this way."

"But I do care for you, David. Almost more than anyone. You're the only person who ever really cared enough about what I thought to get mad at me for it."

He laughed at that. "Here, hold this," he said, giving me the ice-cream tub and, carving out a spoonful with his right hand, he offered it to me. "Eat it. It'll make you feel better. You know I'm right. It's why we eat ice cream. It cures what ails us."

"Oh, David, I'm sorry," I said, and started to weep, turning my head into his shoulder.

"For Pete's sake, Sal, don't get my dinner jacket all sodden. I had it cleaned once this month already. Look, people's feelings land where they land. Just because you're not stuck on Heydrich, I shouldn't have assumed I was next in line."

"You are, but . . ."

"I know. Listen, there's more to this. I mean, about you. Your innocence."

I lifted my head and looked at him. "My what?"

"Innocence. Don't get mad. I know people hate being called that, especially when they're nineteen."

"I'm twenty."

"All right, twenty." He put a spoonful of ice cream into his mouth, bowl-side first, and sucked on the spoon as though it were a Popsicle. "You are pretty well educated, well-read, well-traveled, you dance good, speak excellent German, play a damn fine piano, and, I guess, fence like Doug Fairbanks, but you don't know damn-all about men. Now, that's not strange. Probably when you're fifty, you still won't know much. I sure as hell don't know much about women."

"You're not fifty," I said, starting to take the tub back to the icebox.

"No, but you catch my drift?" He caught my arm, dug out another spoonful of ice cream and let me go.

"Anyway," David went on, "what I mean is, you are so romantic, Sally. You look at the world with those big blue eyes as though it were all shiny and perfect."

"And you're going to tell me it's not." I went to the sink and turned on the tap. He followed me, pulling the spigot over to him, and washed his hands.

"Wouldn't dream of it. Got a towel? Thanks." I stood facing the sink, leaning against it, feeling the hard, cold porcelain under my hands. I could feel the cold night air through the glass of the window. They had taken off the double windows just the week before. It was April.

"Kid," said David, touching my face. I turned to look at him. "You're high on my list and I worry about you. Not like your father would or if he had any sense should, but as a friend. I worry about you and that wide-eyed look of yours and the way you believe people, accept what they say.

"Your friendship with Heydrich especially worries me. And don't get huffy. I'm not your father. I'm not out to protect your morals or your standing in society or whatever fathers do for daughters. That's their job. Look, if Heydrich weren't who he is, I'd say, fine, have an affair with him. An older married man is a good choice. Girls ought to have a little adventure before they settle down. But not with him.

"I think you know he's a dangerous man. I think if you'd be honest with yourself, you'd admit that that's one reason you keep seeing him. You're attracted to that. But listen, Sal, don't be." I started to deny what he had said. He shushed me.

"I know you don't want to believe me. Maybe I'll be proven wrong. Maybe he will value your innocence and keep you safe. But I doubt it. So, here's my advice, kid: Just be careful. Be wary."

"Wary?"

"Yeah. Like a rabbit is when she knows the woods are full of dangerous creatures that want to eat her. She can't stay in her warren, because life's outside. But it's dark out there, Sally. Believe me,

237

I know. Real, real dark. Especially here. Especially now."

I looked out the window, seeing the trees at the bottom of the property. They faced onto a deserted military academy and looked like the dark, dangerous woods David was describing. I shivered, knowing he was right, not wanting to admit it.

When we were on the train back to Berlin, I had told my father about running into Christian in Munich. If Daddy had asked what Christian did, I knew I would have to tell him. But Father didn't ask.

Finally, he turned his head and, in a mild voice, asked me about Herr Professor Mayr.

"Oh, Daddy, didn't I tell you? Christian told me at Christmastime. It's awful. His father killed himself." My father was visibly shocked, although he kept his usual controlled demeanor. His lips tightened and he turned his eyes back to the window.

"I would not have expected it of him," was all he said. So, I never had to tell him either that Christian's father had killed himself when the Nazis gained control of the country, or how.

About a quarter of an hour later, my father said, into the silence of our compartment, "Do you expect to see young Mayr again?"

I looked up from my book, a new Agatha Christie. My father's serious blue eyes behind the wire-rimmed glasses would not be lied to. "I hope so, Daddy. He is an old friend. And we have so much to talk about. Also, I'd like to see his mother. She's in Denmark with Ursula, who married a Dane. Do you remember? I think she was married by the last time we were at the lake. Marta, the second daughter, is teaching German in England, at a fancy girls' school. And Annaliese, the youngest—do you remember her?—she's in Vienna at school. Art, music, or something." My chatter had its desired effect; those intelligent eyes glazed over. My father's patience for small talk was minuscule.

The day after my dinner party, I was flying up the stairs to change into dinner clothes after a long tea for some charity—Daddy and I were going to a dinner at the British embassy. I was looking forward to it, because I knew Sydney would be there, as would Ivor Novello, the composer and actor, who was sure to play and sing for us. I had a beautiful new dress, black velvet with a huge white satin off-the-shoulder collar, a cuff at least seven inches deep. It was late in the season for velvet, but still so cold out, I thought I might get away with it.

My mind was on the dress and getting ready, so I nearly didn't hear my father's soft voice below me. I stopped and turned on the stairs, looking down at him.

"Yes, Daddy."

"Could I see you for moment, my dear?" he said.

"I've got to change, and you do too."

"I know, but this is important."

In his study, Daddy went behind his desk and indicated that I should sit in the chair to his right. I suddenly felt apprehensive.

He folded his hands on the blotter. His desk was covered with files and papers, but all in tidy piles. "Sally, I am concerned about your choice of friends. Please don't say anything until I am finished. Hear me out." He thought for a moment, trusting in my obedience.

"I have lived all my adult life among intellectuals, scholars, so it is strange to see the difference between men and women of the mind and those I am forced to deal with now." He smiled at me wanly. "I have left you alone to live your life here, trusting in your judgment, in your sense of yourself as your country's representative. I have also felt I owed you this, after taking you away from your life in California."

"Such as it was," I added.

"Be that as it may, I have treated you as an adult, have I not?"

"Yes."

"Not placing borders or restrictions on your activities. Not asking after you or demanding reports of where you were and with whom. In short, I have trusted you, have I not?"

"Yes."

"I do not blame you. I blame myself. For my lack of knowledge about you. I did not realize how inexperienced of the world you are. How innocent of the darker aspects of men's behavior."

"Funny, David Wohl said something like that to me last night."

"Did he? He is a bright young man, that is obvious. A young man I would have been pleased to have as a student. But, like many of his kind, he is impetuous and politically romantic, espousing radical causes. Added to this is the fact that he is a newspaper reporter from a third-rate New York paper, and I think you can see how he is not a suitable companion for the daughter of the Ambassador of the United States."

"Are you telling me not to see him any longer?"

"No, but I wish you would not see him alone. That you would not single him out for attention. I fear for your reputation."

"And you don't mind if I spend evenings with the Heydriches?"

"Yes, I do. I was coming to that. It amazes me that you have taken up with such disparate people. And now young Mayr."

"Daddy," I said, trying to stay calm, knowing emotionalism would make him discount anything I said. "I will not stop seeing David Wohl. You will just have to trust me that I will not run away and marry him or cause a great scandal that will embarrass you and the President." I stood up. "What I would like to know is why you don't forbid me the company of the Heydriches."

"I would prefer that you not see them."

"All right. I won't. Although I hope you will let me taper off. I don't want to be rude."

He looked at me a long time, then stood and pulled out his pocket watch, opened it, and read the time. "I believe it is time to change." He snapped the cover of the watch shut. "Very well, my dear, I will trust you this much farther. I think you understand my concern."

"Oh, yes, Father, I do," I said, and left the room.

I was angry with his strictures, but I thought I might be able to get around them. All I had to do was make sure there were lots of people around when David and I were together. Besides, the fact that Heydrich had not talked to Christian about me when he had said he had, made me distrust him. I would miss the music, but it would not be too distressing to allow that relationship to wither. Still, I felt bleak. Here I had met all of these interesting people and my father was going to force me to spend all my time with the likes of Mrs. Bushmuller. Damn.

After dinner that evening, Sydney invited me to go with a small group of people, who were taking Ivor Novello—as charming a man as he was handsome—to a new club.

We were a party of eight and when we were being shown to our table, I dropped my purse. I bent down for it, but a man quickly picked it up for me. When I straightened up, I saw it was an SS officer. He bowed and clicked his heels as he handed me the purse, his eyes frankly appreciating my bare shoulders. I thanked him, and went to take my seat at our table.

Someone made a joke about him. We all laughed and forgot about the incident. The club was very elegant, although it was done in that ocean-liner style the National Socialists seemed to like. But the scale was small and intimate, the lighting low, and the service efficient.

Later, I excused myself and made my way through the tables to the ladies' room. I was thinking about Ivor Novello and how he had played and sung after dinner with such casual ease, most of his attention on us, as though his piano accompaniment were an afterthought. I wished I could be as nonchalant a musician.

"Sally."

I gasped, startled. Christian, in his uniform, stood in the little foyer of the club. "Hello. I didn't expect to see you."

"Nor I, you. What are you doing here?" I asked.

"He's accompanying me," said Heydrich, coming up behind Christian. "Good evening, Sally. What a pleasant surprise. Won't you join us? We'd love to have a pretty girl along, wouldn't we, Mayr?" Then he reached out and, before I could move, slid his index finger along the rim of the wide collar of my dress, across the top of my breasts. I backed up, shocked and embarrassed.

"I'm sure Miss Jackson is with a party, sir," said Christian, his face as unmovable as granite, all hard planes and angles.

Heydrich, who I realized was drunk, stared at me, perhaps considering whether to argue or not. Fortunately, he straightened up, bowed to me and said, "Of course, Sally, of course. I should have known. Come, Mayr, where's our table? We'll have to find some other female companions. Perhaps at Missy's."

He stopped and turned to face me as he said this. "You have heard of Missy's, my dear Sally?"

I knew at once he was speaking of the place where I had seen him drunk on the stairs on Thanksgiving. "Never, Herr Obergruppenführer. Never." I don't know why I used his German title; perhaps to distance myself from him even further than by my courtesy, which I hoped was cold enough to make him go away.

"Ah, too bad. Perhaps Mayr will ... no, of course not. He's too much of a prig, is he not?"

The word I had used on the telephone to David. I lifted my chin, smiled at the general, and turned and swiftly kissed Christian's cheek.

"Yes, he is," I said, smiling at my old friend. "He's always been. I don't mind. It makes it easy to tease him."

"Hard to bed him, though. But, there it is. Good evening, Sally." And he turned and walked away, stopping a few yards away to call out in a low voice: "Mayr."

"I'm sorry," said Christian, taking my hand, as he moved in the direction of the voice. "He's drinking too much again." He walked backward so that he could talk to me, our arms stretching out between us.

"Why are you here?"

"I'm his nurse this week. To be sure he doesn't kill himself. Or someone."

"Poor you."

"Yes. Nice to see you, though." Our arms were at full length, our fingers still entwined.

"Mayr!" came the icy high voice again. Christian grimaced and let go of my hand, turning to follow, then turning back. "Want to go for a drive tomorrow?"

I nodded. "Good. I'll come by around noon. Take you to lunch, okay?"

"Okay."

"You do look beautiful." He smiled at me and then turned and was gone. I watched him weave his way through the tables to where Heydrich and the other SS officers were seated, to the right of the little bandstand, behind a column. Poor Christian, having to shepherd Heydrich around town like that. And I wondered if he would have to follow him to Missy's. I frowned. I didn't like the idea of my old friend in such a place.

A CHANGE OF PLANS

The next day Christian drove me to an old inn, deep in the Grünewald, the huge wild park sprawling through western Berlin and Spandau. He turned up in a little yellow car, a British MG, with the top down.

"Do you mind?" he asked, and I shook my head. The day was nice, warm for the first time that spring.

He drove very fast, especially on the roads inside the woods, keeping one hand lightly on the steering wheel, the other resting on the side of the car. He looked very happy piloting his little car, which was old and slightly battered, through the shadows under the trees.

"Is this yours?" I asked, indicating the car.

"Bought her from a friend."

I asked him a few more questions and he answered me with short, almost curt replies, so I stopped. If he didn't want to talk, I wouldn't force him, and I spent the drive watching the scenery pass.

We stopped at an inn and had a huge delicious lunch—pork chops and apple sauce, with chunks of apple in it, and more apples in the cake afterward. We ate everything and he seemed more relaxed. We talked about our summers at the lake, skirting any mention of his father. He brought up his brother, Kurt, but carefully avoided any reference to Herr Doktor Mayr. Still, we had fun remembering the old days, our shared childhoods, the icy water and the hot sun.

During coffee, Christian apologized for Heydrich again.

"Does he get so drunk very often?" I asked.

"More now than before."

"And you, the men who work for him, you shepherd him around?"

"He expects us to."

"It must be hard."

"Yes." I waited, but he didn't say anything more. We sat in silence again, this one touched with a sense of anticipation.

"Missy's is a funny name for that place," I said, lifting my coffee cup to my lips. It was a wide cup, of fine, thin china.

"How do you know about it?" I sensed a tension in him as he

asked me the question, as though he were afraid of my answer. Quickly, I told him about my Thanksgiving foray into the Berlin nightclubs. I considered whether I should tell him about catching sight of Heydrich and decided to, omitting, however, my whispered conversation with the woman.

"Have you been there?" I asked, and, to my surprise, Christian blushed. "Oh, no, I didn't mean—" I stopped and considered. "Well, yes, I do. Have you? Tell me."

"Yes." He set his coffee cup carefully into its saucer. "Following the general around. Sally, it's not a subject for conversation. And besides, it is too private."

"You have, haven't you?"

"There. You see, you do not want to know the truth. Come, on, let's take a short walk," he said, reaching across the table for my hand.

After he paid the bill, we walked outside to a flagstone path until we came to a low wall. We stopped and, without a word, sat side by side on the wall, turning our faces to the sun. He did not touch me, his hands in his pockets, his legs stretched out and crossed at the ankles. And, as before, he was silent.

It was all right. His company was enough and I sensed he felt the same about me. It was restful to sit in silence, in the sun, with Christian next to me. I yawned and stretched my arms.

"Perfect time for a nap. I wish I were a cat and could curl up right here." He nodded lethargically.

"We'd better get back," he said after a while.

In the lobby of the inn, the innkeeper asked if we were staying.

"No, we are not," Christian said firmly, a faint expression of disapproval on his face.

My father came out of his study as I entered the house with Christian behind me.

"Hello, Daddy," I said cheerily. "Good. I wanted you two to meet again. Christian, you remember my father, Lowell Jackson. Daddy, it's Christian Mayr."

The men shook hands and seemed genuinely pleased to see each other. I could see Daddy's cold politeness warm into pleasure.

"My boy," he said, "Sally told me of your encounter. I am glad to see you again myself."

"Is it time for tea?" I asked. "Or cocktails?"

"Dinner, I think," said my father.

"Oh, my goodness, you're right. I didn't realize it was so late."

"Frau Brenner was concerned."

"It was my fault, sir," said Christian. "I took Sally to lunch at an inn in the Grünewald." And he named the place, letting my father know all was open and honest between us. "I am sorry. It took longer than I expected to get back. The traffic."

"Of course. Well, no harm done. Why don't you stay and have dinner with us."

"Thank you. I would like that." Christian smiled at my father, then at me.

At dinner, and after, we talked of the past. The safe, happy, rosy past, adroitly avoiding present politics, the deaths in both our families, all the unhappy subjects. I was pleased that my father and Christian seemed to be enjoying each other's company.

"I do hope we will see you again, my boy," said my father, as the three of us walked to the front door where Vittorio stood with Christian's coat and hat.

"Thank you, sir. Good night, Sally." Christian kissed my cheek, and took his hat and coat from Vittorio.

"You understand, sir," he said seriously. "I am very interested in your daughter."

My father, surprised by the blunt statement, merely nodded, a bemused expression on his face. Just as surprised, I just stared at Christian stupidly.

"Good," continued Christian, looking at me. "I just wanted to be clear about that." Then he grinned at me, put on his coat and hat, and was gone before I could say a word.

"How long has this been going on?" asked my father mildly.

"He just made it up. Nothing's been going on. He's got a swelled head, thinking I would just—there's nothing going on, Daddy."

"I see," he said, and without another word, went off to his study.

The next morning, we met at breakfast. We were going to a reception and dance at the French embassy that evening and I had an appointment with the hairdresser.

"I liked young Mayr," said my father.

I nodded. I had decided that Christian needed a good talking to. He needed to be told that some girls just wouldn't fall into his arms when he snapped his fingers and bought them lunch. I guessed that because he was so damned handsome, he was used to girls' doing that, but I had decided that this girl wasn't going to.

Still, and I wouldn't have admitted this to anyone, I was very pleased at his forthright announcement. I was glad that he was interested in me, after the coldness of our first meeting. In short, I thought about Christian as a normal boyfriend, as though we lived in the States and he were simply a friend of Eddie's or the boy next door.

My father brought me back to reality.

"He's in the SS." Overnight, somehow, Daddy had done his research on Christian.

"Yes."

"You knew that."

"Yes," I answered, on the defensive. Daddy buttered his toast, the sound of his knife across the dry toast almost deafening in the sudden silence of the dining room.

"He seems to work in an office, in intelligence. For General Heydrich." Carefully, my father put the knife down and, after a small pause, the toast. He picked up his napkin and wiped his fingers, then sat back in his chair. He was going to tell me not to see Christian.

I folded my hands together in my lap, and met my father's gaze. I had won the fight over David; I could win this one.

"I think," he said, "you ought to ask him to accompany you to the reception this evening. And then, I think, you ought to tell him that you are going away for a while."

"Going away? Going away where?"

"The States. I need to go to Washington. Edward will be in Newport during May and we can see him. Maybe take a house nearby for the summer."

"When?"

"We'll leave in two weeks—actually, ten days. I've asked Bancroft to make the arrangements. We can sail from Le Havre. You will want to do some shopping in Paris before that."

"Then, later? After the States?"

"A well-deserved holiday. We'll go to Italy, as I mentioned before." Maybe he had. I didn't remember. "And I would like to go to Prague and Budapest, cities I've always wanted to visit. I've heard they are quite unique. Beautiful."

It was a bribe. The shopping, the chance to see Eddie, a house on the beach, Paris, Budapest, Italy. I frowned. "Daddy," I began, wanting to argue, but I looked into his eyes and fell silent.

I saw how much he wanted me to accept this plan and I saw something else. That he was afraid I would fight him and let this develop into something ugly.

I bent my head. Maybe he was right. Maybe it would be better to stop before I really fell in love with Christian. I hadn't thought through the consequences, and it occurred to me, with a flash of sadness, that my father had.

"Do you really have to go to the States?" I asked. "Or is this an excuse?"

"I do. I have written to the President about this new government. How I have been having conversations with men from various countries, sounding them out, trying to see how the rest of Europe feels about the new Germany—which side they will be on when Hitler leads them all into war. But it is delicate information to send through even our most secure methods. I need to see FDR in person. It is important that he fully understands what I believe this government is doing. Last night, I actually spoke to him by telephone and he agrees. And, while I am there, I will also be meeting with other men in the government, the military, and so on. And, of course, the Secretary.

"My dear, this is important and I would go regardless of personal circumstances, but I would probably not leave until June in order to appear to be merely spending our well-deserved holiday time. But I will also tell you that, however much I like this young man, I cannot allow you to become involved with him. I can only hope that you will understand."

"I do understand, Daddy. All right. I'll do as you ask. I'd like to see Eddie. And be in the States for a while. When would we be back? Can you stay away that long?"

"I would only be gone a month or two. But you might also rent a house in Italy in July and August, if you like, or even on Lake Sebastian. During the warm months. At any rate, you would be gone until September. I would come and go as I saw the need."

September. It was the first of April now. I'd be gone six months. Time enough to forget. September. Well, it wasn't the first time I had left a place I liked, friends. Christian.

"All right, Daddy. It sounds fine. Just fine. I'd better go now. I have plans to make. Telephone calls." I hurried from the dining room.

I came down the stairs that evening to find Christian, in his silver-and-black dress uniform, waiting for me. He wore slacks and dress shoes, not jodhpurs and boots.

"Thanks for making it on such short notice," I said, holding out my hand.

He took it and leaned toward me to kiss my cheek. I moved my head out of his range and removed my hand from his.

"You take a lot for granted, Christian."

His face went blank and he nodded once, but he recovered quickly and smiled at me. "You have a closet of these ball gowns?" he asked, teasing, back on our old terms.

"I do. It's my job, you know. How do you like it?"

"It is pretty."

"Did you like the black-and-white one I wore the other night?"

"It was very sophisticated. But I liked the one you wore at Christmas. The burgundy one."

"I'm surprised you remember."

"Of course. The dress you're wearing now reminds me of the one you wore when we went dancing at the lake."

The dress was pale, pale-pink satin, with large organza sleeves and a full, bias-cut skirt. It had a small collar embroidered with pearls and made me look very sweet and innocent. I had chosen it in anger.

"But," continued Christian, taking a step closer to me, "the burgundy dress made your hair look very dark and your skin glow. You looked beautiful, which surprised me, because I did not remember you as beautiful. Pretty, yes, but not beautiful. In this dress, you are pretty again." He smiled at me. "I do not mind, you understand."

"I do," I laughed. "I think."

The dress proved to be a good dancing dress too, although Christian teased me about the large sleeves. We danced a great deal. He was a good dancer, much better than the last time we had danced. Now he was taller, stronger, more sure of himself. He must have danced with many women to be so. That was all right too.

"Christian," I said, after dancing for a while, "I've got to talk to you. I've got something to tell you." Slipping my hand into his, I led him to a small sofa in the wide hall, far enough away from the other dancers to speak privately.

I told him what Daddy was planning and I told him why, because of the SS, the politics. I had thought it through and I was calm and matter-of-fact. I don't know what I expected him to do. I didn't really know this grown-up Christian well enough to know how he would respond.

He sat forward, his elbows on his knees, so that I couldn't see his face. I studied the line of silver cord, the black fabric, the white shirt along his neck, below his hairline. His hair was short, but not shaved up the sides, Prussian-style, the way the enlisted SS-men wore it. I liked the way the curve of his hairline looked and had a sudden, almost irresistible urge to put my hand there, to feel the contrast between his skin and hair. I looked away.

"We're being parted again," he said calmly. "It's too soon, Sally. I didn't expect this."

"It's business, mostly. Daddy has to talk to the President."

"After Italy . . . then will you be back?" he asked, anger starting to surface in his voice.

"I think so, but my father . . ."

"What about you? Will you do as he asks?"

"Yes, Christian."

"But you are a grown woman."

"What are you asking? That I defy my father? I could harm his career. He'd like me even less than he does." I heard the hurt in my own voice.

Christian sat back, one hand on the sofa between us. I looked down at it, at my own hand so close to it, but not daring to touch.

"He sends—takes—you away because of me. Because I am SS."

"Yes."

"But this is not—" he began. I held my hand up to stop him.

"Please, Christian, don't," I said gently. "Daddy is the ambassador. He stands for America and for the President who sent him. He can't let me see you—because of the SS, but especially the SD."

"What do *you* think about that, my job?"

I was silent for a moment before I answered him. "It is hard for me to separate what I think. I mean, you are you, aren't you? In spite of what your job is."

An emotion flickered across his face, relief or gratitude or a mixture of them both. "I'm glad, Sally."

"But my father likes you, too, Christian. It's just politics, his position."

"Not yours? You don't believe as he does?"

"Of course I do, but I don't know enough. Daddy is a Democrat and I guess I am too. I just don't know. He's the ambassador, Christian. It's the best thing that has happened to him since my mother died. He asked me to come, you see? I can't . . ." My voice ran down and we sat a moment in silence.

"I do see. But I think he wouldn't approve of me regardless of what his job were. His feelings toward the government are well known. Oh, yes, Sally, it's true. I've heard discussions. Everyone knows the American ambassador is a formidable opponent. Just last week—do you know about this?—a man, an American citizen born here, was arrested for something. Your father had to be talked out of going down to the Prinz-Albrecht Strasse himself to get the fellow out of jail."

"I'd hadn't heard that." I couldn't imagine my father storming into Gestapo headquarters. "They must be exaggerating."

"I heard it from a reliable source." He stood up. "Want something to drink? Champagne?" I nodded, and as he went to find some, I thought about what he had told me.

"Christian, what is your job?" I asked when he returned. "That you should hear such things about my father?"

"I work in intelligence," he said, sipping the champagne. "I can't tell you much, Sally."

"Are you important?"

"No. I write reports. I put facts together and write reports."

"That sounds important."

"No. I work in a big room with four other men. All the same rank."

"Obersturmführer," I said, remembering.

"Lieutenant," he translated.

"Like my brother."

"No, navy ranks are different . . ."

"You always said you didn't want a military career . . ."

"This isn't. It is a civil service job. The SS is constructed like the military, but it is more."

"Do you question people? I mean"—I shrugged, trying to trivialize what I was asking him—"like police do. Ask criminals questions?"

"No. I told you. I work with paper."

"Do you spy? Are you spying now?"

"Against the French?"

"Against me?" I said very softly.

He smiled, the corners of his mouth curving slowly upward. He leaned forward and brushed my cheek and hair with his smiling mouth. "Yes, of course," he breathed into my ear, his warm breath making me tremble.

I shifted away from him. "Well, what does it matter? I'm leaving." Why did he do that to me? Making me feel like that was useless. I suddenly felt such conflicting emotions: anger at him, pity for us, regret for myself, and disappointment at the lost chance. Here, I suspected, was a great romance. He was not as bright and witty as David, but I liked Christian's solemnity, his grave expression, the flash in his blue eyes when he was angry, and, especially, the curve of his mouth when he smiled. And I couldn't bear the idea of leaving him again.

"Yes, I remember. You're leaving," he said. "I accept that there is nothing to be done here."

"Yes, there is," I said, standing up, holding my hand out to him.

"What?" He looked up at me apprehensively.

"No, I'm not going to start a revolution. I just want to dance with you."

Without a word, he got up and, keeping my hand in his, walked with me back into the ballroom. There weren't many dancers left and we turned and faced each other. I went into his arms, just as I had all those years ago, in my memories and dreams.

We danced to a waltz, sweet and romantic, and we didn't speak again of the future. Then he took me home, where my father left us alone. As soon as Daddy had disappeared up the staircase, Christian put his arms around me and kissed me. The heat of his hands on my back and waist seared through my dress. I thought I would cry and I lowered my face and hid it against his chest. He laid his hand along my cheek, letting me hide.

"Sally," he whispered, his mouth moving against my hair. It was a good-bye kiss, just as our first kiss, all those years ago, had been.

I had so much to do before we were to leave: packing, arranging for the house to be looked after, and, finally, letting people know we were going.

I telephoned David and had a very unsatisfactory conversation with him. I was still embarrassed by my father's attitude toward David, and by my own reaction, even though David knew nothing of it. I felt there was too much left unsaid between us, but he wished me a happy vacation and rang off.

Sydney I met for coffee at her flat the day before I left. I had told her some of what had happened between Christian and me and she agreed that my father was right.

"I wish he weren't. It's been so strange, Sydney. Everyone behaving so well. And I don't know how I feel about Christian, so I don't know how sad to be."

"If you stayed and fell in love with him, then what would you do? Marry an SS officer? You couldn't, Sally."

"He's not like that."

"Doesn't matter, darling. He wears that uniform, the SD diamond on his sleeve. You just can't have anything to do with him."

"Can't. Can't. Can't. Can't what? Nothing happened. We saw each other a few times. Nothing happened. We barely talked."

"Then count yourself lucky. You're out of it unscathed." I

looked at her, cool and elegant in a gray sweater and skirt.

"I guess so."

"Of course I am. Now, tell me about your trip to Italy. Brian and I are going this summer as well. We should arrange to meet you. You know, at noon on the twelfth of August, in front of the Fontana di Trevi. I'll be the one in the big hat."

"I'll be the one with my feet in the fountain," I said, and we both laughed. I cheered up as we planned a rendezvous. It made me feel I was not cutting myself off from everyone I had met and cared for in Berlin.

Maestro was not pleased that I would be missing five months of fencing and I could not promise him that I would practice. But I did promise to return, and also to visit a certain shop in Rome. There I would buy an Italian foil. Maestro gave me the address and I left the salle thankful that Daddy had suggested the trip to Italy. It promised to be the salvation of the summer.

Finally, I telephoned Lina Heydrich. She was sweet and enthusiastic about my travel plans and promised to pass them on to Heydrich, relieving me of the necessity of talking to him.

I hadn't spoken to him for almost a month, since our last musical evening. I wondered if he knew about Christian and me, if he knew already that I was leaving.

Daddy and I were settling into our compartment on the train, when an SS man on a motorcycle roared up the platform outside our window. I watched him find the conductor, who pointed out our compartment. The SS man quickly entered the train and, after a moment, knocked on our open door.

"Yes," said my father, who had not paid attention to the man's arrival outside.

"A letter for Fräulein Jackson," said the man, holding out a plain white envelope.

"What is it?" said my father, reaching for it.

"It's for me, Daddy," I said, holding out my hand.

He hesitated, then allowed me to take the envelope. The SS man saluted and left. I put the envelope away. Daddy made no comment, only raised his eyebrows. I took it out later that night, when I was alone in my berth.

I ripped open the envelope and looked at the signature: RH. That surprised me. Up until that moment, I had truly expected the letter to be from Christian. I imagine my father had as well. If he had known from whom it was really, he would never have allowed me to keep it.

> Sally—
> I am glad you let Lina know you are leaving for America and Italy. I understand that you plan to visit your brother; that will be pleasant for you. I trust we can continue our music in the fall.
>
> RH

That was it. Nothing I couldn't have let my father see. But I was upset that Heydrich knew we were visiting Eddie, when I hadn't mentioned it to Lina. Well, the rate at which rumors traveled in Berlin no longer surprised me, nor did the fact that Heydrich seemed to know everything.

I folded the letter to put it away and stopped. There was more writing on the back. The spiky writing was hurried, sloppier than that of the body of the note.

> Sally—a quick thought—there comes a point in all our lives when we must reject the constraints put on us by our parents—the future is ours!

No punctuation, just the fast thought, written in haste before he stuffed the note into its envelope. It was a familiar Nazi slogan: "Awake! The future belongs to us!" It was clever of him to use it in a way that would appeal to me, in a way that would let me know he knew about my father's disapproval of Christian. I put the note away, turned out the little light next to my head, and pushed up the blinds so I could see the flat plains of Middle Europe rushing by in the moonlight. It was cloudy that night, and I watched the light and shadows alternately reveal and conceal the world. I fell asleep, Heydrich's words still in my mind.

Daddy's plans went forward as he had arranged. We spent all of April in Washington, although I didn't see much of him. We took the train up to visit Eddie in Rhode Island in the middle of May. My brother looked happy in his handsome navy whites and well satisfied with his career. He took us all over the ship he was serving on—a small, trim cruiser—and introduced Father to his captain.

The beach house Eddie had rented on Newport for us was not far from his base and he came to visit as often as he could. I enjoyed seeing him. Daddy was still busy in Washington, most particularly, with a two-week series of meetings at the War Department. I think it was very difficult for him, as certain factions in both the War Department and the Department of State believed he was nothing more than an alarmist. He came to stay with me for one long weekend and spent all of it writing. At the end of the month, he went to see his old mentor, a professor at the University of Chicago, and came back more determined than ever to tell the story of the new Germany as he saw it. It was his job, he told me. The reason the President had sent him.

At any rate, I was mostly alone in the house on the beach, and I welcomed Eddie's company.

He came up unexpectedly one Friday evening, riding in the cab of a huge, noisy truck. I was sitting on the front porch of the house, watching the ocean change color as the sun set, drinking a gin and tonic.

Eddie yelled at me and leapt down from the cab. He was wearing khaki and was very excited about something. My birthday was coming up and I had been feeling sorry for myself. Eddie hopped up the steps and hugged me.

"What the hell are you wearing? You look terrible."

"I'm on vacation," I protested, my hand automatically going to my hair, which was curlier than usual in the damp air. "I went swimming and—where are you taking me?" He dragged me down the steps toward the truck.

"I brought you something—for your birthday," he cried, hauling me around to the rear of the truck. He pushed aside the canvas tarp to reveal a piano.

"Eddie, you're crazy."

"Didn't buy it, don't worry. Rented it. This fine fellow"—he waved toward the driver, who was watching the two of us from the front—"will return in three weeks to take it away. Right?"

"Right," said the man, smiling. He obviously thought my brother was nuts.

"What do you say, sister?"

"You're nuts," I said affectionately. "But thank you, thank you very much. Now, how do we get it into the house?"

"No sweat. We've got it all figured out. Here, you carry the bench. Bet you thought I'd forgotten it."

The men took care of it, waving me out of the way. They turned the truck around and, using heavy boards as a ramp and a couple of dollies, they manhandled the little upright into the dining room. I wanted it there because the room faced the sea and I liked the idea of looking up from the keyboard and seeing the ocean. Well, looking over from the keyboard, the piano was too tall to see over.

Eddie paid the driver and went out with him. I sat at the piano and opened it, trying a few tentative chords. I hoped it wasn't too badly out of tune; it wasn't, although there were a few keys that made me cringe. Still, it was better than no piano.

"Okay?" said Eddie.

"Very okay," I replied. He came to stand next to me, and his hand lightly caressed my shoulder.

"I could use a drink. Got any? I'll fix us both up. Meet you on the veranda and you can tell me about him."

"Eddie," I said, stopping him in the doorway. "How do you know it's a him?"

"Instincts. And Dad told me. A little."

"Oh," was all I answered and let him go fix us drinks. I sat for a moment, feeling tired, but better, lighter. I put my hands on the keyboard. My fingers felt stiff, but I tried the first few measures of the Haydn concerto I had played with Heydrich. I was rusty, but felt good, and didn't stop. The tone of the little piano was nothing like the Heydriches' Bechstein, but I didn't care. I didn't care about anything for the minutes I played, not even the mistakes I made, nor the darkening room, nor the wide, empty, dark world outside.

When I finished, I heard applause. Eddie. I turned on the seat and bowed.

"Here, you deserve this. Might be a little watery by now," he said, holding out a gin and tonic.

"Thank you." I rose to take it.

"You're really good," he said. "Even on that old clunker."

I flushed at the compliment. "Let's go outside and fight the mosquitoes for a while. Then we'll go get changed and hike into town for dinner."

"Sounds good."

It was good to be with him. We hadn't ever been alone together as adults and we were getting to know each other and discovering that we liked each other. It was very good.

He complimented my piano playing again. I thanked him again for his thoughtfulness. We talked about Daddy and I told him what I knew of Daddy's conferences with FDR and the Secretary. We did not talk about Berlin or "the guy."

Later, after a long, messy meal of lobster, French bread, and beer, we tottered back along the sand dunes to our house. Finally, sitting down in the sand to watch the moon and the dark ocean, I told Eddie a little about Christian, warning him before I did that there was really little to tell.

255

"You always were crazy about him," he said. "Even when you were little. Following him around. I think you've got some weird fixation on him."

"My brother the psychiatrist."

"Well, I sympathize. But I gotta tell you that I think Dad's right. If Christian's a Nazi, you're better off without him. Even if he is someone you've known forever. Makes it tough, though. But . . ." he fell silent.

"Go on," I urged him.

"Well, you might not like this, but have you ever been in love before?"

"Just with him."

"Yeah. So you're lucky. If he's a Nazi, you know he'll do you dirt. Sal, you're so young yet. There'll be another guy."

"I know. I know you're right. Everybody's right about this. I know Nazis are thugs. I know I'm young. I know there'll be another guy. But how will I know him, if everyone keeps shielding me like this?"

"He'll come, sis. You're too pretty to be alone. Now that you've brushed your hair."

I smiled, enjoying his teasing, but there was more I wanted to say. "Eddie, the strange thing is, by taking me away, Daddy has made happen what he was trying to avoid." I felt my throat close and knew I was going to start crying. I fought it.

"I've been sitting here for days, staring at the sea, missing Christian, thinking about him. How we had to leave each other before. Everyone makes fun of me for my infatuation with him. But it's not just an infatuation. I know the difference. It feels different."

"You're only a kid."

"I'm old enough, Eddie. And now here I am, in love with him, again, in spite of everything. In the same stupid position of being a world apart, and it's lucky that I'll probably never see him again. I know I mustn't be in love with him. I accept that. But now I'll have to spend all this time getting over him again. It isn't fair."

"Oh, sis, sis," said Eddie, putting his arm across my shoulders. "It's tough, but it'll get better."

He stayed until Sunday, and before he left he invited me up to Newport the next week.

I went to visit Eddie and we had a lot of fun. He found us dates, and we went dancing. His date was Barbara, his future wife. And when the truck returned to haul the old piano away, I felt I was ready to return to Europe. I could face it now, even Berlin.

* * *

I was tested sooner than I had expected. On the eve of our sailing, Daddy received a notice that he should return to Berlin immediately. There was a crisis brewing, a possible coup by the SA, it was rumored. He wanted me to stay in the States, but I refused.

"I'm coming with you," I said. "I want to get back to a decent piano. And, besides, if there is a crisis, you might need me."

I could see the thought had never occurred to him, but he agreed, impressed, it seemed, by my newfound good sense.

A WEEKEND IN JUNE

We arrived back in Berlin on the last Thursday in June. The house was stuffy, the draperies pulled against the sun. Vittorio was still in the house, but the other servants were on holiday. Daddy went immediately to the embassy and I didn't see him again to talk to for several days.

Saturday morning, I woke to a hot summer's day. I had put off organizing any housework until the rest of the servants returned, and I knew I couldn't stay in the house all day. I called Sydney, who, surprised to hear that I was back, invited me to a swimming outing the next day. I happily accepted.

The next morning, Sunday, Sydney, Brian, David, and I drove out to a private beach at Wannsee to swim and sunbathe. I was very happy to see them all, especially David. I kissed his cheek and he grinned at me.

"You look good, pal," he said. "Life in the States must agree with you."

"I had a good time. I spent a month sitting on an island, staring at the Atlantic. Played the piano a lot. I feel just fine." I smiled at Sydney, knowing she understood what I meant.

It was a hot, clear, breezy summer's day and on the drive back into town, Sydney and I fell asleep amid the damp towels and paraphernalia of the backseat. The last thing I remember before dozing off was David's voice. He and Brian were talking about the rumors going around about Röhm and the tension surrounding his SA.

"He is a fag, and an embarrassment despite the fact that he's Hitler's oldest friend. Friend. Ha!"

The car stopped and I awoke to hear Brian say, "Now what's going on?"

The car upholstery was unpleasantly scratchy against my sunburned arms and legs. I pulled my sunsuit as far down under my legs as it would go to protect myself. Sydney, still asleep beside me, had wisely spread a towel under herself.

Looking through the front window, I saw we had stopped at the end of a line of cars approaching an intersection. There were uniformed men checking each car before allowing it to pass. As we watched, a driver was pulled out of a sports car and roughly taken out of our sight behind a large truck. A soldier got into his car and drove it out of the line.

"Those are SS," said Brian, inching the car forward.

"What the hell is going on?" said David. He patted his sport-shirt pocket, pulling out a battered pack of cigarettes.

"Sydney?" said Brian.

"She's still asleep," I said.

"Why don't you wake her up," Brian said quietly.

I shook Sydney gently. "We're coming to a roadblock," I said. She sat up, running both hands through her hair. She said nothing, but leaned forward, putting her hand on Brian's shoulder. I reached down in my big blue-and-white-striped beach bag to find my comb and tried making sense of my hair.

"Where are my dark glasses?" Sydney asked, and I pulled them out of my bag and handed them to her.

"Don't know how they got in there," I said, not taking my eyes off the activity in front of us.

The car reached the roadblock. There were half a dozen SS enlisted men spread across the road, while an officer checked papers. The men all held guns across their chests. Brian pulled the registration papers out of the glove compartment, as the officer walked to the front and studied the license plates.

Just then two troop carriers, loaded with men, some of whom were carrying machine guns, roared through the intersection.

"Jesus," swore Brian softly.

"Who's declared war?" I said, only half-joking.

"I've got to get to a phone." David was drumming his fingers against the dash, nearly quivering with suppressed energy.

The officer, dressed in a well-fitted black tunic, bent very slightly from the waist and asked Brian politely for our passports. We passed them to Brian, who added his own and handed them out the window to the SS-man. He compared each photograph with each passenger carefully before returning the passports and waving us on.

Brian drove quickly through the almost empty streets. "I'll take Sally home first," he said.

"Stop. Stop here!" shouted David. "I can take the S-Bahn. It'll be faster. Shit—sorry girls—this is a big one. I can feel it." He jumped out of the car before it had fully stopped. "Bye, kids," he cried and disappeared into the subway station. I didn't like losing sight of him. I wanted us all to stay together.

As we drove up to my house, I was surprised and frightened

to see two marines outside the wrought-iron gates, which, for the first time, were closed.

"Is it all right if I leave you out here?" said Brian, impatient himself to get to his office.

"Sure," I said. "Sydney, do you want to stay with me?" I asked as I quickly gathered my things together, hoping she would say yes.

"Thanks, love, but I'd better get on to our embassy. Lady Harcourt-Greves will need me, I imagine."

I kissed her cheek. "Telephone me, please?" I said and left the car. I called to the marines through the bars of the gate. "I'm Sally Jackson, the ambassador's daughter."

"Yes, miss. I know. Pleased to meet you, miss," he said and touched his index finger to his cap before he pulled the gate open far enough for me to slip through.

"What's going on?" I said.

"Can't say, miss," he answered in a soft drawl.

Inside, I handed Vittorio my beach gear. "Is my father around?" I asked, not expecting that he would be. "Do you know what's going on?"

"No, signorina," he answered. "His Excellency left word that you should telephone him at the embassy directly you came in. I'm very glad to see you."

"Thanks, Vittorio." I headed for Daddy's study, to use the telephone on his desk. The one in the little cabinet under the stairs was uncomfortable in the heat.

Sitting on the edge of the big desk, I asked the operator for the embassy. Told that I must wait a few minutes for the connection to be made, I hung up. It was very quiet in the room, in the whole house. I ran my fingers through my hair, feeling a sudden chill against my sunburn. The draperies were drawn and the room was gloomy.

When the phone rang, it startled me so much I knocked the receiver out of the holder. Retrieving it, I put it to my ear. It wasn't my father, but his secretary, Bancroft, who told me the ambassador would be glad to know I was home and that I should stay there.

"What has happened?" I asked. "Has war been declared?"

"No, a putsch, it seems."

"Röhm?"

"So the Nazis say. We suggest that you stay inside until further notice."

I hung up and sat for a moment, rubbing my hands over my chilled arms. I wished Daddy were here or, at least, that I had been able to speak to him. I got off the desk and crossed the room to the window, pushing aside the heavy draperies to look outside. The two marines stood, guns slung over their backs, looking through the wrought-iron bars of the gate down the street. I let the draperies fall and went upstairs to take a shower. Perhaps it would cool my prickly skin.

After my shower, I changed into slacks and a white shirt and decided to go on the terrace to dry my hair. As I went down the stairs, I almost tiptoed, the house felt so empty. I wondered where Vittorio was and went to the music room, where I stood at the side of the closed piano for a moment, stroking the glossy wood. Outside, I could see the long, smooth lawn running down to the trees that bordered our property.

As I turned to go, I heard a distant sound—a crack, like a car backfiring. I stood listening for more, but there was only silence and I left the room.

The entry hall was silent and cool, the flowers under the mirror drooping in the still, hot air. I pulled a dead blossom out of the arrangement and fussed with the leftovers. It looked tired. Leaving the flowers, I wandered to the sitting room. When I opened the doors, I saw that the curtains were all drawn.

Because of the color of the draperies, the room was dim with a melancholy blue light. The sheer curtains on the far French door to the terrace moved gently and I stopped, frightened. The French doors were open. I listened carefully, but could detect nothing. Perhaps Vittorio had left them open.

Slowly, I walked through the shadowy room, past the square of sofas, to the door and moved the curtains aside just enough to see out. There was no one on the terrace, so I went out. I immediately felt better, outside in the sunshine.

There was that sound again. I turned toward it, searching the trees, but saw nothing. I heard several pops—uneven cracks. Then I knew what it was, although I had never heard it before, except in movies. It was gunfire. I walked to the stone balustrade that edged the flagstone terrace. The noise was coming from beyond the trees, from the deserted military academy. Perhaps someone was chasing rabbits or shooting bottles. Then the pops stopped and I let out my breath, which I suddenly realized I had been holding.

I turned my back on the lawn and the trees and the noise and felt my hair. It was still damp and I pulled my comb out of my trouser pocket and sat cross-legged on the broad stone balustrade. Bending my head forward, I combed my hair off my neck. The sun felt good, not too hot.

The gunfire started again. I raised my head and faced it. I felt

261

a chill and climbed down off the wall. For the first time, I wondered where Christian was. The noises I could hear coming from the academy, the absence of the servants, and the beauty of the day—Führer weather, Goebbels's papers called it—frightened me. There was something dangerous out there beyond the trees, under the clear blue summer sky.

I slapped my comb against my leg and waited for another shot. I wished Daddy were home. I wished I knew what was going on. If there had been a coup and I was left here alone in this big house, helpless and forgotten, what would happen to me? What if someone came over the fence behind the trees, carrying a gun?

Hurrying back to the French doors, I forced myself not to run. Maybe it was silly, but I knew the noise was gunfire and I was scared. I pulled the doors toward me, and was attacked by the silky curtains billowing in the breeze. They enveloped me and I panicked, fighting the thin, moving fabric as though it were a living creature.

I almost fell into the dark room, momentarily blinded by the contrast with the bright outdoors, my heart hammering, my breathing jagged.

A harsh voice came out of the dark room, barking at me in German: "Halt!"

I froze, clutching my comb in both hands, barely feeling the tines dig into my fingers.

"Move. Turn around. And get your hands in sight. C'mon. Move it."

I obeyed, turning slowly toward the sofa, and saw a gun. Nothing but a gun pointed at me, ready to kill me. I stared at it, at the evil, black-blue sheen, too frightened even to swallow. It wavered, the black hole shifting, filling my vision. In an instant, it had become my entire world.

"Oh, my God." The gun lowered and I saw it was Christian. He had leveled the gun at me over the back of the sofa. "Sally, I couldn't see who it was."

I didn't move. "What are you doing?" I whispered in English, afraid to speak too loudly and risk startling the gun into life.

"I'm sorry," he said, not looking at me. "I fell asleep and could not see . . . with the light behind you." He wiped his face with both hands, but did not let go of the gun. "I thought you were someone else."

I nodded, not understanding his words. I could translate the German, but the meaning was beyond my comprehension. Near the French doors there was a straight-backed chair and I sat carefully on it, the comb still in my hands. I needed something to hang on to.

Christian swung his legs onto the floor and dully I realized that he had been stretched out on the sofa. I had walked right past him. Now he leaned back and closed his eyes. I looked away, still frightened by the confrontation with a gun.

For several minutes, we sat in silence. Slowly, I felt my sense of reality return, and I began to think and look again. And, looking at Christian, I was shocked.

He looked exhausted, his skin pale, with dark shadows under his eyes. His hair hung lank over his eyes and he was unshaven. His black uniform was a mess: stained and rumpled, buttons undone. Even his boots were dirty and caked with mud. I hated the idea of those dirty boots on my sitting-room sofa. I hated the way he looked, so strange and unlike himself.

An image of how he had looked the last time I'd seen him, at the French embassy dance, flashed through my mind and I wondered irrelevantly if he had several sets of that black uniform.

"What has happened?" I asked. "You look so . . . how did you get in? Are you okay?"

"Yes, of course." He answered me in English. "I fell asleep." He opened his eyes. "Can I have a drink? Have you got something in here?" He looked around the room vaguely.

He watched me as I got up and crossed to the cabinet against the wall. "Will this do?" I asked, holding up the first bottle I put my hand on, a half-empty bottle of Daddy's I. W. Harper.

"Yeah. Anything."

I poured him a shot of bourbon, then handed him the glass across the back of the sofa. He gulped it down. I could see how dirty his hands and fingernails were. I watched him warily as he got up and walked past me to the cabinet. Pouring himself another shot, he knocked it back as quickly as the first, then stood leaning his hands on the cabinet, his arms straight, his full weight on his arms, his gun still in his left hand. He looked at the end of his rope, in spite of the gun.

"Are you hungry?" I asked. "Can I do anything?"

"Listen," he said in German, not turning around. "Who else is here, in the house?"

"Well, Vittorio. The other servants are on vacation." I answered in German.

"Where is your father?"

"At the embassy." I remembered the marines at the front gate. "Oh, there are the two men at the gate. Christian, how did you get in past them?"

He dismissed my question and the marines with a wave of his

gun hand. Taking hold of the bottle, he carried it to the French doors. He drank from it, wiping his mouth on the back of his gun hand. There was another distant crack and his head jerked up.

"Listen," he said. He took another long drink. "When is your father coming home? Soon?"

"Is that gunfire? Please, tell me what it's about. I've been so frightened."

He looked at me, ignoring my question again. "Your father?"

"I don't know," I said abruptly. "I don't know when he'll be home. I mean, he didn't tell me. I didn't even talk to him. Nobody tells me anything. And I'm left alone." I heard myself and stopped. Taking a deep breath, I said, "There seems to be . . . trouble."

He laughed a short, ugly laugh. Taking another swig of bourbon, he waved his arm toward the window. "Do you hear that?" He tipped his head back to drink and, overbalancing, began to fall. I started around the sofa for him, but he righted himself, dropping the bottle, which bounced gently on the carpet.

He did not drop his gun.

Christian stared for a moment at the open French doors, where the soft breeze pushed the curtains to and fro. He started toward them.

"Listen, it hasn't stopped. Hear it? You know what it is? Do you know?" He glared at me, gesturing wildly with his gun. "It's gunfire. My squad's relief. At the old military academy. And do you know how I know? I was there. I . . . I know." He rubbed his face with his arm. His voice was harsh, as though he were hoarse from shouting. "It's been going on since this morning—no, last evening. Since Friday evening—what is today?" He was facing the door, and from where I stood, I could not see his face. "It started last night. Is this Saturday? It's been a long weekend," he said, with another barking laugh.

"It's Sunday," I said in a small voice. He paid no attention.

"You must understand. My squad has been at it all day: we were called in as relief for another squad. Relief . . ." His voice was soft, reasonable, and I could barely hear him. "This morning, early, they gave us the rifles and told us some of us had live ammunition and some of us had blanks. They thought it would be easier for us if we did not know for sure which of us had done it, which gun the killing bullets came from. That's supposed to make it easier for us to . . . do this to our comrades. I suppose it makes sense." He shook himself and pulled his shoulders back.

"The Obergruppenführer saw to it. The Obergruppenführer thinks of everything. Goddamn him. There were six of us. When it

264

started we piled into a truck and drove out to Wannsee and—you won't believe this—but we got lost. When was that? Friday? Yesterday? No, the day before. Anyway, we got lost." He tried to laugh. I remembered with a shudder the truckload of SS men we had seen on our way home from the beach earlier.

"Hell. It was our first time. In fact, that's what the fucker said." He stood straight, with his gun in his hand, to imitate Heydrich. I could recognize the high, light voice. "Men, it's your first time. You are virgins. This is your first blooding." Christian shook his head and looked about for the bottle. "The goddamned Obergruppenführer. He told us he wished he could go with us. The bastard. Where's the fucking bottle?" His foot hit it and he picked it up and drained it.

"Oh, shit, oh, shit." He wiped the back of his gun hand across his face again. He was breathing heavily and muttering to himself. "Why did his wife get in front of him? Stupid woman. We have no battle against women and children. Only against . . . against . . ." He turned and looked at me.

I stood, as I had since the beginning of his incredible speech, absolutely still, my arms wrapped around myself. I was very calm, seeing and hearing him through the thick blue air of the darkening room. He grimaced and, for the first time, looked me in the eyes. He studied me for a long time, searching my face for something.

I felt as if he were receding down a long corridor, and I heard his whisper slither its way back to me.

"I swore when I joined the SS to obey; my honor is . . . my honor. Do you understand?" He kept eye contact with me until, unable to nod or say anything, I turned away from him. I guess he lost his balance; I heard him land abruptly on the carpet. He caught his breath, then said, "Nobody understands. You don't. Father didn't. My mother tries, but . . . oh, shit. I believed the Chief. Christ, I have to, don't I?"

He leaned his head back against the sofa and closed his eyes. He stayed that way for several minutes and I thought perhaps he had fallen asleep. I took a few steps, thinking I would sneak away.

"My boots are so fucking filthy. I'll never get them clean again. Have to have them spit-shined, fucking boots. That's what the Scharführer told us. Funny, he never screamed at us, like Kurt told me his did. But they want those boots clean. Brains, blood, shit. It'll take me forever to get them cleaned." He bent his head, presumably looking at his boots.

I turned around. The boots. Those boots on my sofa, oh, God.

"Go away," I said, but he didn't hear me, or, if he did, he ignored me.

"I swore, Sally. But I didn't expect . . . I told you. A job. That's what it is. The fighting . . . I never expected . . . They taught us about tactics, taught us to march. God, we are great marchers. You know how they trot us out at every opportunity, the pretty boys. No fighting, no violence. Just fancy marching. Hans teased me about that. Hans . . .

"It is natural for boys and men to fight. But I discovered I didn't have to. I fought . . . you know, how boys fight with each other, games, but I've never . . . I've never. I've never had to fight to get what I wanted. My bloody looks got me whatever . . . pretty boy. Even things I didn't want."

He took a breath. "I never fought in the streets as my brother had. Look what happened to him. I never believed that striking out in anger accomplished anything. No, this is wrong, not anger. There was no anger.

"I felt nothing," he said, shaking his head. "No anger. Nothing. I was just doing what I was told, do you see? Do you see? Hans Behrends—remember, you met him in Munich? We went to the beer hall." He let his hands fall uselessly into his lap and stared at them. When he spoke again, it was in a whisper.

"They brought him out to the courtyard early this morning with four other SA—all junior officers. I hadn't known he was there, being held. Maybe if I had known, I could have done something. He saw me—his eyes looked straight at me. He was so fucking brave. I wanted him to say something to me—to curse me, or beg, or forgive, but . . . nothing. He looked right at me and raised his arm in salute to the Führer. Until he fell." Christian stopped, still staring at his hands. "The bullets almost cut him in half. Right across his chest. The blood . . . I've never seen . . . he was my friend.

"Perhaps, if we had been alone for a moment, he might have said something to me, but out there in that yard . . . we were all the same. We didn't dare look at each other. They were all our comrades that we were killing.

"We were warned that our sacrifices would be large, but we never imagined . . . I never . . . these were our friends." His voice rose at the word. "Friends. Hans. Not Communists or Jewish bankers or . . . or enemies. God, Sally, what have I done? What have I done?"

With a violent jerk, he threw the gun across the room. "Shit, I thought to speak to your father . . . my father . . ." His voice faded away. "I wish my father were here." And finally, he was silent.

266

I looked down the room, toward the door, wishing I were out in the sunshine, away from this room and the words he had let loose in it. I wanted him gone. I turned away and covered my face.

In the silence behind my hands, I saw him that summer we were fourteen, sick and pale in his narrow bed. I remembered how I had knelt by his bed, focusing all of my energy, hope, and love onto him, that he should not die. And he hadn't. He had grown healthy and brown, all golden and toast-colored in the sun, his long arms warm around me as he teased me. I remembered how he had talked to me, telling me of his fears of the future. Of the future that was here now. Which had turned out so differently for us, for him.

I lowered my hands. For the sake of the boy and for the man I had loved, who I knew could never do the things this new, grown-up stranger had done, and for my own sake too, knowing I would never forgive myself if I abandoned him when he was in so much pain, I tried calling his name, the boy's name: "Christian."

There was no answer, so perhaps he had left. Just to be sure, I tried once more. "Christian?"

Still no answer. He was sitting, like a lost child on the floor, with his long legs pulled up against his chest, his arms around his knees, hiding his face in his arms.

I was tempted to flee the room silently and leave him and his terrible story behind. I could not connect him with what he had told me. That is, I could not connect the boy I had known with what the man had said. I could not believe he had pulled the trigger; that he was capable of pulling the trigger.

"It can't be," I said aloud in English, and I knelt in front of him. "Christian," I whispered, reaching out to touch his hair. He was warm. Somehow, I had expected him to be cold. Dead. I caressed his head. His bright, golden hair was dull and tarnished.

"Come, love, come," I whispered in German. And like a desperate child, he turned to me, his arms going around me so tightly I could barely breathe. He started to cry, holding on to me for dear life. I held him, rocking back and forth as he sobbed against me.

A man who cried like that, I thought, cannot have done such things. Will not do such things again. Look how it has hurt him. I held him, stroking his back, his head, as though I could make the bad past go away with my touch.

I felt him grow calmer, relax against my breast, his hold on me slacken. We sat awhile quietly in the blue light of the room as the sun went down. I looked toward the French doors, and as I did, I felt his head move against me, turn to nuzzle, then kiss my breasts through my blouse. His body changed; his hands were touching me,

267

searching under my blouse, his lips hungry against me, licking at me through the cloth. He lowered me to the carpet, supporting my head with his hand, the other fumbling with the waistband of my slacks.

I moved my hands to stop him, suddenly frightened, but he moaned, "Please, oh, please," and I let him. He took me then, quickly, more quickly than I thought possible. I felt almost nothing, my mind taking in this shock as one more in an afternoon of shocks. From outside my body, I somehow watched him roughly pull my clothes out of his way, fumble with his own clothing, and raise my legs so that he could more easily enter me.

He paid no more attention to me than he would have if I were a stranger he was raping. He was fast and brutal, holding my shoulders as he pumped himself against and into me. It was not pleasant, but I let him do it, not looking into his wild glazed eyes. It did not take long. I was glad when he was finished.

He lay heavily on me, a deadweight, making it difficult for me to breathe. I said his name, and when he didn't answer, I realized he was asleep. I pushed at him but he was too heavy and I panicked, my legs quivering with the strain, the middle of my body feeling split and raw. I managed to roll him off me and scrambled out from under him, crawling across the carpet, until I could stand on my shaky legs and straighten my clothes.

I walked out onto the terrace. The sun was nearly down and I glanced at my watch, surprised to discover it was nearly seven thirty. Daddy might be home soon and I had to change. There was no time for regrets or emotion and I quickly turned and went back into the house.

Christian was still asleep on the floor. His face was the same. He did not look different. He seemed to be who I had thought he was. And I had let him.

All right, I thought. I will not cry. I will ignore my shaking and I will not cry.

I knelt next to him. "Come on, Christian. Christian," I called softly. He opened his eyes, staring at the ceiling. "Let's get you upstairs into bed. You can sleep as long as you like. You'll feel better with some sleep." And keeping up a continuous litany of maternal patter, I hauled him onto his feet.

"I'm all right," he said groggily and, noticing that his pants were undone, managed to close some of the buttons, to pull down his tunic. He didn't look at me. "I got to go. Where's my hat?"

"You're not going anywhere. You have to sleep. Sleep first." I didn't want him leaving there like that, thinking it would be best for my father and me, and for Christian, if no one were to see him in this condition.

"All right," he said and let me support him out to the hall. We were in the foyer, at the foot of the steps, when Vittorio came around the corner. Where had he been?

"Signorina!" he exclaimed softly. "I did not hear the door."

"He came in through the back, Vittorio. He is in trouble."

"And perhaps a little drunk."

"Yes. Very drunk. He needs to sleep."

"Of course, let me." And he led Christian up the stairs. I went back to the sitting room to retrieve Christian's cap and the ugly gun, and toss the bottle out. I turned on the lamps and plumped up the cushions on the couch. Standing in front of the fireplace, I looked around, the gun in one hand, the cap in the other. Everything looked as it should; but everything had changed.

And there was no time for me to think about it. I went up to my own room, where I put the gun on the small, overstuffed chair in the corner, hiding it under his cap. I was exhausted but I felt filthy and I ached all over. I took a fast shower, and could barely stay awake long enough to pull on my robe and make it to my bed. I lay on my side, my knees pulled up, my hands clasped palm to palm between them, and fell asleep.

I was awakened by a gentle knock on my door. Across the room, the death's-head emblem on Christian's cap stared at me. I got up quickly and went to the door. It was Vittorio, warning me that my father was home and dinner would be served in thirty minutes.

"Dinner?"

"Don't worry, I have taken care of it."

"Thank you, Vittorio. I'm sorry I left it all to you."

"It is all right, signorina. Oh," he added, "Obersturmführer Mayr is still asleep. I have cleaned his jacket and boots. Should I awaken him?"

"His boots?"

"I was in the army, signorina," he said, and made one of those expressive Italian shrugs that can mean everything and nothing.

"I see. Well, we'll leave him. Bring his things up for when he awakens. And perhaps you could keep some food warm for him?"

I put a dress on and brushed my hair. Then I picked up the cap and gun and went to Christian's room. I heard my father cross the hall below and go into his study. I wanted to talk to Christian and see what he would make of what had happened between us. I knocked softly, and when I received no answer, opened the door.

The room was dark, but light from the hall spilled across him.

He was lying on the bed, still fully dressed except for his jacket and boots, his back to the door. I tiptoed over to him. He turned quickly.

"Hello," I said, putting his cap and gun on the bureau. The room still smelled of new furniture.

"Sally?" He raised himself onto his elbows. "I couldn't figure out where I was." His voice was still hoarse, but soft, friendly. He was himself again.

"You're here," I said, waving my arm in the air.

"Why?"

"You were exhausted."

"Yes. Yes, I was. I have a headache too."

"That must be the bourbon. I'll get you an aspirin." I did so, bringing the tablets and a glass of water back from the bathroom. I turned on the lamp next to the bed and shook out two pills into Christian's hand. He took them and the water I gave him, drinking down the entire glass. I had not met his eyes, had not even looked at him once I knew he was awake.

Suddenly, I felt very shy, and I started talking to cover it. "Are you hungry? We're having dinner. Well, almost immediately. But we could wait for you. Daddy's home, too. I don't know what we're having. Usually I do. But Frau Brenner is very good. Oh, I forgot. She's gone." I laughed at myself. "I wonder what Vittorio has arranged. I'd better go check." I stopped as he put his hand around my wrist.

I took a step away, but he didn't let go of me. Still I didn't look at him, could barely look at his hand on me, remembering what it had done to me that afternoon.

"Are you all right?" His voice was serious.

"Me? Why shouldn't I be? I'm fine," I said, looking everywhere but at him.

He let go of me and sat up. I moved toward the door. "Vittorio took your boots and jacket. He's bringing them. If you like, you don't have to get up, you know. In fact, you could stay here overnight if you like."

"Thank you. But I'm all right now. And I'd like to come down to dinner, if I may."

"Yes, yes, of course." I had my hand on the doorknob. It was a narrow wave of brass, brand new and slick under my touch.

"Sally," he said. I stopped. "Thank you."

"For what?" I couldn't turn to face him, sure he would mention, at last, what had happened between us.

"For taking me in. I don't remember everything. I was pretty done in. I don't know what I told you. And I apologize for it, if it upset you." He waited for me to say something, but I was silent. "It's been . . . I didn't even realize you were back from America. I knew your father was and I just wanted to talk to him."

"Well, now you can," I said and left the room quickly.

He didn't remember. He did not remember that he had done that to me. I leaned on the wall outside his room, trying to control my shaking, trying not to cry—or laugh.

He didn't remember. That tremendous, brutal thing had happened between us and he didn't remember. I covered my mouth, sure I was about to make a great deal of noise, then saw Vittorio coming down the hall with Christian's tunic and boots.

I told him our guest was awake and I'd go down to tell my father that Lieutenant Mayr would be joining us for dinner. I could not imagine how I would be able to sit through a meal with him. But I did, of course.

He sat opposite me, looking pale and tired, his face drawn and grave. His manner was subdued and he and Daddy talked about what was happening to Röhm's men. I watched Christian, looking for the change in him, but saw nothing. He was neat, well-groomed again, if his uniform was not quite up to his usual standards. He spoke intelligently in his customary deliberate manner. My father, of course, accepted him, and was obviously impressed with Christian's assessment of the events, of his calm distress over the violence.

They were both so calm that I couldn't stand it. Finally, I interrupted them.

"Are you going to quit?" I said, leaning into the table, finally meeting Christian's eyes.

"What?" he said, a polite, confused smile on his face.

"Leave the SS? After what's happened. Aren't you going to quit?"

He looked from me to my father and I think we both saw that the thought had never occurred to him. Christian looked down at his dessert, a slim, rich piece of torte. He lay down his fork.

"I don't think I can. It would not be honorable," he said slowly.

"Honorable!" I snorted. "And what about Hans? Whom you killed?"

"Sally." My father was shocked. Christian hadn't told him about Hans or the executions.

"No. It is all right, Excellency. She is right to question me. Sally is, I think, my oldest friend and has never been afraid of asking me anything. I value this." He smiled sadly at me.

I wondered what he would say if I asked him why he didn't remember what had happened on the carpet in the sitting room that afternoon. I wanted to smash his handsome face in.

"It is the sacrifices that are important. Germany is in such danger, in such despair, that each of us who has a chance must make sacrifices. Must be strong for our country. Especially those of us in the SS who have made this oath. We have sworn loyalty to the Führer, and what good is that oath if we run away at the first sign of trouble?" He spoke carefully and quietly and then, just as carefully, just as quietly, laid his napkin next to his plate and stood up.

"I thank you both for your friendship and for helping me through this very difficult time. And for the dinner."

"But you haven't finished your dessert," said my father.

"I cannot."

"Another sacrifice?" This was from me, as nastily as I could say it.

He ignored me, and continued speaking to my father. "I think my staying here any longer would be an embarrassment to you, Excellency. I know you do not wish me to see Sally. I accept this"—and now he looked at me with his clear blue eyes. "I wish it could be different. Please, believe that. And I hope someday . . . Well, for now, I think I must leave." And saying that, he bowed—he bowed!—and left the dining room.

I stared at my plate, at the uneaten torte.

"Sally," said my father, reaching for my hand.

I jumped up and ran into the hall. Daddy didn't know everything, barely knew anything, what I had gone through alone at the beach house, what I had gone through, almost alone, here this afternoon.

Christian was taking his cap from Vittorio. He had his gun back in its holster. I hadn't noticed that at dinner. Vittorio went to the front door.

"You won't come back?" I said, pressing my hands together.

"No." He shook his head.

"You can't . . ." I started to say, but my voice was too loud.

"Sally." My father had come out out of the dining room.

I stepped back from Christian. "You're right. Of course. I was just wondering if you had anything to say to me."

An expression passed quickly over his face, but he merely shook his head. "I think it is best this way, Sally. I am sorry."

"You bastard," I said, my teeth clenched to keep them from chattering. I had started to shake again. But it didn't stop me from slapping him as hard as I could, leaving his cheek and jaw bright red.

He flinched, but did not raise his hand, either to me or to his face. Behind me, I heard my father gasp and Vittorio say something in Italian.

I turned and left the three men behind me to sort things out.

Later, lying in bed, trying to sleep, I found that my strongest memory of that unreal day was that Christian smelled bad—of sweat and damp wool and gunpowder, and of something else I could not identify.

Years later, in the destroyed and blasted city, whose canals and sewers were full of the dead, I would recognize the smell again. It was death itself. He had brought it into my elegant sitting room and had told me of it, warning me of its power. Its attraction.

THE LACE SHOP

During that weekend at the end of June, in the summer of 1934, the Nazis, with the SS doing the dirty work, managed to rid themselves of all sorts of bothersome people, including Ernst Röhm. Many of the murdered were old party members who had, for one reason or another, fallen out of favor. The numbers of people actually murdered ranged from seventy, according to Hitler, to several thousand, according to the rumors the foreign correspondents heard and relayed in the bars.

Himmler, with Heydrich, had consolidated the power of the SS and his new concentration camp at Dachau was full to bursting. With hindsight, of course, I can now see that the weekend was the start of the ruthless brutality and violence, sanctified by the state, that would come to overtake all of us. But first, Hitler let the evil loose on his own followers.

When I heard of an officer's wife who had been cold-bloodedly killed as she threw herself between the assassins and her husband, I knew just how terrible had been the price Christian paid for his new job, his position, and whatever else it was he thought the SS could give him.

Just days after that brutal weekend, I ran into David as I came out of Wertheim's, the big department store on Potsdamer Platz. I was leaving for Italy in a few days. David offered to walk along with me, as I had only one more errand left. I happily accepted his company. The store was being picketed by thugs in makeshift uniforms, not SA. I didn't know which was worse, the organized violence of the storm troopers or this new threat from what seemed to be common street gangs.

"We'll have a martini at the Adlon after. I know I deserve it after listening to all that crap." He gestured back at the picketers.

I put my hand in the crook of his arm, wishing I could confide in him. He would hate it, I knew, and he might even hate me because of it. So I stayed quiet, trying to keep up with him as he strode along the street. We turned the corner.

"Poor old Wertheim's. Bet it goes downhill fast."

"I know. I hoped to get in there before the takeover, but it was so crazy, I just left. Now I'm looking for a little shop, a little lace shop."

"A what?"

"A lace shop. A shop that sells lace, dear dimwit. Let's see. It should be right along here." I was looking for the address on a slip of paper and didn't see the danger.

"Uh-oh," said David, stopping. "More thugs."

"What?" I asked, then, looking up, I saw the four SA men ahead of us. "Oh, come on, David. Don't be such a coward." And laughing, I pulled him forward with me.

"Listen, Sally," said David, dragging his feet. "If I don't live through this, will you write my little ol' white-haired mother in Brooklyn?"

"Don't be silly. They're probably not even picketing the store I want. Sydney told me it's just a hole in the wall."

But as we drew close to the four men, I saw that they were picketing the lace store.

"Damn," I said, taking David's arm, and walked right by them. They were SA men, all sturdy young fellows, out proving their allegiance to the government that had just emasculated their organization.

"I'm glad you are so reasonable," said David, as we neared the corner. He stuck his hands in the pockets of his brown tweed trousers and jingled his keys.

I stopped, looking across the street at a tall, narrow poplar tree. Then I turned around and started back down the block.

"Whoa, I, where're you going?" cried David, starting after me.

"Back to the store. Sydney said they had the perfect collar for my new suit's blouse, and I won't have a gang of thugs spoiling things for me."

David grabbed my arm and stopped my march down the sidewalk. "Wait . . . I . . . you don't know these guys."

"Better than you imagine. Oh, David, you can't tell me they'd hurt *me*. I'm an American, they can't touch me." I didn't believe it, but I was sick of being frightened.

"Sweetheart, they won't care if you're Eleanor Roosevelt." He looked down the block where the SA men were watching us curiously. "They are not fooling."

"If you don't want to come with me, then don't, but I'm not going to let a few bullies tell me what to do." And freeing my arm from David's hand, I walked on.

"I'll go get a taxi in case you have to make a run for it," he called after me.

I laughed bravely and continued until I reached the men. I could see the narrow window of the shop. It was covered with swastikas and anti-Jewish slogans admonishing loyal Germans not to trade with the scum inside. I was more angry than frightened by now and the anger gave me strength to confront the picketers.

Smiling sweetly at the four men in their khaki uniforms and jackboots, I walked right through them to the recessed door of the little store.

"Hey, miss," said one fellow in German.

"Yes," I said in English, turning around, leaving one hand on the door.

"It would be better if you were to do your shopping elsewhere," he said in German.

"I'm so sorry," I said, still in English, "but I don't understand you." I smiled at them, still sweetly. "I thought all of you had been killed off," I added, daring them to understand me.

"A fucking foreigner," said a dark-haired man near the curb. "Guess they don't have Yids in England."

"But nobody is supposed to go in," argued the first man. "More money for the Yids."

I was furious and almost said something more, but instead, I turned and yanked open the door, quickly closing it behind me. A bell tinkled inside. The SA men did not enter the store after me.

I stood looking around the room I had risked my neck to enter. The store was very narrow—a glass case took up nearly all the space. Behind it and opposite to it, from the floor to the ceiling, were shelves full of small bolts of lace and boxes. There were no lights on, the only illumination came from the curtained window, and that was obscured by the crude slogans scribbled on the glass.

Looking out the window, I saw the SA men were talking energetically to each other. Perhaps they were deciding who should come in and drag me out.

It was very quiet in the shop. Then I heard whispering behind me and I turned to find a handsome, dark-haired young woman with the greenest eyes I had ever seen standing in the curtained doorway. She wore a dark print dress with white collar and cuffs of much finer stuff than the fabric of her dress. Her eyes shone in the dimness of the little shop.

"We are not open," she said.

"The door was."

"I was coming in to lock it. Now, I will do so after you leave."

"Yes, all right," I said and turned to go. At the door, I stopped. I could see the smudged shadows of the men outside. One of them stepped up to the door. There was a heavy bolt at about eye level and, quite instinctively, I pushed it into place. The man tried the door, rattling the handle. I backed into the shop, watching until he stopped and moved away.

"What did you want?" The young woman's voice was still incredulous.

"A collar for a silk blouse—to wear with a black suit, very smart," I said, turning to face her. "And probably buttons. Do you have buttons?" I looked around.

"Wait a moment, please," she said and disappeared back through the curtains.

I turned to look through the display-case glass and rubbed out a circle. My white-gloved finger came away black.

"It is very dirty. I am sorry, Fräulein," said another voice. I turned. The young woman was back with an older woman. She was very short and dressed all in black, her white hair arranged on top of her head. She also wore beautiful lace at her throat and wrists. She move behind the counter and smiled at me.

"We have been closed almost a month now," she said. Then she made a little gesture with one hand, waving away the minor difficulties.

"You need a collar, Fräulein? For a silk blouse?"

"Yes," I said.

"Good, good. I can help you. It will be perfect. But first, tea." I started to demur. "Please. Marlene, tea for the Fräulein," she called. She had a sweet voice, but was very brisk, a woman used to her own way.

She led me through the curtained door. "The light is better here," she explained. She didn't have to add that we would be hidden from view.

Through the curtain was a small sitting room with deep-green walls and a fine green-and-cream Oriental carpet. A small sofa and two armchairs were upholstered in green, pale yellow, and cream stripes. Everything here was clean, and there was ample light from a lovely, delicate chandelier. It looked like all the best shops, where quiet salesgirls carried or modeled the items one at a time. I realized that it had indeed been an exclusive little shop, and I was angry anew at the stupidity of the waste.

Tea arrived and the old lady and I drank and chatted about pleasantries as though four young men did not hover threateningly outside on the sidewalk.

Marlene, though, was tense and remained suspicious of me, giving me hard looks as the older woman served the tea and dry biscuits.

"Sugar?" asked the old lady.

I started to ask for it, then saw the level of sugar in the bowl. "No, thank you," I said.

"Don't Americans take sugar? As the English do?"

"I suppose it depends."

"They drink coffee, Mother," said Marlene from the door.

"Oh, I am sorry," exclaimed the old woman.

"No, please. This is lovely." I put my cup down. "This room. And your kindness. I didn't expect . . ."

"We're Jews," blurted out Marlene.

I stared at her. "I know," I said softly. The older woman held up a thin hand.

"Marlene," she said emphatically. Then she smiled at me. "We will not speak of it. You are here for a purpose and we will help you. Now to business."

The tea tray cleared, the swatches appeared, and Marlene passed back and forth between the two small rooms with samples of lace. Some were actually collars wrapped in tissue paper that the old lady's slender fingers peeled carefully away.

I shook my head. "I don't know," I said, laughing. "It is all beautiful. I can't make up my mind."

The old woman delicately rubbed her fingertip against her lip, thinking. "Ah," she said, her faded blue eyes lighting up. "I know. I will get it myself." She rose from her chair and left the room, rustling in her long, old-fashioned skirt.

Marlene stood against the other door with her arms folded in front of her. She watched until the curtains stopped moving, then quickly crossed to sit next to me.

"You are really an American?" she asked. She spoke hurriedly, just above a whisper.

"Yes."

She took a deep breath. "You are very brave to come in here. Will they hurt you when you leave?"

"I don't know." I brushed my navy skirt. "I guess I'll find out." I smiled at her with more bravado than I felt.

"What is your name?"

"Sally Jackson."

The other woman repeated it. "I will remember," she said.

I looked around the room and saw a wedding picture in a silver frame atop a small table. I rose and walked to it.

"Is it you?" I asked.

"Yes," answered Marlene. "My husband is in Switzerland."

"Oh, working?"

There was a pause before the answer. "No. He had to go."

I turned to face her. "Had to?"

"Yes." Marlene's green eyes bore steadily into mine, daring me to ask more questions.

"But you stayed here."

"My mother-in-law wouldn't leave her lace," said Marlene in a tight bitter voice. "And I have a little girl."

"A child," I exclaimed, wondering and somewhat afraid at where this conversation would lead.

Just then the old lady came back into the sitting room with a long fold of tissue paper in her hands.

"Here it is," she said and reverently laid her find on the low table. The little room was silent except for the crinkling of the tissue paper as she carefully folded the layer back from the treasure within.

I gasped. "This is beautiful," I whispered and looked up at the woman. "But it's too . . . too much. It's exquisite. And it must be very valuable. A piece of lace like this . . ." I reached out, reluctant to touch the gossamer lace. Here and there tiny seed pearls were scattered amid the flowers of the pattern.

The old lady picked it up with both hands. "Come," she said and led me to the mirror over Marlene's wedding picture. She arranged the lace, a length of about a yard, around my neck, creating a V-shaped collar.

"There you are," she said, holding on to the two end pieces at the back. "Isn't it beautiful?"

"It's perfect," I said, thinking of the dress the lace should rightfully adorn. Then I saw Marlene's face in the mirror.

She was looking at her mother-in-law and her expression was one of utter resignation, of sadness, of defeat.

"Madam, I couldn't. It must be too expensive for me. And it is too beautiful and rare for a suit blouse." I lifted the lace gently off my shoulders and carried it back to the tissue-paper nest.

"I will give you a good price. Because I think you are a young lady who appreciates beautiful things."

"How much?" I asked doubtfully, keenly aware of Marlene's eyes on me.

The old lady named a figure.

"Oh, no," I cried. "Madam, this piece is worth ten times that. I would be robbing you."

"Money," said Marlene. Distracted, I glanced at her.

"I would rather you had it than one of their fat wives," said the

279

old lady fiercely. She stood very straight, looking at me with her chin up.

"And we could use the money," said Marlene slowly.

I looked from one to the other, then sat down and grabbed my purse. Opening it quickly, I pulled out my wallet. I had about fifty dollars' worth of German marks. I counted out almost all of it.

"Here. I'll just keep this to get home." I handed the bills to Marlene. "That's for the lace. Now," I said, looking up at the old lady, "I need a small, more ordinary piece. And cuffs, too." And I pulled my emergency fund out of one of the wallet pockets—two fifty-dollar bills. I placed them on the table, still folded. It seemed so little.

The old lady, unhappy at my ploy, was silent, but her daughter-in-law jumped up.

"Yes, I'll get them."

Marlene returned with several pieces of lace that were quickly wrapped in tissue paper and placed next to the first.

The old lady fingered the paper around the treasure. "My mother brought it from Vienna when she married my father. She said it was a scrap from the Empress Elizabeth's wedding gown." She looked up at me and smiled. "I doubt this story, but it is romantic and I like to think it is true." She took her hand from the paper-covered lace. "Marlene, will you wrap this, please?"

"Madam," I said. "May I give you my card? If you have something else you think I would like." I pulled one of my calling cards out of its silver holder. "Or if I can be of any help to you. Please." And I handed it to the old lady. "I'm going away, but I'll be back at the end of the summer."

"Thank you, Fräulein. That is most gracious of you. Here, Marlene, my dear," said the woman, handing my card to her daughter-in-law, who was waiting to usher me out.

Gathering my gloves and bag, I saw Marlene's face as she read the address. I said my good-byes to the older lady and passed into the outer shop.

"The embassy?"

"My father is the ambassador," I said. Marlene handed me the small oblong package of brown paper and string. I tucked it and my purse firmly under my arm. "If I can do anything . . ." I said.

Marlene nodded and smiled briefly, then she faded back toward the curtains. I took a deep breath, forced a smile onto my face and opened the door.

I was out onto the pavement before the SA men realized it, and walking toward the corner. I heard them call me.

"Hey, girl. Miss Englishwoman."

I continued walking, wondering if they would follow. They did. I heard running feet behind me.

"Hey, stop. Hey, you." Their voices were very loud.

So I stopped and turned toward the men.

"Yes," I said in English. "What do you want? Why are you yelling at me?" I asked in an even tone.

The first man to reach me grabbed my arm and, outraged, I jerked it away.

"How dare you?" I yelled, even angrier than I had been when I entered the lace shop. "Don't you dare touch me or you'll have the government of the United States of America to deal with."

"America," he said. "You're an American?"

"What kind of a country is this that women are accosted on the street in broad daylight? You think you can just do anything? You're barbarians. All of you. You take one more step toward me and you'll be sorry!"

The young men looked at me in consternation. I suppose they were not used to being treated like that. I didn't care, I was furious at them. At that moment a taxi pulled up in the street next to me. Its brakes screeched, startling the SA bullies.

"Jesus Christ, Sally," said David, flinging open the door of the taxi. "Get in here—quick!"

"Go away, David," I said, "I'm all right. Oh, shut up," I yelled as an SA man started to speak. "You just shut up, all of you. I've had enough of this, being pushed around in this wretched country."

David appeared next to me and took hold of my arm, trying to steer me into the car. People were starting to gather. "Sally, come on, kid, this is getting out of hand."

"This used to be a wonderful place, but you and your damn Führer have spoiled it." I was yelling in English, but the crowd picked up on "Führer" and their mutterings began to grow louder. David grabbed both my arms, spun me around and pushed me into the taxi, jumping in and closing the door after us. He yelled something at the driver and the car sped off.

"Damn it," I said, beating my fists against my thighs. "Damn it, damn it, damn it! I hate this country!"

"Here, kid," he said, when I had calmed down, offering me a cigarette. My hands were shaking so badly, I could barely hold it in the flame of his lighter. "So, did you get your lace?" he asked. I held the package up. "I hope it was worth it." I nodded and placed the package carefully on my lap, smoothing out the paper.

"Whew," said David, "what a gal."

"I made a real spectacle of myself, didn't I?"

"Sure did. But it was magnificent."

"This is awful. How can you smoke these things?" And I thrust the cigarette at him. He took it and put it out.

When the taxi stopped, he put his arms around me and gently helped me out.

"Where are we?" I asked, looking around. It was a wide street, and treeless, which was strange for Berlin, the buildings all huge gray monoliths.

"I live up there," he said, and not giving me a chance to comment, led me into the courtyard of his building and up the five flights of stairs to his little flat. Three rooms, no kitchen, with two windows facing the courtyard. The small sitting room was empty of furniture except for a table and two chairs and a bicycle propped up on its kickstand, with a pair of aviator goggles hanging from the handles.

"I'll get you a drink," he said. "The bathroom's in there and I hope you appreciate the fact that I have one." He waved in its direction. When I came back he handed me a glass of very good brandy. We stood by the dirty windows. It was warm and stuffy in the room, and I unbuttoned the jacket of my suit.

"What's wrong, kid?" he asked. I shook my head. "You can tell me. We're pals, right?"

I looked at him, considering, but I knew I couldn't tell him what Christian had done to me, what I had let him do. I felt so guilty and angry about that afternoon, I could hardly think coherently about it, let alone explain it to someone, especially to David.

"Is it Heydrich?" he asked, handing me another glass.

"Oh, no, that's all over. My father didn't like it and we all agreed. Before I went to the States." I drank, then looked around the room. "How can you live here? It's so depressing."

Moving closer to me, David said, "It's dirt cheap. I don't get paid much. And I'm seldom here. Hold still, you've got . . ." and using his thumb, he gently wiped something away from under my eye. His hand was soft and cool on my flushed face.

"I look a mess," I said, raising my hand to my face. He caught my hand, palm to palm with his.

"Not at all," he said, spreading his fingers, letting my fingers coil around his. My thumb ran over his, our hands parted, the fingers stroking and parting, clasping and letting go.

I leaned against him as I watched our hands intertwine. Finally, he brought my hand to his mouth, lightly brushing my fingers with his lips. I felt a stirring inside me and raised my face to his. He kissed me, holding my face, holding me close. I'd never felt such physical closeness with another person, not even with Christian, and it made me breathless.

I backed away—just a step or two—from him. He searched my face for a long time, and when he was satisfied with what he saw, he leaned forward, bridging the space between us, and gently kissed me again, his lips barely touching mine, making me lean, in turn, toward him.

Still without a word, he led me into the tiny bedroom. We lay down together and he held me, until I lifted my face and he kissed me. It was dark in the room and I liked the darkness. I liked being able to feel nothing but his lips and tongue and that he needed a shave, and I could smell the sun his shirt had been dried in. I liked not thinking. I liked his kisses. I liked his lips on my breasts, soft and insistent, pulling and sucking, his hands gently cupping and molding me as though he were drinking me in. I unbuttoned his shirt and touched his bare skin and found I liked that too, especially the feel of his nakedness against my breasts. I liked everything he did to me there in the dark. And my mind finally was at peace.

Until I felt his hand between my legs. He'll know, I thought instantly. If I let him make love to me, he will know I am no longer a virgin. And I knew he would know who had had me. And he would hate me.

I sat up abruptly, wiggling out from under his hands and mouth. I pulled my skirt down and folded my arms over my bare breasts.

"What is it?" His voice was thick and husky, his hands were on my back.

"Where are my things?" I said. "I need my things. I should go home."

I expected him to be angry. Instead, he did a terrible thing. He tried to understand me in terms of that innocence he had talked about in the kitchen that night.

"Oh, God, kid, I'm sorry." He put his arm around me. "I shouldn't have let it go so far. You're so sweet, I just couldn't stop. I'm sorry. Shhh, that's okay. Sally, you're such a sweet kid. I'd never do anything to hurt you. I'm just nuts about you. Ever since we met. Remember how we necked in the taxi? You looked so fresh, like the girls on Fifth Avenue in the fall, all dolled up in their new autumn duds, ready to take on the world."

"Oh, shut up, David," I cried, jumping off the bed, grabbing

283

my shoes, pulling my clothes together. "None of you knows anything at all about me. It's driving me crazy."

I hurried into the bathroom, and when I came out he was back by the window, fully dressed, smoking.

I stood by the door and tried to apologize. He waved his hand. "Forget it, kid. I'm the one who's sorry. But tell me this, what'd you mean, 'none of you'? You talking about the blond again? Did he make a pass at you too?"

I looked at him a long moment, tempted to tell him, just to shock him, to prove how wrong his notions about me were, but I didn't. "I didn't mean anything. I was talking about him, yes, and you, and my father. All of you." And with that lie, I left. I wouldn't let him take me home but he insisted on coming downstairs to get me a taxi.

When he leaned down through the open window to give me a kiss, I did something I have regretted ever since: I turned my head so that his lips just grazed my cheek. I know he knew that it wasn't an accident, but I couldn't look at him. I couldn't tell him why. It was awful.

I spent the rest of the summer in northern Italy, looking at paintings and statues. My father, who was finding his position more and more difficult, joined me in Florence, and we took a small villa in Fiesole for two weeks in August. There were jackboots and uniforms all over Italy too, but I pretended they weren't there, loosing myself in the glories of the past.

There had been repercussions about my scene with the SA at the lace shop. Word had gotten back to the embassy. Father told me that I had been wrong, that I should not, could not, interfere in the internal affairs of our host country. "But," he said to me, "I am proud of you, Sally."

I ducked my head, flustered. Pleased. He asked me about the people in the lace shop and I explained, telling him everything, showing him the lace, which I had brought with me to Italy, not wanting to let it out of my sight. He told me to let him know if he could do anything, but to remember that, officially, he was not allowed to help.

"FDR didn't hire me, Daddy," I said to him.

"No, my dear, he didn't," he replied, and laughed, his tired face finally relaxing.

Though Italy under Mussolini was not nirvana, we both felt wonderful to be out of Germany. I had seriously considered not returning, but after that moment with my father, I knew I could not leave him alone in Berlin.

I had nightmares about what Christian had told me and what I heard from other people, Brian and David especially. David, with whom I had an uneasy Bon Voyage dinner, had seen one of the execution sites: a row of four tall stakes in a courtyard of an old stable. The stakes had been splintered away by bullets and the old stucco wall behind them had been splattered with blood that wouldn't wash out. As he described the scene to me, all I could think of was Hans Behrends being cut in half by the bullets of Christian's gun.

In Italy, I tried to put those horrors behind me, although I felt a deep, dark sadness in my heart that would not go away. I think it must have been for Christian. I mourned him, not only for myself but for the man he had been and wasn't anymore. I didn't think about David. I felt too treacherous, too much the liar.

I had told no one about that afternoon. There were many reasons, not the least of which was what had happened between Christian and me. But I also felt some obscure need to protect Christian, although any protection of mine was obviously useless against the real danger he was encountering, against the things he had done. But I knew that Heydrich would be enraged if he knew Christian had told me about Hans Behrends and the others and the rest of it. Perhaps I should have told my father of Christian's crimes, but they were too terrible. I kept the secret. If I told one secret, the other might slip out too.

I began to think seriously about my future and what I might do with myself. I hated the things that had happened to me, the way I had behaved. Here I was, twenty-one, and I was not at all the honest, straightforward person I imagined myself. What Christian had done to me was very close to rape, except I had allowed it to happen. Then I had rejected David, who obviously would have been gentle and loving. I hated knowing this about myself and I resolved not ever to let any man near me, until I met the man I would marry. Who that would be, I couldn't imagine.

Then I found out I was pregnant.

I was terrifically stupid about such matters, but I did know, from college dormitory conversations, what missing my periods meant. When the weeks went by in July, I hardly noticed, what with the traveling and all, but by the last week in August, when nothing had happened, I realized I had missed two months.

I even remember where I was, sitting in the Piazza della Repubblica, in Florence, trying to write a postcard to David. I was flipping through my appointment book, looking for the dates Sydney and Brian would arrive, when, I guess, the squares of days, all laid out neatly, reminded me. Quickly, I thought back to my last period and then I almost started to laugh at the absurdity of it all, the stupidity, the absolute wrongness of it. I tore up the postcard. How could I ever look David in the face again? I gathered up my things and went back up the hill to the hotel. I needed help, that was obvious, and the only person I could trust to give it to me was Sydney.

She and Brian arrived in Florence the next week. As soon as I could, I got Sydney alone and told her. She was wonderful, gentle and understanding, never condemning.

"You know what the very worst part of this whole thing is?" I asked her. I was sitting on the floor of my room in the hotel, leaning against the bed, my shoes off. She was in the corner, next to the window, curled in a large armchair, smoking. Brian had gone off to take pictures.

"What, love?"

"It's that it happened and it was nothing. You'd think, being pregnant as I am, I would know something now about—you know, *it*. God, I can't even talk about *it*."

"He didn't make love to you, is what you mean."

"Yes. But David . . ."

"Don't tell me you and David—"

"No, but close. I . . . oh, Sydney, I deserve this. If I had been decent and moral, this wouldn't have happened to me."

"Don't be silly." She blew out a stream of smoke. "I'm going to ask you a question, and you don't have to answer, all right?" I nodded. "Are you sure this baby is Christian's? Are you sure, whatever it was that happened between you and David, this could not be his child?"

"I'm sure, Sydney. I know what's supposed to go where." Talking about it embarrassed me and I couldn't look at her.

"All right, love, I just wanted to ask. Because, of course, David would marry you in a flash. Not that he would be the most suitable, but he'd be better than—I don't suppose you'd consider marrying David anyway?"

"Oh, Sydney, how could I? Can you imagine how that would hurt him? I wouldn't let him make love to me because of Christian.

286

He'd hate me, Sydney. He'll hate me anyway, when he finds out." And I started crying again.

"There, there, love," she said, sitting down next to me, putting her arm around me. "Pull yourself together. We must decide what you should do. You haven't got much time. Now, another question. Tell me, do you love Christian? Now?"

I took a moment to answer. It was a question I had been asking myself. "I don't know. I haven't seen him. He doesn't seem to still care for me. But I don't know."

"What about marriage?"

"With him? It would mean staying here. The politics . . ."

"Sally, sometimes I think all of that is so unimportant," she whispered. "Men become so overwhelmed with power and who's got it and what they're doing with it, don't they? I think of myself as a reasonably well-educated, modern woman, and I can manage myself well enough with conversations about foreign affairs or the Treaty of Versailles, but I wonder, really wonder if all of it's not just nonsense."

"Love isn't."

"No. Nor are men and women loving each other and having children and taking care of them." She sat next to me, her long legs reaching beyond mine. "Of course, the politics become highly relevant when the result is roundups and camps."

"And wars."

"Yes, and wars."

The conversation made me think again about Christian's sobbing that day, about his pain. And I began to think I should tell him. Besides, he had only said he didn't want to see me again because he didn't want to embarrass my father. He had never said he didn't want to see me because he didn't care for me. Things would be different if we were married. If he would marry me. If he believed that what had happened had happened.

I leaned my head back against the bed. "Oh, Sydney, I don't know what to do." I got up and went to the dresser, picking up my brush. "It's Christian's baby, and he should know." I ran my hand over the hard bristles of the brush, back and forth.

"Have you thought about an abortion?" Sydney had gotten up and was sitting on the bed, her eyes meeting mine in the mirror.

"No." I looked down at the brush. "Yes. It frightens me. You hear such horror stories."

"Well, the first thing you must do is be sure. I know a doctor—he's discreet and very kind. He's Jewish and has been

287

very helpful to me. Brian and I are trying to get him a visa. Well, he doesn't want to leave. He won't be able to practice in England."

"What have you been going to a doctor for?"

She raised her hand and smoothed her hair away from her face. "The opposite of your problem. I want to be pregnant and can't seem to achieve it." She grinned at me. "No matter how hard we try. It's one reason we came to Italy. The romance."

I flushed and managed a smile, turning back to the mirror. I started brushing my hair. I knew so little. I felt so ignorant, so out of control. This thing had happened to me and a baby, another being, might be inside me right now as a result. It was hard to understand, hard to accept. I should have let David make love to me. At least, then I would have an idea of what it could be. I continued brushing my hair, until the static made it leap out from my brush. I couldn't look myself in the eyes.

When I returned to Berlin in early September, I went to Sydney's doctor. I told him the truth, without telling him the details. He was kind, if disapproving. I said I wanted to be sure before I told the father. He sighed and, patting my shoulder, told me to get dressed.

I was indeed pregnant and once I knew that, I knew I would tell Christian. I wasn't sure I wanted to marry him, but I was sure I wanted him to know what had happened. Then I would decide what to do.

"Sally?" David's voice was rushed and excited. "The boom has been lowered . . ."

It was late afternoon, the day after my doctor's appointment, and I had just returned from a visit to a girls' school with Mrs. Bushmuller. I was exhausted and nervy and had nearly caused a scene when I had spoken harshly to a girl who, dressed neatly in her German Maiden's League uniform, had presented us with flowers.

"What is it?" I tried to interrupt David, but he shushed me.

"Quiet, kid, I don't have much time. I'm at the office. There are two goons here in leather raincoats who are going to escort me to the train station."

"Oh, David," I said, sinking onto the hard cushion of the booth's chair. "Are you all right?"

"Sure."

"What can I do?"

"Pack my stuff. I'm taking the four-forty to Paris—oh, God, I gotta admit I'm not sorry about getting out of here. Can you go to my place and bring my stuff to the station? The concierge'll let you in. I'll call her. Just pack what'll fit in my suitcase and the carry-all. I've got some books, maybe you could send them later. There's not much, as you saw. If it doesn't fit, throw it away or keep it. Can you do that?"

I assured him that I could and hung up. Then I took the time to call Sydney at the British embassy. Sydney wasn't there, or not available, and I left a message. I tried her home and there was no answer. I was still wearing my hat and gloves, so I just ran out and got in the car and gave Rick the address.

David was right. There weren't many personal things to pack. I had his clothes packed in no time, trying to slip books and a photograph of an old couple, his parents, I guessed, in among the clothing. Quickly, I checked through all the drawers and under the bed, ignoring the memory the sight of it caused. Everything was very tidy, which I hadn't noticed on my last visit. He had a bottle of brandy under the sink and I tucked that into the carry-all.

A desk under the window in the second room was covered with papers and books. I went through the drawers, finding blank paper and some pens. I gathered it all up. Under some paper, I found a small notebook. Pulling it out, I opened it, but quickly closed it again. I had seen my name. I hesitated for a long moment before stuffing the notebook into the bag. It didn't feel right handling his personal things; I didn't have to pry any further. A glance at my watch settled the question. It was four o'clock and I had to get to the station.

Rick hauled the cases downstairs, and I handed over the key to the concierge, telling her to take whatever was left in the apartment. At the station, I let Rick take care of the bags, and ran on ahead. The traffic had been heavy, and my watch, which sometimes ran fast, said four forty-five. I bought two platform tickets, gave one to Rick, and hurried out, relieved to see the train was still there. Several cars ahead, I saw two men, wearing leather raincoats as David had described, standing below a window. I ignored them, searching the train windows for David.

"Hello, kiddo," said the familiar voice. I looked up to see David sticking his head out of the open window.

"I've got your bags," I said, gesturing toward Rick, who was hurrying up behind me.

"You're aces."

I explained to the raincoats that they were David's bags and finally they agreed to let the cases on the train.

"Where are you going?" I asked, looking up at him. He was smoking a cigarette.

"Paree, France."

"What happened?"

"They didn't like what I wrote. Didn't you read it?"

"David, I've been away."

"Oh, yeah. Well, see what happens when you leave."

"What's going to happen now, with you gone?" I felt my eyes filling with tears. I reached my hand up to him. He took it, lacing his fingers through mine. He smiled at me, and I knew he was thinking of our hands that day. "David, I wanted . . . there are things I wanted to talk about."

"I know, kid."

"Please, don't hate me. I don't want you to hate me."

"You, kiddo? Not possible. Not possible. Honest. We're pals, right?"

"Forever."

Conductors started shouting and slamming doors shut. The raincoats backed away from the car, their work almost done. I let go of David and took a step back from the train. As the train started to move, I walked along with it, holding my little straw hat on in the gusts.

"Write me, please?" I cried.

"Will do, kiddo," he said, tossing his cigarette away. "Remember about the dark woods!" He raised his hand.

The train picked up speed and I stopped walking with it, watching as it, and my friend, disappeared to the west. I stood staring after that damn train for a long time. It had all happened so fast, and I wondered if I would ever see him again. When I turned to leave the platform, the two raincoats were standing off to one side, watching me. Rick was farther away, and I ignored the goons and went up to meet him.

All the way home, I thought about David and how much fun he had been and how much he had cared. I remember how he had fought with me and rescued me from the SA guys and how he had been so fierce about things and people he cared about. I thought of his kisses. And how I had lied and lied and lied to him.

I looked out of the car window at the busy streets. People were hurrying home in the dusk to dinners and families. I felt so alone, even though I was, in my turn, hurrying home to dinner. At least,

I thought, he won't be here to see whatever happens to me and this baby.

At home, there was a message from Sydney. I called her back and we had a good long talk, both of us crying a little. I remember what she said, just before she hung up.

"Maybe it's time for us all to leave, love," she said. "Now that the summer is over."

CHRISTIAN'S OFFICE

O n my return from Italy, I had found a two-week-old letter from the proprietor of the lace shop, asking that I come to see her as soon as I could.

Worried that too much time might have passed, I did as she asked the day after David left. The shop was no longer picketed by SA men, but it looked even more abandoned and forlorn than before.

Madam was there, and Marlene's little daughter, living in the rooms in back. I started to ask about food, money, but she waved me to silence. Her daughter-in-law had been arrested.

"Two weeks ago?" I said, horrified to think of Marlene in the hands of the Gestapo all that time.

"No, thank God. That message I sent you then was to ask for a loan. You see, Marlene's husband, my son, Joseph, sent us money to come to him, but it wasn't enough. I managed to raise some more. We had enough to pay—to buy—our visas, when, just yesterday morning, they came for her."

"Why? What had she done?"

"Done, Fräulein Jackson?" said the old lady. "It wasn't for anything she had done, it was for what she is."

"I'm sorry. Yes. What can I do? Can I do anything?"

"Get her out."

"But I can't. My father cannot interfere. The President has been quite clear . . ." I stopped. "I know someone who can. Yes. I can do that." And I turned and started to leave, then came quickly back to give her the money I had brought with me. "For food. Anything. I can get more, so don't worry," I said and left.

I had the choice of going to Heydrich or Christian for help, but I knew I could never ask the general for anything.

"Christian? It's me."

"Sally? Is that you? Where are you?"

"I'm home. Here, in Berlin." I sat in the small phone box, twisting the cord around my fingers, my heart pounding.

"You were in Italy." His voice, coming through the line, was formal, distant.

"Yes. Christian, I need to see you. Could I come see you?"

"When?"

"Now. This afternoon. It is an emergency." A double emergency, with time running out on both, but I couldn't think of my personal problem right then. I put it out of my mind.

"All right." And he told me where to go, how to find him in the SD headquarters on the Friedrichstrasse.

He had moved into his own office, with two men in an anteroom and a girl banging on a typewriter.

"Obersturmführer Mayr," I said tentatively. The room was large, with the three occupied desks plus an empty one in the corner.

"Do you mean Hauptsturmführer Mayr?" said one of the men snootily, looking up from an open file.

"Yes. I meant that." A promotion to captain. For his work on that bloody weekend? I nearly backed away, but thought of Marlene and straightened up. I also remembered I was not an unimportant person.

"I am Ambassador Jackson's daughter and I have an appointment with Hauptsturmführer Mayr. Would you please tell him I am here." I could be snooty myself.

The man picked a telephone and spoke into it and immediately the door to the inner office opened and Christian came out. He was in his shirt sleeves, his tie loosened. He came to me, his hand out. We shook hands politely, almost as strangers, greeting each other with meaningless pleasantries. Then he led me into his office.

It was a mess, with cartons piled around, bare empty shelves, and the smell of new paint. There was, as well, a large window with new blinds, a handsome desk, and a good carpet on the floor.

"It's all new," he said, removing a pile of files and paper from a chair, indicating that I should sit. "I just moved in yesterday."

"Your promotion?" I said.

"Yes." He sat on the edge of the desk. "You look well. Your travels have agreed with you."

"Yes." I crossed my legs, covering my knees with my skirt as I did so. I felt him watching me.

"How is your father?"

"Well. Tired."

"Ah." He laced his fingers together nervously. "Did you know my mother is back?"

"No."

"No," he said at the same time. "Of course you didn't." His

booted leg was in my line of vision, swinging back and forth. I remembered his boots covered with dirt on that summer's day, and stood up.

"Christian." He smiled at me, a stranger's smile, guarded, wary. He stopped swinging his leg as he watched me. "It's strange seeing you here," I said.

"Please." He indicated that I should sit again. "It is nice to see you. I wish I had something to offer you, a drink." I sat down and he moved around to sit behind his desk. "Now, tell me what you came for."

I told him about Marlene, pushing aside my nerves and my shyness at seeing him. He listened, his elbows on the desk. When I had finished, he reached for a pad of paper.

"Tell me their names. All of them." He wrote down the information as I gave it to him. "And the woman was arrested. . . ?"

"Yesterday morning."

He reached for the telephone. When he hung up, he smiled at me, or almost did. "There. She's found. They'll bring her here. No. Sit down, Sally. We'll wait here. It's better."

"Is she all right? Will they let her go?"

"Yes to both questions."

"Just like that. They'll let her go, just like that?"

"Just like that." His eyes were steady, looking at me, frankly as though to say: This is what I can do. This is the power my uniform, my promotion, my position have given me.

"Do you still work for the general?" I asked.

"Of course. Everyone in this building does."

I fell silent and we just sat, almost without conversation, for the quarter hour until the phone rang. The prisoner was downstairs, waiting to be released into his custody. Christian took his tunic off the back of his chair and buttoned himself into it as he led me from the room. He grabbed his hat as we passed a shelf and we went down to the ground floor.

An SS man opened a door. Marlene sat on a chair in the middle of the small room. Her head was bowed, but jerked up when we entered. She stared at us without seeing. She had on a dress with short sleeves and I could see bruises on her upper arm where someone had grabbed her roughly, but other than that she looked all right.

I went to her and knelt next to her. "Do you recognize me, Marlene?"

Her eyes met mine. Her beautiful green eyes were empty. Dead. I recoiled slightly from her, from her frightening eyes. What had they done to her? Then she recognized me. I could see the knowledge fight her fear.

"The American. Sally."

"Yes. Sally. Your mother-in-law sent me. I've come to take you to her. And your daughter."

"Annie."

"Yes, to Annie. They're waiting for you. Will you come?" and I stood up, my arm around her waist, pulling her up with me. Her body stiffened. I looked to see what had happened: she had seen Christian standing at the open door. He smiled at us, his face kind and guileless above the uniform. "No, no, it's all right. He's a friend," I murmured to her. "He's helping. He had you released. He's a friend."

She looked sideways at me, disbelief in her face. "You will stay with me?" she said.

"Of course I will. Right to the train."

We drove to the shop, where we collected the old lady and the little girl and took them all to the station. I had telephoned Marlene's mother-in-law to warn her that she must be ready to leave as soon as we arrived. She had a case packed for Marlene, and I gave the young woman my purse, with money for practicalities and comb, brush, and lipstick for her morale. Her daughter, though, was the best tonic, and I was relieved to see Marlene's face soften as she embraced her little girl.

After all the rush we were early, and Christian shepherded us into the station café, buying coffee and cakes for us. The little girl fell asleep and, in the end, he carried her to the train, where Marlene turned to take her from him. I think she hated seeing her daughter in his arms, but she managed to smile and thank him.

He went away, saying he would wait for me, and I got onto the train with the women to settle them into their compartment. Finally, there was nothing more for me to do and I left too. I waited until the train pulled away, watching it disappear.

Christian waited for me at the entrance to the platforms, smoking. He was relaxed and his eyes were on me all the way.

"Thank you for doing that," I said.

He flicked the cigarette away and turned to leave the station. I followed alongside him. "What's the matter?" he asked, putting his arm lightly over my shoulders. "Did you think I was such a monster that I'd refuse to help?"

"I didn't know what you could, or would do."

"You know me better than that, don't you?"

I looked at him and his head turned, catching my glance. "Yes, I do, I guess," I said, wondering if I was right.

"Thank you for the confidence," he said, his arm dropping from my shoulders.

"I'm sorry, but things have changed. You know they have changed. You can't deny it. Things have changed between us. We . . ."

"Yes?" he said, interrupting, wanting me to continue.

I couldn't. "You know," I said. "You must know." We had stopped, still in the busy station, the people flowing around us, avoiding us. I walked away. I still couldn't believe he didn't remember what had happened between us.

"Sally, I'm sorry. Wait." He reached for my arm and I swerved away. He didn't try again. Didn't speak again. Just walked with me to the car. He opened the door for me and closed it after I got in. He leaned down to the open window. "He'll drive you home."

"Don't you need. . . ?"

"I've got a meeting. I'm fine." He stood up, his hand still on the door. I leaned forward to speak, so he would hear me.

"Thank you, Christian. Thank you."

He didn't say anything. Just lightly tapped the door and waved to the driver, who moved the car away.

I didn't turn to look at him, but I thought about him all the way home. It took a long time, through the rush-hour traffic.

Christian had helped. And he had done it for me. Because I had asked him. That much was clear. Our friendship, tenuous as it was, was still intact. If I told him about the baby, though, what would happen then? Could he rescue me as easily?

And his promotion. If we got married, how would I like being the wife of a captain in Heydrich's SD?

I watched the lights blur as we passed th. m, traveling faster now as we entered my neighborhood. But what should I do then? I didn't have much time before I had to make a decision, before I had to tell my father.

I needed help. And that was what convinced me to tell Christian. If I had been pregnant with someone else's baby, in the same desperate situation, I would have turned to him. Because, and this thought shamed me, he wouldn't judge me. He would accept me. He had always accepted me, my stubbornness, my temper, my thoughtlessness. How could I treat him this way? How could I make judgments about him? I didn't know what he had gone through, although he had tried to tell me. And I did not know what I might have done in the same situation.

I needed help. I needed to see him.

The lobby of the gym was empty. The last time I had been there was to watch Heydrich's bout. Then, I had hurried through without noticing the wall of trophies and framed team pictures. The only things that made it different from my college gym were the black banners with the SS lightning bolts and the requisite portraits of Hitler and Himmler. I pushed through the double doors at one end of the lobby. In the dimly lit stairwell, I could hear the distant sound of blades hitting. It was an eerie sound echoing down to me, and made me uneasy and profoundly unsure about my right to be here. I could turn and leave, and no one would ever know.

But I had to find him. I had to tell him. I had gone to his office building in the morning and, after a frustrating conversation with a patronizing reception clerk, finally had been sent here. I went up the stairs, the old wood creaking at my every step.

When I pushed at another door and encountered resistance, I stepped back. The door opened and a young man in a fencing uniform stuck his head out. He was surprised to see me.

"Fräulein?" he said softly.

"Good day," I said. "I'm looking for someone. They told me he was here."

"Who told you, Fräulein?" He was obviously as nonplussed about this encounter as I was.

"At Friedrichstrasse. An officer," I said helplessly.

Patiently, he asked me whom I was looking for. "He's fencing," he said, when I told him. "I'll let him know. Do you want to come in and watch?" He opened the door for me and I slipped into the gym.

Three fencing strips had been laid out at the far end of the gym for the six fencers who were using them. Two men watching the fencers agreed that if I stood there, by the door, I could remain inconspicuous behind the bulk of the bleachers. One of them promised to tell Christian I was there as soon as possible.

The gym seemed much larger with only the few fencers in it. Daylight coming through the long narrow windows along the ceiling turned the walls and floor golden. The footfalls of the fencers echoed down the hall.

One pair of fencers stopped. A hit had been scored, but it was hard for me to see from this distance. The two fencers removed their helmets and I saw that one was Christian. The other was Heydrich. I drew back a little behind the bleachers. The men shook hands and

Christian went to the sidelines. I guessed that he had lost his bout. Heydrich stood and watched the other two pairs. A man in black fencing gear—the fencing master—walked up to him and they talked as they watched.

Christian stood with his helmet under his arm, his blade swinging from his hand, and wiped his forehead with his sleeve. He had never talked about fencing with me. I hadn't even known he fenced. My messenger walked over to him, said a few words and nodded toward where I stood. Christian looked up, searching for me, and I took a few steps forward so he could see me.

His face remained expressionless for a long moment. My spirits plummeted. I had been wrong to come, he was angry. Just then, one of the other bouts came to a climax and Christian turned his head to watch. It took all my determination to keep my feet from carrying me out of the gym. But he turned back in my direction again, and this time, he waved slightly. Then he turned his attention to the fencing master, who was demonstrating a combination.

The last pair to finish their bout were still fencing. One of the men suddenly attacked, ending with a beautiful, clean lunge and retreat. His teammates clapped and he made a brief salute. The losing fencer took a step backward, then suddenly dropped his blade and grasped his hands to his side. The clatter of the blade on the wooden floor drew everyone's attention. The man fell to his knees. One of the other men ran to him and pulled off his helmet. The injured man took his hand away from his side. There was a patch of bright-red blood on his white fencing jacket. He fell forward, one arm extended alongside his head.

The sight of the blood galvanized the fencers. The fencing master moved to the injured man, turning him over, stretching him out. Heydrich sent a man from the gym, presumably for help. The man who had inflicted the injury stood, his blade dropping helplessly from his hand, looking at his partner.

I could hear little except echoing murmurs. The fencing master, kneeling in front of the injured man, blocked my view and I could not see what happened next. But just as two men in white uniforms entered the gym behind me, the fencing master stood up, shaking his head. I pointed down the gym and the newcomers hurried toward the fencers, carrying a stretcher.

They were too late. The injured man had died. I could see him on the ground at his comrades' feet, the red stain across his chest.

It was like a scene from a play, the golden light falling on the young men in white. Heydrich stood over the fallen man, then knelt down and kissed his forehead. The general stood up, said a few words, then raised his arm to salute the dead man. The other fencers followed suit, and the two bearers lifted the body onto the stretcher.

Just then, Heydrich raised his head and saw me. He became very still, staring at me, his gaze seeming to catch me fast. Why had I come? Why? I felt like a fool, no, more than a fool. I felt I had stumbled into some forbidden rite. I should not have been here to see this accident. But here I was, and he had seen me. I waited, unable to free myself from his gaze.

Without turning his head, Heydrich said something that brought Christian to his side, then sent him down the gym toward me. Heydrich turned away, and I backed up and spun around through the swinging doors. I ran across the lobby for the stairs. Behind me, I heard Christian come after me.

"Sally!" he called, but I didn't stop. He caught me at the doors of the main lobby. "Sally, wait," he said, grabbing my arm.

"I'm sorry," I said, speaking English. "I didn't mean to be here."

"Come, please." He pulled me away from the door. I resisted until I realized he was trying to get me away from the door the stretcher-bearers would use. So I followed him through the doors at the other end of the lobby into a gloomy hallway.

I started apologizing again. "Stop, Sally, please," he said, his hand on my shoulder.

"That man's dead. Right there. Dead."

"Yes," he said. His face contorted for a moment, but he controlled it. He let go of me and rubbed his face with his hands, a gesture I remembered from that horrible June day. "What are you doing here?" he demanded.

"I came looking for you," I said, trying to control the shaking that was taking over my body.

"Why?"

"I need to talk to you, Christian," I said. We were facing each other, talking in whispers. I heard activity in the hall. Christian turned his head to look at the closed door between us and whatever was going on.

"In here," he said in a whisper and pulled me a few steps down the hall into a small training room. It was empty except for mats rolled up at one end and gymnastics equipment pushed together at the other. A grimy punching bag hung listlessly to our right. The room smelled of sweat, old sweat, worked into the mats and equipment, into the walls and floors.

"It's so c-c-cold," I stammered, shaking all over. I had my arms around myself and my jaws hurt from my attempt to stop their chattering. "He was a friend of yours? The man who died."

"I knew him."

"How could that happen? I know accidents happen, but not with foils. Not with the tips."

"We don't use tips," he said dully. He hadn't moved from in front of the door.

"That's terrible, irresponsible. Heydrich ought to be arrested for allowing . . ." My voice petered out as I saw his exhausted, sad face.

"What are you doing here, Sally?" he said.

"I'm sorry!" I shouted, flinging my arms out. "I needed to see you."

"Stop apologizing, for God's sake," he snapped. "I'm sorry too. You stop. I'll stop. God, you haven't changed a bit."

"Changed? Oh, I've changed all right." I started to laugh. I think, looking back at my behavior, that I was more than a little crazy that afternoon, wound up tight with fear and insecurity and horror, and feeling my secret, which grew every day, taking over more of me. I couldn't hold it in any longer.

"I'm pregnant," I said, gritting my teeth.

"Congratulations," he said, his face expressionless.

"Pregnant." I translated the word into German.

"I understand you," he said, still in that detached tone.

I turned away from him, feeling sick. "Oh, God, I'm so sick of thinking about you, of dreaming about you. Of missing you. I've spent my whole stupid life missing you." I fought the tears, getting angry instead, and rounded on him. "Why? I don't understand why. There are lots of other boys around, maybe not so damned handsome, but normal, ordinary. Americans, even. Who wouldn't do that to me on the carpet in my sitting room and then *not remember*! Make me pregnant and not even care!" I pushed at his chest and shoved him, pushing him away from me.

"I can't stand it! I can't stand you! You bastard. I hate you." Then I pulled my arm back and swung at him. He stopped me, catching my wrist in mid-swing, grabbed my other arm, and held them both tightly in his hands in the space between us.

"Don't," he said. His hands were wound tight around my wrists, hurting me. I looked up at him. His eyes were intense and fierce. They had darkened almost to gray. I had never seen his eyes like that before. They were frightening. I can hurt you, they said.

I became acutely aware of everything: the pain in my wrists and arms, his tight grip, my awkward position, the distant traffic noises, Christian's breathing. For a long minute we were frozen there, hanging on the brink of something, the currents between us deep and swift. His jaw clenched and his fingers moved on my wrists, as though unsure whether to push me away or pull me toward him.

I looked down. Instantly, his hold on me relaxed and I moved back from him, blindly, bumping against a wall. I leaned on it and slowly slid down until I was sitting on the floor. I was exhausted.

The baby. It was still there, a problem to be faced.

"Why did you do that to me that day?" I asked in a whisper.

He thought for a long time, standing where he was in his canvas fencing jacket with the SS sports badge on the sleeve. He stared at the floor until there could not be an inch of the worn wooden boards he had not memorized. Then he raised his head and looked up at the dirty window with the iron grating in front of it. Finally, he spoke, quietly.

"You were there. No," he said, holding his hand out to stop my retort. "I did not mean it that way. I'm sorry, I find it difficult to talk about this—that day." He fell silent again for another long pause.

"I'm ashamed," he said quietly. "Of the whole . . . of everything that happened. I wish it had never happened."

That was it. I pulled my heavy legs up, preparing to stand. My shoes scraped the floor, and at the sound, Christian looked over at me, our eyes catching hold.

He almost smiled, his face softening a little. "You really thought of me all that time?"

I didn't answer, feeling my face crumble as the tears came to my eyes. I pushed myself to my feet, brushing uselessly at the wrinkles in my suit skirt. I started to cry, the tremors coming from deep in my body, and I turned against the wall, hiding my face.

He didn't say anything, but I was too wrapped up in my own misery to care. He might have left and I wouldn't have noticed. But he didn't leave. He put his hand on the back of my neck, slipping it under my hair, cupping my neck.

"What can I do?" he asked softly. "How can I make it better for you?"

I tried to take a breath, to stop the crying. "You can't."

"The baby. It is my baby?" He was leaning on the wall, next to me, and in anger, I moved away, so that I was a yard away from him, my back still against the wall. I needed the support.

"I'm sorry. I didn't mean . . ." he said softly.

"Yes, it's yours. You're the only man . . . you're the only one." I turned my head away from him.

301

"I did not mean that," he said, stretching his hand across the wall to me, touching my shoulder.

"What did you mean?" Still I didn't look at him.

"I want . . . I think I have always wanted . . . to take care of you. I don't think you know this. That time, when we were kids and we took your dress . . . I could not look you in the face. Now, it is the same. I cannot look you in the face. I have violated you. It is a revolting thing for me . . . and I have not acted honorably. I hoped . . . you would go away. Out of harm's way. Away from me. Who could not take care of you. And now, there is my baby."

"Our baby."

"Yes. Who will take care of this baby?"

"No one." I pushed myself away from the wall. I walked to the middle of the floor and picked up my small purse where I had dropped it. I opened it, fumbling with the catch, and looked at myself in the mirror in the flap. I couldn't see anything.

"If I can, I'll get rid of it. Sydney knows a doctor. If it's too late"—I swallowed, fighting the nausea that first statement had made in me—"I'll go back to the States. Have it and put it up for adoption. You don't have to worry about it. I just thought you should know." I looked around the room. "Where's my hat?"

"There," he said, pointing next to a tall pile of folded mats.

I picked the hat up and went to the door. I knew what I had to do.

When I got home, I telephoned Sydney's doctor. It wasn't too late and I made an appointment for the next morning. By this time tomorrow, I thought, my hand still on the receiver, it would all be over. There was some comfort in that.

I had to change. We were dining with the Bushmullers that evening and going on to a concert. Beethoven. I wondered how I could sit through it. Well, I would have to.

I had made my plans and expected no surprises, but when I came down to leave that evening, Christian stood in the center of the entry hall, his uniform stark against the black and white tiles. My father came out of his study to greet him. Daddy was also in black and white, dressed for dinner. Black and white. Everything should be so simple, so black and white. And red, I added, catching a glimpse of Christian's armband. Blood-red.

They both looked up at me as I walked down the stairs.

"Good evening," I said to Christian and waited for an explanation of his presence.

"May I speak to you?" he said.

"All right." I felt lethargic, exhausted, and, underneath it all, fearful of tomorrow morning. "Come with me. Will you excuse us, Daddy?" I started to move away.

"No," said Christian, surprising me, grabbing my hand and stopping me. "I would prefer you to be present, sir. Please."

My father nodded and allowed Christian to lead us both into the sitting room. Christian let go of my hand and walked to the middle of the square of sofas, standing in front of the fireplace.

"Would you like a drink?" asked my father politely, while I just stood where Christian had left me.

"No, no, thank you. This won't take long." The fall afternoon was cool, and Rick had laid a fire. It was burning brightly, the flames reflected in the gloss of Christian's boots.

"I must say I did not expect to see you again," Daddy said, walking into the square. He did not sit down.

"I did not expect to return. I meant to spare you further association with me. But circumstances have changed, and so I am here to ask to marry your daughter."

For a moment, my very articulate father was speechless, but only for a moment.

"How can you believe she would agree to this? Unless you've been sneaking around behind my back," my father said, controlling his anger, turning to face me.

"No, Daddy. I know nothing of this."

"Well, then, Mayr, you see it is useless." I wasn't watching them. To me, the decision was made and any further discussion was a waste of time. I couldn't understand why Christian was here. I could hear pity in my father's voice. "You do see, don't you?"

"I'm pregnant, Daddy," I said softly, not raising my head, speaking to the floor. "He made me pregnant. But it's all right. I'm going to have—I'm going to fix it all tomorrow morning. Sydney found me a good doctor. I trust him. It'll be all right. No one will know. Don't worry. I'll go back to the States afterward. I promise."

I turned and headed for the door, then stopped. "Daddy, I don't feel like the Bushmullers or Beethoven tonight. Could you make an excuse for me?"

"Sally, what has happened?" my father said, coming around the sofa toward me. "What the hell has been going on?"

"Please, Daddy, don't. Not yet. You can yell at me later. Let me get through tomorrow. You can ask me anything then. I'll be good."

I was at the door, my hand on the knob, when Christian spoke.

"I love you, Sally," he said, his voice taking a moment to reach me. It took me another moment to comprehend the meaning of what he had said.

I raised my head and turned. He still stood in front of the fireplace and I walked slowly to him, I grew warmer, as though it were Christian whose presence warmed me and not the fire. I stopped a few feet from him and waited.

"I love you," he said deliberately. "And I want to marry you. I don't want you to abort or give away our child. I want our child, Sally. I want you." He closed his eyes for a moment, and when he opened them, I saw tears.

"I always have."

Still I waited. There was more I needed to hear. His eyes flicked behind me to my father, then back to my face, concentrating on me. "It is why what happened, happened. I am sorry . . . and I am not sorry. Do you understand?"

I took a step toward him, bending my head back to look up into his face. I searched but found nothing but love there.

Then my eyes fell to his uniform, to the collar tabs with the insignia of his rank, the bright red-and-white armband. I raised my eyes to his again and shook my head, although it took all my willpower and resolve to do so.

"I can't," I said. "I can't."

"Do you love me?" he whispered.

"I can't."

"Just answer me. Do you love me?"

"It's not possible."

He put his hand around my face, forcing me to keep my eyes on his.

"Sally."

"Yes. All right, yes."

And then a miraculous thing happened. He started to smile, a smile that started somewhere deep inside him and spread sure and warm into his face, chin, mouth, cheeks, eyes. Not only did he look happy, but pleased with himself, almost, I might say, smug. He grabbed my hands, kissed my cheek, then said to my father: "Excellency, I would like to ask you again for permission to marry your daughter. And to leave as soon as possible for the United States."

"Do you mean it?" I gasped. Never had I expected anything like this. "Do you really mean it?"

"Yes," he said.

"You'll leave Germany?"

"Yes."

"For me?" I said this shyly, still not believing.

"Yes. For you. What do you say?"

"Yes," I said, and went into his arms.

"Christian," I heard my father say. "I am impressed. Are you sure you have thought this through?"

"I have. It is not as difficult as you might think. But it is more difficult to think of letting Sally go." He still held me, talking to my father over my head. "I hope you will approve now. We will need your help."

My father did not quite believe Christian, and he began asking questions—when? why? how? I went off to bed, too sleepy, too emotionally drained to keep my eyes open. I don't think they even noticed when I left the room. Christian stayed a long time, convincing my father that he meant what he said. My father told me the next morning of the many arguments Christian used, of the reasons he gave for leaving his country, of his love for me. That was what finally convinced Daddy in the end: that he loved me.

The next evening Christian and I went to see his mother, who had just returned from Denmark. Lisa hugged me and gently cuffed Christian on his shoulder, then hugged me again. She cried when we told her about the marriage and the baby, and then she sat us down at her round dining room table and made us something to eat. She was, after the tears and cakes, very practical.

"You have to have a civil and a religious marriage here," she said, then turned sharply to Christian. "I hope you do not intend one of those godless SS ceremonies?"

"No, Mama, not if I can help it." We had decided not to tell her yet about our plans to leave Germany. Christian was worried about leaving her behind.

"That would not do," she muttered, folding her hands on the white lace tablecloth. She thought a moment, then looked up. "Here is what I think you should do. You need to be married as soon as possible, with the least amount of interference. Because of who Sally is and your being in the SS, there could be a great deal of hoopla. So you must elope. You must get married somewhere else and tomorrow or the next day if you can."

"But without you or Daddy?" I protested.

"I know, sweetheart, I hate the idea too, but we can have a party afterward. Think about it; it makes sense and will avoid all kinds of trouble. Not that I wouldn't love to arrange it all, but you two have made that impossible. Ah, I'm glad you have enough shame to blush." She smiled at me. "A grandchild," she said and reached out for my hand. "I couldn't think of anyone I would rather have this boy of mine marry, and I am thankful that you will take him in spite of his dishonorable behavior."

"I should think agreeing to marry me is pretty honorable," I said.

"Just barely," she said. Christian was leaning back from the table, his hand playing with his coffee cup. He smiled lazily at his mother.

"I know!" She slapped the table, as though inspired by her son's smile. "I know what you will do. You will go to Lake Sebastian. You will go there and get married in the little church. You remember it? With all the animal carvings? And then you will go to the mayor to have the civil ceremony. I will complain. The ambassador will be outraged. But when you return, I will arrange a reception for you and we will all make up and forgive each other and your father and I will accept the inevitable. We will even call Annaliese home from Vienna. What do you think of that plan? Pretty good, huh?"

"Mama, I never knew you could be so conniving," Christian said. "But it sounds good." His mother looked pleased. "What do you think?" he asked me.

"I like it. And I like the idea of being married at Lake Sebastian. Thank you, Frau Mayr."

"Lisa, now you are almost a mother too." She shook her head. "I haven't seen you in years, and now . . ."

I got up and went to her, taking her hands in mine. "Thank you, Lisa."

"Well, dear one, what's done is done. It will be all right." And as she had always done in my childhood, she put her arms around me.

THE BEST ROOM
IN THE INN

I knocked on the door to my father's bedroom to say good-bye. To keep up the fiction of an elopement, he wouldn't come to see us off. He opened his door and put his arms around me, then, his hands hands on my shoulders, asked me, "Are you sure about this?"

"Yes, Daddy," I said, hoping I sounded it. "I'm sure. I may be crazy, but I'm sure."

"All right. Well, you'd better go."

Vittorio put my bag in the taxi, then opened the back door for me. "Good luck, miss," he said softly in Italian.

"Thank you, my friend," I said. I hadn't told him, or any of the servants, what was going on, but Vittorio seemed to know.

I was to meet Sydney at the station, and I had a bad five minutes waiting for her. She had my train ticket. Finally, there she was, hurrying along in her high heels.

"Here, darling, I had a terrible time flagging a cab. Are you all right? You look super. Tuck these away." She handed me the ticket and a couple of magazines, one a *Vogue*. "I know. You probably won't need them, but when I say good-bye to someone at a train station, I must buy them magazines or chocolates." We found my compartment and sat down for a moment.

"I didn't know what to pack," I said, holding the magazines in my lap.

"Do you have something nice for the ceremony?"

"Yes. And some woolens. I think they'll be warm. Will it snow?"

"That would be romantic, Sally. Just think of it. Much more romantic than our honeymoon. We went to Cornwall, like idiots, and it rained the entire time. The sheets were damp. The room was damp. I swear our shoes grew mold. Hideous."

"Oh, Sydney, I wish you were going to be there. Is this the stupidest thing anyone's ever done?" I blurted out.

"No, of course not. But I think it may be a close second." She smiled at me. "Sally, I have a secret to tell you," she said, reaching across the space between the seats to touch my arm.

"What? Are you going to have a baby, too?"

"How did you guess? You clever goose, you."

"No! Sydney, I was just . . ." I hugged her. Looked at her and hugged her again. "Oh, that's just wonderful."

"I wanted you to know you weren't the only one with unexpected plans."

"Did you just find out? Why didn't you tell me?"

"Just yesterday, promise. Listen, Sally, I must go. I've got to meet Brian."

"Does he know?"

"Yes. We're going out tonight to celebrate." She stood, smoothing and arranging her coat, gloves, and bag. "Oh, here, I almost forgot," she said, handing me a small florist's box.

I opened it and lifted out a small, lovely nosegay of pink roses, white satin ribbon, and baby's breath. "Oh, Sydney, it's beautiful." I bent my head to it to deflect my tears.

"Well, I just thought you should have some flowers."

She left me alone in the compartment and I sat staring out at the increasingly busy station platform, her flowers in my hand, thinking about big, fancy church weddings and dresses with trains and long veils. All the trappings that I was not going to have. I really didn't mind, but I had to admit that I would have enjoyed the fuss, being the center of such a huge production. I would also have liked to have someone with me, a woman, to tell me things. I was, I realized, lonely for my mother. Then Christian slid open the door to the compartment, and I thought, Everything will be all right now.

"Am I late?" he asked.

"No."

"The traffic is insane." He was still in his uniform and he tossed his hat, upside down, into the small space provided for gentlemen's hats.

"I thought you were going to wear civilian clothes, to be less conspicuous."

"Didn't have time. Besides, we'll get better service," he said matter-of-factly.

I turned to look out of the window at the bustle on the platform. The conductors called out, and with a jerk the train started forward out of the station. Christian busied himself stowing away his bag, hanging his overcoat up. I looked up to see him pulling down the shades, closing us in from the corridor. He kissed my cheek and sat down next to me, then jumped up again. I watched the train slide past the station and the yards, suddenly struck by the idea that I was going to marry this man. For a moment the prospect almost terrified me, the idea of being bound to him, being his.

When he sat next to me again, he held something out to me. It was a ring box. I stared at it, then looked up at him.

He laughed. "Yes, it's for you."

I took it from his hand. Inside was a diamond ring, old-fashioned, with chasing on the elaborate setting, but lovely and feminine. It was an engagement ring. I looked up at Christian, who was leaning toward me, his eyes shining.

"It was my grandmother's. I nearly didn't get it back in time from the jeweler. Sydney found out your ring size. Do you like it?" He put one arm around me and took the box from me with the other hand. Carefully, he removed the ring. "You're shaking," he said and held me against him for a moment.

"Now," he said, "what do you say?" He slid the ring onto the fourth finger of my left hand. "Will you marry me?"

"Oh, Christian, it's lovely." I leaned against his shoulder, ignoring the armrest between us.

"You have not said yes," he reminded me.

"Ask me in English," I said. "So I'll know for sure." And he did. I kissed him again, then drew back. "Why?" I asked.

"Why?" he parroted, still in English. "Why? Why do I ask you to marry me? You silly girl, because I love you."

I swallowed. "The baby?"

"Ah," he said, his arms tightening around me. He switched back into German. "Yes, I will not lie. The baby is part of it." He sighed and rubbed his chin against my shoulder. "I am pleased with the baby. And you."

I put my arms around his neck and hugged him. He held me and we stayed like that for a while.

"Yes," I said, pulling back from him.

"What?"

"Yes, I'll marry you." He laughed and kissed me. Pausing to flip the seat divider out of the way, he gently pushed me back until we were both half-lying, half-reclining on the seat. He kissed me, one arm cradling my head, the other hand busy under my skirt. His fingers grazed the bare skin of my leg above my stockings. I jumped.

"Christian!"

"No one will come in," he said, his hand moving up to my panties.

"But . . ."

"It is all right."

There was a knock on the door. Quickly we both sat up. I pulled my skirt down and crossed my legs, hoping my hair and hat weren't too much out of place, grateful for the interruption.

The door opened. "Tickets," said the conductor in a bored, aggressive voice, which immediately changed to obsequious politeness when he saw Christian's uniform. "Heil Hitler, Herr Hauptsturmführer. If you please, your tickets."

Christian reached into his inner pocket for his and I handed him mine, and he casually held them both out to the conductor, who quickly checked them and handed them back.

"Thank you, Herr Hauptsturmführer," he said, saluted with the Nazi salute and was gone.

Christian turned to me, putting his hand on my knee. "Someone came in," he said, looking sheepish but amused.

"I noticed."

"Let's go have a drink and see about dinner." He stood up and put out his hand to pull me up, holding me for a moment.

"This is so beautiful." I lay my left hand against his chest and wiggled my ring finger. "It was perfect of you to think of it. Thank you."

He covered my hand and bent his head to kiss me, but at that moment the train went around a bend, throwing us against the seat. Laughing, we both grabbed for the luggage rack to keep our balance.

We were married early in the morning, having arrived in Lake Sebastian late the night before. For propriety's sake, we stayed in separate rooms, too tired to mind.

The ceremony in the tiny wooden church was short but surprisingly moving and the pastor and his wife treated us to a glass of schnapps, which did nothing to settle my stomach. I carried Sydney's nosegay and wore a pale-gray dress with some of Madam's antique lace at the neck and cuffs. Though it was an old-fashioned-looking dress, I thought it suited this very modern situation. Christian wore his uniform. I'd rather have seen him in a suit, but at that point, I was just so happy to have us married. Besides, he did look handsome in it and I could see people in the town looking admiringly at us as we walked back to the hotel.

We had a lovely lunch at the little hotel, where we were thoroughly spoiled by Herr Mittelstadt, the landlord, and his wife, who remembered both of us and our families well. Then they walked with us to the mayor's house for the short civil ceremony, the Mittelstadts acting as our witnesses. It started to snow as the mayor married us, big, fat snowflakes hitting messily against the windows of his office.

It was the first snow of the year, an early snow, and it continued all through our wedding day.

At last, we were married and alone in our room. I opened my suitcase and fussed with my things, more nervous than ever. I heard Christian come into the room from the hall, but I didn't turn to look at him.

"Let's go for a walk in the snow," he said energetically. "Let's go walk around the lake and look at our old houses."

"Oh, yes," I said, almost hysterical with relief. "What a good idea. Oh, yes." I pulled my wool slacks and sweater out of my bag and went down the hall to the bathroom to change.

It wasn't as cold out as it had been before the snow started, and we walked along, our arms around each other's waists. We didn't make it very far, because passing a drift of fluffy snow, I couldn't resist and lagged behind him to make a snowball.

"Christian," I yelled, and when he turned, threw the snowball at him, right into his face. I clapped for my perfect aim, laughing at his expression. I should have run, because he came after me, grabbing me and dragging me down with him into the snow.

I screamed as he got a handful of snow down my sweater and in my hair. He sat on top of me, holding both my hands in his, and laughed down into my face. I bucked, trying to unseat him.

"Get off, you big lug," I said. "I'm freezing."

"All right, but I just want to . . ." His face changed and he leaned down and kissed me long and hard, his tongue busy against mine. Finally he stood, pulling me up next to him. My jacket and sweater were wet through to my skin and I was very cold. My teeth started to chatter.

"Serve you right if your bride comes down with pneumonia," I muttered as he wiped the snow off my back. I sneezed.

"Don't you dare," my new husband said, wagging his finger at me.

We hurried back to the hotel and I waited, dripping on the wooden floor, while Christian asked Herr Mittelstadt for a hot drink. Frau Mittelstadt came through the curtains from the back of the hotel, where their private quarters were, and taking one look at me, took me off to a hot bath.

She carried away my damp clothes and left me to soak in the steaming-hot water, admonishing me not to let it cool.

"Then you get into bed and have a little sleep. I'll send that rascal husband of yours up later with some tea. My, what a handsome one he is. But I don't envy you, being married to such a good-looking man. I do envy you his future. You'll have everything. Everything." She was still chattering as she closed the door, and I was glad not to have to hear about Christian's future.

I snuggled happily under the huge feather bed and soon fell asleep, a hot-water bottle against my feet. It was the best sleep I'd had since I'd found out I was pregnant. I awoke in the dark, warm room when Christian brought the tea. He walked, tray in hand, quietly across the room. He laid the tray on the table, which was covered with an embroidered cloth, and came to look at me. I struggled up through the puffy feather bed and sat up, running my hands through my hair.

"What time is it?" I asked him.

"You're awake. It's almost seven. How do you feel?"

"All right. I don't think I caught a cold."

"Good. Do you want some tea?"

"Yes, please." I turned on the light next to the bed and arranged the pillows behind me. "You're all dressed again."

"Hmm." He had a cup for me in his hand. "Milk? Sugar?"

"Both. Why are you in your uniform?"

"I got my clothes wet too. Nothing else to wear down for dinner. Do you want one of these?" He offered me a plate of cookies. I nodded and he put one on the saucer, added milk and sugar to the cup, and carefully brought it over to me.

"Thank you. Why do we have to dress up? I don't have anything either."

"Your gray dress."

"That's special now."

"Well, you have to wear something to dinner."

"I'll wear my traveling suit."

"Good, I'm glad that's settled," he said and sat on the bed. "What an interesting conversation."

I grimaced at him. "Get used to it. We'll have many such."

"I've had years with sisters, remember. I can handle myself very well in these situations. Shall we now talk about hats? Here, there are more cookies, and I know you won't want more; however, I do."

I giggled and drank the tea, although I made him put more sugar in it.

"I can't believe we're really here, can you?" I looked around at the wood paneling, the old ornaments on the narrow shelf that ran all the way around the room at about head height. "I woke up this morning and it took me the longest time to remember I was in Lake Sebastian. After all these years."

"Tomorrow, we'll make it around the lake. Are you finished?"

he asked, holding out his hand. I handed him back the cup and saucer.

"I'd better get up and get dressed. I'll have to do my hair," I said, stretching my legs out under the warm covers.

Christian carried the china over to the table. "I know. You don't frighten me. I'll wait. I have eaten enough cookies to hold me."

Again, I was struck with a terrible nervousness about what lay in store for me with this man. He stood next to the round table, towering over it in his boots, tall and handsome, as he picked up the last cookie and popped the entire thing into his mouth. I leaned back into the pillows, my hands folded on the covers, wondering if he would just gobble me up like that too. I didn't want to leave the bed. Nor did I want to be left alone, but I also didn't want to change with him in the room. But most of all I wanted tonight to be over. What if he was sorry? What if he was only marrying me out of pity, or duty, or for . . .

"I'll meet you downstairs, all right?" he said, picking up the tray, interrupting my panicked thoughts. "You look very pretty in that bed."

"I'll be out in a second," I said, flushing bright red. He grinned at me and went out.

I got myself out of the safety of the bed and into my clothes. I brushed and brushed my hair and gathered it back with combs. I looked chic, but very pale. My stomach was aflutter with nerves and tea and I knew I wouldn't be able to eat anything. I had never been so nervous. You're ridiculous, I told myself and went down to dinner.

Our room was warm from the porcelain stove in the corner when we went up after dinner. It was easy to undress, although my hands shook so hard I could barely manage my buttons and I thought the lump of nervousness and apprehension in my throat would strangle me. Christian moved around the room going about his routine. When he left the room, I got my brush and stood in front of the stove to brush my hair, watching the blurry reflection of my arm move up and down in its glossy surface.

Christian came back into the room and moved quietly around, busy at some task, until he stood behind me. I turned. He was naked except for his open shirt and his skin glowed in the dim lamp light, the shirt hiding and not hiding the curves and planes of his body.

I had never seen a naked grown man and the sight of him, so

beautiful, so different, was the most desirable, most frightening thing I'd ever seen.

"You're beautiful," I whispered.

He reached a hand for me and slowly, dreamily, I took it. He drew me to him and kissed me sweetly on my cheek.

"Shall I leave you alone?" he whispered. I felt myself sway toward him and I shook my head. He laughed softly and started to push my robe off my shoulders but I, with both hands, suddenly held the top where it was. He paused, then shrugged off his shirt.

"You too," he said. "It's only fair."

I let my hands drop and the robe followed with a whisper of fabric against fabric. Carefully, he unhooked my bra, then knelt and undid my garters, slowly rolling down my stockings and, telling me to steady myself on him, took them off.

I ran my hand across his shoulder, feeling the skin, the bone, the smooth warm muscle. Kneeling on one knee in front of me, he put a hand on either side of my hips, smiled up at me, and pushed down my final garment.

He stood, his hands gliding along my shoulders, my arms, my hips. "My wife," he said in English, then repeated the words in German. "I always knew this would happen."

"You didn't," I said softly.

"I did, from the moment you came into my room that afternoon when I was supposed to be taking a nap, remember?" I shook my head. "Yes, you do. I was naked, remember? We were six, I think."

I started to laugh, as the memory came to me, of him jumping up and down on his bed, like a skinny, golden imp. "I remember," I said. "I remember."

"You slammed the door and ran away."

"Yes." His hands were warm and soft and moving on my bare skin.

"Will you run away now?" he whispered.

"No," I said. "No, I won't." And very, very carefully, I leaned forward and laid my cheek against his bare chest, then turned my face so that I could breathe him in, my open mouth hungry for him. Our bodies weren't touching, not yet, but I knew, with a rush of happiness, that this night would be as different from that awful June afternoon as I wanted and needed it to be.

DOES GLASS CONDUCT HEAT?

The secret meadow looked so different in its winter guise, covered with of snow, that I hardly recognized it. We paused under the deep dark-green trees, almost black, against the white-and-gray world. Christian turned to me, his face, cheeks, and nose red with the cold. He looked very happy, very young.

"I love this," he said. "Hey, Sally, do you remember?"

And I knew he was thinking of the couple we had watched that night. As I nodded, an image flashed into my head: he and I, naked in the rich, white velvety snow, making love.

Christian began to take huge steps, as a child might, through the snow, destroying the image. He turned and gestured to me with a jerk of his head. Come on! I followed him into the center of the meadow. Looking back, our footsteps were the only marks on the snow.

"Listen," he said, his breath puffing white clouds into the cold air.

"To what?"

"The forest."

"I don't hear anything."

"Yes. The silence. Listen." He closed his eyes and lifted his face to the sun.

He was right. The silence was full of things to listen to—rustling trees, water dripping, snow falling from a branch, his breathing, my own heartbeat. But the snow muffled every sound, coating the branches, covering the ground so that nothing appeared as it was, but was transformed into something white and beautiful, sparkling in the sun.

I dug my hands deeper into my pockets, shifting my feet in the snow. I wiggled my toes, making sure I could feel them through the layers of socks and boots.

Christian laughed. "You poor thing. You don't like the snow, do you?" He put his arm around my shoulders.

"I like looking at it. From a warm room."

"You want to go back?"

"No, let's go on. I'd like to see the house too. I'm just cold standing here."

"Right. Let's go, then."

We left the meadow and tramped around the lake toward the old Mayr house. Herr Mittelstadt had said that no one ever stayed in it during the winter months.

We went up the path to the lawn that faced the lake. One of the two big trees was gone, downed in a storm, we had heard, three years ago. All that remained was a big stump. The house looked very bare in the snowy yard, the sun glittering off its windows, obscuring the inside. Christian wiped the window in the door and peered in.

"Wait here," he said, and ran through the crunchy snow around the corner of the house.

"Christian? Where. . . ?" but he was gone. I turned from the house to look out across the lake. The water was very calm, a deep-gray color. It looked larger, deeper, and very, very cold. Seeing it in winter made me think of the time I'd swum out into the center of it. And I wondered, for the first time, with an adult's perspective, at my youthful impulsive stupidity. And luck. Then I heard the door of the house open behind me and turned.

"Hello. Come in," Christian said smugly.

"How did you get in?" I asked.

"Secret ways. A window off the kitchen. Kurt and I used to sneak out at night. Come on."

"Is it all right?" I was reluctant to enter the closed-up house.

"Who will know? Come on." And he reached out and grabbed my hand to pull me inside. "Don't be so cautious."

"I'm not. Wait, let me kick the snow off." I knocked my boots against the stone step.

"You are timid," he teased.

"No, I'm not. I married you, didn't I?"

He laughed, conceding my point, and closed the door behind us. It was even colder in the house. We walked through the still, icy rooms, hand in hand. The furniture was covered with dust sheets, as were paintings and mirrors on the walls. The entire house was thick with memories of Christian's noisy family, especially the dining room, where we had had so many happy meals. We stood in the door looking at the long table and chairs under the sheets.

I could almost hear the noise of the big family, and I turned to say something to Christian, but abruptly he turned and walked away.

I followed him. He was standing at the bottom of the stairs, his hand on the lintel post, his back to me.

"Let's go upstairs," he said, without turning around. He took the first three steps as one. I followed more slowly.

He went on down the hall, but I turned into his old bedroom, where he had lain, so pale and sick. The door was slightly ajar and I pushed it open farther. The painted single bed was still there, the mattress rolled up on the slats. I heard Christian enter the room behind me.

"Remember how sick you were?" I asked. "How frightened I was. And your mother."

He grunted, running his hand along the carved picture rail. He opened the little wardrobe; it was empty. Brushing his gloved hands together, he came to stand near me.

"Lots of memories here," I said.

He shrugged. "It was good here."

"For me too."

"Perhaps the best time of my life. Everything was simpler. My brother . . ."

"Yes." I didn't know if he meant Kurt, or his older brother, Thomas. I remembered that Thomas's formal portrait had always stood on the mantel downstairs.

"My father was alive." He was looking down at the yard outside the window, and I could not see his eyes, but when he said the words, a tremor seemed to run through him. He would have shuddered if he hadn't controlled himself so well. I felt I had seen something too personal, too private, and I looked away.

"You know," I said into the silence. "I don't think I ever spoke to your father. At least, I don't remember doing so. He was so mysterious to me."

"He wasn't always like that. But he didn't talk much to anyone after Thomas was killed. Not even to my mother. I always wanted . . ." His voice petered out. He stood leaning against the window frame, his arms crossed, bulky in his coat. "I hardly ever spoke to him, either. Until I was old enough to argue with him. God, how we argued."

"That's not unusual, is it? Sons and fathers argue. Like mothers and daughters do."

"I don't think he and Thomas ever did. Did you? With your mother?"

"I suppose so. I don't remember. It's funny, you know. Now I only remember the good things about her. Not how she sort of ignored me, but how beautiful and talented she was. How I'll never measure up."

"You feel that way? So do I. I'll never be as brave, as honorable as Thomas was. I'd never have been able to please my father."

"Do you think that because we've both lost a parent, we are drawn together?"

"I don't know. Why do you need reasons? Besides, you can't please someone who's dead." Christian seemed edgy, and we fell silent again.

I turned my attention back to the room, to the blue-and-white-checked fabric covering the mattresses, the green, faded paint on the bed. I smiled.

"You're remembering when you kissed me," he said.

"You think you're so smart. How do you know what I'm thinking?"

"That smile." He put his arm around my waist. "I have seen that smile before." Gently, he touched my lips with his other hand.

"When?"

"Last night. Last night I saw that smile. I am right. You are blushing."

"No, I'm not," I said, putting the top of my head against his chest so that he couldn't see my face.

"It is all right. I like your blushes. They are sweet. Like you." His arms tightened around me and he rocked gently from side to side, carrying me with him, until he raised my head and kissed me. When he pulled back and looked into my eyes, I recognized his expression, also from last night. I tried to retreat, but he wouldn't let go of me.

"It's too cold in here," I whispered.

He didn't answer, but raised my hands and kissed each one, through my gloves. His eyes never left mine.

"Christian, we'll freeze to death," I giggled nervously.

"No, we won't. Come with me." And taking me by the hand, he led me into his parents' old room. There, he pulled open the inside shutters on the two narrow windows, letting the vibrant sunshine spill into the room where it seemed to set two rectangles of the wooden floor aflame. Taking the rolled-up, blue-and-white-checked mattress from the bed, Christian unrolled it in the sun. He found an old feather bed in a chest and put it down over the mattress. Then he held out his hand to me.

Standing in the shadows by the door, I could barely see him in the glare of the sunlight, which moved about him, the light reflecting off the dust dancing in the air. He pulled his cap off and his mussed hair flared through the moving air like spun gold.

"Come, Sally. It's warm here," he whispered. I could not see his face clearly, indeed, his entire body was blurred in the shimmering light. He seemed to be in another dimension, a warm, beautiful golden place that enticed me as I walked slowly toward him, holding my hand out, hoping I would find him in all the light. When

318

my hand finally touched his, my relief was so great, I laughed. He was not a mirage.

He pulled my mittens off and unbuttoned my coat, tossing everything aside. We lay down and kissed, and somehow, with the kissing and the sunlight, our clothes disappeared and we were lying naked in that cold, silent room, the crazy sunshine pouring over us like a blessing from the lake. I was shy in the light, not of him, but of his seeing me. The light was his natural milieu, creating more light from within him that washed over me. When I closed my eyes, I could see the glow through my lids. And he was right, I was not cold anymore.

We lay spent and happy and he pulled the feather bed over us so that we lay curled together, his body folded around mine. He ran his hand along my hip, down to my thigh, where it lay on my abdomen. I felt so sleepy, so warm. My eyes were still blasted from all that light and I closed them, snuggling into the feather bed, into his arms.

"It's strange to think there's a child in there," he said, his voice muffled.

"We'll bring her here someday."

"I would like that," Christian said. "To show the child where we were children together. I could tell him stories about his mother—"

"Her mother," I corrected him, my hand over his hand. His arm and hand were several degrees warmer than my body and I backed closer against his body. "What stories?"

"How stubborn you were."

"Stubborn. I was never stubborn."

"What about swimming out until you almost drowned? What about stealing a fellow's clothes?" he laughed softly, nuzzling my neck.

"Or tricking girls so that they make confessions. That was evil."

"I agree. But I think I apologized." His hands were on my breasts, his fingers playing with my nipples, and I had to concentrate to speak.

"Insincerely."

"Oh? Well, then." And one hand moved down me. It was so warm under the feather bed with his body, his lips on my neck, his hands, that I thought I would faint from the heat and the feelings.

Walking back through the afternoon, listening to the crunch of our boots on the snow, I sneaked a glance at him. He caught me.

319

"What are you looking for?" he said.

"I don't know." We walked awhile longer in silence.

"God, I'm starving," he said. "Come on, let's hurry."

"Don't you think it's strange?" I said. He had gotten several feet ahead of me and he stopped and turned.

"What do you mean?"

I studied the dirty snow along the road, where a car had passed, turned the whiteness to gray mud. I kicked at the sludge; it was frozen.

"That we were children together." I looked up at his face. "You're so familiar to me—but not. I see my past in you—but you're still a stranger."

He laughed, understanding me.

"I know, I know," he said, putting his arm around me. He leaned his head close to mine, and I could feel his warm breath on my cold cheek. "I like it."

"You just like the part in bed," I said, kidding him.

"And don't you?" He teased me back.

"Never mind."

"Come on, Miss Ambassador's Daughter, you like it too." He started poking at me and I squirmed away, my boots clumsy on the ridges and tracks of the road.

"Stop it," I laughed.

"You tell me," he cried, coming after me.

I ran, slipping on the frozen ground, and he caught me, of course he caught me, knocking me down into a snowbank. He lay on top of me, pinning me in the cold, crunchy, wet snow. I pushed at him. I could feel the back of my jacket and trousers soaking up the cold. He wouldn't move, teasing me, threatening to rub snow in my face.

"Oh, all right, you bully," I said, reaching my arms around his neck. "I like it. And I like you. Now let me up before I catch cold. What will Frau Mittelstadt say when we come back wet and freezing—again?"

"I don't know."

"And why am I on the bottom, in the snow—again? Why couldn't we have gone to a beach somewhere?"

"I like this. You are very comfortable."

"You aren't!"

"How about now," he said, moving his body against mine. Even through all our clothing I could feel him. My body, almost without my commanding it, arched into his, responding to his desire. He lowered his face to mine and kissed me, then pulled me up so we were both sitting in the snow.

"What have you done to me?" he whispered, his gloved hands on either side of my face. The gray winter sky was reflected in his eyes and I wanted nothing more than to be lost in all that blue-gray.

"I love you," I said. I kissed him, feeling my mouth and breath warming his cold face. "Oh, Christian, I love you, but I'm freezing."

He laughed out loud at that and got up, pulling me after him, and we went back to the inn.

In our room, we dropped our wet clothes and got immediately into bed. I was shivering and he wrapped his warm arms and legs around me.

"Now," he said, "where were we?"

We sat in the little dining room after dinner and chatted with Frau Mittelstadt. Her husband came in to turn on the radio.

"Do you mind?" he asked politely. "The Führer speaks to-night."

"Ah." Christian's face was impassive.

Herr Mittelstadt played with the tuning knob, summoning only nasty shrieks from the big set. It had pride of place in the dining room, looming in the center of the sideboard, several circles of doilies under it.

Another couple came into the room. They were obviously locals, the man in a party uniform, his wife in a wool dirndl. He was dark and thin and she was blond and rosy.

Herr Mittelstadt went to greet them, then he brought them over to Christian and me.

"The local bigwigs," muttered Christian as he stood to greet the new people.

"Frau Mayr, Hauptsturmführer Mayr, may I present Kreisleiter and Frau Walther?"

"Heil Hitler!" Kreisleiter Walther bellowed in a voice more suited for the parade ground than a dining room. He saluted vigorously, clicking the heels of his polished brown boots together noisily. His wife also saluted, but with more decorum.

"It is an honor to meet you, Hauptsturmführer," continued Walther, shaking hands with Christian. "May I present my wife." Christian shook the lady's hand, then turned to me, an amused expression on his face, and introduced me.

"Good evening," I said, smiling and nodding at the Walthers.

"May we congratulate you on your marriage," the Kreisleiter

said to Christian, who barely got out a "thank you" before Walther continued telling him how honored the town was to have been chosen by the Hauptsturmführer for his wedding. I could see, in both the obsequious behavior of Herr Walther and the timid but adoring looks of his wife, that Christian was an important celebrity to them. He seemed embarrassed but unsurprised by the attention.

Herr Mittelstadt interrupted the Kreisleiter, whose title, I was to discover later, meant he was the Nazi party leader of the district. He brought schnapps for a toast, pouring everyone a tiny glassful.

"To your best health and happiness," said Kreisleiter Walther, lifting his glass. "It is in marriages such as yours that the Reich finds its strength. May you be fruitful and dutiful and may you be blessed with many sons and daughters for the Reich. Heil Hitler," he finished off, tossing back his drink.

"Heil Hitler," everyone said, smiling and drinking. The room was warm with everyone's good wishes for Christian and me, and I couldn't wait to leave.

They had to have another toast, this one to the Führer. Herr Mittelstadt recharged the glasses and raised his, but stopped when he saw me still seated.

For a moment, I didn't understand his look. Christian looked down at me, with a slight upward movement of his eyebrows.

"Oh," I said, quickly standing. "I'm sorry."

Satisfied, the Kreisleiter turned back to his business. He made a long toast to the Führer's health, which sounded more like a prayer. There was another round of Heil Hitlers afterward and we all saluted. I'd never done it before and felt so clumsy, I almost giggled.

"Now, Hauptsturmführer," said the Kreisleiter, walking to Christian, "I would like to discuss several matters with you. It is so seldom I have a chance to meet someone from Berlin face-to-face. You understand?" He drew Christian away. My husband looked over his shoulder at me, as though to say he was helpless against such enthusiastic fervor.

"Come, Frau Mayr, sit with us," invited Frau Walther shyly.

"I'll make some more coffee," offered Frau Mittelstadt.

"Thank you," I said, "that's very kind of you."

There was a cozy corner niche next to the tall stove, with benches and a table, where we three women sat.

They asked me a few questions, careful not to get too personal, except saying they thought my husband was very handsome. Then they started in about babies and I smiled at them, wondering what they would think if they knew I was pregnant.

A blast of music from the radio startled everyone, stopping

Frau Mittelstadt in a mid-description of some horrible, messy infant illness.

"Ah, the Führer," said Frau Walther, touching my hand and standing up. We moved out of the little niche to join the men in front of the radio. Herr Mittelstadt fussed with the knobs for a moment, then stood back.

"The reception is not so good tonight. Sometimes it sounds as though he were in the next room."

"Oh, my," exclaimed Frau Walther, her hand over her mouth. "Can you imagine the Führer in the next room? It's the kitchen." She started laughing, but a furious glance from her husband silenced her.

"I'm sorry, Hauptsturmführer, my wife is young . . ." he said to Christian.

"Please," said Christian, embarrassed. "Please, it is nothing."

"Nothing! Nothing to make fun—"

"We will overlook it, Kreisleiter," Christian said gently, his eyes on the man, his gentleness not obscuring his command. Another facet of him I had never seen.

"Yes, Hauptsturmführer, of course."

After the little scene with the Kreisleiter, Christian came over to me, slipping his arm around my waist.

"Sorry, darling," he said softly in English. "I didn't realize."

"How long do you suppose this will take?"

"Well, you know the Führer. He can go on at great length."

"May I have a fainting spell?"

"I'll have to stay."

"Don't you want to?" I teased him. We stood very close together, my shoulder tucked up under his. He bent his head.

"I'd rather go up with you," he said seriously.

"See if you can tear yourself away," I said and, moving out of the sanctuary of his arm, went to make my excuses. The two couples were not pleased with me, but my timing was perfect. No one argued because just then Hitler's husky voice filled the dining room. Everyone's attention was riveted on the radio and I quietly faded out of the room, giving Christian a little wave as I passed him.

I had been asleep but woke up when he came into our room. I heard him moving quietly around. He left for a while and I dozed off once more, waking again when he slipped into bed behind me.

"Sally?" he whispered.

"Hmmm?"

"You're awake." He moved up close to me, putting his arm around me.

I turned to face him. "How long have you been?"

"Hours." He kissed my face, my temples, my eyes, running his lips over my cheeks and nose. "It drove me crazy, thinking of you up here in this bed, naked." He ran his hand over my side, down to my hip. "I thought he'd never stop." He started kissing my neck, moving down to my breasts, cupping them in his hands.

"Christian," I said, smoothing his soft hair. "Don't you . . ." I couldn't think how to phrase my question. "Those people," I whispered, "are members of the party."

"Of course."

"They seem to believe everything, to take it all seriously."

"Yes." He was waiting, hovering over me. I could feel the heat between our naked bodies and I wanted nothing more than his skin against mine.

"Didn't you? I mean, didn't you believe like they do?"

He was still for a long moment, then rolled away from me, so that he lay on his back. The covers slid off me, leaving me exposed to the cool air of the room, and I rearranged them, huddling down in the warmth.

"Have I upset you?" I asked.

"No. No, of course not. I'm glad you ask questions. I'd hate it if you were like those women, those good little wives who cower when their husbands frown.

"All right, I'll try to tell you. At first, I did believe that the National Socialists had the answers to Germany's problems. They seemed to promise hope, jobs, and a chance for us to stand up again. And Hitler was—well, you should have heard him speak, back in the old days. Before everything got so pompous. Now I wonder if it wasn't just their energy that I was attracted to. That and the connection with my brother."

"Christian, what about the Jews?"

"Oh, that's all medieval nonsense."

"But the SS . . ."

"It's for the uneducated men, gives them a sense of superiority. I don't need it. I feel superior enough already." He rolled back over on me, propping himself up on his elbows. "Don't you think I am?"

"You're perfect," I said, and pulling him tight against me, opening my legs for him, drawing him in.

I woke the next morning facing him and lay watching him sleep, his face soft in the gray light of the room. It was utterly silent, and I raised my head to see that it was snowing outside. Then I felt his fingers against my arm.

"You're beautiful," he said, running his hand along my arm. I snuggled down next to him, almost believing him.

"I wish we could stay here forever," I said, thinking of how I had to raise my arm last night, just to be polite.

"It's snowing," he exclaimed, sitting up. "Maybe we'll be snowed in. Wouldn't that be wonderful?"

"It would, but I'd rather be snowed in somewhere warm."

He laughed. "You make no sense at all. Hey, I have an idea."

"Where are you going?"

"It's a surprise," he said, getting out of bed. I pulled the covers around me, making up for the heat loss. He got into some clothes and went out of the room. I snuggled into the covers and decided to go back to sleep. I had almost succeeded when Christian came noisily back into the room.

"I've got it!" he cried, waving a piece of paper on which I could see his handwriting. He sat on the side of the bed. "Look," he said, holding the paper up in front of me.

"What? I can't . . ." I held his hand still and read some times and the names of several cities. "Innsbruck? You want to go to Austria?"

"No, but we have to go through Austria to get to Venice. Or Milan. We could go to La Scala. But I think we ought to keep going south and not even stop in Florence. I was there once in November and it was freezing. We can keep on going to Rome."

"Rome. Italy?"

"Absolutely. Roma. Italia. Espresso. Spaghetti."

"Could we really?"

"I don't see why not."

"Oh, Christian," I cried and threw my arms around him, kissing his face a hundred times. He laughed, holding me against him, as he tumbled over me.

"Well," he said, his hands in my hair, holding my face above him. "Is it a good idea?"

"It's a wonderful idea. And you're a genius for thinking of it."

"I thought so," he said, pulling me down for a kiss.

"Wait," I said, resisting. "What about your job? Can you just stay away like this?" I sat up. "And I should let my father know. How long do you think we'll be gone? Are you sure you can do this?"

"Sally, shut up," he said, sitting up behind me, his hands on my shoulders. "We'll telegram everyone when we get there. After all, it is our honeymoon. We won't get another chance for one until this kid is grown and married herself."

I turned into him, giggling, and we fell down again. We kissed, then lay facing each other. He reached for my hand and threaded his fingers around mine.

"Are you happy?" he asked in a whisper.

"Oh, yes." I kissed his fingers. It was strange, the way our hands were woven together, I felt as though I were kissing my own. "Are you?"

"Yes."

"Really? There's so much you're losing. And you'll have me and a baby to take care of."

"I know." He brushed his lips over my fingers, then looked at me with those clear blue eyes of his. "I want to tell you something," he said seriously. "And I want you to promise never to forget it. Promise?"

"All right."

He held my hand tightly. "Whatever happens, I want you to remember that I said this."

"What happens? What do you mean?" I was suddenly frightened.

"Shhh," he said. "Listen to me. This is important. Shhh." He waited to be sure he had my full attention before he spoke again. "I don't know that anything will happen, but the way things are—nothing is sure, don't you see? So I want you to remember that I said to you, here, in this room where we've made love so many wonderful times, that I love you." He lowered his head to our joined hands. I could feel the soft skin around his eyes, his eyelashes against my fingers.

He looked up again. "Will you always remember that? I love you and nothing in my life is as good and true as you are, as we are together, right now. Will you promise to remember?"

"Oh, my love, of course I will." And putting my arms around his neck, I held him against me. "How could I ever forget?" I murmured into his hair, glad he couldn't see how much his words had frightened me.

After a few minutes, he sat up. "Now," he said, "we'd better get organized. Ah, good, it has stopped snowing. See, we are meant to go. Come on, Sally, you aren't even dressed. We have to hurry if we're going to make the noon train, which we must take to make the earliest connection to Zurich."

"Christian?" I said, not moving from the bed, not even sitting

326

up. He turned to look down at me, a soft expression stealing over his face as he did so. "Could we go all the way to Naples? It might really be warm there."

"Of course, sweetheart. We'll go until we find some sun. All the way to Africa if we have to, I promise." And reaching out his hands for mine, he pulled me up.

CHANGING TRAINS

It was past midnight when the train reached the border between Switzerland and the Reich. We were sitting up because we hadn't been able to book a sleeping compartment on such short notice. I leaned against Christian's shoulder, trying to sleep. I felt the train stop and opened my eyes.

In the corner of the compartment was a man in a crumpled suit, who had gotten on at the last stop. He was asleep and snoring, his bullet-shaped head back against the seat.

I felt Christian move and looked up at him.

"Are you awake?" he asked, moving his arm so that I could sit up.

"Didn't think I'd slept." I looked out the window. The platform was forlorn, empty of people, bare under the floodlights. Suddenly, a squad of helmeted guards came purposefully out of the station building. Several men in civilian clothing followed them.

"This might take a while," said Christian, as we watched the men spread themselves along the length of the train. "Depends on who they're looking for. If anyone."

A guard appeared in front of our window, his back to us so that all we could see was his dark helmet, the barrel of his gun. I moved closer to Christian.

"I should have worn my uniform," he muttered, half to himself. "Might have helped expedite matters.

"Say, is there any more coffee?" he asked. Frau Mittelstadt had furnished us with a lunch basket, including a thermos of coffee. We had refilled it at the last stop. We could hear the guards enter the car, filling the narrow hall with their heavy boot-steps.

"I think so." And I bent over to get the thermos out of the basket at my feet. I twisted the top off and handed it to Christian so I could pour him a cup. I laughed nervously. "I feel so guilty."

"I know," he said. "As though we are about to be caught playing hooky. Thanks." He drank the coffee and I replaced the inner top. "Want some?"

I shook my head. "I'm fine." I put the thermos in the basket and stood up to get my coat from the rack. The door to our compartment opened and when I turned around, the small space was filled up with men.

"Hauptsturmführer Mayr?" said one guard, when he read Christian's passport. My husband nodded and the soldier left the compartment. He was back almost immediately with a man in civilian clothes—the guards, as well as the other man in our compartment, disappeared.

"Christian," said the stranger. "I'm glad we found you."

"August. This isn't all for me?"

"Of course not. It's the usual border thing. We just came along for the ride. Is this the new Frau Mayr?"

"Sally, this is a colleague of mine, August Müller."

"Hello," I said, offering my hand.

"Enchanted, Frau Mayr," said Müller, bending over my hand. "Now that I see you, I am all the more desolated that I must take your husband away."

"What!" Christian exclaimed.

"I'm afraid it's true, old man. The Chief wants you back. You know that, ah, project you were working on?"

"I left Oster all the information he'd need to continue."

"I know, but you know the fellow. . . ?"

"Yes, yes. Holtz. You mean Holtz."

"Exactly. Well, he died."

"What? Jesus, what happened?"

"I'm not sure, I was just sent to bring you back immediately."

"Oh, shit," said Christian. "Dammit." He dropped into the middle seat next to me. "Darling, do you see? I'll have to go."

I looked at him, trying to understand what I had just heard. "Someone died? Was it someone you knew? A friend?"

"No, love, no," he said, leaning toward me, taking my hand.

"Then why. . . ?"

"Someone we were working with. A colleague."

"I don't understand why you must go back so quickly."

"Because I .must." He glanced up at August, who was leaning against the door. He was a pleasant-looking young man, with brown hair and hazel eyes. "I can't explain any more. Please understand."

"Then I'll go too."

"I'm afraid that would be impossible, Frau Mayr," said Müller, pushing himself off the door. "We've got a small plane waiting."

"A plane?" I said, looking from him to my husband.

"It's that serious?" said Christian, his eyes on the other man.

"It is. Look, I'll go ahead and send some men back for your bags. You'll have to decide about changing trains. I'm sincerely sorry, Frau Mayr. Truly I am." And with that he left.

"Do you want to go on?" asked Christian, pulling his bag down from the rack.

"Not without you."

"I could join you," he said, getting into his coat.

"But you don't know how long you'll be."

"No. You're right." He stopped bustling around and held me, a hand on each of my arms, and stooped so he could look into my face. "You look as disappointed as I feel."

Tears came into my eyes and I turned my head so he wouldn't see.

"Oh, poor love," he said, and put his arms around me, holding me against him. "Poor me," he added.

There was something I wanted to ask him, but I couldn't think. He kissed me, his hand under my chin, raising my mouth to his. I pressed myself against him, for a moment thinking I could keep him with me if I made him want me.

"Don't, don't. You make it so hard," he said.

"I know," I said, and I lifted my leg so that my thigh rubbed between his legs. He laughed, and I did too.

"What a nasty joke. You never used to joke like that." But he smiled at me and caressed my face.

"Now," he said, turning away from me, picking up his hat. We heard the men in the hall. "Do you want to get off here and wait for a returning train? That could take all day. Or you could go on to Zurich and get a good night's sleep, then come back."

"I don't want to leave Germany. That'd be too far away from you. I'll wait here and follow you back."

"Good," he said, and opened the door for the men to take our bags. I got into my coat and hat and picked up my purse and the basket. It was very cold outside and our breath hung in the frozen air. We hurried into the station building. Christian crossed to the door of the station master's office and knocked. No one answered.

"I wonder where he is."

"You never know in these towns out in the middle of nowhere," said Müller.

"Well, I can't leave Sally here without knowing how she'll get back to Berlin."

"I'm all right," I said. "I can take care of myself."

"There, see, Mayr. Don't be such a nursemaid."

"That's right, Christian. I'm a married woman now, surely I can manage to get from wherever it is we are to Berlin."

"Really?" I could see he wanted to believe me. I could also see

330

he was eager to leave me or, at least, not to have to worry about me as he did.

"Sure. If worst comes to worst, I'll just call my father and he can send the marines for me."

"Good girl," he laughed and hugged me, gave me a quick kiss. "You go to your father's, all right? I'll telephone him when I get there. And my mother. You call her, too, please? She'll worry about you until you she hears."

"Where will you be?"

"I'll call you. Don't worry." He kissed me quickly and was gone.

I looked around the brightly lit station waiting room. The walls were painted brown to about waist-high and then pale green. There were heavy brown benches around the walls and a double row down the center. It was all spotlessly clean.

In one corner was a monster of a stove, cast-iron, unpainted, and ugly, but I could see the glow of hot coals through the grate on the side and I lugged my bag over and sat on the bench nearest it. Opposite me, high on the wall, was a large clock. It was two in the morning. Eventually, I dozed off.

Suddenly, I jerked my head up, peering into the dark room, which seemed full of strange soft noises and odd shadows in the harsh light. I had avoided looking at the bare black windows before, but now I could see the darkness pressing in around the little station building. The clock said it was four o'clock.

The Chief had sent Müller for Christian. I sat up. That was what I had been trying to remember. Heydrich had sent for Christian. But how had Heydrich known where to find him? No one knew we were going on to Italy. We bought the tickets at the station. Could the station master have telephoned him, or the Mittelstadts? He was supposed to have spies everywhere, but the Mittelstadts? It was too outlandish an idea. But I had to face the fact that someone had contacted the general.

Christian had.

No. I stood up. Sat down again, frightened at the idea. Why did I have to think that?

No.

I wrapped my arms around my middle, suddenly chilled. Coal in the stove popped. Please don't go out, I prayed to it.

But why would Christian do that? And I remembered what he had made me promise to remember. I sat back against the hard bench, the tears starting down my face. He had known this was going to happen. He had planned it all. He had known.

331

But why? I couldn't see any reason for what had happened. Unless someone was coming to kidnap me and hold me for ransom. No, that was too stupid. Why would Heydrich want to do that? I was married to Christian, for God's sake.

Had Christian been lying the entire time? I thought of him, touching me so gently, playing in the snow, glowing in the sunlight in his parents' old room. And I couldn't understand what had happened.

It seemed a very long two hours until the station master came to work at six. He was surprised to see me, but he did make me a cup of hot coffee and offer me a fresh bun.

"There were no trains scheduled to stop here last night," he said, fussing with cream and sugar.

"None? This isn't the border stop?"

"Of course not. That's at—" And he named another town I had never heard of.

"Then why did they stop here?" But I didn't need to ask him. I knew why: to take Christian and me off the train.

"Well, now, you sit down there. There will be a train shortly. You'll have to change twice before Munich. Here, I'll write it down for you." And he got out a pad. He also called ahead to book me a sleeper out of Munich for the trip into Berlin.

It was nearing six in the evening when I boarded the train in Munich, and I wanted to get home. I felt I had been traveling for a week, instead of one day. When I settled in my sleeper, I thought of how, just twenty-four hours ago, Christian and I had been so happy, laughing in our compartment. I sat next to the window, not turning on the light, and laid my head back against the seat, giving in for a moment to the sadness and betrayal and confusion.

Then, scolding myself for my self-pity, I got up and turned on the light. I got my sponge bag out of my suitcase and took it into the little bathroom, so I could freshen up before dinner. As I did so, someone knocked on the door.

"Come in," I said, without turning around, thinking it was the porter come to make up the berth.

It was Heydrich.

"Hello, Sally," he said with a smile, closing the door behind him. "How are you? Are you all right after your long ordeal?"

I didn't answer. I couldn't. I just stared at him, as he walked into the compartment and sat down, glancing outside as the train started up.

"Ah, good, we're leaving. Nice of them to wait for me, wasn't it?"

"Will you leave?"

"What?"

"Will you please leave my compartment? Leave or I shall . . ."

"Shall what? What kind of stink do you think you could raise?" I pulled open the door in answer. He regarded the open door, then me, for a long moment. "Close the door, Sally. Close it. I'm not leaving."

"You can't stay in here."

"You're afraid of me?"

"I'm not."

He didn't answer, merely raised his eyebrows. I closed the door, but remained standing.

"I am sorry. I didn't realize how upsetting this has all been for you."

"You should. You made it happen."

"Indeed I did not."

"Oh, stop lying." I spat at him, making a cutting gesture with my hand, nearly throwing myself off balance as the train jerked. I grabbed the wall and steadied myself. "Can't any of you, just one of you, tell the truth?"

"Ah. I see. You think Mayr lied to you."

"You know he did."

"Wait, my dear. How could I know what he said to you in the privacy of the marriage bed?"

"He lied as you wanted him to. But why? I just don't understand why." I almost flung myself into the seat next to Heydrich's. "Tell me. Please. It would make it so much easier for me if I understood. What is happening? I mean, he married me. Why would he do that if he didn't love me?"

"Perhaps because I told him to." He spoke lightly, almost teasing me.

"You told him to marry me? Why?"

"Because I couldn't?"

"Don't be ridiculous." Impatiently, I jerked in my seat, the space too small to contain my frustration.

"Why do you say ridiculous?"

"Because if you wanted me . . . that way, you'd just take me. Besides, I don't believe you think that way about me."

"Why not? You're attractive. Young. And seemingly out of reach. All reasons that make you quite an alluring possibility."

333

I looked at him, but was unable to tell if he was serious. "I'm not your type," I said.

He burst out laughing. He laughed so long and with such abandon that I started laughing with him.

"There," he said, putting his hand on my shoulder, when we had quieted down. "Feel better?" I nodded, unwilling to concede him anything. "Good. Now get changed and I'll take you to supper and we can talk about your new husband. Don't worry, I'll go get us a table and leave you alone."

He was good company at dinner, keeping the conversation to music, telling me about the ups and downs of his father's musical career as an operatic tenor. After coffee, he walked me back to my compartment and followed me in, as though I had invited him. The porter had been there to make up the bed and there was even less room than before.

"It's cold in here," I said.

"Is it? Do you mind if I smoke? Thank you. Please sit." I sat across from him on the berth. He lit his cigarette, said, "I've been thinking about you and Mayr a great deal ever since you ran off to get married.

"That was an impetuous thing to do, and the only reason I can figure out why you did it is that you are pregnant. So I have been trying to work out when he got you pregnant. Ah, you are pregnant, aren't you?" he said, interrupting himself. I said nothing and he seemed to take that for an affirmative answer.

"Well, as I said, I've been trying to work it out, because, unless you were very clever, you hadn't seen each other in several months before you came to the gymnasium on the day that idiot, Werner, got himself killed. So that means, it must have been the weekend of the SA business. Was that it? Christian disappeared for some time that weekend and I have wondered where he was."

"Why don't you ask him?"

"Oh, come now, Sally. There is no need to be snappy with me. You want to keep me your friend."

"Do I?"

He laughed, a tight laugh, raising his shoulders, keeping his mouth closed. "You are spending too much time with your British friend, Mrs. Stokes. You answer every question with another question as the British do."

"Well, let me ask you another question, if I may." I leaned back, crossing my legs.

"Of course, my dear."

"Why did you pretend you didn't know who Christian was?"

"I didn't."

"All right, why didn't you tell me you knew him then, when I asked you if you could find him?"

He lifted his cigarette and took a long drag from it before he answered me. "I should think that would be obvious."

"Obvious? How?"

He looked at me, a look charged with electricity. For a long moment, I didn't understand, and then I couldn't, wouldn't believe what I saw in his face.

"No," I said, almost laughing. "Oh, my goodness, General. You were just joking. I thought you were just joking."

"Why should it surprise you? You're an attractive young woman."

I blushed and looked down at my folded hands. "No, I'm not. Not that attractive."

He leaned forward and touched me, his fingers grazing my cheek and neck, passing through my hair. "You are. And Mayr is a bigger fool than I'd imagined if he hasn't told you so." His hand fell away from me. "But your looks are not all that attract me to you."

His long, horsy face was almost handsome with his energy and his knowing, amused smile. He knew so much about me, he even knew that I was unwillingly flattered.

He sat next to me on the berth. He turned his torso to face me, although he didn't touch me. "You are intelligent, but very young and very naive. I find this interesting mixture very attractive. But I think what I find the most interesting thing about you . . ." His voice was very low and he pushed a flyaway strand of my hair back into place, his fingers never brushing my face.

"This sweet exterior, all this fragile prettiness, is just a facade. I think underneath you are quite different. I think underneath there is passion and curiosity."

"I'm not passionate," I whispered, and shifted away from him.

"Yes, you are." And he finally touched me, using only two fingers to turn my face to him. "And if you do not know that, after a honeymoon, if you do not know that, pregnant with Mayr's child, then Mayr is not doing his duty."

I frowned.

"You don't like me making fun of him, do you? Good, you're loyal as well, not that I'd expect you to be otherwise."

He put his hands on my shoulders. I could feel his long fingers through the fabric of my suit jacket. He did not pull me to him. He just held me there and looked at me, his eyes intent on my face.

"It is in your fencing," he whispered.

"My fencing?" I tried to back out of his grasp, but his fingers kept me in place.

"I've watched you many times, when you didn't know I was there. You fence as I would if I were a woman. I imagine Maestro often despairs of your technique."

"Yes," I whispered.

He ran his fingers along my mouth, tracing my lips. It made me quiver.

"Lina," I tried to say, halfheartedly trying to turn my face away from him.

"That is only a bourgeois concern. I think you are above it."

"No, no, I'm not. Not at all."

"Of course you are. We have made music together. You are curious about me, aren't you?" He took my hand and lowered his head to it, his lips just above my palm. I could feel his warm breath on my skin. "What I might do to you excites you," he said and, using just the tip of his tongue, ran it from my wrist to my fingers. Like an electric shock, feeling followed where he touched me. "You are frightened by me and your fear excites you."

Instinctively, I covered my abdomen with my free hand, as though Heydrich's seduction could harm my child. I could hear my ragged breath.

Just then someone knocked on the door.

"What?" barked Heydrich, lifting his head, his eyes on me.

"General, a message," said the voice through the door.

Heydrich let my hand go, opened the door, and stepped outside.

I sat still, knowing he would be back. I felt as though I had been violated. He had done what he wanted and, what was worse, my body had responded to him. I had been married less than a week and I had already betrayed Christian. And after those few wonderful nights together.

Christian shouldn't have left me. I hated the general. I hated myself for feeling that way, for listening to him. I wouldn't let it go any further.

When Heydrich returned, I turned to face him and very deliberately wiped my hand on my skirt. He flushed momentarily, then his face shut down as he controlled his feelings, his anger. He just looked at me, and I knew I had made a terrible enemy.

I raised my chin defiantly. He took a step toward me as the train began to slow.

"Too bad. I have to go. I just want to tell you two things. One, Christian has not lied to you. I found out where you were in my own way. And, two: Did he tell you he was a murderer?"

"Yes. He was devastated because you made him part of that firing squad."

"Firing squad? Oh, no, my dear. Not the anonymity of a firing squad. Your husband killed those men face-to-face."

"You're lying." I stood up, balancing myself with one hand against the folded upper berth.

"I thought he was weak. So I sent him into the academy basement where we were holding about forty men. He and another fellow, who I also thought needed toughing up, shot all forty."

"You're lying," I repeated, the only thing I could think of to say in the face of this evil.

"They went from cell to cell, putting bullets through each man's head. Some of those men were their friends. I imagine it was a grisly task."

Christian's boots. His boots that he had said were dirty with brains. I turned around, looking for escape. I had drawn the blind when I changed for dinner, and now, turning, I hit it and it flew up with a loud rattle, filling the compartment with the station lights. I pressed my hands against the window.

"I see I must go." Heydrich put one hand on my shoulder, with the other he caressed my cheek.

"Don't," I said, jerking my head to the other side. He lifted my chin. I could see his eyes. I closed mine.

"You must face it. Open your eyes," he said. I did. "Good. You're not a coward. I didn't think you were. I want to be sure you understand what he did. What I asked him to do and what he did. Do you?" I nodded. "Good." He gently moved me away from the window and guided me into a seat, then turned to pull the blind shut. He squatted in front of me.

"You see this?" he asked. I looked. His gun lay in his hand. Instinctively, I drew back against the cushion of the seat. "This is the same kind of gun. It's a Luger, made of good German steel from the Ruhr, which the French have tried to steal from us. It fires nine rounds. Then you have to reload. So, If Mayr had twenty men to shoot, assuming that he killed each man with one bullet, how . . ."

"Twice," I whispered, then cleared my throat. "Three times."

"Good girl," he said, as though I were a well-trained dog. "Be patient, I'm almost done. He shot them in the head, because that's—well, you tell me why."

I looked at him helplessly.

"Why would you shot someone in the head?"

"To kill him?" I said, my voice small and thin.

"Right. And if you do it there"—he touched my temple—"or here"—he touched the back of my ear—"either place should do the trick. I know Mayr knows that because I told him. Now, when you shoot someone in the head, the bullet exits away from you, taking blood, brains, and bone with it. You usually don't get splattered, but it does happen. Maybe the victim moves at the last minute or your aim is off."

He leaned into me, his body against my legs, his arm over my lap, the hand holding my waist. "Brains are gray," he whispered, "like gray custard. Ah, we've stopped. I must go. Good-bye, dear Sally." He stood up and, without another word, left me alone.

I flew at the door and locked it, my hands shaking so badly I could barely work the key. Then I went into the bathroom and threw up.

I sat in the seat by the corner all night. What was the truth? That Christian had killed those men or that he had told Heydrich where we were going or that he hadn't done either thing. Who was lying?

You knew he had killed those men, I told myself, but a firing squad was one thing. A long string of individual executions was entirely different.

I kept seeing, as I'm sure the general wanted me to, Christian's hands and face splattered with gore. I pulled my legs up and sat, my arms around them, in as small a space as I could manage.

I called my father when I got into Berlin. Christian had told him what had happened and that he wasn't sure which train I'd be on. Daddy offered to send Rick to pick me up, but I said I'd take a taxi.

It was good to be in my father's house. I felt safe for a moment and went up to bathe and sleep. I crawled gratefully under the covers of my bed and fell soundly asleep. Until I started to dream. I don't remember anything specifically, just blood and trains and Heydrich's voice. I woke with a start.

The door to my bedroom opened quietly.

"Who is it?" I snapped, turning on the light on my bedside.

"Me," said Christian, coming into my room in his uniform and tall boots.

I pulled the covers up. He sat on the bed and leaned forward to kiss me. I turned my head. I had hoped to have some time before I saw him.

"Your business is finished?" I asked, my voice hard.

"What is it? Sally?" He sat on the bed. "I know you're angry with me for leaving you there. Darling, I am sorry. There was nothing else I could do. And you got home all right. Are you all right? My mother's party is Friday, did you remember that? We have to talk about where we're going to live. Sally, are you all right?"

"I'm fine," I said.

He looked at me, studying me. "Sally. What happened? What is it?"

"I don't want you to touch me."

"Touch you?"

"Yes, I'll say it in German so you'll understand. I don't want your hands on me. Do you understand?"

"Why?" He was utterly astounded. I could see that.

"Because you're a killer."

I wasn't looking at him, but I heard his sharp intake of air at my statement.

"You knew that," he said, his voice so faint I could hardly hear it. "I told you everything."

"Did you? There's a lot more that Heydrich told me."

"Heydrich? Where. . . ?"

"On the train. He was on the damned train."

"Oh, Christ. Did he do anything? Hurt you? Is that why. . . ?"

"Christian, he told me terrible things about you."

"And you believed him?"

"I don't know what to believe."

"You'd believe him before me?"

"Please, Christian, tell me the truth." I sat up, my hands on his arm.

"The truth. What's so bloody great about the truth? I can't believe you'd believe him and not me. Did he touch you? Did he try to make love to you?"

"No, not really."

"What do you mean, 'not really'?"

"Christian, tell me. Don't get off the subject. Tell me."

"What? What did he tell you? Are you going to let me defend myself or condemn me without a hearing?"

So I told him what the general claimed Christian had done on that horrible summer day. "And I remembered how you held your gun. As though it were welded to your hand." I started crying as I spoke. "And your boots, you were so dirty. And frightened. You were so frightened."

He was silent for a moment, turning his face away from me.

"Heydrich sent us out Friday night to make four arrests. To arrest four men. One wasn't at home, two were, and the last one resisted arrest and we had to take him. I didn't, but one of the other men shot him. In the leg. He wasn't dead. At least, I believed he wasn't."

"What about the woman? You talked about a woman."

"A woman?" he said confusedly, turning to face me. "There was no woman. Maybe I meant . . . Oh, I know. At one of the places, the man's wife came out and we had to hold her back. We shut her in the dining room, she was making so much noise. That was it.

"About Hans, Sally," he said, his voice full of pain. "That was true. I wish to God it weren't."

"But going cell to cell, Christian, did you do that?"

"No, I swear it. There's nothing more. I was in the firing squad that shot my best friend. That was all. Isn't that enough? Oh, shit." And he quickly got up, standing helplessly in the middle of the floor. "I am in such a trap. You don't know, Sally."

"Christian."

"Do you believe me?" he asked. "Do you believe me?" he repeated, desperation on his face and in his voice.

"It's not that easy."

"No. It sure as hell is not."

I pulled my legs up and sat there, studying my hands and the pattern of the covers over my legs. He was still for a long time, then he started wandering around my room. It was strange to have him there, large and male in his uniform. I wished he'd leave me alone to sort out my feelings.

"You hate me now, don't you?" he said, picking up a small bottle of perfume from my dressing table, then putting it down.

"No." I loved him. I loved him and I had to believe him.

"But you don't want me to touch you."

"Is it why you want to leave Germany?" I asked softly.

"It is."

"Do they haunt you?" I whispered. He stood at the bookcase next to the door, his back to me. He didn't move for a long time and when he spoke I could barely hear him.

"Except when I sleep with you."

I bent my head and started to cry.

"If only we had gotten to Italy," he said in the saddest voice I'd ever heard. I hated seeing him in such pain.

"Do you believe me? Please believe me. Not him. Don't believe him," he cried.

"I don't. Honest. I promise I don't. I believe you. I love you."

I held my arms out, and looking into his eyes, said again, "I believe you."

"Thank you," he said, sitting down, lowering his face to my shoulder. "Thank you." We stayed like that for a while, then he raised his head. "It's late, I'd better get back."

"You're working?"

"Yes."

"Where are you staying?"

"With my mother. Where I was."

"Maybe you could move in here, with me?"

"What about your father?"

"He won't mind. He's alone otherwise. We can ask him."

He agreed and got up to leave, but stopped at the door and said, without turning around, "I need you. You can see why."

"Yes," I said softly. "Just give me some time."

"Don't let him win, Sally."

"Just a little time."

After a moment, he nodded and went out.

A PROPER SS WIFE

Christian didn't move into my father's house with me; I moved in with him at his mother's. A temporary situation, we all agreed. Lisa gave us a large room at the back of the flat, overlooking her garden. It was several rooms away from her, but I felt strange there, getting into bed with her son under her roof.

That strangeness lasted for two nights. On the first evening, after a pleasant dinner with Lisa, Christian stayed behind to talk and I got ready for bed alone. I pretended to be asleep when he came in.

I awoke in the middle of the night to feel his hands on me. Half asleep, I lay with nothing in my mind but the pleasure of his caresses. He moved closer against my back. I rubbed against him, as though the sleep he had called me from had robbed me of all inhibitions. He moaned and moved me onto my back, lifting me so he could enter me, his hands running over my back and fanny, around to my stomach and breasts. I sat up, leaning back against him, my head against his neck.

"Oh, Sally," he murmured. I could see the pattern of the wallpaper faintly in the dark, shadows of dark and light spilling across the wall like blood. I could hear Christian's breathing. I needed to see his face, so I moved off him and lay down on my back, wanting him on top of me, wanting the weight of him to obliterate the images that were seeping into my mind.

He gasped as he entered me. I tried to stay with him, to feel only, not think. But it was no good. In the end, I turned my head into the pillow.

"What is it? Did I hurt you?" he whispered, his hand on my head.

"Nothing," I said. "I'm all right. It's nothing."

He was gone by the time I got up the next morning. I lay in bed feeling miserable, thinking of some way I could fix things. If only I could unhear what Heydrich had said.

That night, we slept on opposite sides of the bed, like strangers. The worst part was that he was so sweet to me. He touched my cheek gently with the back of his curved fingers and said good night without a hint of rancor.

Sleep would help; sleep will make everything better. I was still exhausted from my terrible train journey. Surely, after I caught up on my sleep, these fantasies would be gone from my mind.

That night I dreamed that I was waiting in a cell to be shot. The cell was horrible, cold and gray and dripping with dirty water. I sat on a chair in the middle of the square floor, a naked light bulb high above me. I could hear footsteps outside and hear doors slamming. It seemed I waited for hours, my terror growing with each passing minute.

Finally, the footsteps stopped outside my door. I tried to stand to face whatever was in store for me, but I was so pregnant, I couldn't get out of the chair.

My baby. They wouldn't shoot me because they'd kill my baby.

I tried to talk, to get out of the chair, to show whomever was behind the door that I was pregnant. I knew he wouldn't kill me if he knew this. But I was mute and crippled and helpless and with all my energy I tried to scream.

And I woke myself up with a feeble bleat, which my terrified scream had turned into. It was enough to make me sit up, hunched over my knees, thinking of Heydrich's gun, of Marlene, of Christian throwing his gun away that day.

Christian turned over and put his hand on my back.

"What is it?" he asked in a voice foggy with sleep.

"A dream," I told him.

"A bad dream?" He spoke in German.

"Yes," I said, "a bad dream. Someone was trying to kill me. In a cell. Someone was coming for me. I couldn't see him."

He sat up, his arm around me, holding me against him. I let him comfort me, but there was a part of me that couldn't forgive him for exposing me to this. We didn't talk anymore. He just held me and then I moved away.

The next day, as if things weren't bad enough, I received a telephone call from Lina Heydrich.

"My dear, you must come to dinner. As soon as possible. I must see you."

"Oh, Lina, thank you, but—"

"I know your mother-in-law is giving a small family party for you, but you must let me do this. It'll be small. Just us and a few of the younger men who are married. The sort of people you ought to be meeting. For Christian's career."

I couldn't reply to that.

"Sally, it is your duty," she said sternly, then added in a softer tone, "and it would give me so much pleasure."

343

So I agreed and hung up the phone, hoping something would happen before tomorrow night, when I would have to see that man again. I wondered if Lina knew he had said those things to me. She couldn't. How could she be so friendly to me if she did? I rubbed my hands over my face. My skin felt thin and dry.

I needed my husband. I needed . . . something. An airline ticket. I almost laughed at that. I leaned my elbow on the little table, my head in my hand.

"Are you all right?" Lisa Mayr stood at the end of the hall, her eyes full of concern.

"That was Frau Heydrich. She's invited Christian and me to dinner tomorrow."

"That's nice." She came down the hall toward me.

I took a breath and wiped my face. "No, Lisa, it isn't. Her husband is a terrible man."

"Oh, my dear, surely . . ."

"He is. And I can't imagine how I'll sit through dinner without screaming."

Lisa patted me and offered to make me a nice cup of tea and I understood that she didn't want to believe me. She hoped it was my condition.

I sat through the Heydrich dinner without screaming. I had gotten through another sleepless night, afraid of dreaming, afraid of asking for comfort, lying stiffly on my back, drifting fitfully in and out of sleep.

I thought I looked tired and old. When I put on my green velvet dress, it seemed to turn my skin gray, and I decided I'd throw it away after this evening.

There was a welcoming fire in the hearth in the Heydriches' sitting room, and the general was mixing drinks, the center of a domestic, cozy scene. Lina bustled in, giving Christian a kiss and me a hug.

"Hello, darlings," she said. And led me away, before the other guests arrived, to say good night to Paul. I liked visiting the little boy. He was above all these adult concerns and I hoped his father's poison would not harm him.

"Sally," Lina said, softly, when we were in the hall. "When I heard about your elopement, I wondered if you were expecting. Am I correct? Is this the reason for the elopement?"

I couldn't look her in the eye, nor could I deny what she said.

"Oh, no, my dear. Do not be ashamed. We do not think less

of you. No, to the contrary, we applaud your courageous choice—and, I might add"—and she put her arm around my waist, hugging me against her side—"I especially think young Mayr has made a fine choice."

"I don't know."

"Poor child. Does your father disapprove? Is that why you eloped? Well, you will be living in Germany now, and those old-fashioned ideas are dead here. The generation of your father is not relevant any longer. They and their ideas are empty. Germany honors mothers," she said in a low, intense voice. "We give the nation our most precious sons so that the fatherland will be strong." She squeezed me. I said nothing, hoping she would stop. "Come, let us go down to our men."

On the stairs, after she finally let go of me, she told me something else to make me feel better about being pregnant before marriage.

"In many peasant societies," she said, "young men won't marry a young woman until she is pregnant. They cannot have a barren wife, you see?"

"We are not a peasant society," I said, as nicely as I could.

"No, of course not. But that is not to say we should not adopt many of the ideals of that simpler life. Here we are, gentlemen."

We entered the sitting room and Heydrich came toward us, a glass in each hand, and handed them to us. But Lina wasn't finished with the subject. "Poor Sally feels guilty and embarrassed about her fertility. Tell me, my dear, how many times did you and Christian have sex before you became pregnant?" She asked me this amazing question sweetly, as though she were asking what kind of face powder I used.

I flushed and ducked my head, aware of Heydrich standing next to me. He and Lina and I were a small, tight circle. Where was Christian?

"Please, Sally," said the general. "These outmoded bourgeois notions of morality are antiquated and useless. They are not for the likes of you and young Mayr. But don't worry, we won't press the issue." He stepped back, turning to include Christian, who had come up behind me, in the circle.

"A toast," Heydrich announced expansively. We all raised our glasses. Lina, standing at her husband's left, was wearing a dark dress patterned with strange flowers, and coral beads. She gazed up at the general happily, the very picture of a perfect National Socialist wife. She had never recited cant to me before, but now I was part of the inner circle.

I wondered if Heydrich talked to her about brains and blood and murder.

Christian's eyes caught mine, and he smiled slightly. It was the first time our eyes had met in three days and I was grateful for the connection.

"To your happiness," said the general. "To your first child; may there be many more."

"Now tell them our news, Reini," said Lina shyly, after we had all taken a drink.

"You are the first to know, even before our parents. We are expecting another child."

"Oh, Lina," I said, "congratulations." Another little soldier, I thought. A son for the Führer's army. An image from a book I'd seen in my college library came to my mind: a wave of doomed young men—I don't remember which side—pouring up out of the trenches to die before the machine guns of the Great War. I drank. It was sherry, which I disliked, but I drank it down.

"Congratulations, sir," said Christian and proposed another toast to our host and hostess. As we raised our glasses, the front doorbell rang, announcing the other guests.

There were two other couples and when they had all arrived, had been introduced to me, and had drinks in their hands, Christian proposed a toast to the Heydriches' news, adding our own announcement at the end. I was not pleased, until I saw that he had given us all a focus of conversation that carried us happily into and through dinner.

On the surface, it was a friendly, even joyous meal, the food delicious, the candlelight making the dining room shine and sparkle. But there was something lurking underneath that happy surface, something dangerous.

Every time I looked at Heydrich, I remembered what he had said to me. I also remembered that he had sent Christian to face Hans Behrends and the other men in that bloody courtyard. And I remembered how proud he had seemed when he told me that. I wondered which was the most heinous act: ordering death, as Heydrich had done, or actually pulling the trigger.

Immediately after dinner, Lina sent the general and me into the sitting room to pick out a piece of music to play while she and the rest of the guests sat awhile longer over their desserts.

I was apprehensive about being alone with Heydrich, but he went straight to the pile of music on the piano.

"I haven't played in weeks," I said, sitting at the piano and opening it up.

"Then we'll find something simple. Ah, here, this little Scarlatti." He set the music in front of me.

"That's not simple."

"I do all the work. You just follow along." He turned to open his violin case, lifting out the instrument. "A, please. A. Sally, wake up."

I hit the note so he could tune up. He did so, then, setting the instrument down, picked up his bow and fussed with it. I studied the music. We had played it before and he was right, the violin did all the work. I played a few scales to warm up my hands.

"You look like hell," he said, startling me.

"Thank you," I said.

"You're not sleeping well."

"No."

"I guess Mayr's keeping you up at night."

"I guess."

He leaned on the piano, studying my face. "Usually, well-satisfied women look healthy, rosy."

"How would you know?" I snapped. He paled but caught himself and smiled, and went to call the others in.

We played the Scarlatti. The audience was appreciative, especially, I'm sure, because the piece was so short. Afterward, Lina took Christian off to get the coffee with her. They were gone a long time, and I wondered what she was telling him. We had to get out of this house. I'd had enough.

Using my pregnancy as an excuse, we were able to say our good-byes less than twenty minutes later. I hadn't even let Christian finish his coffee.

"I thought you were about ready to die of sleepiness," Christian said, as he started the car.

"I lied. I had to get us out of there. We're not going back there."

"You're serious."

"Of course I'm serious. Christian, that man is evil. Don't laugh. He is, and the longer you stay around him, the more evil rubs off on you."

"Sally, we're leaving. In less than a month we'll be gone."

"Look at what he's done to you, to me. How he's lied. What he forced you to do."

"He didn't force me."

I turned to look at him, at his profile etched against the gray

347

window. I felt such a wave of sadness pour over me, I thought I would drown, I thought I could not bear to live one more minute. But I did. Christian had said what he said and nothing changed. At least, on the surface nothing changed.

"Did you want to do what you did?" I asked. He didn't answer until he had pulled the car to the side of the road and turned the motor off.

"No, of course not." His voice sounded as weary as I felt.

"Couldn't you refuse?"

"No. I don't know. I never thought of it. I didn't consider refusal as a choice. Do you see?" He turned to face me.

"No, I don't see."

"They told us all but one of the guns had blanks in them. That there was a putsch. Don't you understand?"

"I'm trying. Please. I love you. I can't bear this."

"You knew it would be hard."

"I didn't know it would be like this. Knowing about that courtyard. I don't want to know how Hans died. I want to love you. I don't want to know. No, don't touch me." I batted his hand away, not wanting his comfort.

"There's nothing I can do," he said. "It's your decision now, Sally."

I thought about my choices: leaving or staying, leaving him, staying with him, none of it simply black and white. What I really wanted was to be someplace warm and sunny with him. It seemed to me that we spent all our time together in the dark, in the cold and dark. I heard the car pop as it cooled off.

"I'm always cold," I said, voicing my thoughts.

"You've never gotten used to winter."

"No. I guess I'm not tough enough to be the mother of future heroes of the master race. You should divorce me for that."

"I don't want to divorce you." He was silent for a moment. "Do you?"

"No," I said. More silence.

"You still love me? You still believe me?"

"Yes, I do. Dammit." I turned my face toward the side window. "Dammit," I repeated, beating my hands in my lap.

"Don't," he said, putting his hand over mine. "You'll hurt the baby." When I didn't respond, he took his hand away.

"I hate the cold," I blurted out.

"Sally," he said, his voice softening, "I could warm you up, if you'd let me. Sally. I love you." I moved tentatively toward him, letting him put his arms around me. We sat in silence again. After a moment, I laid my head against his shoulder and sighed.

"Do you remember what I said to you?" he asked softly.

"I made a promise, didn't I?"

"Yes."

My head was on his shoulder and I turned my face into his neck, smelling him, the wool of his coat, his soap on his skin, potent scents to me in the cold air. I raised my face and he kissed me, holding me, making me warm again. Then I hid again against his shoulder and we sat there, in the cold, in that little cramped car, for as long as we could.

UNWELCOME GUESTS

We had been living with Christian's mother for a week, and already the flat had become too small, especially after the house in Lichterfeld. And as much as I loved Lisa Mayr, I didn't want to live with her. I tried to explain this to Christian late one afternoon at a dreary café near his office where we had met to spend a few moments alone.

"What is bothering you? Look, if you're still brooding about that business . . ." I could hear the irritation in Christian's voice and not wanting to talk about *that business,* as he called it, I interrupted him.

"I'm sorry. I feel edgy these days. We ought to go. We have to go home to get my dress for the party."

"Home?"

"Oh. I meant Daddy's."

"I know what you meant."

"Christian, you can't blame me for feeling that way," I said. "I fixed up that house by myself. It's been my home. My first real home."

"Sally, we can't live there."

"Why not? There's room."

"Your father."

"Daddy would like it, I know he would. He's alone in that big house. And there's room for the baby. If we're still here when the baby comes. Which is the whole point—we're only going to be here in Germany for a little while. Aren't we? Aren't we?"

Christian nodded. He looked away from me, then back, and smiled. It wasn't a happy smile, more one of resignation. He sighed and touched my shoulder, his hand moving lightly down to my arm.

"Have you asked your father?"

"No. I wanted to talk to you first. But I'm sure he'd be pleased. He's so busy that he needs his home to be well-run, and I was doing a good job."

"Just add me to your chores, huh?"

He was smiling down at me so I smiled back and kissed his cheek.

"Miss—excuse me, madam," said Vittorio, when he opened the door for us that afternoon. It was storming, with rain and sleet, and we had run up the steps from the car. "It is good to see you."

"Thank you, Vittorio." I handed him my coat. "Sorry to be so messy. Isn't it terrible weather?"

"Don't worry, madam."

"Is the ambassador home?"

"Sally. Christian." My father, coming out of his study, called to us. "I thought I heard your voices. It is nice to see you both."

"Good afternoon, sir," said Christian, shaking my father's hand.

"I've come to pick up a dress for tonight," I explained, as Christian handed Vittorio his coat and cap. "And we'd like to talk to you, if you've got a minute."

"Certainly. Let's go into the sitting room. Oh, no, my study—the stove is going in there. I think it will be more comfortable."

"Would you like tea, madam?"

"Yes, please. That would be nice. Coffee for me, though," I said to Vittorio, then turned to the men. "I'll be right with you." And I ran up the stairs to my old room.

I went to the closet without turning on the lights, found the dress and the accessories I needed and a dress box to pack them in. I left everything on the bed for one of the maids to fix for me. Good. If Daddy agreed, I wouldn't have to pack all my clothes until we left for the States.

Then I noticed a box on the chair next to the door and turned on the light. It was a white, flat, square box, tied with red ribbon: a present. I picked it up; it was heavier than it looked. There was no card and I suddenly knew who had sent it.

I carried it over to my desk and opened the top cautiously, half-expecting a cobra or horrible spider to leap out at me. It was, instead, a recording of the Haydn concerto that Heydrich and I had played together. Looking for a note or card, I opened the cover, but there was nothing there except the printed list of artists. I left it in the box, and put the top back on it, sure I would never play those records.

Downstairs, Daddy and Christian were being very polite with each other. I paused in the door to ask Vittorio to send Sophie, one of the maids, to me, then went to join them.

"The tea must be ice-cold by now," I said, going around the sofa to sit in front of the tea tray.

"We're waiting for you," said my father.

"Frau Hauptsturmführer?" Sophie called.

"Sally?" My father looked at me. I turned my head. "I think she's asking for you."

"Oh. Oh, I'm sorry. I didn't realize. What a mouthful. Yes, Sophie, please, I left a dress and some things on my bed upstairs. Could you pack them in the case for me? I need to take it with me when we leave." She curtseyed and left and I smiled at no one in particular, glancing from my husband, who stood leaning against a bookcase, to my father behind his desk.

"Please. Both of you. Come sit down here and let me give you your tea properly."

"Are you both sure you want to live here?" my father wanted to know, after I had asked him if Christian and I could move in.

I looked at Christian. He glanced at me, then sat forward. "I do not feel entirely comfortable with the arrangement," Christian said, his elbows on his knees. "But Sally reminded me that it would not be for a long period." He turned his eyes on me and studied me for a moment. Then, finally, he smiled and said, "Your daughter is very determined, and I find myself unable to refuse her when I have nothing better to offer." He looked down at his hands, laced his fingers together, and continued, "I am concerned about our finances. Something Sally and I have not talked of and I would appreciate it if you and I could come to some sort of agreement about it."

"Fine." Daddy studied Christian with an impassive expression. "Yes. I think this arrangement would suit me. And I will admit that I am not averse to having my daughter safely under my roof still."

Christian did not flinch at the insinuation that he could not protect me, but I could see, in the set of his jaw, that he was angered by it.

"Now," said my father, "may I have another cup of tea? And speaking of family, I almost forgot, I received a letter from Edward. He's getting married. To that fine young woman we met, Barbara Livingston."

"Oh, that's wonderful," I cried, pouring his tea. I handed Daddy his cup and asked for more details. Barbara and Eddie were being married in April, in Newport. She came from a navy family and I knew, after my one evening with her, that my brother was a lucky man. "April. That's when . . . we'll be in the States."

"Yes," said my father. "I wanted to discuss your plans. I thought perhaps that Christmas season is the best time for us to leave."

"That would work. People travel at Christmas," I said. "What do you think?" I asked Christian.

He was sitting in the corner of the leather sofa, his elbow on the armrest, playing his fingers against his eyebrows, a nervous gesture I had never seen before.

"There are many considerations I did not realize before, when we were discussing my leaving Germany," he said, his eyes on the floor at the end of his outstretched leg. "My mother, for instance."

"You don't think they would harm her?"

He grimaced and shrugged. "I don't know. But she does travel to Denmark regularly. I thought of talking to her about what her plans were this year." He had been speaking quietly, seriously, and with a burst of energy, he sat forward again. "But I can't believe that I am so important—you know?—that anyone . . ."

"Heydrich," I put in.

"Yes. That. Heydrich would bother."

We sat in silence, listening as the storm began to die down. I picked up my cup, but put it down when I tasted how cold the coffee had become. I nervously twisted my watch, then had to turn it the right way around to look at it.

"Christian," I said softly, "we should go."

"Yes," he said, not moving. He was frowning. "You know, I have seen a great many things happen in the past years. I thought . . . you believe in something . . ." He shook his head, unable to find the words.

"You feel you've lost something precious," my father said.

"Yes." Christian looked across the table at him. "Yes, that's it. I keep hoping things will change. That the promises will be kept. But . . . every day . . ." He fell silent again, then slapped his thighs and stood. "We'd better go. We'll see you later?"

"Of course," said my father.

My father stood next to me in the entry hall, while Rick put my dress box into the trunk of the car. Then, surprisingly, Daddy put his hand on my shoulder. "I hope all is going well for you," he said softly.

"Of course, Daddy, of course." I smiled at him. "And thank you for letting us come here." I would have kissed his cheek but, with a slight smile, he turned away from me.

I wanted everything to be normal and, at least on the surface, things were. But we hadn't made love since the night before I had that frightening nightmare. I couldn't.

In front of other people, we behaved very well toward each other, pretending that nothing was wrong. I knew, too, that it was up to me to speak to Christian, but I couldn't. How could I tell him I was afraid of him? Sometimes, when I thought he wasn't watching, I would study him, trying to see past the pleasant, handsome young man I had known for so long to the man I had caught a glimpse of that day last June when he had pointed his gun at me across the back of the sofa. I knew that man was there, somewhere, crouching inside him, like a monster in the cellar.

He was giving up so much for me, agreeing to live with my father, to leave Germany. I couldn't believe that in such a short time everything had fallen apart, that I could go from being so happy to such utter misery. And there was no one I could talk to about it.

Lisa Mayr had gone to a great deal of trouble over the wedding party for us, and Annaliese was there, as promised. She greeted Christian and me as we arrived by sprinkling colored confetti over the balustrade of the stairs, laughing, giving us her good wishes.

She put her arm around my waist and kissed me. "I must tell you," she said, smiling naughtily at her brother, "this does not surprise me a bit. Although I admit I was surprised to hear that you're pregnant."

I blushed. "Does everyone know?"

"Don't look at me," Christian snapped. "I didn't mention it." And he went into the flat, leaving us on the landing.

"My goodness, he's touchy," Annaliese said, raising a well-plucked eyebrow. "I didn't realize he was so high-strung. Must be all the aristocrats he meets in his dear SS."

"And you, Annaliese," I said, changing the subject. "Do you have anyone?"

"Several," she said, laughing, and we went into the flat after Christian.

The Stokeses arrived early to help, and Sydney knocked on the door of the bedroom Christian and I were using to ask if she could come in.

"No," I said, opening the door, "I'll come out. Pretty dress. New?"

"Yes. Terribly expensive, but I won't be able to buy any pretty things soon, so I thought, why not?"

We walked into the front sitting room just as Lisa pushed open the double doors into the dining room. I introduced Sydney to Lisa. Then I saw Christian come out of the kitchen with Brian, both of them carrying bottles. I watched Christian set the bottles on the sideboard, and I was struck by the realization that my problem was really simple to fix. He wasn't my enemy. He loved me.

He must have felt me thinking about him, because he turned his head. His eyes met mine but were unsmiling. I smiled at him and started around the table toward him. He watched my progress, but seemed uninterested. Anyway, I didn't make it to his side, because the doorbell rang and in came the Bushmullers and my father and we had to go and greet them.

There was a lot of noise and happy chatter as Christian and I stood side by side in the small entry hall, welcoming the guests.

In a lull, I was about to say something, when he spoke. "I think I'll go find a drink. What can I bring you?"

Disappointed, I was brusque. "Nothing." As I was about to go into the sitting room, the doorbell rang again. Lisa's maid opened the door. It was Heydrich.

I didn't move, dumbfounded. He smiled at my confusion and stepped into the flat.

"Good evening, Sally," he said, handing the maid his hat and coat. He was in civilian clothes. "Lina sends her regrets. Paul is ill." He took my hand and bent over it, touching my knuckles with a brush of his lips.

"I'm sorry to hear that. I hope it's nothing serious."

"He's a sturdy lad. He'll be all right."

"Obergruppenführer." Lisa Mayr came in. She glanced at me, probably wondering if I had known he was coming.

"Frau Mayr, I can only stay a moment. But I had to come," he said smoothly, and she led him into the sitting room, while I wondered who had invited him. I followed the general and Lisa into the room, looking for Sydney.

My father cornered me and dryly asked me who the hell had invited our new guest.

"Don't worry, he's just staying a minute. And I don't think anyone asked him." Heydrich turned and came toward us.

"Ambassador," he said, holding his hand out.

"General," replied my father. For the barest moment, he hesitated, as though he were going to ignore Heydrich's outstretched hand. His inbred manners won out and he reached for the general's hand and gave it the briefest of shakes. "Sally, would you get me some salad? And one of those hard rolls. I feel a bit peckish."

My eyes opened wide at that. I had never in my life heard my father use a word like "peckish."

"Go, on, dear, while I chat with the general here." His Western accent was growing more pronounced as well. I went before I started laughing, although there really wasn't anything funny.

In a little while, Heydrich appeared next to me and took the plate from me to hold as I selected food for my father.

"Did you and Daddy have a nice talk?" I asked innocently.

"Your father is not what I expected."

"You met him before."

"Yes, I remember. But I did not talk to him. He seems . . . you Americans are a curious people." He shook his head, as though to clear it of confusing thoughts of my countrymen, and changed the subject. "I understand you are living here."

"Yes, but we're going to live with my father. There's so much room."

He didn't answer, except to say, "Ah." And there's something you didn't know, I thought.

"Did you get the recording?" he asked.

"Oh, yes. I'm sorry. I forgot to thank you." I spooned some potato salad onto the plate. "I haven't listened to it yet. We've been so busy." I handed him the plate, forgetting I had meant it for my father. "Thank you. It was very thoughtful of you. Now I must go . . ." I gestured behind me as though someone were waiting for me and then I hurried from the room. I pushed through a door and found myself in the pantry. Damn. I shouldn't have run away from him.

He opened the door behind me and stepped into the little space.

"I hope you will not give up your playing," he said.

"No, of course not. I practice nearly every day." There were clean glasses arranged on trays on the counter, white tea towels under them. I picked up a wineglass.

"Do you practice the Haydn? That we played together? It is very beautiful and you played it very well."

"Thank you. It is a beautiful piece."

"Yes." And he moved toward me, quietly whistling the melody, conducting with small, delicate gestures of his long, thin hands. "I hope you will listen to the recording, and remember our musical friendship."

I nodded, smiling to cover my nervousness. "I will, General."

"Please," he said, holding up one hand gracefully. "Reinhard. Please. It hurts me that you never call me by my name."

"Reinhard. Thank you, Reinhard," I said, knowing I wouldn't ever address him so. I just couldn't.

Then he leaned forward slowly, bending down toward me from his great height, and, holding my face, kissed me, his lips settling on my mouth so lightly that I barely felt them until the tip of his tongue lapped against my lips insistently. A shock of feeling exploded through me. He drew back and I saw the triumph in his cold, intelligent eyes.

"You look so fragile with those big eyes and that pretty little face," he whispered, still holding my face, his thumbs caressing my cheeks. "I imagine men want to take care of you. Women too. Missy told me she did. But you know what your particular kind of beauty makes me want?" He leaned down to me again, and I felt his lips brush my cheek, my ear. His tongue touched the spiral of my ear.

I jerked my head but he didn't let go of me, blocking me against the counter. He whispered again, his breath hot on my ear and throat.

"I want to destroy you," he said. His tongue touched me again. "And do it by making you want it. As you do now."

Then he let go of me, and left me, trembling, alone in the little pantry, with the wineglass still clasped in my hand.

"No," I whispered to the air. "No."

How I hated myself at that moment.

FURTHER DISTURBANCES

Christian and I began a strange time after we moved into my father's house. We took over two bedrooms, with a bathroom on the second floor, and I changed them to a sitting room and a bedroom for Christian and me. It was comfortable at the house, but Christian was, of course, still working, and he started staying out later in the evening. In a very short time, we developed a routine in which we rarely saw each other. I was very unhappy and I imagine he was too.

One night, after two weeks like that, we had finished dinner with Daddy, and everything was polite and placid on the surface, with Christian and me avoiding each other's eyes. I went upstairs to write to Eddie, but unable to say anything appropriate, I wandered into my old room and noticed, on my desk, where I had left it, the recording from Heydrich.

My father came into the hall just as I stepped out of the bedroom, the recording in my arms.

"Sally, I have to go out," he said.

"Has something happened?"

"An American professor was attacked. He's in the hospital."

"Why, Daddy?"

"He didn't raise his arm when some SS went by and some thugs in the crowd took offense. They evidently beat him up badly. The terrible thing, Sally, is that all this was supposed to stop when Hitler destroyed the SA. It makes me sick, I can tell you. Thank God, you and Christian will be gone by the first of the year." And saying that, he put on his hat and went out.

Eddie was coming to Berlin for Christmas, and the plan was for my father, Christian, and me to leave with him when he returned. Our story would be that we were going to spend New Year's in London, but we'd just keep on going.

I stood there for several moments after my father had left, forgetting the record in my arms. When I remembered it, I went into our sitting room, and, putting the record on the turntable, sat on the floor to listen.

I knew the piece so well and thought Heydrich and I had

played it nicely. But now, played by professional musicians, it was almost unbearably moving. Sometimes my mother's playing had been like that, and as I listened, leaning my head against the cabinet, I missed her badly. If only she had lived, she could have helped me avoid some of these mistakes I had made and kept on making.

No, I thought, raising my head. Christian is not a mistake. He cannot be. And I got up to go find him. First, I changed into my nightgown and robe, a pale-blue set, the nightgown silk, the robe thin wool, its cuffs and neck edged in satin. I brushed out my hair and tied a blue ribbon around my head. Nothing, though, could help the sadness in my eyes. Go, I said to myself, stopping to take the needle off the record.

Downstairs, my slippers clattered on the black and white tiles. Christian wasn't in the sitting room and I went down the hall to look in the music room. He wasn't there. Daddy's study was the only place left—unless he had gone out.

He sat in the big leather armchair that faced the sofa, his jacket open, his tie loosened, a glass of clear liquid held on his chest. He held one hand over his eyes. The light from the hall fell across him. He might have been asleep, he sat so still.

The radio played light classical music, romantic, schmaltzy stuff, and it covered my entrance. He didn't hear me come in and I almost backed out.

But he looked up and saw me, blinking in the light from the hall. He looked away immediately and drank, almost emptying the glass. His absolute disregard frightened me, but I made myself stay. He had a right to be angry, I told myself.

"Why is it so dark?" I said, turning to switch on the overhead light.

"Don't," he said abruptly. "Leave it."

I turned back. He was slouched in the big chair. On the table at his elbow was a half-full bottle of vodka. Slowly he lifted the glass and took a sip, then, returning the glass to the resting spot on his chest, turned his head to look at me.

"Here you are. My bride." He spoke very slowly and carefully; he was drunk. He took another drink. "What time is it?"

"Nearly ten. I'm sorry I've disturbed you." I did not move from where I stood in front of the door. "Christian?" I said softly. "Are you all right?"

Again, he moved slowly, turning his head to focus on me. "You look very beautiful." Very carefully he placed his empty glass on the table next to him, then folded his hands on his chest and, with infinite weariness, closed his eyes.

"What's wrong?" I asked.

"Wrong?" He sighed, seemed to consider speaking, but didn't.

"Is it your work?" I said, the thought suddenly scaring me. "Did you have to—did Heydrich ask you to do something?"

"Heydrich. Do you want a drink? I think I will have another." And he reached for the bottle and his glass. I said nothing and watched as he poured more vodka, clanking the bottle against the glass.

"You'll feel terrible in the morning." I walked around the sofa toward him.

"Ah, yes, I will," he said and drank, nearly emptying the glass. "You know, I've been sitting here, wondering what I did to you that makes you find me so repulsive. I was bad to you, getting you pregnant. I will admit that. But, shit, I married you, didn't I? I thought, at the lake, everything was fine. What did I do? Heydrich . . .

"Heydrich wants to fuck you, did you know that? Of course you did. How do I know? Well, he told me so. God, he told me so. 'Don't be so old-fashioned, Mayr,' he told me. I knew that he was hot for you. I *knew* that. I've watched him often enough go after women."

"Oh, Christian," I said, trying to interrupt him, to stop the words, the obscenities. I sat down.

He, in turn, hauled himself up and stood in front of me, towering over me as I sat on the sofa. He put his hands heavily on my shoulders and leaned down to speak into my face. I could smell the alcohol on his breath. "Have you fucked him already? That's the real question here."

"No, of course not," I said. "Don't be ridiculous. I told you."

He pushed on my shoulders, forcing me against the sofa back.

"But you were friends with him, you went to his house," he said in a harsh whisper.

"We played music. I was friends with Lina and I liked being with her and their son, until she started that Nazi claptrap. But they were both kind to me, recommending the fencing salle, inviting me to play. It was the music."

"Ah," he said, kneeling on the sofa so that he was straddling me. "He was 'kind' to you. Was he 'kind' to you in the pantry at my mother's? Was that what he was doing? You tell me your version."

"Get off me," I said, trying to laugh, trying to defuse his anger. "You're heavy."

"Tell me about how kind he was." He leaned over, crouching above me, his face next to my ear.

"You're being idiotic," I said, getting angry, trying to sit up. He pushed me back.

"Did you let him fuck you?"

"How can you ask me that?" I said furiously.

"Answer me."

"No," I said defiantly. "No, I won't answer. If you won't trust me—"

"Trust?" He laughed. "What does trust have to do with any of this? Jesus, trust—"

"Christian, let me up!"

"So, you wouldn't sleep with him, and you won't sleep with me because of what he said. Do you expect me to believe that crap?" He looked down at me and shook his head. "Maybe you are as naive as he said you are. Are you? Are you a sweet, stupid, naive American girl? Who fucked my boss because he gave you a recording? Maybe? Don't you realize how they were using you? Both of them. Nice. Christ."

He took another drink from his bottle. I struggled to sit up and he shoved me back again, giving me such a hard push that I bounced against the sofa back. He trailed his hand from my shoulder to my breast.

"Don't." I knocked his hand away and he grabbed my hand.

"You know what I think now? I think that you were fucking him and that is why you married me. So you let me fuck you two, three times and then you couldn't bear it any longer. I will give you that, you couldn't keep up the pretense of wanting me. Was it good on the train with him? Is it good?"

"That's disgusting. Stop this, let me up."

"About this baby," he said, putting his hands against my abdomen. "I've heard it is very unusual to knock somebody up on the first time."

"Christian, listen to me."

"Do you know what I think?" he whispered. "I think maybe this baby is not mine at all, but my boss's. What do you think of that?" His hand pressed and kneaded my abdomen, as though he hated what was there. It didn't hurt, but it might, and the threat inherent in his strength frightened me.

I had to get away and I shoved at him with all my might. What he was saying was so obscene that I couldn't have his hands on me a moment longer. The violence of my attempt must have surprised him because he fell back and I found myself on my hands and knees on the floor. I scrambled to my feet and ran around the sofa, heading for the door.

He came after me without a word, out of the study, across the hall, catching me on the stairs. I slugged him as hard as I could. He almost tumbled down the stairs, falling against the railing, catching himself on it. I ran up the rest of the stairs, down the hall to our room. In the room, I closed the door, but he was there, pushing against it. There was no key and I gave up, running to the other side of the room.

He stood in the open door, panting, his hair in his eyes, an ugly expression on his face. Seeing him like that, I felt cold, strangely calm. My head cleared as though the fear blanked out everything that would hinder my survival.

Or rather, the baby's, because for the first time I felt truly aware of it, of how small and helpless it was. I turned and ran into the bedroom, heading for the door.

He caught me, grabbing my wrist, yanking me back into the sitting room. Crying with frustration, anger, and pain, I kicked him, hurting myself because, in the flight upstairs, I had lost one of my slippers. He swore but I don't think I could have hurt him since he was wearing those damned boots.

Suddenly, he lifted me off the ground. The move surprised me so that I stopped struggling. And, after a moment, he lowered me until my feet touched the floor.

He loosened his hold on me, perhaps because I was crying. I immediately tried to jerk away and he let go of one of my hands, although his arm across my chest still held me fast. He pushed his hand gently against my head and, for one horrible moment, I thought he meant to break my neck.

"You're crazy," I whispered, trembling.

He didn't say anything, as he hadn't since we started this incredible fight. Instead, his hand slid down my neck, over my nightgown, to my breast. I struggled again to free myself, but he held tightly to me. Except for that one hand, moving on my breast. He cocked a leg, so that his thigh ran under mine, almost supporting me. I could feel his erection.

Suddenly, perversely, I felt an overwhelming rush of desire for him. There was nothing in me but want, as though the desire was so strong that all other feelings were wiped away. I slumped against him, my head back against his shoulder.

"Oh, Christian," I said, moving against him, feeling his body respond to me. I was more than hungry for him, I was ravenous, and I turned in his arms to kiss him, practically knocking him over. His hands were fire even through my nightclothes, and when he touched my breasts, skin to skin, I moaned in relief. I tore at his shirt buttons as he fumbled with my nightgown and robe. We fell onto the floor, Christian scrabbling with his pants buttons, not bothering to take off any of his other clothing.

Never have I wanted anyone, anything, so much. And I did so instinctively, not thinking, not talking, not doing anything but feeling. And wanting. All of me seemed to be focused in that secret place where, when he entered me, fast and hard, he drove for my center.

The floor was hard but I didn't feel it. His uniform buttons, before he sat up and wrenched his jacket off, gouged me, but I didn't feel them. There was no kissing, no sweet caresses, just the pounding. I wrapped my legs high around him, helping him go deeper, holding him closer. This position meant I couldn't help anchor us, and the force of his drives into me moved us across the floor until he put his hands on my shoulders, to hold me still so he could reach deeper, as he had done that June afternoon, but now it was different. So different.

I arched against him, my arms flying to the side, hitting the floor. He kept up his assault, hammering at me, and I rose to confront him, to meet his every charge.

"No, no, no," he groaned, moving in long, hard arcs into and through me. I felt him wet and hot in me, as though he were growing, until I could feel him against every part of my inner self. The idea of our feeling each other that entirely so moved me that a smaller rush, an aftershock, rippled through me. And him.

His straight arms held his face high above me, until, finally, he slowly sank down onto me, heavy, his bulk hindering my breathing, making me feel exhausted and overwhelmed. I put my arms around him, too stunned to move my legs and shift his weight.

We lay there for a long time, sweaty, in the ruins of our clothing.

I wondered if he was sleeping, his breathing was so regular and calm. His full weight was on me, pressing me into the floor, his shoulder against my chin, almost throttling me. I tried to roll him off. He resisted moving for a brief moment, then let me push him onto his back. He didn't move. He just lay there, one arm covering his eyes, his shirt and pants splayed open.

I got up, nearly toppling over on weak legs, and staggered into the bedroom. I quickly got into bed, our bed, where I fell asleep at once and slept deeply. When I awakened several hours later, my eyes flew open. Something had awakened me and I stared straight up at the ceiling, trying to hear what it might have been. It came from the sitting room and I sat up to listen.

363

Christian. It was him. And he was crying. I got out of bed and padded into the sitting room. The light was still on and I covered my eyes until they adjusted. He was still on the floor, I guess he had fallen asleep on his stomach, his head in his arms. He looked so disheveled, so uncomfortable, so miserable, that I knelt down and took him in my arms.

"Shhh," I murmured, his head on my shoulder. "It's okay. It's okay."

He raised his head to look at me. He looked terrible, his eyes red, unshaven, his hair a mess. "Are you all right?"

"Yes."

"Really?"

"Yes."

"I'm sorry. So sorry."

"So am I." I held him to me tightly. "I'm sorry for everything," I whispered. "I love you."

"Why?" he asked, looking into my face again. "Why do you love me? Nothing is right about it. Look at what I've done."

"I don't know. I have to. Shh." I put my fingers against his lips. "No more tonight. Come to bed. Come to bed with me."

I helped him up, walking with my arm around his waist, and seating him on the bed. We got his boots off and I removed the rest of his clothing, as he fell back against the pillows. When I climbed into bed next to him, his hand came across the sheets for me and he turned over to lie close behind me. I covered his hand with mine.

"I don't believe what Heydrich said," he murmured so softly that I didn't know if he was dreaming or not. Then he was silent. And we slept.

In the morning, I woke late. He was gone and I felt relieved. I wanted time before I had to look into his eyes and see how he felt about me. Then I heard the shower going and realized that he was only that far away from me.

I pretended to sleep as he quietly moved around getting dressed. I heard him swear under his breath when he dropped his cuff link, and I almost smiled. But I wanted to hide from him, so I controlled myself.

He came over to me and stood above me for the longest time, until I was sure he was testing me. He wasn't. He put his hand gently on my head, caressed me, spoke, and was gone.

I waited until I heard the door close before I opened my eyes, staring into the dim room, lit by the morning light that crept in around the curtains and blinds.

"You make it so hard," he had said. I did. I flipped onto my back. It was my fault. He had done everything perfectly: asking me, in the face of my father's displeasure, to marry him; making the decision to leave the SS, his job, his friends, his family, his country. He had killed those men, under orders, but he was trying to extricate himself from ever being ordered to do such a thing again. I sat up. It was so clear. He was trying to save himself and I wasn't doing anything to help him.

I rang for my coffee, determined to change. I would show him that I could give. That's what I needed to do, give back to him some of the love and caring he had given to me. And last night . . . well, I wouldn't think of that, of the way we had been, the feelings.

I blushed as I thought about it, looking at myself in the mirror over the sink. But I smiled, too, remembering how it had felt to be overwhelmed by him. As I took my nightgown off and turned on the shower, I caught sight of myself again in the mirror. How rosy and fecund I looked. For the first time, I looked pregnant. I stepped closer and saw the welt across the top of my breast. Gingerly, I touched the raw skin and dried blood. I hadn't noticed it last night. I hadn't even felt it. I shook my head, not believing the violence of the passion I had experienced.

A PERFECT
GERMAN KNIGHT

P lay for me. You never play for me," said Christian, leaning on the piano, looking across the music stand at me. It was early evening almost a week after our horrible fight and he had just come home. I hadn't felt well and had slept most of the day, coming down to practice around four. I was in slacks and a sweater, my hair in a ponytail. I usually practiced in the morning, after Daddy and Christian left. I was glad to see him and glad he had stopped to talk to me. He had been very careful with me, very distant and polite, and I had missed his company.

"You've never asked me," I replied, rippling out a scale.

"Well, I am asking you now," he said, coming around close enough to give my ponytail a gentle tug. "I remember your mother. In the summers. She used to play those American songs, jazz and the like."

"And the Spanish and Mexican songs. I liked those." I started to pick out the melody of one. It was a beautiful ballad about a man saying good-bye to his girl before he went off to fight in the revolution.

"I remember that one," exclaimed Christian, swinging around to sit next to me.

I found the melody and added some chords and Christian, as he remembered the words, sang softly. I smiled to hear his tentative tenor. I hadn't heard him sing since we were kids. We leaned against each other, playing and singing the song about love and death. When we came to the end of the song we sat in silence, listening to the last overtones of the piano fade away. I let my hands drop from the keyboard.

"This is nice—with you," I said.

"I like hearing you play. Play me something else." He put his hand around me, touching my neck. I turned my head to face him and he kissed me, holding me close and warm against him. He rubbed his cheek against mine, then quickly straightened up.

"God," he said, "look at the time. Are you going to be ready?"

"Ready for what?"

"Sally, you forgot." He moved away from me. "The dinner."

"The dinner? Oh, no—I did forget!" I dropped my hands into my lap. "Do I have. . . ?" I saw his face. "I'll make it. Don't worry." I jumped up and hurried to the door. "When do we leave?"

"Half past or so."

"I'll do it. Just watch me." I returned to him and kissed him. "I promise. Absolutely," I said, and left the room.

The Reichsführer-SS Himmler was hosting a banquet for the officers of the SD to show his appreciation for the work they, and their chief, had done for the Reich. I did not look forward to it, but I had promised myself to do my best to support Christian. It was hard for him to continue, knowing he would be leaving.

I opened my wardrobe, wondering what one wore to such an affair. Sophie was turning back the bed and I asked for her opinion. We settled on a new dress, one I'd bought during the summer in Paris, a black watered silk with sleeves puffed high at the shoulders, tapering to tight columns with ten tiny jet buttons at each wrist. It was otherwise plain, with a full skirt. Sophie took it off for a pressing and I hopped into the shower.

"Right on time," said Christian as I climbed into the back of the car. The window was up, separating us from Rick, and Christian kissed my gloved hand. "And you look perfect."

"Thank you." I checked my reflection in the window. I'd put my hair up in a smooth coil on top of my head and I did look elegant and collected.

The banquet was in a huge gilded hall at the Adlon. There were nearly one hundred men there from the SD, most with their wives. It was a very special occasion, as women were usually excluded from SS activities.

Christian and I sat at a large round table with six other couples. He was seated across from me, and the huge, hideous center-piece—black and silver roses, which probably cost a fortune—effectively cut us off from each other. I did manage a friendly conversation with the man to my left, a major with a high forehead and glasses and an educated interest in music.

After the dinner, which was good, if too rich, there were speeches. Heydrich got up to introduce his boss. There was a micro-phone and his voice sounded very high coming through it.

"I'm not very good at these events," he said with disarming modesty. "Usually, when I'm asked to come, I say: 'Send the boss. He's much better at it than I am.'" Everyone laughed and Heydrich waited for his audience to quiet down. "I'm happier at work, I like to be working. Well, most of you know that." This comment was received with rueful laughter. "So I will now stop talking and leave

the field to Reichsführer-SS Himmler. He *is* better at this than I."
He stepped back from the podium, holding his hand out toward the
Reichsführer, then joining in the applause before returning to his
seat. I had already noticed Lina, in a royal-blue velvet dress, a spray
of flowers in her hair. We had seen each other and smiled across the
large expanse of the crowded room.

I had never actually met Heinrich Himmler, although I had
seen him at a reception the air ministry gave one New Year's. He
was not an impressive figure for such a powerful man. Small and
insignificant in his fancy black-and-silver uniform, he looked like a
skinny kid dressing up or a clerk on his way to a costume party,
hoping to impress someone. I don't remember much about his
speech, except that it was long and mostly about the hard work the
SS had in front of them, making Germany healthy again. He read
from notes, the light catching his round glasses every time he looked
up. But finally he was finished and smiled smugly at the tremendous
applause he received.

Dessert was served with the coffee, and as we were eating,
Himmler, followed by Heydrich and a few aides, made the rounds
of the room. Himmler didn't stop to talk or meet every person, but
as he passed, each table stood to receive him.

So it was with ours. Heydrich introduced him to Christian and
they all came around toward me.

"Frau Hauptsturmführer Mayr," said Heydrich, smiling at me
over his shorter boss.

"Ah, yes, the American," said Himmler, holding out his hand.

I shook hands with him, saying nothing. His hand was very
damp and flaccid, rather unpleasant to touch. I almost giggled, but
held it in, behaving impeccably. I remembered a story I'd heard from
Sydney, who had heard it from one of the German secretaries at the
British embassy, whose sister worked for the SS. Himmler was
known for his damp handshakes, for his boring conversation, and
for his bad breath. Unlike, for instance, Joseph Goebbels, who,
though as unattractive physically, exerted a strong charismatic attraction on most women who came into contact with him.

"Heini arrives at the office with such fanfare and salutes," the
secretary's sister told her, "and nobody goes to look, but when the
Doctor arrives at his ministry, all the girls rush to the outside windows to see him."

Himmler's next comment to me did nothing to dispel my belief
in the truth of Sydney's story. He stared right at my stomach and
asked me if I was expecting.

The rudeness of the question surprised me, but I smiled and simply said that I was.

"I am pleased," he said, lifting his chin. "I can tell you that at first I was not pleased with Hauptsturmführer Mayr's choice of a bride, although the report of your antecedents was impeccable. But one hears such things about American women, doesn't one, Heydrich?" Himmler leaned his head slightly toward his subordinate, but did not turn to look at him.

"One can scarcely believe," murmured Heydrich.

"But now you have proved that my faith in our man was well-founded. I hope your child is a boy, a fine boy. You must let me know immediately. And, of course, if there is anything I can do for you." He took my hand and covered it with his, patting away at me.

I smiled at him and thanked him and finally he let go of me.

"Good. Good. That is fine," he said as he moved on. Heydrich followed, his energy checked, his dominant personality under wraps, like a racehorse pulling a plow. He smiled at me as he passed.

"You were splendid," whispered Christian.

"What did he mean about my antecedents? Did someone do research on me?" I whispered back at him.

"Of course they did. I told you. When we got married."

"What'd they find out? Anything interesting?"

"Sally. Not now." I opened my mouth. "Please," he said and I was silent.

As we all returned to our seats, Christian and I received covetous looks from the others at our table for the attention given us by the Reichsführer. I kept on smiling, trying to behave, trying to remember where I was.

But if I wasn't already aware of it, after dessert when the company stood and sang, I was forced to see the reality. Their rendition was not as lusty as the men in the beer hall, nor did they sing of spilling Jewish blood or bashing Communist heads. They sang of the future, of their quest, of being destiny's men. Himmler quieted them after the song.

He had a surprise for them and held up a yellow telegram. It was from the Führer himself and Himmler read it. It was simple, wishing the company goodwill in their struggle and thanking them for the work they had done, the sacrifices they had made, promising them the brightness that would be theirs in the continuing years of the Thousand-Year Reich.

"You are the best our nation has," read the telegram. "The shock troops, the vanguard, the knights of the Third Reich."

Then they raised their arms and heiled their Führer. Again with dignity and control, unlike the emotional, sloppy practices of their defeated, dishonored, and murdered brethren, the SA.

The men in this room believed they were the best their country could offer, the best-educated, the brightest minds, the finest bodies, the most ambitious, idealistic, and loyal—the elite. They were sure they were exactly what their country needed at that moment in its history: they were the hope of the future, whom all young Germans looked up to.

And my husband was one of them, singing and saluting with the same quiet fervor. I didn't watch him. I sat and stood when the other women did, and hoped I had a rapt expression on my face, but I didn't look at him. I didn't want to see how well he fit in.

I wished there were someone I could share my true feelings with, someone like David. We could have made funny jokes about the singing and saluting, about Himmler's glasses and limp hand-shake, and I would have felt less frightened, less alone. On the other hand, I thought, looking at the straight black-sleeved arms of the men in front of me, maybe this wasn't something to make jokes about. It really wasn't funny.

I had to remember that we were going to leave, that all three of us would be safe and that Christian's intentions were honorable, that he was not a loyal SS man. But still, I didn't want to know what he did during these last weeks. I wanted to see him, and not his uniform.

It wasn't so hard, since I never asked him about what he did and he never told me. He wrote reports; that sounded innocuous enough.

I tried to ignore everything that would threaten us, but it was becoming more and more difficult. Christian himself seemed to be changing in subtle ways I couldn't really put my finger on. He some-times was gone for several days at a time. Never without telling me, but when he returned he was distracted and distant. He was drinking more than was normal for him and not eating well.

Once I came home from a long, boring dinner at the Soviet embassy and found him standing in the sitting room, a drink in his hand, staring out the windows of the French doors. He had turned on one table lamp, which is why I had opened the door, wondering why the light was on.

He turned his head toward me when he heard the door open and smiled at me. Then he drank. I walked to him and ran my hand across his back. He put his arm around me and pulled me against his side, holding on to me, still without a word.

"Did you just get in?" I asked him after a moment. He nodded and drank again.

"It's very clear tonight, isn't it?" he said.

I looked outside; it was.

"Have you eaten recently?" I asked him as he lifted the glass to his lips. "I'll make you a sandwich."

"It's all right."

"Come on. I had dinner with the Soviets and you know what they know about food." I took his hand and led him from the sitting room, telling him about the terrible dinner I'd had, making him laugh.

I could always distract him, it seemed, and maybe that was my most important role in his life at that time. He never said so, but I could see him slowly relax, slowly become more like the man I knew and less like the tall, silent stranger I sometimes felt I was mysteriously married to.

We made love that night and he fell asleep almost immediately after. I held him for a long time, wondering what would happen to us.

A few nights later, we went to a small Italian restaurant for supper before going to the opera. I don't like to eat heavy food before the theater, but the opera was *Lohengrin* and I thought we'd better eat before Wagner.

I arrived at the restaurant, a long, cozy narrow room, before Christian and watched him arrive. He wore a black wool uniform topcoat, the shoulders of which were flecked with snow. He took it off and handed it and his cap to the hatcheck girl, then came down the room looking for me.

He looked so handsome, his face flushed with the cold, his hair slightly mussed above his perfectly tailored uniform. I noticed, and not for the first time, people, men and women both, watching him.

His face lit up when he saw me and he came quickly to me, kissed me and sat down. The waiter arrived and we ordered.

"What is it we're seeing tonight?" he asked.

"*Lohengrin.*"

"Ah, the perfect knight."

"You look like what he should look like but won't." He made a face at me, rejecting my comment. "You're so handsome. How did you grow up to be so beautiful?"

"Men aren't beautiful."

"You are."

"So are you."

"No," I said, secretly pleased at the compliment. "I'm pretty. It's not the same thing at all."

The waiter arrived with our food and we didn't speak for a few minutes. Then Christian, chewing thoughtfully on his lasagna, said, "It's not so easy, you know. Well, you must know this. But I think it must be easier for a girl to be very good-looking than for a man."

I could see it was a difficult subject for him, and I wondered what it was he wanted to tell me.

"People demand things, expect things—just because of the way one looks."

"What things?" I asked tentatively.

He ignored my question. "It's taken me a while to realize they are only seeing my looks."

"Except for me."

He nodded. "Yes. And that's another reason why I love you. Because you knew me when I was just a short, skinny kid." He looked up from his plate, his eyes catching the light from the little candle to his right. His hair had started to fall onto his forehead, as it had when he was a kid, and I reached my hand out to push it back when he spoke, freezing my hand in mid-gesture.

"You knew me when I was young," he said, paused, then added, "and innocent." His eyes held mine, daring me to ask what he meant, to say anything, but I dropped my hand to my fork and smiled at him.

"And the same goes for me," I said flippantly. He let it go. And so did I.

During the opera, I was reminded of our conversation when, on their wedding night, Elsa pleads with Lohengrin to tell her his name. In the next scene, he does, in front of the king and court, and then departs, leaving Elsa to die of woe. She was encouraged to ask the question by her enemies, almost dared to.

As the lights came up for the curtain calls, I glanced at my husband, who was certainly much closer to the embodiment of the perfect German knight than the stocky, middle-aged tenor on the stage.

What were the questions I should have asked him? What were the answers I was too frightened to hear?

Several mornings after the opera, Sophie woke me when she came in with the coffee. Christian was still asleep, his arm over my waist, and I gestured to Sophie to be quiet and put the coffee in the other room.

I extracted myself, still feeling slightly embarrassed at being found in bed with my husband, and, putting on my robe, went into the bathroom and then into our sitting room.

"Good morning, Sophie," I said. "Here, let me take that." She was juggling both the tray and Christian's briefcase, which he had left on the table. I took hold of one of the handles and she let go. The case was heavier than I anticipated and the contents of it spilled to the ground, fanning out in front of us.

"Oh, madam, oh, dear," exclaimed Sophie, kneeling quickly and grabbing up handfuls of papers.

"Here, Sophie, let me," I said, getting down across from her. "You fix the table. I'll do this. Don't worry."

She got up and did as I asked while I gathered Christian's stuff together, trying to keep the papers in order. Fortunately, most of them were fastened into their respective file folders, but there were loose pages that I gathered up and put on top. Then I came upon something different: several photographs of varying sizes. I looked at them.

They were all black and white and all of people's faces, all but one a man. The pictures were not posed studio shots, but candid and rough. It occurred to me that they were blowups.

"What the hell are you doing?" I looked up. Christian stood, in his pajamas, his arms akimbo, in the middle of the room. He was furious. Sophie and I froze at the look on his face.

"Nothing, we knocked your case over . . ." I stammered.

He crossed the room quickly and grabbed the photographs out of my hand. "You have no business touching this. What the hell is she doing in here?" he yelled, turning toward Sophie, who literally cowered in front of him.

"Christian," I said, putting my hand on his arm. He shrugged it off. "Christian, Sophie was setting the table."

"She's going through my things."

"Oh, no, sir, no," said poor Sophie, her face turning red. "I would never . . ."

"Sophie, please go," I said. "I'll explain."

"I know she was going through them," he said. "I saw her."

"No, please, sir. I would never touch the Hauptsturmführer's things. Please." Sophie was sobbing by now, her hands over her face.

"You stupid girl," he ground out, and raised his hand to hit her.

"Christian!" I cried. "Don't. No."

Looking disgusted, Christian wheeled away from Sophie. I moved to her and put my arm around her as I took her to the door.

"I'm sorry, Sophie, no, of course it's not your fault. Please don't cry. You go downstairs, all right?"

"If there is anything to find out here, I will," Christian said from across the room. Sophie's head went up and she stared at him. He raised his arm and pointed at her. "Do you understand, girl?"

She nodded and lowered her eyes. I could feel her shaking against me. I didn't blame her, Christian was frightening me as well. I could see he was trying to control himself, his fists clenched, his mouth a tight closed line. He was wearing navy pajamas and an untied robe of navy, dark green, and burgundy paisley fabric, but his informal dress did nothing to dissipate the effect of his anger.

I ushered the weeping Sophie out the door, then turned to face Christian. He was gathering up the papers and I went to help.

"Don't," he barked. "Just stay away." I took a step away and he looked up. "These are all secret, Sally. I should not have brought them here. I should have taken them to the office last night when I got back to town, but I was so tired. I never imagined to find you and the maid going through them."

"We were not going through them. We dropped the case and were picking them up."

"Which is a clever way for someone to get a look at everything."

"Sophie? Why would Sophie want to look at those papers? Christian, do you think Sophie is a spy or something?"

"It is possible."

"For whom? Against whom? What an incompetent spy she is, to do it in front of me."

"A seemingly innocent ploy."

"Ploy? Christian, you can't be serious," I exclaimed, trying a laugh.

"It is not a joke, Sally. Why do you insist on making everything a joke?" He almost shouted, hitting the handful of papers against his knee. "This is not a joke. What I do is not funny. There is nothing even remotely funny about this." He finished stuffing the papers into his briefcase and stood up.

"I'm not making a joke. I'm trying to make things better. To get you to calm down. I was the one that knocked your case onto the ground, not Sophie. Honestly, Christian, you are just being paranoid."

"Paranoid," he laughed. "Oh, God, Sally, you are so fucking naive. I can't believe it. You are amazing."

"No, you're the amazing one, attacking the maid and me. Me!" I stood up, facing him. "I think you're just feeling guilty because you brought the papers home—what are those photographs anyway? I think you're just afraid of your boss. Well, don't take it out on me. Okay? Go yell at your colleagues in your damned SD and SS and—"

He didn't let me finished, grabbing my shoulders and giving me a hard shake. I gasped.

"What did you see of them?" he said, his voice low and tight. "The photographs. What did you see of them? Tell me," he ordered, giving me another shake.

"Christian, you're hurting me." I pulled away, but he moved with me, not letting go of me.

"Tell me, dammit."

"Nothing. I saw nothing."

"You looked at them. I know you looked at them. Tell me what you saw." He pulled me closer to him. "Tell me."

I raised my head and met his eyes. For a long moment, I felt as though he were not seeing me, as though he imagined that he had someone else, a stranger, in front of him. The clamp of his fingers around my arms grew tighter. I was frightened by this change in him, and also fascinated by it. He pulled me up, so that I was on my tiptoes. I let him. He looked so steely, so sharp, all the edges of him defined and clear against the gray morning light. He looked into my eyes for that long moment, and then, letting go of me, turned away.

I rubbed my arms, but said nothing. He took the briefcase into the bedroom and in a minute I heard the shower start.

Sitting down at the table, I tried to pour myself a cup of coffee, but my hands were shaking so badly that I couldn't. So I stared out at the foggy morning, at the gray mist on the lawn and trees, hiding the gardens from me.

When Christian finally came out of the bedroom, dressed in his uniform, I didn't look at him. Keeping my head turned toward the window, I did not speak to him, and he went away without a word.

THE BLUE PARROT

Christian came up to our rooms as Sophie was pinning a silver net around my hair, making a neat chignon at the nape of my neck. It was the day after he had yelled at her, and she concentrated on her task as he stuck his head around the bedroom door, smiled at me, and disappeared. Sophie's eyes met mine in the mirror and I could see she was still upset, even frightened of him. I gave her a reassuring look. Christian and I were going out, alone, for dinner and dancing and I had a daring new dress and wanted nothing to spoil the evening.

"Were you held up?" I called to Christian, turning my head to look at the arrangement of net and hair. Sophie held up the hand mirror so I could see the back.

"It looks nice, Sophie. You did a good job."

"Thank you, madam. I hope the Hauptsturmführer likes it."

"He will. Now you'd better go on. Christian?" I walked into the other room. He was sitting in the armchair, a comfortable one I had had covered in flowered blue chintz. His arm was propped on the arms of the chair, his fingers laced in front of his face. He looked up at me, glanced at Sophie as she left, bobbing a curtsey by the door, then he smiled.

"How pretty you look."

"Thank you." I waited for him to say more. I was still angry about the way he had badgered Sophie and me, but he seemed depressed about something. "Do you still want to go out?"

"Yes, of course. But could I have a drink first?"

"All right." I went to the little cabinet where we kept a few bottles and pulled out a bottle of vodka and one of Scotch. I held them out so Christian could see.

"Scotch," he said.

I poured his drink and carried the glass over to him. He sat forward, his elbows on his knees, his head bent, and sighed. "I talked to Heydrich today about our trip to London. He brought it up. He had my visa application on his desk. Didn't refer to it, of course. Just put it where I could see it." He looked up and noticed me standing there, his drink in my hand. "Thanks," he said, taking the glass and drinking. I walked away, fidgeting, wandering around the room, as he talked. I straightened the edge of the rug with my toe, smoothing out the pale fringe over the parquet.

"I've seen him do the same thing with other people, people he was interrogating, for God's sake. He asked me when I intended to return from London. I said after the New Year. He asked if you and your father were coming back then. I said you were and then he asked if your brother was too or if he was going straight back to the States and his wedding. God, I'm a lousy liar. I got flustered because he knew about your brother coming and the wedding. How does he know about Eddie's wedding? Somebody's talking to him about us."

"Oh, that can't be. How could. . . ?"

"The servants. Perhaps Rick. Or Sophie."

"Sophie!"

"I told you I was suspicious of her. Heydrich knows. He knows everything, the bastard." Christian drank the rest of his Scotch, then put the glass on the small table next to him.

"He can't know for sure. He must just suspect."

"That's enough for him to do something."

"Do something? What do you mean?"

"And you know what was the worst thing this afternoon, as I stood in front of his desk? He has a huge, fancy desk so he's miles away from you. Makes you feel like a delinquent student in front of the principal. But the worst thing is I wanted to tell him. I wanted it to be over. He's going to find out, if he doesn't know already, and I want it to be over."

"Christian, he'll only find out when we don't come back . . ."

"Jesus, I'm brave. What a man you've married."

I stood across the room, next to the record player, and I nervously picked up a record and returned it to its jacket. It was Brahms, one of the symphonies. It frightened me that he was frightened and I didn't want him to know that.

"My, that's a sexy dress. It must be new, because I would certainly remember you in it." His voice was very soft, very gentle.

"Do you like it?" Responding to the tone of his voice, I put the record down and turned, showing off the dress, which was very sexy, and very bare, a mere slip of heavy silver beading. It was cut very cleverly so that it seemed to swirl around me, rather than hang straight. I walked closer to him and turned sideways, running my hand down my stomach. "Do I look too fat in it? Is it too bare? I feel like it barely covers me and I look too pregnant. Not that I shouldn't."

Christian reached out and took my hand, drawing me toward him. "You look luscious. All rosy, round, and fertile."

"Fat, you mean."

"No, luscious." He pulled me in front of him, between his knees, his hands on my hips. "I'll bet if you bent over, I could see right down the front."

"That's so immature of you," I said, batting him lightly on his shoulder, glad that his sad mood had gone.

"What do you have on underneath? There's barely room for anything."

I had one hand on his shoulder and he carefully traced the edge of the dress under my arm up along the curve to my neck. Then he leaned forward and kissed the bare skin exposed by the plunging neckline. I shivered, swaying toward him.

"I just did my hair," I said, my voice husky with my feeble protest.

"I don't want to touch your hair. I promise." He continued to kiss and lick me while he gathered up the skirt until he could reach under it. I hadn't put my stockings on yet and he pushed down my panties, then leaned back to undo his buckle, the buttons on his pants.

"Is there room here?" I asked, turning my head to be sure the door to the hall was closed.

"We'll make room," he said, pulling me toward him. I stepped out of my underpants and sat on his lap, folding my legs on either side of him. I wasn't quite able to fit myself to him, and he put his hands under my skirt, touching me, making me ready to receive him.

My long silver dress flowed down over us, covering our naked-ness and what we were doing. He brought his hands out from under the dress, touching my arms, my waist, laughing at my expression. I bent my head to his shoulder, feeling him inside me. I gasped.

"You like that, don't you?" he whispered.

"No—I'm—mad—at—you." Up and down, I spoke with my breath.

"Why?" His voice broke. I held still, my hands on his shoulders.

"Yesterday."

"Oh. Don't stop. I'm sorry. Don't stop. God, you're a witch. Don't stop." He tried bucking me back into movement, but I grabbed his shoulders and shook him.

He laughed at me, and dropped his hands from my waist. "Okay. I give up. Whatever you want. I'll do it."

"Promise?"

"Yes. Yes, now, please, before it's too late."

"All right." And I experimented, moving this way and that.

"Oh, God," he sighed, leaning his head back against the chair. "What do you want? What can I give you, my dearest, sexy witch?"

I didn't answer, concentrating on moving, amazed by the feeling of him. "Do you feel that? How does it feel?"

"Wonderful. The best feeling in the world." His head was still back and he closed his eyes. I watched his face, gauging his reactions. Somehow, I had never really understood my effect on him. Sex had, so far, been something he had done to me. I was excited by the turnabout and I watched the tension rise in him as I moved faster and faster until, finally, his eyes flew open, his head came up, and his hands grabbed my waist, pushing me down onto him, pushing him farther into me, in one long shuddering movement. He laughed weakly, dropping his hands over the side of the chair, letting his head fall back against it.

Still feeling my power, I leaned forward very slowly and kissed him, feeling his lips with my tongue, as he had done to me earlier.

Someone knocked on the door.

Our heads flew up at the same time, turning instantly toward the sound.

"Sally?" It was my father and I started to get up, but Christian held me still. I looked at him in a panic. He grinned naughtily.

"I'm dressing, Daddy," I called. Christian, still with that naughty look on his face, pushed the straps of my dress off my shoulders and leaned forward to kiss my breast. I tried to brush him away, but he kept on kissing me.

"I'm sorry to disturb you," continued my father. "I'm leaving for my dinner now and wondered if you wanted me to ask Rick to come back for you?"

"No, thank you, we'll take a cab." I tried backing off Christian's lap, but he put his arms around me.

"Good. Well, good night."

"Good night, Daddy," I said. "Stop," I whispered, pushing against Christian's chest.

"Don't you. . . ?"

"Stop, please," I said, unfolding my legs, managing to get out of the chair. I got tangled in my skirt and nearly fell. Christian leaned to catch me, but I avoided his hand. "I'm okay. Just shaky." I pulled the straps of the dress up and walked into the bathroom.

I was drying myself when he knocked on the door. I opened it. He was leaning against the jamb, one hand clutching his undone pants, the other dangling a pale-gray satin pair of underpants. "Yours, I believe?" he said.

I snatched them from him and slammed the door. He laughed.

I sat at my dressing table again and Christian began to change into his dress uniform, piece by piece.

"Is this the way it's supposed to be?" I said in a very small voice. In the mirror, I watched him pull on and button his pants. He looked over at me as he took a shirt out of a drawer. He put it on over his head, leaving the buttons done up, then came over to me, the cuffs flopping about his wrists.

He put his hands on my shoulders. "What do you mean?"

"I don't know," I said, after thinking for a moment. I met his eyes in the mirror. "It's not the way I imagined."

"How was that?"

I searched for a description of something I could hardly explain to myself. "We're so . . . wild."

"It's all your fault, you're so luscious."

"That's the baby," I said, letting go of him and turning around.

"I know." He leaned over me, slipping his hand down the front of my dress, fondling my breast.

I twisted toward him, not to dislodge his hand, but to lift my arms to bring him down to sit next to me and kiss me.

"This is crazy," I murmured.

"I know," he said again.

"Maybe we should give up."

"Stay home."

"For days."

"Get it out of our systems."

"We won't be able to when the baby comes."

"No," he said, pulling back from me. "And we won't be able to get all dressed up and go dancing."

"You're right." We laughed at each other and he got up to finish dressing and I turned around to face the mirror and repair my makeup.

We should have stayed home, but we thought we had time, you see. I paused, the lipstick tube in my hand, remembering what he had said about his application for a visa for London sitting on Heydrich's desk. I watched him buttoning his cuffs and was heartened by the ordinariness of the sight.

I didn't know that we had run out of time.

We went to a tiny new, very chic nightclub called the Blue Parrot. It was done, as expected, in bright blues and greens. The waiters, all handsome young men, wore midriff shirts with big ruffled sleeves and tight pants. An aviary filled with exotic birds, including some blue parrots, comprised one wall. I had heard—from Sydney, I think—that the floor show was very erotic, but tasteful. We didn't see much of it, although it was in full feather as Christian and I were shown to our table. A trio of dark-skinned people, two men and one girl, as far as I could see, were doing some sort of dance to drums and a flute. They were dressed in feathers and body paint, and not much of either.

I laughed and covered my face and Christian, amused at my embarrassment, leaned across the little table. "You're a fine one to be blushing."

"Oh, shut up," I laughed.

"Look, we should try that. All you need is a feather. Ooo, I wonder if that hurts."

"Christian, stop. That's terrible. Turn around. Don't look." I waved my hand at him and he turned back to the table, laughing with me at our silliness. Even if the girl hadn't come along and taken our photograph I would remember that moment so clearly, the teasing, the attraction we felt for each other, and how handsome he was, how beautiful he made me feel when he looked at me. I think he was happy, as he leaned forward, his elbows on the table, holding my hand in both of his, about to kiss it.

"Good evening, my dear young married friends."

And we both looked up to see General Heydrich standing before us, blocking our view of the feathers. Christian stood up, instantly sober and distant.

"Good evening, sir," he said.

"I am happy to see you are enjoying yourselves," Heydrich said, enunciating the English very carefully. His eyes were very bright and he stood very straight, very controlled. But as straight as he stood, he leaned at an angle, as though the floor weren't flat. "I am alone," he continued. "May I join you?"

"Of course, General," my polite husband said, raising his hand to attract one of the waiters so another chair could be brought.

"Thank you, Mayr." Heydrich sat down in Christian's chair. "What are you drinking?" He grimaced when I raised my champagne flute. "Whiskey, faggot," he said to the bare-midriffed waiter who had brought the extra chair. The waiter flushed, but faced with Heydrich's uniform and rank, turned away quickly.

Christian seemed about to reach after the man, but stifled the gesture. We exchanged bland but meaningful looks: dismay, irritation at not left being alone, and caution.

"You two are rarely seen these days. Is this a special occasion? Or are the pleasures of the married bed beginning to fade?"

A funny noise escaped my mouth, a snicker, and I covered my mouth.

"Hardly," said Christian, his jaw hardening.

"Ah, I see," said the general, looking at us, one at a time, with eyes as cold as a snake's. The waiter arrived with his whiskey and Heydrich knocked it down and shoved the glass at the young man's stomach. "Another. Well, how nice that you are so happy." The word "nice" was said with a sneer.

"Where is Lina?" I asked.

He shrugged. "At home, I suppose. I often go out without her. She does not enjoy the kind of . . . relaxation I require. Not every husband is as assiduous about taking his wife about in public as Mayr appears to be. Of course, you have been married a short time only and we will not be able to see just what kind of a husband he is until some time has passed. He may revert back to form then." He leaned forward. "Your husband accompanied me often on my evenings out. He was very handy, being so damned handsome. I have missed him in recent forays, but I understand how he is demanded elsewhere. Oh, but how stupid of me, he is leaving the country with you, is he not?"

"For a holiday, General. We're going on a family holiday at New Year's. Is that a problem?"

"No, of course not. A holiday. Is that really all it is, Mayr?" He leaned toward Christian, who couldn't look at him.

"Yes, General," he muttered.

"And you'll be back at your desk, bright and chipper, all spit and polished, the following week?"

"Yes, General."

"Ah, good. Good." Heydrich swung around and focused on me. "Now, my dear Sally, I'm not saying I don't believe Mayr here, but I just want to congratulate you. Just in case."

"For what, General?"

"If—just if, mind you—Mayr doesn't come back . . . well, what a love affair. He would be giving up so much—his job, his country, his honor. I hope you're worth it." He drank the rest of his drink and raised his hand for another.

"It would be very un-German of Mayr to abandon his country because of a girl, however good a lay she is. We are a romantic people, I grant you, but our greatness comes because we never allow sentiment to get in the way of our true vocation."

"And what would that be?" I asked icily.

"Sally," said Christian warningly.

"Power, my dear," said Heydrich. He put his arm on the table, extending his hand to touch me lightly with his fingers under my chin. I jerked my head away. "The pursuit of power, the wielding of it." He dropped his hand to his glass, noticing with irritation that it was still empty. "It is, of course, my error. I believed young Mayr to be as driven, as hungry, as I was as a young man. It was my error, but I must confess, I hate making errors." He spat out the word "hate."

"We all do sometime, General," I said, as though this were a normal conversation.

"Yes, my dear, Sally, we do." And he looked at me with such venom that I drew back from him. I remembered what the woman at the whorehouse had said, about his hurting the girls.

Heydrich held up a hand. "Ah, listen, a tune I recognize. 'I Only Have Eyes for You,' isn't it?" He stood and bowed slightly from his waist to Christian. "May I dance with your wife? She and I have things to discuss."

He held out a hand out to me. He frightened me and my fear made me angry. I nearly refused. A glance at Christian didn't help. He wouldn't meet my eyes, picking up his glass and draining it, and I thought that Heydrich's accusations about losing his honor and running away had hit their mark. I reached across the table and touched Christian's hand. He glanced at me. I tried to convey without words that I was strong enough for this encounter.

Giving my hand to Heydrich, I followed him through the crowd to the tiny dance floor, which was as packed as the rest of the club. The patrons were a mix of uniforms, with dinner suits sprinkled among them. The women, mostly young and well-dressed, displayed the makeup, red fingernails, and curled hair that Himmler continually encouraged his men to reject.

"You look very beautiful, Sally," the general said, not looking at me.

For a moment, I thought I had not heard him, he spoke so kindly, even with sweetness, as though he really meant what he said. "I think you are very happy, aren't you? It shows. And, of course, your pregnancy is making you look lovelier, at least now. It's interesting how some women blossom and others look as though they have been invaded by parasites that sap their strength."

He pulled me closer, but not much, not enough for me to protest. He was, as ever, a very smooth dancer, piloting me through the many other couples, his hand on my waist guiding me expertly.

"Have you given up your fencing?" he asked.

"Yes. It's not safe."

"Of course. Tell me, how is he in bed?"

"What?" I jerked back from him; he held me in place.

"How is Mayr in bed? He must be keeping you happy, but I imagine he's a, well, uncomplicated lover. He seems to lack imagination. Am I right?"

I tried to pull away and he held me even more tightly. "Calm down, for God's sake. It is a mystery to me how prudish you are. I suppose it's your being an American. Tell me—if you enjoy sex so much, as I think you do, why are you so squeamish about talking about it? You can understand why I am interested. You won't talk, reacting like an outraged virgin, yet you seem obscenely complacent with sexual satisfaction. I wonder if your husband can handle you."

I stopped dancing, dropping my hands from his shoulder and hand. "This is none of your damn business." I spun around, my beaded skirt slapping heavily against my legs. I started off the dance floor.

Heydrich grabbed my arm and turned me around, pulling me back against him. People watched us warily, out of the corners of their eyes. I twisted my head to see if Christian was watching, but there were too many people between us.

"My dear, you shouldn't be so sensitive. I know everything about you already. More than you imagine. Do you think Mayr would have approached you in the first place if I hadn't told him to? He's a fine young man, but let's face it, he has no—"

"Don't you dare say anything against him," I said, snarling at him. "And let go of me. You're hurting me. I can't see why you need to ask me questions if you know everything already. Let go of me or I will cause an enormous scene. Believe me, I would love to. I may be prudish and naive, but I am the daughter of—"

"I *am* sorry," he said, smiling, stopping my flow of words, but letting go of my arm. He then ran his fingers lightly over the bruise he had left, making me shiver. His eyes glittered, the pupils huge, the whites edged with red. There was nothing else wrong with the way he looked, his hair was combed, his shave close, and he smelled faintly of his usual lemon after-shave. But, his eyes were all wrong. They were chilling, especially when he smiled. I stood up straighter.

"Your loyalty is commendable. I wish his were. I see where the backbone in your marriage comes from. Ah, there, I've done it again. Insulted him. Now, let's finish our dance. I promise not to say anything more to upset you." He held out his hand again, and I looked at him defiantly. "Come along, Sally. Dance with me. I promise to behave. If not, I'll start a scene. And believe me, you would not want that."

We finished the dance and the next one, and he said not another word, holding me properly, guiding me smoothly. As long as he was silent, all was well. He confused me, flashing back and forth between charm and cruelty. And although I would never admit it to anyone, this seesaw of his behavior interested me almost as much as it frightened me. Or perhaps it was because he frightened me that he interested me. Interested. Hell, enthralled me. If I admit that, my own guilt in what happened is all the more evident. I could have walked away from him anytime during that evening, but I didn't. I let him say those things that shocked and upset me. Still I thought I was safe.

"You like to manipulate people, don't you?" I said.

"Oh, yes." He looked down at me and smiled. "It's always interesting with you because I never know exactly how you'll react. It's why I've pursued our, ah, friendship, shall I call it. I usually don't make friends with women."

"I guess I shouldn't take what you say personally then."

"Oh, but you should. I mean what I say, don't doubt that."

We danced a few minutes in silence and then he said very softly, "You know, accidents can happen anywhere. Here or there, even out of the Reich. Wouldn't you agree?"

I didn't answer, waiting to hear what he was driving at.

"I understand that you will all be coming back after the New Year, but if you're not . . . A medical problem, for instance, and you have to rush home to America, and naturally, your husband has to go with you. Your father, still the ambassador, would have to come back alone, wouldn't he? Don't, my dear. Listen calmly to me, I'm trying to help, to offer you a suggestion."

"You are threatening my father."

"No, I am not. I am merely discussing possibilities and pointing out to you that there might be something you could do to ensure the safety of the people you care for, as well as your own. Ah, the end."

The music had stopped, although I hadn't noticed. He let go of me, perhaps thinking I was ready to listen to his proposition. But I could listen to no more from him, ever. I had reached my limit and I didn't care, I could listen to no more. I turned and walked away from him.

"Think about it, Sally," he said softly, his voice carrying straight to me as I maneuvered through the crush.

"What is it?" Christian said when he saw my face.

I picked up my bag. "We'd better leave."

Blessedly not asking any questions, Christian stood, threw some money on the table and followed me out. I walked straight out of the club and stood freezing, while I waited for Christian to bring my wrap from the checkroom. I smoothed my long gloves up my arms. My hands were shaking. And, for the first time in months, I thought of Marlene and her elegant mother-in-law and the little girl. What had her name been?

"Here, love," Christian said, putting the wrap over my shoulders. It was a white mink cape I had bought, the most expensive piece of clothing I had ever owned, but at that moment I only noticed that it was warm.

"What happened?" said Christian, tucking the ends of his scarf into his overcoat.

"Do you remember that family, the women and the little girl, we put on the train for Zurich?" He frowned, thinking. I couldn't believe he had forgotten them. "The young woman was arrested and you got her out."

"Oh, yes, the Jews," Christian said.

I stared at him. Yes, the Jews, dear, sweet husband. I closed my eyes. I felt as though there were a crack in the universe, in my universe.

"Let's walk a little," I said, wanting to get away. I set off at a brisk pace and Christian hurried to catch up with me.

"Sally, tell me what happened. Did he do something to you?"

"No, no." That's good. Heydrich. Think of him, not Christian or the little girl. She was safe now, with her mummy and daddy and grandmother, safe in Zurich. "He just talked. Oh, Christian," I said as the memory of Heydrich's poison came fully back. "Did he tell you to . . . see me? Did he? What's it matter. Oh, damn him, damn him." I stopped and half-turned in a tight, unfinished circle of frustration.

"God, Sally," Christian said, his breath white in the cold. "What did he say?"

"All sorts of things. He said all sorts of things. Annie!"

"What?"

"Annie was the little girl's name. Remember, you carried her onto the train. You were so sweet with her."

"What the hell are you talking about them for. Christ, it's too cold to talk out here."

"He wants to hurt us. He hates us."

"What did he say?"

"I wasn't really afraid before. I am now. I think he'd do anything, say anything. Why? Christian, why?"

An ugly expression crossed his face. "Oh, shit. Sorry. Come on, down here." He put his arm around my waist and led me quickly down the street toward the lights of a small café.

A tiny brightly lit den welcomed us, the green walls decorated with photos of film stars torn from magazines. There were three small tables covered with musty-looking oilcloth covers. The proprietor, talking to a heavyset man when we came in, looked disapprovingly at Christian in his dress uniform and me in my white mink and silver dress, but they said nothing.

Christian got us coffee and we sat at the table the farthest away from the two men and the window. I kept glancing at the window, fearing to see the general's tall, thin silhouette appear.

"Now tell me what he said," Christian said, and I did, omitting, without thinking, the part about there being "something" I could do. I'd think about that later. "Oh, damn," he swore again, when I had finished.

"Are we in trouble?" I asked.

He smiled a funny, lopsided smile and took my hand, kissing my fingers, then softly rubbing them against his lips. "I'll bet no one, at least not in several years, has spoken like that to him. That was wonderful of you. I've often wished I could do the same. But," he said, putting down my hand, "I still wish you hadn't done it."

"He's a bully. You have to fight back," I said. "I should have done so earlier. I let him just because I was afraid of making a scene."

"Sally, those things I said to you that night, about this not being my baby, and all. He was the one who told me, who suggested that you and he had—"

"I know, I can see that he would," I interrupted him.

"And the other, about him putting us together, I guess that's partly true. I'll be honest with you, Sally. I didn't want to tell you. But he told me to see what I could do, what kind of progress I could make with you. I figured it was because he felt he had no chance with you himself. He told me that very first time, when I thought you were his mistress. God, I hate talking about this."

I sat back in my chair, feeling the hard metal of it even through my thick fur cape. "Even back then?"

"From the beginning," he said, then cocked his head at me. "Now, Sally, don't tell me you believe I still am merely following orders?" He leaned toward me. "My love, you know that's not true. You know it. And you did not arrange to get pregnant."

387

"How do you know?" I raised my chin, trying to make a joke.

"Because of the way it happened. Neither of us expected it, did we?" He smiled at me.

"Did you marry me because you felt you had to, or did the general tell you to? Did he give you permission?"

"Neither. None of those reasons, I swear to you. Listen, Sally, I love you. God, what do I have to do to prove it? I plan to leave this place and go with you and take care of you and our child and have other kids. I swear I do. You must believe me. He's a liar. You know he is. He likes to play with people. You know that. Don't listen to him—listen to me. To what we did this evening together."

I looked from my hands, twisted together in my lap, to his clear, warm blue eyes. I studied his face, his beautiful cheekbones and the arches of his thick, pale eyebrows that perfectly framed his deep-set eyes. "I know," I said, trying to believe I did. I had to believe him. If he were lying, my whole life would be unthinkable. "It just hurts to think of him . . . meddling so. He makes everything sound so vulgar and wretched. I hate him having anything to do with us. Oh, Christian, I can't wait until we're out of this city, away and on our own. It'll be so wonderful not to have to worry, be afraid."

"Don't be afraid, my love," he said, folding my hands in his between our coffee cups. "Besides, he did get us together."

"So we should be thanking him?"

"Exactly. And he's probably behaving so badly because we didn't invite him to the wedding. He probably expected to stand up with me."

"He got himself invited to your mother's party, though. Did you ask him?"

"No," said Christian, watching his thumb stroke the back of my hand. "I figured he invited himself. He wanted to see you, you know."

"I know." I was looking down too, and decided now was the time to tell him of Heydrich's suggestion. But he went on, not giving me a chance.

"About my exit visa, if he knows our plans, then we should think of something else. I'd feel a lot better if we changed them. So, I think . . ."

"Christian, the people I mentioned, the woman, the little girl? Do you know if they made it?"

"Who? Oh, those other . . . Sally, never mind them. Did you hear what I said?" I nodded and he got up and pulled his chair around, sitting next to me, his arm around my shoulders.

"I know we'll be all right," he said. "We'll be all right." We sat like that, oblivious to the others in the café, gaining strength from each other the way animals do when they bunch together in the cold. He picked up my hand and kissed it.

"I wish it were summer," I said.

"Sally, I think you ought to make plans independent of me. I'll talk to your father. But make reservations for you—and Eddie too. That'll be good, with him there. And don't tell anyone. Don't even talk about it in front of the servants."

"You don't need to talk about this. I'm not leaving without you. I won't."

"My dearest love, you must help me. I—I don't know what I can do to protect you, me, except to urge you to do this."

"And what about you? I won't leave without you."

"You won't have to. Everything will go as planned. This is just in case."

"I won't go without you, Christian, I won't. I need you. I'm so frightened of everything without you—myself, other people, doing the wrong thing."

"I'm the one who's the coward," he said. "If I were really a man, I'd go in and tell Heydrich to fuck off, and damn the consequences."

"Don't be silly, that would be ruinous. That's not bravery, that's stupidity, Christian." I turned and grabbed the front of his coat. "Leaving Germany with me is the bravest thing you've ever done, that you could do. Don't you see that?"

"Maybe. Maybe. You don't know all of it, Sally."

"What do you mean?"

The door to the café crashed open, startling all of us, bringing in icy air and three men, two in dark coats and slouch hats and one in an SS uniform and helmet. He had a large gun in his hands. They headed straight for us.

"Hauptsturmführer Mayr?" one of the men in coats asked.

"Yes," Christian said calmly.

"Come with us, please."

"Why?"

Instead of answering, the man grabbed the back of Christian's collar and hauled him to his feet. Christian tried shaking the hand off and the man hit him, hard, across his face, bloodying his nose. I jumped up with a cry. The SS man swung his gun on me, cocking it, and I froze.

"All right, gentlemen, all right," said Christian, raising his hands. "Let me say good-bye to my wife."

Not giving them a chance to protest, he leaned over me, brushing the side of my face against his, his lips near my ear.

"Get to your father," he murmured in English. "I love you."

"Come along, Hauptsturmführer." The same man grabbed Christian's shoulder and pulled him violently away from me.

"No," I yelled, holding on to him. "Please, where are you taking him?"

One man raised his hand and Christian pushed me away, out of range.

"Stay there, Sally." He spoke in German, so they would understand that he was warning me. "They'll hurt you. Please, Sally. Please."

I stopped and looked at all three men and their impassive faces. One of them grinned at me and I backed away a step from them, my arms folded protectively across my stomach.

"Good girl," Christian said. He started to say more, but they shoved him toward the door. As one of the coats went to open the door, Christian turned to look at me. He smiled just as the SS man hit the back of his shoulder with the butt of the gun. Christian was turned completely around by the blow. The gun came down on him again, against the side of his head. A sound escaped from him and he was bleeding. I screamed and reached out for him, but the gun turned toward me, freezing me in my place. Christian disappeared out the door, the goons surrounding him.

I ran out the door in time to see the car pull away from the curb. I stood staring after it.

Questions. Hundreds of questions. Only one question. Oh, God, Christian. Oh, God. Would I ever see him again? Would he be alive? And I found myself talking to Heydrich, almost as though I were praying to him. Don't hurt him. Please. Don't hurt him.

"Come in, lady. Come in." The two men from the café had come after me, to lead me back inside. They sat me down, gave me more of their dreadful coffee, and finally had me telephone home.

I felt so helpless, waiting for Rick, who might or might not be in Heydrich's employ, to come, and, when I got home, waiting for my father to call people. I paced his study, refusing Vittorio's offer of coffee.

At some point, I went upstairs and changed and, at the memory of dressing, at the sight of our room, I nearly broke down completely. I went into the bathroom and threw up until there was nothing left but bile. I cried, hanging wretchedly over the bowl.

No, I told myself. Get up. Not now. Later I could fall apart. So I got up, washed my face, and put on pajamas and a robe, more because it was four in the morning than because I expected to sleep. Daddy was talking to someone on the phone in German when I came back downstairs.

He hung up as I entered. "No one knows where he is. We can't get through to anyone because of the hour." He walked over to me and took my shoulders. "Sally, go to bed. There's nothing more we can do. There's so little I can do, really. But we'll find him. We will."

"Oh, Daddy," I said wearily, "I don't doubt that. But will we get him out of wherever they put him?"

"Hang on, Sally. This will be hard, but hang on. Don't give up."

"Daddy, I need him. I'll die without him. I'll die inside. I don't have any other choice but to hang on." And I turned and went upstairs.

Lying on the bed, I felt the room was too large, too full of his presence, and I got up and went into my old room and, without turning on any lights, crawled under the covers. I was exhausted, but my mind wouldn't shut down, continuing the incessant, silent plea to Heydrich. Don't hurt him, don't hurt him, don't hurt him.

It wasn't until I woke up that I put it all together and knew what I had to do. It was really very simple. It had been the shock of Christian's arrest that had kept me from thinking clearly.

It was simple.

WAITING

I didn't tell anyone where I was going, and I slipped out of the house even before Daddy came down for breakfast.

I waited all day to see Heydrich, sitting on a bench in the hall outside his office on Friedrichstrasse. His assistants were polite, even offering me coffee, but they wouldn't let me near him. He was playing with me, of course. I knew that. He wouldn't make any step of this process easy for me. I didn't care. Just so he didn't hurt Christian. Finally, at five thirty, one of the men came out to tell me the general had left already and was sorry he hadn't found the time for me.

At home, my father was frantic with worry because I hadn't told anyone where I was going. Mrs. Bushmuller was there, and so was Daddy's secretary, Mr. Bancroft, and they all fussed and worried at me. Sydney had come too. She broke past them, and putting her arm around my waist, sorted everything out. Before I knew what had happened, Daddy, Sydney, and I were having a drink alone in the study, and I told them about my wasted, frustrating day. My father was trying to talk me out of repeating the experience the next day, when Vittorio brought word that Frau Mayr was here. I hurried into the hall.

"What has happened to Christian?" Lisa asked, without a word of greeting. "I telephoned his office today. They were very strange. They would not tell me where he was."

"He was arrested last night, Lisa."

"And you did not tell me?" She was calm, her face pale, clutching her black leather handbag in both hands as though it were an anchor.

"We thought we would have him back by now," said my father, who had come up behind me.

"And you have not?"

"No."

"Why was he arrested? What has he done?"

"He's done nothing, Lisa," said Daddy.

"Nonsense. People aren't arrested unless they've done something." She turned to me. "Is it this plan of yours to leave Germany?

392

Is that it?" I didn't answer, but she found her answer in my expression. Her shoulder slumped, the energy that had brought her here to this house spent. "He is my last son. And you . . . I love you like one of my own daughters. Your marriage made me so happy. But he told me about leaving just days ago—that things were difficult for him. Is that why he was arrested?"

"I don't know, Lisa. But we'll get him back," I whispered, touching her arm.

She nodded. "Of course, of course."

"I promise, Lisa. I can't let them have him either."

She nodded, but she didn't believe me, I could see that.

I told Daddy where I was going the next day. Naturally, he was not happy about it, but I insisted, not even listening to his protests.

"As long as they let me in the building, I'll go sit there," I said, and went up to dress. "And I'll go alone."

He had suggested that one of his embassy people go with me, but I knew it would be even more humiliating to have some smooth-faced Harvard man there to watch me beg.

After another sleepless night, I looked terrible, although makeup helped cover up the circles under my eyes. I felt hollow inside, in spite of the baby, and very close to a loss of control I knew would be disastrous to Christian's rescue. So I put on my blue suit and white blouse with the pleated, asymmetrical collar, pinned a hat on and went back to the SD headquarters.

That day I only had to wait until lunchtime, when the double doors to Heydrich's office opened and he came out, followed by his retinue. Snapping orders left and right, causing a great deal of efficient, quiet scurrying, he headed down the shiny, cold marble floor.

I stood slowly, feeling no nervousness, no fear, just an overwhelming exhaustion. Heydrich looked at me—as though I were a surprise—and veered off his course, coming smoothly up to me and taking my hand.

"Sally, I am so sorry. I understand you have been here some time, waiting for me." He kissed my hand.

"Two days," I said quietly, glancing at his flock of black uniforms, waiting discreetly out of earshot.

"I am sorry. What is it about?" He covered my hand with his.

"You know what it's about," I said. My hand lay limp in his.

"Do I?"

I raised my head to look into those cold eyes of his. He looked amused and interested.

"I'm sorry, but I am too tired play your games."

"Games, my dear, Sally? I don't have time to play games, as charming as such an amusement would be with your company. The Führer has returned unexpectedly from Berchtesgaden and I find my hands full with his security."

"Please, Reinhard," I said in a low voice, not wanting his flock of crows to hear. "You said the other night that I could do something about the situation. I didn't understand what you meant. All right, now I do. You've made it very clear. What do you want? What can I do?"

His eyes flicked over me, then away as he seemed to consider my proposition as though it were a new idea. As though he didn't hold all the power in this situation, as though I were proposing a trip for a chocolate cake at Horcher's.

"You look like hell, my dear," he said and, taking my arm, led me down the hall, farther away from his entourage.

"Am I to understand that you are offering yourself for your husband? Is that what you are saying?" He sounded utterly surprised, and even shocked.

I nodded. "Of course, it's irrelevant if you don't know where he is, isn't it?" I said, my voice as tired as I felt.

"Are you all right? You sound quite ill."

"No, I'm not all right!" I blurted out, then clamped my jaws shut to control myself, turning away from him to lean my shoulder against the black marble wall. I laid my hand against it, to feel the coldness, to concentrate and to keep from crying. I needed all my wits about me.

He came up behind me, leaning solicitously over me, a hand on my back. "Dear Sally. I have enjoyed playing with you, but I see your love for that rather useless young man has rendered you quite gutless. So, tell me about your offer. Would you truly do anything for him?"

"Yes. As long as the baby isn't harmed."

"Ah, I see." And leaning so close to me that his lips touched my ear, he started whispering to me, describing the things he would do to me, which became increasingly perverse. "We can go to Missy's," he said. "I am known there. I believe you are as well. There are places there, and girls to help us. Have you ever—no, of course, you haven't. Something else I can introduce you to. If you say yes to me, my dear, dear Sally. What do you say?"

My face aflame, I wrapped my arms around my middle, trying to ignore the nausea his filth was causing in me.

"What?" he said. "I can't hear you."

"Yes," I said, almost impatiently. "All right, anything—just let him go."

"Ah. Very interesting. I wonder, would you let me piss on you? They say the Führer indulges in that particular practice."

"Oh, stop it." I threw my hands up, nearly hitting his face. "You don't mean any of this, do you?"

He grabbed my hand, squeezing it tightly. "Perhaps," he laughed softly. "I am very curious to see how far you would go to save your husband. I must say I envy him, although I imagine he would not be pleased to know you had planned to debase yourself, even for his sake. Of course, I tried to tell him about you and that Jewish newspaper flunky, but he wouldn't listen. Perhaps now he will. So. Yes, I do know where he is."

"Is he all right? Did you hurt him? If you hurt him . . ."

"Sally, be quiet." He tightened his grip on my shoulder and I did as he commanded. "You are not in a position to make even the most timid threat against me. But because I am fond of you, I will overlook it. I am fond of you. Which makes it doubly hard for me to refuse your offer. I would enjoy taking you to bed. I do have a reputation in these matters, and I admit to warranting most of it. However, I have never raped anyone and I don't intend to start with you. My sexual appetites, although large, are quite normal—simple, really. But I have never been to bed with anyone who did not want to be there or was not paid, at least. You understand what I am saying, my dear? Do you?" He massaged my neck, his hand moving to my shoulder. I could feel his cold fingers flash against my skin.

I nodded. "Is there nothing I can do?"

"I'm afraid not. You might have. Don't cry. I can't stand sniveling." His fingers dug hurtfully into my neck. "Especially for such a hypocritical reason. Because, Sally . . ." He was very close to me, his body against my back and side. He reached across with one hand and cupped my chin. It was a strange gesture, almost paternal. "Because you wanted me. I could feel the effect my kiss had on you. It has really hurt my feelings, you and your stupid . . ." He didn't finish his sentence, but dropped his hand from my face and stepped back from me.

"What are you going to do to him?" My voice sounded strident to me. It made my head ache.

He pursed his lips. "I don't know. I'll think of something. Ah, one last thing. I wonder if you would sacrifice everything for him? Your own life, for instance. Of course you would. But what about the child?" he said, putting his hand on my stomach.

"There's an idea. I confess to not liking the idea of fucking pregnant women, as handsome as you are now. Lina quite revolts me. But if you got rid of the child, then . . ."

I didn't hear any more, but slid down to the ground in a faint, the fear and lack of sleep, his evil whispers, all of it finally allowing me this escape.

I came to quickly, with Heydrich and his men fussing about me. "Leave me alone," I demanded, my tongue thick, my mouth full of an unpleasant metallic taste. "I want to go home. I'm all right." I wouldn't let any of them touch me, waving them away from me, snatching my handbag from someone's hands.

"Webber," Heydrich ordered of one of his men, "take Fräulein Jackson—I'm sorry, Frau Hauptsturmführer Mayr—home. She doesn't feel well." He reached out and someone handed him his cap and he put it on. "Good-bye, Sally," he said, touching two fingers to the bill of the cap and smiling at me. "Thank you for dropping by."

I stood and watched him walk away. Please don't hurt him. Please don't hurt him. The refrain was so loud in my head that I was sure Heydrich could hear it; certainly the man Webber, standing next to me, ready to escort me home, could.

"Will he kill him?" I said to him.

"Please?" He cocked his head, as though I were speaking gibberish. Perhaps I was. "Shall we go?" And I let him lead me out of the building.

What was I going to tell Lisa?

"It's no use, Daddy," I said, my hand on the banister at the foot of the stairs. "The general won't help. I even went to see his wife, but she wasn't there." I had had to invoke my father's position to convince Webber to take me. Lina hadn't been home and the maid who answered the door said she and Paul had gone to her parents. I reached up and pulled my hat off, drawing my hair across my face. "I've got to sleep." I climbed the stairs, not waiting for a reply.

I awoke at four in the morning. It was still dark outside, still dark indoors. I knew I couldn't sleep anymore, so I got up and drank some cold water and washed my face. I looked as bad as I felt, tired, old, and frightened. I'd have to go back to the Friedrichstrasse today. It was all I could think of to do.

"Madam? Are you awake?" It was a maid at the outer door.

She was knocking excitedly. I dragged a hand towel from the rack and stepped into the bedroom to call to her.

"Yes, I'm up."

She opened the door—it was Sophie—and bounced into the room. "He's here. The Hauptsturmführer's back."

I didn't need to hear any more. I dropped the towel and flew down the stairs, barefoot and in my nightgown.

He stood, still in his dress uniform, flanked by my father and Vittorio, both in dressing gowns and slippers. One of the marine guards from the gate was at the open door. I didn't pay attention to any of them, but ran straight into Christian's arms. Never in my life had anything felt so good as my arms around him, his closing around me, warmth and familiarity. I closed my eyes, shutting out everything except the feel and smell of him.

"I'm sorry to wake you all up," Christian said, touching my face, his hand moving to my neck.

"Sir, are you hungry?" asked Vittorio.

"What can we do for you?" asked my father.

"I'm very tired. They . . . they wouldn't let me sleep. I'm afraid I don't even know what day it is."

"Sleep, then," I said, taking over. I asked Vittorio to have Frau Brenner fix something later, when Christian awoke, and, my arm around his waist, led my husband to the stairs. Daddy patted his shoulder and promised to telephone Lisa Mayr.

Upstairs, I helped Christian undress and get into his pajama bottoms. The front of his shirt was filthy with dried blood. It seemed an eon ago since he had put it on.

"I should wash," he said, dropping the jacket to his pajamas. It just fell from his fingers, as though he didn't have strength enough to hold on to it. He was nearly asleep on his feet.

"You can do it later," I said.

He sat heavily on the bed, sinking back on top of the blankets, and he was asleep before I could pull the quilt over him. I looked at the bruise on his forehead, but decided it would keep.

It was a dark November dawn outside; I could hear the wind start up. I lay down carefully next to him, as he slept curled on his side, one hand like a child's on the pillow next to his face. Never, had I loved him more, or would I treasure him as much as I did that morning. I couldn't believe that another human being's presence could make such a difference in my life. That I should *need* him so much that I felt literally sick without him was a revelation to me.

How crazy it was that we should be together, that I should be carrying this child; yet, there it was. We are almost a family. The thought made tears come to my eyes. There was no reason or logic to how I'd ended up married to him. And I knew, more than anything, that I wanted to be. I wanted him. Our child. A life together. We will have it, I resolved. We will have it. And with that resolution, I slept.

I woke several hours later and got up, found a skirt and sweater in the dark room and put them on. Then I went downstairs and telephoned Sydney. When I came back into our bedroom late in the afternoon, Christian was, I thought, still asleep. I suppose I made a noise, pushing the door open, because he started.

"It's me," I said softly, and walked around the bed to look down at him.

His eyes were wild and he was trembling. I sat on the bed and felt his forehead. It was cold and clammy.

"It's not fever," he said with a valiant touch of humor. "It's fear."

"Oh, Christian." I laid my cheek against his shoulder, putting my arms around him. "You've nothing to be frightened of now."

"I'm sorry," he said, shaking.

"Shush. It's a reaction to the shock of what you've been through. But you're safe now." I pulled the blankets around him, tucking them in on either side of him.

"I don't think I'll ever feel safe again."

"Shhh." I stroked his face, holding him until he calmed, until he was able to catch his breath. He tried to laugh.

"God," he said, turning onto his back. "That was embarrassing."

"Don't be silly. It's only me." I leaned over to kiss him, but he held his hand up between our lips.

"Can't let you kiss me until I'm clean. I smell awful."

"I don't care," I said, tears filling my eyes. "A bath then; I'll go run it." I got up and headed for the bathroom.

"Sally?" I stopped at the door. "How are you?"

I smiled at him. "Now? I'm fine."

"How's the baby?"

I patted my stomach. "She's doing fine too."

I left Christian alone in the bathroom, although I found it hard to be out of sight of him, and sat in front of my dressing table, next to the bathroom door, staring into space. Daddy sent up a drink for Christian, and, glass in hand, I knocked on the door.

"You want your back washed?"

We went down to dinner with Daddy, and afterward Christian went to telephone his mother. When he was out of the dining room, Daddy asked me how he was and I said he seemed all right. But there was something different about him. I had seen it in his eyes—how frightened he had been, how he had curled up instead of sleeping as he normally did, stretched out.

"Has he told you anything of what happened?"

"No."

"Well, he's home. That's the main thing."

"Yes." I looked down at my plate. There was a pork chop left on it—I hadn't been able to eat it—and I fought to keep from crying. My fingernails jammed into my palms, I practically suffocated trying to keep my emotions under control. And all the time, I looked down at the damn pork chop. My father reached across the corner of the table toward me.

"Don't, Daddy. I can't. Not yet."

"He is home, Sally. Remember that. I think you both ought to leave as soon as possible. Don't wait for Edward."

Christian came back in and sat down again.

"I'll bet she was glad to hear from you," I said.

"Yes." He played with his napkin, loosely folded next to his empty plate. He had eaten everything he had been given.

"Do you want some more?" I asked.

"No. No, thank you. Sally, would you mind if I spoke to your father without you?"

"Why?" I looked from him to Daddy and back. I tried a little laugh. "Will you tell me later? I think I ought to know."

"Of course," he said, his eyes not meeting mine.

In bed and nearly asleep when he came upstairs, I listened to him puttering around between the bathroom and bedroom, taking forever to get into his pajamas and turn off the light. Finally he got into bed, but he did not touch me or reach for me. We said good night to each other and lay side by side without touching. It was so strange that I had to say something.

"Are you all right?" I asked, touching his shoulder.

He laughed, not happily, but a short, hurt-filled bark. "No. No, I'm not."

"Can I help?" There was silence, and I raised myself on my

elbow to look down on him. I could see the gleam of his eyes in the dark shape of his head against the pillow. "Is it what you told Daddy?"

"No. I talked to your father about our plans. Sally"—he reached to touch my arm, then let his hand drop—"I want you to be safe. I asked your father to make sure . . . even if . . . I can't."

"Can't what?"

"I'm such a coward," he whispered.

"What? No. What do you mean?"

"They say these kinds of experiences help you find out just what sort of man you are. I found out. I'm a weak man, Sally. Not worthy of you. Not worthy of you at all and I'm going to let you down."

"Why do you say that? You're not. What did they do to you?"

"No, nothing. It's over."

"Can't you tell me? Let me help."

"You'll hate me."

"Never. I promise. I'd never hate you."

He started crying and I quickly turned on the night-light on my bedside table. It gave me enough light to see him by as he lay on his back, his arm over his eyes. I tried to put my arms around him, but he sat up, away from me. I leaned against the headboard, confused and increasingly frightened.

"I'm despicable," he said.

"Why? I've seen you cry lots of times. The first time when we met and I knocked you down, remember?" He grunted and I reached my hand out and touched his head. His clean hair was fluffy and soft and I stroked it, enjoying the feel of it. "You were smaller than I was, remember, and you tried to push me—"

"The cell was spotlessly clean," he said in a toneless voice, interrupting me. "The mattress on the cot was clean blue ticking. I remember thinking it wasn't so bad. There was a light bulb, the light never went off, but that wasn't so bad. The door had a window in it. Someone looked in every hour, but I ignored him. I slept.

"My biggest worry was about you, whether you got home all right. I thought that Heydrich would let me out in the morning, that he was just trying to scare me.

"No one came in the morning. I could hear breakfast being distributed, but no one came to me. I thought that meant I was going to get out. I waited all day. Every time I heard a footstep, I thought, now. Now, they'll let me out.

"The window kept opening all day. Sometime in the afternoon, I began trying to get the guard to talk to me. I couldn't see his face, the screen was too dense, but I tried to talk to him. To get him to tell me what was going on. Nothing.

"I slept again. Not well. The light. The window opening and closing, quietly. The noise. The footsteps out in the corridor. But I slept. Something woke me up. The light was off. Someone was in the cell. I could hear him breathing . . . could *feel* his presence. I lay without moving. Not speaking. The door, the place where the door was, was black. It might have been open." His voice trembled. I lay very still.

"Then they were there." He stopped, took a deep breath, then continued, "In the darkness. In the cell with me. They were there. No one spoke. The sound, small sounds, then they . . . they . . ."

"Who was it? What, Christian?" I leaned over him.

It took him several tries to get the words out, but he did, finally. "They . . . took . . . they . . . raped me."

"What?" I gasped. My heart stopped. Everything stopped.

"They raped me," he repeated. "That's what they did. They raped me."

"But how. . . ?"

"Please, Sally. Shut up. I don't mean . . . please, just be quiet."

I lay next to him, feeling helpless, wishing there were something I could do, anything, to make this terrible thing go away. He let me take his hand, and I clasped it in both of mine on my breast. It was all I could do. He held on to me tightly.

"I saw . . . there was a light, quick, on and off, maybe in the corridor. I saw one of them was wearing an SS uniform. He straightened up and I could see his collar tabs. Not his face, just his collar tabs. A Scharführer. SS, Sally. *He* sent them.

"It's made everything different, Sally," he said after a while. "I'm different. Everything is different. I just . . . I just can't. I'm sorry." And he took his hand from mine and turned over, his back to me.

"Christian," I said softly, and put my hand lightly on his back. "I love you. I'll always love you. I promise." Slowly, I felt some of the tension in him fade. His breathing slowed until he slept and I let my hand drop.

I couldn't imagine all that had happened to him, but I felt his pain and humiliation. And his fear, his fear frightened me and angered me. SS men had done that to him. Heydrich had sent SS men to destroy him.

God, how I hated that man. I wanted to kill him, hurt him as much as he had hurt my husband, as he had hurt me. He had debased us both and Christian was right. Things had changed.

A horrible thought occurred to me. I opened my eyes in the darkness. What if Heydrich had succeeded in destroying Christian's resolve to leave Germany?

I wondered what that man would do next, because I knew he wouldn't leave us alone.

Later, Christian awoke, needing to talk, and let me hold him. "You must hate me. I must revolt you. I revolt myself."

"You're wrong. I love you."

"No, I mean the way we . . . I just—I almost raped you that day."

"It was different." I rubbed my cheek against his hair. "You didn't mean to hurt me. And I could have stopped you. Especially after you threw away your gun." He didn't laugh at my stupid joke.

"But the way you shied away from me after we came back from Lake Sebastian . . ."

"Christian, stop. Don't say any more. It wasn't you. It was me. I was being childish. And I am sorry. Oh, my love, I'm sorry for all of this."

"It's not your—"

"If I hadn't gotten pregnant . . . If you hadn't married me . . . If I hadn't met Heydrich . . ."

"If. If. If. Well, this is it. Now. I'm not what you think anymore. I don't know if I've ever been who you think I am. You have a picture of me that is false. You've had it for years."

"I know. I know that now. Don't you think you did too?"

"Maybe. All right. You're a lot tougher than I imagined. You make me ashamed."

"Oh, no. Please, don't say that. Christian, a terrible thing happened to you because of me."

"Don't be ridiculous."

"He wouldn't have had you arrested and put somewhere like that if I hadn't . . . oh, I don't know. I flirted with him. I was nice to him. I played music with him. And the fact is, if I had slept with him during one of those practice sessions, he wouldn't be interested in me anymore. I'm right, aren't I?"

"Yes," he said and we were silent. When he spoke next, I was almost asleep. "Let's go away," he said softly.

"We're doing that."

"I mean, now. Alone. Let's go hide somewhere for a short time, a day or two." His voice, coming out of the darkness next to me, sounded strange asking me this simple thing.

"All right. I'll find a—"

"I know a place. An old inn on an island in the Havel. You'll like it."

"How can we go away? Won't he stop you?"

"We'll go on the weekend. What's wrong with that? Just a weekend with my wife."

"You've already planned—"

"While I was locked up. I thought about it. You'll come with me? We'll go Saturday. Please, Sally, let's go away. Just a day or two. What do you say?"

PEACOCK ISLAND

In the Havel River, near Potsdam, is an island named after the peacocks raised there for the royal owners who came to spend languid summer days fishing and shooting. The Kaiser's old hunting lodge had been turned into an expensive and very exclusive weekend retreat. Because it was November, we didn't have any trouble getting a room when Christian called that Saturday morning. Or at least, that was what he told me.

Rick drove us to the ferry and left us, promising to return Monday morning. Christian hadn't said anything further about Rick, about whether he might be spying on us. I vaguely wondered why; perhaps it didn't seem important any longer.

It was a gray, sullen morning, and the Havel River, although flat, was forbidding. The entire vista was empty of human habitation, and I wondered why Christian had chosen such a place. I would have much preferred a night in luxury at the Adlon, right in the middle of town.

A man waited on the other side of the river for us, dressed in a green-and-black-striped jacket, a valet's garb. He carried our two small suitcases up the path through the bare trees. Somewhere a crow cawed.

"That's not a peacock," I joked.

"No, ma'am," said the man. "You'll hear them at night."

Christian strode along beside me, his hands in his coat pockets, his eyes on the ground. He was still depressed. I put my hand around his arm. He didn't say anything, but pressed his arm against his side, capturing my hand.

The hunting lodge had been built in the early sixteen hundreds and renovated at the turn of the century. The manager assured me there was hot and cold running water and electricity. There seemed to be no other guests.

As Christian signed us in, I looked around at the paintings of dogs, horses, and dead game. The walls were whitewashed and very plain, although the wood floors were inlaid with an intricate, beautiful pattern. Through a broad arch, I could see a reception room with Oriental rugs scattered about and heavy furniture. The effect was spare but comfortable, and very masculine.

Our large room was at the back of the building, facing the Havel. It was on the second floor and had three large windowed doors, heavier than conventional French doors, which opened onto a long, narrow balcony. I walked out onto it, but the cold wind drove me back in quickly. The doors were uncurtained and allowed the gray light to fill the room.

The bed, canopied with dark-green-and-brown-patterned hangings, was so high off the ground that steps were provided to help one into it. A large dark-green enameled stove stood in the corner, its tiles decorated with running stags being chased by dogs. Christian tipped the man who had carried our bags up and grimaced at me.

"Picturesque, isn't it?"

"I'll say. Have you been here before?"

"No. But I've heard of it. It seemed a perfect place to hide in. You won't mind, will you?" He smiled at me, touching my head.

"No. As long as you're here."

We went out for a long walk, running before the rain on our way back. We had a large, delicious lunch—there were two other guests, both men, eating silently at separate tables. It started to rain hard just as we moved to the big reception room for coffee. We sat in front of the largest fireplace I had ever seen. A huge log as big around as a giant redwood roaring in it, sending sparks flashing up the chimney.

Christian went to find a newspaper, leaving me contentedly watching the fire, my feet tucked up under my skirt, thinking he had been right about our getting away. Then I fell asleep and I don't remember much after that.

No, I do remember.

I remember dreams and flashes that weren't dreams, almost as if I was neither awake nor asleep. I felt cold and warmth, but mostly a strange detachment, as though I weren't in my body, but only watching it.

The dreams—because that's the best way to describe what I experienced—were good and bad, pleasant and frightening, starting with voices echoing against the sound of the pouring rain. At one point, I was sure I was awake, my eyes open, looking into the darkening room at General Heydrich and Christian, but then they changed into animals, deer, with strange contorted antlers.

I felt cold in my dream and whimpered when I discovered that I was naked and out of doors and it was night, although everything was blue, dark blue. I sat under a tree and looked up to see a peacock standing fearlessly in front of me. He was displaying his beautiful feathers, turning around so that I could see all sides of the fan.

I remember I was embarrassed to be naked in front of the bird, and sat with my legs drawn up tightly, hiding myself as well as I could. He screamed, a horrible, terrifying scream that seemed to come from the depths of me, seemed to be my scream.

Then I was in a room. A large, empty room, also filled with that same blue light. In the middle of it was a platform, about the size of a single bed, with a step going all around it.

Dressed now, I sat on the step.

Christian came toward me. He was twelve or thirteen, dressed in shorts and shirt, his hair in his face, as he was then. He smiled at me, recognizing me, although I was an adult.

"It's cold, isn't it?" he said.

"Not too bad," I answered. "Although it may be too late for stringing the lights."

"Is that all right?" he asked, his hands in his pockets.

"Oh, yes. Fine. Don't you think?"

Then he leaned toward me and kissed me, his hand against my face. It was the kiss of an adult, not the boy he seemed in the dream, and it made me feel a tremendous desire for him. Which disturbed me, because he was a boy.

"It's all right," he whispered, putting his knee between my legs, rubbing against me, making me shudder with desire. I wanted the climax, the ending, badly, and we seemed to be there for hours, but finally I fell away, unsatisfied, into darkness.

I think that was real. Not Christian being a boy, but our attempted lovemaking. I think it was real, but somehow I changed him, or saw him as a twelve-year-old.

Time passed.

Through my closed eyes, I saw a light, a yellow light. In my dream—or awake, I don't know which—I opened my eyes. It was candlelight, from a single candle in a low, silver holder. I stared at it. I had never seen such a warm, beautiful light before. There was a hand holding it. And a face. I knew whose face that was.

I knew he would be here. I was expecting him. He sat on the bed, putting his hand on my hip, sliding it down to my knee and back, up my arm. I was naked again, but warm and unafraid, my hair spread out on the bed underneath me, like the peacock's fan, but much longer than my hair really was. He very slowly leaned over and kissed my breast, then sat back up again.

"You aren't surprised to see me?" he asked, raising one thin

406

eyebrow. He wore a black robe with a high collar, almost like a priest's cassock.

I shook my head.

"Are you afraid?" Heydrich, still looking at me, ran his hand lightly over me, from my shoulder to my knee. He lifted the candlestick high above me and slowly tipped it. A tear of melted candle wax slid off the saucer and fell through the shining air toward my thigh.

It landed, a small, hot meteor. He touched the wax with his middle finger, delicately smoothing it, leaving his fingerprint on me.

I laughed, remembering, even in the dream, how as a child I used to cover my hand with candle wax, let it cool, then watch it crack as I flexed my hand. Then I realized that he wanted to encase me in the wax.

"It'll take so much," I said to him.

He nodded at me, acknowledging the truth of what I'd said. Gently, with one hand, he pushed me so that I rolled onto my stomach, my shoulder brushing against his thigh. He ran his hand along my back, up over my buttocks. He did something to me and I squirmed, not sure if it hurt. I giggled into my hair.

He bent over me, his hand between my legs, lightly, disturbing, almost painful.

I turned to look over my shoulder and saw the candle, another drop of wax . . .

"No-o-o-o," I said, laughing, rolling away from his hand, and the hot wax, rolling myself into my hair. "You can only do that on your hand," I laughed. The candlelight went out and I felt nothing.

Nothing.

Then voices, men's loud voices, harsh and full of violence. Real voices, one of which I recognized as Christian's as I lay half-awake, half-asleep. I felt heavy and limp, my head as groggy as if I had slept for days.

I woke up completely. It was night. The rain had stopped and moonlight was pouring in through the huge windows. I sat up, straining to hear, but there was silence. I was naked under the heavy covers.

And I was alone.

"Christian?" I called out in a panic. The room was large and the moonlight painted all the furniture silver. It stood out stark and skeletal. "Christian."

The door opened, spilling warm, yellow light from the hall into the room, and Christian walked in.

"How are you?" he said, his voice full of concern, coming slowly to the bed. He wore the same pants, shirt, and sweater he had been wearing earlier in the day.

"Were you talking to someone?" I asked.

"No. Oh, yes, another guest. We were saying good night."

"What happened?" I rubbed my face, pushing my hair away with one hand, holding the sheet in front of me with the other.

"You fainted." He looked over the bed, almost as though he were searching it. His eyes returned to me. "Are you all right?"

"I fainted?" I sou ded as incredulous as I felt. "Did you undress me?"

"Who else would undress my wife, but me?"

"I fainted?" I asked again.

"I guess so. I had to carry you upstairs. I'm sorry I didn't put your nightgown on. Do you want it now? Are you all right?"

He sat on the bed and ran his hand over my head, my shoulder, as though he were searching for wounds.

I shivered. "I had such a strange dream. You were a boy, eleven or twelve, and you . . . you made love to me."

"Good for me." He spoke gently.

"No. It was . . ." I shook my head. "I felt so guilty."

"Guilty?"

"Because you were so young. And I was . . . like now."

"Seducing boys. You ought to be ashamed." He put his arms around me, holding me against his sweater. The feel of him, his reality, made me happier.

"And Heydrich. He was here, in my dream, touching me." I shuddered.

He said nothing for a long time, and when he spoke, his voice seemed to come from far away. "What did you do?" he asked carefully.

"I think I fell asleep."

Christian laughed, throwing his head back, and laughed as though it were the funniest joke he'd ever heard.

"It's not that funny," I said, irritated. The dream had been upsetting and not at all amusing to me.

"It's perfect," he said, still laughing, hugging me hard. "It's just perfect. God, I love you." Holding my shoulders, he held me so we could see each other's faces.

"You know I love you, don't you, you crazy, wonderful girl?"

"Yes," I said, confused by his mood swings.

"Good," he said, nearly hugging the breath out of my body. "Good, great." And letting go of me, he hopped off the bed. "Don't move. I'll be right there," he said gaily. He sat next to me, pulling off his clothes, dropping shoes, socks, sweater, on the floor. He pulled his shirt over his head without unbuttoning more than the first few buttons.

"I'm sick of worrying about all of this. I'm going to stop. You too. I order it. Here you are, naked in this huge, funny bed, and I intend to pay attention to nothing else." He unbuckled his belt, then leaned back, nearly lying down, and tugged his pants off, along with his underpants. He was naked.

He stood up and walked around the bed, pulling the canopy curtains, closing us in, except for a narrow strip of moonlight that fell in a clear, almost glasslike, column diagonally across the bed. Then he got onto the bed.

"Let's forget everything. Let's just forget it. We'll just shut out the rest of the world, all of them. We're alone here. We don't have to worry about anything else." He crawled to where I sat up against the pillows and tugged the sheet down, uncovering my breasts, and, bending his head, touched the nipple of one breast with his tongue. He looked up at me, his light eyes catching the silver column of moonlight. "Let's just make love to each other, please," he whispered, melting my nerves, my backbone, my very soul with desire. I knew that what I had felt for the boy in my dream was nothing compared to this—to what I felt for the man.

He saw his answer in my face and bent to lick the other breast, then returned to the first, moving back and forth between them. My head fell forward and I held his head, reveling in the feel of him, his mouth, his hair, his breath on my skin.

He pulled the covers down and stretched out on top of me, holding my wrists and extending my arms full length from my body. "You're not afraid anymore, are you?"

"Oh, no," I breathed.

He moved on top of me, working his way between my legs, entering me without using his hands, slipping into me easily, not letting go of my hands, his body flush against mine.

"You feel how ready you are for me?" he whispered.

"Yes, yes," I replied, as I welcomed him, spreading my legs apart for him, loving the feeling of his power, my lack of it.

Suddenly he stopped, withdrawing abruptly, letting go of my hands, letting me move.

"Christian, no," I crooned, reaching for him. He slipped down in the bed, laughing softly, kissing my belly. He rubbed his face against my skin, whispering in German to the baby. I laughed too, my hands lightly on his head.

His hands brushed my stomach and thighs and in between, making me tense.

"It's all right, Sally. Please, don't be frightened. Not of me." His voice was very soft. I pushed his hands away, and he came up to lie beside me, his eyes level with mine.

"Why don't you like me to touch you there?"

"I don't know." It embarrassed me, even as naked as we were, to talk about it. So I told him: "It embarrasses me."

He laughed and kissed me, little feathery kisses, making me raise my head for more. He kissed me for a long time, his lips sweet against my eyes and forehead, my neck and ears. That made me giggle. I almost didn't notice his hands, busy on their own, until a finger found its way inside me. I became very still, all my senses focused on this new sensation, waiting, waiting . . . he raised himself on his elbow and watched me. He smiled and I turned my head into his chest, my body making my decision, telling me to wait no more. He kissed my ear.

I trembled, feeling more naked and exposed than I ever had with him. His finger inside of me seemed to be breaching my defenses in ways that his penis did not.

"Open a little." He gently pushed my legs apart.

I closed my eyes and followed him faithfully, giving in to him and the feelings he caused. He was all there was to trust in that world. His love was evident, and I let him tumble my last defenses because I felt that if I did not trust in his gentleness and love, I would be lost. And, in the back of my mind, I knew that thing that had happened to him in jail was hurting him and that my capitulation would help him heal. But, most of all, I wanted him so badly that tears came into my eyes.

"Please," I whispered, my hands on his head. He raised it to look up my body at me. "I want . . . please."

"Tell me."

"I want you in me. To feel you." I held my arms out to him, wanting the weight of his body on me, the feel of his skin, his hair, his breath, his masculinity, him. I felt so close to him, so very close, as though we were sharing the same skin and blood.

In the end, all either of us had to give—or hold back—was ourselves.

He lay with his head on my breast, one arm across my stomach. Strangely, I was not cold, although I lay uncovered on the bed, the sheets, blankets, and feather quilt pushed to the edges of the bed.

"I don't think I'm a virgin anymore," I said.

Laughing, he raised his head. "You're so beautiful," he said, his hand on my face, touching my cheeks, feeling my eyebrows, my lips. "I love you, love you, love you," he said.

"You make me beautiful," I said, my arms around his neck.

We dozed that way and when we woke to see that the shaft of moonlight had moved almost entirely across the bed, we pulled the covers over us. There, in the warm and friendly darkness, we talked about our past, reminiscing about our long friendship, retelling stories of our love, our private mythology.

The next morning, I woke up in bed with Christian beside me. The closed curtains around the bed encased us in the warm, cozy darkness. I could hear birds outside and I pushed the canopy back to see that it was a bright, sunny day. I turned over to face my husband, wanting to kiss him, not wanting to awaken him, I contented myself with touching his hair and slipped out of bed.

I was in the bathroom brushing my hair, which was badly tangled, when I heard a loud knocking on the door. I opened the bathroom door just as the door to the hall flew open and three or four men carrying guns burst into the room in an explosion of violence and noise.

"No," I screamed, racing into the room, hairbrush in hand, my robe billowing behind me. "No, please."

Christian was out of bed, behind the curtains, and one of the men hit him. I couldn't see, but I could hear the sound of the gun landing against him and his exclamation of pain.

I ran around the bed toward him, kneeling next to him. Someone picked me up around my waist, tossing me aside as though I were a stray cat. "Stay out of this, lady."

"Don't hurt her, dammit. I'll come, I'll come," Christian yelled. "Just don't hurt her."

"I'm all right," I cried to him.

"Get dressed, Mayr," said one of them.

Christian got up, heading for the wardrobe. I crouched on the steps at the foot of the bed and I watched him, devouring him with my eyes, as he dressed. He didn't have much to choose from, passing around me to get the pants he had dropped on the floor last night. I reached to touch him, my hand grazing his bare leg. I don't think he felt me. He pulled his pants and sweater on, then, as he picked up his jacket, his eyes met mine.

411

He faltered for the first time and looked quickly away. It confused me that he didn't want to look at me. Perhaps he was afraid of breaking down in front of these men. I knew he was afraid. I was. I was stiff with fear.

When he was dressed, his overcoat over his arm, his hat in his hand, he came to me, leaning over me, his hands on my shoulders.

He kissed me and looked at me, an expression of great sorrow on his face. "Go home," he whispered in English. "Take our child home to California. Tell her I love you both more than—more than anything. Anything."

I moaned, my hands reaching for him, but he was gone, leaving me along in that big, hateful room. The whole thing had taken no more than five minutes. And he was gone.

I didn't cry. I didn't fall apart or scream or tear the bed apart or hurt myself, everything flashing through my mind were things I could do.

No. Don't. This was it. He'd never come back from this. I could see that. I could hear it in his good-bye.

Never. No. There must be something . . . there must be someone . . . something I had to do.

I dressed and went downstairs and called home. It took forever for someone to answer and I asked to be put through to Daddy. I got Vittorio and asked him to send Rick to meet me with the car, then I called the embassy. Daddy wasn't there and I spoke to his secretary, telling him the news briefly.

"They took him again," was all I said, hanging up before Mr. Bancroft could ask me any questions. I packed, Christian's things too. Then asked for and got a cup of coffee and a roll. I knew I couldn't fall apart as I did the last time. This time it would take longer. I had to be strong.

Finally, I went downstairs. I had to pay our bill and I didn't have enough money. I laughed at that, my laughter nearly turning to hysteria until I clamped it down. I arranged for the manager to send the bill to the embassy. He was polite, but his eyes never met mine, as though he did not want to look on one as disgraced as I, as though he, too, were afraid.

When I was a very little girl, living with Daddy in Rome, I remember being sad all the time. I missed my mother, who had gone back to the States without me, and I couldn't understand why she would take Eddie and not me, unless I had done something wrong, had made her unhappy. I began to forget her, remembering her in general, forgetting her voice and face and how she sat and walked and touched me. I was too young to understand such things, and I got used to living with a dull ache inside me, yearning for her half-remembered presence.

I remember finding a sweater of hers, permeated with her smell—perfume, linseed oil, and cigarettes—up in the big studio of the villa in Rome. I hadn't know the room was there and had stumbled on it in my lonely wanderings around the place. I was very young, and I remember how high up the room seemed. I don't remember how I had the courage to climb all those stairs to reach it.

The room was just as my mother had left it, her painting things in neat rows, her brushes clean and sorted, a canvas she had been stretching still in its frame. I looked at everything, not daring to touch anything, until I found the green cardigan sweater hanging on the back of a chair.

I sat in the middle of the floor, under the hard winter light of the skylight, and cried, cradling that old sweater in my arms, wrapping myself in it, crying until the tears made the light spin into cartwheels of stars. That was the first time I mourned her. It was the smell of her sweater that brought my grief rushing back, the smell I had forgotten, like a kitten taken too soon out of the litter. But that old sweater reminded me of her so vividly that my heart broke. I know it did. A child couldn't feel such grief without her heart breaking.

In many ways the second time, although horrifying, was easier. I think because I understood it more. I saw her die. I watched my mother die. We were on a street close to our house in New York. It was a rainy Saturday and she and I were running errands. We had just come from a pharmacy across the street. She realized she had forgotten the things we had bought, and, without thinking, she ran back, into the path of a car, slipping in the rain. Although I hated her for running so stupidly across that street, I knew she hadn't done it to hurt me. She hadn't meant to leave me.

I knew by then that although I wasn't her perfect ideal of a daughter, she was beginning to see me for myself. She was, I think, beginning to like me.

Now I lay on our bed, Christian's and mine, in our dark room, too tired, too numb to cry. I had lost him too in my childhood, but it had been a natural parting. But this, this was insupportable. That he should die because of one evil man's lust for power was impossible. Why I was so sure he would die, I don't know. I just felt it.

Images from that June weekend, images he had told me about, of firing squads and guns, haunted me. A stake chewed up by bullets, a wall splattered by blood, made me cry out and sit up. Who had told me that? David. David had told me. No, Brian.

Oh, God, I thought, don't let him hurt him. Please don't let him hurt him.

I lay down again, turning on my side, my face coming to rest against his pillow. I reached for it, smelling him on it, but I couldn't cry. All I could do was rock back and forth, thinking, Please, don't let him hurt him. Please-don't-let-him-hurt-him. Until, finally, I fell asleep.

Sydney was there when I awoke, with a tray of soup and bread-and-butter sandwiches, along with a strong cup of tea, which she made me drink.

"Don't talk," she said, "just eat. You'll be amazed at how much better you'll feel. And, Sally, there's still the baby."

"It doesn't matter, it doesn't matter. I don't want the baby without him."

"Sally. You know you don't mean that. Don't say that. Eat." And so I did, not noticing how my rash statement had upset her.

It was early evening by then and I went downstairs with her and sat with her and Mrs. Bushmuller in the sitting room, until Daddy and some other men, Consul General Bushmuller, I think, certainly Mr. Bancroft, who had been in Daddy's study, joined us. My father had gone that afternoon to see Göring, who, while sympathetic, hadn't promised much.

The problem was, as my father tried to explain to me, that Christian was a citizen of the Reich and not under the embassy's protection. The American ambassador really had no business concerning himself with the fate of a German native, the Reichsminister had told him.

"But he's done nothing wrong," I protested. "What are they accusing him of—crimes against the state, or some such nonsense?" Daddy believed Heydrich had arrested Christian because he had found out Christian meant not to return from London. I couldn't tell my father the real reason Heydrich had Christian arrested again, and, actually, I didn't know. I didn't really know what had happened the night before, or was it the day before that? Was it that that dream perhaps wasn't a dream? I think I understood without admitting it that I'd been drugged.

"Aren't Germans supposed to be so logical?" I blurted out. Everyone looked at me as though I were crazy. Maybe I was. "There must be something we can do."

"I know, Sally. I know. Please, we're doing everything we can. Believe me, I want that young man safe and well almost as badly as you do. I've grown fond of him and I've come to admire his courage." Daddy sat next to me, not touching me, but sitting close. "I don't want my grandchild to be without its father any more than you do."

"Can I get you anything, dear?" Mrs. Bushmuller asked.

"No, I'm fine, thank you," I replied politely.

"Well, we'll go then," her husband said. "If you don't need us any longer?"

"That's fine. It seems all we can do is wait," my father said, rising to walk them from the room. I remained, hunched forward on the sofa, thinking.

"The trouble is," I said to Sydney, sitting across from me on the opposite sofa, "I haven't been able to think clearly."

"It is a shock."

"Yes. I felt like I was the one getting beat-up. Sydney, he told me what they did to him before . . ." I closed my eyes for a moment, trying to block the image. I jumped up and walked to the fireplace. "The worst thing is, I can't help but think I could have easily saved him, prevented the whole thing."

"How do you mean?" Sydney asked. I hadn't told her about Christian and Heydrich and me and the things that had happened.

I turned to look at her, cool and impeccably clothed in a rose-colored dress, smoking a cigarette. She looked tired too.

"Can I have one of those?"

She raised her eyebrows, but got her case out of her handbag and held it out to me. I lit a cigarette with the silver table lighter.

"Are you okay?" I asked, then wrinkled my nose at the cigarette. I wasn't inhaling, but the activity, as small and useless as it was, helped. "You look tired."

She shook her head. "I haven't wanted to tell you, to add to your worry."

"Sydney! What? You're not sick, are you?"

"No." She leaned forward and snubbed out her cigarette in the ashtray and calmly leaned back again, brushing nonexistent lint off her skirt. "I lost the baby."

"Oh, Sydney, I'm sorry." I sat next to her. "I'm so sorry." I put my arm over her shoulders.

"This wasn't the first time."

"Oh, Sydney."

"Yes." She smiled sadly. "I don't know if I can bear to try again. Although Brian says it's because of this country. Nothing good can grow here now, he says."

"So, are you leaving?"

"How on earth did you guess we were?"

"I'm not usually so insensitive to other people, just now."

"Darling, I understand. Really I do." She put her arm over my shoulder. "Brian's being transferred to the East, Delhi, I should think."

"That's so far away."

"Yes."

"When are you leaving?"

"By Christmas. We're going to England first, to see my parents."

"Oh, Sydney. I'll miss you so. Is it a good job for Brian?"

"Yes. He's very excited about it. He loves India, spent several years out there already."

We sat for several minutes in silence, my arm over her. I felt a great deal of comfort from her presence, her support. She had been a rare friend to me, nonjudgmental and accepting of me, and I knew that I'd probably never have a better friend.

The door opened and my father came back in the room. He stopped when he saw me. "I didn't think you smoked, Sally."

"I just started," I said, smiling at him.

"My influence, I'm afraid," said Sydney.

"Hector is going around to talk to Reichsführer Himmler tomorrow morning. He just telephoned to say he was able to make an appointment." Hector was a German in their foreign service, with whom Daddy had developed a friendly relationship.

But I was staring at the remains of the cigarette; I had an idea. "I remember Heydrich saying Hitler has just returned from Berchtesgaden. Has he?"

"Yes, he has." My father stood up. "Sally, you're not going to approach Hitler?"

"No, Daddy. Not yet. But there's someone else who might be able to help. If she's here." And I changed my refrain to: Please, let her be here. "How do we find Eva Braun?"

Sydney had heard my story of meeting the little blonde in Munich and she stood up too. "Do you think she would help?"

"Could she help?" asked my father.

"If I can find her, I'll ask her."

"Brian will know," said Sydney, already on her way out of the room.

"Don't tell anyone, will you?" I said, looking at each of them, thinking of what Heydrich would do if he found out about my flanking movement.

* * *

Sydney contacted Brian and he called her back in record time with the confirmation that a Fräulein Braun was staying at the Chancellery. And when Sydney wondered out loud how I could contact her, Brian suggested that I simply telephone.

We all looked at each other stupidly when Sydney relayed Brian's suggestion to us. My father led me into his study, with Sydney following. Daddy's secretary was just hanging up the phone.

"Get the Chancellery, Bancroft," my father directed. "Please ask the operator to connect my daughter. Use her maiden name."

"Yes, sir," said the young man, mystified. When the connection was made, he held out the receiver to me without a word.

I took it. A polite man's voice asked me what he could do.

"Hello? This is Sally Jackson Mayr. I wonder if I might have a word with Fräulein Braun?" I covered the mouthpiece with my hand. "He's put me through, without a word."

"Hello?" It was a woman's voice.

"Fräulein Braun?"

"Yes? Who is this?"

"Sally Jackson. I don't know if you remember me, but we met last spring in Munich, well, in the ladies' room . . ."

"Oh, yes, of course, the accident with the glass of water." She laughed, sounding so happy and carefree, I could have throttled her. "How are you, Fräulein?"

"Well, actually, I'm married."

"You are? How lovely. I know. To that young SS man, the handsome one, yes?"

"Exactly right. We're expecting, too."

"Congratulations."

"He's a Hauptsturmführer, Fräulein, at the SD, a loyal, hard-working man."

"He sounds perfect. But, Frau Mayr, if everything is so great, why are you phoning me? I gather it's not just to say hello," she said somewhat archly.

"You're right, Fräulein. I'm sorry. Fräulein, I hate to bother you in the evening, but it is about my husband that I wish to speak." I turned my back on the other people in the room. I barely noticed that they were leaving, so completely was all my attention focused on the voice on the telephone.

I explained, as briefly as I could, the situation, leaving out any direct condemnation of Heydrich, although I lied and told her that he had told me that he had Christian locked up.

417

"General Heydrich," she said softly. "I met him. Once. I did not like him." She laughed.

"Well, you're a better judge of people than I."

"Oh? But, Frau Mayr, if the Hauptsturmführer has done something wrong . . ."

I debated for a fast second if I should tell her of Heydrich's proposition to me, and since the entire conversation was a gamble, I did so, briefly, without any details.

"And," I added, "Fräulein, I had been a guest at his home, met his wife and child. Did you know he has a little boy and that his wife is expecting another?"

"Frau Mayr," she said, "you have given me an idea. I think I know someone who would like to make some trouble for the Terrible Twosome." She laughed and added: "Heydrich and Himmler. That's what we call them. I will ask this friend this evening—he is coming for supper—and then I will call you back."

"Oh, thank you, Fräulein."

"It will be late. The Führer likes to stay up very late and I will not bother him with this matter. You understand?"

"Yes, of course. I would rather you did not. Thank you."

"Good-bye," she said and rang off.

I walked into the hall. Everyone was there and I smiled at them. The silence was intense. "She's going to help. She remembered me and she doesn't like Heydrich and knows someone else who doesn't and who could do something. She's going to call back. She's going to help."

"Thank God," said my father.

I sat heavily in a chair, suddenly exhausted. "Please, everybody, we can't do anything more right now. Why don't you go home, Sydney?"

"Are you sure, Sally?" she asked.

"Sure. Go tell Brian what's happened and I'll phone you when Fräulein . . . when my friend . . . calls me back."

"Okay," she said, and took her leave.

Daddy dismissed his secretary, and the two of us settled down to wait for the phone call.

It came around two in the morning. I was in my pajamas and robe again, seated in the big leather chair in the study, trying to read a novel. Daddy came in with a cup of hot chocolate for me.

"Shouldn't you try and sleep?" he asked.

"I've heard Hitler stays up till three or four in the morning."

"Yes. I've heard that as well." He sat behind his desk and

opened a file, closed it, opened his date book, closed it, and finally just sat.

"I've been thinking about Mama," I said. He didn't say anything, but I could sense that he was listening. In all the years since my mother died, my father and I had barely mentioned her. "I've been thinking how much I miss her." I bent my head. "I wish she were here, but I'm kind of glad she's not because she'd be so disappointed in me."

My father was silent for a long time. I had finished my chocolate before he spoke, in a voice I had never heard before, soft and warm.

"The day you were born was one of the best days of my life. We loved Edward dearly, but you were such a delight. You came at a point when . . ." He swallowed. I didn't dare look at him for fear he would stop talking. "Your mother and I loved each other, but sometimes things were difficult. She was an extraordinary woman. You must remember that. But when you were born, things were good, we were happy. I was writing my book. She was painting. Your brother was a healthy, lively child, and then there was you. You were perfect. You made everything perfect for us."

"She always seemed so disappointed in me."

"She had high expectations, which life usually could not meet. But I know she adored you. I'm sorry you didn't feel that. Perhaps it was my fault, as well." I looked at him. He sat with his hands folded on his desk, his head bent forward.

I put my cup down and started to speak. The telephone rang. I leapt out of the chair and snatched the receiver. My father stood up.

"Frau Hauptsturmführer Mayr?" It was a man's voice.

"Yes. This is she."

"A mutual friends of ours, a young woman, asked me to telephone you to tell you this message." He cleared his throat. "She believes everything will be as you asked." I sat down, my legs giving out, pulling the telephone with me. "Frau Mayr, are you there? Did you hear me?"

"Oh, yes. Yes, I did. Is there any more?"

"Just this—will you have tea with our friend tomorrow afternoon to let her know that things did turn out?"

"Of course. I'd be honored."

"Come to the entrance on Leipzigerstrasse at four. I will be waiting for you. And, Frau Mayr, I too will be very interested to hear your news."

"Thank you. I look forward to meeting you, Herr . . ."

"Good night, Frau Mayr," he said firmly, not responding to my invitation to learn his name.

"Good night. Thank you."

I filled in the gaps for my father. He, too, was very curious about who the man on the telephone had been but I was too overwhelmed even to speculate.

"Oh, Daddy," I said, "we have to leave tomorrow. As soon as he is out. We have to leave. We can't stay in this country a minute longer."

"We'll arrange something tomorrow, Sally. But now you ought to go to bed," he said, clumsily patting my shoulder. "I'm sure you're very tired."

"You too," I said and got up.

He shrugged, dismissing his own exhaustion, which I could see in his face. "Tell me how you thought of Fräulein Braun," he asked.

"The cigarette that Sydney gave me. And your reaction, your surprise to find me smoking. In the bathroom of the restaurant, when I met her, she smoked a cigarette. She said something about sneaking it."

"Fancy that," said my father and patted my arm again. "Sleep well, Sally."

"You too, Daddy. You too." I hesitated, wanting to say more, but he appeared to be more interested in polishing his spectacles. I turned away.

THE END

I was awakened the next morning by Sophie, who was knocking on the door to say there was a telephone call for me.

"Who is it?" I called, jumping out of bed, throwing on my robe.

"Maestro von Hohenberg," said Sophie.

Maestro? I couldn't imagine why he would be calling me. I hadn't seen him since I went to the States. I had sent him a note explaining my situation, although I hadn't told him I was expecting a baby, of course. But so much had happened, he seemed to belong to another life. I wondered if I would always divide life into before and after the arrest. I was wrong about that, but not by much.

"Please, Sally, would you come visit me this morning? Is it too late to ask?" His voice sounded very old and frail.

"Are you all right? Are you ill?"

"No, no, nothing of the sort. I understand there is some trouble and I would like to talk about it with you."

"Oh, I think that's over now or will be soon."

"Yes? Well, perhaps you could come talk about it anyway."

He sounded so strange and so insistent, quite unlike his usual self, that I agreed. I felt uneasy as I hung up the phone—as though there were a tremor far away that would ripple until it reached me. But maybe this was the way Christian would be released. Maybe Fräulein Braun's friend had involved Maestro, to keep things more discreet. Maybe Christian was, even now, waiting for me at the salle. I hurried upstairs to dress.

In less than an hour, I was on my way to the fencing salle, dressed in my navy coat over my royal-blue suit with the black velvet buttons. I wore my black velvet hat, just a small round circle, with a long blue tassel in the middle of it, that fell down over one ear. I looked cockier than I felt.

The day was crisp and clear and cold, and I waited, impatiently, for Rick to bring the car around.

"Come back inside and wait, please. It is too cold," Vittorio pleaded.

I laughed at his fussing. "I'll be fine," I promised. "You will call my father and tell him?"

"I'll go do it immediately," he said.

"Good. Good," I said, bouncing up and down, not minding the cold, not minding anything, sure I was about to see Christian, and that everything was going to be all right.

Maestro was at the end of a lesson. Horst had told me to go on into the fencing hall and I stood for a moment outside the door, watching Maestro and his partner finish a bout. Maestro won, but barely, as the man almost managed a hit.

Everything looked as it had the last time I was there, over six months ago. Even Maestro's saber and foil, laid carefully over two chairs, his white towel folded precisely over the back of one, his small brown ceramic jug of water with the cork in the top, in case it was knocked over—were all the same. I missed fencing, and being back in Maestro's pretty hall made me nostalgic. Maybe later, in the States, after our baby was born, I could start again. I breathed in the air, enjoying the smell, the sound of the blades clashing.

I pushed the door open and slipped in. Maestro and his student, a dark-haired young man, flushed and smiling, saluted each other and the young man left the hall.

"Sally," said Maestro, turning to greet me, transferring his sword, an epée, to his left hand so that he could stretch his right out to me.

"It is nice to see you, Maestro."

"Yes, my dear one. How are you?" He peered at me anxiously.

"I have been better."

"And will be again, I trust. Now, my dear, I must tell you I miss you." He had not let go of my hand, drawing me close to him. He looked worried.

"Maestro, you have something to tell me? About my husband?" I spoke softly, the mirrored wall at the end of the long room made it look as though there were people overhearing our conversation. Of course it was only our reflections, Maestro's and mine.

"Oh, dear Sally," he said mournfully, patting my hand against his chest. "The things I have seen." He shook his head. He was making me very nervous. "I am sorry. This is a terrible thing." He glanced behind me, then back to my face.

"Yes. But you called me . . ." I said, my voice sounding high and young. I looked around the hall, at the stacks of gold chairs, the high windows, the gleaming floor. There was no one there, but the white-and-gold plasterwork suddenly seemed sinister. I did not want to stay there any longer.

"Look, my dear," he said, his voice more energetic. He stepped back from me and held out the epée. "It is new. Today was the first day I used it."

"It's beautiful," I said perfunctorily, angered at his obvious change of topic. He was stalling.

"Yes. Look at the line. Here, feel the weight. The way the hilt leans into your palm." Maestro handed me the blade. I did as he asked; it did, indeed, feel perfect in my hand. "You have training in the epée?"

"Just a little. Certainly not enough to warrant a blade like this." I took hold of it in my left hand to grasp the pommel and hand it back to Maestro. I wanted to leave.

The door to the entry hall of the salle slammed and I turned around to see Heydrich, in his SS uniform, striding across the hall, his boots thumping against the wooden floor. The general was angry, his face almost bloodless, his lips pulled in until they were only a single thin line in his face.

I glared at Maestro and turned to leave. Heydrich's voice came after me.

"Sally. I want to talk to you."

"I don't want to talk to you." I had carefully kept all thoughts of him out of my mind, my imagination. I could not understand, or even remember clearly, the dreams I'd had on Peacock Island. Any fascination I'd had with Heydrich had disappeared on the dance floor of the Blue Parrot.

"Now," he barked.

I stopped and turned. "What about?" I asked, although I had a good idea.

"I think you know," he said. "You know very well."

"If it's about Christian," I said, a lot more bravely than I felt, "then it's none of your business any longer. I have taken care of that."

"Get out!" Heydrich snarled at Maestro.

"Sir," said the older man.

"I said GET OUT. NOW!" Heydrich's face was white with rage. He looked huge in his black uniform.

Maestro, with an agonized look at me, backed slowly away. He raised his hands in a strange gesture, as though he were stopping traffic, then turned and left.

Heydrich turned his anger on me. "You bitch," he said from behind his clenched teeth, as close to completely losing his temper as I had ever seen him. He took a step toward me but Maestro's epée was in my hand still, and instinctively I held the blade up against him.

Heydrich stopped, his eyes on the point, which had, of course, a safety tip. His eyes slid from the tip to meet mine. He smiled. Slowly, he reached out to push my blade away with the back of his hand. I didn't let him touch the blade and he stopped his hand movement.

He laughed. "Dammit, Sally, you *are* amusing."

"I don't think you want this to go any further, General Heydrich," I said. "If you wish to speak to me—"

"I do indeed," he said. He relaxed, standing with his hands on his hips. He took his hat off and smoothed his hair back.

Cautiously, I lowered my blade. He inclined his head. "Thank you," he said, "it is hard to talk over a blade. I am sorry to have been so precipitate." He smiled again. His smiling was beginning to make me nervous. He walked over to the spectators' platform and laid his hat on it. Then he began to undo his belt. He took it off and put it next to his hat. His tunic and tie went next and he turned to face me in his shirt sleeves. "Now," he said. "I want to talk to you about a certain mistress of a certain powerful man." As he spoke he walked back across the hall and picked up Maestro's saber.

"I think you know to whom I am referring?" he asked. "Of course you do. No, this wouldn't be sporting," he said, holding the saber up parallel to his body, then laying it back on the chair and picking up the foil. "There."

He walked over to me, stopping several feet away, and smiled again. "It amazes me that you have gone to such lengths to free Mayr. I almost envy him. And I must admit I admire your determination—and imagination. But I cannot allow you women to interfere, no matter who you are. Fräulein Braun I can do nothing about—yet. But you, my dear Sally, I can." As he spoke he tried several advance-and-retreat movements, then a parry or two in the air. I stood and watched him. Watched him as I would a circling shark.

"I will admit also that you have consistently surprised me. I thought you to be as malleable as young Mayr. Have you asked him about his father's death? But, instead—" He suddenly lunged at me. I froze as his point landed gently against my coat, over my heart.

"Instead," he continued, "you appear to have a heart of finer stuff than poor Mayr." He tapped my coat and pulled back out of his lunge. "So, the question is: What am I to do with you?" His hair, which was quite long on top, had fallen over his forehead and he swept it back with the crook of his blade arm. "I truly thought the other evening would be the end of it. And then, there is this babe of yours." On the last word he waved his blade in a circle in front of my abdomen. I took a step backward.

"I did not believe you were truly pregnant and I wasn't going to wait for you to balloon out. Are you sure the kid isn't the American Jew's—that reporter's? You did spend at least one afternoon at his place, rumpled, dirty sheets and all. No, I think there is nothing to do but to ask you, politely, of course, to leave."

"Not without Christian." I ignored what he had said about David. David was safe; Christian was not.

"Ah," said Heydrich, pulling into the attention position, feet in a perpendicular line, his left hand on his hip, his right holding his foil angled to the floor. "There you are then. Salute."

"What?"

"Salute," he said and brought his sword up, then down, using the formal salute that begins a fencing bout. "Do it," he growled at me.

"No," I said. "This is stupid." And I began to walk away from him toward the doors. "I'm leaving."

"No, you're not," he said and lunged, his blade cutting through the air, just inches in front of me. I stopped, turned and tried for another direction, but he was there, cutting off my retreat with his sword.

I faced him. "This is crazy," I said. "I can't fence you."

"Why not?" he asked, and lunged, tapping his point against my shoulder. "A hit," he said.

"I'm pregnant."

"Not my fault." He tapped his blade against mine. "Come on, Sally, get it up."

"You're bigger, with a longer reach than I have."

"Yes," he said, lunging at me again. I ducked out of the way of his blade. "You're cheating," he said.

"You'll beat me just because of your size and strength."

"Yes," he said, slicing the air near my right ear. I flinched.

"Stop it!" I cried, dropping my sword and raising my hands as though I could bat away his blade like I would a pesky bee. "It's not fair."

"No," he agreed. "But then, what is? By the way, those other Jews? The family you got Mayr involved with?" He put his tip under the hilt of my sword and flicked it up, causing it to fly through the air. "Get it!" he ordered. I grabbed the epée by the blade, almost without thinking. "Good girl," Heydrich cheered. "See, you have good reflexes."

"What about those people? What about them?" I let the tip of my blade fall to the ground.

"They didn't make it to Switzerland. Did you expect them to? Up, up," he said, waving his blade at mine.

"What did you do to them?"

"Got rid of them. Put your blade up, Sally."

"Got rid of them? You mean, you . . . you killed them? What do you mean? Annie—the little girl too? Why?"

"Oh, for God's sake. They were nothing. Who cares? Put your blade up. Now." He put so much venom into his order that I complied.

"You will do well. And remember what you are fighting for."

"What?" I said, transferring the epée to my right hand, grasping the hilt, getting a good grip with my red leather glove. The sword, at least, felt familiar and right.

"Young Mayr—and the child," he said, again lunging at me, but this time aiming for my abdomen. And again, on reflex, I parried his attack, successfully driving his blade away to my right.

"See, I knew you'd do well," he said. "People do when they are fighting for something important."

"And what are you fighting for, General?" I asked. I stood with my right flank, the hand holding the sword, toward him, presenting as narrow a target as I could. It's just fencing, I told myself. The blade is different, the man is terrifying, but it's just fencing. The thought calmed me.

"A good question, little Jackson," he said and thought for a moment. "Power? Because I can?" He shrugged. "Because I want to," he said, and smiled at me. "Enough talk. Whoever scores three hits, wins. You lose and you will meddle no longer in affairs that do not concern you. You will leave the country, first withdrawing your request of Hitler's whore."

"And if I win?" I asked.

"You will get what you want. A docile husband for your kid and safe passage to wherever," he said. "Unless, of course, there is an accident."

He smiled at me, a rapacious smile that froze my blood. Sun burst through the windows at the near end of the hall, throwing our shadows onto the parquet floor in front of us. But I felt no warmth from it on my back, so cold had I become with the knowledge that this man meant to kill me. An accident. It happened. I had even seen it happen, hadn't I? And had accepted it as a tragedy, but an accident.

My mind began to work again. I had to save myself to save

my baby. He was right, people will fight when they have something important to fight for and what I had was the most important of all. First, I would try and stay out of his reach. Second, I would try and get near a door. Third, I would . . . what? I hoped someone would come.

He attacked ferociously, as I had seen him do in the fencing tournament. I was at a terrible disadvantage because his reach was so much longer than mine. I was also very pregnant and in street clothes. I managed to kick my shoes off and shrugged off my coat, letting it fall to the ground. My advantages were that I was faster and younger, but, most of all, I had so much more to lose.

My reflexes were swift and for several minutes kept me out of danger. I could do nothing but react to his powerful lunges, his flurry of sword play. Once his blade caught mine and circled to the inside, aiming for my chest. I managed to disengage the contact and dodge the lunge, the sound of the blades lingering in the silent, sun-lit room.

"Well done," he said. His encouragement of my fencing was beginning to distract me. Which, I realized, he meant it to do. Ignore him, Sally. He let me know he knew about David and me, and he told me about Marlene's family to distract me. Forget them. Forget them all, even Christian.

I attacked, catching him unawares. It was a sloppy movement, my blade slapping against his sword arm. But it was a hit. "A hit!" I cried, and backed up as quickly as I could.

Heydrich's head turned from looking, in surprise, at his arm where my blade had been, to me, and from his expression I knew he wouldn't be falsely cheering me on any longer. His eyes glittered with pleasure, with hunger.

He attacked, not letting up, chasing me, his blade flashing in front of me. I did the best I could, but I knew it was only a matter of time until he reached me. He pressed his attack, perhaps sensing my acceptance of the inevitable. Suddenly, his point flew toward my face, utterly surprising me. I was so used to fighting with a foil, where the face is not a target—and, at any rate, helmets were always used—that to be attacked there disarmed me. I didn't have the technique to parry such an attack. I felt a swift burning on my left cheek, just below my eye, and put up my hand. There was blood on my glove. Blood.

I was breathing heavily and my wound frightened me. If I hadn't moved, he would have hit my eye. My nerve was nearly gone and I knew I couldn't last much longer.

I parried another swift attack, and then another, acutely feeling the months away from the salle, the extra weight of my pregnancy. I was so aware of the child. It slowed me down, but it also inspired me.

My book-learned parry. Heydrich had never actually seen me do it. I ran a few feet away from him and turned to face him. He lunged and I parried, then dropped one knee to the ground, scoring a sound, hard hit against his chest. My tip was not bare, but it hurt him, as he was only wearing a shirt. He backed up, rubbing the spot.

"I'd forgotten that," he said. "Shit, this is fun."

We were at one end of the spectators' platform and I jumped up on it, running along the railing. He laughed and ran to head me off at the center, ducking under the banister, his boots thumping noisily on the hollow platforms. I backed up, managing to deflect an attack. I backed up farther, trying to judge without looking how far I was from the door to the dressing rooms. He advanced, lunged, and I dodged his attack.

I didn't even think then, but threw my epée at him, using it, hilt first, like a javelin. It surprised him enough to make him flinch and raise his hands to bat it out of the way. I didn't stop to watch. I turned and ran, slamming into the dressing-room doors and racing down the hall toward the door that led to the outside.

It was locked. I turned. I could hear him at the door at the other end of the hall. Where was Maestro? I was panting, and my side hurt, but I couldn't give up. I couldn't let him hurt my baby. I started for the dressing-room door, the men's, to my right. The door to the hall swung open, banging into the wall.

Heydrich stood there, silhouetted against the light. That's all I registered, that and the fact that whatever he had in his hand wasn't a sword. I leapt for the door, grabbing and turning the knob. It opened and I fell into the room, as a terrific bang exploded in the corridor. It took me a moment to realize what it was, echoing through the walls.

A gunshot. He had a gun. Where was Maestro? Horst? I scrambled to my feet and ran around the lockers. The men's room was larger than the women's, with four rows of lockers and a large shower room, rather than stalls.

It had something in common with the women's room, though. Something I realized as I stood helplessly with my palms flat against the white tile of the shower room. There wasn't another way out. I leaned my face against the tile, the cold porcelain felt good on the cut on my cheek. I started crying in frustration. I had almost done it. I beat once against the tiles, hurting my hands.

I heard Heydrich's heavy tread behind me and I turned to face

428

him. If I was going to die, I was going to face my baby's murderer.

He was very close to me, breathing heavily, and he grabbed my neck, under my jaw, pushing me back against the wall. His long fingers almost circled my neck, cutting off the air, digging into my throat. His other hand held his gun and he held it against my temple.

"There?" he asked. "Or there?" And he moved the gun to my abdomen. Instinctually, I reached down to brush it away. He laughed. He moved his hand so that the weapon was pointing away from me, toward the ground, and I began to hope.

"I do admire the way you fought me. And you're only a girl. And a pregnant girl, at that. I suppose that's why you fought so hard. And so cleverly. Of course, it wouldn't do for you to beat me. I have my pride."

"You could let me go," I said, trying to get my voice past his hand on my throat.

"A draw?" he said. "No, then I will not get what I want."

"What will you do with him?"

"Don't know. Depends."

"On what?"

"How useful he is after he hears of your death," he said, bringing the gun up. "And it has to do with so much more than Christian, doesn't it? I really can't forgive the trouble you've given me."

"But I—"

"Shhh," he said softly, running the barrel of his gun over my lips. "Don't protest. It's too late for that now." He moved the gun away and kissed me. I could barely breathe with his hand still tight around my throat, his lips and tongue horrible on my mouth.

"Why must you kill me?" I croaked out, when he lifted his head.

"Because you'll win if I don't."

"But if you shoot me, surely you'll be accused."

"Ah, no," he said. "I'm the head of the police. I'll just find someone. An intruder . . ." His eyes changed, boring down on me.

I closed my eyes against the sight, giving up, slumping against the tile wall, waiting. My mind was full of images, but mostly I thought of the child in my womb. I covered her with my hands.

Heydrich's hand on my throat loosened, moving down to my shoulder. I could hear him breathing heavily, a horrible sound. He pulled my skirt up and ran his gun along my thigh and I opened my eyes. He was very close to me and I realized, if he was going to kill me, he was going to do something to me first, something with the gun.

"No!" I screamed and he hit me with the gun, slamming it against the side of my head. It stunned me and I fell sideways, sliding down the slippery wall. Heydrich grabbed hold of my jacket and tugged viciously at it. The buttons gave and I hit the ground, banging my elbow hard on the tile floor. I cried out at the pain.

He ignored me, pulling my skirt up. My head was exploding, but I tried to stop his hands. He hit me again, backhanding me with all of his strength. I felt the cold, clammy air of the shower room on my bare skin. I think I was crying because he hit me again.

"Stop sniveling," he said, speaking to me for the first time in German. "It doesn't become you."

Somewhere in my mind, in the place where it still worked and thought, I was beginning to feel some hope. If he raped me, perhaps he wouldn't kill me. Surely, being raped, as horrible as it was, was better than being dead. Surely, the baby would live through it. His hands were on me and I tried to give in, not to fight, not to feel. He pulled my clothes . . . there was coldness . . . the tiles . . . he kissed me again, hurting my mouth where he had hit me.

Then I felt the gun.

Hope left. Heydrich said something but by then my mind was too full of blood and pain and I couldn't understand his words.

I didn't understand anything, fleeing gratefully down into the darkness, letting my mind go, letting go of my body, of the baby. Good-bye, little girl, my mind cried out, as I fell through the bloody darkness, sinking down and down and down to meet the pain that rose up to greet me, the fear and the pain overwhelming my body and my mind, growing until there was nothing left of me, Sally. Pain. He obliterated me. Turned me to pain. Pain. Is all I was.

Is, sometimes, all I am.

BOOK THREE

BERLIN, 1946

CHAPTER 1

There was silence in the room. Sally had been talking for hours, telling Timothy Hastings things she hadn't told Colonel Eiger. Which was nearly everything. All her secrets. Timothy Hastings knew it all now and she was too tired and drained to care. She would eventually, she knew, but not right now. Right now, her throat hurt from too much talking and too many cigarettes.

She sat on the floor in the front room of Tim's apartment, her back against the wall, her knees drawn up to support her elbows. She looked at her hands. They held a cigarette. They were also shaking. She drew the cigarette to her lips, dropping ash on her shirt.

"What a filthy habit." She stubbed out the cigarette in the metal ashtray, and brushed off her shirt. She wore civilian clothes, a white shirt, navy cardigan, and khaki wool slacks. "So," she said, brushing her hands together and leaning her head against the wall, "that's that."

Tim Hastings lounged in an armchair across the room from her, his legs stretched out in front of him. His hands were folded in front of his face. Sally was lost in her memories, and she didn't look at him. She lightly touched the small, almost invisible scar under her left eye with her fingertips. She never even saw it anymore when she looked in the mirror. Of course, she rarely looked at her face in the mirror.

"Who found you?" asked Tim.

"Somebody. Horst, I think." Sally shrugged. "I don't know. I'd just been raped . . ."

"Sally." Tim tried to interrupt, but she had to say it, had to get the fact out, the horror.

"Raped with a gun, *a gun,* you understand. And now I suppose you've figured out everything, why I'm so . . ."

"Sally," he said again and this time she stopped. She was too tired. "Did you try to contact Mayr?" Tim asked after a long, quiet moment.

She shook her head. "I wrote a note to Lisa after I left."

"So you don't know what happened to him?"

Again she shook her head. "When I got out of the hospital, the bastard doctor who they got to take care of me said he was real sorry but he didn't think I'd ever be able to have kids, considering the damage, well . . ." She made a tight gesture with her hand. "Nothing," she added as though that explained everything.

Tim didn't comment but stood, stretched, and went into the kitchen where she could hear him open the refrigerator and clink glasses. Nice, normal sounds. Sally pulled herself up and went to push back the curtains. It was dark out. The window faced the back of the apartment building and the usual Berlin landscape greeted her: gray rubble, desolation, barren ground.

Like me, she thought. Like I feel.

Sally stared at it, her arms folded, remembering the Tiergarten and the little park in front of the embassy, the linden trees, all the greenery the city used to boast of, all burned and exploded and torn up and plowed under, all gone.

Tim handed her a glass without speaking. She drank. It was vodka and tonic, with a lot of ice, and it tasted delicious. He stood next to her, not touching her.

"Do you think it will ever grow back?" she asked.

"Already is. Weeds first, then, when the rubble is cleaned up, they'll start planting."

Sally looked sideways at Tim, still standing next to her at the dark window. He seemed familiar and comfortable in his baggy khaki pants and his old plaid shirt, the shirttail hanging out, the sleeves rolled up, and what she wanted almost more than a night of dreamless sleep was for him to hold her. But there was another question to ask.

She took a deep breath and made herself move away from him, to the footstool where she sat down, the ice clinking against the glass as she moved.

"Do you think I should forgive him?"

"You've been through a lot," he said, his voice level, friendly, but impersonal. "I think your will to survive is formidable. And the person you really should forgive is yourself."

"Thank you, Doctor," she said nastily. He sighed and they were silent for a while. She rolled the cold glass between her hands, then drained it and put it on the end table next to the easy chair behind her.

"I'm sorry." Sally's apology hung in the air. She looked at Tim, as he raised his glass and drank. He lowered the glass and studied the contents for a moment.

"May I ask you something?" She nodded, wrapping her arms around herself. "Do you still love him?"

"Huh?" she said dumbly.

His gaze met hers across the room. He was utterly serious. "Do you still feel anything—besides anger—at Christian? If he turned up, all in one piece, how would you feel about him?"

"Feel? I feel nothing," she said, hunching forward, a picture flashing through her mind: the inn, how his skin had glowed in the light on his skin after he'd shed the hard, black shell of his uniform. She squeezed her eyes shut, trying to stop the image, hating herself for it. "Nothing."

"I don't think that's the truth."

"Well, too bad." Her teeth had begun to chatter and she couldn't catch her breath. She held tightly to herself, feeling her heart hammering at a frightening rate. "T-T-Tim," she said, trying to look up at him. She gasped for air, panicking when she couldn't breathe. She shook so hard, she could feel her joints grinding together, and the sensation added to her panic.

Tim stood in front of her, speaking to her, but she couldn't hear him through the clashing of her teeth. Terrible sounds were coming from her mouth and she fought them.

He slapped her. Once. Then again.

The second slap registered and Sally's surprised body gasped for breath as she felt the stinging pain against her face.

"Breathe," Tim said, his hand on her back. She sat hunched over her knees. "C'mon," he said, "sit up. Give your lungs room." She obeyed him, still concentrated inwardly, not believing the beautiful, easy luxury of air flowing richly into her lungs. She was still shaking, but not as violently.

"Be right back," Tim said.

Sally stared at the carpet, her mouth open, panting, feeling more at odds with her body than she had since she tried to kill herself. Maybe this was its revenge on her.

Tim was back and knelt next to her. "Open your mouth. C'mon, I've got a tranquilizer. You're okay. It's nothing lethal."

Sally took the pill, holding it on her tongue until she could sip from the glass he held for her. Her teeth chattered against the rim and she pulled back, afraid of breaking the glass.

"Did you swallow? All right, just relax. You're okay." He spoke quietly, calmly, sitting next to her, rubbing her back as though she were a dog spooked by a train whistle.

Sally lowered her head, trying to do as he said. She closed her eyes and leaned against him, feeling her tremors slow down, stop. She suddenly jerked, a last nervous seizure. It embarrassed her.

"It's okay," he murmured.

Sally focused on Tim's hand touching her arm. She remembered feeling it on her forehead in the airport and again on the plane.

"You've tried to take care of me since you first saw me," she said, her words slurring. She passed her fingers over her mouth.

"Why? Don't you think you need it?" he kidded.

"Since—since the airport. The storm."

"Yeah. Well, I was interested in you. And you obviously needed some help. Although you were sure crabby about accepting it. But there you were, your bag under your head, in your brand-new uniform, laid out on that bench. I couldn't resist. And I was curious."

"Bet you're sorry. I've been nothing but trouble to you since, haven't I?"

"You bet," he said, tightening his arm around her. Laying her head against his shoulder, she muttered, "My bones are melting." She closed her eyes. Time flew. Something she had said, about not feeling; what a stupid statement. "You're right," she muttered. "I'm not an unfeeling girl, am I?" She opened her eyes. "Except now. I feel numb."

"I imagine you do."

"Yeah," she giggled, the drug blurring all the edges. "I feel fine."

"C'mon, you better get some sleep." He stood, pulling her up with him. "I'll use the couch and you can have my bed. It's a mess, but the sheets are clean." She let him lead her into his bedroom.

"Can you do this on your own?" he asked, holding up a folded pair of pajamas.

"Um-hmm." She nodded, sitting down on his messy bed. She pushed her loafers off and, bending over, pulled her socks off as well. "See," she said, sitting up, but immediately fell back on the bed. She giggled again. What had he said about love? About loving someone?

"Sally . . ."

"Did you? No, I can . . . see." She unbuttoned her slacks and pushed them down as far as she could reach. "Help," she said, and he obliged by pulling them off her legs. "Thanks."

Sally fumbled with the buttons of her blouse, waving Tim away. As fuzzy as she was, from deep inside her, sober Sally made her do the buttons on her own. Her bra was too much, though, and she finally let him help her after several attempts to undo the hooks on the back.

He leaned her against his shoulder, as he put her arms into the pajama top and buttoned it up. Sally, feeling herself recede into a warm, fuzzy darkness, put an arm around Tim's neck so as not to slide too quickly. That part about her loving someone bothered her. Christian. That's who. Did she still love Christian?

"I don't think it's true, Timmy. Okay?" she muttered. She didn't hear his answer.

The door opened, letting some light into the room, light that sneaked under the covers, into her eyes. She had been crying in her sleep, was still crying and, for a moment, didn't know where she was.

Tim's room. She was in Tim's room. In Berlin. Sally pulled her head up from the pillow. She could see Tim's silhouette against the door. "Timmy," she said.

"I heard you crying," Tim said in a sleepy voice. He sat on the bed and put his hand on her shoulder.

"It hurts, Timmy." She was shaking and she couldn't stop the tears. The pain. "It hurts. I'm sorry," she added, her hands on her face, trying to stop. Trying not to cry, not to feel.

"I know," he said. "I know. Don't fight so hard. Here. You need to sleep." He gave her another pill, then got into the bed with her, wrapping his arms around her. Her back was to him and as he fit his long legs against hers, his solid warmth calmed her. "Shhh," he said, his hand against her head. "It's gonna be all right, I promise."

"Everybody's dead," she said, the words barely making it past her chattering teeth. "Mama. Eddie. My father. Lisa. The baby and Marlene and Marta. Even Hey-Hey . . ." She gave up. "Everybody's dead. The city. All the babies. The trees. Everybody's dead."

"You're not, Sally," said Tim.

"Except . . ." said Sally, pausing to try and control her chattering teeth. A tremor passed through her and she clenched her jaw. "Except him," she finally said.

"He can't hurt you, Sally," Tim said, his hand warm against her cheek and forehead. "I promise." And he kissed her temple. She felt it as though it were a kiss given to someone far away from her, but his concern reached her and she laced her fingers through his and held on to him.

"I don't want to die, Timmy," she said. "I don't want to die. I know how it feels. I don't want to die."

"You're not going to die, sweetheart. Nobody's going to hurt you," he said. "I'm here."

"I'm so scared."

"I'm here."

"Don't leave me, Timmy," she murmured, not feeling him kiss her again.

She slept.

When she awoke, the room was filled with sunlight. She lay on her back in the rumpled bedclothes. She felt awful. Tim was gone. She turned her head, using all the energy she could muster to look at the small clock on the dresser across the room. It was eleven o'clock. She closed her eyes. Her head felt full of sand and she ached all over, from her jaw to her ankles.

The door opened and Tim came in. He wore the khaki pants he'd had on the day before and a clean but wrinkled white shirt. He was barefoot, his hair tousled, and he carried a coffee mug.

"How you doin'?" He put the mug down on the dresser and went over to touch her cheek. His shirt was unbuttoned and she could see his bare chest.

"I should get up," she said and swallowed hard. Her throat hurt.

"Don't worry about it. It's Sunday. You want some coffee? You hungry?"

"I should get up."

"Sally, stay. I don't mind having a half-naked woman in my bed. Even without me. Stay. Let me wait on you. Makes me feel useful. What do you want? Coffee? Toast? Steak? Caviar? Gin?"

"Coffee would be nice. And could I have some water?"

"Your wish," he said, bowing, "et cetera, et cetera. Oh, I found you a clean towel, which was a major accomplishment, and it's on the sink in the biffy. Which is thataway. I think there's a glass in there, too. Those pills do make you thirsty."

He left the door slightly ajar so that Sally could hear him in the kitchen. It was comforting, hearing the sound of water running, of someone moving around in another room. Sally sat up, pausing to let the wooziness in her head pass. She waited a moment until it cleared, then she went into the bathroom. She considered a shower, but hadn't the energy, so she washed her face and brushed her hair, hoping Tim wouldn't mind if she used his brush. Finding some tooth powder, she used it on her finger to clean her teeth. She drank two glasses of water.

She looked in the mirror, meeting her eyes; she felt old. She didn't care. Something was different, she could see it in her face. She bent her head, admonishing herself not to cry.

In the bedroom, Tim was straightening out the covers. Sally crawled back into bed.

She managed only a few sips of the coffee he had brought her and handed the cup back to him. "I'm sorry, Timmy, I feel so . . ." She closed her eyes for a moment, overwhelmed by a sense of sadness and exhaustion. And again she slept.

When she opened her eyes again, it was dark in the room. She lay still, thinking: Tim's room . . . she was still in Tim's room. She wondered how long she had been sleeping, how many days. She got up and felt her way into the bathroom. The light didn't work. A power failure, then. She used the toilet, and ran tap water over her hands, cupping them to sip. She was very thirsty. She felt around for a towel, but couldn't find one and used her pajama top.

Hands out in front of her, she slowly made her way across the bedroom, feeling clothing under her feet, to the door. Along the way she hit the corner of the bed.

"Whoops!" she whispered.

The living room was dark but there was light from the nearly full moon, slipping in through the patterns of the curtains. Sally could see the sofa and the long shape of Tim's body.

She hesitated, then sneaked through the room to the kitchen, closing the door carefully behind her. She was starving and hoped there was something to eat.

The food in the fridge was still cold so she knew the power hadn't been off long. She pulled out something wrapped in wax paper—half a cheese sandwich—and gobbled it as she studied the rest of the contents of the refrigerator.

"Aha," she whispered, spotting a beer. She grabbed it, then searched for an opener, muttering to herself. Just before she drank, she remembered the pills Tim had given her. That was hours, days ago. And she drank. The beer tasted heavenly.

On top of the fridge was half a loaf of bread. By the moonlight from the window, she searched the cabinet and found a precious jar of peanut butter from the PX. She twisted off the top and stuck her finger into it, scooping up a mouthfull. It tasted almost as good as the beer did.

Then, getting an idea, she spread peanut butter on the bread and found an apple to cut up the and lay the slices on top of the peanut butter. She took a big bite.

Then thought: a shower. She'd like to be clean. Clean. That would feel so good. She finished the beer and the sandwich, then sneaked back through the living room to the bathroom.

Because the lights were still out, Sally had to take her shower in the dark. It didn't bother her until she started feeling around the bathroom for a towel. Her hands met terrycloth. Who needed the light? Nothing here she wanted to look at. She used the towel to dry her wet hair, before dropping it on the floor. She shook her head, spraying droplets of water all around herself, like a dog after a swim. I feel good, she thought. And the surprise of it made her laugh.

Back in the bedroom, she realized she didn't have any clean clothes and the thought of putting on the clothes she had been wearing was unpleasant. She headed for Tim's closet, when she had another idea.

She pulled the top sheet off the bed and wrapped it around herself, throwing the end over her shoulder as though it were a sari. She ran her fingers through her hair, shaking the damp curls, and wondered if there was anything else to eat in Tim's kitchen.

Halfway through the living room, she was stopped by a noise from Tim, a sort of groan that ended with a sputter. It was a wonder that he was asleep, she thought, considering how terribly uncomfortable he looked. The sofa was a wide one but it wasn't long enough for him and he was sleeping on his stomach, his face squashed into the pillow on one arm of the sofa, one foot propped up on the other. His covers were twisted tightly around him, exposing most of his back and one leg that had come to rest over the edge.

Thinking to make him more comfortable or at least to cover him up, Sally moved toward him. And stopped as pale moonlight moved across his back. He wasn't wearing a top and the leg that hung over the side of the sofa was bare as well. She became terribly aware of her own nakedness under her sari, wondering what her breasts would feel like against the shadowed skin of his back.

Sally reached a hand for his shoulder, then retracted it. She knelt next to the sofa, sitting back on her heels. And Tim opened his eyes and looked straight at her, as though he had known she would be there when he awoke.

He didn't move or speak and neither did she; both of them watching, wondering what she would do. Then Sally broke her gaze away from his and raised herself up so that she was kneeling again. She paused, still not looking at him. She could stand or she could . . . and once again she acted before a thought could stop her. She leaned over and kissed him.

They kissed for a long time. Then Sally began to touch him, running her hands along him, feeling the roughness of the hair on his arms, the smoothness of his chest. She ran her fingers across his face, feeling the soft skin under his eyes and the brush of his mustache, the stubble on his cheek, the silkiness of his hair. She stopped, her hand coming to rest on his chest. He covered her hand with his.

"That was nice," he whispered.

"Yes," she answered, also in a whisper.

He rubbed her hand, the palm of his hand pressing hers against his chest. "Is that all you want?"

"No," she said, the word like a breath. She wished she could see his eyes more clearly, but the moonlight had disappeared. She felt his heart under her hand, and in the stillness of the room, she could hear his breathing.

"Well," he said, no longer whispering, "why don't we go in the other room?"

Sally nodded and he got up, then he tugged her up from her kneeling position so that she stood before him. Lightly he touched her shoulders, brushed his hand just as lightly across the top of her breasts. He tugged gently at her makeshift sari.

"What have you got on?"

"Your sheet."

"My sheet." He tried to push the top down but it was wrapped too tightly. "Maybe we oughta put it back on the bed. What do you think?"

In the bedroom he held her close to him as he unwound the sheet. When he was done he dropped it behind them onto the bed and put his arms around Sally.

"Are you sure?" he asked.

She didn't let go of him, but pushed back far enough to be able to see his face. His body against hers felt almost unbearably good. "Oh, Timmy," she breathed and, putting her hands on either side of his face, kissed him.

She awoke several times during the night, unused to sleeping with someone, and whenever she did, Tim seemed to sense it and although he didn't wake up entirely, he held her close to him. When she did sleep, she slept without dreams. The miracle of his warm skin against hers was enough to chase the ghosts away.

She opened her eyes to see the gray light of dawn through the blinds. If this was all there ever was with him, she knew it had been worth it just for the closeness, which she had fooled herself into thinking she could do without. And the sex, too. She had been crazy to go without it all that time. And she turned her head into Tim's warm shoulder.

When she next woke, he was dressed, showered, and shaved. She watched him as he was tying his tie in front of the bureau mirror, enjoying the way he expertly flipped the ends of it around, the way he looked all spick and span and masculine. He must have felt her eyes on him because he turned his head.

"Hi," he said.

"Hi," she replied.

"What are you looking at?"

"You."

He turned back to finish his tie, then looked at her again, his eyes searching her face, the hills and valleys she made in the covers.

"What are *you* looking at?" she asked. He didn't answer, but tucked his tie into the front of his uniform blouse, patting it down, checking in the mirror. Then, satisfied, he turned and walked over to her, sitting down on the bed. He smelled wonderfully, of soap and whatever he used to shave with.

"I'm looking at you," he said, finally answering her question. He touched her face, her hair. "I can't believe you're here, naked, in my bed."

"I must look a sight. My hair always sticks straight up." And she ran one hand through it.

"Yes," he said, "it does. But you look beautiful."

"No, I don't." That she'd never believe.

"Yes, you do." And gently but firmly, he pulled the sheet off her breasts and kissed each nipple, reminding her of things he had done to her in the night. He replaced the sheet. "Beautiful breasts, too."

She sat up and put her arms around his neck, rubbing her face against his, kissing his smooth, clean-smelling cheek.

"Hey," he said softly, his hands against her bare back.

"Why are you dressed?" she asked. "What's today? Isn't it Saturday? Or Sunday?"

"Neither. It's Monday. You lost a day."

"I should get up . . ." She moved as though to jump out of the bed, but he held her still.

"No, you shouldn't. You are officially on sick leave, so take it easy. I mean, if you want to stay, I'll be back around seventeen hundred or so. I'll bring some food. You must be hungry."

"Yes."

"Good. That's healthy. There's toast and coffee in there, maybe even a roll or jam. Well, you can look. I'll leave my car keys if you want to go home. If you want to go . . . I hope you don't want to leave. Do you?" Sally shook her head. "Great," he said, kissed her quickly and got up. At the door, he stopped to look around at her. "Say, how do you feel?"

"Fine. I feel just fine," she said.

"What's happened to you?" Tim asked, taking the cigarette from between her fingers.

"You," she said, knowing what he meant. She propped her head up on her hand and looked down at him. He was lying flat on his back, one arm under his head, the other holding the cigarette. The room was lit by several candles. The lights still had not come back on. Sally touched Tim's chest gently, reveling in the ease between them. "And what's happened to you?"

"I don't know. You. Those pills I gave you or something."

"Or something. And I think I kissed you." Sally stretched up and kissed his jaw, then relaxed back next to him. "Oh, I don't ever want to leave this apartment, this bed. Can I stay here forever? Will it be different then? I haven't thought of . . . any of that. Those photographs."

He ran his hand over her shoulder, her waist, down to her hip. "Don't worry about them. They're all still there and you don't even have to think about them until you're back in the office."

"What do I have to think about?" she asked, stretching under his hand, his gaze.

"Me," he answered and his smile crinkled around his eyes.

She touched his mustache with her index finger, then kissed it.

"I'll shave it off if you don't like it," he said.

"No. Don't you dare. Don't change anything," she said, reaching for him, drawing him to her.

"Hey, look, the light's back on," Tim called, as he went into the bathroom sometime later.

"Rats," muttered Sally. Part of the dreamy quality of the past hours in his apartment had been because of the candlelight. She turned on her back and pulled the covers over her. She had found a clean set of sheets that afternoon, before Tim came home, and had changed the bed. She had also washed the dishes and had picked up her own clothes, but she had very carefully avoided moving any of Tim's things.

An image: Herself, in a blue wrapper, feeling wifely, picking up Christian's shirt and socks, hanging his uniform tunic in his wardrobe.

Memories from the past. The first one in almost, what? Forty-eight hours. She covered her eyes with her arm, fighting the feeling that was creeping up inside her, threatening her newfound sense of peace.

She felt rather than heard Tim standing next to her. She reached her arms out for him. He sat down on the bed, holding her.

"You all right?" he asked softly.

She nodded, then leaned back so she could see his face. "I don't want always to be like this. Needing your comfort. I liked being happy."

"Well, let's see what we can do to keep you that way. You know what I wish?" Getting under the covers, he stretched out next to her so she could feel the bristly hair on his long legs. She liked it, the feel of his male body, the way he made her own body feel.

"What?" she asked.

"I wish we could get dressed and go out and find San Francisco outside. We could walk to a cable car and ride down to North Beach and I could take you to this little Italian place where we could have rigatoni and red wine."

"Sounds great," Sally said, tracing his collarbone across the top of his torso, running her hand over his shoulder, down the muscles of his arm.

"Then we could go listen to some jazz. Do you like jazz? There's one place with a great combo, a piano, bass, and singer. They'd let me sit in late on Saturday nights."

"With your clarinet?"

"I liked playing there. It was difficult at home when the kids were babies. Irritated Nancy. And I never had time to practice anyway." He fell silent, and Sally watched his expression as he dwelt for a moment in his memories. She drew his face down to hers and kissed him gently. Very gently so as not to wake him too abruptly. "Oh, Sally, Sally, Sally," he said, holding her to him, his voice full of yearning.

She could understand how the past held and caught at you at unexpected moments. Suddenly, she had a feeling, so strong, that she never doubted the future it promised, of Tim and her together, the past finally left behind.

The next morning, Sally got up very early, as planned. She had to return to her room to change, so she put on her clothes and left without awakening Tim. In the living room, she found a pad of yellow foolscap and wrote him a quick message: *Good morning.*

Hated to leave. See you later. She hesitated, then added, *Love, S.*

She propped the pad up in the middle of the floor against a couple of books and stepped over it to leave the apartment. Tim had left her the car keys and she drove quickly through the silent morning streets. It was strange to be outside again but she found the destruction of the city didn't upset her as much as it had before. She wondered why but didn't take the time to figure it out, her mind and heart full of Tim and their long hours together. Her body ached in secret places and her nerve endings felt acutely alive. She felt alive.

At work, she left her bag and coat in her office, and went down the hall to see the colonel. The door to Tim's office was closed as she passed, although she could hear his voice and Nelson Ambrewster's inside. She didn't stop.

She saw Tim several hours later when she entered the conference room for the weekly meeting of D-6. He sat at the far end of the table, as he usually did, slouched in his chair. She could feel his eyes on her as she fielded questions from the other men about how sick she'd been. They teased her, covering up their concern with light banter, and she was grateful for the distraction. She wondered how long it would be before they figured it out and what they would think of her then.

After the meeting ended, Sally walked down the hall with Doug Finkelstein, who was telling her about an interview he had done with a boy who had survived four years at Dachau. Both of them were startled by Tim's voice. He was right behind them.

"Sal," Tim said casually, "you got a minute? I've got something to show you. Just take a minute." He held a file but Sally knew it was just a diversion. She made an excuse to Doug and followed Tim down the hall to her office.

"Lieutenant," he said, opening the door. She passed in front of him to her desk, putting her papers down on it. Tim closed the door and, without a word, they went into each other's arms.

"This is stupid," Sally whispered.

"Stupid? Am I being insulted?"

"No. I mean it's wonderful, but stupid. I was just with you a couple of hours ago."

"Hours and hours ago. We're not used to each other yet." He kissed her again, his lips and tongue delicately touching hers. She backed away from him.

"God, I don't think I'll ever get used to that," she said in mock horror.

"Sure you will. We'll get so used to each other, we'll fall asleep without making love." He was teasing, but Sally could see the hint of a shadow in his eyes.

"In the same bed?" she asked.

"You weren't married long enough to find out," he said lightly. An experiment.

"No," she answered, just as lightly, "I wasn't." And was relieved to see how easily both of them had come through this latest exploration. She kissed him, then gently pushed him away. "Now go. I have to work."

"You want to have dinner tonight?"

"You don't want any time alone?" Sally cocked her head and looked at him. "Be honest."

He thought for a moment, then grinned. "Nope. Not yet anyway."

"Okay. But you tell me."

"Fat chance," he said, and was gone.

It was funny. Seeing Tim, hell, living with him, she was surprised to find herself able to look at her days with Christian in a more realistic light. She could see just how those days had been colored by a quiet desperation.

There had always been such a sense of crisis about their love: the baby, Christian's lies, the situation with Heydrich, all of it. And she began to understand that she had never really gotten to know him. Except, perhaps, toward the end, after his first arrest. Remembering the night on Peacock Island, she could see with the clearer vision of hindsight that Christian had been more vulnerable, and more needful that night. She even could believe that he had loved her that night.

But she also believed that their visit to Peacock Island had been a setup by Heydrich for his own purposes and that Christian, in spite of his love for her, had been involved, perhaps against his will, perhaps not. The Gestapo had come for Christian the next morning. Unless his arrests had been setups as well.

Well, Heydrich had nearly killed her and she had been tricked and lied to by both men, whether Christian had been coerced or not. She had thought never to allow another human being close to her again. Until Tim.

After fighting her attraction to Tim, she realized that her feelings for him—she didn't yet define them as "love"—but her feelings were calmer, less romantic, and, at the same time, more complex. He was her lover, but also her friend, colleague, and co-worker, and he continued to treat her as such. She came to understand that he, too, was reluctant about becoming too intimate. Perhaps the most important revelation, Sally thought, was the knowledge that she made Tim happy. She didn't think, if she forced herself to face the past, that she had made Christian happy.

But there were other ghosts to confront.

She arrived at Tim's apartment building, one blustery evening several weeks later, to find one of his neighbors, an extroverted British woman married to an American, struggling to haul her six-month-old daughter, a string bag of PX groceries, and a large paper-covered package up the stairs. Holding her arms out, Sally meant to take the package. But the woman handed over the baby, and Sally held the infant in her arms.

She carried the child up the stairs without looking at her face, until she couldn't stop herself. The little girl slept, her eyelids almost translucent, the dark down on her head soft as clouds. Sally stood in the middle of the hall waiting as the mother opened the door of her apartment, staring down at the child, studying her.

"Thanks, dear," said the woman.

Sally looked up. The woman was impatient, eager to go inside. "Oh, I'm sorry," said Sally and handed the baby over, her arms bereft as the weight and small bulk left them.

In Tim's apartment, Sally hung up her coat and tunic, kicked her shoes off and went into the kitchen and poured herself a slug of vodka, something she hadn't done in a couple of weeks. She knocked it back and waited for the liquor to hit her stomach.

It didn't help and she fixed herself a vodka and tonic and sipped that standing at the kitchen sink. Instead of calming her, the alcohol made her more upset, and she started to cry.

"Shit," she swore out loud and went to find a cigarette. By the time Tim got home, she was better. She had changed into her slacks and sweater and had half a chicken from the PX roasting in the little oven.

Tim came into the kitchen and kissed her neck while she stood peeling carrots. Just as though we were . . . but she didn't finish the sentence. She smiled at him, trying to hide her depression, and nearly did so.

Until they were in bed and, for the first time, she pushed his hand away. He immediately sat up and turned the light on. Sally tried turning away from the light, but he bent his head to look at her. Then, still without talking, he got a cigarette and lit it.

"Want one?" he said. She shook her head and turned on her side, facing away from him, sick about shutting him out, but unable

447

to explain. He smoked awhile in silence, then, for the first time, he talked about his wife.

"That was how it started with Nancy. Silence. We'd go to bed mad. Push each other gently away. So we just stopped talking. We lived in this little house—her dad had given us the down payment when we got married—it was nearly outside of town, nearly in the prairie. In front were oak trees, the road, a fence, and out the back we had a little bit of yard. But you could see past the fence, to the prairie rolling to the horizon. I used to get up in the middle of the night and stare out the kitchen window, till I felt that silence inside of the house, inside of me.

"Sally, I don't mind you not wanting to make love every time I do. Well, yes, I do. But I'm grown up enough to accept it. But, don't go mute on me, Sal." Though he said it in an even voice, she knew him well enough to hear the hurt he kept covered up.

"I'm sorry," she said, not turning. "You still miss her, don't you."

"No. I missed my life for a time, but now I just miss my boys." She moved to him, laying her head on his chest, within the circle of his arms. He was quiet and she almost dozed off, her breathing rising and falling with his.

"What was it?" Tim asked. "You been thinking of him?"

"Oh, no, Timmy," she said, opening her eyes. "Not at all. No."

"Tell me, Sal."

"It's stupid. Sentimental nonsense."

"Tell me."

"I helped Sergeant What's-his-name's wife up the stairs. She gave me her baby to carry. I don't know . . . I . . ." And she sat up against the headboard, pulling her knees up so she could lean her elbows on them, her hands over her face. "Stupid."

"What happened?"

"Nothing. The kid just lay there, all pink and with that damn smell babies have when they're clean. Oh, shit." She beat her fists against her knees.

"Oh. Oh, I see. Come here," he said and sat up next to her, his arm around her. "I guess it's a lot easier forgetting about Christian than your lost baby?"

"It felt so good. Her weight in my arms. The smell of her. I feel this sadness all the way to my middle, where my baby was killed. It's the worst of it all. The worst, that I couldn't protect her. I should have protected her. I should have."

"What . . . what could you have done?"

"I don't know." She pulled away from him, rolling to the other side of the bed. "Fought back."

"You did."

"I lost and he killed her."

"Might have killed you. And I, for one, would have hated that."

"It's not just her, it's what that doctor told me."

"Do you know for sure you can't conceive?"

"He told me."

"And all these years you've believed him? I don't understand. You're intelligent. Why didn't you have a doctor in California check you out?"

"And what if he said yes?" she said, starting to cry again. "And then if by some miracle I could, who? Who would want me, after what's happened to me? Christ, listen to me moan. All I've done for the past month is moan and cry. Do you have anything to drink? I want something—don't, I'll get it." And she walked into the kitchen and poured a shot from the vodka bottle.

When Tim came after her, she was sitting on the floor in the dark, leaning against the cabinet. He sat down next to her and she leaned against him. The pain was there, but he made it better.

"I lost my kids, too, you know," he said. "I know how you feel."

"Yours are still alive somewhere. That must help."

"Yeah. I do know they're safe. Yesterday, I heard this man, a father talking about losing his kids in a selection at Auschwitz. You know, on the platform. Of course, he didn't know they were going off to the gas chamber, but he soon realized. Yesterday, as he tried to tell me about it, he was tied up in knots, he was so angry, so frustrated, so full of hate. A lot of it at himself. And you know what I felt? Profound gratitude that my boys are safe in the States, that they were never in this kind of danger."

"Do you hear from them?"

"No. They were so young and I thought a clean break would be easier for them."

"Oh, Timmy." She sighed, letting the sadness ripple through her, not fighting it. "What's happened to us all?" She touched his face, gently pushing his hair off his forehead.

He laughed, sadly. "Thank God for sex," he said. "Thank God for you." And he kissed her, putting his hands under the pajama top she was wearing. His hands slid along her bare back, down her and around her, touching her breasts. He pushed up the pajama top and, bending down, put his mouth to her body, his mustache, his lips, his teeth making her quiver. She folded over him, her fingers in his soft hair, holding him against her, lifting his face to her mouth and tongue, wanting him in her everywhere. He lowered her to the floor and entered her and she wrapped her legs around him. They made love there until the floor grew too hard and the kitchen too cold and the night too long and they fled back to bed and comfort, to hold each other and sleep, the demons at bay once more.

CHAPTER 2

I don't mind your going without me," Tim said, pushing his dark glasses up his nose. "I just worry about your going into the Russian zone alone."

"It's in the middle of the day. I'll wear my uniform, and besides, if I get into any trouble, you can contact Annaliese's Russian colonel. What is his name? Sorin. He seems a fellow who likes to rescue women." Sally had been invited to a party at Annaliese's, to meet someone, who, Annaliese said, "knew something."

Tim didn't answer, just grunted. He and Sally were walking through the huge black market that flourished under the Brandenburg Gate.

Sally stopped to look at a nearly complete set of china displayed on an old sheet. She crouched to pick up a plate. "Wedgwood," she said, turning the plate over to check the mark. "My mother had this color. I think. Or maybe it was the green." The seller, a middle-aged man in a neat black coat and hat, smiled hopefully at her. Carefully, she put the plate down and stood up, brushing her gloved hands off. "I really hate this," she said, walking away.

"What?" asked Tim, loping after her.

"This," she said, waving her hand at all the people. "It's so damned depressing. People trying to sell their little bits and pieces for nothing."

"It's buying and selling," said Tim, taking her elbow. "A basic human activity. So who else would be at this party?"

"I don't know. Friends."

"Not yours."

Sally studied Tim, who, dressed in civvies and his uniform top-coat, looked so clean and healthy and very American. She turned toward a table of crystal and picked up a bowl.

"Look at this. How much?" she asked the seller in German, and shook her head when she heard the price. "Peanuts. Peanuts."

"Why don't you buy it?" asked Tim, taking the bowl from her hands. He held it in both of his and turned it from side to side. Sunlight hit the carving on the sides and turned into multicolored prisms, spilling onto the ground.

Sally shook her head. "I don't want it. What would I do with it?" She wandered toward a display of used books. The seller had put a blanket on the ground and arranged his books, nearly all large German medical texts, on it. Sally bent down and opened the cover of the first book she saw, but quickly closed it, not wanting to look at colored illustrations of skin disorders.

She noticed a man looking at her, down at the end of the row of sellers. He was tall with light hair, and when he saw her notice him, quickly turned and disappeared into the crowd.

Sally stared after him, wanting to chase him, knowing it would be ludicrous to do so. She didn't believe it could be him. But still, she suddenly felt the cold, in spite of the sunshine, and she turned to find Tim.

He had come up behind her and Sally, not noticing, turned right into him. "Whoa, girl," laughed Tim, holding a bulky package, wrapped in brown paper, out of harm's way.

"Sorry. What's that?"

"It's for you." He thrust it at her.

"It's the bowl." She held it in both hands, feeling the weight of it. "Why?"

"'Cause I wanted to."

"Timmy, that's sweet, but what am I going to do with a crystal bowl that weighs fifteen pounds?"

"Use it as a door stop? Hell, I don't know. I gave it to you. You figure it out. Save it for your vine-covered cottage."

"Can you see me in a vine-covered cottage? Honestly, Tim. And now I have to lug it around."

He smiled at her, a closemouthed smile, and said, with perfect, irritating patience, "Then I'll carry it for you." He took the package back. "C'mon, let's go get a beer."

They went to the Basement Dive. Doug Finkelstein was standing at the bar talking to Willie, the bartender. A man was picking out a tune on an old upright at the other end of the bar. It took a moment before Sally identified the song he was trying to play as "Maresy Doats."

"Hiya, Tim, old boy," said Doug jovially, slapping Hastings on his shoulder. "Sally. Where've you two been? Come on and join me."

"I'm going to sit down," Sally said, still irritated about the bowl. Without waiting for the men, she sat down at a table. She really should just go home and be alone, she thought. Tim brought her a beer and she thanked him, trying for a pleasant expression.

"Think I'll talk to Doug for a while," he said.

"Fine," she said to his back. She picked up the beer. So much for trying to be pleasant. He had left the bowl, clumsy in its paper wrappings, on the table, and she fingered the brown paper.

"Hey, Doug," she called, "where did the old piano come from?"

"Did you know Sally played?" Tim asked Finkelstein.

"No, I didn't. Say, Willie," Doug called to the bartender, "where'd you dig up the piano? Sal, you ought to play us something."

"I'm out of practice."

"There's nobody here," Finkelstein said. "Please. Do you know any good stuff?"

"Good stuff?" she laughed, putting her mug down.

"Yeah. Chopin. Schubert. That good stuff."

"I used to, but I haven't played in years. Literally."

"Well, Sal," Tim said, "now's the time to start."

She dropped her eyes from him to her hands, aware of what he was saying, resenting a little his correct assessment. Music had been such an important, rich part of her life, a good part, and she had pushed it aside with everything else, making it part of the bad things that had happened to her. She stretched her hands in her lap and wondered if they remembered how to play. It would feel good to play. She stood up.

"You guys stay here."

The man who had been playing, just fiddling around, really, got up as she approached. He was a lieutenant, young. "It's all yours," he said. "But watch the low E and F. They're pretty dicey."

"Thanks, Lieutenant, I will." Sally sat down. There wasn't a regular piano stool, just a bar chair, and it felt strange. She stretched her foot to the pedals, tried them, then sat still for a moment. The beat-up old instrument looked, she thought wryly, as though it had gone through the wars.

The worn ivory keys were rubbed bare to the wood through the middle register, but they felt good to her fingers. She tried a few chords. From a C to a D, back to C. The sound was tinny and she imagined that if she looked, she'd find the pads on most of the hammers as bare as the middle keys were.

Oh, well, hell, so what? And she started to play a Chopin nocturne. She stopped and started again. Her hands remembered, but were clumsy and unable to do what they used to do. It was frustrating, but she didn't mind. Not really. She felt as though she had come home.

Tim came and stood next to the piano after a little while to ask

453

if she'd like another beer. She shook her head, but smiled at him, not stopping or minding anymore that he had been so right about this. He touched her arm and went away.

When she finished, the men applauded.

"Thanks," she said. "God, I'm so rusty."

"It's been a long time," Tim said, grinning at her.

"Oh, don't look so smug," she teased him, then got up and joined the two men at their table. "He has this project," she said to Doug. "He's rehabilitating me. My own little denazification."

Tim whistled. "Phew. Just trying to get some music into my life. Meanwhile, I think I'll just move over here, out of range."

"Coward," she called, as he went off to the bathroom.

"You and him," said Doug, nodding his head in the direction Hastings had gone. "You an item?"

"Yeah," said Sally. "When he's not playing doctor. Can't you tell? I think I'm a project."

"There are worse things to be. I mean, you look, you both look, a lot more relaxed. Nothing like a good lay. Whoops," he said, his face turning red, "sorry, Sal. I forget sometimes you're not a guy."

And Sally smiled at him, a smile that started small and grew until she had to laugh, making Doug laugh with her. "He buys me crystal," she said, patting the paper-wrapped bowl. "Look at this, some poor bastard's Waterford."

"Well, *he* probably stole it from some Jew," Doug said.

Sally stopped laughing.

"What?" he said. "I can't joke about it? Listen, kiddo, if you can't joke about it, you might as well go belly-up."

"You're probably right." But she fell silent, thinking.

"Course I'm right. Anyway, I'm glad for the two of you. It's nice, you know, that you found each other."

"Nice? No, it's more than that. I'm Tim's project. Aren't I, Tim," she said to Hastings as he sat down again.

"Aren't you what?"

"Your project."

He smiled, tilting his head so that she couldn't see his eyes behind his glasses. But he didn't say anything and she thought maybe she had made him angry.

"Why do you say things like that?" he asked her when they got back to his apartment, after a silent car ride. She had said that maybe she would go back to her own place, but he had taken her by her wrist and pulled her gently in his door.

"I don't know," she said, sulking. "Because it's true. You do treat me like a patient."

"I don't have sex with my patients."

"Is that all it is? Good, because I'm the perfect lay. I can't get pregnant . . ."

"Probably can't," he put in.

"Never did in a year of screwing around. Anyway," she continued, "I'm tough, so you don't have to worry about breaking my heart. Actually, I don't think I have one anymore."

"Sally."

"Well, isn't that the way it is? You don't have to love me, you can just take care of me like a good doctor and have sex with me without responsibility. I'm probably totally incapable of loving anyone." She dropped her bag on the ground and fell onto the sofa, not looking at him. "You're not the first one to figure that out. And, after all, a good lay's a good lay."

"Oh, for God's sake. Don't talk like that. Why do you talk like that? How many guys told you that, Sally? How many?" He turned quickly away from her and, making his hand into a fist, hit his forehead. "Jesus, I can't believe this. Look, I don't care."

"Yes, you do."

"No, I don't. Do you? Do you care about the women I've slept with?" He sat on the table in front of her.

"No." She studied the arm of the sofa. "Yes. Just one."

"Yeah, one, right. You got it."

"Your wife," she said sadly.

"Your husband," he echoed.

She saw the truth in his face, the fear he had of the hold Christian still had over her, the hold she let him have.

"I was young," she said.

"So was I."

"Was she pretty?"

"Yes," he said. "A brunette with big dark eyes and a great figure—big breasts, tiny waist. Small, came up to here on me." He indicated on his shoulder, then sat down next to her on the sofa. They didn't look at each other.

"Are you trying to make me jealous?" Sally asked.

"Yes," he answered. "As jealous as I am."

"Well," she said, playing with the loose threads on the arm of the old sofa. "I guess we're both jealous then."

"Good," he said, picking up her hand and kissing it. "So, anyway, I enlisted when I found out she'd left."

"How'd you find out?"

"Came home from the clinic and she was gone. After med school, we lived in this little town, Salina. I told you about it, the prairie out the back door. Nancy came from Wichita, her folks were still there. Now Wichita's no metropolis compared to New York or even beat-up Berlin here, but Nancy wanted to live in Wichita. She also wanted someone else. She hated our little house, Salina, and me. She'd waited through med school with me, thought I'd set up a practice somewhere swank. That she'd finally get her reward. Instead, I wanted to go home and live in a small town and raise our boys. That was my dream. Thought hers was the same. It wasn't. So she left. I should have listened to her, I guess. Paid more attention. I found out later that she had been seeing the guy for almost a year when she was visiting her parents.

"So she left about a week after Pearl Harbor, and I decided to fix her. I'd go enlist and get myself killed. So I joined up, not telling anyone I was a doctor, and before I knew it, I was on a troop ship on my way to North Africa. Actually, until then, I'd liked being in the army. Never had to think about her or anything else.

"Well, after we landed, what with one thing and another, it was pretty tough. Tougher than I had imagined. In fact, I discovered I didn't like fighting at all. Now, some guys did, do. Some revel in it. You know, the adrenaline starts pumping, you do crazy things, great things. But not me. My inclination was to turn and run back into the sea.

"I didn't though, I kept on. It wasn't that I was afraid. I was, but that wasn't it. It was that I just didn't like it. Here I was, a doctor, and I was killing people. It didn't make sense.

"The thing came to a head when my unit, moving behind Patton's tanks, captured a German tank crew. They were still next to their tank, which had burned, and one of the guys was lying on the ground. He looked dead. The other guys surrendered. We were taking their guns, trying to talk to them, when the dead guy shot at me. Because I was closest, I imagine. The corporal shot him, but didn't kill him. I tried to help the guy. He was badly burned. I asked if anyone had any sulfa or morphine or anything.

"The corporal said to leave him. I said I couldn't. He ordered me. I refused. We got into an argument. God, it was crazy. I don't know why I wouldn't budge. The poor kraut kid was going to die anyway. I don't know much about burns, but I could see that.

"So I was arrested for refusing to obey an order. And aiding and abetting the enemy." He let go of her hand, but she left it lying in his.

"Why didn't they hang you as a traitor?" she asked.

"Colonel Eiger, Major Eiger then, was my CO, and he did a remarkable thing. He actually asked why I'd done what I did. The upshot was he found out I was a doctor. Boy, did he hit the roof then. Said I was criminal, not letting the army use my skills where they would do the most good."

"So that's how you wound up in Hawaii?"

"Can you imagine a better place to sit out a war? But that's the whole sorry story of my military career."

"Doesn't sound so bad. All you were trying to do was help people."

"Don't make me sound like Albert Schweitzer." He laughed and raised her face so that he could kiss her. Which he did with great intensity, pushing Sally back so that she lay under him. She let him, moved with him, wanting their passion to clear the past away. He kissed her ear, her throat, her breast, and the feeling made her forget everything except his body against hers.

They were on the floor when it happened. Tim was above her, his arms straight, holding him up as he moved slowly into her. She watched his face and his eyes met hers and she came in a long, slow explosion of feeling. Reaching for him, she pulled him down on top of her, to hold him close. He moved quickly to his own climax, gasping against her shoulder. She tightened her arms around him, almost overcome with the feelings he engendered, the affection and trust and satisfaction.

And then, out of all this feeling, her face buried in his shoulder, her mind and heart completely focused on the man she held in her arms, Sally murmured *his* name.

Only it wasn't his name she said, it was Christian's. She clamped her lips shut, but it was too late. The word was out of her mouth.

Tim became very still. She could feel his body withdraw from her. Then, with a burst of energy, he was up and away from her, leaving her half-naked, alone.

"Tim?" she said, getting up.

He stood at the end of the sofa, staring out the window. He was naked, his weight on one leg, his arms folded across his chest. Sally moved tentatively toward him.

"Tim, I'm sorry. I don't know—" she said.

"Stop. Just stop." He cut her off with a brusque gesture.

"Tim," she tried again.

"Sally, shut up. Don't say anything. Just shut up. Because if you don't, I will probably hit you and I have never hit a woman in my life. And I don't intend to start with you. Although, now that I

457

think of it, maybe that's what I ought to do. Would you like that?" He turned to look at her, a frightening expression on his face.

"How could you think that?" she whispered and turned and left.

In the kitchen, she looked around helplessly. What should she do? What could repair the damage she had done?

Nothing, she thought, falling onto the closest wooden chair. Nothing. She folded her arms and rocked forward, then back. Nothing. She was hopeless. It was hopeless. The damage could never be repaired. She would only hurt Tim, perhaps even worse than she had done just now. She had already forgiven his reaction, knowing he hadn't meant it.

She sat in the chair for a long time, as the kitchen grew dark. She thought she should get dressed and leave, but she did nothing.

Until she heard music. She raised her head. Someone was playing a clarinet. Tim. The music was low and mournful, then suddenly began to build in pitch and intensity. Sally stood.

Tim sat on the end of the bed. He'd put on his slacks, but no shirt or shoes. The room was lit only by light spilling out of the open bathroom door. He ignored her, or perhaps he didn't hear her, lost in his music.

She stood near the door, listening, her heart aching with the music as it ebbed and throbbed.

He stopped and lowered the instrument, his fingers still on the keys. "Do you think he's still alive?" he asked, his voice steady.

"I don't know."

"Tell me."

"All right. Yes, maybe he is," she said quietly.

"You've seen him." It was a statement, not a question.

"No," she said quickly. Then, softly: "Maybe. Someone like him. A ghost."

"And if he's not a ghost? What then?"

"If he's the guy in that photograph, he'll be arrested."

"No, I mean, about us."

"Us? Tim, I didn't—"

Again, he cut her off with a gesture. "Do you still love him?"

"You asked me that before," she accused him.

"You had an anxiety attack instead of answering."

"That's not fair."

"So, answer me. Tell me. Be fair to me. Let me know if my competition is some gorgeous blond superman." He began to take the clarinet apart and fit the sections in the case on the bed next to him.

458

"What am I? A game? A battle?"

"Oh, come, on, Sal. Just answer the question. Do you still love that monster?"

"No, and don't call him a monster."

"Christ!" He slammed the case shut and stood up. "How can you stand there and say that. You're not a stupid woman, Sally. You know those photographs are of him. You know it, but you refuse to acknowledge it. Why? I'll tell you why. Because you still love him, or, at the very least, still want him."

"I don't."

"You coulda fooled me, doll." His voice was full of contempt and anger.

"Don't, Tim."

"Tell me, did you think I was him all the way along? Were you really screwing him? Was that what you were doing?"

"Don't." She turned away. He moved across the room, grabbing her arms, and shook her.

"Don't? Do you know what you did? Do you know?"

"Yes. Yes. I'm sorry. Please, Tim." She started crying. "I didn't mean it. It was a stupid mistake. I didn't mean it." With that he let go of her and she leaned against the doorjamb, covering her face with her hands.

"Why did you say it, Sally? Why did you say his name? There, like that, while I was making love to you? Why?"

"I don't know," she cried. "I don't know where that came from. I don't know. Stop asking me. You ask me so damn many questions. Stop. Can't you just stop?"

"All right." His voice was low and quiet in the room after her outburst. "I'll stop. And you'd better go."

"Good. All right. If that's what you want."

"It is," he said, and when she met his eyes she understood that he meant what he said. She got dressed and left his apartment.

Sally lay on her bed in the dark and smoked. She wondered if she wasn't the biggest fool who ever lived, and she thought about how to do what she wanted to do. If Christian was alive—and she had a gut feeling that he was—she needed to see him. She needed to see him, because until she did, or until she knew for sure he was dead or beyond her reach, he would stand between her and Tim. He would stand between her and everything, life.

The next morning, though she'd had no sleep, she went to talk to Colonel Eiger. He didn't approve of Sally's idea, nor did he like the personal aspect to it.

"But this *is* personal, Colonel," said Sally, hoping he hadn't heard anything about her and Tim. "If Christian is the man in the pictures, there is no escaping that fact. Please, Colonel." She sat forward in her chair, placing both hands on his desk. "Please help me do this."

He leaned back in his chair, playing with the ubiquitous pencil, and regarded her. "Lieutenant," he said. "You got another plan here? A secret revenge or some such?"

Sally sat back in her chair. "No, sir, of course not," she said, trying to laugh. Her head hurt like crazy. "Nothing."

Colonel Eiger studied her, then grunted. "Okay. If he's the guy who commanded that 'special action,' I wouldn't mind nailing him."

So Sally's plan went into effect.

It was simple.

All she had to do was convince Annaliese that she wanted to see Christian and that she would be no threat to him.

CHAPTER 3

Sally heard the party sounds as she climbed the stairs to Annaliese's flat. The laughing and happy conversation evoked a strong pang of shyness in her and she hesitated before knocking. She wished she had not come, already feeling guilty about the lies she would have to tell Annaliese. Annaliese opened the door.

"Sally! Where have you been?" she cried.

"Hello," said Sally, allowing herself to be drawn into the entry hall and divested of her coat and hat. It was warm in the flat after the cold hall and the colder fall afternoon.

"It's good to see you," Annaliese said, adding Sally's things to a pile of wraps. "What is that?" she asked, nodding toward the bag Sally carried.

Sally held it up. "Bourbon."

"Very good," said Annaliese. "We don't have any of *that*. Lots of vodka, of course. Come in. Let me introduce you to everyone." Annaliese, her arm around Sally's waist, took her into the sitting room. "Quiet, everyone," she called. "Quiet."

The room was full of people, sitting on chairs, the sofa, and the floor. To the right, Sally could see others standing around the table, where the remains of a large buffet were spread out. The guests fell silent.

"This is a dear old friend of mine," Annaliese announced, her arm still around Sally's waist. "We've known each other since we were little girls . . ."

"Just last year, Annaliese?" cried a young man with wire-rimmed glasses and curly brown hair.

"Shut up, Klaus," said Annaliese, laughing. "Anyway, as I was saying, this is Sally Jackson. And, yes, she is an American, but be nice to her anyway. Look, she brought a big bottle of bourbon." Annaliese held up Sally's gift.

Sally laughed along with the group, who started talking among themselves again. Behind her, she heard a small voice call her name. She looked around and saw Klara running toward her. Happily, Sally knelt and held her arms out to the child.

"Hello, pumpkin," she said in English. Klara laughed at the endearment, which Sally had used on an earlier visit.

461

"I'm not a pumpkin," Klara said in German, but using the English word.

"Of course you are," Sally said, touching Klara's nose. "You're as round and rosy as one."

"Klara, come," called Annaliese.

"You come too," said the child, grabbing a handful of Sally's skirt.

"I will, but you go before we both get into trouble."

"Yes," said Klara, and turned and whirled off, leaving Sally alone.

"Hiya, kiddo." Surprised, Sally looked around so quickly, she almost twisted her neck. She saw a very skinny, very tanned man, who was probably her own age but looked ten years older. He wore steel-rimmed glasses, a yellowed shirt at least a decade old, and he needed a haircut. In each hand he carried a glass, mismatched, of liquor. He grinned at her.

"Hi," she said hesitantly.

"This is for you," he said, holding a glass out. He was missing his ring finger and the top joints of his middle and little fingers. A soldier. "Down the hatch."

"Thanks," she said, taking the glass.

"Cute kid, ain't she?" he said.

"Yes," agreed Sally, trying not to cough after a sip from the glass. It tasted like first-run vodka and she was sure it had stripped her vocal cords.

"Christ," he said, seeing her reaction. "That shit too strong for you?"

Sally shook her head, then nodded. "I mean, yes," she said, wiping her eyes. She looked at the glass. "What is it?"

"You know, homemade hooch. You gotta drink a couple o' glasses before it goes down easy."

"Right," Sally said and took another sip. "Where'd you learn your English?" she asked.

"I was a POW," he said. "In New Mexico. Out in the middle of the fucking desert. My name's Kurt." He pronounced his name as an American would: Kirt.

"Hello, Kurt," said Sally, shaking hands with him. "My name is Sally. Have you been back long?"

"Two fucking days," he said.

"You must be glad to be home."

"Glad? Glad? Shit. This dump's a fucking morgue. Thank God I don't live in the Reds' sector, but Christ, I can't wait to get the hell out of here. No, this country's had it; I'm going back to the U.S. of A."

Over his shoulder, Sally saw Annaliese, in the door of the kitchen, gesturing to her. "Our hostess," she murmured and slipped past him, wondering how some snotty American sub-consul would react to Kurt's peculiar English.

The people she passed on her way to the kitchen parted before her and she realized that it was the first time she had been alone in a group of Germans since she had returned to Berlin. Alone with the enemy, even though the shooting was over. A man and a woman were deep in conversation, blocking the door to the kitchen.

"Pardon me," said Sally, and was dismayed by the venomous looks they gave her as they moved quickly away. She thought of the cigarettes in her bag, her leather shoes and bag, her camel's hair coat, all valuable commodities on the black market. She chided herself for her paranoia, but was glad she hadn't worn her uniform.

"How did you like Kurt's American English?" Annaliese asked. "He's very proud of it." She handed Klara a slice of bread and jam. "Here, sweet; now be good."

"Sally, would you come play with me?" Klara asked, her mouth full of bread.

"Not now, sweetie, I have to talk to your mama. Maybe later. Okay?" Sally blew a kiss at Klara, who sent one back. Then she giggled and ran from the kitchen. Sally turned to Annaliese. "Kurt's English is very idiomatic," she said, dryly. "I take it he learned it from GIs?" She searched in her bag for her cigarettes. "Want one?" she asked, holding out the pack to Annaliese.

"Thanks," Annaliese said, and held a match out for Sally before she lit her own cigarette. "Sally, wait here," she whispered. "I've got someone who said he knows where my brother is."

She walked to the door and came back in a moment with a tall man, whom she introduced to Sally as Günther. Like Kurt, he was very thin, and dressed in pre-war clothing, but his dark hair was cut and neatly combed and he wore his old clothes with an air of sophistication. His skin was pale, almost white against his black hair and eyebrows.

He smoothly bowed over Sally's hand. "Fräulein," he said. "You were interested in news of Annaliese's brother? May I ask why?"

Sally studied him for a moment, then looked past him to Annaliese, who stood at the sink with her back to them. Sally gestured at the cigarette pack she had left on the table.

"Thank you," he said, and took one out of the pack.

Annaliese turned with a bottle in her hand to pour them each a drink. "Here you are. Now I had better go see if my guests have robbed me yet." And she left them alone.

There were no chairs in the kitchen—they had probably been commandeered for the sitting room—so Sally leaned against the table.

"I knew Annaliese's brother before the war," said Sally. "In the early thirties." Silence. "Did you?" she asked.

Günther took a long pull on the cigarette, releasing the smoke through his nose. "Yes," he said.

"I see," said Sally, remembering Heydrich's habit of monosyllabic answers. She smiled grimly. Günther said nothing but raised one eyebrow, questioning. "You remind me of someone," she said.

"An unpleasant memory," he said. "Not Mayr?"

"No," said Sally. She took a chance. "His boss. The Chief."

Günther's face was poker-straight, then a flicker of understanding showed in his eyes. "The Chief. You knew him?"

"Yes."

"How?"

"We played music together."

"Ah. He was reported to be good."

"He was."

"About Mayr—is he wanted for a crime? Would he be tried?" Günther asked in a flat, bored voice. He was leaning against the ironstone sink.

"I don't know," said Sally. "That's nothing to do with me. I want to know about him for personal reasons. I'd like to know if he's alive. At least to know that."

"You cared about him?" Günther asked, still in that calm voice.

"I did," said Sally, looking into his eyes. She didn't have to lie about that, but the pretense of the situation was making her very nervous. She was sure this man could see through her. He held her eyes for a long time and then sighed.

"The last time I saw Mayr was in April or May of 1944," he said.

"That long ago." Sally was disappointed. He hadn't believed her. She picked up her glass. He watched her, his eyes, eyes as dark as his hair, unreadable.

"Were you in the SS?" Sally asked bluntly.

Günther barked a short, unamused laugh. "My dear Fräulein," he said, shaking his head. "You don't suppose I would tell you if I had been?" She smiled, joining in his unfunny joke. "But no, I was not. I was in the Luftwaffe. I met Mayr on leave.

"You knew him before the war? You were lovers?" he asked matter-of-factly.

"That's none of your business," Sally said sharply.

"Ahh," he said, and she knew she had given everything away.

"What were you doing in Berlin?" he asked, standing close enough to her so that she could smell him. Or his clothing, which stank of the harsh cleaning fluid that could not camouflage the sweat and smoke and other smells that had sunk into the very fibers of the cloth. He himself was clean; she could see that. But his clothing would never be.

"My father was the ambassador," she said for the millionth time. It would be the perfect epitaph on her grave. "My father was the ambassador."

"I see," he said.

She smiled sadly. "Christian never spoke of me? I would have thought . . ." Her voice trailed off and she picked up her purse. The tears were not hard to summon and she pulled a handkerchief out of her bag. "I'm sorry," she said. "I just hoped . . ."

"I'm sorry, Fräulein," Günther said.

Sally hitched her bag over her shoulder and, thanking Günther, walked to the door.

"If . . ." he said, stopping her. "If I think of anything else, or if I hear something, how would I contact you?"

Sally turned slowly and stared at him a long moment. He stared back impassively. She handed him her card.

"I came back to find him," she whispered. "Please, help me." And she sounded so convincing, she wasn't sure at all that she wasn't telling the truth.

Sally stood on the front steps of the apartment building pulling on her gloves, glad to see that her jeep was still there. The cold afternoon was quickly fading into an even colder night. She walked down the steps, noting that there had been further repair done on them since the last time she had visited Annaliese. She heard the front door of the building open behind her.

"Fräulein Jackson." Sally turned. Günther came down the steps toward her, hurriedly buttoning his coat, a Luftwaffe overcoat, the insignia removed and the metal buttons exchanged for ugly flat wooden ones. "I have something that would interest you." He spoke casually.

"And what would that be?"

"Something to show you," he said, with a charming smile.

"What?" she asked, irritated by his manner.

"A photograph. At my flat. If you would drive us?" She hesitated. "I am helping you with your investigations," he offered.

"Yes," she conceded. "All right. But I'll stop at the checkpoint to let my CO know where I'll be."

"A prudent action," he said, his black eyes twinkling in secret amusement, even as his shoulders hunched against the cold.

After the telephone call at the checkpoint, Günther directed her to an apartment building in what was once the fashionable section of Charlottenburg. Sally followed him into a large entry hall and up a white marble staircase that corkscrewed majestically up under a leaded skylight, now glassless. Gray evening light slid down through the squares of battered lead, barely touching the walls, throwing shadows into the corners and down the long empty corridors. It was icy cold and their breath showed in the still air. On the fifth floor, they walked down a long hallway where the carpet had been ripped up and the paneling torn from the wall.

"The Russians," he said, waving his hand at the torn-up walls, "used it for firewood." He stopped in front of a double door and pulled a key out of his trouser pocket.

"Did you live here before?" asked Sally, thinking how elegant the place must have been. Even in its present unhappy state, it still retained an air of fashionable sophistication; as Günther himself did.

"Before?" he said, looking up from fitting the key into the lock.

"The war," she said. What else would she mean?

"I am disappointed in you. I would think you understood that questions about those long-ago halcyon days before the war were forbidden," he said, and pushing open the door, he stepped aside to allow Sally to enter. "I, of course, remember nothing of them. I find it more comfortable that way."

Sally gave him a look and walked past him into a small square empty entry hall. The walls were white with an elaborate plaster frieze around the molding. Or rather, they had been; now, they were dingy, gray, and the molding was chipped and cracked.

Günther closed and locked the door behind them, then led Sally through a double door, passing quickly through the next room.

"I live only in here now. It's easier to heat," he said, opening another door.

It must have been a library or study, the walls were covered with empty shelves. There were two tall windows, one boarded up and one boasting half of its glass panes, allowing some waning evening light into the room. Facing the windows was a fireplace with what had once been a beautiful black marble mantel, now horribly disfigured by several gouges and one huge crack.

"Please," Günther said, "sit down. But I'd advise you to keep your coat on. It's chilly in here. I'll get the fire going and make us some tea."

Sally stood resolutely in the middle of the floor. "I'd rather you showed me the photograph right away. I can't stay."

"Please," he said, spreading wide his hands. "You are my first guest since . . ." He paused to think. "I can't remember how long."

"I am not your guest," she said firmly. "Please. The photograph."

"Very well." He reached into the inner pocket of his jacket and carefully pulled out a photograph. Wordlessly he held it out to her, and just as silently she took it, angry that he had been able to trick her so easily into coming to his rooms. Still, the photograph was real, and tilting it toward the gray light from the window, she saw it was of a group of people. Günther leaned over her shoulder.

"I took this my wedding day," he said softly. "This is Mimi, my wife. She is dead now." He pointed to a pretty, youthful woman in a stark suit and a tiny, veiled hat. Next to her, arm in arm, was a handsome dark-haired woman, also in a suit and with a chic turban over her hair. And next to her, with his arm around her waist, looking forthrightly into the camera, his chin raised, looking older and thinner than she remembered him, was Christian. He wore the gray SS uniform issued after the war began, and the way he stood prevented her from identifying his rank. Automatically, Sally turned the photograph over. Nothing. She wished she could study it without an audience.

"Perhaps some tea now?" Günther asked, turning on a light and startling her.

"No, thank you," she said, holding the photograph out.

Languidly, he took it from her and put it on the cracked mantel of the dead fireplace. Then, again, he reached into his jacket. "I have something else you might be interested in," he said, bringing the object out of his pocket. It glittered in the light.

From his hand dangled a gold chain with a small charm, which caught the light, winking, bright and warm in the cold, gray room. Sally walked slowly over to Günther, holding out her hand until the charm, a small gold heart delicately enameled with white and pink flowers, came to rest on her palm. As he let go of it, the thin chain whipped around Sally's hand.

It was the locket she had given Christian that last summer at the lake. She had forgotten about it. She opened it, knowing what was inside. Not a picture, but a small dried leaf, a piece of their

467

beloved Lake Sebastian, which she had put into the locket so that Christian might carry it with him always. Had he?

Even to Lezaky?

"Where did you get this?" she whispered and looked into Günther's dark eyes, vivid in his pale face.

"You recognize it."

"It was mine, from my brother, when I was a kid. I gave it to . . . did Christian say when, where? You could have taken it from his body." Günther's face was still expressionless. "He gave it to you to prove to me that he's still alive, didn't he? Didn't he?" Sally's voice rose as she repeated the question. "He knew I'd understand . . ." Her hand closed around the chain and she looked into the shadows of the room, at a screen covered with faded green silk standing in the corner, her senses stretching for a clue, the sound of a foot sliding across the floor, of a man breathing.

"Please, Günther, tell me. Please. Is he here? Is there a room back here? Is he in it?" She headed for the screen, determined to force the issue.

"Why should I tell you?"

"Günther, this"—she held up her fist, the gold chain looped around her wrist. "This was a secret between him and me. It is, I think, a token from him. To make me think of those days."

Sally slipped the locket into her coat pocket, then sat on the bed so that she was knee to knee with Günther. "Let me give *you* something. I have a picture too. A photograph taken in Czechoslovakia, after Heydrich's murder—during the actions. You know?" She saw from his eyes that he understood what she was alluding to. "If it is Christian, he will be in terrible danger."

"But you are the only one who can identify him in this picture?"

"No, I have other photographs of him. We're using those as well. The Czech photo shows his rank and outfit; the coloring and size of the man is the same as his. It's just that the face is not entirely clear. We are very busy and would not be spending so much time on him if the incident weren't so awful."

"And if you were not personally involved," added Günther.

"Yes," Sally said slowly, "you're right. Look, I don't have to see him. It would be better if I didn't, but please, can't you tell me if he's alive and well? That's all I want. Tell me, Günther. I don't blame him. I don't want revenge." She frowned and again avoided his gaze.

"We were young," she said, and shrugged as though to forgive some trivial youthful indiscretion. "I don't know what he

468

did afterward, or if he was in charge of that action group. All I know is, I loved him once a great deal. And the anger, the bitterness—it's gone. But I want to know what happened. Where was he? What happened afterward? Why didn't he ever contact me or my father? I loved him, Günther," she repeated. "I should think he'd want to know that."

For a long time, Günther studied her, then, finally, answered with one word: "Yes."

A long exhalation of breath escaped Sally, as though all these years she had been holding back, holding on to something, and now it could be released. "I knew it," she whispered.

Günther held up his hand, his index finger extended like a stern father's. "I will answer no more questions about his whereabouts. Understand?" Sally nodded. "I do not believe that you could still care for him, after the things he put you through." Günther smiled at Sally's expression. "Yes, he told me. He said—"

"I don't want to talk about that. It was a long time ago. It is over," she said sharply, interrupting him. She picked up her handbag. "I'd better go. I've stayed too long."

"Tell me one thing," said Günther, standing behind her. "Would you help him? If you could?"

Sally stood, her hand poised above the top button of her coat. "I don't know. I don't know." She turned to face him. He was very close to her. She could smell the cleaning fluid on his clothes again.

Günther smiled at her, a horrible, lupine smile, his lips pulled back over his teeth, which looked yellow in contrast to his pale, bluish skin. Sally took a step back from him.

He touched her arm. "We all knew," he whispered. "About Heydrich and Christian and you. We all knew. We listened to the stories as though they were a serial in a ladies' magazine. Christian didn't know we did. I can tell you, we were disappointed when it ended the way it did. He did not mean for it to, but he lost his temper. He had a terrible temper."

"Who?" whispered Sally, leaning away from him, but held by his hand on her arm and by her horrified fascination in what he was saying.

"The Chief, of course," replied Günther.

"You *were* SS."

He didn't deny her accusation. Sally tried to take a step away from him, but his hand closed around her arm, stopping her. "We had a very difficult time cleaning up after him generally, but your

469

case was a particularly messy one. We were all sorry about it, truly we were. It was not supposed to end like that."

"How? How was it supposed to end?"

"On the island. Heydrich would finally have you and be done with it. With you and Mayr, that is. Then he could engineer the scandal he needed to undermine your father."

"My father?"

"Your father's criticisms of the government were becoming untenable—he had to go. Well, the Chief certainly accomplished that. And shall I tell you something else about Mayr? The Chief had to order him to start the affair with you. It wasn't you, personally. Just women. You understand?"

Sally shook his hand from her with a brusque movement. "No, I don't want—you're lying." Sally backed away from him. "I don't want to talk about it. You're wrong. That's crazy. Listen, just tell him what I said. But stay away from me. All of you. You're revolting. Stay away." And with that she turned and fled, leaving Günther alone in his empty, cold rooms.

"Well, Sally," Colonel Eiger said, when she telephoned him to report the events of the afternoon, leaving out the more personal parts. "It looks like now all we can do is wait."

"Yes, sir."

"But, Sally"—his voice was full of concern—"don't go *anywhere* alone. You got that? No more gallivanting around by yourself, into the Russian sector or elsewhere. That's an order."

"But, Colonel," she said, "if he's going to try and contact me, and I'm never alone, he won't do it."

"If he needs to contact you badly enough, he'll find a way. These men are SS, Sally. Remember that. God knows what these guys are up to or what they'll think they have to do. You do what I say, Lieutenant. That's an order."

So Sally promised and went back to her room. She sat on her bed, still in her overcoat, her hands sunk in her pockets, missing Tim, wishing for his arms around her. Her fingers closed around the little necklace and she pulled it out of her pocket.

She twirled it around her finger. It was one of the few things she had ever received from her brother. And she had given it to Christian because it was her favorite possession. She couldn't believe she had forgotten about it. She also couldn't believe that Christian had kept it all these years.

As for what Günther had told her, she would ignore most of

it, unable to sort out the truth from the lies. Günther hadn't known Christian as she had. He hadn't seen her husband fight with the choices and decisions he was faced with. She could accept that Heydrich had meant to have sex with her on the island, had had her drugged, but she had spoiled that plan. And Christian? Had he been what Günther said?

She wished she were at Tim's, in his bed. She wished she could be done with this.

CHAPTER 4

"Hi," Doug Finkelstein said to Sally, as they met in the foyer of their office building. She stood at one of the two tall windows that looked out at the barren garden at the rear of the building. It was late November and the much-battered place was cold and clammy, the space heaters the army provided doing little against the years of miserable weather the old building had endured.

"Morning," Sally replied. "What a dreary view. You ready?" They were going over to the hospital to see Mala, the young woman who had photographed the pictures of Lezaky.

"She's not there anymore."

"What? What happened? She didn't. . . ?"

"No. She's alive. They've sent her to a bone man in Zurich."

"Have you heard about Mala?" said Max Tobin, coming up behind them.

"Yeah. I was just telling Sally."

"We were supposed to go visit her," said Sally.

"Well, let's get some coffee instead," Tobin suggested, and the three of them went down to the cafeteria in the basement.

The place had recently been scrubbed, disinfected, and painted. The furniture was army issue, gray, metal, utilitarian, but someone had put up yellow-and-white curtains on the high, narrow windows, and they helped warm the place up.

"I wish I had had a chance to thank her," Sally said, after they had gotten their coffee and found a table. "For those photographs."

"I wouldn't think you'd want to," said Doug.

She looked at him, surprised and a little hurt by his remark. "Why do you say that?" she asked. Doug shrugged and picked up his cup, almost hiding behind it. "Identification in such situations is always difficult."

"Maybe you don't want to," he said.

"Would you? If he were someone you had known?"

Doug shrugged again, sipped his coffee. "Christ, this stuff is awful. You'd think they could at least do that right."

"Those photographs have caused you a lot of heartache, haven't they?" Tobin said in a mild voice.

"Yeah," said Sally, "all of them. I wish, though, she had been able to get his face. I wish I knew for sure."

"Oh, speaking of photographs," Doug said, pulling a letter out of his pocket. He handed it to Sally. It was from *Life* magazine and it was addressed to Sally, in care of the unit hospital. "Sergeant Dolan asked me to give it to you."

"It must be about her pictures?" Sally said.

"Maybe they want to buy them." After a discussion with Mala, via the translator, the unit, that is, Sally, had sent a few of her photographs to David Wohl, care of *Life* magazine. She hadn't said much in the letter, not knowing if David was still at the magazine or if he would be in a position to help.

In all the years between that afternoon when Sally had said good-bye to him at the train station and this letter, she had seen him just once. It had been during the bad days in Los Angeles and she and David had drunk the night away. He had been divorced and a father and although his dark hair was graying, it was still curly and disheveled. After that meeting, they had written on and off, but that had petered out after Sally's return to Palo Alto.

When she was well again, she had followed his career, keeping track of him through the news of his award and his work as a broadcaster. She had even heard him on the radio, reporting from the Soviet Union before the German invasion, his sharp New York voice reaching her across the thousands of miles that separated them.

"Open the letter, Sally," said Max.

A check fell out. Sally picked it up. "Oh, God, look at this," and handed it to Doug. "This is great. She'll be so proud. I'll bet she never sold any before." She read the letter. It was short and well typed:

Hey, kid: Imagine hearing from you, after all this time. And from Berlin of all places. Hear the Adlon's a hole in the ground. Listen, the photos are great stuff. Are there any more? My pal, the photo ed., agrees and we shook a check loose for the girl. They'll want to know more about her. Meanwhile, maybe I'll see you one of these days. Love,

And he had added his signature in pen. Sally felt pleased to hear from him and with such fantastic results for Mala. Maybe she would see him again one of these days.

"That's why she brought them to us," Tobin said, looking over Finkelstein's shoulder at the check. "Terrific."

"Here," Finkelstein said, handing Sally back the check. "You can get her address in Zurich from Sergeant Dolan." Both men watched her put it back in the envelope and tuck it away in her purse. "So, Sal, you going to the Thanksgiving wingding? I hear there's going to be a live band."

"No. Are you?"

"Sure. How 'bout you, Max?"

"Too old to jitterbug. I'll go for the dinner, though. I hear they're importing turkey and all the trimmings."

"You're kidding," said Doug.

"Nope. Carl, the supply sergeant over at the Officer's Club, told me."

"God, I'd love some real mashed potatoes," Doug mused. "With real butter."

"I'd like two real scrambled eggs," said Max. They laughed and enjoyed a torturous fifteen-minute conversation about food.

Later that day, Nelson Armbrewster knocked on Sally's office door and when invited in, asked her to the Thanksgiving party.

"I'm not a bad dancer," he said. "And I look rather good in my dress-up. Oh, which reminds me, you do have a dress, don't you?"

"Yes, Nelson, I do have a dress. And I'd love to see you all dolled up."

"Good. I'll even pick you up at that convent you live in."

Sally looked at herself in the little mirror over her sink. She had brought one dress with her, a black velvet with a halter top and low back. It was pre-war and had a full skirt. She wore elbow-length black lace gloves with it. Afraid that she looked pale, she put on some bright-red lipstick. There. That was better.

Unfortunately, she didn't have a dress coat and had to wear her camel's hair, but then so did everyone else. The halls of the "convent," as Nelson had called it, were noisy with women getting dressed, and Sally smiled at the female confusion, the voices calling out to borrow earrings, or stockings, the smell of treasured bath soap and perfume and the glimpses of colored dresses, pinks and blues and lavenders, instead of the usual olive drab, dark brown, and nurse's white.

Nelson was waiting for her in the foyer, looking distinguished in his dress uniform. She kissed his cheek and told him so.

"Thanks, old girl," he said. "You look pretty stunning yourself. Smell good, too."

They could hear the band as they pulled up outside the Officer's Club. There was a traffic jam in front of the club, as guests arrived, so Sally and Nelson left the car with the enlisted man who was acting as valet.

As they walked down the stairs into the main room, which was decorated with brown and orange crepe-paper streamers and three precious yellow chrysanthemums, on each table, the music, noise, and perfumed air hit them. Sally laughed. Nelson lifted an eyebrow.

"Oh, Nelson," she said, tucking her hand into the crook of his arm. "It's so nice."

"It looks rather like a school gym to me," he said.

"It does. It does, but isn't it wonderful? So normal. The flowers. Oh, I love it. Thank you for asking me. I appreciate it."

"I don't date for charity, Sally."

"I know, but Doug put you up to it, didn't he?" She smiled at him when he didn't answer. "That's okay. I just hope you're not going to disappoint some other girl."

"She wouldn't be able to attend."

"A Fräulein?"

"Yes. Actually, a countess."

"Of course she is. Well, we'll have a good time, Nelson, and you can tell her about it and laugh at the hokey decorations."

He patted her hand, and led her into the room to find their table.

"Hey, guys, over here," cried Doug, standing up and waving at them. He was sitting with the pretty redheaded nurse, Margie, whom he introduced to Sally and Armbrewster.

"I know Margie," said Sally, "we share a bathroom. I didn't know you two knew each other."

As they chatted, Sally was relieved to note that there were only four places at their table. If Tim was there, at least they wouldn't have to sit together. But she couldn't help looking for him.

The band stopped playing and the leader made an announcement that they would return after dinner.

"Oh, good," said Doug, rubbing his hands together, "turkey time."

An hour or so later, as the waiters cleared the tables, the band returned and launched into "In the Mood."

"C'mon, Margie," Doug said, standing up and holding his hand out to his date. "Time to cut a rug."

"Would you like to?" offered Nelson.

"I think we have to," laughed Sally. "Although I must warn you I haven't danced in years."

"Who has, my dear? Who has?"

Sally danced for hours. She hardly sat down, except hurriedly to gulp some champagne, before someone else asked her to dance. She danced with strangers, with Doug and Nelson, and even two dances with Colonel Eiger, who, surprisingly, was a great dancer, smooth and surefooted. He was just inches taller than Sally, and he held her close so that they danced cheek to cheek. She didn't mind. She loved moving to the music and the smells of perfume and after-shave and the happy crowd of people in their best civvies. It was so different from the everyday world they inhabited. In here, with no outside distractions, they could forget the bombed city and the hungry conquered people. So she just stopped thinking and let herself dance, as though she were in a crepe-paper-hung dream.

"I'll Be with You in Apple Blossom Time" came to an end and she leaned back to smile at the colonel.

"Where'd you learn to dance like that?" she asked dreamily.

He was about to answer, when someone came up behind Sally. She saw Eiger's eyes register the new arrival just as the band started into the first long, low, sensuous chords of "Moonlight Melody." The colonel let go of her and stepped back as Sally turned to face her new partner.

It was, of course, Tim.

They stood and looked at each other for a long moment, as the dance floor filled with dancers, drawn by the seductive, nostalgic music.

"Want to dance?" he asked.

"Yes," she answered and went into his arms. He folded their hands together on his chest. She could feel his cheek against her hair, his heartbeat under her hand, and closing her eyes, she let him lead, happy to move as he directed, the music swirling around them.

"We've never danced together," he said.

"No." She kept her face against his shoulder.

"I thought we should." Sally nodded. "Sally?" His voice sounded husky. She leaned back in his arms so that she could see his face. "I've . . . how have you been?"

"All right. And you?"

"Fine. Fine." He gently pulled her back against him. They

danced a few moments before he spoke again. "Actually, I've been lousy." She waited. "I miss you."

Sally stopped moving, separating them. "Tim, I didn't mean . . . I've been so worried."

"Sal, stop. I'm all right. I overreacted."

"No, you didn't. You were perfectly right. What I did was—"

"It was just a mistake."

"But it was cruel. I hurt you. Timmy, I didn't mean to."

"Hey," he said, putting his arms around her, drawing her close, "you're not crying, are you?"

"Of course not."

"Good, because this is supposed to be a party." When the music stopped, he held her a moment longer, then let her go. "You want to have dinner with me some night?"

"Some night?" she asked.

He smiled and touched her face. "After I get back from Nuremberg? My place?" Sally nodded. Taking her hand, Tim led her back to her table.

"Hello, Hastings," said Doug. "Sit with us."

"Thanks, can't," Tim replied, pulling out the chair for Sally. "Have to get back to my date." He waved one hand vaguely.

"Oh? Who is she?" Doug stood halfway up, craning his neck to look.

"Nobody you know, don't worry," Tim said. "Good night, all."

"Night, Hastings," said Nelson.

"Night, Sal. Thanks for the dance. See you." Tim's hand landed for a moment on her back, then he was gone. She'd see him next Friday and the anticipation bubbled through her. She didn't even care that he had brought someone else tonight. They'd be together next Friday.

It seemed to Sally, as she stood and looked out the rain-splattered window of her office on Monday morning, that it had been raining forever. Here it was almost December and no sign of Christian. But she'd see Tim this Friday and she closed her eyes for a moment, remembering the feel of his arms around her.

What if she were to telephone him right now and ask him to come by her office? Sally ducked her head, laughing at herself, at her hunger. Her eyes fell on the carton of photographs Mavis had left her.

They had come to rest there, under her window, weeks ago. She had meant to do something with them, but had been unable to force herself to open the flaps again. And she had been busy.

Just last week, Sally had received a letter from Mavis, now in Washington, D.C., and a member of the brand-new United Nations agency for refugee relief, asking about the photographs. She had enclosed an address of a refugee center where Sally could send the photographs.

She'd pack it all up, the list and the photographs, and send everything to the center, Sally decided. Someone there would have the time and someone there wouldn't be so spooked by the pictures as she was.

Pulling Mavis's list out from under a pile of papers, she went over to the box and dragged it away from the wall. The pictures were nearly to the top of the box and she could see that they'd need to be more carefully packed if they were going to survive the mails. Maybe she could find a stronger box.

Absently, she picked up a photograph and turned it over. Nothing. How impossible this would be! She put it back into the box and picked up another one. This one had something written on the back but in nearly illegible writing and the ink had faded. Impossible without the proper equipment and staff. She tossed the picture back and started to fold up the flaps again.

A face looked up at her and she stopped. Huge eyes peeked up from behind the picture she had just thrown back into the box. Gingerly, she pushed the top picture with a finger so that she could see more clearly what had caught her attention.

It was a snapshot of a girl, probably about seven years old, in a sweater and skirt, her light hair cut in a chin-length bob, one side held back with a big bow. She looked mischievously at the camera and her cocky expression made Sally smile. She turned the photograph over. In clear, precise writing it read: Katrina van der Lee, and underneath, 3/5/35. There were some more words, in Dutch, Sally presumed, since she could recognize the word "Amsterdam." Katrina was a little Dutch girl.

Sally turned the photograph back. The little girl stood, arms akimbo, head cocked to one side in a garden so sunny that light glared from the photograph, obscuring much of the background detail.

March of 1935. Perhaps it had been her birthday, perhaps her father had cajoled her into the garden for a photograph. March of 1935. Wasn't that . . . Sally sat back on her heels. That was the month her child should have been born.

She tensed, waiting for the familiar rush of pain that always accompanied thoughts of the loss of her unborn baby, but instead of the sharp stab, she felt a soft sadness. When had that happened?

She looked at the picture of little Katrina van der Lee. Maybe the girl's mother or father had carried the photograph onto the train, maybe Katrina, who would be almost an adult now, was still in Amsterdam. Or maybe she had been forced onto the train with her parents . . . maybe she had survived. Maybe. There were happy endings. There were. Not everyone had died. The Nazis and the war had not killed all the children.

Sally stood up and walked to her desk, carrying the photograph, which she propped against the lamp. Katrina's face that March day so long ago was full of life and self-confidence, the self-confidence that comes to children when they are secure in a loving family.

What would it be like to make a child look like that? To raise an energetic daughter like Katrina? Maybe, Sally thought, it was time to forget old pain, maybe it was time to . . .

The telephone rang.

She picked up the receiver.

"Sergeant Sanchez, Lieutenant." Sergeant Sanchez had replaced Sergeant Taveggia at the front desk.

"What's up, Sergeant?"

"There's a cable for you, Lieutenant."

"A cable?" There is no one left to die, was her first thought.

"From Manila."

"From Manila, in the Philippines, Sergeant?" Something, a thought, a feeling, pinged way off in the distance. She became very still, as though she were trying to hear the sound, identify the feeling. Was it pain? Anticipation?

"Seems to be, Lieutenant," answered Sanchez. "Where my people were from."

"Oh," said Sally, "I didn't realize that." Manila. Someone might be alive! She dropped the phone on her desk and ran from her office.

Standing in front of the sergeant's desk, Sally ripped open the cable with shaking hands. It was from the Army Command in Manila. She read the message, then reread it, her brain refusing to understand what her eyes saw. Someone *was* left alive.

Eddie.

Eddie, her brother, was alive.

"Bad news, Lieutenant?" asked Sergeant Sanchez.

"Oh, no, good—very good—news," said Sally, grinning at him,

tears in her eyes, on her cheeks. She rubbed her face with the back of her arm.

Tim.

And she ran across the room, surprising the sergeant, startling the German secretary, practically knocking over a major on the other side of the door to the hall.

"Excuse me, sir," said Sally, saluting quickly, not stopping. She ran down the hall, skidding around the corner. The door to Tim's office was open. He was sitting at his desk, his feet up on an open drawer.

Sally stopped in front of him. She stood, gasping for breath, holding out the crumpled cable.

"Timmy, Timmy, look," she said, and laid the cable on the blotter, smoothing it out.

"What?" Startled, he dropped his feet and sat up.

"Read it, read it," Sally ordered.

He let out a whoop and was up and around his desk before Sally could move, enfolding her into a hug. She burst into tears, crying and laughing and saying over and over, "Eddie. He's alive. He's alive, Tim." Tim held her and laughed with her, and wiped her tears away. He reached behind her to push his door shut, then led her to his chair, pulling her onto his lap.

She sighed, her arms around his neck, and kissed his cheek.

"I'm happy for you, Sal."

"It's a miracle."

"What happened?"

"I don't know beyond what's in the cable." She reached out and picked it up off the desk. "He's in a naval hospital."

"I've heard stories of guys being saved by guerrillas. Maybe that's what happened."

"He's alive. He didn't die on that road. He didn't die. It makes me feel so . . . so . . ." She searched for the word.

"Hopeful," he offered, his cheek against her hair.

"Yes. Hopeful. And, you, Tim?" She moved so that she could see his face. She touched his mustache as though to make sure it was in place.

"What about me?"

I love you, she wanted to tell him. The words appeared in her mind as though from deep inside her and she opened her mouth to say them, but stopped. Instead, she reread the cable.

It was spare: Eddie was alive and in a hospital where his condition was stable, although he was not well enough to be moved yet. Please advise.

"I'd better go get him," she said. "Take him home. Or stay with him." And Tim's arms tightened around her, reminding her that sometimes nothing is gained without an attendant loss. "Oh," she said, putting her arms around him in return.

Then she remembered. "I can't, can I? Not until all this other business with Christian is over. Dammit." She stood up, grateful for the anger that kept away the idea of saying good-bye to Tim. "Damn."

"Talk to Eiger," Tim said, his voice flat.

"Yeah," said Sally, walking to the door. "I'd better go do that right away." She stopped and said, her back to him, "All those photographs I've been looking at for six years, of all those people who've died, but now, someone's alive! I'd never have believed anything like this could happen, something good."

"Sally?" His voice was hesitant. She faced him, but Tim said nothing else, just looked at her, then smiled, releasing her. "Better go talk to the colonel," he said gently.

"He's all the family I have left, Colonel," Sally explained when she showed Eiger the cable. "And tracking down an ex-husband who may or may not be implicated in a crime is suddenly not a priority with me."

"I'm surprised at you," Eiger said.

"I'm not saying the crime shouldn't be investigated and the man punished, but, oh, Colonel, don't you see . . ." She leaned forward, her hands on his desk. "That is the past. I mean, it's all to do with death. All of this, being here, in the army, us, we're all working to avenge the deaths of so many innocents. A thing that should be done. But, please, give me a chance to a future, to finding life. Even if he . . . if he's too banged up to move, or a vegetable or whatever, he's still alive. Alive!"

"I think you ought to go," Eiger said in a mild voice. "I can't argue with that." He pulled a bottle of bourbon out of his bottom drawer and poured them both a drink to toast the miracle of Eddie's return from death. Sergeant Dolan came in and joined them, then left to make the arrangements for Sally's trip.

"The Mayr business is simple," Eiger said. "You just need to tell the sister, ah, Annaliese? Just tell her that you're leaving immediately. Tell her why."

"All right," Sally agreed. She reached for the phone and asked that the connection be made.

481

"I hope Annaliese is there," she said to the colonel as they waited for the call to go through.

She was.

Sally told her the news and was gratified, and guilty, over Annaliese's emotional response. "Oh, Sally," she said. "To have someone come back. Oh, my dear, I'm so pleased and happy. And I'm so glad you've told me. It makes me feel better to hear of such good news."

"I also want to tell you, Annaliese," continued Sally, "that I'm leaving."

"Leaving?"

"Yes. I don't really know what condition Eddie's in, and I'm the only family he's got. He doesn't even know about his wife and kids. I've got leave to fly out there."

"All the way to the Philippines?"

"Yes, I'm leaving Friday," Sally improvised. She wanted it to be over.

"Sally," cried Annaliese, "that's so soon."

"I know. I was lucky to get on a flight. As it is, it's going to take me a week, at least. It'll be a horrible trip across Turkey, India but it'll be worth it."

"Oh, I'm sorry you're leaving so soon, I guess we won't be able to see each other?"

"No. And Annaliese, I don't think I'll be back either," said Sally slowly.

There was silence. "What will you do?" said Annaliese in a small voice.

"I don't know. It depends on Eddie's health," Sally said, speaking the truth. "But listen, I have your address and I'll write when we reach San Francisco. Please keep in touch. Send me pictures of Klara. I'll miss both of you so much. And if there's anything I can do later, if you—I don't know—want to come to the States or need anything, don't hesitate to write. Promise?"

"Promise," agreed Annaliese.

"Good, well, I'd better say good-bye," said Sally.

"Wait, Sally," said Annaliese. Sally froze the receiver against her ear. "It's about Christian . . ." Annaliese began.

"Tell him," said Sally, with a quick glance at the colonel, who raised his eyebrows. "Tell him what's happened and that I hope he'll be happy for us. I think he liked Eddie. Tell him I got the locket and understood the message and . . . I'm sorry."

"Sorry?"

"Yes, just tell him that I'm sorry," said Sally and, saying good bye again, hung up, putting down the receiver as though it were hot. She hadn't liked making the call, deceiving Annaliese.

"All right. Now," said Colonel Eiger, "we set up the trap." He reached for the telephone. "That bit about leaving Friday was chancy. We don't know if she can get word to him in four days."

"Guess we'll find out," Sally said, her stomach aflutter with nervousness.

CHAPTER 5

"I f you stick close to me, Christian won't be able to contact me. Besides," Sally added, "he would have to get past Sergeant Sanchez up here and the guards downstairs. Which means he probably won't come. I really think I ought to take long walks or some such thing."

"Absolutely not," Eiger said. He had called the rest of the unit in that morning to tell them Sally's news and to make the plans necessary for her safety.

"He's not going to hurt me," Sally said.

"You don't know that," Max Tobin said in his usual mild manner.

"Not if he's the guy in the photos," Finkelstein added.

"Lieutenant," Eiger said. "You are a United States Army officer, working for a military intelligence unit. You have the photographs of him committing a criminal act, a war crime. And what's more, you can identify him personally."

"I guess so." She was aware of Tim, seated at the end of the table next to the colonel. She didn't like being the center of attention.

Sally looked across the table, above Armbrewster's well-groomed head, to where the sequence of photos were tacked up: the officer aiming his gun, the crumpled body of the child on the ground under the tree, the officer wiping his brow, his arm shading his face.

Heat. Summer. That day in late June, during the bloody weekend of the Röhm Putsch, he had worn his uniform. Then, later, after the meal, he had stood in the hall, his hat in hand, saying good night. She had slapped him. He had put on his hat and gone away. She shivered, remembering the redness of his cheek, the stiffness in his body as he reacted to her slap, and, most clearly, the shadow the hat had cast on his face.

"You're right," she said, "but it's hard," she added under her breath.

"We don't want you hurt," Max Tobin said.

"He wouldn't—"

"Sally," Tim said, interrupting her. "He's dangerous. Whatever he might have been—whatever you were to him, he's different now. You must accept that, Sally."

She looked around the table at the faces of the men, so full of concern for her. She tried smiling at them. "He's probably in Buenos Aires by now. He probably won't show."

"Sure, if he knows what's good for him," Finkelstein said, in a mock-tough voice.

"Now, let's arrange her pickups to and from work until she leaves," Eiger said.

"You do remember that Tobin and I are due in Potsdam at noon today?" Armbrewster said. "Perhaps we can do our bit later in the week."

"I've got Friday," she was glad to hear Tim say. With all the new developments, she had wondered if their date was still on.

"I can do it the rest of this week," Finkelstein offered and he and Sally agreed that he should come by her office at 1700 and drive her to her quarters.

As the men got up to leave, Max Tobin put his hand on Sally's shoulder and squeezed it as he passed her. When they were alone, Tim leaned toward her and touched her knee.

"Did I tell you I was going to Nuremberg tomorrow morning?"

"Yes," she answered unhappily. How much time would she have left with him?

"Otherwise, I'd stick to you like old gum. Drive you anywhere you wanted to go."

"Thanks, Timmy."

"I'll miss you, Sal. I wish . . ."

"No," she said, standing up, moving out of range of the hurt in his warm eyes. "Let's not talk about it. Maybe later. After . . . I can't think about that now. I mean . . ." She turned quickly, afraid she had said something stupid again.

"Don't worry, kid, I know exactly what you mean and I only wish I were going to be here all week to watch over you." He got up and went to her, putting his hands on her upper arms.

"I'm not that helpless," she gently chided him.

"I know. I know." He brushed her lips with his. "I'll see you Friday. We'll talk about things then." At the door, Tim paused. "Sally, he is dangerous. Don't take any chances."

When he had left, Sally sat for a long time studying the photographs on the wall, her emotions in a turmoil of excitement and sadness, resignation and anticipation, so that she had to struggle to focus on the pictures. Only Mala's were there; the private photographs that belonged to Sally were in the colonel's safe. Some of the prints had lost their tacks and their edges were curling up, so she tidied them up.

Christian was in her mind often that week. Not the adult in his black-and-silver uniform everyone said was a danger to her, but the boy from the lake. He was with her, all brown and golden, as she went about her work, as she waited for him to appear. She began to feel a heavy foreboding and hoped he would stay away from her.

Sergeant Dolan had achieved the impossible and gotten her a flight for the following Monday. He also started the paperwork for her discharge. Sally had a busy schedule: to clear her desk, finish the reports she could, and hand over those she could not.

As promised, Doug Finkelstein ferried her back and forth from her quarters and even hauled her footlocker off for shipment to San Francisco. Everyone, including Sally, assumed she was not returning. It was a bittersweet few days as she got ready to leave not only Tim, but the colleagues she respected and the work that had saved her sanity through so many long years. No one asked her what she would do in San Francisco and she did not think beyond getting Eddie there and taking care of him.

Thursday afternoon, she wrapped up the box of photographs taken from the camp victims for shipment to a refugee center, slipping in the snapshot of Katrina van der Lee. She made a silent apology to Mavis as she did so, but she just could not look at one more photograph of one more tragedy.

Nor would she go back into the conference room to look at the photographs of Christian, knowing too well what she would see: the implicit violence, the stark black-and-white shadows. They were just a few more of the many pictures she had been living with all these years, pictures of a world gone mad, pictures she didn't want to look at anymore.

"Sally, you ready to go?" Doug asked, startling her. He stood in the open door of her office with several manila envelopes in his hands.

"Oh, my. What time is it? Sorry. I've been a little distracted. I didn't realize it was that late. Can you give me a minute?"

"No problem. I've got this mail to drop off, then I'll get the car. You can meet me downstairs. You have any mail to go?"

"I sure do. If you wouldn't mind lugging a box down." She pointed to the box of photographs. "Is it too much to carry?"

"Nope." Finkelstein picked up the carton. Sally put his envelopes on top of it and, thanking him, opened the door.

"See you," he called, going down the hall. She watched him push through the swinging doors until they stopped moving, then looked at her watch. It was just after five o'clock, a dark, cold December afternoon. She wondered what the weather in Manila would be like and reminded herself to ask Sergeant Sanchez.

Standing at her desk, she separated a report from its carbons and put the original into a file and locked it in her bottom drawer. She clipped the carbons together and, glancing again at her watch, decided she had enough time to run them down to Nelson's office.

The hallway, lit at intervals by bare, wire-caged light bulbs, was quiet. The door to Nelson's office was locked and she continued down the hall to Sergeant Dolan. She could hear the wind come up outside, rattling the old windows, whistling in through the bomb-damaged closed-off offices. She looked down the hall at the series of doors, all nailed shut. There was nothing behind most of them but a three-story drop to the basement. But as she looked, one of the doors rattled, startling her.

Spooked, she hurried down to Dolan's office, wondering which Nazi ministry had used this place, anyway. Scolding herself for her foolishness, she opened the door to the sergeant's office. He was typing. It was a comforting sound in that long dim hall, with its row of closed, secret doors.

Sally handed Dolan the report for Nelson Armbrewster and they discussed her travel plans. She admonished him for staying so late.

"I am about ready to leave," he assured her. "I don't like to leave work overnight."

"Sounds like a storm is coming up," she said. "You don't want to get caught in it."

"No, ma'am, I do not," he agreed seriously.

Stopping in the rest room, Sally washed her hands and glanced at herself in the mirror to check her hair. Her eyes were enormous, with dark smudges under them adding to her pallor. She smiled at herself, trying to relax, but in the glare from the overhead light, the smile only made her look worse. What the hell did Tim see in her, anyway? She certainly wasn't a beauty anymore. She thought of his lips on her breast and shivered with anticipation, knowing there was nowhere on earth she would rather be than in his bed, with his arms around her.

Well, she'd be there, or at least in his apartment, soon, tomorrow night. Only twenty-four more hours to be gotten through.

Christian had probably been too far away for Annaliese to contact in time. And Sally realized how much she hoped that was true. She did not want to confront him. Not now. Not ever. Giving her bangs a brave fluff, she left the rest room and went to pick up her coat and bag.

Pale, watery light seeped through the blinds on the windows of her office from the streetlight outside. It had started to rain and she felt the cold wind that made its way into the room through the cracks in the window frame. It felt cold enough for snow. Sally leaned across her desk to pick up her bag, and stopped.

The desk light had been on when she left.

She froze just as she was, off balance, leaning toward the lamp, one hand outstretched, trying to decipher the sounds, the lights, everything blurred in the rush of the storm, the floating shadows.

She turned her head toward the window and, out of the corner of her eye, she saw something move.

He was here. Her brain knew it before her body could respond.

His hand covered her mouth as he pulled her back against him. He held a gun to her temple, the barrel cold and hard against her skin. The feel of the gun made her stomach turn.

She was very still, frightened by the gun.

"You feel this?" said the voice, his voice, in German, a tense, thin whisper, barely audible above the rain. "You feel it?" he repeated, pushing the barrel hard against her skull. She nodded, trying to quell the panic that rose in her. "You will be quiet, yes?"

She could do nothing, not move, nor speak, but he seemed to be satisfied, and taking the gun away, let go of her. She rubbed her temple to get rid of the feel of the cold metal.

A gust of wind hit the windows and she started. The storm battered the windows, drowning out the sounds of the rest of the world.

"Hello, Sally."

She turned. He was barely visible, except as a tall shadow, striped in the moving, undersea light seeping through the blinds.

The gun, shining dully, pointed at her. It scared her, but her curiosity was stronger than her fear, and she searched the darkness for his face. The shadow put his hand on her shoulder, spoke. "You stay quiet and do what I say, and everything will be fine. Yes?" he said. She nodded. She was shaking.

"Good. Good." He kneaded her shoulder, as though to calm her fear. "Believe me, I do not want to hurt you, Sally, I do not. So," he said, still in that thin whisper of German. "Here we are. Not as you imagined."

"Christian," she tried in a weak voice.

"Quiet." His voice was gentle but firm. His fingers flicked across her cheek. "I will speak and you will listen and no one will be hurt." Pushing on her shoulder, he moved her to the window. He parted the blinds and was striped by the headlights of a passing car. Quickly he shut the room back into rainy darkness. Sally caught an impression of his face, of hard thinness and deep lines alongside his mouth.

Again, he leaned down to her ear. She could feel his breath on her cheek. "You have pictures. I want to see them. The pictures you say you have of me." His voice was calm and reasonable, as if he were speaking to a child.

"There is only one."

"There are four. I want to see them. You will not argue with me, you will do as I say. I do not want to hurt you. Don't make me hurt you."

"You sneaked in here for that? You can't destroy them. The negatives are . . ." He put his hand on her face, the fingers splayed across her mouth, silencing her.

"I told you to be quiet, didn't I? Not to argue. Now, you will take me to see the pictures. Shhh, no more talk. No more. Remember what I said." He spoke calmly and only the tense grip of his hand on her face betrayed how much self-control he was exerting. His hand hurt her but she neither moved nor made a sound.

They had gotten used to the sound of the wind and rain and immediately were alerted to a different sound: footsteps coming up the hall toward Sally's office. Instantly, Christian was across the room to the door, where he turned the key and waited, gun raised.

Men's voices. Doug and Sergeant Sanchez were talking about her, wondering where she was, why she hadn't met Doug downstairs. She wanted to cry out.

As though he anticipated her impulse, Christian gestured her to the floor. She went down, instantly, afraid of the gun. She still could call to Doug and the Sergeant, but if she did, and they forced their way into the office, Christian would shoot them. So she kept silent, watching his still shadow by the door.

Someone knocked on the door. She forced herself not to cry out, not to make a single noise. She couldn't keep herself from shaking.

"Doesn't look like she's here," Doug said.

"Light's off. She must have gotten past me." This from the sergeant.

The door rattled. "Locked. She must have gone. Come on, Sergeant, let's go check downstairs again." And their footsteps receded into silence. Christian waited several minutes before he moved, and she waited, too, hunched down uncomfortably across the room from him. The rain ceased and everything became absolutely still.

He moved. Her head came up.

"Now," he said, squatting down before her, the gun hanging loose in his hand. "Where are the pictures?" When she did not answer, he put his hand under her chin, cupping it. "You must do this."

"Yes," she said, hating the silence and the darkness, the feel of his hard hand on her face. If only he would turn the light on. Was Sergeant Dolan still in this office? She hoped not.

"Where are they? They are not in his office."

"How do you know? How did you get in here?" Maybe she could get him to talk and Doug and the sergeant would come back.

He slapped her. Once. He slapped her hard, knocking her sideways so that she hit the floor. Shocked and stunned by his brutality, she lay breathless, her face stinging, hating her helplessness.

"You see?" Christian said in a reasonable voice, not whispering anymore. He touched her arm. "Come along, get up. You will show me the pictures. I will look at them. And then I will go away and you will be safe forever. I promise that."

She could see the light from Sergeant Dolan's office under the door. He was still there, still working on her orders. She stopped, her arms wrapped around her middle.

"Who is it?" Christian whispered.

"The colonel's clerk. We have to go through his office. He's still here. You won't hurt him?"

Mayr's only response was to push her forward, but she wouldn't move, gun or no gun. He shoved the gun against her and she twisted away from it. Or tried to. He grabbed her shoulder, tightly.

"Sally," he said in a warning voice.

"Don't hurt him."

"Go," he said, squeezing her shoulder painfully.

"Don't—"

"Now, you be calm. No one will be hurt if you stay calm." He let go of her.

Not believing him, but having no choice, Sally let the gun push her forward. She stood before the door, her arms at her side until the gun prodded her and she opened the door to the office. Dolan's head came up from the work he was doing, a look of surprise on his face.

"Lieutenant Jackson!"

"I'm sorry, Sergeant."

"No, ma'am. I just didn't think anyone . . ." He trailed off as Sally was propelled into the room. Christian closed the door behind them, and with as little fuss as he would expend on any mundane chore, he turned, and shot the sergeant twice.

The first shot hit the sergeant's head in an explosion of blood, bone, and brain, and the second opened his chest into bright-red sunbursts, the force of the bullets driving him back against the wall, knocking over his chair.

Sally stood transfixed, unable to move or cry out. Black and white. She'd seen it all in black and white but never in color, never in such terrible colors.

Still absolutely self-possessed, Christian walked around the desk and shot the sergeant again. Sally could not see the sergeant anymore, hidden as he was by the desk, and she began to moan, like a wounded animal, raising her hands to her face.

Christian, finally hearing her, turned and raised the gun and, without aiming, pulled the trigger again. The bullet went into the wall above the file cabinets, clearing Sally easily. She screamed and backed straight into the wall.

"Shut up," he yelled. "Shut up. I told you to shut up. You see what you made me do? You shut up or I'll kill you too. Do you understand? I'll kill you too. I don't care!" He screamed the last words, the veins in his neck standing out against his red skin, the hand holding the gun visibly shaking.

Through her own panic, Sally recognized his and saw it was much more dangerous, and understood that she was very close to death. She lowered her trembling hands and held them out, palms toward him, placating.

"Yes, yes. Shhh, I'm quiet. Shhh, I'll do as you say," she murmured until he lowered the gun. He paid no attention to the body in its grotesque position between the blood-spattered desk and wall and went to the conference-room door.

He opened it, saw it was dark and motioned for Sally to enter. "Is this it? Turn the lights on." She hurried in front of him and did as he asked. "Hurry up," he yelled, hitting the door with the gun as she waved her hand in the air under the hanging lamp, searching for the cord. "What the hell are you doing? Turn the fucking lights on. NOW!" He roared the last as her hand came in contact with the cord. She pulled it and the light came on.

491

He slammed and locked the door. "Where are they? Answer me!" he demanded.

"They're there. There, on the wall," she said, pointing, and quickly turned on the lights above the corkboard, illuminating the rows of photographs. As he went to them, he put the gun in a pocket of the gray overcoat he wore.

"Where am I?" he asked impatiently.

"The four at the end."

"Which four? Where?" She heard the hysteria build again in his voice and she hurried around the table to show him. "That's me?" He sounded incredulous and this so astonished her that she snapped back at him without thinking.

"You were there. You were the commander. Look. Look, Christian. Look, goddamn you." She jabbed her finger at the sequence of pictures she knew so well. The child, the officer, the child's body limp and obscene on the ground as the officer wipes his brow. "This *is* you. *This is you.*" She pointed at the blowup.

"That's not me," he said, stepping back from the wall. "You think that's me?" He studied the photograph, then shook his head. "No. But I know who that is."

"Who?"

"Doesn't matter. He's dead now."

"Oh, for Christ's sake. Look at him. It's you."

And again he leaned forward to study the blowup of the officer. He shook his head. "What year was this?"

"1942. After Heydrich's death."

"A happy day for all," he muttered. "A long time ago."

"You can recognize yourself, surely."

"It was a long time ago." But still he stared at the pictures. "What a mess. What a mess." He was silent for several moments, then seemed to rouse himself. "Well, is that it?"

"I don't believe you. I can't believe that you can deny that you did that, you murdered that child, as surely as you murdered Sergeant Dolan out there."

"As I might murder you if you don't shut up." His voice tightened. "I should kill you, Sally. It was stupid of me to shoot him, and now I'll probably have to kill you. I don't want to, but . . ." He took a step toward her, and she backed away, her eyes on his face—on his blue eyes that had become empty and dead. "You'll come after me, won't you? All of you, with your shiny new guns and your well-pressed uniforms over your well-fed American stomachs. You'll hang me like you did the others. Except for Fat Her-

ann. Ha! He had the right idea. Fooled you all too with that
yanide capsule."

Sally turned toward the door, forgetting that he had locked it.
Ie came up to her slowly, standing behind her, his fingers circling
er throat, pulling her gently back against him.

"I should kill you," he whispered. "I should. Though, I'm so
ck of it all." His fingers pressed into her larynx. She gasped. "But
ou leave me little choice." His hand fell to her breast, covering it.

"Don't," Sally said, suddenly more angry than frightened, and
ith a quick gesture, knocked his arm loose, broke away from him.
he rounded on him and shoved him as hard as she could, sending
im stumbling against the locked door. But there was no place to
o. She turned to face him. He had the gun out again.

"Don't. No more," she said, her voice sounding too loud and
trident to her ears. "Please, Christian, it's over."

"You will accuse me. They'll believe you."

"Go. I won't stop you. I promise. Go, now."

"You will come after me, hunt me down."

"No."

"To kill me. To hang me like some stupid little Russian."

She stared at him, stunned at his words, at the image they con-
ured up to her. "A Russian, Christian? Did you hang Russians after
zechoslovakia? I've seen photographs of the Russians the SS
anged. Did you do that too?"

"Shut up." He waved the gun at her. She didn't care.

"And the child, the child hiding in the tree? Christian? The
hild hiding in the tree?" she repeated. He slowly lowered the gun.
he took a step toward him, the table still between them. "It is you,
n't it?" But still he did not speak, turning instead to sink into a
hair, his back to her. "I recognized you, the line of your jaw under
hat damn hat. I recognized you. I loved you once and I recognized
ou. How could you do that? A child, Christian, a child."

"It's not me." His voice was weary, exhausted, his hands moved
ut she could not see what they did.

"Oh, for Christ's sake," she cried, and sank into the nearest
hair. Had they been in this room for hours already? Days? He
noved again and she turned to watch. He brought the gun up,
ointing the barrel toward his face, as though he were studying it.

"Christian?"

At the sound of her voice, he stood and shoved the gun into
is pocket. "What are you doing?" she asked.

"Stop asking me questions." He went to the door and unlocked
t. She jumped up and ran to him, grabbing his arm.

"No. You can't leave."

"Leave me, Sally," he said, pushing her away. "I've been her[e] too long already."

"No." She grabbed him again, pulling him around to face he[r.] He tried to grab her hands, push her away, but she wouldn't let hi[m.]

"Sally, stop it." He hit her. Not as hard as he had hit her i[n] her office, but hard enough to bring tears to her eyes.

"I hate you so much," she said, leaning against the wall.

"I know. Doesn't matter. It's too late."

"No," she said, insisting, taking his arm again. "You're here. [I] want to know things. You have to answer questions."

"Sally, don't."

"No. I have to know. So many things. For instance, have yo[u] been following me? Have you?" she repeated. He gestured with h[is] hand, which she took as an admission. "Well, good. That means [I] wasn't losing my mind."

"Calm down." He shook her hand loose and turned away. Sh[e] quickly got between him and the door.

"No. You must tell me. You owe it to me. You know you d[o.] Tell me about us. Not Czechoslovakia. I want to know what hap[-]pened between us. Please. I can't stand it." She started to cry. "D[o] you know what you did to me? How you destroyed my life? Did h[e] tell you to? Do you know what you did to me? He nearly killed m[e.] Why? Christian, why?"

"Stop crying." He tried to push her aside again but sh[e] wouldn't let him, slapping at his hands. He caught her wrists. "Stop[,] Sally. Stop. I will not have this. I will not." His hands were vises o[n] her as she tried to twist away. He shook her hard. "Stop. You sto[p.] Don't make me—"

"You're revolting. I hate you!" she yelled at him, strugglin[g] against his hands, trying to kick him, hurt him. "I hate you."

He slammed her against the wall, holding one of her hands i[n] each of his, pressing her wrists to the wall, his body against hers, h[is] knee between her legs, making her nearly immobile. He put his fac[e] against hers, not kissing her, just holding his cheek against her[.] Then, when she stopped struggling he began to speak, his voice lo[w] and tense, the words coming fast from him, tumbling out of him [as] he held her pinned between his body and the wall.

"We were pawns to him. Everyone was. I was his favorite. Th[e] perfect knight, he called me and, yes, he fucked me. Not that he w[as] a fairy. He just fucked anything and everyone, because he could. T[o] prove that he could. He was such a shit, spreading his shit aroun[d] until it covered everyone. And you, that family shit. You were s[o]

494

naive. Playing music with him, thinking your father's position could save you from the corruption, not knowing it was your father's position that attracted him. You were so innocent, so stupidly naive and trusting. God, you were trusting. You trusted everyone. Him. Me.

"And me, I wanted—you know what I wanted? To save you. I wanted to save you from him, from me. You trusted me." He stopped and stepped back from her, releasing her hands. Tenderly, he put his hands on either side of her face and studied it. She found it difficult to look into his eyes, they were so cold, so many fathoms cold. She held very still as he looked at her.

"I loved you," he said. "I loved you all my life and I let him ruin us, hurt you."

"Why?" she asked, her need to know stronger than her fear of what he would tell her.

"I thought I could make a deal with him. That I could outwit him. It really is amazingly funny, when you think of it." And he started to laugh, moving away, his laughter loud and horrible in the room lined with Mala's photographs. "There I was, a twenty-year-old boy, thinking because he'd made me an Obersturmführer . . . and you know why he did that? It wasn't for my industry and National Socialist ideals, believe me. But I thought I could manipulate him, and what's really amusing about it is he let me think I did." He slammed his fist into the corkboard, breaking a hole in it.

"'Marry the girl, Mayr,' he told me. 'Best of luck. Just one little thing, Mayr, one little thing, one fucking little thing.'" Christian kicked a chair, knocking it to the ground. "'Don't forget to come to the office on Tuesday afternoons, and, oh, Mayr, by the way, your little wife, how is she? Tell me about it. Does she do this and this?' But telling him wasn't enough to keep him away from you, so, my dearest, darling little Sally, you know what happened?" He paused and smiled with such bitterness, with hate, yes, hatred, that Sally backed a few steps away from him. He grabbed her arm, pulling her toward him.

"I hated you," he whispered, "because I loved you. I felt it was your fault. Isn't that crazy? It was so simple—all you had to do was sleep with him and he'd leave me alone. But you wouldn't, keeping your precious innocence to yourself, hoarding it, while the rest of us sank into the shit. Of course, if you had slept with him, I would have had to kill you. The idea of his hands on you made me crazy. So he had me either way."

"Why did he arrest you?"

"Ah, well, that's easy. I wouldn't do what he wanted. I was so fucking noble. For about five minutes, until he sent his boys in to take care of me. I gave in. And after all of that, after getting you out there and drugged . . . he liked the idea of the drug. He wanted you nice and soft. After all of that, all I went through, you fell asleep." He started laughing again. "I mean, you have to appreciate the man for not taking you anyway. He could have. I've seen him beat the shit out of whores and fuck them anyway. But he wanted you awake while he took that innocence from you."

He ran his hands over her face, covering and uncovering her eyes, her nose. She stood stiff and unyielding in his arm. His hand cupped her face again.

"Oh, Sally, he wanted to see your eyes as he corrupted you, to see you enjoy it. Which you would have. All of us did."

"Christian, why did you let him?"

Christian dropped his hands from her. There was a strange smile on his face. "That's right, you don't know. Now, this is the best secret of all."

"What? What, Christian?"

"I killed my father."

"Your father committed suicide."

"No. I killed him. Shot him. The first time I visited him after I received my commission. Shot him with my brand-new officer's sidearm."

"Why? Christian, your father—"

"Was an honorable, old-fashioned democrat, of all the bloody, stupid things. He believed in the Republic. He hated the National Socialists. He hated me."

"No, he couldn't. He was a good man."

"Absolutely. Too good to live. He raised his walking stick to me, so I shot him. Then I did the worst thing of all, I told Heydrich. He covered it up. Took care of me. That's when it all started."

"Christian?"

"Christ, can't you stop?" He began pacing, making wild gestures, and then he stopped, standing at the end of the table. And again he took out the gun. He held it in both hands and studied it.

"You know, what I really wanted to do there in that canopied bed? After we made love? I wanted to kill us both. To end it all right there. To keep you safe forever. I should have. Death is the only safe place left. Believe me, I know."

Sally watched him study the gun. He didn't look like a monster. He looked like a tired thin man in a shabby, ill-fitting suit. His cheekbones were very pronounced, as were the lines from his nose to his chin. His nose had been broken, adding to his worn appearance. He was still handsome, but there was a hardness about him now, and that deadness in his blue eyes.

His head came up. He heard the noise outside before she did. Someone calling her name. Men's voices coming along the hall. A door opening and slamming shut.

"Christian, you can still give yourself up."

"Stop, Sally. It is too late." He pointed the gun at her. She didn't move.

"No. No. It's not. Please, Christian. Don't do it. No more. It's time to stop. No more." She ignored the men calling her name.

"Please, Christian." She took a step toward him, toward the gun. It hovered just a yard away. She didn't care. She reached her hand for him, to stop him from using the gun this time. "It has to stop."

"I loved you, Sally," he said, his voice infinitely weary, infinitely sad. "And," he continued, "I will not die at the end of a rope."

Without another word, he put the barrel of the gun into his mouth and pulled the trigger.

CHAPTER 6

B lood splattered on the wall, the floor, and arced up to hit the ceiling. She saw the blood. On his boots. On the wall behind the stakes. In the shower room. The long gashes in the plains where the bodies toppled into the graves, spilling blood in the dirt. An explosion of blood and bodies and steel and water and death in the plains and oceans and jungles. Like the salle's shower room. The shower rooms filled with blood.

"No!" she screamed, her arms stretching toward him. There was blood on her sleeves, on her hands.

Christian's body stood, swayed, supporting the thing that his head had turned into, then, slowly, almost gracefully, he crumpled to the floor, folding up as he fell. Sally followed his progress down, landing hard on her knees, falling forward onto her bloody hands.

Why couldn't she save him? She had loved him enough, hadn't she? Why couldn't she save him from the blood?

Someone was at the door, calling her name, but it sounded miles away. Her world had narrowed to the space between herself and the bloody ruin only feet away from her. Her friend. Once upon a time, he had been her friend.

People burst into the room, but she ignored them.

Christian. She had to concentrate on him. Dead. He was dead.

"It's so cold," she said.

She became aware that someone was touching her, trying to get her to stand. Christian's arm had fallen across his chest, blocking her view of his shattered head. She looked at his left hand, flung aside, palm up, as though he were sleeping. He slept on his side, she remembered.

She shook away the person touching her and crawled the short distance to Christian's hand. Reaching out very carefully, she covered his fingers with her own. His hand was still warm, but it was dead and unresponsive.

"Oh, Christian," she said softly. She laid her cheek against his hand, her tears falling onto his long, thin fingers. "I'm so sorry," she whispered. When she raised her head, the tears had stopped.

She sat back on her heels and looked up into Tim's face. He

put his hand out to help her up, not minding the blood. "Thank you," she said, taking his hand. She walked out of the room with him, not looking again at the body.

Sergeant Dolan's body was gone. Colonel Eiger was on the phone at the sergeant's desk. He turned to watch her walk by. At the door, Doug Finkelstein was talking to an NCO.

Sally stopped. "Doug? Where is Chester?"

"They took him away, Sally," Doug said gently.

"Someone should call his family. Where are they?"

"Atlanta, I think. Max is taking care of it. How are you?" he asked, touching her arm.

She frowned. "I'm okay, Doug," she said, looking around distractedly. Where was. . . ? What was she looking for? Tim put out his hand. She gratefully took it, holding on tightly. "I want to go outside."

"Of course," he nodded and walked with her down the hall, past her office.

On the top step outside, they came to an abrupt stop.

"Would you look at that?" Tim said, his voice full of wonder.

It had snowed. The rain and wind had turned into snow, which lay quiet and clean, covering the black ruins of the city. The night was clear and crisp and cold, and above, the stars shone as brightly as the lights on the Unter den Linden of Sally's memory.

"It's too cold, sweetheart," said Tim, his arm around her, gently steering her back inside.

"No," she said. "I don't want to go inside there."

"Well, then, I'll go get your coat. You wait here, all right?" He waited until she nodded, then moved away. Sally turned back to look at the city, all white and glistening in the moonlight and starlight, no longer, or at least not until the snow melted, a haphazard jumble of rubble.

All the ugliness was covered up for a moment. And, seeing it Sally realized that she didn't want to leave. She would, but she didn't want to leave Berlin. Not now, when it was in ruins, when children still lived in the hospitals and camps and needed so much help.

It didn't make a lot of sense, but this city was home to her more than any other had ever been and she did not want to leave it. Or perhaps because of it. Berlin was where she had been the happiest and the most miserable, where she had learned and lost the most. There it was, a truth, ugly or not. And the Berliners, the enemy, who had done these terrible things, were they so different from her? She had known. She had seen, but she had closed her eyes and refused to acknowledge the evil. That was a truth too.

The truth. She'd never know exactly what happened and maybe Christian was right. It had all happened a long time ago. And hadn't they both paid the price? As for Mala's pictures: they were a version of truth that needed interpretation.

All right. That was her job and she was good at it.

She believed Christian had killed that child, and commanded the action group that destroyed the village. He had told her the officer was dead. That was true too. Christian, even before he pulled the trigger of his gun, had been dead inside, dead all through because of the things he had done. And now he was out of the reach of any retribution.

It was over.

He had become a monster. She was there and saw it start, but she still couldn't explain why. He was a monster she recognized, a monster whose death moved her. A monster she had once loved and wanted to have children with.

Death solved the problem of his guilt. But she, Sally, was not dead. She raised her head to the winter sky, glad to feel the cold air against her face, cooling her flushed cheeks.

She was alive.

She thought of his family, his mother, whom she had loved, and his father. How terrible for Christian to have lived all those years with that awful crime. There had been so much death: his brothers and sisters, their unborn child, Eddie's family.

Sally looked at the stars. Once, somewhere, she'd heard a folktale that said that the stars were the souls of babies, twinkling clear and bright and pure up in heaven. She had held their child in her heart all these years, the child she had never held in reality. It was time to let them both go. It was time to look to the future.

Sally lowered her eyes and hugged her arms across her chest. So, here she was, thirty-three years old, childless, parentless, but not as lonely as she had been. Christian was gone for good now, and she would mourn the loss of him, but . . . she swallowed hard.

How tired she was; she couldn't think about it any longer. She stood up straight, fighting the exhaustion.

Eddie.

She had to go find her brother and take him home and do whatever she could to help him. Thank God, there was money and the promise of quiet days in San Francisco. She would take Eddie there. And then? What would she do then?

Years ago she had stood in her pretty, lacy negligee, looking down onto the bustling, twinkling lights of Unter den Linden. The lights, the bustle, had covered a deep, destructive evil, but evil doesn't last forever. Surely, the fire and destruction had cleansed the soul of the city. Surely, with all the deaths, both of the guilty and the many more innocent, some of the debt had been paid.

And her own debt? Gone, she hoped, taking a deep breath. She had been blind, but now she saw. That had been her greatest sin. That she had loved him. That was no sin. Never. Because it was all there against death. The blood. The monsters. Even against the lies. Love was all there was, fragile and rare and incomprehensible.

Someone put a coat around her shoulders and she turned. "Timmy," she said.

"Here, put your coat on. You must be freezing."

She nodded and slipped her arms into the sleeves of her coat.

"You ready to go?" he asked, still behind her, his hands on her shoulders.

She nodded.

"I like it before it gets muddy," he said, gesturing toward the snowy street.

"I've been thinking," said Sally. She stuck her hands deep in the pockets of the coat, her fingers closing around the little gold locket.

"What about?" Tim asked.

"How much I loved, love, this city." She pulled her hand out of her pocket and looked down at the little necklace.

Tim was silent, standing next to her, his hands in his pockets.

"It's such a waste, isn't it?" he said.

"Yes, a waste," she said, looking at the beautiful white, ruined streets, thinking of her childhood friend, the slender boy with the golden hair and clear blue eyes, eyes as blue as the sky above the deep, cold lake. He was receding from her mind already, sinking down into the lake. He'd be safe there and she let him go. She'd remember him as he was then, when they were fourteen, all those years ago. And she pulled her arm back and threw the locket as far as she could. She couldn't see or hear where it landed.

Tim watched her, but said nothing. She had never shown him the necklace. It didn't matter now. It was over.

"Well," Tim said after a moment, "do you want me to take you home?"

"Yes," she said in a soft voice. She held out her hand, he took it, folding it between both of his.

"Do you want to come home with me? We do have a date tonight."

"Is that tonight?"

"Yeah." He raised her hand to his lips and kissed it, his moustache soft against her cold fingers. She sighed and turned her face into his shoulder. It would be the easiest thing in the world just to stay there in his arms.

"I think you like me," he said softly, his arms tightening around her. "Just a little bit."

"Just a little bit," she murmured. How could she leave him?

"I don't know, Sal."

"What?" she asked, leaning back so that she could look into his face. How could she leave him? His eyes met hers. "What?" she repeated.

"Your going. How can I let you go?"

"I have to go," she said. She could hear the pain under his words.

"I know. But, maybe . . ."

"Timmy," she said abruptly. She figured she should be the one to speak since she was leaving, since she had always been so frightened. It was hard and she touched his lapel, fussing with it. "I don't really cook at all. Well, I guess you know that. There are a lot of things we would have to decide. I mean . . ."

"Sally . . ."

"Work and Wichita and I have to take care of Eddie too. And you know how slowly the army moves. It could takes months. But I could meet you or wait somewhere. I just can't lose you . . ."

"Sally," Tim said, breaking in on the flow of words. He put his warm hands on either side of her chilled face. "Sally Jackson, are you asking me to marry you?" And when she nodded, he began to laugh, wrapping his arms around her, rocking the two of them back and forth, his laughter echoing off the silent buildings on the snowy moonscape of the block.

NAZI EPILOGUE

Sally watched the seam of the nurse's white stockings flash under the hem of her uniform, above her crepe soled shoes. Her own civilian shoes tapped noisily on the linoleum as she followed the nurse down the long ward to the lone patient at the far end. The beds they passed were all empty, the white covers tight on the white mattresses, the white mosquito netting draped neatly above. There were long windows the length of the room, open to the outside, their wooded shutters propped open, and at intervals, doors that opened out on to the veranda.

"He's in the last bed," the nurse, said quietly. From behind them, they could barely hear the radio that sat on the desk at the nurses' station.

Eddie lay on his side, his hips and shoulders making sharp mountains in the white sheet that covered him. Sally gasped when she saw him, he was so thin, so fragile. They had shaved his head and the shadow of his hair accentuated his skull, his gaunt cheeks.

"He's asleep," said the nurse. "We'd better leave."

"No," whispered Sally. "I want to stay. We've come a long way."

"It'll be all right," Tim said, moving forward, putting his arm lightly around Sally. "We won't disturb him."

"Well, all right. But let him sleep as long as he needs. He is very weak. He doesn't sleep well at night," the nurse whispered and then went away.

"I'll get you a chair," Tim said.

She sat for a long time, watching her brother. Tim left her for a while, touching her shoulder as he went out the door at the end of the room to smoke a cigarette on the veranda.

The doctor had told them that Eddie was suffering from malnutrition and dysentery and a few more exotic infections. He had appeared out of the jungle, six months ago, carried by two Filipino commandos. Evidently, he had spent most of the war with the commandos. He had been delirious when he was admitted to the hospital. The two men who had brought him in had only known him by his first name and praised his bravery. He had been in a Japanese

503

prison camp and he'd escaped. Beyond that, they could tell the doctor little. It wasn't until recently that Eddie had become lucid enough to identify himself.

At first, the doctor, a young Navy man, didn't know if Eddie would live.

Sally studied her brother's thin face. He looked like the POW's liberated from the camps in Europe and she prayed that his experiences hadn't been as harrowing.

There were so many things to ask, so many things to say. Eddie didn't know about his family, or their father. He didn't know about Tim. She looked out the door at her husband. He was leaning easily against the narrow railing around the veranda and, sensing her gaze, turned his head and smiled at her.

Eddie moved restlessly, his arm twitching on the sheet. He began to perspire heavily. Sally leaned forward, alarmed. "Tim," she called, quietly. Tim came quickly to the other side of the bed and reached down to gently pick up one of Eddie's bone-thin arms and feel for a pulse.

"His pulse is racing," Tim said. "I'd better call the nurse to get his doc."

Just as Tim put Eddie's arm down, Eddie opened his eyes and saw Sally. He looked at her for a long time and she began to fear that he didn't recognize her. His expression was so strange. He didn't look at all like himself, he was so terribly fragile. And his eyes—those dear, familiar eyes—were shadowed with the memory of experiences she could only imagine.

Then he smiled.

"Hello, Sally," he said, his voice a hoarse whisper. "Long time no see. Who's the guy?"

Without a word, she left her chair, kneeling on the floor, her head close to his, covering his thin hand with her own.

"No, c'mon, Sal. Don't do that." He touched her face. "It's all over now, Sally. It's all over. It's all over."

"I'm not crying, Eddie," she said as she raised her face to show him. Sally knew as she smiled at her brother, and then looked across him at her new husband that Eddie was wrong. It wasn't all over. She looked into Tim's green eyes and knew it was just beginning.

504

AUTHOR'S NOTES

In placing my story against the tumultuous years between 1933 and 1946, I have tried to be consistent and faithful to the historical background. My sources? Well, I started reading about the Third Reich nearly twenty years ago, long before I ever thought about writing a book. I've read scores of books: histories, biographies, picture books, novels, and memoirs. I also watched documentaries and other films, and have actually seen Reinhard Heydrich move across my television screen and shake hands with an official of the Vichy government in footage shot in 1941. Heydrich was real, an elusive figure in the Third Reich hierarchy who was, by the time of his assassination in 1942, seriously considered to be the natural heir to Hitler.

Sally Jackson is a fictional character, but her existence is based on the fact that the U.S. Ambassador, William E. Dodd, did indeed have a young, pretty daughter named Martha. She wrote a memoir of her family's experience in Berlin and after her father's death, she and her brother edited his very dry diaries.

It was one scene in Martha's memoirs that I read, years ago, that caught and persisted in my imagination. During the weekend of the Night of the Long Knives, as the Röhm Putsch came to be called, an SS officer, an acquaintance of the Dodd family, wound up crying on their sitting room sofa. How he came to be there and what else happened I can't remember. All I can remember is how incongruous the idea of an SS man crying on the American ambassador's sofa, and I started making up a story to explain his behavior.

OTHER BOOKS AVAILABLE